Theresa Monsour lives in Minnesota with her husband and two sons. A journalist by trade, she has reported on working mothers, crime, courts, education and city life. When she is not writing she enjoys fishing, cross-country ski-ing and cooking.

Also by Theresa Monsour

Dark House

THERESA MONSOUR OMNIBUS

Clean Cut

Cold Blood

Theresa Monsour

SPHERE

This omnibus edition first published in Great Britain in 2009 by Sphere

A CIP catalogue record for this book
is available from the British Library.

ISBN 978-0-7515-4158-8

Printed and bound in Great Britain by
Clays Ltd, St Ives plc

Sphere
An imprint of
Little, Brown Book Group
100 Victoria Embankment
London EC4Y 0DY

An Hachette UK Company
www.hachette.co.uk

www.littlebrown.co.uk

Clean Cut

This book is dedicated to my husband, David, with all my love.

ACKNOWLEDGMENTS

Thanks to my:

husband, David and our sons, Patrick and Ryan, for supporting me in this great adventure;

mentor, John Camp, who encouraged and helped all along the way;

doctor friend Marilee Votel-Kvaal and nurse sister-in-law Rita Monsour for their medical advice;

brother, Joseph Monsour, and sister, Bernadette Monsour, who have faith in me;

father, Gabriel Monsour, and late mother, Esther, for raising me right;

police pals Sergeant Mark Kempe and Officer Randy Barnett, who answered my questions;

agent, Esther Newberg, and editor, Leona Nevler, for being wonderful to work with;

past and present editors, reporters and other colleagues at the *St. Paul Pioneer Press*, for creating a newsroom that nurtures writers.

ONE

Despite the rain, Finch stayed.

All day ninety-degree heat had cooked the garbage cans behind the restaurants that lined the street. The stink of discarded food mingled with the smell of the prostitutes' sweat and perfumes. Musk and pickles. The men who usually drove up and down the street hunting for hamburgers and hookers had stayed away. At dusk came the rain, making a sizzling sound like meat hitting a hot pan. One by one the women left their corners, a parade of bored sentries abandoning their posts.

But Finch stayed.

She was the only daughter of western Wisconsin dairy farmers. At fifteen, she had been crowned princess in a county pageant and waved from a paper-flower float. Even then she knew she wasn't the prettiest, that she got by on her hair and her breasts. On her seventeenth birthday she decided that even though she was only a little pretty, she shouldn't have to put up with all the farm crap. All the family crap. She scribbled a three-word note to her mother and thumbed her way to St. Paul.

Now twenty-three, she waved to johns from the city's sidewalks. She wasn't even a little pretty anymore.

"Hey, Finch. Call it a day?" asked Charlene Rue. She and Finch shared a corner and were always the last to leave the street; their pimp wouldn't have it any other way. He told them the ugly ones had to stay out later because he couldn't stand looking at their faces in the daylight.

Together, the pair ducked under the awning of a secondhand store. A sign in the window said ANTIQUE PARLOR, but it was a junk shop, specializing in chipped dinner plates and broken table lamps. Rue took one last drag down to the filter and flicked her cigarette into the gutter, where a stream of water carried it and a string of French fries into the sewer. She was fat, and older than Finch. She'd dressed up her short brown hair with a garage-sale braid clipped to the back of her head, but the rain made the hairpiece stink like a wet dog. Rue yanked the braid off and stuffed it in the back pocket of her shorts. "Come on," Rue said. She set her umbrella down on the sidewalk, pulled another cigarette out of the pack tucked in her bra and lit up. "Let's pull the plug. I'm drownin' and so are you."

"I can't go yet," said Finch, using the bottom half of her pink tank top to wipe the water from her green eyes. The rain made her pale skin appear shiny and translucent, like the inside of a seashell.

She took a pull from Rue's cigarette and handed it back to her. "Gotta turn one more trick."

"Whatever you say, darlin'," Rue said. She slipped in and out of an accent that was vaguely southern. She handed Finch her yellow umbrella. It had a busted spoke and sagged at one end. "Don't lose it and don't get sick, or Sully'll beat your bony behind."

"What about you?" asked Finch. The ugly ones looked out for each other.

Rue spotted a rolled-up newspaper resting on the junk-shop stoop. She picked it up, unfurled it and held it over her head. "I'll make a run for the house," she said. Finch watched her go and smiled; the braid in Rue's back pocket looked like a tail.

As soon as Rue was out of sight, Finch folded up the umbrella.

2

The thing was useless. The rain had already soaked her through to her skin, and her long, red hair hung in heavy strands. She felt like she was wearing a wet mop on her head. On nights like this, she thought about slicing it off, getting a dyke cut like some of the other girls. Sully liked her hair and wouldn't allow it, said she'd be even homelier if she cut it. "Who'd want you then?"

He used to call her pretty. She sometimes wondered when she'd crossed the line. Had there been a particular day when she'd woken up suddenly ugly? Or had it been a gradual thing, like aging? Had there been a middle stage when she could have rescued her looks? Would her face have lasted longer on the farm, or faded even faster? It didn't matter. Now all she had was her hair and her breasts.

Sully had long red hair, too. He kept it pulled back in a ponytail to show off the diamond earrings that studded his lobes. When they were out together—buying condoms at the pharmacy or beer at the liquor store—people mistook them for siblings. She hated that but Sully got a kick out of it. Called her "Sis" and pinched her ass in public, and watched their faces.

If they'd seen what he did to her in private . . .

When they didn't bring home enough money or when they mouthed off to him or when he was drunk enough or high enough or feeling mean enough, Sully LePlante beat his whores with plastic clothes hangers. The white one was for the white women, the black one for the black women. He saved a special red hanger for Finch.

"To match your hair, baby," he said when he used it on her, and he used it on her a lot. Some of the other pros called her "Flinch" behind her back.

She hadn't yet met her quota for the evening and she wasn't anxious to feel the sting of that hanger against her buttocks and thighs, so she stayed on her corner after Rue and the other hookers had left.

Finch stepped off the curb and tried to make eye contact with the driver of a maroon station wagon. It sped by, kicking up a jet of water that barely missed her feet. Several minutes passed. A semi rumbled

3

up the street. She waved; he slowed and honked but didn't stop. Window-shopper. Two men in a pickup truck followed.

"Get off the street, you stupid cunt!" one of them hollered out the window. They steered into a puddle, splashed her legs and laughed.

A white van crossed the street. The front passenger-side window was missing. A plastic Target bag was taped over the opening. She recognized the car. Didn't waste her breath. They were from the neighborhood, and people from the neighborhood would like to run her over. Run all the pros over. She fiddled with the umbrella and popped it open again, for something to do.

She figured it was raining on the farm. Since it was June, the lilacs would be done. Her mother's pink peonies would be in full display, the dark green stems bending from the weight of the heavy flowers. She fingered the crucifix hanging around her neck, a Confirmation gift from her parents. Instead of throwing it away with the rest of her past, she clung to it like a drowning woman clutching a life ring. She never took it off, even when Sully complained that it spooked the johns. Like a thousand other nights, she thought back to the note she had left in her mother's sock drawer. Finch wondered if she should have left clean. No note. No nothing. Those three words. What good were they? They only kept her from ever going home again. Three words. Ten letters: "Dad raped me."

She saw another car coming down the nearly deserted road. One last john, she thought. One last trick.

He peered through the windshield of his black Chevy Suburban. The wipers struggled to keep up with the downpour. The car radio was tuned to a hard-rock station: Friday night, and a weekend of the Rolling Stones had started, kicking off with their *Exile on Main Street* album. He bobbed his head to "Tumbling Dice" and brushed a shock of hair from his eyes. *GQ* handsome, but with an angry edge. Whenever he entered a room, he looked as if he'd just come from an argument. He wasn't a wheat-colored blond with blue eyes. He was a winter blond: gray eyes and almost white hair. He favored dark or neutral clothes. Color photos of him looked identical to black-and-white ones.

He came to a red light and stopped. What was that noise? He turned down the radio and held his breath so he could hear it again. Buzzing. The fly was back. Damn. Deal with it, he told himself. Handle it. He inhaled deeply and gripped the steering wheel. The wedding band on his left hand bit into his flesh. He imagined he was wrapping his fingers around the submissive throat of a tiny woman. He exhaled. Slowly.

The light changed, but he didn't notice. The driver of the car behind him honked once and then pulled around to pass him. He snapped to attention and stepped on the gas. The St. Christopher medal and coach's whistle, both dangling from chains draped over his rearview mirror, swung wildly and smacked against the windshield. In the rear storage area of the big vehicle, a half dozen soccer balls bounced around.

Driving west toward the Minneapolis city line, he scanned the corners but found nothing on the drenched, darkening streets. He braked at a traffic light and looked to his right through the windows of a Burger King restaurant. Maybe they were inside, drying off and waiting for the downpour to let up. All he saw through the window was an old man in a T-shirt hunched over his coffee cup like a human question mark. The light changed. He drove on, searching.

"Jesus Christ," he muttered to himself, not in prayer but in frustration. He stopped himself. He looked at the religious medal hanging from his mirror. He knew the engraved words by heart: "St. Christopher, protect us." He wondered if he swore too much, then set aside his moment of Catholic guilt. His life was neatly compartmentalized and piety belonged in another box, to be opened later.

The buzzing again. He turned up the radio, let the guitar riffs drown it out.

He thought back to the accident of several weeks ago, in the spring. That's what it was, an accident. He had gotten too rough. If she hadn't liked it rough, Miss Accident, what was she doing hanging out in that

5

kind of bar? She had been a slut, anyway. Deserved it. Like that nurse in the incident during his fellowship. Miss Incident. Neither had been his fault, really. As long as it hadn't been deliberate, then there was nothing to confess. Nothing to reconcile. He was clean. Blameless.

Certainly he was usually more in control than he had been with those two, able to take things to a certain point and then pull back. Sometimes he miscalculated the boundaries of the women he laid, especially the bar pickups and the prostitutes. With strangers, you don't know how far you can take it. He always tried to ease them into it. He would start with a little rough handling. A couple of slaps. Some shoving. He'd grab their hair. Couldn't keep his hands off the hair. Before he was really satisfied the way he wanted to be satisfied, they were pulling on their clothes and sobbing or screaming at him.

"You sick bastard! What's your problem?!"

He laughed and repeated the question out loud: "What's your problem?"

Miss Accident and Miss Incident had gone beyond miscalculations. They'd died on nights when his life's problems had sent him spinning out of control. Miss Incident had been the night his father succumbed to cancer. Miss Accident happened after his wife miscarried his son. That same anxiety he'd felt those other two nights was working his gut now, but he didn't know why. There'd been no new train wrecks in his life, no new catastrophes. Yet for some reason, in the back of his throat, the coppery taste of adrenaline mixed with the smoky flavor of Scotch.

For some reason, the buzzing in his head was worse than ever.

The rain refused to let up. He was ready to quit the hunt and go home to his bottle of eighteen-year-old Macallan and forty-year-old wife. On any given day he far preferred the former to the latter. A bottle of single malt didn't whine or complain or ask where he was when he should have been coaching the kids' soccer game. It didn't demand to know why he hadn't come home all night or ask for explanations when

6

there were buttons missing from his shirt and mud on his shoes. Scotch didn't ask for much, save the occasional splash of water.

He was pulled from his whiskey reverie when something caught his eye. A flash of yellow, a beacon in the rain. She was soaking wet and the only thing more pathetic than her skimpy pink outfit was her broken umbrella. She was petite. He liked that. He could see her nipples under her saturated shirt. He liked that, too. She had hair that reached all the way down to the small of her back. He liked that best of all.

He navigated the Suburban to the curb and rolled down the front passenger-side window. Standing on her toes, she poked her head in, dripping water onto the leather interior. The last of her mascara was running down her cheeks in brown rivulets; they looked like muddy tears.

"Hey, baby, lookin' for a date?" she asked.

He hated hooker-speak. Why not call it what it is? How about the direct approach: "Hey, mister, want to pay me to wrap my mouth around your organ?" Or "Hey, big guy, I charge reasonable rates for sexual intercourse."

"Get in," he said flatly.

She folded the umbrella and shook it a bit. She jerked open the door, climbed in with a little hop and slammed it hard. He winced but said nothing as she leaned forward and squeezed water from the hem of her shirt onto the carpet. Like most whores, she looked prettier from the curb. Up close, he could see the freckles fighting the acne for space on her face. The pimples were winning. There were tired circles under her eyes and fine lines creeping across her forehead. By the time she hits forty, her face will need a lot of work, he thought. Still, she had fabulous, long hair.

Then he noticed the small crucifix around her neck. Catholic. It made him uneasy. She saw him staring at it and quickly tucked it under her tank top. She turned around in her seat and tossed the umbrella on the car floor behind her. She spotted the lab coat he had thrown on the backseat.

His jaw tightened as he watched her eying his name tag. Damn, he thought. He should have stuffed the coat under the seat before leaving work for his excursion.

"You a dentist or somethin'?" she asked.

"Or somethin'," he said.

He sounded snotty and sarcastic, and sarcastic customers made her feel stupid. She wanted a sharp comeback: "What's the *A* on your name tag stand for? Asshole?" She laughed.

He didn't like it at all. He was supposed to be in charge, piss her off, make her mad. The bitch was the one laughing. In a smooth move that was almost reflexive, he slapped her across the face with the back of his right hand.

She yelped. "What the fuck was that for?" she cried, holding her left cheek with her hand. He could see it was red, see the stripes from his fingers. Her skin marked easily, and that aroused him. He could also see she had her right hand on the door handle, ready to open it. He didn't want her to leave. Things were getting interesting.

"I'm sorry," he said, slipping into his best altar-boy face. "God, I don't know what got into me. I had a really bad day. Stay. Please stay."

He sounded genuine; the sarcastic snot was gone. She slid her right hand off the door handle and looked at him. She noticed how handsome he was, how well built. He had to be at least six feet tall. She guessed he was in his mid-forties. He smelled good. Clean. Most of her customers were paunchy old men who, on their best days, smelled like Old Spice and onion rings. Still, he had hit her. Only Sully could hit her. She straightened her back, sitting as tall as she could with her slight frame. "You had a bad day. Big deal. Join the fuckin' club. That's no reason to haul off and . . ."

"Look, let me make it up to you," he said, quickly interrupting her. "Whatever you usually charge, double it."

The rain was slowing. He pulled away from the curb, veered into the left lane and made a squealing U-turn around the concrete median and headed east, back toward downtown St. Paul.

"Hey, where're we goin'?" she asked, an edge of panic in her voice. "I've got a parkin' lot one street over."

"I want something more than a blow job," he told her. "Don't worry. I'll pay for it."

"Where are you takin' me?" she asked. She was frightened. She couldn't read this guy. Couldn't get past the pretty hair and eyes.

"What can I call you, anyway?" he asked, trying to lighten things up. "What's your nickname? Please don't tell me it's 'Red.'"

She laughed nervously. "Finch. That's what the other girls call me. Finch."

"Finch? Well, that suits you," he said, his voice smooth and soothing. "You are a delicate little bird."

"Okay," she said. She had to get down to business. "Where's the cash?" she asked. "I haven't seen any paper yet."

When he stopped for the next red light, he reached into the right pocket of his windbreaker and pulled out a money clip stuffed with folded fifties. He peeled off three of them and threw them on her wet thighs. "You'll get the other half when we're through," he said. "Okay, Finch?" She picked up the bills and paused with them in her hands. It looked like she was doing some adding in her head. Math probably wasn't her best subject in school, he thought sardonically.

She was mentally tallying what her total day's earnings would be with his contribution and dividing it by her hours on the street. The little game she played with herself made her feel better. She thought of herself as a contracted professional paid by the hour, as opposed to a common prostitute paid by the sexual act. "That's cool," she said, stuffing the bills into the pocket of her shorts. She leaned forward and turned up the radio volume.

They cut through downtown St. Paul and drove south across the Wabasha Bridge, crossing the Mississippi. They took a right after the bridge and passed a recreation area along the riverfront, following the Mississippi until they were in the thick of Lilydale Regional Park. "I don't like it here," she said. "It's too creepy." She told herself she'd messed up; it was too late to bail out. On one side of Lilydale Road were thick woods that ran along the river. On the other side were tree-covered bluffs dotted with caves, where teenagers partied all summer and homeless men hung out.

He pulled off the road, turning into a sandy clearing on the river. The rain had stopped. Some daylight was lingering. Without saying a word, he turned off the ignition, slipped the keys into his pants pocket and got out of the driver's seat. He slammed the door hard behind him. Finch sat for a minute, reassured herself he was tame— he wore a lab coat with a name tag, for God's sake—and followed him outside.

A lone picnic table in the middle of the clearing was covered with carved initials and messages. "Black Magic Woman 7-24-95." On one side of the clearing was a railroad bridge that crossed the river and snaked through the park. On the other side were four massive concrete pillars anchoring the tower of a high-voltage power line. Spray-painted in script on the pillars: "Well-cum to my garden! Black Magic Woman." Down a small hill that led to the river's edge, a decrepit fishing boat moored close to shore. The boat appeared dark and unoccupied. Across the Mississippi was an old power plant.

He was in back of the vehicle with the gate open, rifling around for something. Several soccer balls rolled out. He quickly picked them up and threw them back in. He pulled out a picnic blanket with wool on one side and waterproof canvas on the other. He shook off some cookie crumbs and laid it wool-side-up on the wet, sandy ground.

"Strip," he said.

"What?"

"Take off your clothes."

"It's your money," she said with a shrug. She kicked off her sandals, stepped into the middle of the blanket and started peeling off her damp tank top.

It had stopped raining and the heat had returned. He wiped sweat

10

from his forehead with the back of his jacket sleeve. He took off the jacket and tossed it on top of the picnic table, and then sat down at the table to watch her as she wrestled with the wet shirt. The straps were tangled in her hair.

"How 'bout giving me a hand here?" she asked.

He didn't answer or move. He watched. She pulled the shirt hard over her head. Her necklace flew off and landed on the ground at his feet. She didn't notice. He thought about picking it up for her, but didn't want to make the effort. He decided at that moment she was stupid and clumsy, and he didn't like stupid, clumsy people. She dropped her shirt in a wet knot on the blanket. He stared at her breasts. Small, he thought, but nicely shaped. He got up from the table and started toward her.

She was looking down to unzip her shorts when he slapped her so hard she thought his hand was a brick. She fell backward, stunned. She scrambled to her knees to get up and run, and he slapped her again and again. She couldn't catch her breath enough to scream. When she finally sprawled flat on her back, he leaned over her smiling, grabbed her by her hair and pulled her to her feet. He held her an arm's length away from him, by the hair on top of her head. For an instant she couldn't feel the ground; her toes swung in the air. She regained her footing and whipped her arms around like a cockeyed windmill, finally finding a voice to scream. "You son-of-a-bitch!" she shrieked.

He laughed. She couldn't believe he was laughing. She had been slapped around by johns before, but not like this, not with such perverted relish. "You goddamn sick bastard! Nut case! What in the fuck is your problem?"

"I knew you had a good fight in you," he said. "Redheads always do."

"Fuck you!" she said, and spat in his face. The spit was mixed with the blood oozing out of her nose and split lips. He didn't like being spat upon. Didn't like it at all. He pushed her backward onto the blanket and fell on top of her.

II

She screamed.

"Go ahead," he said. "Who'll hear you?"

She pulled her right arm out from under him, reached up and gouged his face with her nails. Deep, bleeding scratches. He didn't even grimace. He looked right through her, as if she didn't matter. She retreated to the one place she had left. She shut her eyes and started praying under her breath. "Our Father, who art in heaven, hallowed be thy name . . ."

This wasn't what he wanted to hear. This wasn't the time or the place for prayers. He wanted screams. Screams muffled the buzzing.

"Thy kingdom come, Thy will be done . . ."

The walls separating the different sections of his compartmentalized life were losing their structural integrity, threatening to collapse. He had to shore them up. Shut her up.

"Stop it!" he growled. "God doesn't give a damn about whores." He wrapped his right hand tightly around her throat and with his left, pulled down her shorts. He put his mouth to her ear:

"The fly shall marry the bumblebee," he whispered.

At the water's edge, in the waning daylight, another man watched through the fishing boat's porthole.

TWO

Paris Murphy rolled over with a groan and reached for the ringing cell phone, inadvertently knocking it off the nightstand. "Aww, man," she mumbled.

Under the bed and still ringing.

"Answer the phone," the naked man said into his pillow. He was sprawled out facedown, taking up three-quarters of the bed. At six-three, he couldn't help it.

It kept ringing. She stretched her arm down and felt around the floor with her fingertips.

"*Please* answer your fucking phone," he said.

The phone stopped ringing. She rolled back over to look at him. He's pretty damn gorgeous, she thought. Curly brown hair, broad shoulders, smooth back. Men don't realize how much women appreciate a nice back, she reflected.

The naked man flipped onto his back and opened his soulful brown eyes. "What if it's your mother? Do you want her to come knocking because she didn't get an answer? All we need is for her to find me here, screwing her daughter."

"Number one, my mother doesn't come knocking. She thinks my

house could sink and she doesn't know how to swim," Murphy said, running her fingers through her hair.

"And B, she would be thrilled if you and I . . ."

"You mean number two," he said, smiling and scratching his crotch.

"What?" she said, resting on her elbow.

"The last time I checked, babe, number two followed number one. B doesn't follow number one."

"I'm trying to make a point," Murphy said, laughing.

"That point would be?"

"That point would be that my mother would be thrilled to find out we're sleeping together," she said. "You *are* my husband."

"But we're supposed to be separated," he said, pushing her down and rolling over on top of her.

"This doesn't feel too separated to me," Murphy said. She gently raked his back with her nails.

"Give me a minute and I'll show you some real separation," he murmured, forcing her thighs apart with his knees. He kissed her. His tongue darted into her mouth.

The ringing resumed.

"That could be work. I'd better get it," she said, rolling him off her and getting out of bed to search for the insistent cell phone. She found it and sat naked on the edge of the bed to answer it. "Hello . . . Ah, man. Not Finch. Shit. Did anyone pick up LePlante on this? . . . No kidding? What time Friday?"

Her husband reached over from behind and cupped her left breast with his left hand.

"Damn it, stop it," she told him, putting her hand over the mouthpiece.

"Look, I'll be right down there," she said into the phone.

She set the cell phone on her nightstand and stood up.

"Have I told you lately how much I hate your job?" asked her husband as he lay back in bed.

"Not for at least five minutes," she said. She yawned, stretched her arms over her head and walked over to her dresser.

Murphy was tall for a woman, at five feet ten inches, but small boned, giving the illusion she was petite. She had a small waist and narrow hips, but larger than average breasts. She worried they made her look fat. They didn't. She carried herself like a hockey player. Quick. Graceful. Ready to slash. She never smiled at strangers. Most men kept their distance. Even though by her age—thirty-six, six years her husband's junior—most women need makeup, she didn't need a thing. Her eyes were almond-shaped and colored violet and framed by lashes so long and thick they looked fake. Her olive skin was a gift from her Lebanese mother, as was her long, black hair. She usually wrestled it into a ponytail behind her head for work, but sometimes, in her off-hours, let it go free.

There weren't too many off-hours for her—or her husband, an emergency-room doctor at a downtown hospital. They knew it was one of the many problems in their on again–off again marriage of eight years.

More ringing—

"That's *your* phone, Jack," she told her husband. She pulled a pair of panties out of her dresser drawer and stepped into them.

He groaned and reached over to the nightstand on his side of the bed, and picked up a cell phone. "Jack Ramier here."

Murphy always liked the way that sounded. "Ramier here." She smiled to herself. God, she missed having him around regularly, especially at night.

"Yes . . . yes," he said into his cell phone. "No. No. Don't worry about it. It's not a problem," he said, smiling at his wife. He put down his cell phone.

"I thought you weren't on call this weekend," she said. She scanned the floor for her jeans. They were under the bed. She pulled them out, shook off the dust balls and wiggled into them.

"I'm not, but they need some extra help in the E.R. They're stacked up in the hallway like firewood," he said. His clothes were folded in a neat pile on the nightstand. He sat naked on the edge of his side of the bed and pulled on his socks.

Mr. Methodical, she mused, starting from the bottom and working his way up. That's how he did everything. It drove her nuts. She wished he'd put his baseball cap on first. Just once. For variety.

"It must have been one hell of a Friday night around town last night," he continued, slipping into his boxers. "What's your Saturday-morning mayhem, my desert flower?"

She loved it when he called her that, even though his tongue was firmly planted in his cheek.

"I've got a dead hooker," she said distractedly as she rifled around in her dresser drawer for a bra. Her own insensitivity gave her pause. She didn't like it when the job did that to her. She didn't want to be another prickly homicide cop. Too many of those already.

"Knew her?"

"Yeah. Wisconsin girl," Murphy said. "Sexually abused as a kid. Ran away. Ended up on the street."

"Ended up dead," said Jack.

"Yeah," said Murphy. "Ended up dead."

"How about dinner back here, tonight?" Murphy asked, as they walked down to their cars.

They stopped in the parking lot. She looked down and dug in her purse for her car keys; she didn't want him to see her face when he answered. A "Yes" wouldn't necessarily mean much of anything, other than that he missed her cooking. A "No" would speak volumes.

"Absolutely," he said. He opened his car door and slid into his silver BMW. "I'll bring some champagne."

She looked up and smiled. An "absolutely" accompanied by champagne was very promising.

"Meet you back here at six," he said. He smiled back at her and pulled on his baseball cap.

"Here" was her floating home, a houseboat moored on the

Mississippi below the Wabasha Bridge, across the river from downtown St. Paul. She'd bought it after she and Ramier had split the first time. He kept the Dutch Colonial they had purchased together in St. Paul's Macalester-Groveland neighborhood. She'd hated cutting the grass and doing routine home maintenance, but what he didn't know was that she would mow a football field now to have him back. The riverfront had its charms, but it couldn't match the heat of his arms and legs wrapped around her at night.

The riverfront also had its dangers, as poor Finch had discovered Friday night, Murphy thought as she rolled down Lilydale Road in her Jeep Grand Cherokee. She snapped on the radio. Her favorite rock station was playing some old Rolling Stones tune. "Let's Spend the Night Together." She flicked it off impatiently. She hated the Rolling Stones.

Snaky Swanson curled up in the bowels of the fishing boat and wept. When he went off his Risperdal, he imagined snakes were following him. These were not ordinary snakes. Schizophrenics rarely suffer from dull delusions. They sang, read poetry—William Blake—and when the St. Paul Saints were at home, delivered play-by-plays of the baseball game. This wasn't always a bad thing. Sometimes Swanson found his slithering pals good company. They could be entertaining and even made him laugh out loud on occasion with their dry, reptilian wit. He found their observations on the human condition to be insightful. Mostly he found the snakes annoying, however, and so stayed on his antipsychotic medicine as well as he could while living on the streets. The Risperdal made him tired, a problem when you're moving from one home under a bridge to another. Sometimes he started doing so well he forgot why he was taking the medication, and stopped.

He had been taking it lately, however, and that was why he was weeping. He was perfectly sane and healthy, and clearly remembered that the night before, he had watched a man murder a woman along the shore. He had been too terrified to do anything, even yell, as he peeked through a grimy porthole. He felt weak and vulnerable himself and was certain if he tried to stop the killer, he would be the next victim. All he could do was watch while the woman tried to fend off her attacker, her skinny white arms thrashing. When she screamed, he covered his ears. He hardly slept that night, feeling guilty for his inability to help.

Come dawn, he heard a train screeching to an emergency stop. Not much later, sirens. He looked through the porthole. A lone train engineer standing over the white, waxy figure on the ground. It wouldn't be long before the cops would arrive, swarming around the body and the riverfront like blue vultures. They'd find him on the boat and blame him. At the very least, he had done nothing to save her, and he was trespassing to boot. He could be arrested and thrown in a jail cell, and he didn't like sharing such close quarters with his slithering friends.

"What am I gonna do? What am I gonna do? Oh, God, help me!" he whispered to himself. He wrapped his arms around his backpack as he continued to watch through the window and listen to the sirens. Louder, closer. Finally the engineer turned to take the steps back up to the train. That was his chance. Swanson threw his backpack over his shoulder. He slipped into the brown water, waded the short distance to shore and ran into the woods.

He had one person in the world he could trust with his secret, and he wasn't sure it was her weekend to work at the soup kitchen.

Four squad cars and a hearse from the medical examiner's office blocked the dirt turnoff leading to the murder site. Beyond them were vans with call letters belonging to three television news stations and behind them was the beat-up Ford F150 pickup truck belonging to the *Pioneer Press* police reporter. No company name or logo decorated the sides of the cop reporter's truck—it was his own—but a bumper sticker clearly reflected the owner's attitude: SOME PEOPLE ARE ALIVE ONLY BECAUSE IT'S AGAINST THE LAW TO KILL THEM. Murphy pulled up behind the truck and dodged the television cameras and reporters. Two uniformed patrolmen were keeping them on the paved road, away from the dirt turnoff. A television news helicopter hovered overhead.

"Hey, Murphy?" hollered the newspaper reporter, a tall man in his late twenties with a shoulder-length brown mop and John Lennon eyeglasses. "Who creamed the dairy queen?"

"Lose the attitude, Cody," Murphy said as she brushed past him. He was dressed in his usual Hawaiian shirt and jeans.

The murder scene was deceptively festive in its yellow color scheme. Yellow police tape was staked around the body, a crime-scene photographer in a yellow polo shirt snapped pictures, all pulled together by a yellow Union Pacific train stopped on the railroad bridge at the side of the clearing. A glum train engineer sat in the middle of the steps spanning the twenty feet from the railroad bridge to the ground below. Erik Mason, an investigator for the medical examiner's office, was talking to a couple of uniformed patrolmen. Evans Bergen, the night guy in homicide, was standing around with his hands in his pockets. Murphy thought he was a worthless turd. He was the master of under-time—got to work late and left early. He was young, short and had blond hair that was already thinning on top.

Then there was the body itself. Finch was on her back on a plaid wool blanket. Her face was battered and bruises dotted her throat. On the blanket next to her was her tank top, and on the ground next to the blanket were her sandals. Her shorts and panties were tangled around one leg. A wad of bills was sticking out of her pocket.

"Finch," said Murphy, carefully stepping over the police tape. She crouched down to get a better look at the hooker's body. Mason started toward her. "Semen?" Murphy asked, without looking up.

"Yup," said Mason.

"Hair?"

"Got some."

"Skin?"

19

"Loads of it. She clawed a good chunk out of him."

"Good," she said.

"We'll give her a full workup," Mason said. He was a tall, athletic-looking man in his late thirties with short, walnut brown hair and hazel eyes. Like Murphy, he was a runner. She hadn't worked with him for a while and she was glad. He attracted her and she didn't need that. He drove a sapphire XK8 Jaguar convertible, a $75,000 car. Rumor was that he bet the horses.

"It won't take a forensic genius to figure this out," said Murphy, standing up.

Bergen walked over. "Why does the media give a crap about this case?" he asked, nodding toward the road where the crowd was gathered. "Since when do they give a damn about a dead whore?"

Murphy cringed. To be reduced at life's end to two hard words, *dead whore*, was cruel. "Finch tried to leave the life," said Murphy. "The newspaper did a profile of her. She grew up on a dairy farm. She even won a beauty pageant."

"Bergen says her pimp has an airtight alibi," Mason said, peeling off his latex gloves as a couple of other staff from the M.E.'s office started loading Finch into a body bag.

"Yeah," said Murphy. "Airtight." LePlante had been in a bar on West Seventh Street most of Friday afternoon, shooting pool and boozing it up. He cracked a cue over another drunk's head and spent the night in detox. He was still sleeping it off Saturday morning. "He doesn't even know Finch is dead, not that the sleazebag would give a rat's ass one way or the other," Murphy said. She looked over at the M.E.'s staff guys as they pulled a bag over Finch.

"Hey—wait!" she yelled. "What the hell?"

She knelt on the ground next to the bag and carefully lifted Finch's head.

"What's wrong?" asked Mason. He crouched down next to Murphy.

"Finch never cut her hair. That asshole, Sully, wouldn't let her. Ever," said Murphy. "I saw her on the street a couple of days ago.

She was bitching about how this hot spell was miserable with long hair."

"So?"

"So someone gave her a pretty shitty haircut." She turned Finch's head so Mason could see that a wide section of the young woman's long red hair had been sloppily chopped from the back of her head.

"Now *that* is weird," said Bergen, looking down with his hands still in his pockets. "Hair fetish?"

"I'd say so," Murphy said.

Mason stood up. "I'll give you a call when I have something. You'll be out on the street all day?"

"Yeah. I have to talk to some of the other ladies," said Murphy, setting Finch's head back down. "I'll give you my cell-phone number."

She stood up and looked around the immediate area. She'd have some people sweep it, but it wasn't very promising. This ratty part of Lilydale was especially isolated. When she was a uniform, she'd occasionally come across a teenage couple pulled into the clearing. Busted up a kegger along the shore here once. She looked down the small hill to the river. The power plant and the fishing boat were possibilities. Street people set up camp anywhere they could.

Bergen shuffled next to her. "Need anything from me?" he asked. "I want to file my end of the paperwork and hit the road."

"Go," Murphy said, waving him away. "I'm on it."

THREE

Dr. A. Romann Michaels used his hands to wipe the steam from the mirror. He was damp and pink after a few Saturday-morning laps in the pool and a long, hot shower. He still had a slight headache. Nothing too serious. He'd had much worse, and he had something to take care of it. He took a drink of Scotch and shuddered. Hair of the dog. He set the glass down on the bathroom counter and leaned closer to the mirror. "Bitch," he said. He ran his fingers lightly over the scratches on his left cheek and glumly studied the three red stripes. They were deep and wouldn't fade quickly.

He needed a story for his family.

His two girls were attending a soccer camp in Denmark, and his wife had decided to stay longer at their Lake Superior cabin. The two of them had just spent a week there, joined by the queen mother. The entire vacation was an unpleasant haze. He couldn't stand being alone with the two of them for such a long stretch, even with Scotch as a buffer, so he'd driven back early. Work was a good excuse. Plus he did have a soccer tournament coming up. As the coach, he had to show up whether his daughters were around to play or not.

As far as the clinic was concerned, he'd come up with something by Monday to satisfy his gossipy staff. He could tell them he'd taken a spill into some bushes while biking. Something like that.

More bothersome than the scratches was the burning knot in the pit of his belly. Things had gotten out of hand last night. He was sure no one had seen the girl and the park would be empty by dusk. Despite being drunk, he still had managed to collect his souvenir. He had to wash her hair, of course. God knows what kinds of things could be crawling around in it.

"What's your problem?" he asked himself in the mirror. "Hell, what problem? I don't have any problem." Then, more honestly, "Maybe a couple."

He slipped the red hair out of the plastic bag.

Michaels's problems, like nearly everyone's problems, could be conveniently blamed on crappy parents.

His parents were rich.

He'd played on the lawn of a Summit Avenue mansion that had been in his mother's family for two generations and eventually passed on to him. The place was a rambling 1880s Queen Anne with a high-pitched roof and gables, turrets and towers. A greenhouse squatted on the east side, a sleeping porch on the west and a swimming pool in the basement. The house was in a neighborhood bordered by two Catholic colleges and sprinkled with churches. He and his parents walked to mass together on Sundays, strolling past other historic Victorian homes.

He was an only child and his mother and father lavished *things* on him. A massive train set complete with a miniature Bavarian town, a hand-carved rocking horse imported from Italy, radio-controlled cars and boats and chemistry sets. Private French instruction, private fencing lessons, private tennis classes, private everything. He attended Catholic elementary and prep schools in Minneapolis and plush summer camps in northern Minnesota.

He wanted for nothing, except sane parents. Behind the wrought-iron fence, behind the leaded-glass windows, behind the Irish lace curtains, the banker and his pious wife fought like demented dogs.

As a boy, he would sit watching as his father and mother hurled insults and objects at each other. He learned to study the level of Scotch in their glasses to anticipate the severity and duration of the evening's fight. They drank out of tumblers with painted pheasants on the side—funny how those fragile items were always spared in his parents' mad scramble for ammunition—and when the booze covered the hen resting on the ground, it would be a brief battle. When the whiskey reached as high as the cock in flight, the boy knew it was time to take cover behind the couch. They would slap and punch each other, scratch and claw, kick and flee to opposite corners like spiteful children. The banker usually won. He once dragged his wife all the way up the stairs to their second-floor bedroom by her long, golden, beautiful hair. The son loved his mother's hair.

Their battles always ended in the bedroom, finishing the fight with a good fuck. They never shut the bedroom door.

Michaels coped. When he was very young, he saw a television report about a girl who fell down an old well. Her playmates ran for help, leaving her alone. The girl said she wasn't afraid until she looked up and saw daylight beyond her reach, so she stopped looking up. She imagined she was sitting in a cardboard box in her bedroom. He'd admired the girl's survival technique and, as it turned out, spent his life using it himself. As long as he didn't look up and see the daylight, as long as he properly boxed his life and compartmentalized his world, he could keep everything under control.

When he was a child he looked up from the hole at times, and it made him envious and angry. Once he was sitting in the backseat of the car after a dinner party. His father was driving, half in the bag and yelling at his mother. His mother was drunk and crying. They were at a stoplight in downtown St. Paul. It was winter and snowing. A family was standing outside the bus depot—mom, dad, three kids. Each carried a suitcase held shut with twine. They were laughing; he wanted to be them.

The older he got, the more Michaels isolated himself. He didn't go to other kids' houses because their families were normal. He didn't bring friends home. He stayed on the fringes of social circles at school. His only playmates were his cousins—most of them had equally screwed-up families. He participated in sports that emphasized individual events; he was not a team player.

He decided to braid the red hair before he washed it so that loose strands wouldn't be lost down the drain. That would be wasteful. He fished a rubber band out of one of the bathroom drawers and wrapped the band around one end of the twist of hair. Then he carefully separated three sections and started braiding. The work relaxed him. Calmed his nerves. He used to help his mother brush and braid her hair. In her sober moments—she used up most of them when he was young—she held him on her lap and let him play with her long braid while she read nursery rhymes:

"Fiddle-de-dee, fiddle-de-dee,
The fly shall marry the bumblebee.
They went to church and married was she.
The fly has married the bumblebee."

He and his mother laughed over that one. She nicknamed him Buzzy and he called her Bee. He imagined he was a fly walking down the aisle in a tuxedo, with a bee bride on his skinny fly arm. Sometimes the bee had his mother's face and hair. Sometimes it looked like his favorite cousin. The one from Iowa. A little younger than he. Long blond hair and gray eyes like his. She'd let him play with her hair, wash it, braid it, tie ribbons in it. She was the only other person who called him Buzzy. She liked the rhyme. His daughters used to like it too, but they pushed him away as they got older. Said they were too old for nursery rhymes. Too old to let him do their hair.

Despite the drinking and the fighting he could have turned out normal, or a little screwed up the way most people are a little screwed up. But then she killed herself, Bee did. Michaels blamed himself. He thought he should have said yes. The fly should have married the bumblebee.

He was a junior in high school. He had gotten home late from swim practice, the smell of chlorine still hanging in his hair. Michaels found her in his bedroom, sitting on his bed with one of his childhood books. The nursery rhymes. "Buzzy, come sit on Bee's lap," his mother said. His father had slapped her around and then left to find a hooker, something he'd been doing more and more. The boy had heard his father tell his mother she wasn't pretty anymore. Her face was puffy. Her figure was gone. Her hair had thinned. Her beautiful hair.

"Buzzy," she said, patting the mattress. "Come." He stood in the doorway and stared. One sleeve of her dress was torn and hanging by a thread on her shoulder. Blood oozed out of the corner of her mouth. Her lipstick was smeared around her upper lip like a pink moustache. His father had really done a number on her this time. The boy walked into the room. She smelled like Scotch. She was lit. Of course.

He stepped closer. "Mom . . ."

"No. Bee," she said.

"Bee, maybe you should go to your own . . ." Before he could finish, she pulled him down next to her and kissed him on the mouth. Lipstick and blood and whiskey. He felt like vomiting. She pushed him down onto the bed and crawled on top of him. His mother's soft form pressed him against the mattress. Repulsion and panic locked his limbs. He shut his eyes, opened them again and rolled her off him. "Jesus Christ!" he yelled, bolting up from the bed.

"Don't swear," she said drunkenly. "It's a sin."

"A sin? You're coming on to me and you're worried about my swearing. You're fucking nuts."

"No, Buzzy." She sat up and grabbed his wrist with both hands, trying to pull him back onto the bed. He wrestled his arm away from her, drew it back and slapped her. She fell back on the mattress, crying.

He ran out of the house, his face hot and red with rage and shame. He drove to the side of town where he expected to find his father cruising the streets, and instead found his first hooker. He didn't kill her, but he beat the hell out of her and got away with it. That made him feel better. More in control.

When he got home early the next morning, four police cars and an ambulance were in front of the house. The neighbors stood watching on the sidewalk and in the street. Michaels's father sat on the front steps, his arms wrapped around his bowed head as her body was carried out on a stretcher. The garbage man had found her floating facedown in the backyard pool. She'd emptied a medicine cabinet into her stomach.

Michaels never told anyone what had happened the night before.

His father filled in the backyard swimming pool.

When he got to the bottom of the red braid, he took another rubber band and wrapped it tightly around that end. He filled the bathroom sink with warm water and opened the cupboard below to look for shampoo. A tangle of curling wands and electric hair rollers fell out, a reminder that his oldest daughter had staked a claim to the hallway bathroom in an annoying burst of adolescent independence. They had long blond hair, his daughters did, and had strict standing orders from him never to cut it short. He didn't give a damn about what they wanted. His wife got a short haircut once and it made her look like a lesbian, he thought. It had sent him into a rage. Jennifer's long blond tresses were the best part of her, the only part he could tolerate. She grew it back, promised never to cut it again.

He squirted a dab of shampoo into the sink, swished it with his fingers and gently turned the red braid around in the sudsy water. He rinsed it under the tap and patted it dry with a towel. He picked it up and sniffed. It smelled nice and clean. He rubbed the braid against his cheek. So silky. He shut his eyes, cradled the braid in one hand and stroked it with the other. Michaels thought about the redheaded whore. She had gotten to him. Her crucifix startled him, and her desperate recitation of the Lord's Prayer almost stopped him. Almost. Something about her was gnawing at him in an unfamiliar way. What was he feeling? Was it genuine remorse or simply fear of getting caught? Isn't guilt some awkward combination of the two? Is it immoral when there is too much of the latter and not enough of the former? Is one emotion worth a trip to the confessional and the other not?

He'd have to think about it. He set the braid down and took another drink of Scotch. He noticed a strand of red hair caught under his wedding band. He pulled off the hair and tossed it in the toilet. The ring had never felt comfortable on him in all his years of marriage. It seemed too tight, binding. Such a nuisance and so meaningless, he thought. He soaped his hands with a squirt of the shampoo. He twisted and pulled until the band came off. He held his wedding ring in the palm of his right hand for a moment, reflecting on its weight and shape and color. A simple gold circle. It felt light in his hand. Insubstantial. Like his marriage.

He set his ring down on the counter and caught his image in the mirror, the wild-eyed naked man staring back at him. "What's your problem?" he said.

He waited for an answer.

"No, seriously, I really want to know!" he shouted. "What is your problem?"

He threw the last bit of Scotch into the face of the angry man. The amber liquid ran down the mirror like dirty tears. A whore's tears. He found the image disturbing. He filled the empty glass from the tap and hurled some water at the dripping Scotch. It fell short of the mirror and splashed all over the counter. "Pathetic," he mumbled. He filled it again and threw the water harder. The glass flew out of his hand and struck the mirror, shattering it.

Now I have to think up a story for this as well, he thought.

He tucked the braid into a fresh Ziploc bag. He sealed it shut part-way, squeezed the air out by pressing it against his chest and zipped it the rest of the way. Still naked, he tiptoed around the broken bits of mirror on the bathroom floor, walked down the hallway to the attic stairway, and up.

Treading barefoot on the wood floor, Michaels navigated his way around a rocking chair and an end table. Though it was morning, it was already warm in the attic. His feet left damp prints that quickly evaporated and disappeared in the heat. He bumped into a child's red bicycle, knocking it over. His old bike. He bent over and picked it up. There were still playing cards in the spokes. He squeezed the bike horn. Nothing. He was disappointed. He glanced at the collection of ancestral portraits stacked against a large trunk and steered clear of an unsteady-looking tower of coffee-table books. "We need to get rid of some of this shit," he muttered under his breath.

He stared wistfully for a moment at an infant's highchair. The back of the seat was decorated with the crooked decal of a clown holding a bunch of balloons. He remembered when his older daughter, as a toddler, had sloppily plastered the sticker on the chair to surprise her younger sister. Now the edges were peeling. He tried to press them flat but they curled back up.

Small windows at each end of the attic let in the morning light and illuminated the dust hanging in the musty air, making it look like a swarm of fireflies.

From a corner laced with cobwebs, he pulled out a Victorian hatbox decorated with roses and violets. Cherubs danced among the blooms.

He lifted the cover and placed the bag of hair inside, next to the other bags of hair.

FOUR

"Jesus!" Rue said in a muffled voice as she breathed in and out of the lunch bag. There were greasy stains on it. "What is this?"

"Liverwurst and Miracle Whip," Murphy told her. "That's what he eats every other day. Liverwurst and Miracle Whip."

Rue looked at the way Murphy's partner bit into the sandwich and laughed. The bag expanded with the expulsion of air. She pulled the bag away from her face and wiped her eyes with her hands, smearing dark mascara under them; she looked like a raccoon. She felt the back of her head to make sure her braid was still clipped in place. Rue took her lit cigarette back from Murphy and puffed, trying to compose herself as much as a hooker can with two cops questioning her.

The owner of the lunch bag, Gabriel Nash, took another bite of his warm, aromatic sandwich. He had thirty years on the force and two clean kills; he'd been shot once himself, in the shoulder. Murphy trusted him with her life, but not with a hooker's feelings. She waved her partner over. They backed against the hood of Gabe's rusty Volvo station wagon, which was parked in front of an adult video store. For some reason, observed Murphy, the Volvo looked as if it belonged there.

"I told you not to yell at her," Murphy said.

"Big deal. I raised my voice. What the hell did she get so worked up for?" Gabe asked. He looked over at the hooker. She was sniffling and tugging nervously at her black shirt. The top was too tight and too short, and revealed a doughy, white expanse of midriff.

"I don't want to tell you how to do your job, Gabe, but you don't seem to get it," Murphy said in a low voice. "Rue needs a soft touch."

"Oh, pardon me. A sensitive hooker. That's a good one. What kind of name is Rue, anyway?""

"Charlene cooked it up herself," said Murphy. "Sully told her she needed a street name, so she came up with Rue. It's French for street."

"Pretty fucking cute. What's up with the ratty hairpiece?"

"The braid? She got a couple of them from a garage sale," said Murphy. "When she wears them both at the same time she looks like Heidi. Maybe you should compliment her on it."

"Nah," said Gabe. "It looks like shit and it doesn't match the rest of her hair. Who the hell is Heidi?"

Murphy sighed.

One of Rue's Saturday regulars pulled up to the curb behind the Volvo. He was a fat man wearing a red polka-dot tie with a short-sleeved white shirt. The top of his head was bald and red from the sun, but gray hair the texture of steel wool stuck out at the sides. He was driving a yellow Cobra convertible, with the top down—like a circus clown who got lost looking for the Big Top.

"Hey, Charlene?" he yelled from the car. He was drunk and slurring his words. "Is this a fuckin' bakery line, or what?"

"Get lost, asshole." Gabe took another bite of his sandwich. The driver looked at him and rolled away.

Murphy pulled some tissues out of her shoulder bag and walked over to Rue. "Your mascara is all over the place, Charlene." The hooker threw down her cigarette and took the tissues, dabbing her eyes with them. "Okay, Charlene," said Murphy, "what were you saying about this yellow umbrella?"

Rue said nothing but continued fussing with her face. She extracted a small mirror and a mascara wand from the pocket of her skirt and applied a stroke or two of mascara to her eyelashes.

"Forget the umbrella!" said Gabe, his voice rising. He wiped his mouth with the sleeve of his sweatshirt and walked over to Murphy and Rue. "Did you recognize Finch's last trick? What kind of car was he driving?"

Rue opened her mouth to answer, but nothing came out. Her eyes were starting to tear up again. She dabbed at them with the tissue. Murphy gave Gabe the eye. "Okay, okay. I'm sorry I yelled," he said to Rue. "Now tell us about Finch and the goddamn umbrella."

"I didn't want her to get sick from the rain. We watched out for each other. We had the same birthday. Did ya know that? We were both born on Christmas Eve. I'm quite a few years older than Finch. I looked younger than her, though, 'cause I have such fine skin. Finch had pimples, poor darlin'. She wouldn't mind me tellin' ya that, God rest her soul." Rue quickly made the Sign of the Cross.

"Okay," said Murphy. "So the last time you saw Finch alive, she was standing alone in the rain on her usual corner . . ."

"*Our* usual corner," interrupted Rue.

"She was standing alone in the rain on the usual corner you two shared, and she was holding your yellow umbrella," Murphy continued. "Is that right?"

Rue nodded her head again.

"You didn't see her get in any car or go with any john?" Murphy asked. "Is that right?"

More nodding.

"All the other working gals had turned in for the evening?" asked Gabe.

"Except for me," said Rue.

"Do you remember about what time that was?" Murphy asked patiently, as if questioning a frightened child. "Was it nighttime? Was it dark out yet?"

"No, it was gettin' there, but it wasn't dark yet," said Rue. She pulled a cigarette from the pack stuffed in her shirt. "Now I told ya everythin' I know," she said, lighting up with shaking hands. "Can I go now? Please? It won't do my business no good if I'm seen talkin' to you two. No offense, darlin'."

Rue turned to walk away. "Charlene," said Gabe.

"Yes, Sergeant," she said, turning around.

"You dropped your hair," he said, pointing down. Rue bent over and picked the brown braid off the sidewalk. She clipped it back on and gave it a little tug to make sure it was secure. "It looks very nice on you," said Gabe.

Murphy usually worked alone because it was in her nature. She felt comfortable around men, but also felt hemmed in by them. She had grown up a middle child in a house with ten kids; she was the only daughter. Her parents owned a bar on the Mississippi that catered to barge workers. They made enough to pay the bills, but a big house was out of the question. The boys slept two or three to a bedroom. So she could have her own space, she dragged her mattress into the root cellar and claimed it as her room; her brothers called her "Potato Head." The day after she graduated from high school, she moved into an efficiency apartment. All through college at the University of Minnesota, she worked at two jobs so she could squeak by without a roommate. The solitude was glorious. Even during her marriage, she insisted that she have a room of her own—a small library filled with dozens of cookbooks.

As a patrol officer, she drove alone. As a vice cop, she walked among the hookers and johns by herself. Now as a homicide investigator, she almost always worked solo. The other cops thought she was spooky for wanting to work alone, but not Gabe. He'd known her half her life. He'd watched her handle rowdies at the family bar and talked her into police work. So when the head of homicide asked her to team up with somebody on this very visible case, she recruited Gabe.

*　*　*

33

"What have we got? We've got a girl standing alone on a street corner in the rain," Gabe said as they drove back to the cop shop in Gabe's Volvo. The car was a wreck. The mustard yellow leather seats were grimy, apple cores and empty pop cans rolled around on the floor, and the air conditioning was out. It smelled of cigarette smoke. All the knobs for the radio were missing; Gabe used a pair of pliers to work the controls. The front passenger seat leaned so far back, Murphy felt like she was in a reclining chair.

"We've got more than that," said Murphy, struggling to sit up straight despite the reclining seat. "We've got a girl standing alone on a street corner in the rain, holding a yellow umbrella."

"Jack shit," said Gabe, scratching his gray head. "And Jack hopped the last train outta town."

"Look, we didn't find the umbrella with the body. Right? So where is it? Find the yellow umbrella and maybe we have the killer."

"Yeah, and maybe we find the yellow umbrella and all we have is the yellow umbrella," said Gabe. "Maybe she dropped it on the street when he grabbed her, and somebody else picked it up." At a light, he reached into his pants pocket and pulled out some smokes.

"Thought you were trying to quit," Murphy said.

"Want to finish this pack," he said, lighting up. He took a long pull and blew it out the window.

Murphy opened her mouth for her "you're going to have a fucking heart attack" speech when her cell phone rang. She fished it out of her purse and leaned back to talk, abandoning her efforts to sit up in the broken seat. "Murphy . . . Yeah? Okay, we'll run over there. Ask Sister to keep an eye on him. He has a snake thing going on and if they start bugging him, he'll take off. Okay? . . . Yeah! . . . Snakes." She shoved the cell phone back in her purse.

"Snakes?" Gabe asked.

"Over to Sister Soup," she said.

"I am not a snake fan," he said.

* * *

Snaky Swanson was sitting alone at one end of a cafeteria table wolfing down a steaming plate of mashed potatoes and gravy. The potatoes were piled so high, they resembled a grade-school science project on volcanoes, with gravy lava running down the sides. Snaky looked like an end-up dust mop, with hair he kept tied into a ponytail with a shoestring. His jeans were filled with holes and he wore an army-surplus jacket with some other guy's name sewn on the front pocket. He kept his backpack on his lap under the table while he ate, occasionally touching the backpack with his free hand to make sure it was still there. He was twenty, but could have passed for fifty. His beard was streaked with gravy.

"Eats potatoes," said Sister Ella Marie DuBois, a petite black woman who met Gabe and Murphy at the door. She was wiping her hands on her white apron. It covered the simple navy blue, knee-length dress that served as her religious order's habit. Instead of a nun's veil, a cook's hair net covered her close-cropped gray-and-black hair.

"How's the snake situation?" asked Murphy.

"Under control," said DuBois, looking back at Swanson's table with her hands on her hips. "He's terrified this man is going to come after him."

"He taking his meds?" asked Murphy.

"Yes," said the nun. "I think he saw what he says he did."

"Thanks," Murphy said. The two detectives walked over to the table.

"I'm not going to go to jail, am I?" asked Swanson, looking up from his plate and wiping his mouth with his hand.

"Why the hell would you be going to jail?" asked Gabe, taking a seat on one side of Swanson. Gabe wrinkled his nose and leaned away from Swanson. He reeked of urine and mildew, like a parking-ramp stairwell. Murphy took a seat across from them.

"I didn't help her," Swanson muttered. "I didn't help her." He dropped his spoon and covered his face with his hands. DuBois walked over and put her hand on his shoulder.

"Samuel, you are not going to jail," said Murphy. "You couldn't have gotten to her in time to help her."

"I could have yelled," Swanson said, looking up. "I could have yelled. I could have yelled. I was afraid."

"That's cool, being afraid," Gabe said. "This freak *should've* scared you. He'd scare me."

"So, Samuel—what'd you see?" Murphy asked. "Was it only the one guy?"

"Yeah, one guy," Snaky said. "A white guy. Big. With blond hair."

"Long? Short? Curly?" asked Gabe.

"Short. Straight."

"Keep going," said Murphy.

"He drove a black car. One of those SUVs."

"Rust on the sides? Any big dings or dents? Busted lights? Busted-out windows?" Gabe asked.

"New," Snaky said positively. "Loaded."

"Did you see the license plate?" Murphy asked.

Swanson shook his mop head.

"Even a couple of letters or numbers?" she asked.

"I wasn't close enough, and it was getting dark."

"Anything weird about his face? Big nose, scar, anything?" she said.

"I told you!" Swanson said, anxious again. "I wasn't that close and . . ."

"Okay, okay," said Gabe.

"He had a jacket on, but he took it off."

"Color?" she asked.

"Light brown, beige, something like that."

"Good," said Murphy. "That's good. Any other details about the car or the man that you could see from the boat? Can you think of anything else that might help us find this bastard?"

Swanson frowned, concentrating. "Soccer. When this guy opened his Suburban, a bunch of soccer balls rolled out the back."

*   *   *

"Here's what we've got," said Murphy, as she and Gabe drove to the cop shop. Gabe was steering with one hand and trying to adjust the car-radio volume with the other. The pliers kept slipping, causing the radio to suddenly blare or go silent. "Would you quit messing around with the radio and listen to me?"

He dropped the pliers.

"Here's what we've got," said Murphy. "A white guy who drives a black Suburban and coaches soccer. A family man. He probably makes a good living—Suburbans ain't cheap."

"Motive?" asked Gabe.

She thought for a moment. "He's crazier than shit?"

"Works for me," Gabe said.

Murphy's cell phone rang as they were pulling into the police head-quarters parking lot. "Yeah, Murphy . . . Okay. We'll be waiting. I just pulled into the cop shop with Gabe . . . Yeah, he's still an asshole." Gabe gave the phone the finger. Murphy smiled and continued. ". . . I can't tonight. Let me take a rain check on that. Thanks. Later." Murphy shoved the cell phone back into her purse.

"Erik said Finch's hair was cut with a very sharp tool," Murphy said as they got out of the car. "He found a nick on the back of her neck near the hairline."

"So what are we dealing with? A mad barber? A crazed stylist?"

"Maybe not," said Murphy. "Erik said it was probably a scalpel."

"Good," said Gabe. "A whacked-out surgeon. I'd hate to think it was someone stupid who we could catch."

As they stood together in the dusty parking lot, the sound of week-end traffic droned from the nearby freeways. Gabe reached into his pocket and pulled out his pack of Winstons.

"How many left in that pack?" she asked.

"Not enough," he said.

"I've got three ideas on how we can find this guy," said Murphy, rummaging around in her purse for her car keys. When she didn't want to wear a belt or shoulder rig, the purse was also her holster, and carried a .40 caliber Glock Model 23 in a special sleeve.

"Number one, we might want to scope out the parking lot at a couple of soccer tournaments on this side of the Twin Cities," she said, pulling out her keys. "That is assuming the son-of-a-bitch is from around the East Metro area."

"Why do we think that?"

"Because only a local would be familiar with that isolated clearing in Lilydale."

"I'll do an Internet search for tourneys," offered Gabe. "Gotta be a state soccer association that keeps a schedule. Number two?"

"Well, number two is a long shot, but we should . . ."

"Check out Finch's funeral," said Gabe.

"You taught me that," said Murphy. The lesson was that sometimes a killer would go to the victim's service to observe his handiwork or, on rare occasions, to express remorse.

"What's three?"

"Well, I hate doing it and I'm a little old for this stuff, but I could spend a night out on the streets as a decoy. We might want to do it on a weeknight, since that's when he nailed Finch. It's another long shot."

"Your hubby sure as hell isn't going to like that idea." Gabe knew they were trying to get back together.

She remembered, looked at her watch. "Shit. I gotta go. I'll call you tomorrow morning after church."

She turned to go to her car, but Gabe grabbed her by the arm. "Hold on," he said. "What was that rain-check thing about with Mason?"

He pays attention to little things, thought Murphy. "Nothing," she said. "He wanted to get a drink. As friends. We're both running in the Twin Cities Marathon this fall."

"Hmmm."

"Oh, Gabe, come on," Murphy said. "Drinks."

"Yeah." He took one last drag and threw his cigarette on the ground. "Bullshit."

FIVE

Murphy stopped at a Lebanese grocery on the West Side, rifled around on the floor of the car and found an issue of *Bon Appétit*, and dashed into the small market. The place smelled of cumin and onions. Braids of garlic hung from the ceiling. Middle Eastern music twanged in the background, and Murphy immediately recognized it. Her mother played it, patiently translating the Arabic lyrics for Murphy or any other listener who didn't understand the language: "He loves Lebanon, even though the land is afire with war . . . She waits for him, but he has gone away, so she withers away in the cold winter . . . The moon is our neighbor and his house is behind our hills . . . A boy she knew was lost in battle . . . Even after we die, the flute continues to wail and cry." Murphy found it depressing; she preferred her father's Celtic tunes.

Standing in front of a mound of produce, Murphy flipped through the magazine. She needed pine nuts for a rice pilaf. The main course would be lamb kebabs with mint pesto. Instead of her usual standby salad of tabbouleh, she opted to try a cherry-tomato-and-artichoke salad. Jack would have to have her hummus, of course, and it was a simple enough recipe:

Six to eight cloves of garlic, peeled
One lemon, juiced
A half-teaspoon of salt
One fifteen-ounce can of garbanzo beans, drained but the liquid reserved
Two tablespoons of tahini (sesame seed paste)

Mix the garlic with the lemon juice and salt on high in the blender until white and foamy. Add the beans. If the mixture is too thick, add a little of the reserved liquid and keep blending. After a smooth paste forms, add the tahini and blend thoroughly. Chill and serve with Lebanese flatbread or pita.

Gonna be good, she thought.

"Larry, can you cube a couple of pounds of lamb for me?" Murphy asked the man stationed behind the meat counter.

"Sure, honey," he said, reaching into the glass cooler and pulling out a leg of lamb. He slapped it on a butcher-block table behind the counter and started carving. "Got a big date tonight?" he asked.

"Let me guess," said Murphy. "My mom and pop were in here."

"You got it," he said, laughing and encasing the lamb in white butcher's paper. "Got the latest news on your love life, hot off the presses."

On her way home, Murphy puzzled over how her folks had found out; she and Jack were trying especially hard to keep things under wraps this time. Jack hated it when her big, loud clan weighed in with marital advice. He was the only child of two university professors. Whenever she visited his folks' house in St. Anthony Park, she felt like she was in a library. When Jack joined her family for dinner, he had to shout to be heard over her brothers. "Your family wears me out," he told her more than once.

She pulled into the parking lot of her river neighborhood, with its assortment of houseboats tied up at the St. Paul Yacht Club across from downtown St. Paul. She was proud to be part of the odd collection of people living on the Mississippi. Her closest neighbors included a wildlife artist and his photographer wife, a dentist, a bartender and his teenage son, a psychic reader, an architect and a garage-door salesman who played the sax.

Each river residence was a miniature-house, with a compact galley, small living room, bathroom with shower and one to three bedrooms depending upon the size of the craft. They even had washers, dryers and furnaces. In the winter, the exteriors were shrink-wrapped in plastic to keep out the cold. It looked goofy, but it worked. Most owned their houseboats and took great pride in them, keeping them well scrubbed and neatly painted. Murphy's needed some work. The outside paint job was peeling, the deck looked weathered and gray and sections of the deck railing were wobbly. She'd socked away some money for needed repairs, but had blown it all on upgrading the galley. She was content to live in a rickety houseboat as long as it had a great kitchen.

She spotted Jack's car in the parking lot. Great, she thought, the champagne should be chilling already.

She slid out of her cool car and into the stifling parking lot. Still well into the high eighties and humid. She wondered if this was the summer she would be forced to buy an air conditioner. Living on the river wasn't like living on a lake, with refreshing breezes coming off the water. As she walked toward her boat with a bag of groceries, she inhaled the Mississippi air and found it more putrid than usual. She nervously eyed the brown water around the dock. The last time it smelled this bad, there had been good reason. She'd found a rotting leg floating alongside her boat. Turned out it belonged to a towboat worker who'd fallen overboard and been run over by his own craft. The leg was late for its owner's funeral by a good two weeks.

Jack uncorked the champagne and poured them each a glass while she threaded the meat on long metal skewers. She carried the skewers out onto the deck.

"Gonna make some hummus?" Jack yelled from inside the boat. "Gotta have hummus if we're gonna have lamb."

"I'll make hummus," she yelled back.

"Make sure you put in enough garlic," he said. "Last batch was on the wimpy side."

"How did a white boy like you develop such a taste for garlic?" she asked.

He laughed and walked out with the drinks. "Here ya go, Potato Head." He handed her one glass and plopped into a chair with his.

Murphy slapped the meat on the grill, a shaky old Weber. One of these days she'd have to buy herself a new gas grill, she thought. Another item on the houseboat wish list.

The sound of a sax drifted from the water. Murphy turned and looked over her railing. Floyd Kvaal was in his canoe with his sax and his three-legged dog. Nearly every Saturday night in the summer he paddled up and down the shoreline, stopping to serenade whoever was out on their boat deck. Sometimes people tossed dollar bills into his boat. Sometimes they tossed him a beer and the dog a steak bone. The whole thing was weird, but Murphy thought everyone who lived on the river was a little warped and that's why she liked it.

"Hey, Paris, will play for food," said Kvaal. He set the sax down to paddle closer to her deck.

"Meat's not done yet," said Murphy, leaning on the railing. "How about some flat bread?" She tossed Kvaal a round loaf; he caught it, ripped it down the middle and gave half to the dog.

Jack stood up and peered over the railing.

"Oh, Jack. Hello. Didn't see you there," Kvaal said.

"I'll bet you didn't," Jack said. He sat back down with a frown. Kvaal saluted Murphy and continued his paddling, heading for the psychic reader who was also grilling on her deck.

"You could try being friendly," Murphy said to her husband.

"He's hitting on you," Jack said.

"He's being neighborly," she said.

"Bullshit."

"I'm ten years older than he is," she said.

"So what?"

"Jesus Christ. You think everyone is hitting on me," she said.

"I don't care for that mangy dog of his, either. Barks when I'm on the dock."

"Tripod's better than Brinks. That's his 'stranger on the dock' alarm. He knows you don't live here. He has other talents, too. He can pee against a tree while standing on two legs."

"Which two? Never mind. Don't want to know. Lamb's burning."

"No it isn't," she said. "It's perfect." She turned the skewers.

The meal was good and so was the lovemaking. She molded her back and bottom against his front as they rested on their sides and took in the night view from the bedroom windows. Across the river sparkled St. Paul City Hall and the Radisson Riverfront Hotel. The illuminated Wabasha Bridge looked decked out for Christmas. "I love it here," she whispered.

"So do I," he said, and curled tighter against her.

Sunday morning, she slipped out onto the deck, sat in one of the lawn chairs and deposited the newspaper on the seat of the other. The sun hadn't yet baked the mist off the Mississippi. She read the food section and came up with a new omelet to try on Jack.

"*Mmm.* Bacon," he said, shuffling down from the master cabin up in the boat's penthouse. He lowered himself into a chair at the kitchen table. Murphy poured him a cup of coffee. "I can at least pour my own java," he said with mild irritation. "Stop being such a good waitress, would you?"

After years of helping her mother cook for her father and brothers, and flipping burgers for barge workers at the family bar, Murphy couldn't break the habit of waiting on males at her table. It annoyed the hell out of Jack.

"Do you want to make the omelets, too?" she asked with a smirk. Jack couldn't cook.

"Never mind," he mumbled. She slapped a plate in front of him. He took a forkful. "Needs salt," he said. She put a plastic camel on the table with one hump containing a salt shaker and the other a pepper shaker. He raised his eyebrows. "This camel collection is getting out of hand. I counted six new brass ones in the living room."

"Shut up about my camels."

"You need to get in touch with your Irish roots. Why not leprechauns? Camels are so ugly."

"Are you trying to start a fight this morning?"

"How about a leprechaun riding a camel?"

She laughed and walked over to the refrigerator. The front of it was plastered with paperwork—bills, shopping lists, photos, postcards and reminders of medical and dental appointments—precariously held up by a variety of magnets. She scanned the mess and found the mass schedule she wanted under a magnet shaped like a miniature police badge. "How about the cathedral this morning?" she asked.

Murphy dipped her fingertips in the marble holy-water font inside the cathedral doors, made the Sign of the Cross and steered Jack toward the front of the church. Taking a pew up front was her habit. She was also one to enthusiastically participate in services, singing every hymn—albeit badly since she was tone deaf—and happily following along in the book. Her husband, on the other hand, had to work hard at keeping his place in the missal. He had been raised by parents who were lazy about religion. They went to mass on major holidays, but slept in most Sundays. Jack tried to do better to please Murphy, but his church attendance remained sporadic.

Before the mass began, Murphy drank in the lavish ornamentation of the cathedral—stone carvings, metal grillwork, imported marble. Massive statues of St. Mark, St. Luke, St. John, St. Matthew. Enormous, round stained-glass windows in a design reminiscent of a dial telephone. She never tired of the place. Every time she went to mass there, she discovered some detail she'd never noticed before. This time it was the words carved into the stone wall, over one of the cathedral's many doors:

"Conduct Me, O Lord, in Thy Way and I Will Walk in Thy Truth."

SIX

A mile away, in a smaller Catholic church, Michaels was also at morning mass. His attendance was better than sporadic, but his participation was cynical and self-serving. He took a pew in back and neither glanced at a missal nor sang the hymns. Sometimes he wondered what he was doing there. Church had provided comfort during the darkest periods of his life. The weeks following his mother's death, when he walked into his bedroom and thought for an instant he saw her sitting on his bed. "Come, Buzzy." The months watching powerlessly, a medical eunuch, while cancer shrank his father to a mumbling skeleton. The colors on the altar seemed more vivid, the ritual richer, coming on the heels of his personal dramas. As the pain and turmoil faded, so did his interest in the mass. He kept going anyway because he had been raised Catholic and believed in God and heaven and hell. He wasn't sure about the devil. Sunday services, he figured, were his insurance policy.

His mind drifted, but he was usually able to pull it back to catch some of the words floating from the front of the church. He often spent the hour glancing at the other parishioners and assessing them, measuring them. Sometimes it was a judgment based on their physical appearance, sometimes on their dress. Occasionally he found an especially attractive woman sitting near him, a woman with long hair, and spent the hour fantasizing.

This Sunday his mind was wrapped around Friday's poor outcome. That's what he decided to label this latest killing. Medical speak. Miss Poor Outcome. She was different from Miss Accident and Miss Incident. Something new was devouring his insides, setting fire to that knot in his stomach that could only be loosened with four or five or six glasses of Scotch. He couldn't put a name to it. Was it guilt or remorse? Was it the nagging fear of getting caught? He methodically dissected his emotions as he sat in back of the church. The words of the priest, the responses of the congregation, the hymns sung by the choir, and the incense carried by the altar boys all flowed ineffectually around him like muted music in a department store.

"My brothers and sisters, to prepare ourselves to celebrate the sacred mysteries, let us call to mind our sins."

What was bothering him? Was it fear of getting arrested?

He thought about the evidence he had left behind. First, there was the blanket. He realized Sunday morning it wasn't in the Suburban when he was rifling around in back for his windbreaker. He had remembered to grab the jacket off the picnic table, but he didn't recall picking the blanket up off the ground. Stupid mistake. Then there was the semen he'd left behind. He should have used a condom. Very stupid mistake. The police could use that, but they needed to match it with the DNA of a suspect. He was not a suspect. He had never been arrested for anything his entire life.

"May almighty God have mercy on us, forgive us our sins and bring us to everlasting life."

Was he conscience stricken for killing her? Is that what was eating at him? Did he feel bad that he had killed her? Contrition was

47

unnecessary, he reasoned. Miss Poor Outcome had been a prostitute—a whore who had forced his hand, made him lose his temper. He figured she shared the blame for her own death. Still, he couldn't deny there was something different about this one, this Finch. She'd prayed before he took her life, before he strangled it out of her. The others he had taken used their last breath to curse him, swear at him. Maybe killing a woman—even a hooker—with the Lord's Prayer on her lips was an abomination beyond simple rape and murder. Had he committed a sin for which there was no name? No forgiveness?

Suddenly the old man seated to his left thrust a basket in front of him. Already time for the collection. He reached into the right pocket of his windbreaker for his money clip, slipped out a folded bill, and tossed the money into the basket. He passed the basket on to the old woman seated to his right. When he shoved the money clip back into his pocket, he felt something else inside. A chain of some sort. Where had that come from?

"Lord, I am not worthy to receive you, but only say the word and I shall be healed."

He pulled the chain out of his pocket and stared. How could this be possible? He didn't remember removing it. It wasn't even broken; it was still clasped shut. He would remember having slipped it over her head. He certainly would have remembered fumbling with such a tiny, cumbersome clasp if that was how he had taken it off the body. Why would he have wanted it in the first place? Jewelry wasn't his usual sort of souvenir. He felt the blood drain from his face. An icy sweat enveloped his body. The pounding in his head drowned out the background noise of the mass.

"Excuse me," someone said to him. They were lining up. Time for Communion. People were sliding past him in the pew to go up to the front of the church for the Eucharistic bread. He was motionless, ignoring them, as he stared into his right hand.

In his palm he cradled the murdered woman's crucifix.

He quickly shoved his hand back in his pocket, as if those around him would see the necklace and immediately know. He slipped out the back before the mass was over and ran to his car, pulling his jacket off as he went. He left the crucifix buried in the windbreaker and tossed it on the front passenger seat of the Suburban. During the drive home he kept glancing over at it, as if it were an unwanted rider in his car. He contemplated driving over the High Bridge and chucking the jacket out the window. He imagined it floating over the bridge railing and into the water, but that was dangerous. Someone could find it.

He pulled into his driveway. He left the jacket in the car and went into the house. He stayed inside with the shades down and the music turned up. The phone rang a couple of times. He didn't care if it was work or his wife or even his daughters calling from camp. He couldn't trust his own voice and what it might reveal in its unsteadiness. It took the entire day, but he calmed himself, kept the fly from busting out.

He swam laps in the basement pool until his arms and legs were numb. He walked naked through every room in the house, something he did when he was home alone. He forgot to eat, but he remembered to drink. By nightfall, Michaels had it all figured out. Wondered what he had gotten so worked up about. In his study, alone and in the dark, he stretched out naked on the couch. He loved the feel of soft Italian leather against his back and legs. He loved the smell of leather, the earthiness of it. From one of the surviving pheasant glasses, he sipped what remained of his fourth glass of twenty-five-year-old Glendronach. He rested the cool glass on his stomach, right over the spot that burned inside. He needed a game plan, he thought. What was tormenting him the most was not his fear of getting caught or guilt over her death. What was troubling him was the nagging possibility that he had committed a sin for which there was no absolution. Surely a priest—the right priest, at least—would offer him absolution in the confessional.

He needed to shop around, that's all. A suburban priest wouldn't do. They'd listened to too many boring confessions of working mothers guilty about swearing at their children. A guy like that might freak out. He couldn't go to a priest in his neighborhood; his voice might be recognized. Though what goes on in the confessional is secret, he still didn't want to take any chances. What he needed was a sophisticated city priest who'd handled a nice rich smorgasbord of sins. Adultery. Sodomy. Thievery. Incest. Rape. Hell, the right guy had probably dealt with a murder or two. Probably got a couple every year.

Confessions weren't generally heard Sunday nights and he didn't want to wait until the traditional Saturday afternoon. He might be able to find a church with weekday offerings of the sacrament. A church in Minneapolis.

There, he thought; it's all settled. He sat up on the couch, rejuvenated. He decided to go for an evening drive, cruise a bit with the windows down and the warm night air in his face. He pulled on the meticulously coordinated clothes—white silk boxers, taupe Egyptian-cotton slacks, ivory short-sleeved linen shirt and taupe Italian loafers—that he had deposited in a pile next to the couch earlier in the day. No socks. When he could get away with it, he went without socks. He liked the feel of leather against his feet.

As he slipped into the driver's seat of his Suburban he looked over at the windbreaker, a heap of nylon material on the front passenger seat. "Fuck you!" he said angrily. "I'm not afraid of you." He reached over and grabbed the jacket. Even though it was too warm for it, he slipped it on defiantly. He took the chain out of his jacket pocket, wiped the crucifix clean with the edge of his shirt and carefully put the necklace back in his jacket.

*　　*　　*

He glided down Summit toward the river and wondered when his wife would get home and ruin his fun. As far as he was concerned, she could spend her entire summer at the lake. God, he loved being alone in his house, without a nagging, nosy bitch yelling after him, "Where are you going now? Do you know what time it is?"

He laughed. That was such an inane question. He stopped at a light. "Do you know what time it is?" he said out loud in a high-pitched voice. "Do you know what time it is? Do you know what time it is?"

The light changed and he continued driving west and thinking about his wife. His Jennifer. Mrs. Perfect. He'd somehow ended up marrying a little mommy. Not his mommy. God knows his own mother never gave a damn how late he stayed out or where he went. How had he ended up with someone so sickeningly sweet and good when what he needed was someone as scarred as he? As a teenager he'd gravitated toward girls who were loose or damaged in some way. Girls who were not judgmental. His tastes for such women intensified after his mother's death with one additional requirement: They had to have long hair.

Jennifer's hair was what drew him to her in the first place. From across the campus mall he spotted her, so pale and petite and perfectly proportioned. She looked like a Barbie doll that had been left out in the sun. Her blond hair reached down to her butt.

He'd assumed too many things about Jennifer. While they were dating she'd have a glass of wine with dinner or a bottle of beer on the boat, so he thought she'd be okay with his drinking. Instead, she became a teetotaler with the birth of their children and nagged him about his drinking. He'd carefully watched her with her father, saw the way he hugged her and kissed her on the corner of the mouth, and assumed incest. Whenever he saw parents kissing their kids a little too much or a little too close to the mouth, he assumed incest. Beyond a quick peck on the forehead, he rarely kissed his own daughters. He figured Jennifer would open up to him after they were married, spill all the sordid details. As it turned out, he was wrong about his wife's father. She came from a normal, loving family, and he resented her for it.

He reached the end of Summit and turned onto River Road.

At least her father had died of cancer the way his had, slowly and miserably. That offered Michaels some consolation.

SEVEN

"Paris, I don't think you're ready for a single."

"I can handle it."

"Why won't you ever listen?"

Jack and Murphy were inside the stucco boathouse of the Minnesota Boat Club on Raspberry Island, a sliver of land downstream from Murphy's houseboat and accessible from a bridge on the banks of the Mississippi. The Monday-morning sky was pink with dawn.

"Are you going to help me or not?" she asked.

"Do I have a choice?"

"Not if you want to get laid tonight." She reached for a twenty-six-foot boat.

"Jesus. Not that one," he said. "That's a racing shell. Here. Let's take this seventeen-footer." She took the bow and he the stern. They held the boat over their heads and walked the long, narrow craft out of the boat bay, down the ramp and onto the dock in front of the clubhouse. They gently flipped the boat into the water. Jack was a competitive rower and had belonged to the boat club since high school. After years of listening to him talk about "sculling" and "sweeping," Murphy had finally started a beginning-level rowing class and found she loved it.

"Why can't we do this after work?" he asked.

"I'm gonna be busier than hell today working Finch's murder. Might not get out in time." Murphy stepped into the hull, sat on the sliding seat and strapped her feet to a stationary platform. Jack looked down at her from the dock, frowning. She smiled at him. "I'll be fine."

"Let me take a boat out with you."

"No. I want to try this solo."

"Keep your hands . . ."

"I know, I know," she said. "Keep my hands on the oars at all times."

"They balance the boat and if you capsize, they'll keep you afloat," he said.

"I don't intend to capsize."

"Lots of people do their first time out in a single," he said. "Be careful of the barges and towboats. If they get too close . . ."

"I'll lift up my shirt and flash 'em."

"You're hilarious this morning. I'm so glad you dragged me out of bed for this."

"Look, this whole rowing thing was your idea," she said. "If you didn't hate running so much we could be pounding the pavement together right now. Safe and dry and on land."

"I thought this was something we could get into together. I didn't intend for you to take a single out by yourself after a couple of lessons. Can't ever do anything halfway, can you? Always out to prove something. This river isn't anything to mess with; it's a dangerous body of water."

"Stop worrying." She shoved off, smiling at him as she glided upstream toward the High Bridge.

"Stubborn," Jack mumbled.

She passed the Ramsey County Detention Center. The Science Museum. It was a good workout. She used the muscles of her legs as well as her arms and back to pull the oars. Her rowing instructor— a college kid with a tattoo on his shoulder of crossed oars—was surprised Murphy took to the oars as quickly as she did. She found it an easy movement that she could do with little thought. The river was quiet early in the morning. The solitude was even better than when she ran. No cars to dodge or pedestrians to step around. She had time to think about Jack and her marriage.

She wondered if they'd get anywhere this time, or if they'd follow their usual pattern. Jack called it the three F's—fucking, fighting, fleeing. She hoped she wouldn't be the one to blow it this time. She missed him, missed their marriage. No question they loved each other and wanted to be together, but they aggravated each other. It didn't help that their demanding jobs kept them flying out the door in different directions. She couldn't resent his work the way he hated hers. Jack was a top-notch E.R. doc at Regions. He'd led the push to make the hospital a Level-I Trauma Center, so they'd be equipped to handle the worst of the critical-injury cases. Mangling car wrecks. Shootings. Stabbings. Sometimes, when she was accompanying a victim or a wounded suspect, their paths crossed in the emergency room. Jack always looked at her the same way, and she knew what he was thinking: "Paris, this could be you on the table."

"I'm careful," she told him. "I don't take chances."

"Bullshit," he said. "You're a gambler. You get high from taking risks."

He was right. He was the careful one. The methodical one. They were so different from each other, and those differences pulled them apart. Her father had called children the glue that keeps marriages together. Was it time for glue?

She set the thought aside and returned her attention to the river. After the High Bridge, the shores turned green and wild. It was a river view of Lilydale she rarely got to see. For a moment, she forgot it was where Finch had been murdered and simply thought of it as a wooded park along the Mississippi.

She turned around a short way into the park; she and Jack had to get to work. The return trip wasn't as peaceful. A barge. A wall of metal that towered over her in the water. It stayed in the middle of the river and she stuck close to shore. Murphy held her breath, clutched the ten-foot oars and steadied the bobbing boat as best she could. She exhaled as the barge cruised by her. "I did it," she said under her breath.

She was almost back at the dock when a speedboat, ignoring NO WAKE signs posted along the shore, zipped past her. The shell capsized and Murphy tumbled into the water.

"Dammit!" she sputtered, spitting out brown water and pushing her wet hair off her face. She looked toward the dock and saw Jack shaking his fist at the speedboater.

"You were right," she said as they walked the boat back into the bay. "I wasn't ready for a single."

"You were doing great until that asshole kicked up the water. You're a natural."

"I feel more natural on land," she said. "I'm gonna stick to running for a while. But thanks for not saying it."

"Saying what?"

"'I told you so.'"

"You will never hear those words from my mouth"—he looked at his watch—"this morning."

EIGHT

"The cat got me," he told them when he arrived at the clinic Monday morning.

"A cat? I didn't know you had a cat," said one of the nurses. "What kind is it?"

"It's an alley cat; a red one," he told her, enjoying his private joke. "Maybe I'll take it off your hands."

"You don't want her," Michaels said. He could win an Oscar. "She's a nasty stray I found on the street last Friday during the rainstorm. She's probably diseased. Let the Humane Society deal with her."

He walked toward Exam Room Three to look at another set of pendulous breasts. He did it all—rhinoplasty for those who wanted a new nose, mentoplasty for patients who desired a reshaped chin, blepharoplasty to fix baggy eyelids, otoplasty for protruding ears, chemical peels for superficial wrinkles and face lifts as the ultimate age eraser. Hair transplants were becoming more and more popular with men, and everyone was lining up for liposuctions and tummy tucks. He really shined with breasts. He could make a flat-chested woman look like a centerfold; and for women wanting to go in the other direction, from a bulbous DD to a perky B, there was reduction mammaplasty. Michaels loved the whole idea of carving up women and reassembling them to his own specifics.

One thing he wouldn't take was birth defects—cleft lips, cleft palates and the like. They weren't big moneymakers. He referred those cases to one of his do-gooder colleagues, claiming they had more expertise in that area. That was a lie, of course. No one had more expertise. No one. He was the absolute king of the hill. Over the years he'd been courted by several large practices and turned them all down; he liked being alone and in charge of his own show. In fact, he'd even thought about opening a couple of his own satellite offices around the Twin Cities, but he was already too busy.

He did manage to squeeze in some volunteer work. He didn't care about the pathetic indigents he dealt with—dumb women damaged by violent boyfriends and husbands—but donating his time polished his reputation. More important, that voyeuristic side of him, that little boy hiding behind the chair, was aroused by the stories of domestic abuse that accompanied these patients. He pushed them:

"How did he set fire to your nightgown? What did he use? A lighter? A candle?"

"Describe the knife he used to cut your face. Did he get it out of a kitchen drawer?"

"Did you cry when he broke your nose? Did you fight back?"

"Who started the argument? Were you drinking? Doing drugs?"

His curiosity was regularly rewarded; the details were delicious.

He had difficulty keeping his mind on his work this Monday, however. He was preoccupied with finding a priest to hear his confession. Michaels wanted reassurance, redemption, release from the nagging fear that he had paved his path to hell. He shut his office door during lunch and flipped through the Minneapolis yellow pages. He called a dozen Catholic churches until he found one that offered confession on Monday evenings.

Father Ambrose shifted his weight a bit and tried to find a comfortable position in his seat in the confessional. He was unsuccessful. He felt sore all over. What a great weekend he had had. Fishing at a parishioner's cabin all day Saturday and the better part of Sunday. Good steaks on the grill. Cold beer. All he had had to do was slip off the collar and slide into some shorts and a T-shirt and everyone relaxed, almost forgot he was a priest. He shouldn't have gone water-skiing, though. That was a mistake. He'd wanted one turn around the lake. It had been years since he'd been behind a boat and he wanted to see if he could still get up on one ski. He did, and now his hips were paying the price. He knew he would need hip-replacement surgery down the road. They'd been bothering him off and on since his foot-ball days at St. Thomas. Still, he'd waited this long and he could wait longer. He had plenty of time.

He sat in the dim, tiny room in back of the church and waited for his first penitent. The priest's portion of the confessional looked like a closet, with an out-swinging door and a chair inside. On either side of this tiny room was a booth, each with heavy maroon drapes hanging in the doorway serving as a privacy curtain for penitents. Inside each booth was a kneeler facing the priest's room, as well as a screen above the kneeler. The penitents knew it was their turn when the priest slid open a window covering the screen on their side.

Ambrose flexed his hands and examined his palms. They were sore from hanging on to the towrope. He smiled. Yes. It had been an outstanding weekend. He again tried adjusting his position a bit. No dice. His hips still ached. He knew he really needed to lose some weight, especially since his heart attack months ago. He wasn't ter-ribly fat. He was husky. Defensive-lineman husky. Even dropping ten pounds would help. Then there was that ulcer of his. Perhaps the cook at the rectory could come up with a tasty low-fat, heart-healthy diet that was compatible with his ulcer. Lord, what a dismal thought. He'd be eating Cream of Wheat and applesauce all day.

He ran his fingers through his hair and rubbed his beard. So quiet in the shadowy, cool church. You'd think people would have a lot to confess following a weekend, but that apparently wasn't the case. Monday nights were frequently slow. Every time he tried to trim the confessional hours to only Saturdays, parishioners complained. People don't like change. Especially old Catholics. So set in their ways. Some were still whining about the nuns dumping the long habits. He was all for it. Nothing wrong with seeing a little leg.

"Time to get down to business," he said to himself. Ambrose reined in his mind from its wanderings as he prepared himself to hear the sins of the faithful. Someone stepped into the booth to his right. He slid open the window covering the screen on that side and tipped his ear toward the penitent. The screen allowed him to hear the sins but not clearly see the sinner. He waited. He heard paper shuffling. A child. Some kids scribbled their sins on bits of paper so they wouldn't forget.

"Bless me, Father, for I have sinned." A little boy. He sounded anxious. "It's been two months since my last confession."

A long pause. Ambrose heard more paper shuffling. A long silence. "Son? Are you still there?"

"Yes, Father. My sins are, I, umm. I yelled at my little sister. I called her a bad name."

"Yes, son."

"I yelled at my little sister. I called her a bad name."

"You already said that, son."

"I know, Father, I did it twice."

The boy had also pulled the cat's tail. Twice. Two seemed to be this kid's lucky number. For his penance, he assigned the lad two Our Fathers and two Hail Marys. "Be nicer to your sister, son, and leave the poor pussies alone."

The penitent immediately following the boy was undoubtedly the child's mother. She confessed to swearing at her son for swearing at his little sister. One of those "God dammit, stop swearing" moments parents have when they're losing it. Ambrose was bothered that she had booze on her breath. She wasn't drunk; after years of hearing people's voices but not seeing their faces, he could tell after listening less than a minute if someone needed a cab ride home. No, she wasn't drunk, but he could definitely smell the alcohol. She needed the drink either to deal with the kid or to muster up the courage to go to confession.

He wished people didn't dread confessions. Over years spent hearing them, Ambrose observed that an adult's trip to the booth had the same calming influence as a child's "time out" in a quiet corner. In both cases, it was a reflective time to examine one's conscience. Yet some people feared it so much, they went once a decade. Some even saved all the baggage until they got to the end of the road. He'd heard amazing things from the lips of dying people.

Healthy people weren't slackers, either.

The most memorable confessions involved sex. A bride-to-be asked for absolution on the eve of her wedding, after sleeping with her future father-in-law. A teenage boy asked for forgiveness after forcing himself on his sister, at knifepoint. A mother of five confessed to having an affair with one of her children's teachers, a woman. A farmer once drove an hour to the Minneapolis church to tell his sins to Father Ambrose. He didn't want to tell his own pastor that he'd been committing sexual assaults on a weekly basis, against his sheep.

Nothing surprised Ambrose anymore. After thousands of hours spent sliding that window open and shut and open again, hearing confessions had gotten tedious.

At least, up until that Monday night.

After a half dozen additional penitents—mostly lonely, elderly parishioners who seemed more in need of someone to talk to than a confessor to hear and absolve their sins—an extended silence enveloped the church. Perhaps that was it for the evening, thought Ambrose. He checked the luminescent face of his wristwatch, a recent gift from his parishioners in celebration of his thirty years in the priesthood. Five minutes remained of the scheduled half hour for penance. He stood up, shook each foot—the right one was growing numb—and sat down again.

He heard the heavy steps of a man. Someone entered the booth on his left. Ambrose slid open the window over the screen on that side.

"Bless me, Father, for I have sinned. It's been six weeks since my last confession."

Ambrose heard the penitent's breathing. Quick and shallow, as if the man had just finished running a race. He reeked of whiskey and perspiration, the sour-smelling sweat that comes from nerves and fear and guilt. A chill ran up the priest's spine. No minor offense, no venial sin, brought this man to the confessional. He was going to unload one of the big ones.

"I killed a woman, Father. A prostitute."

Ambrose gasped without realizing it.

"I strangled her. Raped her. Raped her twice, actually, if you count after she died. It wasn't entirely my fault, really. She made me mad, spit in my face. She shares responsibility for her own death."

The priest was stunned.

"One other thing, the thing that has really troubled me, kept me up at night . . ."

Good, thought the priest, perhaps now comes a sincere expression of sorrow.

"She was Catholic I think, and she started to say the Lord's Prayer while I was killing her, choking her, and I'm concerned this would somehow elevate the seriousness of this offense."

The man paused. The few seconds of quiet made Ambrose dizzy, as if the silence had somehow sucked all the oxygen out of the confessional. On his side of the wall, the priest's hands trembled and his legs felt wobbly. He didn't think he could stand if he had to. The weakness wasn't from fear, but horror. He wanted to listen and cover his ears at the same time, the way a passing motorist wants to at once gawk at a bloody accident and avert his eyes. His calling left him no choice, however; he had to minister to this man.

"Well, there, I've told you all there is to tell," said the man, breaking the silence. His voice had the casual relief of someone admitting to stealing a box of paper clips.

Ambrose struggled to deal with it; all this asshole wanted was reassurance he wasn't going to hell. "Recitation of one's sins is not enough to obtain forgiveness," Ambrose said. "Without sincere sorrow, confession accomplishes nothing. Nothing at all. Without sorrow for sin, there can be no forgiveness. No absolution. Surely you understand this. Are you not at all sorry that you killed her?"

"No, she was a whore," said the man, expressing it as flatly as someone stating a simple, widely understood fact. The sky is blue. The grass is green. She was a whore. "I realize and acknowledge it was a sin, as it's a sin to take the life of a dog or a bird or . . . a . . . cat."

The priest thought he heard snickering with that last word. This man was nuts. Had to be. "Son, give me permission to go to the authorities with this confession. In fact, let us together go to the police. You can begin your long walk down the road to forgiveness by offering amends to this girl's family and the greater society."

"No, Father. I will not turn myself in. That is not going to happen. Ever. I have too much to lose. Perhaps I'm not making myself clear, Father. She was a prostitute. A prostitute. A whore. I will not surrender my reputation, not to mention my freedom and my life—I have a good life, Father—because of a dead whore. Give me a penance, some prayers, and let me out of here."

"No. You've committed a mortal sin and a horrible crime. You must confess to the police."

"I'll fry in hell first—and drag you along with me!"

NINE

"No way in hell I am gonna let you out of the house. You are not going to do this. Let someone else do it."

Murphy was dressed in a short, sleeveless black spandex dress that hugged her breasts, midriff and waist. It looked like a Speedo racing swimsuit with a tight skirt attached as an afterthought.

"You're chumming the water to attract a murderer, and you're the meat! This is pure fucking bullshit!"

"Stop yelling, Jack. I put a pan of lasagna in the oven for you and there's a loaf of rosemary bread baking in the bread machine on the galley counter. As soon as it beeps, take it out. You can eat in front of the television and watch Tuesday-night baseball or something. Aren't the Blue Jays playing at the Red Sox tonight? That should be a good game."

"Do the words 'Boston Massacre' mean anything to you?" he said.

"Yeah, sure," she said distractedly. "Whatever."

Murphy looked at herself in her bedroom dresser mirror. Jack was sitting on the edge of the bed, still dressed in his blue hospital scrubs. He had gotten off work as she was preparing to leave. While he fumed, she tugged on the dress. She'd be well dressed for a prostitute; most stick to blue jeans, T-shirts and sneakers. She needed to attract attention. At least the attention of this particular man, if he happened to be out.

"Look, I got full backup," Murphy said. "I'm gonna stop at the station and get wired, so Gabe can hear what's going on. There'll be unmarked cars up and down the street. It's all pretty safe."

"Safe my ass," Jack sputtered. "You can't predict what this maniac might do."

"Chances are we'll never see him," she said. "Hell, it was probably a one-time thing, and if he's smart, he won't be out trolling for hookers for a while. This is a shot in the dark. Nothing is going to happen. I'm sure of it."

Actually, she wasn't at all sure. She didn't tell him the Minneapolis cops had an unsolved murder with similar circumstances in the spring. A young woman, a regular at a Minneapolis S&M bar, was found beaten and strangled in a Hennepin County nature center. Her hair had been cut. Minneapolis homicide cops kept the haircut out of the news to preserve a detail only the killer would know. Murphy regretted letting Jack in on Finch's haircut. He'd keep it under wraps—they never violated each other's work confidences—but the twist to the case rattled him. Murphy could feel Jack glaring at her as she grabbed a brush from the top of her dresser and gave her hair a few strokes. She usually didn't wear it loose for work—she thought it looked too girlish and unprofessional—but she knew the hair might be a key. So did Jack. She clipped on some big rhinestone earrings shaped like butterflies.

"Are you listening to anything I'm saying?" he asked.

Impatiently, she kicked off the high-heeled sandals. "How the hell can I walk in these things?" she mumbled. She went down on her knees to rifle under the bed for another pair of shoes. Jack's legs were in the way and he wouldn't budge. "Move. I'm looking for something," she told him, trying to push his legs aside. He planted them farther apart to serve as an even bigger obstacle. She dove between them.

"Even from this angle, I can see your ass when you bend over. Do most prostitutes wear white Fruit of the Looms? Seriously, don't you have a longer dress? How about that blue one you wore to mass on Sunday?"

"I'm supposed to look like a hooker, not a church lady," she said, the sound of her voice muffled under the bed. She found the shoes, stood up and slipped them on. They were dusty. "Much better," she said, looking down at the black flats. "I can run in these."

"Run? What will you be running from? You shouldn't have to worry about running if you have good backup, right? What's this 'run' shit?"

"Jack."

"Don't tell me to fucking calm down!" He stood up, ran his fingers through his hair and paced once around the bedroom. "Don't do this, Paris. I mean it. I worry every damn day if you're going to come home from work in one piece. I can live with that if I have to because I know how much you love your job, but this is purposely putting yourself in harm's way. I have a hard time handling that."

"Jack, it's . . ."

"Stop telling me it's safe. I may be a civilian, but I'm not stupid. I've been sleeping with a homicide cop."

She smiled. "Jack, I love you, but I've got to do my . . ."

He stopped pacing and put up his hand to halt her words. They were standing in opposite corners of the bedroom. Her heart ached. She'd never felt closer to him than in these last few days. She'd even contemplated bringing up the subject of children.

"If you walk out that door, I won't be here when you get back. I mean it, Paris. This is my goddamn line in the sand. Do not walk out that door."

The hair on the back of her neck stood up and her eyes narrowed. If there was anything she resented, it was ultimatums. He knew that. She grabbed her purse and headed out. "Pound that line in the sand up your ass," she said over her shoulder.

"So Jack was okay with this, Murphy?"

She didn't answer; she stared out the window with her arms folded.

She and Gabe were in an unmarked department van, headed to the strip where Finch had last been seen alive. Gabe was driving, a Winston hanging out of his mouth. Murphy was in the passenger seat; she'd been wired. Not far behind them were two additional unmarked cars—Ford Crown Victorias—driven by Chuck Dubrowski and Max Castro, both veterans. They would visually track her and the johns. They carried Nikon F5s in case a particular man or car resembled the one involved in the killing. Gabe had his favorite country-western radio station turned low; Patsy Cline was falling to pieces. The humid city air smelled like rotten eggs.

"Murphy, what's wrong?" asked Gabe. "Talk to me. Come on." They stopped at a red light. He switched off the radio. "You had a fight over this decoy deal, right? I saw this coming a mile away. I knew this was going to be a problem. I predicted it, didn't I?"

The light turned green, but Gabe didn't budge the van. A car behind them honked twice and squealed around them.

"Drive," she told him. "The light isn't going to get any greener."

Gabe drove on, but kept talking: "It isn't too late. We can turn around and wire someone else. One of the women from Vice would love to get in on this. Go home and patch things up. Uncork a bottle of wine. Slide into something sexy. We can forget about . . ."

"Stop."

"Stop the van?"

"No, shut up. It's too late."

"What do you mean?"

"The fight's over, Gabe. The house lights are on. Jack has left the building."

"It's never too late to make nice, Murphy."

"Well, it's too late for at least tonight," she said. "Let's rock 'n' roll."

"Yeah, yeah. Let's rock 'n' roll," he said. He pulled over to let Murphy out on the strip. They looked like customer and client. "Just don't bend over," he said. He flicked his spent cigarette out the widow.

She hopped out with her purse, flipped him the bird and slammed the door.

There's an art to luring johns, thought Murphy. She strolled past a Burger King, then a bar with a neon sign on its roof that looked like a giant tilted highball glass. Next to that was a tattoo parlor with a hand-painted placard posted in the window: "Ask About Our Mother-Daughter Discount."

Enticing johns has nothing to do with clothing, jewelry or hairstyle. It doesn't have much to do with looks. It has absolutely everything to do with eye contact. When a woman standing alone on a sidewalk tries to make eye contact with every male driver or car passenger who passes on the street, she is effectively hanging out her hooker's shingle. Open for business. Come on in. Bring cash.

A husky, long-haired, bearded biker on a Harley drove right onto the sidewalk and stopped next to her. She knew this would freak out Gabe. "It's okay, guys. He's fine," she said under her breath. Still, she was ready to reach into her purse if necessary.

"Hey, mama, wanna get nasty?"

He was wearing so much black leather and silver it was hard to figure out where he left off and his hog began. "I only do it in cars, pal," she said, smiling sweetly. "Sorry."

He threw his shaggy blond head back and laughed. More silver inside his mouth. He was a big teddy bear. "I'll be back with my pink Cadillac," he said, winking at her. He rolled his bike off the sidewalk and went down the street.

There are horny idiots who will approach any woman standing on a street corner. Schoolgirls lugging backpacks are stopped. Mothers pushing strollers are propositioned. Elderly women carrying grocery bags are offered money.

A dumb shit waving his wallet at any and every female standing or walking on the sidewalk doesn't know what to look for, thought Murphy.

He doesn't know how to shop. He wouldn't know a hooker if she sat on his lap and unzipped his pants. These are the obtuse fools who make life especially miserable for the people living in the neighborhoods haunted by prostitution traffic.

When she worked in Vice, Murphy once suggested, only half jokingly, that the morons arrested for propositioning respectable women should be forced to attend a class on identifying hookers. They could be shown flash cards. Hooker. Hooker. Woman carrying laundry. Hooker. Girl waiting for bus. Hooker. Lady walking her dog. Hooker. Hooker. Your grandma. Hooker.

A teenage boy in a metallic-green half-ton Chevy Silverado pickup truck pulled over to the curb. "How much for a knob job?"

Murphy looked through the window. God, was he even shaving yet? Why wasn't he off screwing teenage girls? Don't boys do that anymore? "Get lost, kid. You're jailbait!" she hollered and waved him off. "I don't need that kind of trouble."

"Hey, fuck you!" he yelled, and squealed away.

She took her time and looked at the cars as they passed under the streetlights. She looked particularly hard for black Suburbans, and studied blond men in any sort of car. After all, Finch's killer might be taking the wife's minivan out for a drive this evening and leaving his own vehicle in the garage. Was it a two-car garage in an upscale neighborhood in the city? Was it a three-car garage in some pricey suburb? What was his story? Why long hair? Why murder? Why a hooker?

What drives any man to pay for sex? Working in Vice, she'd heard every theory possible. One Vice cop told her the whole problem was that middle-aged wives wouldn't give blow jobs, so their husbands had to go out and pay for them. Another theory promoted by another Vice cop held that all men supplement the sex they get in marriage or dating. Most do it through masturbation, but those who aren't adept at jerking off get sex on the street or through extramarital affairs. She liked that second theory better than the first.

On Monday, Murphy had put word out on the street that the cops were going to be involved in a sting operation on the strip the following Tuesday night. Pros who wanted to avoid a night in a holding cell were advised to lie low. Murphy thought she had the avenue pretty much to herself. Then she saw a familiar figure sashaying toward her on the sidewalk. "Tia, get your sorry ass off the street," said Murphy.

"Wanna make sure you okay, baby," said the hooker. Tia was a friend of Rue's and looked like a Latina version of her. Fat. Tight skirt. Short top with a brown midriff bulging out. Lots of makeup. Tia's shoes were usually nicer than Rue's, and there was one other difference between the two hookers: Tia was a man.

"Why are you sticking that big nose where it doesn't belong?" asked Murphy.

"You mean this little button?"

"Go home," said Murphy. She noticed that Tia needed a shave.

"No place like home. No place like home. You like my new shoes?" Tia clicked the pumps together. "You ain't in Kansas anymore, Murphy."

Murphy looked down at the hooker's feet. Fire-engine red, with stiletto heels. "How the hell do you walk in those?" asked Murphy.

"They don't care if I can walk, baby. That's not why they pay me the big bucks."

Dubrowski pulled up and rolled down the passenger-side window. "Hey, Tia, how about I give you a ride to the station?" he yelled through the window. "Got a cell with your name on it, in two languages."

"I can take a hint; this munchkin going down the Yellow Brick Road," Tia said, and clacked down the sidewalk.

"Thanks, Chuck," Murphy said. Dubrowski pulled away from the curb.

*　*　*

Murphy stopped under the awning of a secondhand store. It had grand aspirations. ANTIQUE PARLOR said a sign in the shop's grimy window.

A dark sedan pulled up to the curb. A plastic statue of the Virgin Mary was stuck to the dashboard and a half dozen rosaries hung from the rearview mirror. Murphy recognized the car; it belonged to a priest from the neighborhood. He had helped close a strip club down the street by taking Polaroids of everyone entering and leaving the place and sticking the photos on the Web. Called it the Sodom and Gomorrah site.

She walked up to the car and poked her head in the passenger-side window. She saw him, a short, skinny fellow hardly visible above the steering wheel except for his black fedora.

"Sister, why are you selling your body? Are you familiar with the story of Mary Magdalene? It's not too late to save your soul," he said, holding up a Bible. "Jesus tells us . . ."

"Father, give it a rest. It's me," she said, smiling.

He squinted. "Murphy! What are you doing? Thought you'd left Vice for Homicide," he said.

"That's why I'm out here," she said.

"Oh, that prostitute's murder. Poor girl."

"Keep a lid on it, okay Father?"

"Gotcha, Murphy," he said. He reached over and opened his glove compartment and pulled out a religious medal on a chain. He tried to give it to Murphy.

"Father, it really doesn't go with the rest of my outfit," she said.

"I see what you mean. Incognito and all that." He made the Sign of the Cross. "Be careful, Daughter." He pulled away.

Murphy kept walking. She was getting warm in the close-fitting dress. She was glad she had gone bare legged; she would have died in panty hose. She stopped in front of a nail salon. FRENCH MANICURES said a sign in the window. She looked at her own short nails. Even in flats, her feet were starting to hurt. She slipped off her shoes and stood barefoot on the sidewalk; the pavement was still warm.

A skinny guy with curly black hair pulled over and honked. She stepped back into her shoes and walked over to the curb. At first glance, she couldn't tell if his hair was wet or greasy. After a closer look: definitely greasy. He was driving a pizza delivery car. He smelled like onions and sausage.

"Waddya charge for a full-fledged fuck, pretty woman?"

"I don't do guys in paper hats," she said.

He realized he was still wearing his work cap. "Aw, fuck!" he said. He ripped the cap off his head, threw it on the car floor and drove off.

So went the evening, with Murphy getting one offer after another, but clearly drawing no killer. They were almost ready to pull the plug on the operation and call it a night when Rue's clown customer from Saturday pulled over to the curb to make a bid for Murphy. "Nice hooters, baby. Will a couple o' twenties get me a peek and a feel?"

"Gabe," Murphy said under her breath. "Remember this guy? He doesn't know when to quit."

The fat guy in the yellow Cobra extracted himself from his convertible and stumbled drunkenly toward Murphy. He tripped on the curb, but steadied himself and managed to get up on the sidewalk without falling. This time he was dressed in orange Bermuda shorts and a yellow T-shirt. On his feet were yellow socks and black penny loafers. He practically glowed in the dark. The guy clearly needed to dry out— and get a clothing makeover.

"Gabe, get your ass over here," she whispered into her bosom.

The fat man was getting too close. "Come to Papa," he said, holding out his arms and belching. "I got the money you want and the meat you need."

"I don't think you can afford me, honey."

"Bullllshit!" he said angrily, and reached for the wallet in his right shorts pocket. As he pulled it out, a pistol fell to the ground. Murphy recognized the small weapon immediately. Beretta Model 21. Nickel finish. Smooth walnut grip. Accurate as hell. When he bent over to pick it up, Murphy ran behind him and pushed his fat ass as hard as she could with her right foot. He fell flat on his face. She kicked the Beretta out of his reach and pulled her gun out of her purse.

"Don't move, sumo Romeo. I'm a cop and your ass is seriously busted."

Gratefully, she heard tires squealing. All three of the department cars. Dubrowski and Castro jumped the curb and blocked the side-walk on either side of the drunk. Gabe double-parked with a screech next to the drunk's convertible, hopped out of the van.

"What the hell took you so long?"

Dubrowski helped the big man up and Castro cuffed him while Gabe retrieved the Beretta.

Murphy tucked her Glock back inside her purse and walked over to the yellow convertible. A half-empty Vodka bottle sat on the passenger-side seat. Murphy picked it up. "Buddy, you shouldn't be caught cruising around town with this loser friend of yours," she told the drunk as they eased him into the back of one of their unmarked squads.

"Well, I'm hungry," declared Murphy, standing in the middle of the sidewalk under a streetlight, her hands on her hips. She kicked off the shoes, pulled off the rhinestone earrings and marched bare-foot toward the van. "Who wants to come over to my place for lasagna after we give our drunk pal a ride to the station house?"

TEN

Murphy slid out of bed in the middle of the night and dumped two trays of ice cubes into a sheet-cake pan and set the pan in front of a fan. It didn't help. She moved the fan from the foot of her bed to the head, so it blew in her face. She rolled around trying to find a cool spot on the sheets.

At sunrise she got up and dragged herself down to the galley. Murphy opened a can of Diet Pepsi and sipped it while flipping through the newspaper looking for a sale on air conditioners. She couldn't find one. "To hell with it," she mumbled. She went back to her bedroom and pulled on some shorts and a T-shirt. The day was going to be another scorcher and she had to fit her run in before it got too hot.

She walked out onto the dock to do some limbering up. She felt stiff. She hadn't run for a few days and she didn't like that; running cleared her head and lifted her spirits. She stopped stretching suddenly when she heard something thumping against one of the piles beneath her. She walked toward the edge of the dock and looked down into the water. A huge, dead carp. A big chunk missing from its white middle. One milky eye. "Yuck," she muttered.

She got on her back and curled her knees to her chest. She heard howling and turned her head. Teenage boys on a pontoon.

"I'll help you exercise real good!" one of them hollered. His friends laughed.

She'd seen them on the river before, at all hours. She wondered if they ever went home. They gave her grief whenever they spotted her outside her boat. She usually ignored it, but she wasn't in the mood for their crap today. She flipped them the bird. They hooted even louder. "Little assholes," she mumbled to herself. She stood up and ran down the dock toward the road.

She wasn't fast—on her best days she did eight-minute miles—but she had endurance. She ran north up the Wabasha Bridge, glancing below at the Mississippi. A couple of paddleboats were docking along the riverfront across from downtown. In the summer, they made lunch and dinner cruises, and had Dixieland bands.

She passed the St. Paul City Hall and Ramsey County Courthouse. Two blocks later, Marshall Field's department store on one side of the street. Bald mannequins in pale dresses in the windows. On the other side of the street, a string of small shops. Nail salon. Comic-book store. Jewelry shop. Then a bagel bakery. Long line of office workers waiting inside. A deli and market. Signs promising cheap cigarettes. A tiny candy and popcorn shop. Women in brown aprons and hairnets scooping caramel corn into plastic bags. Children's Museum. Street-level storefront crammed with toys, games, puppets.

She ran across the bridge over Interstate 94 and crossed Twelfth Street. Wabasha ended at a grassy mall that led to the State Capitol Building. At the south end of the mall, where Wabasha came to a dead stop, were steps leading to the Peace Officers' Memorial. She wiped her face with the hem of her T-shirt and walked up the steps leading to the large black block that was the heart of the memorial. It sat in a pool, with water pouring from the top and down its sides. Engraved in the stone were words from Matthew 5:9—

Blessed are the peacemakers,
for they shall be called
the children of God.

She turned around and ran south down Wabasha. She thought about her husband. She thought about the case. The night before had done nothing to advance the murder investigation or her relationship with Jack. She needed to make headway in both areas. Time was slipping by quickly. The case was growing colder; so was her husband. By the time she got back to the houseboat, she'd made a decision: the job owned her ass during the day, but she needed to spend some evenings on her marriage. She would call Jack and apologize. Maybe a little candlelight dinner followed by a back rub.

The post-run shower was long, hot and relaxing. She heard muffled ringing as she was drying off. She grabbed the robe hanging from the master-bathroom door and padded into the bedroom. Where was that damn cell phone this time? She checked under the bed. Nope. In the nightstand drawer. No. She lifted up the pillows. "You bastard, where are you?" She found it buried in the bedsheets.

"Yeah, Paris Murphy."

Erik Mason.

"Paris. I hope I didn't wake you." He had a bedroom voice. Even in the morning, in the middle of the week.

"No, no, Erik. I was hopping out of the shower after a run," she said.

"Hey, we should run together sometime before the marathon," he said.

"I'd drag you down, Erik. I'm pretty slow."

"I like it slow," he said, laughing.

"So what's going on? Something with the case?"

"The autopsy didn't turn up anything unexpected. She was strangled and sexually assaulted—probably simultaneously. We found some blond pubic hairs on the blanket. We've got plenty for a DNA profile."

"Bet we don't get any hits out of the database," said Murphy. "I'll bet he's never been in the system."

"One more thing: Finch's parents and her pimp, Sully, say her necklace is missing. A gold crucifix on a chain. She kept it tucked under her top and never took it off. She'd been wearing it since Confirmation."

"I don't suppose anyone has a picture of Finch wearing it?"

"Her folks gave me a copy of her Confirmation portrait," he said. "She's wearing it against a light-colored blouse."

"I'll swing by this morning on my way in and pick it up."

"Better still, Paris, why not meet me for drinks after work and I'll hand it over then?"

"I don't know, Erik. I've got to . . ."

"Come on. Drinks. Besides, I'm busier than hell today. I've got to be in court in an hour."

Jack worked late Wednesday nights anyway, and it was just drinks. One drink. "I can't stay late," she said. "I've got some stuff to do."

That morning, at the cop shop, she picked up a bulletin from the Minneapolis Police Department about a black Suburban spotted leaving the scene of a bizarre crime Monday night. Someone had assaulted a priest, left him for dead on the floor of his church. The night janitor found him and called 911.

"Come on, Curtis! Why the hell did you guys sit on this Suburban for better than a day?" asked Murphy, yelling over the phone at one of the Minneapolis homicide investigators. Curtis Marx wasn't the best detective on the other side of the river, but he wasn't incompetent either. "You know we're looking for a black Suburb. What is this? Son of rim job?"

"We didn't get it until late last night. Honest to god, Murphy," said Marx. "The rectory housekeeper heard tires squealing Monday night and looked out a window in time to see the car tearing down the street," he said. "She didn't think anything of it. Thought it was

77

another jerk burning rubber. She finished cleaning up and went home for the night."

"So . . . ," said Murphy.

"So when she got up in the morning and caught the television news, she flipped," said Marx. "She felt terrible about Father Ambrose—guilty that she hadn't run across the street to check on him. It took her a day to pull herself together. She's crying her eyes out."

"How's he doing?" asked Murphy.

"He's at Hennepin County Medical Center. Got a concussion, a busted hip. Looks like he was choked. He's pretty messed up, the poor guy, but he's gonna make it."

"I don't suppose the housekeeper got a license number," said Murphy. She didn't know why she even bothered asking.

"Shit no. Nothing."

"A look at the driver?"

"Nope."

"Figures. Anything else?"

"One little thing. We're keeping it out of the newspapers."

"Don't leave me in suspense, Curtis."

"It's probably nothing. A parishioner may have dropped it earlier. Chances are it has nothing to do with the assault. We're having trouble getting prints off it."

"A crucifix," Murphy said.

A moment of silence, then, "How'd you know that?"

She pulled out of the station-house parking lot and steered the Jeep onto the I-94 ramp headed west, for downtown Minneapolis. She needed to pry the crucifix out of the Minneapolis cops. It wouldn't be easy; it was their evidence and cops on both sides of the river were territorial. It didn't help that there was new bad blood between the two departments. In the spring, Minneapolis undercover had arranged a meeting with a low-level dealer in a St. Paul park, but they didn't flag St. Paul until an hour before the operation went down. The sting turned sour, ending in a shoot-out and a dead bystander. Lawsuits were still flying over that mess, and St. Paul cops looked as though they didn't know what was happening in their own city. From then on, Minneapolis P.D. called the mess in the park "the unfortunate miscommunication with St. Paul" and St. Paul cops called it "getting fucked in the ass by Minneapolis," or simply "the rim job."

Still, Marx sounded interested. She told him she suspected that the man who killed Finch had dropped the hooker's necklace while trying to murder Father Ambrose, and may also be the man responsible for their unsolved murder from the spring. Marx told her to drive over and pitch it to his boss.

"Come on, Neal, don't you want to add a little more black to your board?" she said to the lieutenant in charge of Homicide. She was sitting under the white board he kept on his office wall. The solved cases were written in black and the unsolved in red. It was already shaping up to be a long, ugly summer in Minneapolis; there was a lot of red on the board.

Neal Olson grunted. He was a big, blond Swede with a whisk-broom moustache and long, yellow teeth.

"I'm not leaving without it," she said, folding her arms across her chest.

Marx, a tall, twitchy man with slick black hair, stood in the office doorway leaning against the frame with his hands shoved in his pockets. "It's not asking too much, Lieutenant," said Marx. "Shit, she's the one who put the pieces together on this thing."

"I'll take good care of the necklace," Murphy said.

Olson grunted again. "You'd better," he said. "Remember whose evidence it is. This is Minneapolis evidence. This is on loan to St. Paul. Fucking *on loan.*"

"'On loan,'" she repeated.

"That means we get it back. Sooner than fucking later." He reached across his desk to hand her the white box. He stopped before dropping it into her palm. "When you gonna come work for me?" he asked.

She laughed, snatched the box from his hand and stuffed it in her purse. "Thank you," she said, and stood up to leave.

"You didn't answer me," Olson said.

"Thanks, Curtis," she whispered to Marx as he stepped out of the doorway to let her through. "Owe you one." He nodded.

"Think about it, Murphy," Olson yelled after her.

Murphy planned to take the crucifix to Finch's funeral for identification by the dead woman's parents, but she didn't want to upset them by showing them some stranger's trinket by mistake. Over drinks with Erik, she would compare the Minneapolis crucifix with the one in Finch's Confirmation portrait. If they looked similar, the necklace would be joining Murphy and Gabe on their road trip to a rural Wisconsin cemetery Thursday morning.

Why did the man who murdered a hooker also attack a priest? Why would a killer go to a priest? She had some theories. Maybe she'd bounce them off Erik. Over drinks. One drink.

Murphy walked into their meeting place, an Eastern European bar and restaurant down the street from the cathedral. When she entered, brass bells hanging from the top of the door announced her arrival. She stood at the hostess stand and scanned the room. To her right was an L-shaped bar with room enough for a half dozen bar stools. On shelves behind the bar was a wide array of vodka. Russian Prince, Polar Ice, Magic Crystal, Stolichnaya. Straight ahead was the restaurant. Modern-looking lights with wide shades hung from the ceiling by silver chains. A paisley fringe shawl covered each shade. The tables were draped with white linen and topped by lamps with red shades.

"Hello, Paris."

She started. He'd walked in right behind her. Erik was dressed in dark pants, a white shirt and a tie. He must have come right from court, she thought. The crispness of the dress shirt emphasized his broad shoulders. Unlike many male marathoners, he looked muscular instead of sticklike. Murphy guessed he supplemented the running with some serious time in the gym.

"Table for two?" asked the hostess, a compact woman with a Russian accent.

"We're not eating," stumbled Murphy. "We're here for . . ."

"Let's get a table," Erik said. The hostess led them to a table in a back corner. Ignoring her whispered protests, Erik guided Murphy by the elbow. "Thank you," he told the hostess. "This is perfect."

He pulled a chair out for Murphy.

"This was supposed to be drinks," she said, sitting down. "In fact, one drink. Period. I feel like I've been shanghaied, Erik. I'm busy. I don't have time for . . ."

"Make time," he said. He sat down across from her. "I know you and Jack have separated again."

"Well, yes," said Murphy, fumbling to form a complete sentence. "Yes, we have."

"I'd like to take you to dinner while the door is open," said Erik. "That's it. Dinner. Really. No need to be skittish."

"I'm not skittish; I'm a little surprised," she said defensively. She was still in her standard work outfit of jeans and a blouse. "I'm not dressed for a nice restaurant. This was supposed to be a work meeting over one . . ."

"I know—one drink. You look fine. Here. I'm not dressed either," he said, undoing his tie, slipping it off and dropping it on the table.

"Yeah. Right. That's much better," she said, laughing.

"The food here is great," he said. "I haven't eaten and you haven't either. I did bring that picture." He slipped Finch's eight-by-ten color photo out of a manila envelope as the waitress came by the table for drink orders. "Martinis are great here," said Erik. "Let me order one for you."

"Fine," she said, and reached across the table for the Confirmation portrait while he ordered.

The picture had been taken against one of those fake-looking nature screens used in department-store photo studios. This one had a spring scene with flowering apple trees. Except for the red hair framing her face, the girl in the foreground was nearly as pale as the blooms in the background. Finch was dressed in a cream-colored blouse with pearl buttons down the front and a prim lace collar. Against her blouse rested a crucifix, hanging from a gold chain.

Murphy set the small white box on the table and took the cover off. "You're not going to propose to me, are you?" asked Erik. She laughed.

"If the necklace inside this box matches the one in the portrait, we're in business," she said. She took the plastic bag out of the box, unsealed it and carefully extracted the gold chain. The crucifix sparkled in the soft glow of the table lamp. Murphy studied the portrait on the table in front of her and then scrutinized the crucifix, holding the chain a little closer to the lamp. "Bingo," Murphy said under her breath.

"Now explain," said Erik.

The drinks came; Murphy sipped.

"Vodka and Drambuie," he said.

"*Mmmm*," she said. "Divine."

"Careful," he said, his eyes twinkling mischievously. "It's sweet, but strong."

"Please spare me." She laughed, almost choking on her drink.

"Tell me about the crucifix," he said.

She recounted the assault against the priest and offered her theory about the same man being responsible for both attacks, as well as a Minneapolis murder early in the spring.

Before she realized it, dinner had arrived. She was so busy talking, she didn't recall ordering. He must have done it for her. Again, his choice for her was wonderful: a Cornish game hen covered in a thyme-scented honey-wine sauce. He ate a bloody filet mignon smothered with mushrooms. Their conversation during the meal was comfortable.

He switched from talking about work to discussing books and movies. She discovered he also liked to cook, and for some reason it didn't surprise her. He didn't ask her about her marriage, and she was glad. She wouldn't know what to say about it.

"Dessert?" he asked.

"No way," she said.

"One more martini?"

"God, no. You'd have to carry me home."

"That's entirely doable," he said. "I live a block from here."

"My home . . . not your home," said Murphy, again tripping over her words.

"We could do that, too," he said, reaching across the table and placing his right hand on top of her left. She quickly slipped it away.

"No. Really. I need to get home."

They strolled down the sidewalk to the parking lot on the side of the building. Night again failed to chase away the heat; warm air radiated up from the pavement.

"Tell me, Paris. Why did Finch's murderer go after a priest? What's your theory on that weirdness?"

"Are you Catholic?"

"No. I could convert."

She laughed. He was entertaining. "Catholics are supposed to go to confession on a fairly regular basis, but many don't. Either they think it's too intrusive or too scary, or they haven't committed any mortal sins and aren't worried about the venial ones."

"You lost me."

"Well, if I can remember the official definitions from my good ol' Baltimore Catechism, a venial sin doesn't deprive the soul completely of sanctifying grace. It's not as serious. Swearing would be a venial sin, for example."

"A mortal sin?"

"A mortal sin is a grievous offense against the law of God. It deprives the sinner of sanctifying grace. Basically, it's a one-way ticket to hell. Murdering someone would put you in the express lane."

They stopped at the Jeep and Paris fished her car keys out of her purse.

"So you think Finch's killer . . ."

". . . Is a practicing Catholic who went to Father Ambrose to obtain absolution, but something went wrong."

"Fascinating," said Erik. He suddenly flattened his body against hers, pinning her against the car, and kissed her on the mouth. His body felt good against hers; she enjoyed it long enough to feel guilty about it. "Would you call this a mortal sin or a venial sin?" he whispered in her ear.

She gently but firmly pushed him away with both hands. "I would call it a bad idea," she said. She opened the Jeep door and got in. "Good night, Erik."

"You don't know what you're missing," he said, leaning against the door. "I do a really good breakfast."

She smiled, shook her head and grabbed the door handle.

"Seriously. Don't write me off, Paris."

"Good night, Erik."

ELEVEN

Michaels followed the news coverage about Finch's murder; but after the regrettable mishap in the confessional, he became preoccupied with the fate of the priest. Killing a whore—even a pious one—could be forgiven by some priest, somewhere, sometime. Murdering a man of the cloth was different.

"Sacrilege." That's what the priest had uttered before Michaels pushed the big man down and wrapped his hands around his throat. After fleeing the scene in a fright—he hoped to hell no one saw him—Michaels looked for a detailed definition of the word that same night.

"Sacrilege. Sacrilege. Where is *sacrilege*, dammit!" As he sucked down a couple of glasses of Scotch to calm his nerves, he frantically paged through a stack of religious reference books he'd pulled from the shelves of his home library and mounded on the coffee table in front of him. His clothes—windbreaker, slacks, shirt, shoes, boxers and socks—were in a heap on the couch next to him.

He lifted the enormous family Bible and immediately set it down again. Couldn't wade through that thing tonight. He picked up the compact Bible his daughters used for homework assigned by their Catholic school and opened it to the back. All he could find was a map index. "Just what I need—'The Division of Canaan' and 'Palestine in the Time of the Maccabees.' Useless." He threw it down.

He saw a slender book, a child's Catechism, and grabbed it from the heap on the table. He looked at the front cover a moment; it had a picture of Jesus holding up an opened book. Written inside the book was "I AM THE WAY AND THE TRUTH AND THE LIFE." He remembered it was his childhood Catechism. He turned it over and looked at the back cover. It had a picture of Jesus on the cross. Under it was written "LOOK AT A CRUCIFIX EVERY DAY. Ask yourself, If He loves me that much, what will I do for Him today? Start going to mass on weekdays? Spend more time in prayer?"

"Stop strangling priests?" he said to himself.

He scanned the index in back of the slender volume: "Revelation . . . revenge . . . reverence . . . right . . . rite . . . rosary . . . sacrament . . . sacramental character . . . sacramental confession . . . sacramentals . . . Sacred Scripture . . . sacrifice."

"Here it is," he announced to himself, taking another gulp of Scotch. "*Sacrilege:* the irreverent treatment, or mistreatment, of sacred persons, places, or things." A very serious offense—the kind that can send a man straight to hell.

"Son-of-a-bitch," he hissed under his breath. "Now I'm in some serious shit." Nothing he could do about it now, he thought. He threw the Catechism on the pile of books, polished off his drink and stood up. He walked back and forth in front of the couch. More immediate than his worries about his soul were his fears about getting caught. Had he left anything behind as he did with Miss Poor Outcome? Not that he recalled; he shouldn't have had so much to drink beforehand. He wondered what other evidence they could have on him. Fingerprints? No. He'd pulled his leather gloves on before opening the priest's side of the confessional. At least he had done that right. What if someone had seen him leaving the church, gotten a look at him or his license plate? It would be easy enough to claim mistaken identity. Suppose the police came knocking? What would they find in his home that would be difficult to explain, that could cause him problems?

He stopped pacing. The hair.

He ran up to the attic, pulled out the hatbox and ran back down to the library. He stood next to the built-in bookcase. It ran the length of the wall and reached to the ceiling. He pulled a shoulder-high shelf toward him, and a section of the bookcase swung open smoothly and noiselessly. The safe room. He reached to the right inside the room and flipped a light switch.

The ten-by-ten space was filled with furs, jewels, paintings and guns—a couple of rifles, but mostly handguns. A sweet little Russian PSM. A couple of Glocks. A collection of SIG-Sauers. A rare Civil War Union officer's sword hanging from one wall and a Picasso painting hanging from another. Michaels appreciated the room itself as much as what was in it. Behind the drywall, fastened directly onto the wall studs, was a system of heavy-gauge steel-mesh and bullet-resistant fiberglass panels. They could stop .44 magnum bullets. The door was similarly reinforced and could be barred from the inside. A cell phone, a radio and a small television allowed contact with the outside world. More than a safe room, it was a fortress, and he had designed it. His wife had argued against it, said it was overkill. He had told her she was naïve, that the world was a dangerous place, especially for the rich.

He walked to the small wall safe, set the hatbox down on the floor and paused, recalling the combination. The wall safe was a new addition to the room, and he hadn't used it much. His wife didn't know the combination and he would never give it to her; he intended to use it for things like this, like the hair. He turned the dial. Left forty. Right twenty-two. Left thirty-six. It clicked. He pulled it open. He felt around inside. Only a few legal documents. He picked up the hatbox and set it inside. He shut the wall safe and spun the dial around a couple of times.

He turned to walk out, but stopped to admire his wife's furs hanging in fluffy panels. He ran his fingers down the length of a Russian lynx stole. He stroked the white fox jacket hanging next to it. He'd lost count of how many minks he'd bought her. Only the best. God how he'd indulged her when they were first married, before he became bored with her, bored with their mundane and sporadic sex life. He slipped his naked body between a couple of long mahogany mink coats. Wonderful. He felt himself starting to get hard and laughed. His wife's coats—dead animals on hangers—turned him on more than she did. He buried his face in one of the coats, breathed into it. Almost as sensual as the hair, but not quite. He sighed and stepped out of the fur. No, it wasn't enough to get him off, but it wasn't too bad. He flicked off the light and walked out, shutting the door behind him.

Two days later, he read a story in the St. Paul paper that said the priest was hospitalized in serious condition. *Not dead.* Perhaps Michaels's soul wasn't entirely doomed. He still could make amends. His reputation could also remain intact. As with the whore's murder, the authorities had no suspects. Minneapolis police detectives were waiting for the priest to improve before interviewing him about the assault, according to the news account. This didn't worry him. Michaels assured himself that the priest's vow to keep confessions private would prevent the father from handing police a description of his assailant. Even if he opted to violate that confidence, he doubted that the priest had gotten a good look at him. The church was dim and it all had happened so very quickly, from what he could remember.

With the concern over the priest compartmentalized—placed in the "worry about it later" box—his thoughts returned to Miss Poor Outcome. He turned to the newspaper's obituary section.

TWELVE

Murphy and Gabe took her Jeep, and she drove, taking the scenic route to Finch's funeral. Murphy had decided to keep the evening with Erik to herself. After all, it was just dinner and Gabe didn't need to know; she didn't want to listen to a lecture all the way to the funeral. Erik had rattled her, but also flattered her; she needed that. She was also attracted to him. It didn't help Jack's case that he wouldn't return her calls. Maybe he wasn't serious about getting back together except in the sack, the one place they never had any problems. Maybe it was all they had left in their marriage. Murphy didn't want to think about that.

She emptied her mind, letting the scenery wash over her as they passed one Wisconsin cornfield after another. "Knee-high by the Fourth of July," she mumbled.

"What?" asked Gabe.

"Haven't you heard that saying? Corn should be knee high by the Fourth of July. Or maybe it's corn as high as an elephant's eye. Something like that."

"It ain't the Fourth yet—and that corn looks crotch high to me," he said.

"How poetic is that?" She laughed. "Crotch high by the Fourth of July?"

"I never said it was poetic."

She laughed again and slipped a compact disc into the Jeep's CD player. He wanted country-western and she wanted rock. They compromised on jazz. The sound of a sax saturated the car, wafting through the interior. "Grover Washington, Junior," she said. "Live at the Bijou."

"Nice," said Gabe.

"Uh huh," she said.

He reached into his pocket and pulled out his Winstons. She gave him the eye.

"Fine," he said, putting them back. "I don't need it."

They drove through the town of Luck. A sign on the side of the road advertised the annual festival. "Lucky Days."

"Look, it says 'Pig Sale. Half Off.' Sounds like a good deal," said Gabe, pointing to a homemade sign stapled to a tree and decorated with balloons. "You suppose that means you get half a pig or . . ."

"I think it was meant to say 'Big Sale,' not 'Pig Sale,' Gabe," she said, smiling. "Part of the *B* fell off."

"Oh, yeah."

Outside of town, a herd of cattle stood in a pond, cooling off. While it wasn't yet noon, the temperature was already well into the eighties. They almost stopped at a roadside stand, where a man in bib overalls was selling enormous wooden sculptures carved with a chainsaw. Gabe eyed a six-foot-long rendition of a muskie.

"Seriously, Gabe. Where in the hell would you put something like that?"

"Yeah, you're right. Keep driving." They did. Cornfields. Farmhouses. Barns. Thick woods. Yellow road sign warning of deer crossing. More farms. Lutheran cemetery. John Deere dealership. Rows of green tractors. Another town. Liquor store. LOWEST BEER PRICES IN TOWN. Farther north, leafed trees giving way to pines. Three more deer crossings. Bigger town. Two liquor stores. LOWEST BEER PRICES ALLOWED BY LAW. COLDEST ICE IN TOWN. Another Lutheran cemetery.

Murphy noticed the dearth of Catholic churches and cemeteries. This hunk of Wisconsin was Lutheran country, with a heavy Scandinavian and German influence. Finch had been Irish Catholic. Her last name was Hennessy. Murphy knew that. It turned out Finch wasn't her real name; it was Fionn. Her middle name was Clare. Murphy hadn't known any of that until Finch was dead. She wondered what the grave marker would read. Fionn Hennessy. Fionn Clare Hennessy. Daughter.

How sad to be ignorant of someone's full name until reading it on a death certificate. Still, a name, while an important detail, is not the full measure of a person, reasoned Murphy. Her mind wandered back to the necklace, now tucked away in her purse. The necklace was a detail. Like the yellow umbrella. Murphy had learned over the years that some details—seemingly innocuous, unimportant details—could make or break a case. Details like a strand of hair. A bit of fabric. A drop of blood. A noise down the street. A couple of gumdrops.

A few summers earlier, a Jane Doe was found murdered and dumped in a vacant city lot. She'd been beaten so badly her face was gone. The Ramsey County Medical Examiner found that she'd been drinking—and also found the remains of a few gumdrops in her stomach. Armed with that unusual detail, Murphy called a bartender. "Do any bars in town put gumdrops on the counter for customers to munch on?"

"No way."

"Are there any drinks served with gumdrops as a garnish?" asked Murphy.

"Anything is possible in the glamorous world of booze," he said. "Let me get my book . . . Yup. Here it is. It's called a gumdrop martini. It's got lemon-flavored rum, vodka, Southern Comfort, dry vermouth, lemon juice and—*taa daa!*—a lemon slice and gumdrops as garnish."

Murphy checked the bars, found one that served gumdrop martinis. After talking to the patrons and bartender on duty the night of the murder, she came up with the woman's identity and the name of the man seen bothering her. After his arrest, he confessed.

Some details were important.

"We're here, Gabe. Wake up." She nudged him; he'd dozed off the last thirty minutes of the trip.

"Yeah, yeah. I'm up," he muttered.

He tightened his gray tie and smoothed his white dress shirt. Murphy wore a navy blue skirt and short-sleeved cotton blouse. Her hair was pulled back into a ponytail, held together with a plain navy blue ribbon.

Murphy turned into a tar parking lot off the road jammed with cars and pickup trucks. "Looks like Finch got a nice turnout," she said, pulling into a space at the corner of the lot. "I'm kind of surprised."

"How many hookers' funerals you been to?" he asked her.

"Umm. I think this is my first." She turned off the ignition.

"My fourth," he said. "No, wait. Fifth. Anyway, here's the deal." Gabe pulled down the visor and looked in the mirror. His tie was crooked and he tried straightening it as he talked. "Just because she was a hooker doesn't mean people won't turn out. In fact, I guarantee you some of them came *because* she was a hooker."

"Like going to a freak show?"

"Yeah." He continued struggling with the tie.

"That's horseshit," she said.

"That's life," he said. He turned and looked at her for help. She reached over and adjusted the tie.

"There," she said. "You look fine."

They worked up a slight sweat crossing the parking lot. The warm tar was soft under their shoes. "Pray for air conditioning," Gabe said as they climbed the sun-baked wooden steps leading to the church's door. Gabe's prayers were not answered. The church was an oven.

Murphy and Gabe walked to the front of the church, where a

handful of Finch's family members gathered in a tight knot around a white coffin. Finch rested against a satin pillow. What remained of her red hair was artfully arranged around her face and neck so only her family—and Gabe and Murphy—would know that a lot of it was missing. A middle-aged couple stood at the head of the coffin. Both had red hair salted with gray. His was trimmed very short, almost Marinelike in its sharp angles. Hers was in a tight bun behind her head. Their son, Finch's younger brother by three years, sat alone in a pew in the middle of the church, his face in his hands. They were all dressed in black.

"Mr. and Mrs. Hennessy?"

"Yes?" said Finch's father. His voice was gravelly.

"I'm Sergeant Paris Murphy and this is Sergeant Gabriel Nash."

"We're very sorry for your loss," said Gabe.

"Thank you for coming," said Mrs. Hennessy. She was a tiny woman with skinny legs; she looked like a crow in her black dress. She took Gabe's right hand in both of hers and held it for a moment. Gabe nodded. Murphy thought he was far better at this sort of thing than she. She felt awkward trying to comfort grieving families; could never find words that sounded real.

"Hope my directions were okay," said Finch's father, shaking Murphy's hand.

"Real good directions," said Murphy. She noticed the farmer's palms had the texture of sandpaper, but his grip was weak. That surprised her because he was such a big man. His shirt collar was tight on his sunburned neck; his biceps looked one flex away from splitting the sleeves of his suit coat.

Husband and wife stood apart, facing the coffin and hardly looking at each other. Murphy sensed hostility between them. Maybe it was the grief. She'd seen it happen after other murders, survivors turning against each other. Murphy thought there was something else going on, however. Finch had never named who'd abused her as a kid. Murphy had assumed it was an uncle or neighbor because Finch had never said anything negative about her folks. Now Murphy wondered if it was the father.

"I have to apologize," said Murphy, pulling the small white box out of her purse. "This may be upsetting, but it's necessary." She feared they'd be even more distraught after the service, and didn't want to wait to show it to them. "I would like you to identify a piece of jewelry," she said, opening the box and removing the plastic bag.

Murphy drew the necklace out of the bag and held it up. Finch's mother gasped. She instinctively reached out for it, as if touching it would restore her daughter. "Fionn's Confirmation crucifix," she said. "You found it. Where? How? Can we have it back?"

"I'm sorry," said Gabe in the reassuring, gentle voice he reserved for crime victims and their families. "You will certainly get it back as soon as possible, but we really can't let you handle it right now. It's evidence in Fionn's case, and may also help solve a couple of Minneapolis crimes as well. You are sure this is her necklace? Take a good look."

Fionn Clare's parents stared at the tiny, gold chain and its cruci-fix. As Murphy held it in front of their faces, it swayed slightly in the warm breeze of the church fans. "Yes," said her father, his voice breaking. "That's our daughter's necklace. I remember the day I put it around her neck."

Murphy caught a glint of hate in the mother's eyes as he spoke. No, worse than hate. Repulsion. He was the abuser.

The church eventually filled to capacity, with some visitors forced to stand in back. So they could mingle more easily, Gabe and Murphy asked that the Hennessys not identify them as police investigators; and they asked that any strangers be pointed out. Gabe checked the parking lot for black Suburbans while Murphy watched the crowd, standing off to the side with some other women. In such situations, she wished she were shorter so she didn't stick out, so she could blend in easier. Such a hot box; she felt the perspiration collecting on her forehead and above her upper lip. She couldn't verbalize what she was looking for as she leaned against the wall and read the faces, concentrating on the blond men. He might appear guilty or remorseful, curious or smug. It could be some combination of those things—or something entirely different.

Is it you? she wondered, her eyes resting on one male face. No. He looked ready to nod off; his wife had probably dragged him here. What about you? No. He was relaxed as he whispered to a knot of other sunburned men. He was a farmer. You? No. Eyes too red and face too drawn. Probably a relative.

She prayed she would recognize the look.

As their eyes met and locked briefly, she thought she saw it.

He was standing in the back, behind some men in jeans. He wasn't overdressed. Gray trousers and a long-sleeved oxford shirt, with the top button undone. Everyone else in the room seemed a little uncomfortable in their church clothes, a little wrinkled and sweaty. He could have been standing under an air conditioner. His clothes were professionally pressed and looked expensive in their studied casualness. He was a big man, but not in the same way as Finch's father. He was tall and well proportioned, and handsome behind his thick, blond hair. Only his eyes betrayed his cruelty. His cool, gray eyes, at once savage and sad. She'd seen that same look in the eyes of pit bulls dragged away from dog fights.

Trying not to arouse his suspicions, she looked away after taking a mental photograph.

His eyes lingered on her quite a bit longer.

THIRTEEN

It never occurred to him that she was a cop. Not in his wildest, wettest dreams.

All he saw were full breasts straining against the white blouse, violet eyes and long, black hair confined by a band of ribbon. With her olive skin, she was more exotic-looking than the other women in the church. She was taller than he usually liked, but small boned with fine, fragile-looking wrists. Michaels wondered what she tasted like, how easily her lips would bruise under his mouth. He imagined undoing that ribbon and loosening her hair, running his hands through it. He was pleased that she had averted her eyes after he caught her staring at him. He found it submissive, and he adored that quality in a woman. She was obviously interested in him. If only he had the time, but this was a busy day. He had had his staff reschedule the morning appointments so he could make it to the service—he'd fed the nurses a story about a sick friend—but he needed to make it back to the clinic for his afternoon patients.

During the two-hour trip to the funeral—he took his gray Lexus sedan thinking it would be more discreet than his loaded Suburban— he'd contemplated what compelled him to attend. He thought back to his father's service. Brief. Formal. Little sentimentality. Pretty much summed up his father's personality when he wasn't drinking. His mother's service, like his mother, was another story. Friday-night wake with sobbing relatives. His mother inside the coffin, a rosary in her hands. Pink lipstick on her mouth. Michaels couldn't look at her without remembering the taste of her blood and lipstick. Saturday-morning funeral and burial that took hours. Flowers. Everywhere, flowers. Neighbors making pilgrimages to the house Sunday. Hot dishes and condolences. Michaels's father stopped drinking that weekend and Michaels started.

No. Michaels was not a big fan of funerals. More than once he almost changed his mind about Miss Poor Outcome's service, almost stopped the car and turned around. Now here he stood, in the back of a hot church in the middle of nowhere listening to the whore's weepy brother recite some shit by Oliver Wendell Holmes.

Her hands are cold; her face is white;
No more her pulses come and go;
Her eyes are shut to life and light;
Fold the white vesture, snow on snow,
And lay her where the violets blow. .

This outing was a mistake, he thought. What had driven him here? What had lured him here? It had to be more than simple curiosity. Michaels thought back to the obituary notice sitting on the passenger seat of his car. During the drive over, he kept picking it up and looking at it whenever he came to a light. It had a small photo of the whore. It must have been taken years ago; she actually looked good in it. Almost beautiful. Almost. Those days were long gone by the time he'd gotten to her, which was unfortunate since he much preferred taking pretty women. Perhaps her funeral interested him because she had been pretty at one time.

He checked his watch. How much longer? He was suffocating. Haven't these hicks discovered air conditioning? Look at them all, dressed up with their prissy wives on their arms. What a bunch of rubes. No wonder this Finch fled to the city. Working as a hooker on the streets of St. Paul had to beat shoveling cow shit out of a barn in the middle of Butt Fuck, Wisconsin.

Michaels sighed and looked at his watch again. He'd already lost an hour of his life, an hour he'd never get back. Screw his curiosity. He contemplated slipping out the door, but it was too crowded. He didn't want to attract attention, although he was sure he was safe from any suspicion. If someone inquired about his relationship to Miss Poor Outcome, he had a story ready. He could say he had provided her with medical treatment as part of his volunteer work on that domestic-abuse program. What a lovely lie. He'd come off looking like a saint. Brilliant. In fact, given an opportunity, he might introduce himself to the whore's family as her bereaved physician. No. That was too risky, and he needed to get the hell out of here as soon as the mass was over. Still, what a delicious joke that would be, he mused. He covered his mouth with his hand as he struggled to stifle a laugh. A woman in polyester stretch pants standing next to him handed him a tissue and patted his arm.

"She's with God now," she whispered.

"Thank you," he said, and lifted the tissue to his mouth.

"Here, take this," she said. She tried to shove a plastic rosary into his hands. This was too much. Any minute now he was going to lose it and laugh out loud.

"No, thank you," he muttered through the tissue, and pushed her hands away. She stared at him briefly and returned her attention to the front of the church.

If any, born of kindlier blood,
Should ask, What maiden lies below?
Say only this: A tender bud,
That tried to blossom in the snow,
Lies withered where the violets blow.

She had only been a hooker. Hell, Michaels thought, she probably hadn't even been good at hooking. Otherwise she would have been working for one of those upscale escort services. Funerals gloss over the bad shit. Someone should stand up and tell it like it is. What would he say? "She was a mediocre prostitute who couldn't give a decent fuck if her life depended on it. Actually, her life had depended on it, and that's why she's dead." He forgot himself and smiled. A fat man with Frisbee-sized sweat stains under his arms glared at him. Michaels stopped smiling and glared back. He wanted to tell the fat turd to stop looking at him. Instead, he turned his face. He told himself to be more careful; sloppiness could get him in trouble.

Michaels checked his watch a third time. Why did the priest let the brother go on and on? This was a funeral, not a Romantic literature reading.

As he finished the poem, the brother broke down, sobbing. His father stepped up to the lectern, slipped an arm around his son's shoulders and helped him back to his seat. Finally, thought Michaels. Let's get on with it and get the hell out of this steam bath.

The mourners spilled out of the church and walked to the adjoining cemetery. Michaels intended to bolt right after the mass, but as he hurried down the church steps he noticed the black-haired woman standing in the grass, watching him. Who was that lout with her? Her father? An uncle? It couldn't possibly be her husband. She wanted him. No mistaking that gaze, so shy yet so intense.

He decided to stay for the burial.

"Gabe, I think that's him," Murphy whispered. She grabbed Gabe by the arm and they flowed with the crowd toward the cemetery, pallbearers leading the way with the casket.

"No Suburban! Not a single one," he said.

"I don't care about the car. He drove his wife's car or something."

"Why do you think?"

"Look at him."

99

"Yeah. Nice pants. He sticks out in this crowd. But I see a handful of other big blonds here who look capable."

"Watch them leave," she whispered. "Get their plates—especially the ones from Minnesota—and make sure you get that guy's car."

"Interesting bastard," Gabe said.

The family sat on folding chairs around the casket. They and the grave were shielded from the sun by a canopy erected over the site. The mourners clustered around the canopy while the priest prayed over the casket.

"Grant this mercy, O Lord, we beseech Thee, to Thy servant Fionn Clare Hennessy, that she may not receive in punishment the requital of her deeds who in desire did keep Thy will, and as the true faith here united her to the company of the faithful, so may Thy mercy unite her above to the choirs of angels. Through Jesus Christ our Lord, Amen."

At the edge of the crowd stood Michaels. Now he realized why he had come, what had drawn him. This interment gave him a satisfying sense of completion. He could slide the cover over this compartment in his life. He smiled slightly.

The priest offered the final petition before the casket was lowered into the grave.

"May her soul and the souls of all the faithful departed through the mercy of God rest in peace."

The doctor looked at his watch. Damn. He needed to hurry if he wanted to be back in time for his afternoon appointments. The dark-haired woman was gone. What a shame. Well, maybe some other time. He walked briskly to the parking lot and slipped into his car.

* * *

"We can rule out your other big blonds," Murphy said. They stood beside the church, behind an evergreen. "Look at my guy's face."

"Motherfucker," Gabe said. "Kiss your ass if those aren't fingernail scratches."

FOURTEEN

As soon as she and Gabe returned to the station from Finch's funeral, Murphy hunkered down in front of a computer and started typing. She ran a check on the Lexus plates.

Dr. A. Romann Michaels.

"A doctor," she muttered.

His place of residence—a Summit Avenue address.

She was familiar with the stretch of homes in that section of Summit. While the entire avenue is gorgeous—called the best-preserved Victorian boulevard in America—the doctor's neighborhood was especially sumptuous. Meticulous lawns and lavish flower gardens protected by wrought-iron fences. Perfectly restored and maintained mansions listed on historic tours of the city. The wealthy who lived in these showplaces were the descendants of the lumber barons, railroad tycoons and politicians who had helped build the city and the state. His last name was also familiar. They were big-deal bankers. Could the murderer really be from the most respectable ranks of the community? Not any doctor, but a member of one of St. Paul's old, moneyed families? Or was she chasing the wrong man?

Murphy tried to brush aside a twinge of self-doubt. It wouldn't be the first time someone wealthy had gotten involved in something seedy. The city's history was peppered with such cases. Many years ago there was the department store heir who'd been sent to prison after paying someone to murder his wife and her lover. A few years back she'd busted a senior partner in one of the oldest law firms in the city; she'd caught him at home as he was masturbating in a room filled with child porn. She'd heard that one high-society matron had been caught picking up male prostitutes in downtown Minneapolis last summer, but that had been kept pretty quiet.

Still, these cases were quite rare, thought Murphy. It's not that the wealthy have higher morals; they have better lawyers. They don't often do something wildly stupid or impulsive; they're too shrewd for that. It doesn't take brains to inherit a fortune and a place in society; however, it does take some intelligence to hang on to both for any length of time.

So what was he doing at Finch's funeral—with scratches on his face?

She did an Internet search using the doctor's name and discovered that his clinic had an impressive Web site. He was a plastic surgeon with an office in Edina. Of course, Murphy thought cynically. That's a suburb with a lot of disposable income for face lifts, tummy tucks and boob jobs. The Web site had some interesting pictures. It showed a drawing of a woman's silhouette before and after breast reduction. It had real photos—with the heads cropped off—of women's chests before and after breast augmentation. Murphy wondered why anyone would want bigger breasts. She found hers a handicap when she ran, and she resented the effort it took to find an adequate sports bra.

The clinic Web site had some personal information about Michaels. It said he was married and had two daughters. He was an avid swimmer and enjoyed sailing, alpine skiing, windsurfing and golf. "Weekend jock," she thought.

He also liked exotic-game hunting. Murphy wondered: "What the hell does he do—shoot elephants and rhinos in his off-hours?"

He had earned his medical degree from Northwestern University Medical School. He had completed residencies in general surgery and plastic and reconstructive surgery at Stanford University Hospital. He had capped his training off with a plastic surgery fellowship at the Mayo Clinic in Rochester. He was certified by the American Board of Facial Plastic and Reconstructive Surgery, was a fellow of the American College of Surgeons and a member of the Academy of Plastic Surgeons of Minnesota. The list of articles he'd written for professional journals was a mile long.

Something else in his background did give her pause. He'd received a prestigious humanitarian award for his work on a local domestic-abuse project. She was familiar with the program, an effort aimed at offering battered women free medical services—including plastic surgery to lessen the physical scars of their abuse. Jack and his colleagues in the E.R. were among the physicians who'd gotten the project off the ground a few years ago. It had received national attention and served as a model for other programs around the country.

Damn. Maybe she was mistaken about this man. But what about his presence at the funeral?

Gabe walked up behind her and handed her a Diet Pepsi. She popped it open and took a swig. "Thanks."

"What'd you come up with?"

"A. Romann Michaels, M.D."

"M.D.?"

"Yup," she said. She took another gulp of pop.

Gabe looked at her screen. "What's this?" he asked, pointing to a foreign phrase at the bottom of Michaels's bio.

Murphy rolled her eyes; she remembered it from her high-school days. "*Nulli secundus,*" she said. "It's Latin."

"It means?"

"Second to none."

"You shittin' me?"

"I shit you not."

"Jesus. The guy's sure got a high opinion of himself," said Gabe, walking back to his desk.

"I'd say so," she replied. She clicked back to the home page and suddenly noticed the clinic's logo up in the corner. A bouquet of roses changing from buds to open flowers, and circled by the words: "Plastic surgery. Opening up a world of beautiful possibilities."

"Give me a break," she mumbled.

Amid the roses, a fly chased a bumblebee.

She wondered if Jack was familiar with this plastic surgeon. It would be a great excuse to call him, try to patch things up. Still, he hadn't returned any of her calls. Instead of applying pressure to the relationship—especially after that nasty fight—maybe it was best to step back a bit. Besides, she knew someone else who had helped launch that program—a guy who witnessed the final results of domestic abuse on the exam table of the M.E.'s office.

"Erik?"

"Paris. I was about to call you."

"Yeah. Right. That's what they all say."

He laughed. "No. Really. I snared a couple of Saints tickets for next month. They're playing the Sioux Falls Canaries. How about it?"

He had caught her off guard and stumbling for cover. "Well . . . I . . . I don't know Erik. We work together quite a bit and maybe we shouldn't . . ."

"As friends, then, Paris. Let's go as friends. I'll even let you pay for the beer and brats. How about it?"

"Yes, that sounds like fun, Erik. Sure. Why not?"

"Great. Let me grab the tickets and I'll give you the date so you can mark it on your . . ."

"Wait, Erik. Let's leave the logistics for later. This is a professional call."

"Sure. What's up?"

"Remember that tip you gave me about the scalpel cut on the back of Finch's head?"

"Yeah, I remember."

"You were right on the mark, Erik. I think her killer is a doctor. A plastic surgeon. I think this bastard who did Finch also assaulted the priest. This morning I showed Finch's parents the crucifix found outside the confessional and they positively identified it as their daughter's necklace. If all that isn't enough, Minneapolis has that unsolved murder I told you about with the same M.O."

"So who is he?" asked Erik. "Who is the murderer?"

"Romann Michaels."

"Whoa! Do you know who he is?"

"I know all about it."

"His uncles own half the politicians in town. He's got relatives up on the hill."

"Yeah, yeah."

"Are you sure about him, Paris? What's your evidence?"

"I don't want to talk about it," she said. "I'm not one-hundred-percent sure he's the one. So keep it quiet."

"Damn well make sure you got your ducks in a row before you go after him. He's very well respected, Paris. He's tops in his field—an artist. Won awards for his volunteer work. He's patched together battered women so they look even better than they did before they got beaten up."

"I wanted to ask you about that," she said. "You were involved in that program, right?"

"I still am, to an extent. So is your ex."

She didn't want to correct him. Jack was not her "ex" anything, at least not yet. "Did you work with this Michaels guy on that project? Can you tell me anything about him?"

"We were both presenters at a domestic-abuse conference held a couple of years ago for medical professionals in Chicago," Erik said. "He had a really slick show. He showed before-and-after slides of the battered women, but, uh, the only thing was, he . . . um . . ."

"Forget the tact, Erik," she said brusquely. "I'm a homicide cop, not a nun. Tell me."

"The thing about him was, he spent a lot of time on the 'before' photos, about the depth of the knife wounds or the severity of the burns, about the pain the women suffered, whether they were raped. He even talked about the genitalia injuries in detail. Way beyond what was necessary. He spent almost no time at all on the 'after' photos, which really showcased his work. He zipped right by them almost as if . . . well . . . like he was getting a hard-on talking about these women getting beaten," said Erik. "Like he was getting off on the abuse. At first I thought it was me. Then a couple of the conference attendees mentioned it, said they thought it was really weird. Sickening even."

Erik paused, thinking about what he had described to her.

"Shit, Paris. I don't know. Maybe you are on to something," he said. "He could be a nut case. I can tell you his conference presentation was disturbing."

"Anything else?" she asked.

"Yeah," said Erik. "The guy really likes his Scotch. The good stuff. Aged single-malt whiskey. He was really putting it away when I talked to him one night in the hotel bar."

"You had a couple of drinks with him?"

"Not really. I sat down at the bar and tried to strike up a conversation. He's a loner. He was more interested in his drink—and in watching the women in the bar."

"He liked the ladies?"

"Sort of."

"What does that mean?"

"He didn't say anything about them or try talking to any of them; he wasn't a pickup artist or anything like that," said Erik. "All he did was watch them."

"Creepy?"

"Yeah, a little."

"Exotic-game hunter," Murphy said softly, almost inaudibly.

"What did you say, Paris? What did you call him?"

"Never mind, Erik. I was thinking out loud."

* * *

His body was as lean as his office. He stood a ramrod-straight six feet, with a build that was muscular yet slender. His skin was tanned and leathery from his hours spent fishing. He tolerated golf and wasn't half bad at it, but he played only when he needed to bend the mayor's ear. His shirts were white, long sleeved and starched. His ties were dark. He wore a suit coat to work, though it was usually left hanging from the back of his chair. His thick gray-and-brown hair never deviated from a disciplined crewcut. His desk was not large—he had purchased it himself rather than make do with the standard-issue metal clunker—but it gave the impression of authority in its glossy oak finish and sharp edges. The desktop was bare except for a telephone, an eight-by-ten photograph of his three blond sons and a brass nameplate: CHIEF BENJAMIN THOMAS CHRISTIANSON III.

Murphy and Gabe had plenty of time to study the chief as they sat in chairs facing his desk late Thursday afternoon. Christianson was on the phone negotiating with the Minneapolis police chief. His voice was at once firm, smooth and convincing. He could have been a diplomat arranging a cease-fire between warring nations. Rumor had it he got the job because of family connections, but he clearly held on to it because of his own merits.

"Look, my people have made impressive headway, and clearly our investigation dovetails with your case involving the assault on the priest, as well as that homicide from the spring."

He paused, listening to his counterpart in Minneapolis.

"No problem there," he said. "I think we're both in agreement on that one."

Murphy briefly wondered what they were in agreement on; probably something in reference to the rim job. Then her mind wandered.

Sitting across from Christianson made her feel like she was back in high school, waiting to get chewed out for mouthing off or skipping class. Except for the lack of crucifixes on the walls, Murphy thought his office could pass for a Catholic school principal's office in its nearly spiritual devotion to simplicity. The walls were painted a flat white and were unadorned, save for a few photographs of the chief shaking hands with police officers receiving awards. Some were St. Paul cops and others wore uniforms from Des Moines, Christianson's hometown and where he'd served as chief before coming to Minnesota. A tall antique oak bookcase—another of the chief's personal furniture pieces—sat against one wall. The shelves were filled with books related to police work: *The Complete Guide to Compact Handguns. The International Biographical Dictionary of Law Enforcement. Homicide Investigation Techniques.* Behind his desk and off to one side, looking isolated and lonely on its own stand, was a computer. It was turned off. He used it only for word processing and e-mail. He viewed the Internet as the slacker's window to the world; he was suspicious of any cop who relied on it more heavily than old-fashioned footwork.

She remembered the last time she'd sat in this chair. She'd reamed out an assistant county attorney for refusing to prosecute one of her cases—her parting words to him were "Kiss my Lebanese ass"—and Christianson had called her in for a ten-minute lecture on cop etiquette. She'd listened to him, thinking he was a Puritan and a perfectionist. Then on her way out, he'd praised her for solving her latest case. She had to admit he did let her cut procedural corners when necessary. The only problem was they often disagreed on when it was necessary.

"Correct. That's all I'm saying," Christianson said into the phone, switching it from one ear to the other and swiveling his chair around to face the windows behind his desk.

Murphy sighed, leaned back in her chair and stretched her legs out in front of her. She hated this politicking and maneuvering; she just wanted to do her job. That's why she'd probably never get past sergeant, and that was fine with her. Sometimes Gabe chewed her out for her crappy attitude, but he wasn't exactly rocketing up the career ladder either.

"You have a talented bunch of detectives over there, but I know you're short on manpower and our load is lighter," Christianson said.

Gabe looked at her and rolled his eyes. She grinned back. The chief's a slick salesman, thought Murphy. That's what Gabe called Christianson behind his back—"Slick." The two men didn't like each other, but at least they had fishing in common. She had absolutely nothing to say to the chief that wasn't work related. Whenever she saw him stepping into an elevator, she took the stairs.

"That's right," Christianson said, swiveling his chair back around so that he faced the detectives. "So why not let my folks lead the investigation into all three cases?" He paused, listening again. He smiled at Gabe and Murphy and gave them the thumbs-up with his left hand while holding the phone with his right.

"Yes. Yes. I understand completely. Certainly. They will work with whoever you give them. We will keep you fully informed. Absolutely. Thank you. Give my best to Delores."

He hung up the phone, leaned over his desk and smiled at the detectives. "Well, we're in business," he said. "You two are running it. Minneapolis will throw a body your way if you need one. Let me know what you need from me and when you need it."

FIFTEEN

He used to look forward to certain Thursdays.

Every Thursday, a bar in Minneapolis hosted an S&M night. They called it "Pins and Needles." He didn't go every Thursday. He didn't want to become too familiar to the staff or the clientele, and he didn't want to become bored with it. So he indulged himself once every few weeks. Told his wife he was meeting old high-school buddies for drinks.

He decided to avoid the place after what had happened with Miss Accident in the spring; he'd picked her up at the bar.

After suffering through the whore's funeral and returning to a waiting room filled with pissed patients, Michaels decided it was time to treat himself.

He wore what everyone wore S&M night. Black. He slipped into a black T-shirt, black jeans and black shoes. He admired himself in the bedroom mirror before leaving the house. Black looked so good with blond hair. He drove the Suburban. More black. As he pulled out of the driveway, he slipped in a CD to get in the mood. Fine Young Cannibals seemed right. "She Drives Me Crazy" rattled around inside the car. He shut off the air conditioner and rolled down all the windows; it was muggy out, but he didn't mind. He took Summit west almost to the river, hung a right on Cretin Avenue and took that to Interstate 94. He wished the drive were a little longer; anticipation was half the fun.

The night of Miss Accident, his drive to the bar had been in a drunken fog. Jennifer had called home. She'd lost the baby while up at the cabin with a friend. She'd delivered the bad news in a flat voice and hung up before he could ask any questions. He'd sat with the phone to his ear, listening to the dial tone and paging through the photo album that would never materialize. Cub Scout meetings. Baseball games. Sailing trips. Michaels had flung the phone across the bedroom and cried for the first time since his mother died. Then he'd grabbed his Scotch and his car keys and driven to the bar with the booze under the seat. He'd pulled the bottle out every third stoplight or so to take a swig. He'd never done that before, literally drinking and driving and drinking and driving.

He promised himself he'd stay sober and in control this visit. Keep the fly at bay.

He pulled into the club's parking lot. Crowded, but not full. By the end of the evening there would be cars parked on the grass. More and more people were discovering Thursday nights at this place; it was a dirty little secret that had grown large and not so secret.

The cold air hit him in the face as he walked into the club. The club's air conditioner was cranked. Then it was always cranked Thursday nights. It kept the women's nipples erect, gave the clothespins something to hang on to, and it hardened the hot wax more quickly. He looked around the warehouse-like room. There'd been a few decorating changes in his absence—he didn't remember that barbed wire along the balcony rails from before—but it was basically the same. Chain-link fencing here and there. Cages. Minimal lighting. Black-and-white posters from old prison flicks.

The real atmosphere was provided by the club patrons themselves. Many dressed as simply and conservatively as he, but others went all out. Women dressed in short, tight spandex dresses that showed every

112

curve of their breasts. Some wore black slips and corsets. Gothics floated in wearing long dresses with black gloves up to their armpits. Lots and lots of leather. The vampire look was popular. He was surprised at how some men could wear a cape with a straight face. There were often surprises at the club from the costumes alone.

He tried not to look startled this particular night when a man walked out of the bathroom dressed in nothing but a white cloth diaper. That man was obviously a doer. There were two sorts of patrons S&M night. The doers and the watchers. Diaper man was a doer. Michaels was a watcher. He enjoyed watching, and thought it was more dignified.

He took a seat at the bar and watched the show onstage. A short, plump woman with spiked hair was dripping hot wax onto another woman's chest. The willing victim was tied to a pole, her wrists bound over her head with pantyhose. She wore a sheer blouse; the wax melted right through it. Next to this couple was a male-female team, with the man tied to the pole with a rope and the woman whipping him. Not too hard. Just hard enough.

"What can I get you?" asked the bartender. Her hair was oriental-looking—long, straight and blue-black. Her lips were painted black and so were her nails.

"Isn't it hard to keep those on all night?" he asked, eyeing the clothespins pinching her nipples under her thin tank top.

"Not at all. It turns me on," she said. She smiled. Black lipstick smudged her teeth. "What turns you on?"

"Don't ask," Michaels said. "You don't want to know." He scanned the greasy whiskey bottles behind her; their selection was usually lousy. "Got any decent Scotch?"

"All we have are blends," she said. "These twenty-somethings don't drink Scotch."

"Aren't you a twenty-something?" he said.

The flattery hit home. She reddened. "Don't ask," she said. "You don't want to know."

Michaels laughed. He liked her. She had big tits and a smart mouth. Her slightly lined neck showed her age. Necks were a dead giveaway, even more so than hands. He guessed she was in her late thirties. Most of the doers were in their twenties; the watchers were in their thirties and forties and fifties. She might be a doer in her off-hours.

"Johnny Walker neat," he said. "A double."

She set it down in front of him. He threw some bills on the bar, grabbed his drink and slid off the stool.

"Leaving so soon?" she asked.

"I'll be back," he said. "Wanna look around." He flashed her a smile. She was his for the taking. He wasn't sure if he was in the mood tonight. Besides, he had to be careful; he'd had enough problems lately. Didn't need to add to the list.

He walked to one of the side rooms, for the real action. For twenty dollars, you could watch while strangers strapped your date to a table and tormented him or her with clothespins, hot wax, whatever. That's where he'd met Miss Accident. Her date had been drunk and had run out of twenties. They'd kicked the loser out of the room. Michaels had stayed. He'd been only too happy to flip for a couple of treatments. She had had a high tolerance for pain.

Michaels pushed aside the velvet curtain hanging in the doorway of the first room and poked his head in. He wasn't interested. They were all too fat and ugly: the one on the table, the one doing the work and the one watching. The next room was empty. He checked his watch: only eleven o'clock, still early by S&M standards. The place didn't start hopping until midnight.

He headed back to the bar. Someone grabbed his arm. He turned.

"Hey, baby," said the woman at his elbow. "Need a slave? I've already been trained." She was tall and emaciated, with a chest as flat as a slab of marble. Her boyish hair was dyed the color of grape Kool-Aid and hugged her head like a purple bathing cap. Not his type. Not even close.

"Let go," he said, shoving her hand off his arm. "I don't want any."

"You sure?" she asked. Her fingers curled around his wrist like white snakes. She smiled; her teeth were gray stubs.

"Never been surer of anything in my life," he said, pulling his hand away. "Now get lost."

"Fuck you," she said. He watched her go. She crossed the room and wrapped her fingers around the arms of a man standing alone near the stage. She'd find some chump, maybe even a good-looking one. Thursday nights, even ugly women got lucky if they were willing to put out—and put up with some pain. She looked more than willing.

He returned to his seat at the bar. The bartender had her back turned to him. Her hair was a dark curtain down her tall, narrow frame. She was mixing a blender drink. She poured the pink slush into a couple of glasses and opened a fridge under the counter to retrieve something. Strawberries. She put one in each drink and took a bite out of a third.

"Don't tell on me," she said. She winked and tossed him one before sliding straws into the drinks. She walked to the other end of the bar and set the drinks on a waiter's tray. The waiter, a leather-clad kid who looked barely twenty, leaned over the bar and said something to her. She turned and looked at Michaels and then turned back to the waiter, nodding. Michaels figured she was telling the waiter she hoped to get laid after closing time.

She returned to Michaels's end of the bar with a big smile on her face. "So how's it look? Not much out there tonight?" she asked, wiping the countertop with a towel. "Or can't find what you need?"

"I don't know what I need tonight," he said. He tossed the strawberry stem into an ashtray and licked his fingers. He watched her watching him do it.

"Maybe I can help you out later," she said.

He studied her face. She wasn't very pretty. Her chin was too pointed, her nose too sharp and long; there was a big gap between her top front teeth. She had her hair going for her, though. Interesting, smooth hair.

"Maybe," he said, taking a drink of Scotch. "Later."

He met her outside after the club had closed. They both leaned against the side of the Suburban. The night air was hot and humid. She had a cigarette between her lips and was taking long, deep pulls. The clothespins were gone. Her nipples looked erect; he wondered if they were still sore.

"Which is your car?" he asked. There were two left in the parking lot, both of them beaters.

"Neither," she said. "I walk to work and mooch a ride home."

"Where's your ride tonight?" he asked.

"I'm looking at him," she said, smiling. He thought about it; he liked laying them on his own terms, and never in their own homes. Maybe it would be all right if he behaved himself, didn't let things get out of hand. Didn't let the fly cut loose.

She tossed the butt to the ground and stepped on it. "I know what you're thinking—that I'm some sleaze who might pull something. I'm really a nice, normal person," she said. "This bar scene is only for the summer. I'm an art teacher at a community college."

"Sure," he said. "Fine." He opened the passenger-side door for her. She hopped in and slammed it shut herself. A little too hard. This one was no frail flower. He slid behind the wheel and shut his door. "How do you know I'm not some maniac?" he asked, turning on the ignition.

She laughed. "Look at you," she said. "You're so clean-cut, it's pathetic."

He smiled but said nothing as he steered his SUV out of the parking lot.

High ceilings, tall windows, dark corners, bare brick walls, drafts every-where. Typical warehouse apartment. Bad art hung from every bit of

116

wall space and was propped up against half the furniture. The oil paintings were all swirls of pastel—pink, yellow, lavender, cream. The Easter Bunny's LSD trip. Nearly every flat surface—every table, chair and countertop—was covered with pink clay sculptures that looked like one sexual object or another. Breasts. Penises. Vaginas. Lots of vaginas. Some of them were crumbling. "Did all this yourself?" he asked.

"Yeah. What do you think?"

"Really interesting," he said. "Different. Lots of pink."

"Titty pink," she said, smiling. "It's my favorite color." She took a couple of paintings off the futon couch so he could sit down. "To be honest, I stink," she said. "I know I do. I still love it. It's a great release."

She disappeared behind a Japanese screen and reappeared with two glasses filled with Scotch. "Sorry. It's another cheap-ass blend," she said, handing him one of the glasses.

"It's fine," he said. He examined the glass; it had smudges on it and a chipped rim. He sipped hesitantly. She set her own glass down on a bare spot on the coffee table and sat down next to him. The hem of her short black skirt crawled up to her crotch. He studied her in the harsh light of the naked bulb hanging from the ceiling. Her hair. It didn't look quite right. Too shiny, too smooth. Much too perfect. "Your hair . . . ," he said, and reached out to touch it. She dodged his hand.

"Let's listen to some tunes," she said, sliding off the couch. She walked over to the CD player sitting on the floor across the room and popped in a disc.

The music was some screeching shit he didn't recognize. Irritating. She saw him frowning and turned down the volume, but not enough. He felt a headache coming on. He took another drink. This could be a mistake, he thought. Maybe he couldn't behave himself. He wondered if anyone had noticed her getting into his car. She'd probably told one of her friends in the club she was leaving with someone, a blond stranger she'd met at the bar. Control yourself. Control.

She walked toward him, smiling. The way her long hair swung was enticing, but not quite right. The ends were too even.

She sat back down and pulled the glass from his hand. "You didn't come for the booze anyway, did you, baby?" she said. She set his glass down, leaned over and kissed him. She smelled like cigarettes and tasted like whiskey and strawberries. She leaned over farther, pressing him back against the couch. Her tongue darted into his mouth, scraping against his teeth. Her right hand slid down to his crotch. "Baby, you are sooo big."

He grabbed her by the shoulders and pushed her away. "I like being the one in charge," he said.

She ignored him and fell against him, burying her mouth in the crook of his neck. She bit him.

"Dammit!" he said. He pushed her face away and felt his neck. She'd drawn blood.

"You crazy bitch!" he yelled. He shoved her off him. She landed on her ass, on the floor between the couch and the coffee table. He stood up to leave. That's when he noticed it. No wonder the hair looked wrong. He grabbed the top of it and pulled it off, throwing it on the floor. Underneath, her head was shaved and ringed by a black barbed-wire tattoo. Hideous. He stood over her, staring in disgust.

"What's your problem?" she said, grabbing the edge of the coffee table and standing up. "You some kind of tight ass? Can't handle something a little different? Afraid? Then what were you doing in the club?"

He wanted to hit her. He really did. Wanted to see her ugly egg head bounce against the wood floor. Wrap his hands around her chicken neck and squeeze. He knew the creepy cunt wasn't worth it, but he couldn't resist. Couldn't hold back the buzzing. The fucking buzzing. He clenched his fists and took a step toward her.

The door opened and the young waiter in black leather walked in. "Hey, teach," the kid said. He shut the door behind him, walked over to the bald woman and stood behind her, gnawing on her shoulder. He had to be fifteen years her junior.

"Hey, lover," she said. "What kept you?"

The kid pulled his mouth off her shoulder. "Some ass wipe poured hot wax on the urinals, plugged 'em real good. Had to stay and scrape it off." He looked at Michaels. "Did we find a new student?"

"What the hell is going on here?" asked Michaels. "Who is this?" He took a couple of steps back; the kid was skinny but taller than he was. His head was shaved and ringed by barbed wire, too. Multiple hoops in both ears and in his nose.

"Josh here is in my art class," she said, smiling at the doctor. "Beginning Oil Painting."

"She's teaching me a few other things, too," the kid said. He reached around from behind and cupped her breasts with his hands. He had crude homemade tattoos on his fingers.

"Josh wanted a classmate," she said. "You looked brave enough, healthy enough."

"It'll be tasty," the kid said. He smiled and then licked his lips, so Michaels could see the silver studs dotting the tip of his tongue.

"Come on," she said. "Don't let the wig thing bum you out. Bet you never had a man and a woman at the same time."

Michaels strained to listen; he could barely hear her above the buzzing. Buzzing. Buzzing.

The woman untangled herself from the boy's arms and walked over to Michaels. She peeled off her shirt and dropped it on the floor at Michaels's feet. The barbed-wire tattoo circled each of her breasts and silver rings pierced each of her nipples. Michaels reached out his right hand and, with his fingertips, traced one of the hoops. He grabbed the ring between his thumb and index finger and pulled. She smiled, creepy cunt. She liked it.

She slipped her arms around his neck and arched her back, grinding her crotch into his. "That's it, Mr. Clean. Give it a try. Get a little dirty."

He was getting hard, but something was wrong. The buzzing was erratic, as if the fly had hit a window. This won't work, thought Michaels. Not two at once. Not a bald woman and a tattooed boy.

Michaels wrapped a hand around each of her bony wrists, peeled her arms off him and backed away. He felt something under his shoe and looked down. The wig. An ugly mound of fake hair.

"Freaks," Michaels growled, and kicked the wig. It slid across the floor like a mad black cat and slammed into the stereo. He yanked open the door and walked out.

"Pussy!" the boy hollered after him.

The bald woman laughed.

SIXTEEN

"Are you nuts, Paris? Do you know who he is?"

Friday's telephone conversation with Jack did nothing to validate Murphy's intention to pursue the plastic surgeon. She had called Jack hoping he could offer some insight into Michaels's background. She also prayed they could get their reconciliation efforts back on track. Instead, Jack lost it.

"You're ready to accuse him of killing another woman in Minneapolis? Let's not even talk about the assault on a priest. He's on the parish council of the oldest Catholic church in town. He's a family man; he's got a wife and two daughters. Babe, you are way off base. You are not even in the right fucking ballpark. How can you do this?"

"I'm not doing shit yet," she said. "I've got a lot of legwork to do, but he's a suspect, and I want you to keep that under your hat."

"No need to worry about that. This is absurd."

"No, it's not—the fact is, you don't know what the hell you're talking about, and I do. I saw him there at Finch's service, with scratches on his face. So did Gabe. Can you tell me why he'd attend a hooker's funeral, one—two hours away in Wisconsin?"

"Maybe she was one of his patients," said Jack. "Ever think of that? Maybe he knew her from his volunteer work."

"I checked with Finch's family—both the one on the street and the one on the farm. They've never laid eyes on Michaels. Finch hadn't seen a doctor for years, and her pimp never beat her badly enough to leave scars. He's far too clever for that. Maybe she knew Michaels. We'll check, but I don't think so . . ."

"Here's a brilliant idea, hot-shit detective. Why don't you call Michaels and ask him why he was there and where he got the scratches?"

"'Cause he'd bullshit me," she said. "But hey, thanks for telling me how to do my job."

"Fuck your shit job. I can't tell you how nuts this seems."

"Erik Mason doesn't think so," she said.

"What'd he say?"

"He said Michaels gave a pretty disturbing presentation at a domestic-abuse conference for medical professionals."

"I remember the conference. Two years ago, at the Drake. I didn't make it to that particular talk. What was disturbing about it? Wait. Don't even bother answering that question. I don't give a shit what Erik Mason thinks. He's got his head way up his ass on this one and so have you."

"Listen . . ."

"I don't want to listen to any more of this bullshit," he said curtly. "I've got to get dressed and go to the hospital. If I allow myself enough time, maybe I can murder a hooker or two on my way to work."

"Jack . . ."

He hung up on her.

"The doctor isn't in. If you need to schedule a plastic surgery consultation, I can transfer you to the appointment desk."

"I'm not a patient. I'm a rep for Texas Surgicare. You guys use our sutures, and we've got some new surgical tape we'd like him to try."

"Maybe you should talk to our office manager, then. Why don't I put you into her voice mail?"

"That's okay. I'd really rather talk to Dr. Michaels. Will he be in later?"

"He's gone for the day. He had a weekend soccer tournament in Wisconsin. May I take a message? Would you like to leave your name and phone number?"

"No, I'm traveling. I'll give him a try next week."

"That's fine."

"Thanks for your help. Have a nice day." Gabe hung up and winked at Murphy, who was sitting on the edge of his desk sipping a Diet Pepsi. On his desktop, ringed with coffee stains in its service as a temporary coaster for his mug, was a printout from a state soccer association Web site. It listed all the teams, their coaches and game dates. A weekend youth tournament was set to start that Friday night across the border in Hudson. Snaky Swanson's tip about the soccer balls had proved invaluable. Michaels was indeed a coach, and his team—one made up of girls ages twelve and thirteen—was scheduled to compete.

Gabe popped the last of his liverwurst and Miracle Whip sandwich into his mouth, chewed twice, swallowed and asked, "How was that?" He wiped his chin with a sheet of computer paper. "Did I sound like a medical-supply salesman?"

"No," said Murphy, sliding off his desk and tossing her pop can into his wastebasket. "You sounded like a used-car salesman. Next time, skip that 'Have a nice day' stuff. I hate people who say that."

"I'll make a note of that," he said.

"So, feel like watching a little soccer tonight?" she asked.

"You betcha."

They were in Murphy's Jeep, but she'd let Gabe drive, an agreeable compromise. Murphy wished she and Jack could work things out in their marriage as effortlessly as she and Gabe did on the job. As they crossed the bridge over the St. Croix River, they looked down at the dozens of boats dotting the water. The early-evening sky above the sails was darkening with storm clouds. The sign at the end of the bridge said WISCONSIN WELCOMES YOU, and bragged about the state's troika of activities: INDUSTRY. AGRICULTURE. RECREATION.

"It should say, 'Cheese. Cows. Beer,'" said Gabe, chuckling at his own joke.

"I'm not exactly sure how to get there," said Murphy, wrestling with a road map. "Maybe we should stop at a gas station and ask directions. I have my cell phone in my purse. I could call . . ."

"I have a pretty good idea where we're going," Gabe said. "Sit back and enjoy the ride." Gabe took Exit 2 and found the soccer fields north of Interstate 94, down the road from Hudson. Eight of them, like checkerboards in the cornfields. They parked between two mini-vans with soccer stickers plastered to their windows and stepped out of the Jeep.

The outside smelled like approaching rain and freshly mowed grass. A game official went by in a golf cart; girls dressed in matching yellow soccer uniforms followed him, giggling and squirting each other with their water bottles. A teenage boy carrying an armload of black-and-white soccer balls went the other way. Every few feet he dropped one and picked it up again, cursing each time it happened. The back of his shirt read: "If I Am Not A Courteous Player, Please Let Me Know. Call 1-800-EAT-DIRT." The sound of cheering spectators and yelling coaches filled the air.

Gabe looked wistfully in the direction of the snack bar at the edge of the parking lot.

"Now what?" he asked.

"Did you bring that printout?" asked Murphy. "It lists the teams and the field numbers."

"Shit," said Gabe. "I forgot it. It's sitting on my desk under some other crap."

"God dammit. All right, you check the fields and see if you can find him. I'll snoop around the parking lot and look for his truck."

As Gabe wandered off, mostly in the direction of a hot-dog stand,

Murphy walked down the rows of cars, looking for a loaded black Suburban or a gray Lexus sedan. She figured he hadn't driven his sports car because it would seem so ostentatious and out of place in the sea of middle-class minivans and station wagons. Dressed in cutoffs, sneakers and a T-shirt, she looked like all the other soccer fans sitting on blankets and in folding chairs along the sidelines.

"Lose your car?" asked a woman cutting through the parking lot with a sleeping toddler in her arms.

"Yeah," said Murphy. "I can *never* remember where I park."

A heavy man in a sweat-stained muscle shirt grunted past her, carrying a cooler filled with bottles of Gatorade. He set it down on the gravel-covered lot for a few seconds, caught his breath and picked it up again. Six boys in matching royal blue soccer uniforms ran past her, heading toward the snack bar. A few drops of rain splattered her arms and spotted her T-shirt. From what Murphy remembered of the tournament printout sitting back on Gabe's desk, the games would not be called because of rain, but would be shut down immediately if there was lightning. She looked up at the slate-colored clouds, but saw no flashes.

She continued her tour. Minivans, especially of the forest green variety, were everywhere. Minivan. Minivan. Minivan. Station wagon. Minivan. Station wagon. Minivan. Minivan. Whoa. Here's a rebel—a full-size conversion van, and painted eggplant purple, no less. She wondered how that one had slipped past the soccer fashion police.

Then a new black Suburban, sharp-edged in the green meadow of gently curving minivans. She reached into her purse for the list of plates, and slipped between the Suburban and a minivan parked next to it. The plates were right. She knew they'd be. She crammed the paper back into her purse.

As the rain grew heavier, fans began running to their cars for umbrellas and slickers. Murphy heard someone crunching on the gravel toward her row of cars. She didn't want to be seen by Michaels, so she ducked to the other side of the green minivan, crouched and adjusted the side-view mirror of the van so she could watch the black Suburban through the van windows.

There he was. Michaels was dressed in khaki slacks and a white polo shirt. His shoulders were broad, and his arms were tan and sinewy. His hands were large. She hadn't noticed that at the church. She assumed surgeons—especially those doing such delicate work as plastic surgery—had small, nimble hands. Not this one. He opened the rear passenger-side door of the Suburban, rummaged inside it, tossed an empty pop can to the ground.

A litterbug, Murphy thought.

"Where the hell is it?" she heard him mutter to himself. "I know I saw the damn thing." More digging and cursing. "There you are," he said. He pulled something out of the car, slammed the door shut and sprinted across the parking lot, heading back toward the fields.

Murphy stood up and poked her head around the corner of the minivan to watch him. Halfway across the lot, Michaels popped open a yellow umbrella. Even through the downpour, Murphy could see. Finch was calling from the grave.

"Son-of-a-bitch," Murphy whispered. "There it is."

SEVENTEEN

He couldn't remember where it had come from. As Michaels slid into the driver's seat of his Suburban after work, he'd noticed it on the floor behind the front passenger seat and was grateful for it. The darkening sky above the interstate signaled the little umbrella might come in handy. He would have preferred his oversized golf umbrella, but he hadn't been able to find it when he was leaving for the clinic that morning. God knows where his wife had stashed it. Hell, she probably gave it to the Salvation Army. She was always giving shit away. She had absolutely no respect for his stuff.

His wife. He briefly wondered when she was returning home with the queen mother. He thought about his daughters and how they might be doing at the camp. He hadn't received a call from them in better than a week. He shuffled the fleeting concerns to the back compartment of his mind as he tried to concentrate on the Wisconsin soccer tournament.

He wanted a drink, but didn't have the time. Too bad. Booze made the tiresome games more tolerable. His assistant coach wouldn't be there. He was vacationing up north. Fishing. What a stupid sport. Regardless, Michaels would have to run the entire show by himself. He especially hated taking charge of the line changes. Parents who thought their precious daughters weren't getting enough time on the field were quick to buttonhole him on the sidelines. They were all a bunch of whiners, but the mothers infinitely more so than the fathers. If the fathers didn't like something, they stood grim-faced and silent with their hands buried in their pockets. They might approach him after the game, mumble something, but the mothers couldn't wait. They practically ran to him during the game to complain. He frequently fantasized about lining them up in a row and slapping each and every one of them right across the face. That one in particular—a tiny, full-lipped brunette with big tits and an even bigger mouth. He'd love to slap her good and hard, leave some red marks on her face. He'd love to make her weep. She probably wouldn't be much of a challenge. Her spoiled crybaby daughter was one to burst into tears at every opportunity; he wished he could really give her something to cry about.

He deeply regretted having gotten suckered into coaching this year's soccer team, especially since his daughters were missing part of the season. On top of everything else, the team was having a lousy year and he would undoubtedly be blamed. Admittedly, some of his extracurricular activities after work had caused him to miss some games and practices. They were a crappy bunch of players anyway, and no amount of drilling and training and scrimmaging would elevate their level of play. He had to admit that even his own daughters were mediocre. If he had boys, that would be different; they would be fine soccer players. Wishing for a son was pointless, of course. The miscarriage had ended that dream.

He turned into the tournament parking lot and pulled into the first space he could find. He sighed as he stepped out of the car and walked to the back of the SUV. He opened the gate and dug out a couple of soccer balls, the water bottles, the goalie jersey and his coach's clipboard. The board was blank. He knew he should have planned his lineup and a couple of plays, but screw it. He'd wing it. The dumb little shits didn't listen to him most of the time anyway. He slammed the gate shut and looked up at the sky. "Come on, God," he thought as he scrutinized the dark expanse over his head. "Give me a break."

His bad luck; all he got was rain. His arms were too full to grab the umbrella on his first trip between the car and the field. The game hadn't started yet and he figured he still had time to retrieve it. He bounded across the parking lot for his second trip to the car and was drenched by the time he reached it. It took some digging around—it had rolled under the back passenger's seat—but he found it. As he ran across the parking lot on his way back to the soccer fields, he opened the umbrella.

"Piece of shit," he mumbled at the tangle of yellow nylon and flimsy spokes. "Don't tell me you're broken, you worthless thing." To hell with it. He'd mooch an umbrella off one of the parents. Maybe that mouthy little brunette would share a corner of hers if he smiled nicely and put her clumsy daughter in as the starting goalie. Anything was better than this defective scrap of metal and material. Where in the world had it come from? He'd never have bought anything so inferior. Disgusted, he tossed it into a muddy puddle at the far end of the parking lot and continued his sprint back to the soccer fields, silently cursing the summer storm that brought torrential rain but no lightning.

Murphy had been following him from a distance by dashing and ducking between cars. Checking to make sure Michaels was well out of sight, she emerged from her hiding place between two minivans. She carefully picked up the soggy umbrella by the edge of the cloth. "Hello, my precious," Murphy cooed at the dripping mess. She ran back to her Jeep with it. Even if no useable prints could be pulled off the thing, it was still valuable evidence. Rue could testify that the yellow umbrella had been in Finch's hands the night she disappeared. Finch had undoubtedly left it in Michaels's car after he picked her up.

After sticking the umbrella in the Jeep, Murphy retrieved her own umbrella from under a pile of magazines and popped it open. Time to watch a little soccer, she thought.

"Sara, get back in the net! You're playing too far out of the goal! They'll get around you! Get back!"

The goalie ran back toward the net in the driving rain, slipped and fell face forward into the wet grass inside the white lines of the goalie box. The left forward for Minneapolis shot from the side and scored the first goal of the game against Michaels's St. Paul team.

"Dammit!" Michaels yelled. "I told you to get back. You can't play that far out!" The goalie slowly rose from her prone position in the grass and promptly dissolved into tears. Bits of dirt speckled her wet face. "Perfect," Michaels mumbled. "Goalie sub!" Michaels yelled and waved the goalie over to the sidelines. "Should I pull you out of the net? There are three girls behind you ready to take your place. I don't have time for bawling," Michaels told her, his right hand gripping her left shoulder. He towered above her. Even in the pouring rain, the girl could see the veins standing out on his forehead. His hand was squeezing her shoulder, hurting it, but she was afraid to say anything or push it away. "Answer me, Sara. Are you up for this or not? Do you want to sit on the bench? Should I put in one of the subs?"

"No," she said, wiping her nose with the back of her right goalie glove. "I'm sorry they got past me. I thought I could get back in time."

"Well, I guess you thought wrong," he said. "Maybe next time you'll listen to me."

The ref blew his whistle. "Are you going to sub or not? Put someone in the net and let's get going!" he yelled. Michaels let Sara back into the goal. The game resumed in the rain, which slowed but remained steady. The frustrated surgeon, soaked to the skin, stood glowering along the sidelines with his arms folded across his chest. He braced himself, waiting for the mouthy brunette to pounce and bitch at him for yelling at her princess.

"Would you like to share my umbrella?"

He turned toward the husky female voice on his right and smiled broadly. He couldn't believe his good fortune. Finally things were going his way. He ducked under her black umbrella. "Thank you," he said. He ran his fingers through his wet hair. "What I really need at this point is a towel."

"I recognized you from the funeral," said the black-haired woman.

Her wet shirt was matted to her skin. He could make out her nipples under her bra. She was even more enticing than when he'd seen her from a distance, inside that country church. Her long hair was unfettered this time and hung in a thick, damp sheet around her face. What a face. Smooth. Flawless. He couldn't improve a single feature. Not one. "Yes, I saw you at the service," he said. "I remember you. Vividly."

"So sad," said Murphy.

"Yes," he said. "Sad."

"The service was nice, didn't you think?"

"Very nice," Michaels said. With a small smile, he added: "Especially the brother's reading."

"I hope they catch whoever did it," she said. She watched his face and listened to his voice for a reaction.

"I'm sure they will," he said evenly.

Not a muscle on his face twitched; he's a cool one, she thought. "How did you know Fionn?" she asked.

"She was a patient of mine," he said, relieved that he had fabricated that story earlier so it quickly popped out of his mouth. "I'm a surgeon," he continued. "I met her through my volunteer work with abuse victims."

"How admirable," said Murphy, impressed with how quickly and easily the lies rolled off his tongue.

One of his players fell. He stepped toward the field to yell: "Come on, ref. Tripping!" The ref shook his head. "Horseshit, ref," he said under his breath. He returned to his spot under the umbrella.

"What about you?" he asked. "Were you related to the poor girl?"

"I'm a friend of the family," said Murphy.

"Oh, I see," he said. "How coincidental bumping into you here. Do you have someone in this tournament?"

"Yes . . . I have a couple of nieces playing for Hudson," said Murphy. "I was on my way back from the car with my umbrella when I saw you."

"Is your father here with you? At least, I assumed that was your father with you at the funeral."

Murphy smiled, amused by the thought of Gabe as her father. "He's here with me, but he's not my father," she said. "He's an old friend."

"It sounds like you have lots of friends," he said, smiling and stepping closer to her under the umbrella. "Any husbands?"

"Not as many husbands as friends," she said. They both laughed.

"What about you?" Murphy asked. She could smell his cologne through the rain. Obsession for Men, a scent she adored but could never get Jack to wear. "Are you attached? You must have children on this team."

"My two daughters. They're in Europe right now."

"You're their coach?"

"Yes. I really enjoy it," he said.

"You must be so busy, being a doctor and all. I suppose your wife helps with the team."

"Their mother and I are . . . no longer together," he said, glad he had removed his wedding band.

"That's too bad," Murphy said. She wondered if he was telling the truth; she couldn't see his ring finger and his face was hard to read.

"Not at all. We're much happier apart," Michaels said.

The parents on his side of the field started yelling over a slide tackle made by the other team. "I do need to get back to the game," he said, stepping even closer to her. He could smell her hair, fragrant from an herbal shampoo. "I'd like to talk with you later, so don't wander too far. I don't even know your name."

A cheer erupted from Michaels's side of the field. His team had scored. He stepped out from under the umbrella, turned toward the field and clapped. "All right!" he hollered. "Way to go, Lauren! Nice goal! How about a couple more of those?"

Murphy stepped back from the sidelines and almost tripped over Gabe. "What in the hell are you doing?" Gabe hissed into her ear. He grabbed her arm. "Have you lost your mind? Have you completely lost it? What are you doing with Dr. Demented?"

"Figuring him out," she whispered. She yanked her arm away from Gabe and continued eyeing Michaels.

"Too fucking dangerous, Murphy," Gabe said. His face was a knot of concern.

"He had the umbrella," she said, stepping farther away from Michaels's field and closing her own umbrella. The rain had stopped.

"What?" said Gabe, looking at the dripping umbrella she had just folded shut. "What are you talking about?"

"Not this one," said Murphy. "He had the yellow umbrella, the one Rue loaned to Finch the night she was killed."

"What do you mean by 'had'?"

"He threw it away and I picked it up," she said. "It's sitting on the floor of my car."

"You have it?" he asked.

Murphy nodded her head, watching Michaels's back as he yelled directions to his players. He wouldn't win any popularity contests.

"First step," Murphy said.

"I'm afraid to ask what your second step might be," said Gabe.

"Get him alone in a quiet place—but a public one. Maybe a restaurant or a bar," she said. "It sounds like he's a big drinker. Maybe I can loosen him up."

"Bullshit," said Gabe. "It's too dangerous. I won't let you do it. No way in hell."

Her eyes narrowed and seemed to change color, going from violet to black. He knew the look. "Fine," he said. "I am going to be there—along with my good friend Mr. Glock."

"You can't," she said. "He remembers seeing both of us at the funeral. I told him we're friends of Finch's family and that you and I are . . . chums."

"Oh, we're chummy, are we? Well chums don't let chums drink alone with murdering rapists," Gabe growled.

She recognized that tone of voice. She wasn't going to change his mind, and he wasn't going to change hers. "Okay, then you'll have to wear a disguise," she said. "Dust off that wig."

"Fine with me. As long as I'm there."

At the game's halftime, Michaels chewed out his team for letting go of a three-point lead. "You're benched for the rest of the game," he told the sniffling Sara. "You're a sieve tonight. I'm going to put Debbie in net."

The mouthy brunette stepped into the team huddle. "Dr. Michaels, I do not like the way you're treating my . . ."

At his sides, Michaels's hands tightened into fists. "Don't tell me how to coach," he told her. "Go sit down with the other parents or you can stay home the next game. You and Sara both." Her face reddened. She shut her mouth and went back to the sidelines. Michaels relaxed his hands. Embarrassing her wasn't as good as hitting her, but it wasn't bad.

He turned around to look for the woman with the black hair. She was standing several yards away, chatting with that friend of hers, but she turned her head and their eyes met. Michaels stepped out of the huddle and walked toward her while her cloddish friend ambled off with a cigarette between his fingers. "Drinks Monday night? How about the bar at the St. Paul Hotel?"

"I know the place," she said. "Very nice."

"Your name?"

Murphy flashed him a smile. "Let's save some surprises for later," she said.

He laughed. "I like that," he said. "I like that a lot. You've got style. Okay, let's trade the formalities over a glass of single-malt whiskey."

"Only if they pour Lagavulin," Murphy said.

"A Scotch connoisseur, too," he said. "Perfect." The ref blew his whistle. The game was resuming. "I'll meet you there at eight o'clock Monday," he said, and ran back to the field.

Gabe came up behind Murphy. "Eight o'clock Monday at the St. Paul Hotel bar," she said.

"We'll be there," Gabe said, as he patted the gun holstered under his sweatshirt.

EIGHTEEN

"Paris, I hate to say it, but Gabe is right. This is too dangerous. He's a head case, and you can't predict what he'll do."

"Gabe will be in the bar."

"For some reason that does not make me feel better about this whole scheme."

"Come on, Erik. I know you aren't exactly president of the Gabriel Nash fan club, but he isn't called 'Nasty Nash' because he's a pushover. Give him some credit."

Murphy and Erik were talking as they ran along Lilydale Road Saturday morning. Murphy usually ran alone, preferring to set her own pace and use the quiet time for sorting out problems or simply emptying her mind, but Erik had called first thing in the morning and asked to join her.

The day was going to be hot and muggy following Friday-night's rainstorms. They ran past Harriet Island, which was already filling with picnickers staking out claims to tables. From the running trail atop an embankment, overlooking the park and the river, they could see a Mexican family hanging a piñata from a tree. Salsa music wafted from a tape player. Closer to the river, they could see several blond children, already pink from the morning sun, climbing all over an enormous ship's anchor assigned permanent shore duty as a park decoration. After the neatly mowed Harriet Island came the disheveled Lilydale Regional Park. The steep bluffs and paved road were to their left. To the right of the running path were thick woods and then the Mississippi River flowing parallel to the road.

Murphy thought about Finch. She wondered whether they should go to the clearing where her body was found. "Why don't we run over to . . ."

"Let's not go there, Paris."

"What are you talking about?" she said. "You don't know what I was going to say."

He didn't answer and kept running a few steps ahead of her. The hum of insects filled the long, silent pause. She could feel him waiting for her to capitulate.

"Okay," she said. "I thought . . ."

"You think too much," he said shortly. "Run . . . Don't think . . . Run."

He was pressing her to do eight-minute miles. Erik was a strong runner; she knew he was holding back so she could keep up. She appreciated his patience. On the rare occasions when she ran with other women, she was usually the fast one and grew frustrated trying to match a slower pace. They ran under the railroad bridge that gently curved through the park—the same bridge that looked over the clearing where Finch's body was found. Graffiti was spray-painted all over the bridge's supports, including words that had been there since Murphy was a kid: THE RIVER RATS RULE. A short distance past the bridge, they turned around and doubled back for the return trip to Murphy's houseboat.

They pounded down the dock. Tripod ran out and barked from his owner's deck. Erik stopped and laughed. "Goofy-looking pooch."

"Tripod."

"How'd he lose his leg?"

"A car, when he was a puppy," she said. "You like dogs?"

"Dogs. Cats. Kids. Like 'em all," he said, smiling at her. "What about you?"

"Take cats off the list."

He laughed and wiped his wet face with the bottom of his T-shirt. They talked and slowly walked the rest of the way to her boat.

"Why didn't you and Jack ever . . ."

"We could never agree on a breed."

Erik looked at her. She smiled. "Sorry," he said. "I was stupid for asking. If you don't want to talk about it, that's fine. It's really none of my business."

"You're right; it is none of your business. I'll tell you anyway. The timing was never right, that's all. We're both perfectly healthy and all that, and we both love kids. But we could never agree on when to start a family. Whenever it was right for one of us, it was wrong for the other. There. Now I've told you twice as much as I've ever told my mother."

She and Erik tripped sweaty and tired into the galley. Erik looked into her living room. "Camels," he said, laughing.

"Like them?"

"Yeah. Camels are cool. I see you have both the one-humped and the two-humped variety."

"I don't discriminate," she said.

He walked to the sink, turned on the tap and stuck his mouth under the faucet.

"God, don't drink that," she said. "It's St. Paul water. I've got some bottled stuff in the fridge."

"Why does everyone piss all over St. Paul water?" he asked in between gulps. "It's fine."

"*Piss* is the operative word here," she said. She walked over to the fridge to get some water and was not surprised to find a note from two of her older brothers, Patrick and Ryan, taped to the handle. "Potato Head: Stopped by with the new boat. Sorry we missed you. Look for us upriver." The message was scrawled on a sheet of stationery from the orthopedic surgery practice they shared.

"Something wrong?" asked Erik, leaning against the kitchen counter with one hand and wiping perspiration off his neck with the other.

"My overachieving brothers swung by with their latest toy," she said, crumpling the note. "We missed them, thank God." She and Jack had been frequently surprised at their Dutch Colonial. Once Jack was standing naked in front of the refrigerator gulping milk when Murphy's mother walked into the kitchen. Jack used the milk carton to cover his crotch. "Shame on you," said the tiny, dark-haired woman, shaking her finger at him. "Go get a glass."

Murphy grew sad thinking about Jack. She contemplated calling him. Maybe making good on that promise of a romantic dinner followed by a back rub could lure him back to her riverfront home. Of course, if he heard about her plan to meet Michaels for drinks Monday night, that could ignite another huge fight.

She was startled from her thoughts when she felt Erik's arms wrapping around her waist from behind. "Got anything going on the rest of the day?" he asked.

"What?"

"I have some ideas about how you could fill your weekend," he whispered in her ear. "Why don't we start with a hot, soapy shower after our run and see where that takes us?"

"No, Erik. I was thinking I should . . ."

"As I said earlier, you think too damn much, woman," he said, nibbling on her neck. "Don't think."

"I thought we were going to be friends," she said, trying to push his arms off her waist.

"Friends can make wonderful lovers," he said softly.

He was hard. She felt him through his thin running shorts as he pressed against the small of her back. He smelled of perspiration and the outdoors; she liked the salty-fresh combination.

"Come on, Paris. Relax. Let it happen," he said. He pressed his body against her back. He slid his right hand up under her sweat-dampened bra and T-shirt and cupped her right breast.

"Do you want me to stop?" he asked. "Say if you want me to stop."

She inhaled sharply. "Stop," she breathed, and pushed his arms off her. She took a step away from him but kept her back to him. "You'd better leave," she said.

"Look at me," he said.

"No."

He stepped in front of her and took her face in his hands. Her eyes were down; all he saw were dark lashes. "You can't, can you? You can't look at me. You want me and you're afraid."

"It's not about being afraid," she said. She pushed his hands away from her face and raised her eyes. "It's about my marriage."

"You've split."

"We're working on it."

"If it takes too much work, maybe it isn't there," Erik said. "You should move on."

"Go," she said. "Go home."

She took a long shower, as hot as she could stand. She wanted to scald the memory of Erik's hands off her. Jack would never sleep with another woman, even when they were separated. He was as consistent and steady in his marriage as he was in his professional life. So was she, up until Erik. She'd never come so close to giving in. Why now? Could it be the physical attraction alone? Was she that weak?

The questions and the guilt burned her worse than the water.

NINETEEN

That weekend, the good doctor also contemplated the cheating heart—his wife's.

Michaels had tried the cabin's telephone over the weekend, starting with a call late Friday night after the dismal soccer game. He'd called again in between the two equally pathetic tournament games on Saturday. When he got home Sunday afternoon from the fourth and final game—at last, a win—he tried yet again. No response, only Jennifer's cloying recorded message: "Ahoy, landlubbers! We can't answer your distress signal right now. We're riding the waves of Lake Superior. If you'd like to flag down the captain or his first mate, please leave a message at the sound of the foghorn!" God, he hated that message. He slammed the phone down and paced around the master bedroom.

"Where the fuck are you? Are you banging someone else? Where are you?" he muttered. He took off his clothes, threw them in a corner and fell back on the bed, a mahogany four-poster that matched the Victorian armoire with the carved door panels and the marble-topped mahogany nightstands on either side of the bed. He appreciated that there was nothing delicate or modest about the room, a cavernous space filled with dark, massive furniture that had been in his family for generations. As much as he loved the bedroom, his wife hated it. Perfectly symbolic of their marriage, thought Michaels.

After an hour, Michaels got up from the bed, walked across the floor to the armoire and threw open one of the tall doors. The inside of the nineteenth-century antique had been retrofitted with an entertainment center that included a television and a stereo system. He slipped a disc into the CD player and turned up the volume on his favorite selection from Dylan's *Blood on the Tracks*.

Bobbing his head to "Tangled Up in Blue," Michaels made his way to the dresser and, from the top drawer, pulled out an old key with a hair ribbon looped through one end. He walked to his nightstand, carefully inserted the key into the lock on the drawer and slowly turned to the left. The drawer was fussy and frequently stuck, but this time it opened with ease. He reached in and pulled out a bottle of Scotch— a twenty-five-year-old limited-edition Tomatin. Next he pulled out a painted pheasant glass, set it on the marble top and filled it with Scotch, well past the cock in flight.

He set the bottle of Scotch down and reached into the deep night-stand drawer to retrieve his oldest memento—a long braid of auburn hair he'd retrieved from the hatbox earlier that weekend. He'd thought about returning it to its hiding place in the safe room, in case his wife returned from the cabin unannounced. He'd decided to enjoy it a bit longer . . .

The twist of hair was held together at each end with a rubber band. He buried his nose in the braid. She'd used a fruit-scented hair spray. He loved it that years later, he could still smell traces of it. He draped the braid over his neck like a scarf and pulled down the comforter so he could rest on the ivory satin sheets, the only furnish-ing he'd allowed his wife to select for the room. With a sigh, he stretched out on the bed again. Next to him on the sheets, he laid out the braid. He handled it gently; it was his first and his favorite.

He gazed up at the bedroom ceiling. If Jennifer was sleeping around on him, where was her mother? Maybe she was out getting some action as well. He laughed at the prospect of his mother-in-law rolling around under the covers with some poor gigolo. Then he swiftly dismissed the disturbing image. "You probably forgot how to do it, you dried-up old bitch," he said out loud. He laughed again, and turned on his side to reach for the Scotch glass. He emptied it and poured himself another tall one, spilling a bit on the nightstand and spotting the sheets. "Where are you, you two bitches?" he said, loudly. He took another long drink, enjoying the warmth trickling from his throat down to his belly. A few drops splashed on his chest, hitting the few blond curls and turning them wet and golden. The scent of his cologne mixed with the smell of the booze, and he liked it.

He scratched his testicles with his left hand and thought about another bitch. A delicious one. That black-haired woman with the flawless skin and full, round breasts. He switched the drinking glass to his left hand, freeing his right hand to wrap around his stiffening cock.

If it appeared that his wife wasn't going to be home Monday night, perhaps he could bring the mystery woman back with him and do her right here, in his bedroom. Then he could fuck his cheating wife on the same sheets when she finally got her whore ass home. That would be sweet revenge. No. It would be satisfying, but far too dangerous. He didn't want to betray too much of himself to the woman. A room at the hotel. Yes.

He continued stroking himself with his right hand. With his left hand, he set the Scotch down and reached for the braid. His soft, compliant lover. The throbbing beat of the music bounced off the walls of the bedroom. The amber liquid in the glass atop his nightstand rippled slightly, like a puddle trembling before an approaching thunderstorm.

The St. Paul was an old hotel with thick walls. No one would hear her screams. He wouldn't hurt her too badly. He didn't need to add to his growing list of mortal sins. He'd keep it to a light beating followed by some vigorous sex. She'd enjoy it. He only hoped she was a good fighter. She'd already displayed some spunk in refusing to disclose her name. Perhaps he should encourage that little game, insist they maintain their anonymity, or exchange first names. He'd make one up. He hated his first name; it was his father's. He didn't like his father.

He'd loved his mother. Bee.

He stroked his hard cock with his right hand. With his left, he caressed the braid, bunched it up, and rubbed it against his testicles. Wonderful. Silkier than the sheets. He shut his eyes and imagined the hair belonged to a woman, a beautiful woman who did what he told her to do. Exactly. "That's it, baby," he whispered. "Like that." He slowed his stroking; he didn't want to come too soon.

Perhaps he could reach his apex with that black-haired woman, finally feed the fly's gnawing hunger that seemed to be occupying more and more of his waking moments and even invading his dreams. Since his return from the cabin, he was finding it increasingly difficult to sleep straight through the night. He would sit bolt upright at two or three in the morning, his head filled with the buzzing. Fucking buzzing. Sometimes it took almost half a bottle of Scotch to lull him into a stupor that resembled sleep.

This woman with the violet eyes and succulent breasts and long hair could finally satiate him. Then maybe he'd make her his last. He needed to wind down his activities. He'd been making too many mistakes, too many bad judgment calls. Look at the mess Thursday night. Yes, maybe he'd make her his last. The fly's last. She'd be a magnificent finish. "Yes, you could be the one," he whispered, picturing her under him, frightened and squirming.

What about the hair? He killed them when he took the hair, and he wanted her hair. He thought about her hair.

Emitting a moan and clutching the auburn braid, he ejaculated.

TWENTY

Murphy stared at her computer screen Monday morning, studying the e-mail that had arrived shortly after she'd gotten to the station house. On an intellectual level, it was rewarding, because it confirmed her suspicions and validated her investigative instincts. She was absolutely correct about this gifted surgeon, respected community member, killer. On an emotional level, however, the information in the electronic message disheartened her and it troubled her that she felt this way. As she sat still and silent in front of the screen, she tried to dispassionately analyze why she was so disillusioned despite having been proved right.

Why am I feeling this way? she wondered. I can't possibly empathize with this bastard. We have absolutely nothing in common. Economically and socially, we come from opposite sides of the tracks. We grew up on opposite sides of the river. Literally. Why do I care? She decided it was his looks. The face. The hair. The body. The whole package was so attractive and hid so much evil. Her job was easier when the bad guys looked the part. Scummy and ugly and capable of doing wrong.

These were shallow, surface observations. She was afraid to probe too deeply into her own psyche for fear she might find the common ground she shared with Michaels. All her adult life, she'd denied those impulses.

During college, she'd found herself gravitating toward athletic partners. She told herself that was what she wanted in bed. Athleticism. Still, they usually disappointed. They were too tentative and gentle, and far too self-conscious. On the rare occasions when she found a man who satisfied her, she never had to tell him what she wanted. He knew. Perhaps it was the way she fought back in bed. Perhaps it was the hoarseness in her voice or the catch in her breath. Maybe it was how she behaved outside the bedroom. How she carried herself. She didn't act like a timid person.

She could never name what she wanted. It scared her that roughness might appeal to her.

Was that what drew her to Michaels, and why he frightened her?

"Murphy, what are you reading so intently? You look like you're going to pop a vein in your eyeball."

Gabe's words jarred her out of her trance. He came up behind her and handed her a cup of coffee.

"I got an e-mail from the Rochester P.D. They have an unsolved murder from several years ago with the same M.O. as our friendly doctor."

"No shit," said Gabe.

"No shit," she said. "A nurse who moonlighted as a stripper was found in a farmer's field—raped, beaten and strangled."

"What makes you think the doc did her?"

"She had this long, auburn hair—I'm talking down to her knees. Sort of a gimmick for her act. She was pretty well known for it around the strip-club circuit."

"So?" said Gabe.

"So someone gave her a sloppy haircut the night she died," said Murphy.

"He's twisted," Gabe said.

146

"He did her while he was at the Mayo Clinic, for his fellowship," said Murphy. "The years match up."

"So what's wrong? You read Dr. Demented like a large-print book."

"Nothing's wrong," she said. "Sometimes when I expect the worst from people, I wish to hell they'd disappoint me."

"Almost never happens, kid. Expect the worst and . . ."

"Hope for the best?" she said.

"No, hope the shit doesn't hit the fan," he said. Then: "Hey, has Mason come up with anything more for us?"

"No," Murphy said curtly, and quickly switched subjects.

"I'm going to give Rochester Homicide a call," she said, picking up the telephone. "I might want to go down there and see what they've got in their files. Do you want to go down there with me? How about tomorrow? We can leave first thing in the morning and be back by dinner."

"Uh, I've got some legwork to do before we talk to Ambrose," said Gabe.

"Forgot. That's right," she said. She was secretly pleased that she could drive her car and play her own music for a change. "Never mind. I'll make a quick trip of it." She started punching Rochester's number, but Gabe took the receiver out of her hand and put it down.

"That can wait," he said, sitting on the edge of her desk. "We need to talk about tonight."

Gabe wasn't a pedantic tutor. He stood vigilantly but quietly in the wings, waiting for his protege to ask for direction. He believed it was best to learn by mistakes, as long as the errors were not life threatening or embarrassingly stupid. When Murphy needed help, she'd ask for it. He remembered when she'd been in Vice and struggling with her first big case. A john was robbing the hookers, and had shot one in the thigh. Still, the hookers refused to cooperate. They gave vague descriptions of the perpetrator and were afraid to say too much.

"I don't know," Murphy had said. "Maybe they don't know me well enough yet to trust me." She had been ready to hit the streets as a decoy, but Gabe steered her in another direction.

"Look, Murphy. Some asshole is dipping into the till at the goody store, right?" he'd told her. "Who do you think really gives a shit? The cashiers at the goody store or the owner of the goody store?"

She'd talked to the pimps and solved the case in no time. "Thanks for your help," she'd told Gabe afterward.

"Thanks for asking for it," he'd said, and he meant it.

"What about tonight?" asked Murphy.

They were in a long, narrow conference room with the door shut. Gabe had insisted their conversation be private. From the bank of tall windows that stretched against one wall, they could see the tangle of freeways that bordered the north side of the cop shop. Gabe took a chair at one end of the long, lacquered conference table. Murphy sat a few chairs away from him, sipping her coffee. She leaned back in her seat and stretched her long legs out to prop her feet atop the table's edge.

"Let's shit-can the entire operation," Gabe said. "Forget about the bar."

She opened her mouth to react, but Gabe kept talking. Quickly. An appliance salesman making another frantic pitch. "This is a bad idea, Paris. Michaels is unpredictable as hell. He's on the soccer field one minute and murdering hookers the next. He's got this weird hair fetish going on. Forget about it. Don't show up at the bar. Okay? Let's forget the whole damn idea."

"Jesus Christ, Gabe! Where did this come from?" She pulled her legs off the table and sat up.

"I'm worried about you."

"He won't try anything," she said adamantly. "It's a public place. I can handle myself."

"You're too sure of yourself, " said Gabe. "You've usually shown a little common sense. I haven't seen that here."

Murphy jumped out of the chair and started pacing along the

windowed wall. "What in the hell are you talking about? Huh?"

"I'm talking about the unnecessary risks you've been taking to get close to this guy. I'm talking about the unnecessary risks you've been taking in your personal life. I'm talking about you and Mason."

She stopped pacing and took a deep breath. She turned away from Gabe to look outside, resting both hands against the waist-high window ledge. She saw the busy stream of cars crisscrossing the highways at the edge of downtown and longed to be in one of those cars, heading north to the woods and lakes, or east to the forests of Wisconsin. Anywhere but here, in this office, having this conversation.

She turned her head to look at Gabe, but kept her hands against the ledge. Suddenly, he looked old and tired to her. There were deep lines in his face she had never noticed before. Even his hands looked old and wrinkled. Maybe it was the harsh ceiling lights in this room, or maybe she was seeing her mentor through more seasoned eyes. A wave of sadness mixed with nostalgia threatened to wash over her, but she pushed it back. She took her hands off the ledge and stood straight, squaring her shoulders.

"Fuck you on the Mason thing," she said. "And this isn't different from any other undercover gig."

"Bullshit, Paris, you . . ."

"Meet me at my place at about seven," she said, pushing her hands into the pockets of her jeans. "Don't forget your trusty wig and beard. Okay?" He sat in the chair looking at her, his coffee cup between his hands. She was suddenly torn. She wanted to win this one. For some reason, maybe to reassure herself he wasn't getting old, she also wanted him to first resist her a little more. Put up more of a fight.

"Okay," he said, sighing.

She didn't want him to see her face, her disappointment. "I've got to call Rochester," she said. She quickly turned her back on him, opened the door and walked out of the conference room, leaving him sitting alone at the end of the long table.

*   *   *

Murphy helped Gabe into his disguise before dressing herself. She brushed his gray hair and pulled it all back into a ponytail held together with a flat barrette. She used a bunch of bobby pins to secure the ends of the ponytail to the top of his head and slipped the blond wig securely over the whole mess. The wig was even longer than Gabe's natural hair and more neatly trimmed. A few gray strands stuck out along his forehead; she tucked them in. She walked around him and studied his head from all angles as he sat in a kitchen chair in the galley. "It's crooked," she said. She tugged it to one side and then the other.

"Ouch."

"Sorry." She stepped back to look at him. "Good," she declared. "Nice and straight. There's no gray hair peeking out from underneath."

She used spirit gum to attach the short, blond beard to his face.

"How do I look?" he asked.

"Like a well-groomed Dead Head," she said, laughing.

"That's cool," said Gabe. "Jerry Garcia is my hero."

"I thought you only liked country-western," she said.

"There's a lot you don't know about me," said Gabe, grinning and inspecting the beard with his fingers. "I'm actually a very complex person. A Renaissance man." He started humming "Truckin'" and tapping his feet to the beat.

"Well, as long as we're onto a Grateful Dead theme, why don't we take it all the way," said Murphy. She ran up to her bedroom and came down with a couple of ties draped over each forearm. "Official Jerry Garcia–label ties," she said. "Pick one, Mr. Renaissance Man."

"Mason's ties?" Gabe asked suspiciously, his eyes narrowing.

"Jack's ties," said Murphy. "Erik won't be leaving any ties here."

"Good," said Gabe, smiling and pointing to the brightest of the collection.

Murphy started to help him secure the tie around the collar of his white dress shirt, but he stood up and brushed her hands away impatiently. "I've been dressing myself for better than fifty years," he said.

He got out of the chair and went into the guest bathroom to look in the mirror while he worked. After knotting the tie, he loosened the belt on his navy blue dress pants. "Gotta drop some pounds," he muttered to himself, pinching his waist.

"Start getting dressed, my sugar magnolia," he yelled from the bathroom.

Murphy ran back up to her bedroom. She scanned her small closet, searching for something in particular. She saw it. She pulled out a simple black slip dress and threw it on the bed. Fishing through her dresser drawers, she found an unopened package of panty hose she had stashed in there for some occasion or another. She ripped open the package, pulled out the hosiery and threw both on the bed next to the dress. She disrobed, tossing her clothes in a pile on the floor, and grabbed the hosiery. "Whoever invented these obviously hated women," she grumbled, tugging one leg on up to her thigh and then the other before pulling the panty portion over her hips and waist.

She lifted a strapless bra out of a drawer. It looked like a giant bandage. She could hardly breathe when she wore the thing, and it crawled down her chest. She tossed it back in the drawer. She slipped the dress over her head. It slid silkily into place. Did she need to shave her armpits? She looked in the mirror and lifted up her arms. No dark shadows. Good. From under the bed, she retrieved a pair of dusty black pumps. She wiped them off with a wad of Kleenex and stepped into them.

She surveyed herself critically in the bedroom-dresser mirror. She frowned and reached behind her head to unfetter her hair. Michaels liked his women with long locks and she needed to show off hers. She shook her hair out and grabbed a brush to give it a few strokes. After she put down the brush, she studied her face in the mirror, searching for the same signs of age she'd spotted in Gabe's. She saw a couple of fine lines around her mouth. No crow's-feet or gray hair. Yet. She touched her face with her fingertips. "Tick tock, tick tock," she muttered into the mirror.

She reached into her top dresser drawer and dug around for some lipstick. She hadn't worn any in ages. She pulled out a tube and read the label: "Killer Coral." She smiled. "That's appropriate," she thought. She leaned closer to the mirror and applied a couple of strokes to her lips.

"How you doing up there?" Gabe yelled.

"Come on up, Jerry," she said. As he came up the stairs, she admired how his conservative slacks and crisp shirt nicely complemented his contemporary hair and tie. Over his arm was draped a dark blazer, a necessary item of clothing to hide the holstered gun hanging from his shoulder rig. Maybe he didn't look so old and tired after all. "You clean up real good, partner," she said, smiling.

He laughed and blushed. "Yeah, right. Tell it to my ex-wives."

"Really. You look very nice," she said. She walked over to straighten his tie; this time he didn't push her hands away. "You look like a music company executive or something."

"You look pretty hot yourself," he said. He noticed her lipstick, and that she wasn't wearing a bra. "A little too hot as a matter of fact. Murphy, are you sure you don't want to . . ."

"Stop, Gabe. We had this conversation."

"Okay, okay," he said, throwing up his hands. "I give up."

"Ready to rock?" she asked.

"Let's rock," he said.

TWENTY-ONE

Back and forth. Back and forth. Michaels stopped counting after fifty laps. A good workout, the best he'd had in some time. He started with the breaststroke, broke it up with the crawl and then returned to the breaststroke. He ended with the butterfly; all he could manage was a few laps, and he thought that was pathetic. It used to be his signature stroke in high school, what had earned him two state trophies. He'd have to work on that. After the last lap he stretched out on his back and floated for a while. The long, white-tiled room was dim, with most of the illumination provided by the lights lining the walls of the pool.

When he was a kid, the basement pool was a great refuge when he wanted a break from the screaming and chaos in the rest of the house; water is wonderful for muffling the senses. When she was in town, his favorite cousin joined him. They'd float on their backs for what seemed like hours, silent and naked, stretching out their arms to touch fingertips. They didn't need to talk; they were partners in purgatory. Her parents were crazy, rich drunks, too.

He finally rolled over, swam lazily to the ladder and climbed out of the water. He pulled a robe over his nude body, slipped his feet into some sandals and walked up two flights.

He dropped the robe on the master-bath floor, kicked off the sandals and, with a sigh, eased his frame into the bubbling Jacuzzi. He leaned back and shut his eyes. He was glad he'd had the time to exercise before the big night; it rejuvenated him and helped him order his thoughts. He had once again packed away his questions about his wife's whereabouts to make mental room for his fascination with the mystery woman. He was so looking forward to meeting her that night at the bar—and possibly taking her up to a room at the hotel—that he had barely been able to concentrate on his patients during the day. He'd left work early, leaving his nurses to offer excuses to the patients remaining in the waiting room.

On his bed he had laid out his clothing for the evening—Italian-made charcoal gabardine trousers and jacket, midnight blue dress shirt with mother-of-pearl buttons, dark blue Hermès silk tie with black diagonal stripes, black Italian loafers, dark dress socks and gray silk boxers. He was taking a chance by going with a more formal look, but he wanted to impress this woman, sweep her off her feet. He looked good in his Wop outfit.

He stepped out of the tub and toweled off. He stood back and inspected his body in the mirror. Broad chest and well-defined shoulders. He still had a swimmer's shoulders. Flat stomach. Strong thighs. Nice, big cock—that crazy barbed-wire bitch from the club had been right about that. He turned sideways. Hard, round ass. He flexed his biceps, felt them with his hands. Not too bad. He needed to hit the weights and the pool a little more regularly. Otherwise, she'd have nothing to complain about tonight. Not one damn thing.

He wrapped the towel around his waist and walked into the bedroom. With the remote-control pad, he flicked on the television in the armoire. He tossed the remote onto the bed, dropped the towel to the floor and started to dress.

A stiff-haired male anchor from one of the local evening news programs was on, giving a promo for the ten o'clock news. "An Apple Valley man leads police on a wild high-speed chase, injuring two pedestrians and another motorist before his car careens into the side of a town house. Legal troubles and criminal charges continue to mount for a Twin Cities psychologist and father of four accused of fondling his female patients. Dutch elm disease makes a comeback in the metro area. Will your favorite shade tree be the next to go?"

After stepping into his boxers, Michaels reached for the remote to change channels. There had to be something else on.

"Tune in at ten for an update on the Minneapolis priest who was brutally assaulted and left for dead in his own church a week ago. What do authorities hope to discover when they question him from his hospital bed this week?"

Michaels froze. The crammed "worry about it later" compartment of his life suddenly burst open, spilling out its unsettling contents.

He waited to hear more from the television news anchor, but the promo ended and a commercial for a fast-food joint paraded some burgers across the screen. He spent half an hour surfing the local stations, anxiously searching for similar promos from the other television news programs. "Will a man of the cloth help police identify his attacker?" asked a breathy female anchor giving a teaser for another news station. "Or does his vow to keep confessions confidential seal his lips? Watch us at ten to learn more about this priestly dilemma."

All the news stations had it. He flicked off the television and angrily hurled the remote across the room. It shattered against the wall, scattering batteries and broken plastic pieces on the carpet and wood floor. "Son-of-a-bitch!" What if the priest did describe him?

He stomped past his wife's dresser, the marble top loaded with perfume bottles, religious statues and silver-handled hairbrushes. In one fluid and rage-filled motion, he knocked it all off with a swipe of his arm. The delicate bottles exploded, releasing a riot of fumes into the air.

He spotted the lone object left standing on his wife's dresser—a small statue of St. Jude, patron saint of hopeless cases. St. Jude was his wife's favorite saint, the one she'd prayed to while her father was dying of cancer. He would hear her whispering in the middle of the night, when worry stole her sleep: "Pray for me, I am so helpless and alone. Make use, I implore you, of that particular privilege given to you, to bring visible and speedy help where help is almost despaired of."

He picked up the small statue, no bigger than his hand, and glared at it contemptuously. At that instant, it represented the crippling emotions that threatened to weaken him and bring his world cascading down around him—the nagging guilt for his mortal offenses, the terrifying fear of landing in prison or hell, and the anxious dread that he was losing control of his life. "When am I going to get this Catholic monkey off my back?" he growled, and slammed it against the dresser top. The statue crumbled, all but disintegrating in a dusty cloud of clay.

He needed a plan, but there wasn't time to think about that now. He looked at the clock. "God dammit to hell," he said, running his fingers through his hair. He needed to finish dressing and get to the bar. Didn't want to keep the mystery lady waiting.

As he hurried east down Summit Avenue toward downtown, his knuckles turned white from the grip he had on the steering wheel of his Porsche. He didn't bother turning on the radio or slipping in a CD. He cursed every red light. The top was down, but the rush of summer air against his face did nothing to cool his temper, or drown out the buzzing in his head.

He picked a dark booth huddled against the wall opposite the bar and sharply ordered the waitress to bring him a double of the twenty-two-year-old Craigellachie, neat.

"Can I get you anything else?" she asked.

She was a tall brunette with short hair, a flat chest and no visible hips. The long black skirt and unfitted white blouse did her boyish figure no favors, he observed, but at least she looked professional.

"Would you like a glass of water on the side?" she asked.

"Surprise me," he said dryly.

She returned with a snifter containing the Scotch and a tall glass tinkling with ice water. "Shall I start a tab?" she asked.

He didn't answer immediately; he was staring straight ahead, lost in thought.

"Sir? A tab?"

"Yes, yes!" he snapped. "Start a tab." He picked up the snifter.

"Enjoy," she said, smiling, and walked away.

He sipped, luxuriating in the gentle burn that trickled from his mouth down to his gut. He drank again. He was starting to feel better. Much better. The fly was settling down.

He scanned the long, narrow room. A quiet night, as he would expect of a Monday evening at any establishment in town. Two fat, bald businessmen in white dress shirts sat bellies up to the bar, one at each end, resting their wide bottoms on tall wooden stools with ladder backs and black leather seats. Their suit jackets were draped over the backs of the stools. One of them puffed on a cigar purchased from the small glass humidor kept behind the bar.

Two male bartenders in white shirts, black trousers and dark ties busied themselves behind the bar polishing martini glasses and wine goblets. They could have passed for twins. Both wore their blond hair slicked back with some kind of gel, giving them a retro look consistent with their vintage surroundings.

The dark bar itself was an impressive slab of L-shaped wood furniture, running half the length of the room and curving around the back wall. It boasted a top that was glasslike in its high-gloss finish. The shiny counter surface was softly illuminated by a couple of green-shaded library lamps sitting on the bar top, one at each end. Behind the bar were glass shelves stacked six high and mounted against mirrored walls, giving the illusion of depth. The shelves were stocked with a mind-numbing array of liquor, but Scotch clearly ruled the day. Auchentoshan, Bladnoch and Glenkinchie from the Lowlands. Clynelish, Glenmorangie, Oban and Tomatin from the Highlands.

Speyside in the north was well represented by Cragganmore, Glenfiddich, Inchgower, Mortlach. From the windswept isle of Islay came Bowmore, Bunnahabhain and Lagavulin. That's what the mystery lady had asked for. Lagavulin. Not a bad choice, thought Michaels. It has a powerful, peaty taste and smell accented by sweet undertones. He favored it after a heavy dinner, with a good cigar.

Where was she? He checked his wristwatch. Still early. He took a couple of slow, calming breaths and settled in to enjoy the view from his dark nook, with its glove-soft leather upholstery. Against the opposite wall and close to the bar's entryway from the hotel lobby was a blackboard with the quote of the day scribbled across it in white chalk. Today's offering was from Hemingway's *The Sun Also Rises*. He smiled as he read it, appreciating its slam against sentimentality: "This wine is too good for toast-drinking, my dear. You don't want to mix emotions up with a wine like that. You lose the taste."

He watched a chesty young woman sashay in wearing a short, black leather skirt, tight taupe sweater and black pumps with clear acrylic stiletto heels. The nice Catholic boys at the prep school he'd attended called those kinds of pumps "Come fuck me" shoes. From her forearm dangled a handbag covered with fake leopard fur. Her short, curly hair was bleached and dyed a hideous shade of platinum. Her makeup looked as though it had been applied with a trowel. She was a cheap piece of work, barely one step up from the whores he found on the street corners.

She hopped onto a bar stool next to one of the fat businessmen and started chattering. He ignored her. She kept yammering. He threw some bills on the bar, slid off the stool, grabbed his coat and left. She moved on to the man at the other end, the one with the cigar. He nodded his head a couple of times and then took the cigar out of his mouth to study the damp end, apparently finding it more interesting than the woman. He put it back in his mouth and pointedly turned his head away from her to watch the baseball game on the television mounted from ceiling brackets above the bar.

One of the bartenders leaned over the counter and said something to her in a low voice. She responded, shaking her blond head vigorously. The other bartender looked at her and put his hand on the phone behind the counter. "Fuck you," she sputtered. "I'm outta here." She hopped off the bar stool, turned on her heel and clicked out. Unruffled, the two bartenders returned to polishing glasses.

Michaels eyed her spiteful retreat. She had fat thighs, he thought, and she was stupid. Everyone in town knew that this bar—and the hotel, for that matter—threw hookers out on their asses. This fact was so well known and obvious Michaels was surprised there wasn't some sort of permanent sign posted at the hotel's glass front doors, right next to the stickers welcoming Visa and American Express. The unwritten law of the land was that this particular bar was a club for gentlemen and their invited ladies. No whores allowed. Michaels agreed with that. Some places had to be off limits. Everyone knew that. Everyone except this ditsy blonde.

As she left, another blond ambled in from the hotel lobby—a man with long hair and a beard. Long locks aside, he looked like a businessman in his white shirt, dark slacks and blazer. The tie was a bit much, however. He was probably involved in the arts in some way. The new arrival took a booth near the door, along the same wall as the bar. Something about the man's barrel body was familiar, but Michaels brushed the thought aside.

He took another sip of Scotch, rolled it around in his mouth and swallowed. A few more minutes went by. He glanced up at the television screen. The Tigers were winning at St. Louis. He was about to check his watch again when he saw her glide in from the lobby, and she was exquisite.

Her black hair hung like a velvet curtain around her swanlike neck. The black slip dress draped temptingly from her smooth, olive shoulders by two thin spaghetti straps. Those straps would be so easy to snap, he thought. The lustrous material glided over her breasts and hips, describing the smooth lines of an athletic but feminine woman.

The hem fell above the knee. Hard, well-defined calves detailed her long legs. She must be a runner, he thought, and that bodes well for her endurance in the bedroom. At the same time, her small wrists and ankles told him she would not be too difficult to contain. That's what he wanted—a woman who could put up a lively fight, but would succumb when he desired.

He smiled to himself, pleased he had reserved a room at the hotel. He had used an alias and planned to pay in cash. In case things got a bit out of hand, as they had been wont to do lately. If that happened, she would be the last. The fly could be put to rest. That's what he told himself.

Good enough to eat, he thought, his eyes caressing her up and down. Good enough to eat, but easy enough to beat.

TWENTY-TWO

Murphy surveyed the room, noting the big man seated at the bar as well as the waitress and the two bartenders. Otherwise, the place appeared empty of civilians. That was good, she thought. She didn't want to run across anyone who recognized her. On any other night of the week, there was the possibility of bumping into a familiar judge or lawyer who might greet her by name or rank. A Monday in a downtown bar should be pretty quiet. She glanced briefly at Gabe, who had a clear view of the entire room from his seat near the door. He pushed back his blazer slightly. Murphy welcomed the private and reassuring peek at the holstered gun hanging from his shoulder rig.

On the wall above her partner's booth were several framed black-and-white photographs of the glitterati who had visited the bar or hotel, or worked at the establishment before they became famous. F. Scott Fitzgerald, Hubert H. Humphrey, Judy Garland, women's golf pioneer Patty Berg and railroad giant James J. Hill. Despite the bow to a couple of female notables, it was a very male establishment, reeking of cigar smoke, expensive Scotch and Italian leather. She'd always felt very comfortable in the place.

Murphy saw Michaels stand up. She hadn't noticed him there when she first set foot in the bar; she was being too slow or inattentive or both. She needed to be at the top of her game tonight. She quickly plastered a smile across her face, taking in his figure as he strolled across the bar's wood floor. He had a deliberate, graceful gait. He was handsome in his almost monochromatic attire, but even those dark blues and rich blacks couldn't coax any warm color from his cold, gray eyes. If you feel yourself wavering, she told herself, simply look into those heartless, soulless orbs. They were probably the last things Finch saw before she took her final breath. The last things the priest saw before he nearly died on the floor of his own church. The last things uncounted other victims saw as the life was strangled from their bodies. Remember Finch, she told herself. Remember Fionn Clare Hennessy, buried in a country cemetery.

"Hello, lady," he said. "You look beautiful. Absolutely stunning."

"Thank you," she said, smiling. "I guess we both like black."

"Black is the color of seduction," he said. "I'm sure you know that already." He extended his right hand. She reached out and took it. Such soft, smooth skin, he thought. He walked her over to his booth against the wall. She slid into it so she faced the lobby door. He sat down across from her. He longed for the feel of her legs pressed against his, but he initially kept his distance fearing such immediate closeness would make her uncomfortable. He had to move quickly but carefully this evening, he thought. She wasn't going to be one of his usual conquests.

The skinny waitress walked over. "What can I get for you?" she asked Murphy.

"The lady will have a Lagavulin," he said. "Neat."

The waitress looked at Murphy, who nodded. This man was used to barking out orders and seeing them followed, Murphy thought.

"Would you like another, sir?" the waitress asked, picking up his empty snifter.

"Yes," he said curtly, and turned his head away from the waitress to stare into Murphy's eyes. Then his gaze moved lower. He could make out the points of her nipples under the dress. She wasn't wearing a bra, and he liked that. What magnificent breasts, he thought.

"Thank you, miss," Murphy said. "Please bring me a tall glass of ice water like the gentleman's."

He is no gentleman, thought Murphy. He's rude, accustomed to treating others like servants. Having money shouldn't preclude politeness. Of course, she couldn't remember the last time she'd come across a well-mannered maniac.

The waitress quickly returned with their drinks. "Let me know if you need anything else," said the young woman. "I'll be back in a bit to see how you're doing."

"Thank you," said Murphy. She looked at Gabe seated near the door. His beer sat untouched in front of him, but he was smoking like crazy. His eyes were glued to the booth she shared with Michaels. The doctor didn't notice because he was too busy studying her breasts; she wished she'd worn the strapless bra.

"Tell me about yourself," he said to Murphy. He took a deep drink of Scotch.

"You go first," she said, smiling coyly. He laughed.

"Why don't we keep names out of it," he said. "I rather enjoy this game."

"Fine," said Murphy. "Then tell me as much as you can about yourself without name-dropping."

"I like that," he said, smiling. "Another rule for the game. Now let me think." He took a long drink and paused, staring up at the ceiling. He drummed his fingers on the table. "I need a cigar in my hands for these deep thoughts," he said. "Do you mind if I grab one? I won't light up yet."

"Please go right ahead. I like a good cigar myself once in a while."

Michaels slid out of the booth, walked up to the bar and pointed to the humidor. The bartender pulled out a fat cigar and showed it to him. The doctor examined the band, shook his head and pointed to another one. He held up two fingers. The bartender handed him

163

a pair of slender cigars. Michaels examined the bands, sniffed them and nodded. He slipped them into the inside breast pocket of his jacket. He's a fussy bastard, she thought.

Michaels was all smiles walking back to the booth. "I got us both a treat for later," he said, and he slid into the booth next to her. She could feel his legs against hers. "Back to our game. I'm a doctor," he said. "I think I can tell you that without giving away too much."

"A gynecologist?" she asked.

He laughed. She felt his left hand on her left shoulder, softly stroking and rubbing her bare skin. She looked over at Gabe. His eyes were wide; he looked ready to jump out of his seat.

"You are naughty," he said. "No, a plastic surgeon. Now your turn."

"I work with food," she said, deciding to invent a career involving something familiar.

"You're a waitress?" he asked, sounding a little disappointed.

"No, a gourmet chef," she said. "I cater private affairs."

"Wonderful," he said. "Tell me about some of your favorite dishes."

He's testing me to see if I'm telling the truth, she thought. "Well, it's hard to pick one or two favorites," she said. "If you're talking appetizers, I prepare a wonderful olive-and-artichoke tapenade. For the main course, I would have to go with my roast leg of lamb with lemon-coriander crust. To accompany that, I might pick grilled asparagus with gorgonzola butter and spring greens with candied walnuts tossed in a raspberry vinaigrette."

"Dessert," he said, picking up his snifter to take a deep drink. "Let's not forget dessert."

"Life would be boring without dessert," she said. "How about a caramel flan?"

"Marvelous," he said, clearly impressed. After putting down his snifter, he rested his right hand on her thigh, only removing it to lift the glass to his lips.

"Are you a gourmet? You obviously know your Scotches and cigars," she said. "Tell me about your other interests, your extracurricular activities." Yes, she thought, describe those special hobbies of yours—rape and murder.

"Golf. Can't be a doctor unless you play golf. I love the water. Swimming. My favorite is sailing," he said. "We . . . I mean, um I . . . I have a cabin and boat on Lake Superior."

"You said 'we' at first," Murphy said, taking a dainty sip of Scotch and following it with a gulp of water.

She is way too observant, he thought. "I owned the boat and the cabin with my wife," he said. He took a long drink of Scotch before continuing. "We've been divorced for some time," he said. "She let me keep both. She isn't much of a sailor." That last part is the god's honest truth, he thought sourly.

That first part is a lie, thought Murphy, who detected the telltale white tan line around his left ring finger. She also noticed how his voice caught in his throat when he said the word "wife." He must despise her, she thought.

"What about you? Hobbies?"

"I run," she said, then decided to throw out another teaser. "I hunt. Small game. Pheasant and grouse mostly."

"How unusual. A woman who knows her Scotches, smokes cigars and hunts."

"I grew up in a houseful of males," she said.

He nodded, finding that believable.

"Do you hunt at all?" she asked. He smiled but didn't answer. Murphy decided not to push the question; she didn't want to make him suspicious.

He emptied his snifter and snapped his fingers to attract the attention of the waitress. He noticed Murphy had hardly touched her Scotch. "Is there something wrong with your drink?" he asked.

"Not at all," said Murphy, taking a longer drink to appease him. She felt a rush of warmth from the alcohol. "What else? Where were you born?"

"Well, I was born in St. Paul but I'm a product of the Minneapolis

Catholic school system," he said. "The discipline was actually fine preparation for medical school. Would you like me to dazzle you with a little Latin?"

The waitress brought him another snifter. He took it from her hands before she set it down. He lifted it as if toasting. *"In vino veritas,"* he said, and nearly drained the snifter.

"In wine there is truth," Murphy said.

"Very good," he said.

"How about this one?" she asked. *"Facilis descensus Averno."*

"The descent to hell is easy," he said. For a moment, the drunken smile faded from his face.

"A favorite of my high-school religion teacher," she said. "A kick-ass Christian Brother."

"Aha! You went to Catholic school as well," he said. The smile returned. He laughed and raised his glass to her. "A toast to our shared misery." He emptied it.

Murphy saw it took quite a few drinks to get him to this stage. He's a heavy drinker.

"They're wrong, you know," he said, running his index finger along the edge of the empty glass. "The descent is anything but easy."

"What do you mean?"

"Are you as tormented by Catholic guilt as I am?" he asked. "What is it about us that drives us to beat ourselves up over normal, human failings?"

"What sorts of human failings do you consider normal?" she asked. Here we go, thought Murphy. This should be as interesting as hell.

He leaned conspiratorially into her ear, nearly putting his mouth on it, and whispered: "How do you like your sex?"

"Straight up and neat," she whispered back. He threw his head back and laughed so loudly the man at the bar and the two bartenders turned around. Gabe stared at them.

"I like mine with an extra twist—a rough one," he said. "Is that so

166

decadent? Is that so sinful? Why do I have to beat myself up over that?"

"You don't have to beat yourself up," she offered, again pushing his hand off her thigh. "Isn't that what confession and penance are for?"

He shook his head. She didn't say anything. She waited for him to say more. She thought he was close to handing her something useful and revealing, something incriminating about his most recent trip to the confessional.

"Tell me," he said, looking into her eyes. "When was the last time you went to confession? Things have changed. Priests aren't what they used to be. They aren't content with laying a few rosary beads on you. They want you to do all sorts of shit."

"Well, the penance depends upon the seriousness of the offense," she said, realizing Father Ambrose must have asked too much from this man. Perhaps he even demanded he turn himself in to the police. "Some things require more than prayer," she said evenly, trying to sound reasonable. "Some sins require . . ." She wanted him to fill in the blank.

"Require what?" he asked, an edge of bitterness in his voice.

"Restitution?" she said.

"Bullshit. Remorse should be enough. Simple remorse."

Keep going, she thought. He stopped talking and stared straight ahead; he seemed to be studying the air itself.

"Enough small talk," he said, sliding out of the booth. "Let's go out in the hotel garden and admire the stars. It should be dark enough by now. We can have a smoke out there."

He threw a wad of cash on the table and held out his hand, but Murphy ignored it. She wiggled out of the booth and walked out with him. When she passed Gabe's table, she tried not to meet his eyes. Her partner wouldn't be liking this at all.

"Great," Gabe muttered. He crushed his cigarette butt in the ashtray, threw some crumpled bills on the table and got up. Carefully staying several paces behind, he followed them into the lobby and out of the hotel. He stopped outside the double glass doors of the hotel entrance, standing nonchalantly next to the doorman.

A black limo pulled into the circular drive at the hotel entrance, spilling out a drunken man in a rumpled gray suit and a sober, somber woman in a blue dress. The doorman, a young man dressed in a period costume, held the door open while the man tripped in ahead of the woman. She stomped after him.

On either side of the circular drive were elaborate English gardens decorating the front of the hotel. The one on the north end of the building was the smaller, less lavish of the two. The larger garden on the south end seemed to grow more elaborate every year, even within its confined urban space. This summer, walking paths wound their way under metal arbors and snaked through patches of yellow snapdragons and peach day lilies. White clusters of sweet alyssum scented the air. Rabbits hopped among the plants.

A tall, black wrought-iron fence separated the gardens from the sidewalk. On the street beyond, a couple of cabs were parked in front of the hotel. The cabbies were leaning against the sides of their cars, having a smoke and talking. One had his radio tuned to the game. Otherwise, it was quiet.

Gabe watched his partner and Michaels walk to the far end of the larger garden. He lost sight of them. He didn't want to get too close, for fear of tipping Michaels off. He pulled out his pack of Winstons. Empty. He strolled down the drive between the two gardens to the sidewalk, giving a sideways glance to see if he could spot Murphy and Michaels from that angle. They were sitting on a bench that backed into some tall evergreens planted against the side of the hotel. He looked straight ahead and recognized the cabbies; he bummed a cigarette off one of them. A large group of people walked through the hotel doors. The cabbies tossed down their smokes and got in their cars, pulling up the circular drive for the fares. Gabe stood alone on the sidewalk for a minute and then walked back to the hotel entrance. He stayed there, one hand shoved resentfully in his pants pocket and the other occupied with a smoke. Under his blazer, his Glock was ready.

After the two taxis pulled away, the only sound was that of an occasional car passing on the street. The night air had turned cool. Murphy shivered. Michaels slipped his left arm around her and rubbed her bare shoulder. "We should go back inside, where it's warmer," she said.

He took off his jacket and draped it over her shoulders. "I almost forgot our treat," he said. He slipped his hand inside the coat to pull out the two cigars, brushing her left breast as he did so. He felt his pants pocket. "No matches. Stay right here." He stood up and walked through the garden to the lobby doors. "Got a light?" he asked the doorman.

The doorman reached into his pants pocket and pulled out a book of hotel matches. "There you go, sir."

Michaels started to leave, but eyed Gabe for several seconds. Gabe stared back, puffing on his cigarette. Michaels thought he looked very familiar, but couldn't place him. "Do I know you?" Michaels asked.

"Don't think so," Gabe said, then turned around to stroll through the smaller garden.

Michaels went back to the bench. Gabe took a hard pull on his cigarette and watched the doctor disappear into the garden; he gritted his teeth. "Bastard," Gabe whispered.

Michaels sat down and tried to give Murphy one of the cigars. She shook her head and pushed his hand away. "Let's smoke them inside," she said. She felt in control since he was drunk and she was sober. Still, this garden spot was far too dark and private. She took off his jacket and handed it to him.

"That bar is dreary," he said. He slipped the cigars back in the jacket pocket, threw the jacket over the back of the bench and leaned toward her. "We could get a room," he said softly.

"You've got to be kidding," she said. She stood up to leave. "I don't even know your name, let alone . . ."

He grabbed her by the arm and yanked her back down to the bench. He pulled her toward him and kissed her hard on the mouth. His left hand cradled the back of her head, his fingers entwined in her hair.

"Stop," she said when he lifted his mouth off hers for an instant.

He didn't respond; he was listening to the buzzing. He pulled her off the bench and onto the ground.

She felt some sort of fragrant ground cover beneath her. His body was flat on top of hers. Through her thin dress, she could feel he was hard. For an instant—one out-of-control instant—she was aroused. Then she was terrified. "Don't," she said.

"I'll take it slow," he whispered. "Slow, but rough. A woman like you, I'll bet you like it rough." He again sealed his lips firmly over hers. He tasted sharply of Scotch. His right hand cupped her left breast. He squeezed hard, his hand slipping a bit on the satiny dress.

She struggled to push against his chest with both hands, but he was too strong and heavy. She tried to scream, but couldn't with his mouth over hers. His right hand moved from her breast to the strap of her dress. He slipped the strap off her shoulder and pulled down the bodice. His mouth moved from her lips to her breast. She emitted a squeak that was the very beginning of a scream, but he quickly covered her mouth with his left hand. With his right hand he grabbed her left wrist and pinned it down on the ground, close to her side. He peeled his mouth off her breast and put his lips close to her ear:

"The fly shall marry the bumblebee," he breathed.

His words made no sense to her, and that frightened her as much as his actions. He was nuts. Her head was spinning. Was she going to be raped by a crazy man in front of this hotel, in the middle of downtown, with her partner yards away? After all the jams she'd gotten out of over the years, was she finally going to be finished by one of her own making? Hell no, she thought. This is not going to happen. She pushed against his chest with her free right hand and bit the meaty palm covering her mouth. He didn't budge. She bore down as hard as she could with her teeth, grinding. He pulled his hand away with a yelp. "You bitch!" he snarled, letting go of her wrist to slap her.

He lifted his body slightly off hers, resting on his right elbow and shaking his left hand in pain. That gave her the maneuvering room she needed. She bent her right leg and kneed him in the groin. He grunted and started to roll off her, but she grabbed him by the shoulders for leverage and kneed him again, even harder. He tumbled off her, rolled into a ball and clutched his crotch.

She scrambled out of the garden, fixing her dress strap as she ran. She almost knocked Gabe over on the sidewalk in front of the hotel. He threw down his cigarette. "What the fuck is going on?" he asked, gaping at her disheveled state. Bits of greenery were tangled in her hair, her dress was askew and she was panting. He saw a red mark on her face; the bastard had hit her. "Did he . . ."

"No, he didn't get that far," she whispered frantically. "Now shut up and get me the hell out of here before he catches his breath. My cover is still good and I don't want to blow it."

"Bullshit," hissed Gabe, looking toward the garden while reaching under his blazer for his gun.

She stopped him, resting her trembling hand on his arm. The doorman eyed them nervously, but became distracted when a taxi pulled up, disgorging two women loaded with shopping bags from the Mall of America. The doorman took a couple of the bags and held the door open for them before following them inside with their purchases.

Murphy pulled Gabe into the smaller garden. "We can get the son-of-a-bitch for assaulting a cop right now," said Gabe. She couldn't see his face in the dark, but she could tell from his voice that it was red with rage.

"It's his word against mine," she said. "He's got all the money in the world to fight it. We need hard evidence on these murders."

"How about I stroll over there and beat the living shit out of him?" said Gabe. "At least let me make that small contribution."

"I'd like to kick the warped bastard's ass myself," she said, struggling to steady her quavering voice. "Right now, as far as he's concerned,

I'm just the one who got away. Let's keep it that way. Besides, he didn't get off scot-free."

"What did you do to him?" asked Gabe.

"Let's say he won't be walking upright for a while," she said.

"Should we stop at the hospital and get you checked?" asked Gabe as they trotted toward Murphy's Jeep, parked on a downtown side street.

"No. I'm fine," she said. "I'm just a little shaky. You drive, okay? You've got the keys in your pocket anyway."

They stopped next to the Jeep. "Go ahead and get it over with, Gabe," Murphy said as her partner fished the keys out of his pants pocket. "Say it." She leaned against the car with one hand while he fumbled with the door lock, taking what seemed like forever to finally open it. She was still trembling like a kicked puppy; her face still burned where Michaels had struck her.

"What are you talking about?" he asked as they slid into the car.

"Say it. I deserve it. I want you to say it. Really. I do!" she said, shouting without realizing it.

"What, Murphy? Say what?" he yelled back.

"Oh, fuck you," she said, slamming the passenger-side door shut.

"Okay," said Gabe, slamming the driver's-side door. "I told you so! I fucking told you so! There. Are you happy? Are you?"

"Yes," she said softly. She touched her sore cheek. "Now don't say another goddamn word about it for the rest of the night."

TWENTY-THREE

She drove alone down to Rochester Tuesday morning. All the windows of the Jeep down. The radio blaring. Tina Turner. "I Might Have Been Queen."

I might have been dead meat, mused Murphy, thinking back to the previous night and the near catastrophe in the dark hotel garden. At a light, she looked in the rearview mirror and checked the small, pale bruise on her face where he'd struck her. She'd covered it with some makeup; it would be gone in a day or two. She knew his words would stay with her longer.

"I'll bet you like it rough."

His words bothered her because she worried that they were true. She wasn't delicate; she was drawn to coarse and primitive things. Even mean things. Did that make her coarse and primitive? Mean? She adored the abrasive nature of police work, with its intimate exposure to the violence of the streets and the rawness of people's emotions. She loved living on the urban shores of the unpolished Mississippi. She enjoyed the rowdiness of her family's riverfront bar, with its clientele of barge workers.

When she was in her early twenties and pouring drinks at the bar one summer night, she slipped out for a stroll along the Mississippi with a Cajun towboat pilot fresh from New Orleans. He had a strangely musical accent that was at once French, Canadian and southern. He was a head taller than she and a decade older, with massive arms, jet-black hair and piercing green eyes. They went to his cabin aboard the boat, got drunk on Southern Comfort and fell into his bed. He was very rough, holding her wrists tight during their lovemaking, grabbing her hair in his fists. It frightened her and, though she would never admit it, excited her.

She didn't tell anyone about that night along the river. Not even Jack. Especially not Jack.

Of course, she didn't want it as rough as rape. No woman did. She had thought she could manage the situation at the hotel, but it had all boiled over into a wretched mess. Why had she fooled herself into thinking she was in control of a clearly uncontrollable situation? Had she been asking for trouble, for rape? No. She had endangered herself and the case with her arrogant overconfidence.

For all her trouble, what had she learned about Michaels? He was a high-class alcoholic who liked his Scotch expensive, neat and in great quantities. He was a womanizing control freak who quickly evolved into a masochistic rapist with the help of his booze. He was a tormented Catholic who felt enough guilt to go to confession, but had assaulted the priest when the penance proved threatening. He was an unfaithful husband who hated his wife. She had managed to assemble a pretty complete profile of the guy in one evening, but almost at the cost of her life. His rape victims didn't live to tell about it.

One thing in the picture didn't fit: his nonsensical words. "The fly shall marry the bumblebee." It sounded like a child's song. She'd have to do an Internet search and see what that pulled up.

Unlike the drive to western Wisconsin, this trip had few stretches of woods and forests breaking up the monotony of farmland. She passed one cornfield and peeling red barn after another, interrupted only by meadows covered by bales of hay rolled up like giant pieces of Shredded Wheat. At least it was a short trip.

ROCHESTER WELCOMES YOU and MAYO MEDICAL CENTER EXIT 4 MILES read two signs at the city limits. From the highway, Murphy could see a cluster of red buildings up on a hill that represented a fraction of the sprawling medical campus. She took the hospital exit and wound her way around the campus until she found the coffee shop where she was meeting a Rochester homicide investigator. She preferred buttonholing colleagues away from their station houses. She found fellow detectives more relaxed and open when they were off site, freed of the distraction of ringing phones and bellowing superiors.

"Sergeant Paris Murphy," she said, smiling and offering her hand.

"Sergeant Daniel Klassen," he said, sliding out of his seat at the coffee shop to stand and introduce himself. He was Murphy's height and in his mid-fifties, with short gray hair and a neatly trimmed moustache. Gold wire-rimmed glasses framed his eyes. A slight paunch pushed out his white dress shirt and draped over his navy blue trousers. He waited until she took a seat at the table before sitting down himself.

The waitress, an older woman with hair drawn back in a bun behind her head, brought grease-stained breakfast menus to the table. She wore a yellow dress covered by a white apron, also grease stained. "How ya doin' there, Sergeant Dan?" she asked Klassen.

"I'm doin' fine, pretty lady," he said, grinning and not bothering to glance at the menu. "What kinda pie we got today?"

"We got apple, strawberry-rhubarb, lemon chiffon, banana cream, cherry, Mississippi mud and chocolate silk," she said. "I put aside a piece of your favorite, in case you came in today. Which you did."

"Which I did," he said, smiling. "Bring on that peach pie, then. Don't forget the java."

"What can we get for you, sweetie?" she asked Murphy.

"Coffee is fine, thanks," Murphy said. "Black."

After the waitress left, Klassen slid a manila file folder across the table. "Here's what I can give you," he said. "You can keep it. It's all photocopies."

The tab of the folder carried the victim's name, last name first. "Magnuson, Roxanne E." A person never wants her name on the tab of a file folder, thought Murphy. It's rarely for a happy reason. "I hope you don't mind if I poke around your case," she said, rifling through the file.

The waitress set down two coffee cups and what looked like half a peach pie, à la mode.

"Hell. If you think you can crack it after better than a dozen years, more power to you," he said, digging into the pie and vanilla ice cream. "We thought some out-of-towner probably did it and then took off," he said in between bites. "When I heard you guys had a case with the same M.O., especially with the weird hair thing, I thought I'd better flag you. Figured after all these years, maybe the son-of-a-bitch resurfaced up in St. Paul. Maybe he got hungry for some city meat."

"I appreciate that," she said, smiling.

"Yeah, but when you called me yesterday afternoon and told me who you were looking at, well, I have to tell you, it's hard as hell to believe one of our doctors did this," he said, wiping ice cream off his moustache. He took a sip of coffee and gave her a tight smile.

"Our doctors." Rochester took care of its own.

"It's just a theory I have," she said, still smiling and taking a sip of coffee. "Do you have any suggestions regarding folks I could reinterview? Any loose ends I could reexamine?"

"Not really," he said. He looked up from his pie; the smile was gone from his face. "We interviewed and reinterviewed everybody and his goddamn uncle."

Murphy realized she'd pissed him off with the suggestion that there were loose ends. A couple of male uniformed officers walked through the café door. Klassen nodded at them. Murphy suspected he would rather be sitting with them than an uppity female cop from the Twin Cities. She wasn't going to get very far asking this guy for help. "Well, thanks much," she said, sliding out of her chair. She reached into her purse to throw some cash on the table.

"Don't worry about it," he said, waving away the money. "Good luck."

"I'll give you a call if we find anything," she said.

"Yeah, you do that," he said. He didn't try to mask the skepticism in his voice.

"Thank you very much," she said again, and left. As she walked down the sidewalk to her car, she could see through the coffee-shop window that he had wasted no time in joining his colleagues at their table—and ordering more pie.

Murphy drove to a lake in the middle of Rochester, parked her Jeep in a lot overlooking the water and studied the file. She rolled down the car windows to enjoy the meager breeze off the lake. Warm, but overcast. The beach off the parking lot was void of swimmers but filled with fat Canada geese; their droppings littered the sand. Several of the big birds waddled up to her car, looking for a hand-out.

Everything seemed to be in order in the file. The autopsy report found that Roxanne E. Magnuson had been beaten and raped, but no semen was found. The suspect had apparently used a condom. That bit of information made Murphy doubt the rapist was a spontaneous stranger. "Out-of-towner my ass," she mumbled, flipping through the police report. The cause of death was strangulation. The report also made a reference to the section of missing auburn hair. As with Finch, the victim had a nick on the back of her neck, probably from the sharp object used to shear off her hair.

The murder victim's housemate, another nurse named Marcia Colvin, told officers her friend had been seeing a married man on the sly. Colvin didn't know the man's name; Magnuson had been very secretive about the relationship. Colvin claimed she saw him parked outside the house one night, dropping her friend off. Colvin happened to be up studying for a medical school entrance exam, having aspirations beyond nursing. The rental house was on an unlit country road and Colvin had been unable to see the car clearly. When Magnuson opened the car door to get out, triggering the car's interior light, Colvin was able to get a good look at the man behind the wheel. Her description was detailed enough to result in a police composite sketch.

Murphy pulled the drawing out of the file and held it up. These things are always so generic-looking, Murphy thought as she studied the sketch. It could be the doctor or any other big, blond guy in Minnesota, a heavily Scandinavian state brimming with big, blond guys.

None of the victim's other friends or co-workers—at the hospital or on the strip circuit—knew anything about Magnuson having a regular beau, married or not. The woman slept around quite a bit— and probably did a little hooking on the side—and was seen in bars around town with lots of different escorts. For those reasons, it seemed investigators eventually discounted the theory that a boyfriend had committed the crime. They decided Magnuson must have fabricated the story about the steady man in her life, perhaps as a cover for the stream of johns and one-night stands.

Murphy read the written report of Colvin's description. She said the man in the car that night was handsome. Strikingly handsome.

"That composite sketch didn't do him justice. He was so handsome, almost beautiful. Do you know what I mean?"

Murphy stood on the front porch of a newer house on the outskirts of Rochester. It looked pretty much like the other enormous single-family homes in the upper-middle-class development. They were all painted taupe, beige or a close cousin. They all boasted three-car garages. The lawns were trimmed and fertilized so meticulously they looked like golf-course greens. White petunias filled every white window box. The entire neighborhood was a suffocating tribute to beige and all other things bland.

The stripper's housemate had stayed in town, and Murphy was easily able to track her down. She was married and had two kids—they kept tugging at their mother's pants leg as Murphy tried to interview the woman—but Marcia Colvin kept her maiden name.

"Poor Roxy," Colvin mumbled as she studied the composite sketch. "How long has it been?" She answered her own question, sounding sadly retrospective. "It's been at least twelve or thirteen years I think. Maybe more," she said. "I can't believe how time flies. We're all getting older, aren't we? I know she wasn't exactly a nun, but Roxy had a good heart. Then don't we all when we're stupid young women?"

Colvin was close to Murphy's age but a few inches shorter, plump and tired-looking. Her brown hair was in the close-cropped, efficient style of a frantic mother. Gray was starting to creep into it, but she was probably too busy even to think about coloring it. The toddlers, two girls, kept her running. Her medical-school plans had fizzled. She was still a nurse and worked at the hospital five days a week, mostly nights. Her husband was an accountant at the hospital with day hours. They took different shifts to avoid putting their kids in day care.

"I'm pretty sure I could still point him out if I saw him in the flesh," she said. "I'm sorry I can't say I'm one-hundred percent sure. I guess too many years have gone by for me to swear on a stack of Bibles, but if I saw him in person, I think I could identify him with ninety-nine percent certainty. He was gorgeous."

Ninety-nine percent isn't too bad, Murphy thought gleefully. "Did your housemate ever drop any names?" Murphy asked. "Even a first name or some dumb pet name she had for the guy?"

"No," said Colvin, shaking her head. "All she ever told me is he was a married man, and that's why they both kept it under wraps. I think the police thought Roxy was fantasizing by telling me she had someone steady, but I believed her, and I did see this guy that night."

"I'll be getting back to you," said Murphy, reaching into her purse. "In the meantime, do me a favor. If anything comes to mind that might help me out—something about the man or his car or something

179

Roxy said—please give me a call. Here's my card. Please don't share anything we discussed. Not even with your husband."

"Son-of-a-gun," the woman said, taking the card and handing the composite sketch back to Murphy. "Imagine catching the guy after all these years. Wouldn't that be a kicker? Son-of-a-gun."

"Thanks for your time," said Murphy. "I'll let you get back to your kids." One of the chubby-cheeked toddlers clutched what looked like the remains of a peanut-butter-and-jelly sandwich. The other one had a fistful of spaghetti noodles and a face stained with red sauce. They were still in their sleepers.

Murphy started to step off the porch and then stopped and turned around. "Hey," she said. "You've got kids so maybe this sounds familiar. 'The fly shall marry the bumblebee.' "

"It's a line from a nursery rhyme. Mother Goose," said Colvin. "What does that have to do with this?"

"Rather not say right now. Can you recite the whole thing?"

"Wait a minute. I've got a book." Colvin disappeared into the house for a minute. The two toddlers stood on the porch staring up at Murphy. The one with the squished sandwich held it up to her. Murphy laughed and shook her head.

"No, thank you."

Colvin reappeared, flipped through the book and opened it to a page with a picture of a fly and a bee standing atop a wedding cake. Murphy took the book and read the rhyme:

"Fiddle-de-dee, fiddle-de-dee,
The fly shall marry the bumblebee.
They went to church and married was she.
The fly has married the bumblebee.

"What in the world can that mean?" Murphy mumbled to herself. She handed the book back to Colvin.

"Who is this guy, anyway?" asked Colvin.

180

"We think he's a surgeon," Murphy said.

"Plastic?"

"Why?"

"That could explain it," Colvin said.

"Explain what?" asked Murphy.

"Well, Roxy made pretty good money between nursing and dancing and whatever," said Colvin.

"Yeah, I'm sure the 'whatever' paid especially well," said Murphy, smiling a little.

"Look, I never gave a darn as long as she came up with her half of the rent and didn't bring anyone home," Colvin said defensively.

"Sorry," said Murphy. "Her lifestyle wasn't your responsibility."

"Well, anyway, she made decent scratch but not enough for something like that," said Colvin.

"Something like what?" Murphy blurted out. "What are you talking about?"

"Well, she had this tattoo on her shoulder," said Colvin. "She got it in high school. A red heart with an old boyfriend's name in it. Ed was his name. I joked with her that she should find a guy named Fred or Ned or Ted. Then all she needed to do was add a letter or two."

Murphy laughed.

"Anyway, she talked about getting it removed, but she made some calls and found out it would be expensive," said Colvin. "It could be done in a doctor's office, but it would take several clinic visits."

"So," said Murphy.

"So suddenly Roxy starts getting the treatments—over weekends," said Colvin. "I asked her about it and she didn't want to talk about it."

"He must have given her a freebie in his office after hours," said Murphy. She didn't share with Colvin her suspicion that it also could have been in trade for Roxy's services.

"That is very good information." Murphy scratched in her notebook.

"Well, good luck trying to nail him, my dear," said Colvin, offering Murphy a firm handshake.

"Thank you."

"Let me know what I can do to help," said Colvin as Murphy stepped off the porch. "Go carefully, Detective. You know, some people think doctors are gods and can do no wrong. That's doubly true for surgeons."

"You sound like someone who knows better," said Murphy.

"Darn right I know better," said the woman, picking up one of the fussy toddlers. "I'm a nurse."

Victorious but drained, Murphy drove straight home from Rochester. Her heart fluttered when she turned into the parking lot of her riverfront neighborhood. "Great," she mumbled to herself. "What is this about?" Jack's silver BMW was there. She was at once excited and apprehensive. She questioned what brought him to her houseboat after a week of ignoring her calls.

One word came to mind: Gabe. She wondered exactly how much her partner had shared with her husband about the last several days, and then decided it was irrelevant because all of it was bad. Some of it was just worse for her marriage. She pulled her key out of the ignition, but sat in the Jeep for a couple of minutes. She drummed the steering wheel with her fingers. She considered starting up the car again and pulling out, going to the cop shop. She had plenty of paperwork she could do. If she stayed away long enough, maybe he'd leave. She pushed the key back in the ignition, but didn't turn it.

Don't be such a chicken shit, she said to herself. She pulled the key out again, shoved it in her purse and slid out of her car. She stopped to take a breath, slammed the car door and walked down the dock and into the houseboat.

She found him sitting in the galley, dressed in jeans and a white T-shirt. He had set the kitchen table with a white tablecloth, china, silverware, candles and a bouquet of Sweetheart roses. She loved Sweetheart roses; he had given them to her when they were dating.

"I'm sorry," he said, getting up and lighting the candles.

"What?" she said, dropping her purse on the floor.

"I apologize for my behavior of the last several days," he said, walking to her and wrapping his arms around her. "I've been a world-class prick."

"I guess we make a great pair," she said. "Who the hell else would put up with our garbage?"

Gabe must have told him about her dangerous encounter with Michaels, but not about Erik. She would have to confess to him sometime, but not now.

"So this asshole is actually a sick pervert who rapes and murders women and then takes their hair as some kind of war trophy. He nearly added my wife to his list of victims."

"He didn't get very far," she said. "He still doesn't know I'm a cop. He assumes I'm some woman he picked up, mauled and let get away. We need to keep him thinking that way. There'll be plenty of opportunity to kick his ass in court, after we nail him on these murders."

"Are you really all right? Gabe said you were okay. You should have let him take you to the hospital to get checked over."

Jack was stroking her hair and she wanted to push his hands away. She felt guilty, like she didn't deserve him. "I'm okay," she said. "Stupid of me to think I could control that situation, manipulate it. Gabe tried to talk me out of the whole dumb operation. He really did."

"The stubborn Irish completely ignored him."

"Why is it stubborn Irish? Why isn't it stubborn Lebanese?" she asked.

"I think the Lebanese in you kicked Michaels in the nuts," he said. "Twice."

"The first hit was a grounder," she said. "The second one was out of the ballpark."

He laughed and then grew serious. "I am so very sorry I doubted you," he said.

"What have you done to my kitchen?" she asked, suddenly noticing the pile of pots and pans in the sink. "What is that awful smell?"

"Um, that was going to be dinner," he said.

"You can't cook," she said, slipping out of his arms and walking over to the sink to investigate the black mess inside the pots. She saw the charred remains of a chicken or some other bird in one pan and burned rice in another.

"I am well aware I can't cook," he said, sounding a little sheepish. "I reaffirmed that this afternoon, with a vengeance. I wanted to surprise you."

"You sure did," she said, picking up one of the pans by the handle and staring inside.

"Maybe this will make up for it," he said. He walked over to the refrigerator, opened the door and pulled out a bottle. He showed it to her.

"Dom Pérignon!" she gasped. "You can't cook, but you sure know how to chill a good bottle of champagne."

He set it on the table and pulled two frosty champagne glasses from the freezer.

"What next?" she asked.

He pulled a box of takeout food from the refrigerator and, with great ceremony, set it down on the linen-covered table.

"Oh no!" she said. "Jack. Honest to god! With Dom Pérignon? The wine police will break down our door."

"Look, I know it's not coq au vin, but what the hell, it's still good food, right?" he said, pulling a chair out for her and motioning for her to take a seat. *"Madame, pour vous."*

"I love you," she said as he took a seat across from her.

"I love you, too," he said, a catch in his voice. "Now tell me," he said, clearing his throat, "do you want regular or extra crispy? Stop eyeballing those drumsticks, wife. I call first dibs on those puppies."

The sound of a New Orleans–style band floated down the Mississippi from a riverboat carrying revelers on a moonlight party cruise. The enormous stern-wheeler sliced a tame wake through the water, gently rocking Murphy's compact houseboat. "Do you hear?" she asked, pausing with dirty dishes in her hands. "Louisiana Two-Step" drifted through the open houseboat windows. "Remember the music coming out of the open doors of the clubs along Bourbon Street? We should do that trip again. Listen to that." She swayed back and forth.

"I can't hear anything but your voice," he said, grabbing her from behind and wrapping his arms around her waist. "Put the plates down and come to bed, babe. We can clean up in the morning."

He was shirtless and shoeless, dressed only in his jeans. She had discarded her slacks and shoes and was clothed only in panties and a blouse. He pulled the china out of her hands and set the pieces down on the kitchen counter. Facing her, he clamped a hand on each of her shoulders and pulled her toward him. He kissed her hard on the mouth, his tongue pushing past her teeth. She arched her back, pressing her body into his, and moaned softly. She scraped her teeth against his tongue as he pulled it out.

"I want to make love," he whispered in her ear.

"I think I'd enjoy that, horny wench that I am," she said, smiling and reaching behind him to push his buttocks into her hips.

He pulled her blouse over her head, not bothering with the buttons. She clawed at the zipper on his jeans. They made love on the living-room floor. He was on top because that's how she liked it. No discussion. He knew what his wife wanted before she did.

"That's what you want, isn't it, babe?" he breathed in her ear as he entered her. She groaned and clutched his buttocks, grating her pelvis against him. "It's what you need," he said hoarsely. "Isn't it?"

"Yes," she whispered.

TWENTY-FOUR

Room One. Rhinoplasty.

"Don't expect instant results, Mrs. Merrill," Michaels said to the woman sitting on the exam table. "This isn't one of those soap operas where the surgeon removes the bandages and you're suddenly a beauty queen."

"I understand."

"You will wear a splint for several days after the surgery," he said. He sat across from her in a high-backed leather office chair.

"Yes," she said, nodding her head. "A splint."

"There will be swelling on the inside and outside of your nose," he said.

"Yes," she said. "Swelling. I understand."

"Your eyes will turn black and blue because of bruising of the loose tissues around the eyelids; it'll look like someone punched you. This is perfectly normal and not a cause for concern," he continued. "The whites of your eyes may even turn red, but this shouldn't alarm you, either. In most cases, it clears up in a couple of weeks or so."

"I understand."

He was dutifully giving her the same lecture he gave his other rhinoplasty patients, but Mrs. Merrill, dressed in a cream-colored Liz Claiborne slacks ensemble, wasn't paying too much attention. Michaels guessed she was stoned on some prescription drug, probably Valium. Her high-heel-shod feet were dangling off the edge of the exam table and she was studying her cream-colored shoes. A black scuff on one of the toes apparently troubled her more than the predicted after-effects of her upcoming surgery. She reached down and rubbed the scuff with her thumb.

"Please realize, Mrs. Merrill, that it may take as long as a year for the final appearance of your nose to become apparent," he said. "That's because normal healing takes place quite gradually."

"I understand," she said. "As long as a year."

"If we don't achieve the results you want, we can make some minor adjustments down the road, a little fine-tuning," Michaels told her. "I doubt that will be necessary. I get it right the first time and rarely have to go back for revisions."

"Scarring?" she asked.

He couldn't believe she had asked a question. "Inside the nose," he said. "It's not visible."

She nodded. She was in her late fifties and still dyed her hair bright red. With her thin frame covered in cream and her fiery shock of hair, Michaels thought she looked like a lit wooden matchstick. She was bored and stoned, and probably depressed because she was getting older. Michaels had already given her a breast lift. Now the nose job. Her husband didn't care, kept forking over the money for the operations. He told Michaels he'd do anything to keep her happy and out of his hair. Michaels figured what she really needed was to get off her ass and get out of the house, find a constructive activity, something other than shopping and surgery. He could probably tell that to half his patients, but he wouldn't make any money that way.

"Here's a brochure," he said, shoving a pamphlet into her hands. "Please read it. A nurse will contact you before your surgery date to provide you with additional instructions."

"Yes, Doctor," she said.

He left the room and headed down the hall.

The last place Michaels wanted to be on Tuesday was trapped in his clinic measuring the pendulous breasts and massive snouts of doped-up matrons. He had a nagging headache. His muscles ached. His left hand was sore from that black-haired woman's bite. His mind was still trying to get a grip on Monday night's fiasco. How had she beaten him? She was stronger than he'd expected, and more coolheaded than he liked. He shouldn't have picked such a tall woman. The small ones were better; they were easier to subdue and seemed to panic and lose control quicker. Would she be able to find him and press charges? He hadn't left anything behind that would identify him. He'd paid for everything in cash. Remembered to grab his jacket off the garden bench. The two of them had never exchanged names.

On the other hand, he decided he had no reason to worry. He could rightfully claim she'd consented and then freaked out when things got a little rough. Hell, he could accuse her of assault. It had taken him what seemed like an eternity to uncurl his body. Fortunately no one saw him stumble out of the garden and wobble to his car. That doorman with the black top hat was preoccupied with late-arriving hotel guests.

Then there was that other side of him, the side that still desired her. Perhaps even more than before, now that he had tasted her mouth and breasts and run his hands over her skin. Now that he had experienced her squirming under him, struggling for release. If he had the opportunity, he would try to take her again. Next time, he'd know what to expect from her and he'd come prepared. Next time, she wouldn't get away from the fly.

Room Two. Reduction mammaplasty.

Clutching the chart, he rapped on the door once with his knuckles and walked in.

"How are you doing, Mrs. Townsend?" he asked the plump blond woman. She'd gone from a sagging 40DD to a perky B in a three-hour operation the month before.

"Well, I'm still a little sore," she said. She was dressed in a blue paper robe and had her chubby arms folded protectively over her chest. She was modest to the point of ridiculousness, despite her forty-five years of age and five children.

"Please open the front of your gown," he said. She didn't budge. "Mrs. Townsend?"

"Can't we skip that part?"

"Mrs. Townsend, I don't have X-ray vision," he said impatiently. "I need to have a look at them." He untangled her arms; their pink flabbiness repulsed him. "I think they're coming along quite well," he said, examining the scars that ran under her breasts. They were thin and would fade even more with time. He was a fucking artist.

"The area around your nipples also looks excellent," he said as much to himself as to his patient. "Yes. Marvelous outcome around the nipples." She was blushing. He imagined screaming the word "nipple" until she collapsed in an embarrassed, jiggling heap on the exam table. "Nipple! Nipple! Nipple!"

"Why don't you try going without a bra for a while longer?" he told her. "The rubbing could irritate your nipples."

"Thank you, Doctor," she said, quickly rewrapping herself in the paper robe.

"Hold off on the jogging for a bit longer, all right?" he said.

"Oh, I don't jog, Doctor," she said, smiling.

She didn't get the joke.

"Should I try vitamin E? My sister-in-law said it works wonders on . . ."

"Is your sister-in-law a plastic surgeon?"

"No."

"I guessed not. Some people believe vitamin E hastens healing and lessens scarring, but there is no solid medical evidence to back that up."

"So should I use it?"

"Do as you please," he said tiredly. "Come back and see me in two months and, again, don't irritate those nipples."

Then there was that other issue involving the priest. He needed to silence the man, one way or another.

To hell with organized religion and all its trappings, he thought bitterly. He'd been a good Catholic all his life, serving as an altar boy, attending Catholic school, marrying a Catholic girl in a Catholic church, making it to mass on a fairly regular basis and even serving on the parish committee. He'd baptized his daughters and sent them to Catholic school as well. He'd donated enough money to the archdiocese over the years to build his own cathedral. Yet the one time he needs some big-time forgiveness, he's told to chuck everything he's worked for and turn himself in to the authorities. Bullshit, he thought.

All he had to show for his devotion to the faith was angst-filled Catholic guilt—and that had done nothing but cause him grief.

He wondered how differently his life would have turned out if he had been born a Lutheran.

Room Three. Tattoo removal.

These were becoming increasingly popular as teenage decisions haunted people into adulthood. A yellow rose that looks appealing on a pert eighteen-year-old butt looks bad on the flaccid ass of a middle-aged woman.

This patient happened to be a man, however, and his skin art was a recent acquisition. He wanted a large tattoo removed from the area over his right shoulder blade. "Let's get a look at what we're tackling here, Mr. Smith."

Michaels pushed aside the paper robe covering the thirty-five-year-old man's back. The patient was a tall, thin, pale man with wispy black hair and faded blue eyes. Michaels took one look at the tattoo and immediately wondered how many drinks had been needed to convince

Mr. Smith that getting this masterpiece was a perfectly sound idea. The coffin was about seven inches long and deep purple in color. The casket lid was slightly askew, revealing a smiling gray skeleton inside. The skeleton's eye sockets were red, its teeth were yellow and it had one bony hand raised, flipping the bird. This had to be a six-drink tattoo, thought Michaels. Maybe even seven. Seven tall ones.

"Out of curiosity, Mr. Smith, what is your profession?"

The patient cleared his throat. "Umm. I'm a . . . umm . . . funeral home director."

"I see," Michaels said dryly. "I have to be honest with you, Mr. Smith. Tattoos are tough to take off, and yours covers quite a large area. There are several removal methods, but they all leave some scarring. People should think about that before they . . ."

"Spare me the lecture," said the patient. "I've already heard it in spades from my wife. Get the thing off. I'd rather have the scar."

"I would suggest a series of laser treatments."

"Great. Let's do it." He pulled the paper robe back over his shoulders and hopped off the table.

"Certainly," said Michaels. "I'll send a nurse in and she can set you up with a treatment schedule."

Driving home after work, he decided he would pay a visit to the hospital later that night, before the police did. There were elegantly simple ways to make it look like an accident.

As he pulled into his driveway, he noticed his next-door neighbor sipping iced tea on her front porch. A sense of urgency enveloped him. He needed to make a dash for the house before she collared him.

He got to the side door off the driveway before she intercepted him. "How are you, stranger?" she chirped. She'd materialized at his elbow.

"Hello, Elaine," he said, setting his briefcase and lab coat down on the steps leading to the side entrance of his home. "What are you up to?" About two hundred pounds, he thought cynically. He found everything about Elaine Roth simply too large and blocky. She was a tall woman, easily matching his height. She was also big boned, with wide wrists and hands. Her long, brown, frizzy hair was streaked with gray and kept back from her face with two large tortoiseshell combs. She dressed like a clerk in a food co-op—long, gauzy skirt the color of mud with a white peasant top and leather sandals with white ankle socks. Elaine was divorced; he decided it had to be because she'd switched teams, turned into a lesbian.

"So where's your better half?" Elaine asked.

"Huh?"

"Your wife. My partner in crime. Where is she? I haven't seen her in ages. Where are you hiding her? Is Jennifer locked in the attic, or what?"

"She's still up at the cabin with her mother," he said.

"Really? We were supposed to go to the Man Ray photo exhibit at the Walker tonight," she said, frowning. "We've been talking about it forever."

"I don't know what to tell you, Elaine," he said, shrugging his shoulders. "She's still at the lake. I've been having trouble getting in touch with her myself. She doesn't seem interested in answering my calls."

"Well, that's odd," said Elaine, winding a frizzy strand of hair around her plump finger.

Elaine probably knows all about it, Michaels thought; she was more up to speed on the state of his marriage than he. Elaine had been the one at the cabin when Jennifer lost the baby. Elaine was the one Jennifer ran to with gripes about him. The two women spent many summer evenings walking and talking, undoubtedly spilling their guts to each other. They made an odd-looking couple—his tiny, slender wife and this tall, imposing woman—as they strolled up the grassy parkway that ran down the middle of Summit Avenue. He once asked Jennifer if Elaine had ever tried to get her in bed; Jennifer told him he was a pig. He wasn't sure if that was a "yes" or a "no."

"Look, Elaine, I'm in a bit of a rush and I don't have time to chat," he said. He picked up his lab coat and briefcase and put one foot on the first step. Without warning, the big woman reached up to touch his left cheek. He started and shoved her hand away from his face.

"What happened there?" she asked, staring at the fading but still visible red lines left over from his encounter with the redheaded hooker.

"Cat scratched me," he said. He brushed past her, ran up the steps and went into the house, slamming the door behind him.

TWENTY-FIVE

Michaels stepped off the elevator and looked to his right and left, scanning both ends of the hallway. He smiled. Quiet and empty, as he knew it would be.

Late at night, hospital hallways become tomblike in their silence, disturbed only by the occasional squeak from a nurse's shoe or the rattle of a lab cart. Sometimes a restless patient hollers for more pain pills or ice chips. Maybe a midnight emergency funnels doctors and nurses into an individual room. Chatter from the nurses' station might carry down the hall a bit. Mostly they are quiet and empty.

He walked down the corridor, looking at the room numbers on the doors. He was praying Ambrose had a private room; a roommate would complicate things. In a room with an open door, an old man groaned loudly and rolled over to face the hallway. Michaels walked past quickly, making sure his head was turned the other way. He was dressed in his lab coat and had a stethoscope draped around his neck. He had altered his name tag, in case he was stopped. Tonight, he was DR. HAEL. He'd thought about removing it entirely, but that could flag an attentive nurse or security guard.

His nerves were steadied by a decent amount of Scotch. Not enough to make him drunk; he needed sufficient sobriety to get the job done.

There could be no mistakes. No screwups. This one had to be quick and clean. The fly had to stay out of the picture.

He'd mentally walked himself through the evening several times and could see a couple of instances where there'd be a danger of leaving prints, so he wore surgical gloves. He kept his hands shoved in his coat pockets, again to avoid attracting attention; doctors didn't generally run around at all hours wearing surgical gloves. In his right coat pocket he had his fist wrapped around his most essential tool, other than his nerves: a syringe filled with a killing quantity of potassium chloride. Such a delicate thing, the chemistry of the human body. Too much or too little of a seemingly unimportant element can kill rapidly and efficiently, often leaving no visible evidence behind.

In his hospital bed late Tuesday night, Father Ambrose slept uneasily in his medication-induced stupor.

His room was small and faced the freeway, but he was as happy as hell it was private. No hacking, wheezing roommate to keep him up at night. The window ledge was jammed with flowers and cards. The children from Vacation Bible School had made a banner that hung on the wall opposite his bed. The kids had used finger paints to put their handprints on it and then each signed it. He could tell which students were suffering through Mrs. White's class during the school year; she really hammered them on their handwriting. Behind her back, he and the school principal called her the "cursive Nazi." Men from the parish council had hand-delivered ceramic mallards filled with green ferns and ivy. The liturgical-music director had surprised him with a planter shaped like an open hymnal. Hokey, but well-meaning.

Boxes of chocolates were stacked on his nightstand. When he was bored, he tortured himself by staring at them. His ulcer was acting up, and he couldn't eat them. He was on blood thinners after his hip replacement to avoid blood clots, a common by-product of inactivity, and the blood thinner was making his ulcer bleed. He was nauseated and couldn't eat in the days following the surgery anyway, so he was on intravenous feeding. He was also on a heart monitor, something doctors considered a wise precaution given his heart attack several months earlier.

His sister had visited him over the weekend. "Jesus Christ," she'd blurted out, staring at all the tubes and wires. "You're all fucked up."

He was, and in ways she couldn't see or understand.

He stirred in his sleep, pushing the covers off his arms. Doubts filled his dreams.

It had been eight days since the attack. In the week following it, he had recovered from near strangulation, a serious concussion and hip-replacement surgery. Ambrose had hoped the police would wait to question him in the comfort of his rectory after his release from the hospital, but they were persistent; they were scheduled to visit him Wednesday in his room. Tuesday night he'd fallen asleep still sorting out in his mind what he should do.

He could say to hell with it, dump the priesthood and tell the cops everything, including that the maniac had confessed to killing a prostitute. He wondered if that was more moral than following the rules dictated by his collar.

Plenty of times, he'd had second thoughts about his choice of profession. Once or twice it was the sight of a beautiful woman sitting in the front pew during mass; the long-legged ones captured his attention. He questioned himself again after he'd failed to save a favorite parishioner's marriage. Then he couldn't talk his own sister out of getting her teenage daughter an abortion. "Mind your own business," she'd snapped. "You don't have kids. What do you know?"

What *do* I know? he'd wonder. Then he'd tell himself: I know I'm a horseshit priest. He'd open up the jobs section of the want ads. He'd manage to snap out of it, regain his footing. Sometimes through prayer. Sometimes with a stiff drink. It wouldn't be so easy this time; nothing had challenged him as much as this mess.

If he stuck by his calling, anything his assailant had revealed in the confessional was off limits. Every priest knew the drill. He could not divulge the sins uttered to him to save his own life or even spare the life of another. He could not reveal them in the name of justice or to avoid a public calamity. No law, no officer, no courtroom could compel him to disclose the secrets of the confessional. The only possible release from this obligation of secrecy would be if the penitent himself granted the priest permission to speak. Ambrose was sure that permission was not forthcoming, especially given the crazy asshole's violent reaction when the priest had said going to the police would be part of his penance.

Maybe he could satisfy his calling and his conscience: Ambrose was certain he wouldn't be violating the Seal of Confession by giving the detectives a description of the penitent—but not his sins—as the man who had nearly strangled him to death on the floor outside the confessional. Father Ambrose had gotten a good look at the mean S.O.B.

His cold, gray eyes were not easily forgotten.

Michaels slipped unnoticed into the priest's room. As he had hoped, the man was sedated and tethered to an IV, but the heart monitor took him by surprise. Damn. He should have thought of that. The old boy was fat and undoubtedly had at least one heart attack under his belt already. The monitor would trigger an alarm when the priest's heart was in distress, alerting the nurses' station. That might give them an opportunity to save the priest.

Worse yet, the EKG on the monitor would show spikes pointing to high levels of potassium. He had no idea if the priest had already given the cops a description of his assailant for a composite sketch. The elevated potassium could point to sabotage by a medical professional, and that might be enough to narrow the focus dangerously close to him.

Still, he had to make sure this priest never made it to the witness stand. Doubts could be raised about a composite sketch, but live testimony would hang him. He had to get rid of this pain-in-the-ass priest and it had to look like a natural event. Like an act of God.

Michaels took the syringe out of his lab coat and gently pushed the tip of the needle into one of the ports in the IV line. He pushed down on the plunger, sending the potassium into the priest's body. It would take about thirty minutes for the potassium to send the father's heart into an unwieldy rhythm.

He checked his watch. He wanted to give the potassium time to do its work before he made his next move.

He studied the five round patches taped to the man's chest, each a different color and each with wires leading to the heart monitor. He looked for the wire from the green patch. This was the ground lead. Unsnapping it would send a low-level alarm to the nurses' station indicating the leads to the monitor had somehow come undone. It would also mask the alarm indicating his heart was in distress.

They would eventually come to the priest's bedside to snap the errant wires back on, but they wouldn't rush. It wouldn't be considered a life-threatening emergency. By the time they got around to it, they would find the priest clinging to life, call a code and start working on him. Hopefully, they would forget about the monitor. They would have no EKG record pointing to a spike in the level of potassium.

Michaels checked his watch again. He needed to wait a bit longer. He didn't want to unsnap the green lead too soon. He was perspiring under the lab coat; he could feel the sweat trickling down his back. He wiped his damp brow with the sleeve of the coat. He wanted to do this and get out of here. He walked to the door and poked his head into the hallway. He scanned both ends. Still empty and quiet. Good. He walked back to the priest's bed.

He had an excuse ready should he be caught in the room—he had been checking on one of his own patients on another floor and decided to look in on the priest, an old friend of the family. He knew it was a flimsy story, and full of holes. He didn't even have surgical privileges at Hennepin County Medical, let alone a recovering patient. If they woke Ambrose to confirm the story, he'd be shit out of luck.

He studied the small room, indirectly illuminated from the freeway lights outside the window. GET WELL SOON, FATHER AMBROSE! read a banner stretched across one wall. The sign was decorated with children's handprints. How saccharine, thought Michaels. There were so many bouquets in the room, it smelled like a funeral parlor. Father Ambrose would be seeing the inside of one of those soon enough, he thought, smiling.

Michaels checked his watch again. Hallelujah. Time to do it. He looked down at the sleeping priest. "Hope you said your bedtime prayers," he whispered. Without hesitation, he unsnapped the green lead and strolled out of the small, dim room.

He walked calmly but quickly down the hall toward the elevators. He pushed the down button and paced in front of the door, waiting for it to open, willing it to open. The thing was taking too long. Maybe there was somebody on it. A late-arriving patient. He scanned the hallway for exit signs. Where were the stairs?

"Can I help you?"

Shit, he thought. He shoved his hands in his pockets and turned toward the inquisitive female voice. She was a nurse—a thin reed with stringy black hair.

"No thank you," he said evenly. "I was checking on a patient on another floor and thought I'd stop here to look in on a friend." The elevator doors opened and he stepped on.

"At this hour?" she blurted out.

The elevator doors closed before he was forced to concoct a response. He breathed a sigh of relief. He looked at his hands. They were shaking. With his trembling right hand, he gripped the railing along the elevator wall, steadying himself during the trip down.

"Ah, shit," said Libby Delmont. "It looks like the leads in twenty-six are screwed up."

"That would be Father Ambrose's room," said Phyllis Jared, a tall woman with short, gray hair.

The two nurses stared at the bank of monitors resembling a stack of miniature computer screens, each bearing a room number. "Where's Tess?" asked Delmont. "The poor bastard is the space cadet's patient tonight."

"She's checking on thirty-two," said Jared.

"Flip ya for it," said Delmont.

"Naah. I'll take it," said Jared. She sighed and stood up. "I need the exercise."

Jared liked Father Ambrose. He was a flirt. She saw him checking out her ass once while she was opening his window blinds. Plus he was an angler, so they had a little something in common. At one time she could have talked religion with him, but she'd quit the Catholic Church years ago. She told him she saw too much misery to believe there was a god. Ambrose didn't try to pull her back into the fold. Instead, they had friendly, invigorating debates about the role suffering and death played in life.

When she walked into his room, she found him struggling for breath, fighting for life. "Father Ambrose," Jared said into his ear, trying to get a response. She couldn't find his pulse. "God dammit to hell!" she muttered.

"Libby! He's in v-tach!" she yelled down the hall, using the short-hand term for ventricular tachycardia, a fast heart rhythm. "Call a code! He's unresponsive!"

"Son-of-a-bitch!" said Jared, looking down at the priest.

TWENTY-SIX

"That murdering bastard. He did it, Gabe. I know he did," Murphy whispered into her cell phone as she sat nude on the edge of her bed early Wednesday morning. She didn't want to disturb the man sprawled naked next to her.

She held the phone to her ear with her right hand and, with her left, grabbed her robe off the edge of the bed. She tiptoed into the bathroom, gently shutting the door behind her. "Wait a minute, Gabe," she said in a low voice, and set the phone down on the bathroom counter so she could slip into the robe. The morning was cool for a change.

"He's going to be all right, isn't he? Ambrose?"

"Yeah, the code team got to him in time," said Gabe, who was calling from the nurses' station down the hall from the priest's room. "They've stabilized him and shipped him over to the ICU. We won't be able to talk to him today; that's for sure."

"He's lucky to be alive," she said.

"Luck had nothing to do with it," said Gabe. He winked at nurse Jared, who was standing at his elbow. She smiled at him and handed him a cup of coffee. He already had her phone number stuffed in his pants pocket.

"So the blood work confirms someone loaded him up with potassium, huh?" Murphy said.

"Sure as shit looks like it," said Gabe. "Then they unsnapped the heart monitor to cover their tracks. Who'd know to do that?"

"A doctor."

"Bet your ass a doctor," he said. "We were idiots. We should have put someone outside his room."

"Yeah, well, that's Monday-morning quarterbacking," she said. "What do we do now?"

"We need to show that it wasn't some medical screwup," he said.

"Right," she said. "That would be the obvious defense—that the hospital screwed up. Did anyone see him? Patients? Nurses? The shift hasn't changed on that floor yet, has it?"

"No, but you'd better get your butt over here pretty soon if you want to talk to them," said Gabe.

"What happened?" asked Jack, shuffling into the bathroom.

"Someone tried to off that poor priest last night," she said, wrestling her hair into a ponytail behind her head.

"No shit?" asked Jack, stepping back to give her room before he got a faceful of black hair.

"I shit you not," she said. She dropped her robe to the floor.

"How?" He picked up her robe and hung it on the bathroom door hook.

"Potassium," she said. She opened the medicine cabinet, grabbed the deodorant off the bathroom shelf and rolled it under her arms.

"You're sure some nurse didn't mess up and give it to him by mistake?" he asked. He squeezed past her and lifted up the toilet seat to pee.

"Tell me something, Jack," said Murphy. She closed the cabinet and looked at him, smirking while she took a good-natured jab. "Why are doctors so quick to blame the nurses?"

"Why are nurses so quick to blame the doctors?" asked Jack.

"In this case, I know it was a doctor," said Murphy. "A particular doctor."

With the car windows rolled down and the wind in her face, she navigated her Jeep onto westbound I-94. The early rush-hour traffic was fairly light on the St. Paul side of the river, but she hit a snarl at the city limits. "Great," she muttered. A logjam around the University of Minnesota exit. "Damn students should take the bus." The tangle loosened, she wove around a slow-moving semi truck, and breathed easier as she took a downtown Minneapolis exit and made her way to the hospital parking ramp.

"I saw a guy by the elevators last night," said Tess Clayton, nodding her dark head. Clayton took a sip of coffee from a Styrofoam cup. In between sips, she picked at the rim of the cup. She was a skinny, nervous type, and needed to keep her hands in motion. "He was gorgeous," she said. "He was tall. I swear to god he had shoulders out to here." She stretched her arms out. "He looked like a model or something. Blond hair. Gray eyes. Icy gray. He looked like a soap opera guy."

Murphy and Gabe had gathered the night nurses together in their break room to ask if they had spotted anyone suspicious roaming their floor Tuesday evening. They sat at a sticky round Formica table marked with brown rings from coffee cups and Coke cans. The room smelled like old coffee, burned popcorn and melted cheese. The nurses kept looking at their watches; their shift was long over.

"Was he dressed like a doc?" asked Murphy. She was scratching notes in a pad.

"He had on a white lab coat and a stethoscope," said Clayton.

"A badge? Some kind of ID?" asked Murphy.

"A name tag. Wait. I'm not sure about the name tag. If he had one, I guess I didn't really look at it."

"Christ," Jared said, rolling her eyes.

"He looked lost or something. He looked like he didn't belong here," said Clayton. "That's why I stopped and asked him if he needed help."

"What did he say to you?" asked Gabe.

"He said he was visiting someone on our floor after checking on a patient of his on another floor," Clayton said. "That sounded like a bullshit story to me. Who visits at that hour of the night? Then he got on the elevator and was gone."

"You didn't report this to anyone?" asked Gabe.

"No," said Clayton, pausing to take another sip of coffee. "I didn't report it."

"Earth to Tess," said Delmont.

"Go to hell," Clayton said. "What was I suppose to do? Tackle him before he got on the elevator?"

"Okay, okay, let's not lose it here," said Gabe.

"Anything else weird about him?" asked Murphy. "Think."

Clayton chewed her bottom lip and peeled another half inch off the rim of her coffee cup.

"This is painful," said Delmont.

"Yeah," Clayton said suddenly. "Yeah. He had surgical gloves on. Why would he need those if he was visiting, right?"

"Right," said Murphy. Across the table, she and Gabe exchanged glances.

"So you know who this guy is?" asked Jared. "Is he a doctor? Are you going to arrest his ass?"

"We're gonna talk about it," said Gabe. "Please don't discuss anything you've heard here. What was said in this room stays in this room, ladies. Got it?"

"Surgical gloves," Murphy said as she and Gabe walked to their cars. "Michaels is getting slyer by the second."

"Guess we can kiss the possibility of prints good-bye," he said.

"Speaking of kiss—you got her phone number?" Murphy asked.

"I got her phone number," he said. "She likes to fish."

"You don't give a damn that she can bait her own hook," Murphy said.

"What do you mean by that?"

"You know what they say about nurses and sex?" asked Murphy.

"No, what do they say?" asked Gabe, perking up.

"I don't know," said Murphy. "I thought you knew."

They stopped in front of Murphy's Jeep, parked a couple of spaces away from Gabe's Volvo, and she took the car keys out of her purse. "We'd better get together with the chief to go over what we have," she said.

Gabe grumbled.

"Look, he's been pretty decent so far," she said. "He's cut us a lot of slack. We haven't been pulled away to work on any pissant stuff and he sent a uniform over to watch Ambrose."

"Yeah, yeah," said Gabe. "He's my new best friend."

"I'll meet you at the cop shop," Murphy said.

TWENTY-SEVEN

Gabe sat back in his chair while Murphy did the shouting. He wasn't surprised by what Slick had to say. It's all circumstantial and we can't arrest someone for appearing guilty. Blah. Blah. Blah. We need more before we can haul him in because this isn't a police state you know. Blah. Blah. Blah. The county attorney will throw it back in our faces without something resembling a smoking gun. Blah. Blah and still more blah.

"What the hell do you mean?" Murphy asked. "We have more than enough. This is bullshit!" Murphy paced back and forth across the carpeted floor of the chief's office, behind Gabe's chair.

Gabe was enjoying the whole show.

"Murphy, sit down," said Christianson.

"I will not sit down," said Murphy.

"If this guy was Mr. Joe Fucking Average . . ."

The *F* word. She hadn't used that in front of the chief in weeks.

"Murphy . . ."

"If this was Mr. Joe Fucking Average, we'd have yanked him off the street with half this evidence. You're only saying we don't have enough because he's a surgeon and because his family is . . ."

Christianson's back stiffened in his chair. "This has nothing to do with his family," he said.

"This has everything to do with his family!" she yelled.

"Calm down," Christianson said.

"I will not calm down!"

"Paris, please," Christianson said, quickly switching to the friendly, first-name approach.

"Don't patronize me!" she said, her eyes narrowing. She looked at Gabe. "Say something, will you? Help me out here!"

"Murphy . . . ," the chief continued.

"Chief, maybe I didn't make clear everything we have on this creep," she said. "Let's go over all of it one more time."

"Oh no, let's not," pleaded Gabe, rubbing his forehead. "Please, let's not."

She shot her partner a threatening look, and he clamped his mouth shut.

"Number one," she said. She saw Gabe cringe and stopped pacing. "What is your problem?" she asked, glaring at him.

"I have no problem," he said, raising both palms defensively. "No problem at all."

"Good," she said. "Now where was I?"

"A," said Gabe, trying not to smile. "I believe you were on A."

"Thank you," she said, and resumed her pacing. "A. We have the yellow umbrella. Charlene Rue, a working girl, is ready to testify the yellow umbrella discarded by Michaels is the same umbrella she handed to Finch—I mean Fionn Hennessy—the night she was raped and murdered."

"We don't have good prints on the yellow umbrella," Christianson said.

"No," said Murphy. "We don't. I saw him remove it from his black Suburban and throw it away."

"Okay," said the chief. "He can say he found it somewhere, picked it up. What else?"

"B. We have a witness who saw Hennessy beaten by a blond man driving a loaded black Suburban," said Murphy. "A Suburban filled with soccer balls. Michaels drives a black Suburban and is a soccer coach."

"Our witness wasn't close enough to see the killer's face or get a license plate, and, unfortunately, happens to be schizophrenic," said Christianson.

"He was on his meds and perfectly sane when he saw the murder," offered Gabe.

"That's all fine and dandy," said the chief. "But you both know the defense attorneys will chew him up."

"We have Sister Ella Marie willing and ready to testify that Snaky— I mean Swanson—was taking his Risperdal at the time and was mentally healthy when he witnessed the killing from the boat porthole," said Murphy. "I'd like to see them poke holes in a nun's testimony."

"Then I suppose we should pray for an all-Catholic jury," said the chief, smiling. "What else have we got, detectives?"

"Three is the necklace," said Murphy.

"Ah yes," said the chief. "The well-traveled crucifix."

"The killer removed it from Hennessy's neck and later dropped it while assaulting Father Ambrose," said Murphy. "It ties the same man to both crimes."

"This assumes the murder victim's crucifix and the one found outside the confessional are indeed the same necklace," said Christianson.

"Her parents will take the stand to identify it as their daughter's keepsake," said Murphy. "If we get hard up, we could even haul in her pimp to confirm it is Hennessy's necklace. He'll testify that she never took it off."

"Wouldn't defense attorneys have a good time taking shots at Sully's credibility?" said the chief. "How long is Mr. LePlante's rap sheet?"

"Pretty fucking long," Gabe said.

Murphy glared at him but continued talking and pacing. "Four,

Gabe and I saw Michaels slinking around Hennessy's funeral service, with scratches on his face. Tell me that is not incriminating behavior."

"As I pointed out earlier in our conversation, the scratches could have come from anywhere," said Christianson, leaning back in his chair and rolling a pencil between his palms. "Michaels offered an explanation for his presence at the funeral, did he not?"

"That was a load of crap," sputtered Gabe. "Finch was never his patient."

"We don't know that for certain," said the chief. "All we have to base that on is the dubious word of her pimp and her prostitute friends."

"Her family also said she was never—" said Murphy.

"A family that hadn't seen her in how long?" interrupted Christianson. "Michaels could easily claim that she was a patient and then refuse to offer anything more detailed, citing patient privacy. I think it's quite believable that he treated her, given his volunteer work with that domestic-abuse program."

"What about Father Ambrose?" she said.

"What about him?" Christianson said with a dismissive wave of his hand. "We haven't even interviewed him yet. We have no idea what he brings to the table. Can he positively identify Michaels as the man who assaulted him? How much is he willing to say about what was revealed to him in the confessional? My understanding is priests are obligated to maintain confidentiality in much the same way a doctor is required to keep patient information private."

"The assault took place outside the confessional," said Murphy. "Therefore, that should be fair game."

"Maybe," said the chief, tapping the eraser end of the pencil on his desk.

"As far as what was said inside the confessional itself, well, you might be right," said Murphy, sounding discouraged. "We might be screwed there."

"Speaking of the priest, we have a witness who saw a black Suburban

209

leaving the scene of the assault at the church," said Gabe, trying to bolster his partner's position. "We have a nurse who can testify that she saw Michaels on her floor the night someone tried to finish off Father Ambrose."

"Being a medical professional, he could offer a reasonable explanation for being in the hospital that night," said Christianson. "Even if it's a bogus excuse, like the one he gave the night nurse, a jury might buy it. He could even claim it was a case of mistaken identity, that it wasn't him at all on the floor that night. Do we have any prints from Ambrose's room?"

"No," said Murphy.

"How's that possible if Michaels is your man?" asked Christianson.

"He was wearing surgical gloves," she said.

"Clever bastard," Christianson said in a low voice.

"What about his connection to previous murders—the ones in Rochester and Minneapolis?" asked Gabe. "They had the same M.O. as with Finch. The killer strangled them and cut their long hair with a sharp tool, possibly a surgical instrument. Murphy even got the Rochester victim's housemate identifying Michaels as the dead stripper's married boyfriend."

"The Rochester murder took place years ago," said Christianson. "The defense will take apart the housemate. More important, where is the hair? We don't have it."

"Let's get a search warrant for his house," said Murphy, who stopped pacing and stood in front of the chief's desk, her arms folded across her chest. "Let's demand a genetic sample from him to compare with the semen found on Hennessy's body and the skin under her nails."

"Not yet," said the chief. "That would be tipping our hand too soon."

Murphy fleetingly wondered if she should tell the chief about that night at the hotel, but quickly brushed aside the dangerous thought. She and Gabe had agreed it was best to keep the entire unsanctioned and ill-advised operation from their superiors.

"You've done some good work here and you've accumulated an impressive amount of evidence," said the chief. "But . . ." His voice trailed off. He put down the pencil and swiveled his high-backed leather chair around to stare outside the row of windows behind his desk. He released a barely audible sigh and turned his chair back to face Murphy and her partner. Murphy thought Christianson seemed depressed and distracted, like after the Minneapolis mess.

"But what, Chief?" asked Murphy. Christianson wasn't looking at them anymore; he was staring at the photo of his sons on his desk. "Chief?" said Murphy, returning to her seat to look Christianson squarely in the eye.

"His family's got deep pockets and lots of friends," Christianson said. "We need more than we've got." The chief spun his chair around again to face the windows. He didn't say anything for several seconds. Then: "Keep working the case," he said tiredly. The two detectives sat motionless, anticipating something more. "That's all," Christianson said without facing them.

Gabe and Murphy looked at each other and got up from their chairs. Christianson continued staring out the windows. Gabe held the door open for Murphy. Before she walked through, she looked at the chief's back and then at her partner, raising her eyebrows. They walked down the hall.

"Christ, what was that all about?" asked Murphy. She stopped at a water fountain in the hallway to drink. She suddenly felt thirsty and tired.

"I knew it wasn't going to be a slam dunk," said Gabe. "I never thought I'd say it, but Slick is probably on target with this thing. Ramsey County doesn't want to screw up its felony conviction rate by prosecuting cases it might not win. He's also right about this guy and his family having the bucks to fight this."

"That's not what I'm talking about," she said, wiping her mouth with her hand. "Who do you think is riding the chief's ass on this case? He sounded whipped."

"Yeah, I noticed that," said Gabe. "Well, it's high profile. The media are doing a number on him. The mayor. Who knows? Probably wishes he was back in Iowa."

The pair walked into Homicide's office and past Dubrowski and Castro, each seated at a desk piled with paperwork, newspapers, old lunch bags and dirty Styrofoam cups. Even though one was of Polish descent and the other Mexican, they had worked together so long they looked alike—curly gray hair, big arms, bushy eyebrows, red necks. They wore identical wire-rimmed glasses and the same brand of jeans. Dubrowski's gut was a little flabbier.

"Congratulations," Murphy told them. They got a conviction.

"Thanks," said Dubrowski.

"How's your case shaping up?" asked Castro.

"Gabe and I are on our way to the conference room to talk about that," she said.

"We are?" asked Gabe. "Oh yeah, we are."

Dubrowski and Castro laughed as Murphy and Gabe walked into the long, narrow room and shut the door behind them. Gabe took a seat at the head of the table while Murphy sat on the edge of the table and planted her feet on the seat of a chair.

"What would happen if we did connect some of the dots for the press, without naming Michaels as a suspect?" she asked. "Let's play that out. What would it do for us if we simply went public with the theory that the three murders—in St. Paul, Minneapolis and Rochester—were committed by the same person, by someone we haven't yet identified? We don't even have to say why we think they're related or reveal anything about the hair jobs. That way we don't tip our hand too much."

"What about Ambrose?" asked Gabe. "What do we say about him?"

"We also leave out the connection between Finch's murder and Father Ambrose," she said. "That way we protect him. Michaels disconnected that lead off the heart monitor to cover his tracks. Let's make him think he was successful. If anyone asks how Ambrose is doing, we simply say he had a heart-related setback in the hospital."

"So Michaels thinks he got away with his second attempt on the priest's life," said Gabe, scratching his chin.

"In fact, let's tell the reporters that before Ambrose had his setback, he met with us and refused to discuss the assault in his church because of the Seal of Confession," she said.

Murphy slid off the table and walked to the other end of the room, where a white, erasable board hung from the wall. She picked up a marker and drew a vertical line down the middle of the board. On one side she wrote the word "PROS" and on the other she scribbled "CONS."

"On the pro side, we might scare up some new witnesses to the crimes," said Gabe. "We could get some new leads."

Murphy nodded and scribbled "New Witnesses" and "New Leads" under "PROS."

"On the con side, we would tip Michaels off," said Murphy. "He might lawyer up. Worse yet, he could skip town."

She wrote "Doc Gets Lawyer" and "Doc Flees" in the "CONS" column.

"On the other hand, he might get smug and comfortable if he thinks we're clueless when it comes to naming a suspect," said Gabe. "He could make some mistakes, mess up big time and really hand us the case."

"Or he might get so rattled that he messes up," said Murphy. "We could lay a real head game on him by running a composite sketch. We'll make it close to his likeness, but not identical."

Gabe laughed. "I like that idea a lot," he said. "That gets my vote."

Under "PROS" Murphy scribbled "Doc gets nervous/comfortable—screws up."

"Then let's watch our suspect," said Murphy. "Let's put him under surveillance, at least for the first few days after the press conference, to see what he does."

"Okay," said Gabe. "Slick might go for that."

"Now wait a minute," said Gabe, standing up and pacing the width of the room with his hands shoved in his pockets.

"What's wrong?" asked Murphy. She stopped writing and turned to face him, the marker still in her hand.

"For us to run a composite sketch, someone has to give us a description of Dr. Demented," Gabe said.

Murphy paused and frowned. She walked over to the conference-room windows and glanced outside as she tried to think the problem through. She tapped on the ledge with the butt of the marker and looked at the traffic below, with cars crawling along the freeway. "We'll say a passing motorist saw him pick up Finch," she said, pointing the marker out the window. "Then we can even run a description of his Suburban."

"That's good," said Gabe, smiling. "A passing motorist. That could be anybody."

"Here's one more for the pro side," said Gabe. "Going public with some of this also takes some pressure off the department. Not that I give a shit about Slick."

Murphy walked back to the board and scribbled "Good P.R." under "PROS."

"I didn't call it P.R.," said Gabe. "That sounds so phony and calculating."

"Well, that's what it is, good public relations," she said. "Really, this whole damn scheme is phony and calculating. So what? Let's make those media dogs help us out for a change."

"Yeah, I guess you're right," he said.

They stopped talking and stared at the blue scrawls on the white board. "Well, it looks like the pros have it," said Murphy. "Let's call a press conference tomorrow, in time for the lunchtime news. They'll replay it for the six o'clock and the ten o'clock. The papers will follow along."

TWENTY-EIGHT

Michaels was suffocating, suspended facedown in a sea of hair. Fragrant, radiant hair. Red hair flaming like a bonfire. Brown hair the color of walnuts. Blue-black hair as dark and glossy as a crow's feathers. Gold hair, braided like his mother's.

Somewhere in the distance, surrounded by the hair, was his wife. She held a baby in her arms, a boy. He started to cry. Jennifer held the wailing infant out to him and laughed. Then she reached up and grabbed a length of white hair. It turned into a rope like the rigging from their sailboat. She wrapped the rope around herself and the baby until he couldn't see them anymore; all he saw was a coil of rigging. The rigging turned into a snake, its head at the very top of the coil. He heard screaming and crying and knew it was his wife and the baby, even though he couldn't see them. An arm poked out from the coil and he saw it was Jennifer's; he recognized the diamond wedding ring on her finger. Another arm poked out; it was a chubby baby arm. The snake reached down and bit off each of the arms. It spat out the finger with the wedding ring still on it. It wasn't Jennifer's ring anymore; it had turned into his gold band, and the amputated finger was his own.

Michaels looked at his hands. His ring finger was gone. He tried to swim toward the amputated finger, struggling to maneuver his naked body. Ribbons of hair twined around his arms and legs and waist, pulling him down, down, down. The hair had a will of its own and had a mind to kill him. It promised to be a soft death. He forgot about his wife and the baby and the snake and the missing finger. He stopped struggling. He surrendered and relaxed his limbs, letting the locks pull him deep into an abyss. The pit didn't have a name, but he knew it was hell, and he didn't care.

Then panic replaced submission. He twisted and turned as he fought the tangle of hair. The bands only tightened their grip. He felt a swatch of hair tighten around his penis and another wrap around his throat. He tried to scream, but all that came out was a buzzing noise.

Michaels woke facedown in his pillows. He rolled over and sat upright in his bed. The sheets were tangled around his legs. He kicked them off. His head burned and throbbed like an open wound. His damp body shivered uncontrollably. He covered his face with his hands and released sobs that rocked his shoulders. His breakdown lasted a few minutes. Then he wiped his face with the corner of the top sheet and angrily punched the mattress with his fist. "I'm weak. I'm a coward," he said.

In the dark, he fumbled around but couldn't find what he needed. He pulled the chain on the lamp atop his nightstand. The lampshade's colored glass cast a comforting glow. He yanked the bottle of Scotch off his nightstand and poured a modest amount. With great effort, he wrapped his shaking right hand around the glass and lifted it to his lips. He drank until the glass was empty. The heat trickling from his throat to his gut smoothed his nerves. He poured himself another, taller drink and finished it as quickly as the first.

He sat on the bed, his knees pulled up to his chest, his arms wrapped around his knees. He thought about the priest and wondered if he was dead; he'd heard nothing on the news about him. He thought about the nurse who'd spotted him by the elevators; he hoped she'd bought the story he fed her. He thought about his unreachable wife; he made a mental list of the men who could be fucking her at the cabin. He thought about the black-haired woman; he silently berated himself for letting her get away.

He checked the clock next to the lamp. 11:22 P.M., but he briefly forgot what day it was. He thought hard. Wednesday. 11:22 P.M. Wednesday.

"I can't even remember what day it is anymore," he whispered. He stretched out flat on his back, grabbed a pillow to hug to his chest and stared up at the ceiling. His compartmentalized existence was collapsing around him. The killer and the doctor, the husband and the rapist, the Catholic and the heretic were coalescing like a palette of watercolors left in the rain.

"I have to remember who I am," he said. He knew what that meant: no more holding back the fly.

He threw off the pillow and jumped out of bed. He yanked on his boxers, jeans and a polo shirt. He slid his bare feet into his loafers. He was still damp and shivering, so he put on a summer blazer. He sifted through the car keys piled on top of his bedroom dresser and selected the set for his Porsche. He shoved the keys into his right blazer pocket. He opened the top drawer of his dresser and retrieved his driving gloves. Before he slipped them on, he looked at his fingers and laughed. Of course they were all still there. He pulled on the gloves, wiggling his fingers a bit and enjoying the tightness of the leather. From under a stack of clothing in the same drawer he extracted a little kit he hadn't used in a while: a scalpel and a plastic bag. He wrapped the bag around the surgical tool and shoved the package into his left blazer pocket.

The top was down on the Porsche. He inhaled the night air as he shifted gears. He needed to do a little shopping, and what he craved couldn't be found along the well-lit highway. Being in a convertible made him more exposed, vulnerable. Under the driver's seat he kept a hand-gun, a 9mm SIG-Sauer. Black matte finish. Trigger with a click as smooth as that of a Minolta camera. He took a roundabout route to his final destination so he could cruise down University Avenue in a calming exercise before the chase. On University Avenue you could have your palms read, buy a used pinball machine, fix a flat tire and find a decent bottle of Scotch. Even in the middle of the week, on a Wednesday night, there were things to see and do on University Avenue.

He stopped at a red light and looked to his right. Several well-dressed people were spilling out of a nightclub. They were laughing. A couple of the men in the group were weaving drunkenly as they walked along the sidewalk.

The light changed. He drove on.

Another traffic light. He looked to his left, at an all-night convenience store. Teenage girls were clustered around a pay phone at the edge of the store's nearly empty parking lot. Two teenage boys were skateboarding in the middle of the parking lot, probably hoping to attract the attention of the girls, but the pay phone apparently had more magnetism. Such lovely girls. One turned her head, looked admiringly at his car and then at him. She smiled and he smiled back. Such beautiful, long, blond hair. So like his daughters' soft locks. He felt an ache in his crotch, a catch in his throat. He'd never taken such a young thing before. Her body would be so firm, her breasts so fresh. She'd be so tight, maybe even still a virgin. She wanted him; he was sure of it. He could tell by the way she looked at him. Perhaps . . .

The light changed. He hesitated, wondering what would happen if he took a left into the store parking lot. A car behind him honked. He drove on, reluctantly.

Enough sightseeing, he thought. He glanced to the right at the Porsche's clock. Midnight. He piloted the car to the fringes of town, to a stretch of avenue with boarded-up storefronts, fast-food joints, bars and video shops offering hard-core porn. "Sex and the Single Clown" read a poster in the filmy window of one adult-video store. It depicted a white-faced, red-nosed clown in a circus costume with his arms wrapped around a woman. Another poster displayed nothing but a woman's feet, with red-painted toenails. "Toe Job" was the title. Michaels laughed and shook his head as he drove past the shop. Some people have such strange fetishes, he thought smugly.

He surveyed the sidewalks on both sides of the street. The pickings were slim late at night in the middle of the week. Across the street, on his left, he saw a fat blonde dressed in tight white shorts and an equally snug white T-shirt. The car in front of him—a blue Ford station wagon sporting a bumper sticker that read, "Driver Carries Less Than $20 Cash. He Has Teenagers"—made a frantic U-turn and stopped at the curb next to the woman. She walked over to the car and leaned into the open front passenger-side window. She and the driver exchanged words. She nodded her head and got in, slamming the door hard. At the next intersection, the car took a right turn. They were headed to a dark side street, where she could give the family man a blow job in the front seat of his station wagon. He apparently carried enough cash for that. Or maybe he only had enough for a toe job, Michaels thought wryly.

The doctor drove on, hungry and hunting. He found himself driving toward the corner where he'd picked up that little redheaded whore, the source of all his recent problems.

There, on that very same corner, was a prospect. Standing under a streetlight with a cigarette hanging out of her mouth. She was short but heavier than he usually liked. Her tight jean skirt stretched across her wide hips and seemed on the verge of separating at the seams. Her close-fitting tank top accented the roundness of her doughy shoulders. While it was difficult to see clearly in the yellowish haze cast by the streetlight, she at least seemed to have a nice creamy complexion. He guessed she was in her late twenties or early thirties.

He almost kept driving when he got to her hair, noticing how short and lackluster it appeared. Then he spotted the thick braid in back of her head. "She'll do," he muttered to himself.

. He pulled over and she strolled over to the Porsche, doing nothing to hide her childlike admiration for the car. "Nice ride," she said, running her fingers across the red finish. She smiled at him. "Lookin' for a date?"

"Get in," he said, leaning over the passenger's seat to open the door for her from the inside. She dropped her cigarette into the gutter, slid in and gently closed the door. How unusual, observed Michaels. A thoughtful whore. "Let's talk business," he said, pulling away from the curb. "What do you charge?"

"Well, darlin', that depends on what you want," she said, inspecting the Porsche's instruments with her fingertips.

"What if I want a full fuck?" he asked coarsely. She seemed to cringe at the word *fuck*. A thoughtful, sensitive whore.

"We need to go to a particular motel for that," she said. "I provide the protection and you pay for the room, as well as for my services. If you don't want to use a rubber, you're gonna have to pay more."

"How much for your services, with a condom?"

She opened her mouth to answer and he cut her off. "It doesn't matter what you charge. I'll pay for it. Okay? Tell me where to turn."

"A man who knows what he wants," she said, smiling. "It sounds like you done this before, darlin'."

He threw his head back and laughed. He felt good. Very good. Very much in control. Something he hadn't felt in a while. "Is it down this street?" he asked.

"The next one," she said.

"What's your name?" he asked. "I like my *dates* to have a name." He turned right and headed down the dark road that led to the motel.

"Call me Miss Rue," she said. "That's French for street, you know."

He steered the car around the potholes in the motel parking lot and parked the Porsche at the far end. Rue had turned down the visor over the passenger's seat and was checking her makeup in the mirror. She wrestled a mascara wand out of her skirt pocket and applied a few strokes to the upper lashes of each eye. She snapped the lid back on and returned the wand to her pocket. She reached in back of her

220

head and felt her braid, turning her head a little to look in the mirror.

He was impatient. "You look fine, Miss Rue," he said. "At least for my purposes."

"What's that supposed to mean?" she asked, looking at him quizzically.

"Never mind," he said. He threw a couple of twenties into her lap. "Go pay for the room," he said, nodding toward the motel office at the opposite end of the lot. "I've got to raise the top on the convertible."

She stepped out of the car, and with an exaggerated sway of her hips, walked toward the office. The shack was detached from the motel but a few steps from the closest rooms. "Be sure to get a room at this end," he said after her. "I want some privacy."

"You betcha, darlin'," she said over her shoulder. "I'll bring back the change."

I'll bet you will, thought Michaels, shaking his head. He wondered how someone so childlike had lasted so long on the street.

The Magnolia Manor was a dreary, dirty place and exactly what he'd expected. The building was two stories high and covered with pink aluminum siding. At one time it had probably been a bright pink, but it had long ago faded into something resembling a pale flesh tone. A set of rickety wooden stairs at the end closest to the motel office provided access to the rooms on the second floor. Black wrought-iron fencing provided a railing for the rooms on the second story. A black coach lamp was mounted next to each door of the dozen motel rooms, but only a couple of them worked. No attempt had been made to match the A-frame office to the motel. It had the long, steep roof and tall windows of a typical A-frame building. Faux stone covered the sides of the office, giving the building a north-woods look. This was furthered by the sickly pine trees planted on the sides of the building.

The only other vehicles in the tar lot were a beat-up Honda motorcycle—probably belonging to the innkeeper—and a Chevy Nova with busted-out windows and four flat tires. Both were parked outside the motel office. After raising the top on the Porsche, Michaels moved the car to the side of the motel, next to a stand of birch trees and overgrown bushes. The street traffic was thin at that hour, but he didn't want to take any chances.

In a feeble and condescending tribute to decorating, a poster for *Gone With the Wind* hung on the wall above the bed's brass headboard. It was mounted in a black plastic frame and was covered by scratched acrylic. It showed Scarlett O'Hara in the arms of Rhett Butler while Atlanta burned behind them. "That's my favorite movie," said Miss Rue, as she entered the motel room ahead of Michaels.

"Figures," Michaels said.

She stood studying the poster for a moment while Michaels shut the door behind them and locked it. He slid the security chain in place as well. "If I seen it once I seen it a hundred times," she said wistfully, as much to herself as to Michaels.

With his black driving gloves still on, he fiddled with the clock radio on the nightstand next to the bed, finding an agreeable rock station. He stopped when he hit some Tom Petty and the Heartbreakers. "Even the Losers."

Rue walked into the bathroom and checked her face in the mirror. She pulled a tube out of her skirt pocket and applied a stroke of pink to her lips. "Jesus Christ," Michaels said, watching her through the doorway. "I want to fuck you, not marry you."

"You're a strange one," she said. He laughed and walked over to the bed and sat down on the edge.

She turned and checked her braid in the mirror. Satisfied, she walked out of the bathroom. She looked around the room; it wasn't her usual. She took her johns to the room closest to the office. She sat down on a metal folding chair—the only other furniture besides the bed and nightstand—and peeled off her shirt. Michaels leaned back against the headboard and watched. "Why ain't you undressin'?" she asked as she stood up to wiggle out of her tight skirt. "It takes two to tango, darlin'." She folded her clothes and set them on the seat of the chair.

He stood up, removed his blazer and laid it on the end of the bed. He walked to the nightstand and turned up the volume on the radio.

It wasn't as loud as the buzzing in his head.

"Tell me," said Michaels, stepping toward her, "do you like the way Rhett sweeps Scarlett off her feet?" Before she could answer, he grabbed her by the shoulders and pulled her toward him. He pushed her backward onto the bed and fell heavily on top of her soft form. Her eyes were wide but calm. She'd had rough johns before.

Not this rough.

He wrapped his gloved left hand around her throat and squeezed. With his right, he grabbed a fistful of hair on the back of her head. Suddenly his face contorted in a mixture of confusion and rage. "What the hell!" he yelled. From behind her head, he pulled the brown braid. He held it for a moment, staring at it in the gloved palm of his right hand. It looked like a dead animal.

"You bitch!" he snarled, looking down at her frightened face.

"What?" she squeaked. She was clawing his left arm with her fingers in an attempt to dislodge his left hand from her throat. She tried to raise her knees against him and push him off, but she couldn't; he was too heavy.

He dropped the braid on the floor and released his grip on her throat. He rolled off her and slid off the mattress, standing on the floor next to the bed. He looked down at the whore gasping for air. Brown mascara mixed with tears ran down her cheeks. All the fury and frustration of the previous two weeks bubbled to the surface, spilling out onto the writhing female figure sprawled out on the dirty bedspread. He drew his arm back and punched her in the stomach. She wheezed sharply and curled into a ball. With his left hand, he pulled her to a sitting position on the bed by the top of her hair. He swung his right arm back and slapped her face hard, all the while keeping a tight clamp on her hair. He slapped her until his hand hurt.

Blood oozed out of her nostrils. She fought for breath to scream or cry, but found she had none. She scratched at his left arm with the fingernails of her right hand in a weak attempt to release his hold on her hair. She raised her left arm in front of her face to try to fend off his blows.

He let go of her hair. She fell back on the bed, panting and sobbing. He fell on top of her again and wrapped both hands around her throat. She pulled at his shirt and then used her chubby fists to beat at his back. He laughed at her.

Her eyes rolled to the back of her head as she slipped into unconsciousness.

He didn't rape her. He decided Miss Rue, a hideous fraud, wasn't worth it. He peeled himself off her sweaty body and walked to the end of the bed. From the pocket of his blazer he withdrew the plastic bag and scalpel. He unwrapped the scalpel and laid the plastic bag on the nightstand. He bent over her and grabbed the top of her hair with one hand. In the other, he held the scalpel. Her eyes fluttered open. He looked down at her and smiled. Amazingly, she smiled back, weakly. He put his mouth to her ear and whispered: "The fly shall marry the bumblebee."

He slit her throat in a single, deep stroke. He wiped the blade on the bedspread and shoved it back in his jacket. He inspected his gloved hand, the one he had used to strike her and then slit her throat. "Disgusting," he said, and wiped his glove on the bedspread. The leather was smeared with her pink lipstick and blood.

Pink lipstick and blood. For an instant, he saw his mother sitting on the bed, patting the mattress. "Come, Buzzy."

"No," he said. "No, Bee." He blinked and his mother was gone. The buzzing was fading; he could hear the radio again.

He looked around on the floor. Where did it go? He found it; he'd accidentally kicked it under the bed. He picked it up and dropped it into the plastic bag. He would keep the braid—not as a valuable souvenir, but as a reminder of his own stupidity.

He would call this one Miss Mistake.

TWENTY-NINE

A row of reporters and photographers assembled like a firing squad in front of Christianson's desk Thursday morning. Before the press conference, Christianson had set down some ground rules for the reporters: he would take a limited number of questions after reading a prepared statement; only he could be quoted directly; the two detectives could provide background, but couldn't be named or pictured in the print or television news accounts.

Murphy and Gabe stood in the back while the chief gave a statement outlining the theory that the three murders were connected. A couple of the reporters' mouths dropped open, but they kept scribbling in their notebooks. The bored-looking newspaper photographers stood straighter and snapped pictures. A routine press conference had turned into a good story.

"We are asking the public to assist us in solving these crimes," said Christianson. "If anyone has spotted this man, we're asking them to call us here at the station. He may be driving a newer, black Chevrolet Suburban."

The chief's public-information officer, a nervous bald man with a wispy moustache, handed out composite sketches of the suspect. The reporters nearly ripped the sheets of paper out of his hands.

"Is he armed?" asked Glory Harding, a bug-eyed public-radio reporter who looked as though she'd come straight out of college. "Should he be considered dangerous?"

"No, you should invite him over for dinner," Gabe whispered to Murphy. She smiled and rolled her eyes.

"His weapon is chiefly his hands," said Christianson. "Each victim was strangled and beaten. As far as being dangerous? I'd say so."

"Chief Christianson, who provided you with a description of the suspect?" asked Cody, elbowing his way to the front. "How do you know he drives a black Suburban?"

"Sergeant Murphy, Sergeant Nash. Would either one of you like to answer that question?" said the chief.

Murphy stepped forward, but stayed behind the cameras. "A passing motorist saw Fionn Hennessy get into this man's car shortly before she was killed," she said.

"Can we have the name of the witness, get a few quotes?" asked Cody.

"Not a chance in hell," said Gabe. "You know that."

"A guy's gotta try," said Cody.

"Is he a john?" asked Foster Jones, the *Minneapolis Tribune* reporter, a black, salt-and-pepper-haired veteran with a big gut. He and Gabe were fishing buddies.

"Is the passing motorist a john?" asked Gabe, trying not to grin.

"No, no," said Jones, laughing. He knew Gabe was pulling his leg. "I'm wondering if the killer is a john. Well, I suppose the motorist could be a john as well. My question is . . ."

"I know what you're asking, Foster," said Murphy, smiling. "We don't know if this man was one of Fionn's tricks. It's certainly possible."

"Why do you think these murders are related?" asked Cody. "Beyond the strangulation thing, what else about the killer's M.O. connects the three of them?"

"We can't discuss that," said Christianson.

"As long as we're all standing here, how about an update on Father

Ambrose?" asked Jones. "Is he talking about his assault?"

"Father Ambrose is unable to help us at this time," said Gabe. "He had a setback in the hospital. Some kind of heart trouble."

"I still don't understand why St. Paul P.D. is taking charge of a Minneapolis case," said Mimi Englund, an A.P. reporter. "Is this some sort of weird payback for that Minneapolis shoot-out in St. Paul? What do you guys call it?"

"The rim job," offered Foster, grinning.

"Ouch," Murphy whispered to Gabe. "That one had to piss off the chief."

Christianson didn't blink. "We've already explained we're not in charge," he said. "We're simply lending a hand to our overloaded colleagues across the river."

"That sounds a little too warm and fuzzy to be the whole story," said Englund, planting her hands on her hips. "Is there a St. Paul angle to the case you're not sharing with us?"

"No. That's all for today, ladies and gentlemen," said the chief. "We'll keep you apprised as more information becomes available."

"That went okay," said Gabe as he and Murphy left the chief's office. The public-information officer herded the media pack down the hall to the elevators.

"I guess," said Murphy. "Do me a favor, though. The next time you and Foster are out in the boat, watch what you say in front of him as far as work goes."

"What do you mean?"

"Rim job."

"Oh yeah," Gabe said. They both laughed as they walked into homicide.

"I hate to wreck your jolly mood," said Castro, putting down his telephone. "One of your witnesses turned up dead in a cheesy motel."

"Ah, man," said Murphy as she parked across the street from the Magnolia Manor. "What a crappy place to die."

"What the hell were you expecting?" asked Gabe.

"The Hilton!" Murphy snapped. She turned off the ignition and threw open the car door. "I figured Rue was going to get croaked at the Hilton."

Yellow police tape blocked the entrance to the motel parking lot, which was dotted with a half dozen marked and unmarked squad cars. Tia and a couple of other pros stood outside the tape, craning their necks to see what was happening. A group of neighborhood kids on bicycles pulled up next to the hookers. "You get the bastard who done Charlene! You hear me?" screamed Tia as Murphy and Gabe ducked under the tape. "You assholes fuckin' do your job!"

Some of the kids laughed. "Fuckin' do your job!" one of them repeated. They all picked up on it and chanted: "Do your job! Do your job! Do your job!" More laughter. Murphy and Gabe kept walking across the parking lot.

Murphy stepped into the motel room ahead of Gabe and immediately noticed how the hooker looked more elegant in death than she ever had in life. She was flat on her back, making the curve of her stomach appear gentle rather than bulging. Her limbs looked smooth, pale and graceful in their final repose. Her head was thrown back against the bed, as if in some fanciful pose struck for a painter.

Her face and throat told the true story. Dried blood snaked out of her nose and crusted her nostrils. Her cheeks were battered and streaked with mascara. Her lips were split and pink lipstick was smeared around them as if from a sloppy kiss. Her throat was a congealing, red smear. A large, dark stain started at the pillow under her head and spread under her in a large, elliptical shape.

The crime-scene photographer had come and gone. Murphy and Gabe chased the uniformed officers outside; it was so crowded in the motel room they could hardly turn around. The radio was blaring. "That was on when we got here," said a young patrolman, one of the last uniforms to leave. "We didn't touch it. We didn't touch anything."

"Good," said Gabe, holding the door open for him. "Now take a hike."

"He probably cranked it to cover the noise," Murphy said.

They stood at the side of the bed, looking down at Rue's nude body. "Murphy, this really doesn't fit," said Gabe.

"It can't be a coincidence," she said, shaking her head. "It would be too convenient for him, too lucky."

For different but closely related reasons, both detectives were apprehensive upon finding Erik Mason at the scene as the investigator for the medical examiner's office. "Paris, I have to agree with Gabe," said Erik, standing at the foot of the bed.

"Pinch me," Gabe said. "I must be dreaming."

Erik flipped him the bird and continued. "This isn't Michaels's M.O. He likes a nice, clean strangulation and this is a bloody mess. He goes for women with long hair and you said yourself that Rue kept her hair short. We'll do a workup, but so far it doesn't even appear she had sex with whoever did this to her."

"You know how the Doc favors some sex mixed with his murder," added Gabe. "I mean, that's what floats his boat."

"I know, I know," said Murphy. "With the coup de grâce being a crappy haircut for the victim."

"Rue's clothes are even neatly folded on that chair over there," Erik said. "It really looks like this was some customer gone sour. Nothing more."

"A customer gone sour? Nothing more?" Murphy sputtered. "Whoever it was beat the hell out of her and then sliced her throat. Even if this isn't the work of our doctor pal, it's pretty horrible stuff. Whoever did this is an impressive maniac in his own right."

"Yes, yes," said Erik. "I wasn't trying to make light of what happened here. I was . . ."

"Never mind," she said, rubbing her forehead. "I know what you were saying. I'm saying . . . I don't know what I'm saying. I'm a bitch today, okay?"

Murphy and Gabe stepped away from the bed while the two somber-faced men from the medical examiner's office loaded Rue into a body bag. Murphy studied the dead woman's hair until the zipper finally made its way to the top, sealing in the battered face. In the recesses of her mind, she could see Rue alive and laughing, tugging on a skirt that was always too short and too tight, fussing with her makeup. Something about her hair. Something recent. A blurry image. Murphy struggled but couldn't bring it into focus. "Something is wrong with this picture," said Murphy. "When you mentioned Rue's short hair, something clicked."

"What?" asked Erik.

"I don't know," she said distractedly as she watched the men lift the bag onto a stretcher.

"How do we find her people?" asked Gabe, stepping to the side as they wheeled her out. "Have we got phone numbers for them down south?"

"What do you mean, 'down south'? She's from northeast Minneapolis," said Murphy.

"Really? What was that half-baked accent about?" said Gabe. "You know, all that 'darlin'' stuff."

"Rue wanted to be someone else," said Murphy.

"You mean she didn't want to be a prostitute?" asked Erik.

"She wanted to be a more glamorous one," said Murphy as she stared out the motel windows and watched Rue's body being loaded into the medical examiner's hearse. "She picked up that silly southern accent because she thought it made her sound exotic."

The hearse pulled out of the parking lot. As it did, Murphy saw Tia collapse sobbing into the arms of the other prostitutes. The neighborhood children pedaled off on their bicycles, laughing as they chased the hearse down the street. One threw a rock at it.

"How sad to have no greater goal in life than to be a more alluring hooker," said Erik.

"Yeah," said Murphy. She turned and looked at Erik. "Sad."

"Hey, Paris, how about drinks tonight?" asked Erik as he and the two investigators stood in the motel parking lot. "We still need to firm up stuff on that Saints game."

Murphy gave Gabe the eye. He raised his eyebrows but said nothing as he took the hint and walked toward their car. He smiled to himself. After the way Murphy had snapped at Erik in the motel room, Gabe was confident she wasn't going to be too long. Still, he wanted to keep an eye on things. He crossed the street to the car and leaned against the side of it, turning the driver's-side mirror out a bit so he could watch what was happening in the parking lot without being obvious. He took a pack of Winstons out of his pocket, peeled off the cellophane top and pulled out a smoke.

"Erik, I'm back with my husband," said Murphy. "I'm sorry. I should have called you."

"I'm a patient man," Erik said. "You two have tried this before." Erik looked across the street to make sure Gabe wasn't watching them. He stepped closer to Murphy, grabbed her by the arm and pulled her toward him. "I know what you like, maybe even better than Jack does," he whispered into her ear. "You'll be back."

Murphy looked up at him and started to say something in response. Instead, she shoved his hand off her arm, turned on her heel and walked away. She ducked under the police tape and saw that only Tia was left standing in the street. The other hookers had returned to their corners. "Want a ride?" Murphy asked.

"No," said Tia. "I want Charlene back."

"Me, too," Murphy said tiredly, and crossed the street to Gabe. He was standing outside the car, leaning against the driver's-side door with a cigarette between his fingers. She fished the keys out of her purse and tossed them to him. "Your turn to drive," she said.

Gabe didn't look at her as he got behind the wheel with the cigarette between his lips. "Thought you were gonna quit after you finished that last pack," she said.

"This is the same pack. Got a couple left," he said.

231

"Yeah. Right. Roll down your window. I don't want to smell that shit."

He rolled down the driver's-side window.

"Better straighten out that side mirror," Murphy said.

"Huh?"

"Don't pull that innocent crap on me," she said.

"Jesus Christ," Gabe said. He pulled the cigarette out of his mouth and flicked it outside. "What is your problem this morning?"

She didn't answer. As they pulled away, Murphy looked into the rearview mirror and saw Tia still standing alone behind the police tape, staring at the motel.

Murphy braced herself for questions about Erik and was grateful that Gabe instead held his tongue. They said nothing to each other as they headed back to the station. Murphy closed her eyes and rested her head against the car window. Her mind shuffled back and forth between Rue's body sprawled on the bed and her own body under Michaels's. In the background, she could hear Tia's words mockingly repeated by the neighborhood children. "Do your job. Do your job."

THIRTY

She was on her back in bed, but couldn't feel any support beneath her. The room was too bright, as if the sun had come indoors. Still, she couldn't make out his face when he came to her. He flashed a long knife in front of her face. With her fingertips, she felt along the blade and recognized it as one of her own kitchen carving knives. He pushed her hand away and slipped the tip of the knife under the bodice of her nightgown. With one pass, he slit the gown down the middle and it fell off her body. She shivered and he crawled on top of her. He was fully dressed, but suddenly his clothes melted away and she felt his warm nakedness against her own. He stretched out so his body rested flat against her body. His legs on top of her legs. His stomach against her stomach. He didn't move for a while. He rested. At first he felt light, but he grew heavier. She sensed his chest rise and fall with his every breath; she felt the beating of his heart. Somehow she knew he was Jack, and that made her comfortable. She strained to see his face, but it was turned away from her and buried in her hair.

"Look at me," she said. Her lips didn't move, but she could hear her own words. They echoed, as if coming from inside a cave. "Look at me. Look at me." The face buried in her hair laughed, and she knew it wasn't her husband. Instead she wrapped her legs around him and clawed at his back. His skin came off in her hands. It felt dry and lifeless, like parchment paper. She bunched it up in her fists and released it. The flesh fluttered into the light, turning into a swarm of bees. Hundreds and hundreds of bees.

"I really hate you," she heard herself say. "Hate you. Hate you."

"Then you love me," he said. His breath burned her ear and the white walls turned red. He lifted his face off her hair and looked at her with his gray eyes. Michaels.

She screamed.

"Paris. It's okay. Paris."

She opened her eyes and shuddered. She turned her head and looked at the clock on her nightstand: 3:07 A.M. She pulled the covers up around her neck, even though it was warm in her bedroom. For a moment, she was afraid to turn her head to see who was in bed with her, consoling her. She did turn her head, and was relieved. Jack. Of course.

"Must have been quite a dream," he said. He rolled over onto his side and rested on his elbow as he talked to her in the dark. She stayed flat on her back, clutching the sheets with clammy hands. "Do you remember what it was about?"

"No," she said, lying. "Why?"

"You were yelling in your sleep," he said.

"What did I say?" she asked.

"You said, 'I hate you. I hate you.' Pretty weird."

"Yeah," she said. "Weird."

He fell back asleep, but she stayed awake another hour, staring at the ceiling. She finally shut her eyes and went back to sleep after the lights from a passing barge cut across her bedroom walls, reassuring her that she was safe in her bed and not lost in another bad dream.

* * *

"Potato Head, wake up."

Murphy rolled over onto her side. Morning already, and she was wiped out. Jack shoved a phone into her hands. "It's your mother," he whispered. "I picked up your cell phone by mistake. I guess we're busted."

"Never mind," Murphy mumbled, struggling to sit up in bed while Jack flipped onto his stomach.

"What did you say, honey?" Amira asked on the other end of the phone.

"Nothing, Imma," said Murphy, using the Lebanese term of endearment for mother. "What's up?" Murphy glanced at the clock. Not yet seven. Instinctively, she covered her naked top with her pillow and pulled the edge of the bedsheet over Jack's bare bottom, as if her mother could see them through the cell phone.

"You take such a nice picture, honey," said her mother.

"Thanks, Ma."

"I wish you would do something with your hair."

"Yeah, Ma."

"Otherwise, the photo in this morning's *Pioneer Press* looks lovely. I sent Papa out to buy some extra copies. I'll save one for you."

"Thanks, Ma." Murphy paused for a moment, then realized what her mother had said.

"Shit!" Murphy said. "Shit, shit, shit!"

"Watch your language, young lady," said her mother.

"Sorry, Ma."

"I'll bet your mother told you to watch your language, didn't she, young lady?" Jack muttered into his pillow.

"It's . . . those lizards!" Murphy said angrily, running her fingers through her hair.

"What lizards?" asked her mother, alarmed. "Do you have lizards on your boat, honey? I told you not to live on that filthy river."

"Ma."

"What, honey?"

235

"Can I call you back later?"

"Sure, honey. Kiss Jack for me. Tell him to put some clothes on before going into the kitchen. He could catch a cold."

"Okay, Ma. I'll tell him."

"Please. Think about doing something with your hair, Potato Head."

"Okay, Ma. I will."

"You can't keep pulling it into a ponytail. You're not a twelve-year-old tomboy anymore."

"Okay, Ma."

"I love you, honey."

"I love you, too. Bye." Murphy put down the cell phone, not knowing whether to laugh or scream. She released some visceral combination of the two. *"Aaahhh!"*

"What happened?" asked Jack, rolling over onto his back.

"Cody, you bastard! I thought I could trust you!"

"What did I do, Murphy? What in the hell are you talking about?"

"You know damn well what I'm talking about, you lying piece of garbage," Murphy shouted into the phone. "You ran my photo and name in the paper today, asshole. That's what I'm talking about. You're going to ruin this entire investigation."

"I don't know what you're talking about," Cody sputtered. "Let me get a copy of the city edition."

She heard paper shuffling. While she was on the phone, her partner walked over to her desk and dropped his copy of the *Pioneer Press* on her desk. He looked grim faced.

"Shit," said Cody, back on the phone. "You know, this isn't even my story. It's a wire story we picked up from the Associated Press. It's got Mimi Englund's byline on it and it's not about the murders. It's a short update on the priest based on what you and Nash said yesterday. Our copy desk must have pulled a file photo of you to run with the wire story. Shit. I'm sorry."

"Gabe and I were not supposed to be quoted directly about anything we said during that press conference," she said. "The chief made that clear."

"Well, I'm not defending what Englund did," he said. "I think there was some misunderstanding. I suspect she thought you couldn't be quoted about anything related to the murders. You've been quoted before about the priest's case."

"Yeah, but I was never pictured," she said. "Today you used my name and my photo, making it crystal clear who I am and sending up flares for the killer."

"You know who he is, don't you?" asked Cody.

"Don't change the subject," she said angrily. "Even if it's not your story, you ran it. With my photo. Did the *Tribune* run the A.P. story, too?"

"Yeah, but they buried it on the inside and didn't run a head shot of you," said Cody.

"I suppose TV is going to pick it up, too," she said.

"I doubt it," said Cody. "Not enough visuals."

"Did the photo make it into your on-line publication?" she asked.

"Probably not. Let me check," Cody said.

Gabe sat down at his terminal and also logged on to the Internet. She heard Cody and her partner both typing frantically on their keyboards. Gabe looked over at her and shook his head.

"No, we didn't run a photo on line," Cody said.

"Well, that's something," she said.

"You know, we only ran the photo and story in the city edition," Cody said, trying to reassure her. "If he doesn't live in the city, maybe he didn't see it."

She didn't respond.

"He does live in the city," said Cody. "You do know who it is! Come on, Murphy. Give me something."

"Drop dead, Cody," she said, and slammed the phone down. Murphy picked up the paper and frowned at her photo on the front page of the Metro section. Gabe walked over to her desk and sat on the edge of it.

"You know, to be fair, Slick should have made the ground rules a littler clearer," he said.

"Since when are you the great defender of the Fourth Estate?"

"All I'm saying is . . ."

"Well, it's neither here nor there now," she said with a dismissive wave of her hand. She threw the newspaper in the wastebasket. "Our friendly plastic surgeon knows who I am, and I'm sure who you are as well," she said. "We really need to pull that surveillance operation together pronto. God dammit!"

Her phone rang. Erik:

"I think I have some good news for you. At least, I think it's good news. Relatively speaking. Why don't you get Gabe and come on over?"

The public face of the Ramsey County M.E.'s office was a neat, modern, bright conference room off the front entrance. Erik was waiting there with a plastic bag. "That's what I couldn't remember," said Murphy, grabbing the bag containing a brown braid. "Rue did have long hair recently—when she wore those secondhand hairpieces."

"When that Puerto Rican friend of hers came by to identify the body . . ."

"Tia," said Murphy.

"Yeah, Tia told me about them," said Erik. "Rue had two of them. Sometimes she wore pigtails. Usually, when she did wear the hairpieces . . ."

". . . It was clipped to the back of her head," finished Gabe. "Now I remember, too. One fell off while we were interviewing her."

"I had Tia come back with this one," said Erik, pointing to the braid in the bag. "She wore the other one the night she was killed. It's missing."

"I know exactly where it is," said Murphy, taking a seat at the conference table and putting the bag down in front of her. "It's in

238

Michaels's trophy case. I was right, wasn't I? He did do poor Rue."

"The wound across her throat was made with a very sharp tool," said Erik.

"A scalpel," said Gabe, sitting next to Murphy.

"I don't understand why he changed his M.O.," said Erik, pacing the width of the room as he talked. "He doesn't strangle her. He slashes her throat. He beats her, but he doesn't rape her. Instead of finishing off with his signature haircut, he takes home a ratty braid."

"That might be why he did Rue differently," said Murphy. "He only gets his rocks off on longhaired women. Maybe he didn't know it was a hairpiece until he got her inside the motel room."

"After he discovered the hair was fake, he couldn't rape her because he couldn't get it up," said Gabe. "All he could do was slit her throat."

"The braid must have really pissed him off," said Murphy.

"Then why did he take it with him?" asked Erik, who stopped pacing and took a seat across the table from the two detectives.

"Who knows? I'm not a psychologist," said Murphy. She stared at the braid. "Maybe he couldn't stand leaving empty-handed. He had to take some sort of souvenir with him, even if it was a lousy braid."

"What do we tell the press about Rue?" asked Gabe. "Should we connect the dots for them on this one?"

"Forget it. I'm out of the dot-connecting business," said Murphy. "Let them figure it out for themselves or make up whatever they want."

"We can't say much official anyway because this is all conjecture," said Erik. "We didn't find anything in the autopsy that you didn't see in the motel."

"Of course not," Murphy said. "That's how this entire case has been going! It's not that he's a brilliant professional killer, but he *is* very careful. I'll give him that. No one noticed him or his car at the motel that night. He had Rue go to the office to pay for the room. He didn't leave a weapon and probably left no prints. The thing is, he's also very, very lucky."

"Tough to fight," Gabe said. He stood up to leave, but Murphy stayed in her seat, looking down at the braid in the bag.

"Rue told me she talked the woman down to five dollars for both."

"What?" asked Erik.

"The woman running the garage sale wanted five dollars for each and Rue got her down to five dollars for the pair," said Murphy. "Charlene was pretty proud of that bit of bargaining." She slid the plastic bag across the table to Erik and stood up. "It really sucks to think a life can turn on a two-for-one hairpiece, doesn't it?" she said.

THIRTY-ONE

Michaels was trapped in surgery the better part of Friday with one breast reduction after another. The last one went badly because of excessive bleeding. Hester Hanson had disobeyed his orders to stay away from alcohol and garlic for two weeks prior to her operation. In fact, she'd had enough wine that she'd thinned her blood so it wouldn't clot properly. To make matters worse, she took aspirin the morning after her drinking for her hangover. This had happened before with other patients, though not to this extreme. Most denied the transgression. In this case, however, her husband, Zachary, claimed they'd never received such preoperative instructions from him.

"Doctor, I swear we never heard any such thing," said Zachary Hanson as he and Michaels argued outside Hester's room. "Why would we ignore something so important? Do you think my wife wanted to bleed to death so she could have a couple of glasses of wine and some chip dip?"

Michaels knew it wasn't a couple glasses of wine. A bottle perhaps. "Mr. Hanson, I assure you the situation was not that dire," said Michaels. "She did not come close to bleeding to death."

He didn't like the Hansons. They were nouveau riche ex-farmers who made money by selling their farm parcels on the southern edge of the Twin Cities. They still dressed and talked like farmers. Every time he saw Zachary Hanson, he was in the same flannel shirt and baggy-ass blue jeans. Like he had just stepped off the soybean field.

"I also want to assure you, Mr. Hanson, that I did indeed give you instructions warning against the consumption of alcohol, garlic and aspirin in the weeks prior to surgery," Michaels continued, his face reddening in contained anger. "Your wife set a new standard among my patients. She managed to use all three!"

"Bullshit!" said Hanson. "That is a crock! You didn't warn us about jack shit!"

Michaels was tired. He had a headache. He wanted to go home to a hot bath, a cold steak sandwich and some good Scotch, in precisely that order. "Look, Mr. Hanson, I tell all my surgical patients this personally and I have my staff pass along written instructions as well. I know I told your wife. Positively no alcohol, garlic or aspirin for two . . ."

"You're covering your ass," snarled Hanson, sticking a fat, ruddy finger in Michaels's face. Two surgical nurses walked past them in the hospital hallway, still dressed in their scrubs. They looked back as Hanson's voice continued to rise. "You're one lucky son-of-a-bitch that she made it through the surgery. Here everyone says you're the top tit man in town. I'm still waiting to be impressed. That's for damn straight!"

The doctor felt the muscles around his jaw tighten. No one questioned his skills, his talents, his gifts. Especially not some ignorant rube riding high on his newfound wealth. He grabbed Hanson by his shirt collar and shoved him flat against the wall. "Look, you hick jerk," he growled lowly. "I *am* the best in town. In the country, for that matter, and don't you forget it! It's not my fault your dopey wife can't follow some simple instructions."

The two nurses stopped at the end of the hall and turned around wide-eyed to watch. Michaels released Hanson, who looked genuinely frightened. "The nurse will send you home with some post-op instructions tomorrow," Michaels continued. "If there are any problems this evening—and I'm sure there will be none—they will page me. Is all that clear?"

Hanson nodded but said nothing.

"Now why don't you go down to the cafeteria and have a cup of coffee?" Michaels said evenly.

The smaller man nodded, turned and walked quickly down the corridor, brushing past the two nurses. The pair watched him step onto an elevator. As the doors closed behind the startled man, the two women turned and stared at Michaels. The taller of the two leaned toward the other and whispered something. The shorter one nodded. Michaels glared at them. "Nosey cunts," he hissed under his breath.

He didn't get to the newspaper until Friday night, as he was stretched out naked on the bed with a glass of Scotch on the nightstand.

He inhaled sharply when he unfolded the A section and read the headline stripped across the top of the front page: MAN SOUGHT IN THREE MURDERS. Police had made the connection between the murder of the redheaded whore and the deaths of women in Minneapolis and Rochester. How did they find out about the one from his fellowship? How? Miss Incident was years ago. He fought to control his trembling hands as he held the newspaper. With great effort, he forced himself to read slowly and carefully, even though his frantic eyes demanded he skip ahead to find anything that clearly pointed a finger at him. His hands dampened the edges of the newspaper as he held it. He turned to the continuation of the story on page three. A composite sketch—of him!

The buzzing. Not now. He dropped the newspaper and covered his ears with his hands. "Calm down," he told himself. "Fucking calm down." He shut his eyes and took deep breaths, and it stopped. He opened his eyes and lowered his hands from his ears. Good. The fly was back in the jar.

He picked up the newspaper again and studied the sketch carefully.

It could be anyone, he told himself. Anyone. The police chief was asking for the public's help, according to the story. Anyone seeing the man in the sketch—possibly driving a newer black Chevy Suburban—was asked to call authorities. Shit. They had the color and make and model of his car! How? He kept reading.

Supposedly, someone saw the whore get into his car. Bullshit! The streets were empty that rainy night. He remembered that clearly. This was conjecture on the part of the police. Nothing in the story revealed why they thought the three cases were related. Nothing. The news account also failed to make the connection between the murder of the whore and the assault on the priest. It had no mention of his most recent and disappointing outing. Didn't the fat whore make it into the paper at all? Surely someone had found Miss Mistake's body by now.

He threw the A section to the floor and grabbed the Metro section, quickly flipping through it until he found a short story on the back page about a woman's nude body found in a motel room. Her name was being withheld pending notification of relatives. That was it on Miss Mistake. No cause of death. No mention of whether the police were looking for anyone.

On the surface, the police appeared stumped. They had bits and pieces, but they didn't have the entire puzzle assembled. Very far from it.

He wasn't so naive. He suspected they knew much more about him than they were letting on. Perhaps they even knew his name. So why were they claiming they needed the public's help? They were tormenting him, challenging him. He was sure of it.

How had they gotten the information they did have?

He dropped the Metro section on the bed and reached over to his nightstand to grab his Scotch glass when a photograph on the front of the section caught his eye. He picked the section up again and nervously unfolded it.

He was stunned. "God dammit," he said. "You had me."

That evening rendezvous with her, with this Detective Paris

Murphy—finally a name to the beautiful face—had been a net cast for him. He knew he should be furious, but instead he was pleased.

He took a sip of Scotch and mulled over what he had said to her that night; it was hazy. He had had too much to drink, but he hadn't said anything that implicated him in any of the murders or the assault on the priest on the floor of the confessional. He was safe there. Something else about that evening, something that had nagged him that night at the hotel. What was it? He took another drink and it came to him. That familiar-looking man on the hotel steps, the one with the long hair and the beard. He was part of the scam. Now Michaels remembered where he'd spotted that barrel figure and Cro-Magnon posture before. He was that so-called friend of hers from the funeral and soccer tournament, dressed in a lame disguise. Must be her cop partner.

"Such a cool liar," he said. He studied the photo. So professional, with her dark hair pulled back sternly from her face. She had high cheekbones; he hadn't noticed that before for some reason. Those eyes. He lost himself in those eyes. He stroked the photo with his finger-tips and smiled. That night in the hotel bar and garden had been a trap set for him, but she was the one who was almost snared. She yielded for an instant. He felt it as his lips sealed over hers, as his mouth tasted her breast. She could have surrendered. She would surrender if he had an opportunity to be alone with her again.

He read the story under the photo. A short update on Ambrose. The priest had refused to talk to the police because of the Seal of Confession. It also referred to a heart problem the father was suffering from in the hospital. Was it possible he had managed to slip the potassium into the old boy without anyone spotting it? No. He would have to be incredibly stupid to believe that. The police knew about it.

They were baiting him with these stories filled with half-truths, teasing him, hoping he would make a revealing mistake. They were buying time. They needed more evidence before they brought him in, especially with his family's influence around town. That's what all this was about. His father's youngest brother, a downtown developer, had bankrolled the mayor's reelection campaign and another uncle, a downtown banker, had the governor's ear. Cousins in the legislature. So many powerful, moneyed cousins. Blood ties and wealth. Unbeatable. His relatives would come through for him. Most liked him. The ones that didn't like him wouldn't want the family name dirtied.

He grabbed his cell phone off his nightstand and held it for a moment, debating which uncle to tap for help. Maybe he'd start with another relative. Someone especially well positioned to help him. Someone who'd take his side no matter what. He punched in the number. She answered.

"Hello, cuz," he said into the phone. He lay back against the pillows. "It's been too long."

Michaels set down the phone and smiled. The relative front was in order. He hopped out of bed and paced across the floor. Now he needed to get out of town for a while, let things settle down. A trip to the cabin would be good. He'd leave in the morning. He needed to talk to his wife, anyway; time for some serious ass kicking. Maybe he'd spend a week or two up north. Screw work. He could have his staff reschedule his appointments and surgeries.

He wanted to pay someone a visit before he left town. He wanted her to know he was on to her little scheme. He wanted her to know he still desired her. Most important, he wanted her to know he was fully aware that she desired him.

He ran down to his home office and logged on to the *Pioneer Planet*, the on-line news publication of the *Pioneer Press*. He went into the newspaper archives and did a search using her name. He came up with dozens of hits. It seemed Detective Paris Murphy was an investigative star of sorts. She got all the tough cases. A satisfied smile stretched across his face. "I suppose I should be flattered you're pursuing me," Michaels muttered. He pulled up one police story after another, but what he needed was some personal information.

Here it is, he thought. A recent profile from the newspaper's feature pages. He rolled his eyes at the title: "Murphy's Law." "Who writes this shit?" he grumbled. He quickly scanned the piece.

She usually preferred working without a partner, but sometimes teamed up with a veteran detective, Sergeant Gabriel Nash. "So that's the ugly fuck's name," Michaels said to himself. She came from a large Catholic family and had attended Catholic schools. Her hobbies included running and cooking. "So you didn't lie about everything," Michaels said in a low voice. He found no mention of hunting and he clearly remembered her asking him if he liked to hunt. That was obviously a ploy to pull something out of him about his favorite pursuit. Michaels was pleased to read she was separated from her husband, an emergency-room doctor. The newspaper story didn't name him. She lived in a houseboat on the river.

That last bit of information was what he needed, and he knew exactly where that floating neighborhood was docked. He went back upstairs, opened a dresser drawer and pulled out some clothes.

THIRTY-TWO

"Tell her it's him all right," Castro said, peering through his binoculars. "He's leaving by the side door and walking down the driveway toward his garage."

"Actually, it's a carriage house, converted into a garage," Dubrowski said, correcting his partner.

"Fucking excuse me," Castro said. "Then tell her he's walking down the fucking driveway toward his fucking carriage house, converted into a fucking garage." Castro sat behind the wheel of the unmarked squad car—a dark blue Crown Victoria—parked across the street from Michaels's house on Summit Avenue on Friday. In the passenger seat next to him, Dubrowski was on a cell phone speaking to Murphy. She had asked them to call her at home that evening if the surgeon left his house during their surveillance.

"What a long driveway," Castro mumbled. "I'd hate to shovel that puppy in the winter."

"What did he say?" Murphy asked Dubrowski. "Michaels has a shovel?"

"No, no. He said he'd hate to shovel that driveway."

"He's opening the garage door," Castro said, picking up his burger to take another bite but still watching through the binoculars.

248

"He's opening the garage door," Dubrowski repeated to Murphy.

He paused in his narration to pick up his fish sandwich and finish it off. He wiped his mouth with a paper napkin and started sucking on his shake. The front seat of the car—littered with crumpled paper napkins, empty paper bags and paper cups—looked like the tabletop of a fast-food restaurant. The floor of the backseat was covered with newspapers and pop cans. Sitting on top of the backseat was a cardboard box across which was scrawled in black marker: "Detectives— Clean up after yourselves, assholes. Dump trash in here." The inside of the box was the cleanest spot in the car.

"Now what's he doing?" asked Dubrowski.

"I don't know," said Castro. He popped the last wedge of burger into his mouth and wiped his hand on his pants while continuing to look through the binoculars held in his other hand. "I don't have a clear view because part of the garage is tucked behind that big mother house. He's probably in there choking the bishop. Actually, I'm pretty sure he's . . . Whoa! Wait a minute. Wait a minute. Yup. Here we go!"

He threw down the binoculars. "Gentlemen, start your engines," Castro said with a grin, turning on the ignition.

Michaels rolled out of the driveway and sped down Summit. The Crown Victoria pulled away from the curb and went after him, keeping a discreet distance. "He's headed east toward downtown," Dubrowski said into the phone.

"Stay with him," Murphy said.

"He doesn't have a private plane at the downtown airport, does he?" Dubrowski asked Murphy.

"No, he doesn't," she said.

Castro saw Michaels look in his rearview mirror. The Suburban stopped at a light. Castro slowed and let another car cut between the squad and the Suburban before he stopped.

"What the hell are you doing?" asked Dubrowski.

"I don't want to ride his ass the whole time," said Castro. "He'll get wise to us."

"We're gonna lose him."

"The hell we are. How long have I been doing this? I ever lose anybody?"

"What's going on?" asked Murphy.

The light changed. The car ahead of Castro took a turn and the squad was again behind the Suburban.

"Castro almost lost him, but now we're okay," Dubrowski said into the phone. Castro flipped his partner the bird.

They followed the Suburban through downtown St. Paul. "He's headed toward the Wabasha Bridge," Dubrowski said into the phone.

"The West Side isn't his usual hunting ground," said Murphy.

As if dropped from the sky, a white limo cut sharply in front of the Crown Victoria and Castro hit the brakes. "Shit," he muttered.

Up ahead, the Suburban turned south onto the bridge.

"Now we're going to lose him for real!" Castro said. He honked at the crawling limo. A black airport van pulled up next to the limo. Both lanes were blocked. He couldn't pull around both the van and the limo with opposing traffic zooming by. "Oh great! Fucking great!" said Castro, pounding the steering wheel with his fist.

"Can you still see Michaels's Suburb?" she asked.

"No, but I'm sure he's over the bridge by now," Dubrowski said into the cell phone.

"Where is he going?" Murphy wondered aloud. Suddenly it occurred to her. She inhaled sharply.

"Murphy, what's wrong?" Dubrowski asked. He heard only her breathing. "Murphy, what is it?"

Then it also occurred to him. "We gotta get to Murphy!" Dubrowski said.

"Get out of there!" he yelled into the cell phone. "Get out of there now!"

The silence on the other end of the phone made him fear it had gone dead. He held the cell phone tight to one ear and plugged the other so he could hear more clearly.

The airport van pulled up. Castro squealed around the limo and took a right onto the bridge.

"Murphy! Murphy!" Dubrowski yelled. "We're coming. We're on the bridge."

A long silence.

"It's too late," she said. She heard a car pull up and then Tripod barking wildly. Stranger on the dock. "He's here." She stood in her living room, with the sliding glass door leading to the deck wide open. Beyond the deck was the Mississippi. She stared at the flat, brown water and tried to draw a sense of calm from it.

"I'm going to radio some backup for you," Dubrowski said. "I'm calling Gabe."

"Hurry," she said. She switched the phone to her left hand and with her right pulled her gun from her purse. "Don't come in too soon. I want to hear what he has to say. Stay in the parking lot."

"Murphy, there is no way I am going to leave you alone with that head case," he said.

"It'll be okay," she said.

"Hello, Paris." She turned around and looked into his face. She pulled the cell phone from her ear, but continued gripping it tightly. She stood in the living room, behind the counter that separated it from the galley. He stood on the other side of the counter in the galley.

"Are you going to kiss me or kill me?" he asked coolly.

"Neither," she said evenly.

"Your neighbor, the amazingly untalented sax player, was kind enough to direct me to the right houseboat after his mutt tried to take my arm off," he said. He scrutinized the galley and living room. "Nice place you have here. Just like you."

"I'll take that as a compliment," she said.

"I meant it as one," he said. "How big is it? How many bedrooms?"

"One," she said.

"*Hmmm.* How about a little tour?"

251

"No," she said flatly. "What the hell do you want, Michaels?"

"Please call me Romann," he said. "I think we know each other well enough, especially after our intimacy in the hotel garden."

"Fine," she said. "What the hell do you want, Romann?"

"You're not a gracious host," he said. "Aren't you going to offer me a drink?"

"I'm fresh out of Scotch."

"The wine will work," he said, crossing the galley's wooden floor; he took a bottle of Cabernet Sauvignon from the wine rack. He studied the label, frowned and slipped it back into the rack. "Not nearly complex enough."

"I'll bet you've got some nice Chardonnay chilled," he said, and walked to the refrigerator. He eyed the collage of bills, postcards and photos plastered to the front of the appliance. "It's such a Catholic thing," he said, surveying the mess. "We have this need to cover the entire front of our refrigerators with scraps, as if we're trying to re-create those paper stained-glass windows we made in grade school." He yanked open the refrigerator, stuck his head inside and rummaged around. He emerged with a bottle of white wine. He slammed the door shut and set the bottle on the counter. He grabbed two wineglasses off the open kitchen shelf next to the wine rack. He held them up to the ceiling light to inspect them for spots. Finding them satisfactory, he set them down on the counter next to the bottle of Chardonnay. He pulled open a couple of kitchen drawers, but couldn't find what he needed. "Do you want me to open it with my teeth?"

Still keeping the gun and her eyes on him, she set down the phone, opened a drawer under her side of the counter and fished out a corkscrew. She threw it to him and he caught it. With great finesse, he opened the bottle, sniffed the cork and poured each of them a glass. He carefully recorked the bottle and returned it to the refrigerator. He noticed he had spilled a drop of wine on the counter. He grabbed a sponge from the sink and wiped it up.

"Are you always so careful about cleaning up after yourself?" she asked slyly.

He looked at her but said nothing as he tossed the sponge back in the sink.

"Why don't we enjoy this with a river view?" he said, a stem in each hand.

"After you," she said, nodding toward the deck. He acquiesced, walking around the counter and across the living-room floor. He stepped through the open sliding glass doors that led outside. She followed him.

"Quite a view," he said, scanning the riverfront. On the shore across the river, a crane groomed itself from its perch on a rock. A pair of ducks bobbed on the water a yard from her boat. The sky was purple and the air was warm and dead still. He handed her a glass. She took it with her left hand. In her right, she continued holding the Glock. "Can't we sit down?" he asked, nodding toward the deck chairs.

"Fine," she said.

"Ladies first," he said. She slowly lowered herself into one chair and he sat down in the other.

He took a sip of wine. "Nice," he said, smiling. "It's a low-end California, but nice."

She studied his face. His gray eyes. His broad shoulders. The muscled expanse of chest. Fleetingly, she wondered why the most venomous snakes were also among the most dazzling.

"That was an interesting game you played with me," he said, smiling and taking another sip of wine. "You had me fooled, but in the end, you only fooled yourself. Don't you agree?"

"Why?" she asked warily.

"We're so much alike, you and I," he said.

She laughed dryly. She took a drink of wine—her nerves needed it—and set the glass down on the deck.

"I'm serious," he said. "You lied to yourself. You told yourself you were doing your job, pursuing a suspect. What you really wanted—and what you almost had—was a soul mate."

"That's ludicrous," she snapped.

"Hear me out," he said. He paused and took a sip of wine. He frowned thoughtfully, staring at the liquid in the glass. He sloshed it around a bit, admiring the way it lightly coated the sides of the goblet. "We're both loners by choice, you and I," he said softly, his eyes still trained on the wine. "We're both ambitious and headstrong, which adds to our sense of isolation. Then there's that whole Catholic guilt trip that colors everything we say and do and think. It's like this additional, hovering presence in our lives, constantly watching us and waiting for a misstep so it can judge us. It's almost like our third parent. A mean, suffocating parent."

As reluctant as she was to give any weight to his words, she couldn't deny the slivers of truth in them.

"We both value a sense of control over our lives. 'I have everything under control.' How many times do we say that to ourselves? It's almost our mantra, isn't it?" he continued. "We're not in complete control, are we? We both suffer this uncontrollable thirst. There's a yearning inside of us, a nagging hunger we can't identify or put a name to. It comes from this shadowy, passionate corner deep inside of us. We're genuinely afraid to go there."

She felt as if she was looking into a cracked mirror. Her reflection was looking back at her through him, but she hated what she saw: something ugly and splintered.

"We almost went to that place together, that night, in that hotel garden," he said, his eyes leaving the wineglass to take in her face and read her eyes. "I felt it. I felt you soften. You came so close to giving in."

"No."

"Yes," he said. "I could have given you something you've never had before. I could still. Right now. Let's go back inside. You can keep the gun on me. I find that exciting."

She shook her head again.

"I know you want it," he whispered.

"No," she said. "No, I don't."

"Oh yes you do," he said in a low voice. "You're getting weak and your head is spinning thinking about it."

"No," she breathed.

"Come on, Paris," he whispered, leaning toward her intimately. Conspiratorially. "No one has to know. It will be our filthy little secret."

"Stop," she said sharply, raising the gun barrel. "I know what you're trying to do, you sick son-of-a-bitch." She stood up. She felt dizzy and momentarily grabbed the back of the deck chair for support. The wine. "Is this how you did it? Is it? Was the poetry this pretty? What did you say to Rue before you beat the hell out of her and slit her throat?"

His eyes widened.

"I know about Rue," she said, still pointing the barrel at him. "I know about Finch and Roxanne and that woman from the club in Minneapolis."

He stood up. "Sit your ass down!" she barked. "I'm not through with you yet."

He hesitated, staring at her face and then the gun, wondering whether she would really shoot him. He looked at her face again and lowered himself back into the chair.

"Tell me about the hair," she purred, walking back and forth across the deck in front of him. "Why is it so important to you? Why do you have to take it? Is there a name for that sort of fetish?"

"I don't know what you're talking about," he said, lowering his eyes and staring into his wineglass.

"Oh, sure you do," she said. She slipped the ribbon off her ponytail, threw it into his face and shook her hair free.

He stared at her but said nothing. He took a long drink of wine, finishing the glass. He fingered the ribbon as he held it in his lap and wondered if he could overpower her. Raping her would be satisfying; he started to harden thinking about it. His hand tightened around the ribbon.

"What do you like about long hair? Do you play with it at night, roll around naked in it?" she asked tauntingly, running the fingers of her free hand through her own hair. "Where do you keep all that hair you've so carefully collected? Under your pillow? Maybe you suck your thumb while you're holding it, like a baby and his blanket."

"That's enough," he snapped.

"Oh, no. I'm just getting started," she said. "Bet it really pissed you off when you discovered Rue's hair wasn't real. Did that make you angry? Is that why you did her differently from the others? Is that why you didn't rape her? I suppose you can't get your rocks off with fake hair."

He bolted out of his chair. She took one last poke at him: "'Fiddle-de-dee, fiddle-de-dee. The fly shall marry the bumblebee.' What does that mean, Michaels? Are you the fly or the bumblebee?"

His face turned ashen. "Do I look like a fucking bug?" he asked. He angrily threw his glass overboard, but he held on to the ribbon. "I'm leaving now," he said, his eyes angry slits.

"Don't break my heart," she said, a small smile on her face. Though she had failed to extract anything resembling a confession from him, though she had learned nothing new in the case, she'd won. He'd barged into her home to rattle her and he was the one leaving in an emotional tangle.

"This isn't over, Paris," he said, his eyes locked on hers, his fist wrapped around her hair ribbon. "We still have some things to resolve, you and I. I will be back."

Murphy heard Tripod barking again.

"Paris!" bellowed a male voice from inside the houseboat.

"Out here," she yelled.

Gabe ran through the doors onto the deck with his gun drawn. Behind him were Castro and Dubrowski. Gabe reached for his cuffs.

"No," Murphy said, putting her hand on Gabe's arm. "Let him go."

Gabe looked at Michaels's face; Michaels stared back in disdain. "Are you sure you don't want me to fuck him up a little?" Gabe asked. "That pretty mouth is begging to get busted."

"Sign me up for a piece of that," said Dubrowski.

"No," Murphy said. "I just want him out of here."

Gabe stepped out of Michaels's way. Michaels walked through the open patio door past the other two detectives. Castro pursed his lips in a mock kiss as Michaels went by. They heard Tripod barking and then Michaels's SUV squealing out of the parking lot.

"You okay, Murphy?" asked Dubrowski.

"Fine," she said. "Thanks, you guys. Thanks a lot." He and Castro holstered their guns and went back outside.

"What happened in here?" asked Gabe.

Murphy stuffed her gun in the waistband of her jeans and sat in one of the deck chairs. "Nothing happened," she said, shutting her eyes and breathing in the river air.

"Did he give up anything?"

"Jack shit," she said, opening her eyes again.

"Want me to hang around for a while?" asked Gabe. He shoved his gun back in his holster.

"Nah. I'm okay. That asshole won't be back." She noticed her wineglass at her feet. She picked it up and took a long drink. "A low-end California."

"What?"

"Nothing," she said, and emptied the glass.

THIRTY-THREE

Michaels drove home and, after pounding down a couple of tall Scotches, collapsed exhausted into bed. He slept fitfully. He found himself getting progressively less sleep every day. The worries were piling up on him like bricks, and it was taking more and more energy to keep the fly tucked away.

He woke well before dawn with his face buried in his pillow and his sheets kicked into a heap at the foot of the bed. He was still tired. He checked the clock on his nightstand and saw her hair ribbon next to it. He grabbed the ribbon and flopped over on his back. He tried to go back to sleep with the ribbon bunched in his right fist, but instead he stared at the ceiling for twenty minutes. He rolled out of bed, threw the ribbon back on the nightstand and ran down to the basement. He lost track of how many laps he did; he swam until his legs and arms ached and his eyes stung from the chlorine. He went back upstairs, took a long, hot soak and pulled on some clothes. While he was dressing, he glanced out the bedroom window that faced Summit Avenue.

There they were, parked across the street from his house. They were wedged between a couple of other cars, but not hiding themselves. He probably should have expected some sort of tail. Fuck them, he thought angrily. The getaway up north was more and more appealing. Let them tail him all the way to Duluth and beyond. What did he give a shit? Nothing for the cops to see at his lake home, except for his whore wife and her witch mother—and for all he knew they were on the sailboat, tied off somewhere along shore. He still couldn't reach them by phone, or his daughters at camp for that matter.

He called his office and left a message on the machine for his staff, curtly ordering them to reschedule his appointments and surgeries for the next several days. A death in the family, he said; he didn't try for a neat excuse.

From his closet he grabbed a black leather bomber jacket. It got cold around the lake. He walked over to his dresser for his car keys and caught his reflection in the mirror. His eyes were bloodshot and there were dark, puffy rings under them. He resolved to take better care of himself. He'd been denying the fly what it needed and was losing sleep as a result. Now he was nothing but a knot of tired, frustrated nerves. He shut his eyes and deliberately conjured up a satisfying image. "I can still make it happen," he said to himself. "I will make it happen." He opened his eyes, scanned the collection of car keys on his dresser top and scooped up the set for the Porsche. Might as well let them get an unobstructed view. He'd ride with the top down. He wanted to look them straight in the eye and make them fully aware that he could also see them. He pulled open the top dresser drawer, took out a pair of black driving gloves and shoved them into the jacket pockets. From his nightstand, he took her ribbon. He sniffed it; it smelled like her herbal shampoo. He smiled, curled it into a neat circle in the palm of his hand and slipped it into his pants pocket.

He ran to the library for one last essential. He pulled open the bookshelf and walked into the safe room, flipping on the light switch. He wanted a second gun in addition to the Sig, for insurance. He popped open a gun case, eyed his Browning automatic but instead picked out his Smith & Wesson, shoving it in his pocket. He turned around to shut off the lights but before he did, he looked back at the wall safe. He'd stashed the scalpel in there after its last use. He thought about taking it and the hatbox with him.

He walked over to the wall safe, opened it and pulled out the hatbox. He lifted off the cover. The ugly brown braid and the scalpel were both sitting on top, each in its own plastic bag. How had Paris Murphy connected him to Miss Mistake and to the others? She was taunting him. Teasing him. If she had some hard evidence on him, she wouldn't have let him walk away. What he had in his hands would qualify as hard evidence. If the cops ever found the hatbox and its contents, he'd be in some serious shit. An army of uncles and cousins couldn't save his ass then. No. Better to leave the souvenirs home, where they'd be hidden and secure. He reached into his pants pocket, pulled out the circle of hair ribbon and set it on top of his collection. He looked at the ribbon. A taste of things to come. He put the cover back on the box and set the box back in the wall safe. He shut the safe, gave the knob a couple of spins, turned out the lights and shut the door.

He walked to the middle of the library and turned around to study the bookcase. There were no major gaps between the shelves; there was no unevenness in the woodwork. Nothing gave it away, especially if you weren't looking for it. It would take the cops forever to find it. His valuables would stay well hidden. He turned around and left.

Evans Bergen and Pete Sandeen had been parked in front of Michaels's house since five in the morning, relieving the surveillance team that watched the house all through the night and into the early-morning hours. On the seat of the car were an empty doughnut box, crushed juice cartons and balled-up paper napkins smeared with chocolate glaze.

"I can't believe the union isn't gonna fight the chief's bullshit plan," said Bergen, licking glaze off his thumb.

"Which bullshit plan would that be?" asked Sandeen, a union steward. He was a head taller than Bergen, twenty years older, and had a thick head of white hair. "There's so many you've got to be more specific."

"That crap where he's eliminating the lieutenants and captains and replacing them with a handful of commanders. There's no place to advance after you make sergeant. What's the point of bustin' your ass?"

"We filed a grievance," said Sandeen, bumping off his coffee and tossing the empty Styrofoam cup on the seat of the car.

"I know the commanders get paid a hell of a lot more than the lieutenants did, but you can't make it unless you kiss the chief's ass," said Bergen.

"Quit pissing and moaning and join the grievance committee if you want something done," said Sandeen. "Otherwise shut the hell up and let the thing wind its way through the process."

Bergen grumbled.

"What time is it?" asked Sandeen. He was behind the wheel. He punched the dashboard clock with his fist. "I swear to God the clock on every fleet car is busted."

Bergen checked his Dick Tracy wristwatch. "It's almost seven," he said, yawning. "Time flies when you're having fun, don't it?"

"Whoa—that's him!" said Sandeen. They saw Michaels exit his house through the side door and walk calmly but purposefully to his garage. Sandeen turned on the ignition. "The horses are out of the gate," he said as the Porsche darted out of the driveway, heading east down Summit Avenue.

"Nice wheels," said Bergen as the Crown Victoria followed. "What do you suppose those go for?"

"Too much," said Sandeen

At a stoplight, Michaels turned his head and looked behind him. He made eye contact with Sandeen, gave him a little smile and a wave. He turned back around and slipped on his sunglasses. "He knows we're on his tail," said Sandeen. "Arrogant bastard."

"Big deal," said Bergen.

The light changed and the Porsche pulled away, with the Crown

Victoria close behind. "You'd better wake Murphy and Gabe," Sandeen said.

Bergen sifted through the pile of debris on the seat and pulled out the cell phone. "Hope he ain't going far," he said as he punched Murphy's home number.

"Who the hell knows?" said Sandeen. "Life is one long orgy for this guy. Maybe he got a bead on some new whorehouse specializing in longhaired hookers."

"Do you suppose there is such a thing?" asked Bergen.

"Somewhere—probably in L.A.," Sandeen said wisely.

"Yeah, in L.A.," said Bergen, nodding in agreement as he waited for Murphy to answer her phone.

"There's no answer at Murphy's or at Gabe's," he said.

"It's early, but they might be at the cop shop already," said Sandeen. "Give them a try there."

Gabe picked up the call from Bergen; his partner was on her line talking to Michaels's neighbor, Elaine Roth.

"I really should have called yesterday when I saw that composite sketch in the newspaper; it's hard to believe someone you know could do something like that," said Roth. "He looks exactly like that man, and he drives a black Suburban, like the story said."

"We appreciate the tip, Ms. Roth," said Murphy.

"On top of all that, I remembered those scratches I saw on his cheek when I talked to him earlier this week," Roth said in a breathy voice. "He said a cat scratched him. I know for a fact they don't own a cat. The girls are allergic. I started to put two and two together. Then when I heard him tearing out of his driveway early this morning, I knew I couldn't wait any longer."

"Has his behavior been unusual in any other way lately?" asked Murphy. "Have any of his family members or other neighbors mentioned anything to you?"

"He has two daughters and they're both at a soccer camp in Europe," said Roth. "His wife . . ."

"His wife?" said Murphy. "Isn't he separated or divorced?"

"No, no," said Roth. "Although she really should dump him. He drinks like a fish and he's so verbally abusive. They're forever fighting and have nothing in common but their children, and sometimes he seems barely able to tolerate his own daughters. He wanted sons, you know, but she was glad they had girls. She was afraid the boys would turn out like him. That's why she . . ."

Roth hesitated.

"Why she what?" asked Murphy.

"Nothing. Never mind."

"You were saying something about his wife's whereabouts."

"She's still up at their cabin with her mother," Roth said.

"Have you ever been there?" Murphy asked. "Can you tell me where it is?"

"Sure," said Roth. "Jennifer and I have had a couple of good weekends up there."

While Murphy jotted the directions to the cabin in her notebook, Gabe leaned over her desk, scribbled a note on some scrap paper and shoved it in front of her face:

"THE DOC IS ON THE RUN."

"Thanks, Ms. Roth," Murphy said quickly. "We'll call you if we need anything more. Good-bye."

"So where is this place?" asked Gabe after they hit the highway.

"It's outside of a North Shore town called Castle Danger," she said, studying her notebook containing the directions Elaine Roth gave her.

"Castle Danger?"

"Roth said it's named after the formations along the shore and a ship named *Castle* that sank on the rocks."

"But Jesus. Castle Danger?"

"Look, it could be worse."

"How?"

"We could be headed to Climax."

263

Her cell phone rang. She fished it out of her purse, assuming it was Jack or her mother, and quickly answered it. "Paris Murphy here," she said.

"Hello, lover."

She shivered. "How did you get my phone number?"

"You really shouldn't leave your bills out for anyone to see," he said, his voice dripping with smug pleasure at catching her off guard. "Someone could steal your charge-account numbers."

"I'll be more careful next time," she said. "Won't let any scum into my kitchen."

He laughed. "I miss you already, and we've only been apart twelve hours."

"Then why don't you stop and turn around, save us all a long road trip?"

"Can't do that," Michaels said. "I'm tempted to slow down so you can catch up. On the other hand, I don't want to make this too easy."

"Easy would be boring," she said.

"I assume you're already on the interstate," he said.

"Yeah. Coming up," she said.

"I'll put the coffee on," he said, and hung up.

THIRTY-FOUR

The bright Saturday-morning sun quickly burned off the gray mist. Michaels looked below to his right as he entered Duluth from Interstate 35, taking in the city's industrial area and the harbor beyond it: massive ships coming and going with their cargo. Grain elevators. Railroad tracks. Steam pouring from factory stacks. Small, working-class homes in muted colors huddled under towering power lines. Out of Duluth, the highway hugged the Lake Superior shoreline, crossing the rivers running down to the lake. Hardwoods and pines punctuated the shore and the adjacent ridgeline.

He pulled into the marina before stopping at the cabin; his sailboat was still there. It didn't look like it had been taken out since he'd last used it and that angered him. If they weren't out on the boat, why the hell weren't they answering the phone?

The cabin was forty miles north of Duluth outside Castle Danger. The summer home sat atop a hill overlooking the lake. Michaels pulled the Porsche down the driveway; his mother-in-law's silver Mercedes sat the end of the drive. They must be home. He parked behind the Mercedes, yanked off his sunglasses and stepped out of the car.

"Would you look at this shit!" he said aloud. The grounds were low-maintenance by design. Giant hosta lined either side of the driveway with clumps of orange daylilies and yellow black-eyed Susans. Native evergreen and oak trees required nothing in the way of attention. The only real maintenance necessary was lawn care. Rather than hire a garden service, Jennifer insisted they pay some neighbor boys to cut the grass. Apparently she hadn't bothered calling them. The lawn hadn't been touched since he'd left two weeks earlier.

He thought back to that week he had spent at the cabin with his wife and her mother. He'd drunk too much—parts of it were completely obliterated from his memory. He could summon blurry images and faint words to fill in a few of the blanks. He and his wife had had a fight his last night at the cabin. A big one. It started in the house, spilled out into the yard and ended up in the carriage house. Her mother walked in on it. Then the three of them were yelling. What was it about? Something about a bill. He remembered holding it in his hand. A fight over a bill sounded reasonable. She was always spending too much. There was something else, wasn't there?

The front door was unlocked and slightly ajar. That didn't feel right. He pulled the gun out of his pocket, pushed the door open and walked into the house. He stood still in the foyer, listening. Silence. He called out their names. Nothing. He walked through the house filled with arts-and-crafts pieces from the early 1900s. The thump of his shoes on the wood floors seemed amplified by the emptiness of the cabin and stark simplicity of the furniture. He made his way from one room to another.

Almost unconsciously, he ran his hand across the top of an oak sideboard in the dining room. All the dust on his fingers. Strange. Not like his wife to let the housekeeping go like this.

In the study, he critically eyed the surface of a desk that sat under an open window. The early-furniture piece was made of quarter-sawn oak and was one of his favorites, but now the top was marred with water stains. It had rained up at the cabin in the last two weeks and no one had bothered shutting the windows. A breeze pushed out the curtains, made them billow over the desk. He walked over to close the window and looked through it to the water. Whitecaps. A rough day on the lake. He walked into the kitchen. Everything clean, no food left out. He checked the sink. One glass. He picked it up. A Scotch glass, his. Was there any booze left in the cabin? No, he'd finished it all that last night. He set the glass back in the sink and walked out of the kitchen.

His survey of the first floor found nothing missing; there had been no burglars or robbers or other intruders. He slipped the gun back into his pocket and walked upstairs, each footstep producing a creak with its own unique sound. When he reached the top of the stairs, he stopped and again called out their names. No one answered. He inhaled deeply and exhaled slowly. His mind was starting to clear. He continued his solemn inventory of the house, knowing he would not find them but still hoping they were there.

He looked inside his younger daughter's room, her bed mounded with stuffed animals. Children. That struck a cord. The fight had had something to do with children. Had it had to do with his daughters, perhaps some spending on their account? No. That wasn't it.

He walked into the hallway bathroom. Nothing amiss. He pulled back the shower curtain and looked into the stall. Bone-dry, with a spider crawling around a web in one corner. He reached up and swiped it with his hand. They'd been gone long enough for a spider to spin a web. How long does that take? He felt sweat collecting on his forehead. He grabbed some toilet paper and wiped his brow and the back of his neck. He caught his reflection in the mirror. He looked like a lunatic; a lunatic worried about spiders' webs. He dropped the tissue on the counter and quickly walked out of the bathroom, shutting the door behind him.

He poked his head inside each of the other bedrooms. Nothing seemed out of place. All the beds were made. Jennifer did the beds herself, as soon as everyone was up. She said she felt her home was in order if the beds were all made, and they had to have hospital corners.

Hospital. The argument had something to do with a hospital. Was he spending too much time at the clinic? No, she didn't give a shit about that. Something else. It would come to him.

He stopped in the doorway of the master bedroom. Out of the corner of his eye he saw Bee sitting on the edge of the mattress, waiting for him. "Come," she said through her mouth painted with pink lipstick and blood. "Come, Buzzy." He turned his head quickly and she was gone from the bed. "Leave me alone, Mom," he said tiredly. "Fucking leave me alone." He turned away from the bedroom and went back downstairs.

As he walked through the kitchen toward the back door, a piece of paper caught his eye. A bill or statement sitting on the library table by the back door. He reached for it and paused briefly before picking it up. He knew what it was now; it was a bill from a medical clinic. The fight came back.

It wasn't a miscarriage. His wife had aborted their third child, his son, at a Duluth clinic during a vacation at the cabin with Elaine. She had planned to intercept the bill when it arrived in the cabin mail, but he found it first.

"I'm forty," she said. "I'm too old to have another baby."

"I'm tired," she said. "You're never around to help."

Finally it came out: "I don't want to bring another like you into this world."

That's when he slapped her. She ran from the yard into the carriage house and he followed, drunk and hurt and angry. Behind him ran her hysterical mother, horrified at what her daughter had done, terrified of what he might do in retribution.

Clutching the bill in his right hand, he walked out the back door of the cabin and crossed the yard to the carriage house. He hesitated, and then pushed open the heavy oak side door of the windowless building and stepped inside the blackness. The odor turned his stomach.

He ran back outside, slamming the door shut behind him. He fell to his knees in the overgrown grass and vomited. The acid from his stomach burned his throat on the way up. He continued retching after there was nothing left to bring up, his body vibrating with dry heaves. He didn't bother going back inside the carriage house. He knew they were both dead—his wife and her mother. He had strangled his wife with his bare hands and caved her mother's head in with a shovel as she crouched crying over her daughter's body.

Still kneeling, he dropped his face into the sheet of white paper that had ignited his rampage and wept. He cried not for his loss, for even now he could not pretend he had ever loved her. He cried not for the aborted son, for the child was an abstract thought or dream fragment, and not an infant he had held and loved. He wept only for his own lost body and soul. He was doomed to life in prison and an eternity in hell. It was one thing to kill a collection of whores and sluts and leave their bodies in anonymous public places; that left open the possibility that the acts could be blamed on random strangers. But in his murderous rage, he had sloppily killed his wife and her mother and left them to rot under his own roof. In his intoxicated state, he had even cut his wife's blond hair as a souvenir, adding it to the collection of hair he had tucked away in the hatbox. The evidence against him would be overwhelming. He had handed the cops everything they needed to lock him away forever. He was a drunken idiot and a weakling.

"Stupid! Stupid! Stupid!" he chanted through his sobs.

In his mind, the buzzing drowned out his own cries.

Minutes passed. He wiped his eyes with the sleeves of his shirt and slowly rose to a standing position. He dropped the balled-up medical bill into the tall grass. He heard the crashing swells of the lake, and it beat back the buzzing in his head. He shut his eyes and listened, deliberately slowing his panic-stricken breathing to match the calmer pace of the pulsating surf. "I can still do it," he whispered.

He opened his eyes again and started pacing. "Okay. What are my options?" he muttered. "What? What? What?" He paced until he left a flat rectangle in the tall grass. He briefly considered burying the bodies or dumping them in some isolated area in the surrounding woods for the animals to finish. How about the lake? The cold, deep lake. He concluded that he couldn't bring himself to touch the decomposing corpses. Besides, there would be other evidence not so easily disposed of, such as the blood on the floor of the carriage house. From what he could recall, his mother-in-law hadn't died easily.

He remembered the gun. He pulled it out of his pocket and looked at it, running his fingers along the barrel. One pull on the trigger and it was over. Maybe it was the only way they'd ever stop hounding him, the only way to finally silence the fly. Still, it would be an even bigger sin than the one he had committed here, and where would it leave his daughters? He didn't have the stomach for it; he loved his life too much. No. It wasn't an option, now or ever. He shoved the gun back in his pocket.

He had his wealth and his medical talent. He could fight it or flee, or do both. His relatives could help, and his daughters would forgive him in time. They didn't need to know everything anyway. He could tell them it had been an accident or the work of a burglar. How could he explain away the hair collection? Given enough time, could the cops or someone else find it? No. Impossible. Still, he shouldn't have left it behind.

He checked his watch. He'd wasted valuable minutes stewing over his own stupidity. Now there was simply no time to cover his tracks. They'd be here soon. He didn't bother locking up the house. He didn't give one look back to the carriage house as he rolled the Porsche out of the driveway.

THIRTY-FIVE

"There it is," Murphy said.

"Got it."

The Crown Victoria pulled up behind the silver Mercedes. "Fuckin' quiet," Gabe said.

Michaels was dead meat: while Murphy and Gabe were on the road, Dubrowski and Castro were conducting an early-morning interview. Although he refused to release details of Michaels's confession, Ambrose was able to identify the man who had assaulted him outside the confessional. The chief had given them the green light to pick up Michaels.

"This isn't his," Murphy said, studying the Mercedes as she stepped out of the car. She peered through the windows. Nothing inside. She touched the hood, ran her fingers over it. "Covered with dust. Dammit! He could be on his way to Canada for all we know."

"Easy," Gabe said. "Let's look around, okay?" He moved a bit stiffly as he stepped out of the car. It had been a long, tense drive, with Murphy vocally second-guessing herself the entire way. Gabe had never seen her this edgy.

"Grass hasn't been cut in a while," Murphy said as they walked toward the house with weapons drawn.

"Some cabin," said Gabe, walking a few steps ahead of her. "Where in the hell is the outhouse? I say it ain't a cabin unless there's an outhouse."

"I see a carriage house," she said.

"That doesn't count."

They reached the top of the front steps and saw that the front door was ajar. Murphy raised her eyebrows and looked at Gabe. He gently pushed it open farther with his left hand and walked through. "We don't have a search warrant," Murphy said under her breath, at the same time stepping in directly behind him.

"Fuck the search warrant," whispered Gabe, looking to his left and right as he went inside. "He invited us."

"Yeah, right. For coffee," Murphy said dryly.

"Nice cabin furniture," said Gabe, surveying the dining room.

Both stopped walking and listened. All they heard was the churning lake. Murphy nodded toward the ceiling, indicating that she planned to look around upstairs. Gabe lifted a hand and they split up.

Murphy went up the stairs and methodically walked through the second floor. The door to each bedroom was wide open. No dresser drawers were pulled open. Nothing seemed out of place. Even the beds were all made. Only one door upstairs was shut; she figured it was the bathroom. She put her ear to the door, held her breath and listened. Not a sound. She gently pushed the door open, walked in and looked around. No one inside. She spotted a wad of tissue on the bathroom counter. She picked it up by the edge. Still damp. She sniffed. His sweat and cologne.

"He was here all right," she told Gabe, who was waiting at the bottom of the stairs.

"He must have left in quite a hurry," said Gabe, returning his gun to its holster. "He didn't even take time to lock up."

"Let's quick check out the carriage house," Murphy said. She slipped her Glock back in her purse.

They walked through the kitchen, out the back door and across the yard. On their way to the carriage house, Murphy noticed a flattened strip of grass and a ball of paper in the middle of it. She bent over and picked it up. She unfolded it and studied it as they continued walking to the side door of the carriage house.

"Do you think his wife and his mother-in-law are on the run with him?" asked Gabe as he pushed open the heavy oak door. The overpowering stench on the other side of the door hit them in the face.

"No," Murphy said.

Gabe pulled the collar of his shirt over his nose. Murphy dug a kerchief out of her purse and held it to her face. She felt a chill as she worked her flashlight around the room. "Dammit!" she gasped. "All four of them."

"Bastard!" Gabe growled.

"His daughters," Murphy said. Her light rested on two small figures sprawled next to each other, blond hair matted with dried blood. "He even did his daughters."

Cops and sheriff's deputies were crawling all over the cabin and woods by the time he called. This time, she knew who it was when she answered her cell phone. "Hello, lover," he said smoothly.

She resisted the urge to rip into him, played it as cool as he. "I thought you'd *be* here," she said. "I might go dance with someone else."

Michaels laughed.

Gabe was inside the carriage house with the Lake County coroner and his staff. She was outside the side door, standing in the tall grass with the medical statement in her left hand and the phone in her right. "Quite a mess you left here," she said. "It's so out of character for you not to tidy up after yourself."

"What are you talking about?" he asked.

"Come on," she said. "Don't bullshit me. We looked in the carriage house. I got a whiff of your cologne in the cabin."

"Obsession for Men. Like it?"

273

"I used to," she said.

He laughed again.

"You must have been very hurt, very angry, when you found the clinic bill," Murphy said, trying to muster a sympathetic tone.

"Now you're patronizing me, Paris," he said.

"No, I mean it," said Murphy. She shoved the medical statement into the pocket of her jeans and tromped a path through the tangled grass as she walked back and forth outside the carriage house. She plugged her left ear so she could better hear from her right above the sound of the crashing waves and the television news helicopters overhead. "I don't have kids of my own, so I can only imagine how it would feel to lose a baby. You deserved better." She stopped talking. She heard his breathing. It sounded slightly labored. She deliberated, and then tossed one last piece of well-chosen chum into the water.

"Was it a baby girl?" she asked. "Or was it a boy?"

"A son," he said. "That's why she did it. She didn't want a boy because she knew I did. For years I wanted one. She said she never wanted to bring another like me into the world."

He stopped talking for several seconds and Murphy didn't attempt to fill the silence. She wanted him to do it.

"I hoped to continue the family name," he said. "Wanted someone to share my interests, my life."

"Why did you stay married to her for as long as you did?" she asked.

"It wasn't easy," he said in a low voice. "We stuck it out for Stephanie and Alexandra."

"Your daughters?" she asked.

"Yes," he said. "I'll admit to being a horse-shit husband, but I am not a bad father. I love my daughters . . ."

His voice trailed off with the word *daughters*, as if he were falling asleep midsentence. Murphy thought he sounded tired, genuinely anguished and confused. Very confused. The self-assured sexual demon was slowly slipping beneath the surface, being replaced by a weary, lonely man. "Why don't we meet and talk?" she offered. "How about it? The two of us, over that coffee you promised me."

"Talk about what?" he asked warily.

She took a chance, risked having him hang up on her: "Romann, what does that rhyme mean? Who is the fly and who is the bumblebee?"

His answer was barely audible: "My mother read that rhyme to me."

"Your mother is . . ."

". . . Dead. Killed herself. A long time ago. She was the bee. I pretended she was the bee."

"And you were the fly."

"Yes."

"I'm sorry." Murphy stopped talking for several seconds. Something more had happened between mother and son. Murphy didn't want to probe any deeper. He was already on the edge. She switched gears: "Aren't you tired of all this? Aren't you tired of the sleeping around and paying for sex, the killing and the lying and . . ."

"I want you to know something, Paris," he said, interrupting her. "I want you to know I never meant to . . ."

She pressed the phone hard to her ear. She thought he was going to utter something resembling a confession or an expression of remorse, but he abruptly stopped himself.

"I didn't do it," he said. "I didn't kill them. Someone, a burglar probably, killed the two of them sometime after I left the cabin to go back to . . ."

"Killed the *two* of them?" she asked.

"Yes, dammit! I didn't do it. I don't give a shit if you believe me or not. You don't have anything on me. Nothing."

"We'll see," she said. "We're searching your house back in St. Paul right now."

"I think it's safe to say you won't find a thing," he said.

"What about the hair?" she asked.

He paused, then laughed. "As I said, it's safe to say you'll come up empty-handed."

"We'll catch up with you eventually," she said. "You can't run forever."

"I don't plan to," he said.

"Romann . . ."

"Don't try to find me, Paris," he said. "I'm leaving the country. Remember, *vita brevis, ars longa.*"

"What the hell does that mean?" she asked.

He hung up.

Gabe came out of the carriage house and ran to her side.

"Him?" he asked.

"Who else?" she said.

"We'll trace it," he said.

"He's on his way to Canada," she said. "I know he is." She slipped the cell phone back in her purse.

"We've got checkpoints set up all along the highway," Gabe said. "The sheriff sent deputies to the marina, in case he slips past them to get to his sailboat. We're bringing in some dogs."

"He's smart," she said. "He'll get across and disappear."

"We've alerted the border cops," Gabe said. "We'll get him."

"We're gonna lose him," she said. "We've already lost him."

"Murphy . . ."

"Another thing," she said. "I think he's completely lost it. Completely."

"Shit. What makes you say that? The pile of bodies he left behind?"

"I don't think he has a handle on exactly what went on here," she said, nodding toward the carriage house.

THIRTY-SIX

The phone call was traced to International Falls; Murphy figured he was well into Canada by that night. Dogs. Helicopters. State troopers up and down the highway. Border checks. All turned up nothing. Over Murphy's protests, Christianson told the two detectives to forgo a trip to the border and stay in the Duluth area to help the local cops process the murder scene.

Murphy and Gabe trudged soaked and exhausted up the steps of their cabin at eleven o'clock Sunday, their second night in Castle Danger. The temperature had dropped and the wind had picked up. The drizzle had matured into a steady rain. The cabin was one of six that sat atop a steep hill at the water's edge. The collection of log homes was the only tourist accommodation in Castle Danger. Gabe and Murphy had an end cabin, with the woods on one side of them. By the time they'd come in for the night, the interiors of all the other cabins were dark.

The instant she flicked on the lights her cell phone rang; she started and looked at Gabe. "Want me to take it?" he asked, holding out his hand.

She shook her head and reached into her purse for the phone.

Christianson: "You two pull up stakes and come back in the morning," he said.

"Chief?"

"Michaels is long gone and there's no point in you and Gabe hanging around," Christianson said. "The Lake County sheriff can wrap up without you." Murphy thought he sounded exhausted and stressed-out.

"What about Canada?" she asked.

"The authorities there have a handle on it," he said.

"The hell they do," she said. "Let me and Gabe go up."

"Forget about it. I want the two of you back at the station."

"Chief . . ."

"You've got plenty to keep you busy right here," he said. He hung up.

"Fuck," she said. She shoved the phone back in her purse and threw it on a couch. She plopped down next to it and put her face in her hands.

"Murphy?"

"He wants us back in St. Paul," she said through her fingers.

"You okay?"

She lifted her face out of her hands and nodded. "Yeah. Just tired." She rubbed her arms. "Jesus, it's freezing in here. What do you say we start a fire and warm the place up?" She stood up and shuffled over to the stone fireplace along the front-room wall. She pulled some dried, split logs and old newspapers from the wicker basket next to the fireplace. She stacked the logs in the hearth, shoved some newsprint in between a couple of them and struck a match to the paper. "I don't get him," she said as she kneeled in front of the fire.

"Who?"

"Christianson."

"Let it go," Gabe said as he rubbed his wet head with a kitchen towel.

"He's acting like a dick in the biggest case we've ever had, and I'm supposed to let it go."

"Let it go for tonight. We've got a roof over our heads, a roaring fire and a six-pack of beer. What else do we need? I suppose I could have picked up another six-pack, but I figured you weren't a big beer drinker so . . ."

"Gabe, never mind the beer," she said, grabbing a poker out of the basket to jab the logs. "We forgot the food. I don't know about you, but I haven't eaten all day. I'm starving."

"I'm kind of hungry, too," he said, tossing the towel in the sink. "I'll run out for pizza." He grumbled as he checked his pants pockets for the keys to the Crown Victoria. "I suppose I should fill up the tank while I'm in town, too." He walked through the kitchen.

"If you smoke in the car, roll down the windows," she yelled after him.

"It's raining out," he said.

"Fine," she said. "Go." She waved him away. He exited out the cabin door, shutting it tightly behind him.

She propped the poker against the wall and stayed kneeling in front of the fire. She shut her eyes and listened to the surf as the blaze baked her face. She concentrated, trying to read the lake's rhythm. It seemed every seventh wave was a big one that dashed against the bedrock beneath the cabin. She counted again. Yes. Every seventh one. Then she heard a splash that seemed out of sync. Perhaps she only imagined there was a pattern. She started counting again. On the fifth wave, she heard the door in the cabin's kitchen open. Against her back, she felt a chilly gust from the outside. "What did you forget now, Gabe?" she asked tiredly without opening her eyes.

From behind, a large hand clamped over her mouth and a muscular arm snaked tightly around her waist. She opened her eyes wide and pulled frantically at the arm as she felt herself being yanked quickly to her feet. "Hello, lover," he whispered into her ear. "I dropped by for a visit on my way back home."

He pushed her against the cabin wall next to the fireplace, flattening his body against her back. He bit hard on her neck while she struggled, her angry protests muffled by his left hand.

"Are you cold?" he breathed. "Why not let me warm you from the inside out." He forcefully ground his pelvis into her back. His right hand reached around from behind, slipped under her shirt and bra, and roughly cupped her right breast. "Your nipples are hard, lover," he murmured. "Could it be I excite you?"

She turned her head. He'd colored his hair brown. She writhed and he crushed her even harder against the cabin wall. She felt as if all the oxygen was being pressed out of her body. His breath, reeking of whiskey, made her sick to her stomach. She tried to bite his hand; he was wearing leather gloves. He laughed. "I'm ready for your bullshit this time, Paris," he said hoarsely. "It's useless." He groaned as he rhythmically rubbed his pelvis against her. He released her breast and slipped his right hand into the front of her pants. She felt his fingers under her panties, against her skin. Into her ear he whispered those words. Strange words. "The fly shall marry the bumblebee." She knew he was about to move in for the kill.

He eased his body off hers slightly, giving him more maneuvering space. She discovered that her left arm was loose, no longer pinned tightly against the cabin wall. She reached over with outstretched fingers and snatched the fireplace poker resting against the wall next to their bodies. Gripping it tightly in her fist, she jammed it down as hard as she could into his instep. She felt it hit pay dirt through his athletic shoes.

"Bitch!" he snarled. He released her and stumbled backward. She whirled around, grabbed the poker with both hands and swung, catching the side of his head. He grunted and fell flat on his back.

She raised the poker to stab him in the chest as he was sprawled on the floor, but he wrapped both hands around the tip and yanked it away from her. It clattered to the floor next to him. She tried to run past him, but he rolled onto his stomach and lunged for her ankles. She fell flat on her face with his arms locked around her legs. She extracted one foot and slammed the bottom of her shoe into his face. He howled and grabbed his nose.

She scrambled to her feet, ran through the kitchen and threw open the cabin door. She tripped down the wet, wooden cabin steps and fled through the dark, with the rain cutting her face and the waves roaring in her ears. She ran toward the neighboring cabin, setting her sights on the light cast by a wall sconce mounted next to its door.

He was on her heels. He tackled her and they both tumbled down the rocky hill to the icy water's edge.

He stood up, blood oozing out of his nose. She rose to her knees and tried to stand in the surf, but stumbled. She felt something warm and wet trickling down her forehead. He grabbed her by her hair and pulled her to a standing position, only to slap her hard across the face and knock her back down onto the rocky shore. "Get up, bitch, so I can hit you again!" he hollered above the waves.

"Are you crazy?" she screamed.

"Fuck yeah!" he yelled, and pulled something out of his jacket pocket. Over the sound of the waves, she heard a crack. In the glow cast by a yard light outside her own cabin, Murphy could make out what was in his hands. Her heart sank. A gun.

He fired another shot over her head. "Don't!" she screamed. "Don't shoot!" She managed to get up on all fours on the shore while he stood over her at the water's edge, his back to the lake. Her feet and hands were growing numb.

"Come on," he growled as he pointed the pistol toward her head. "You can do better than this!"

Count the waves, she told herself. Count the waves.

"You disappoint me! This is way too easy."

That was five, she thought.

"I like you like this, on the ground, like a dog! Maybe we should do it doggie style."

That was six, she thought.

"Or maybe I should blow your fucking brains out!"

She paused patiently. Now! she told herself. She charged forward like a linebacker and rammed him hard below the knees as the seventh wave roared up on shore behind him. Between the force of the wave and her hit, he lost his footing and toppled down into the water. She heard a thud and hoped his head had hit a rock. She sprinted away as the surf boiled over him.

As she crawled up the rocky hill in the rain, blood dripping from a gash in her forehead, Murphy prayed that Michaels had drowned.

THIRTY-SEVEN

They found a beat-up truck down the road from the log-cabin resort. Michaels had driven up to International Falls after fleeing Castle Danger, and then swung back down through the Iron Range, trading in the Porsche along the way. Murphy and Gabe couldn't figure out why he'd returned, other than for revenge.

She was at work by Thursday, with stitches in her forehead.

"Nothing," Murphy said, hanging up the phone.

"That's not a surprise," Gabe said. "Superior doesn't burp up bodies until it's good and ready. Don't worry. Lake County said they'd call us and they will."

She stood up and walked to Gabe's desk. The dark rings under her eyes troubled him. "You came back too soon," he told her.

"I'm fine, really."

"Still having nightmares?" he asked in a low voice.

"No," she said.

"He's gone, Murphy. You have to believe that."

"He's resourceful," she said.

"He's dead," Gabe said.

"He knows the North Shore," she said. "He knows how to swim."

"He knows. He knows. He knows. Now all Michaels knows is the bottom of the lake." Gabe stood up, grabbed her by the elbow and pulled her toward the conference room. Castro and Dubrowski, both standing by the water cooler, watched them go.

"She's losing it, I tell ya," Castro said, shaking his head.

"Paranoid," said Dubrowski. .

Gabe steered her into the conference room ahead of him. He saw Castro and Dubrowski staring and whispering. He flipped them the bird and shut the door.

"Why won't you believe?" Gabe asked.

"He could be hiding," she said.

"We looked, the cops up there looked," he said.

"So where's the body?" she asked. She folded her arms across her chest. "Show me the body."

"He's fish food," Gabe said. He sighed and sat down on one of the chairs. He shut his eyes and ran his fingers through his hair. "You're giving him way too much credit. He wasn't sane enough to save himself. He was flipped out. All that fly and bee bullshit."

"Crazy people can't swim?" she said, and walked over to the windows to look outside at the morning sun ricocheting off the cars on the freeways.

"You need some time off; you need a vacation," Gabe said. "Why don't you and Jack take a little trip? You've been talking about going back to New Orleans. Throw some shit into a suitcase and go."

"Louisiana in June?"

"Okay. Bad idea this time of year." He looked at her back, expecting her to turn around and say something. She stood staring out the windows. "How about you two driving to my fishing shack in Hayward and kicking back on the lake for a week?" he offered. "I've got electricity up there now. Television. VCR."

She didn't answer.

"You and your hubby could rent some porn flicks and screw your brains out."

No response.

"Paris!"

"Huh? What did you say?"

"Might as well use some of that comp time you've got on the books before Slick gets on your ass about it," he said. "How many weeks have you got?"

A knock at the door. "Yeah?" Gabe yelled.

Castro opened it a crack and poked his head into the room. "Chief wants you guys. Pronto."

"Speak of the devil," Gabe said, getting up from the chair. "Murphy . . ."

"Coming," she said, turning around and following him out.

"Wrongful death?" Gabe sputtered. "You have fucking got to be kidding!"

"We knew this lawsuit was coming," said Christianson. "They're trying to clear up the family name."

"What about the family he slaughtered?" asked Gabe. "What about his wife and her mother and those little girls?"

"Michaels's relatives are claiming we got it all wrong, that someone else killed them. A burglar or whatever," said Christianson. "They're launching their own investigation."

Murphy laughed. "Their *own* investigation?" she said. "That'd be hilarious if it wasn't so disgusting. They're buying Michaels an alibi. Postmortem. I could puke."

Gabe stood up and walked back and forth in front of Christianson's desk. "Don't let them near the house," he said.

"It's still sealed tight," said Christianson. "I just wish we'd found more inside. We can certainly pin the priest's assault on Michaels, and of course the attack on Murphy. The deaths in Castle Danger are not our problem."

"'Not our problem,'" Gabe said dryly.

"You heard me correctly, Nash. *Not our problem!*" Christianson snapped. "We needed more to tie Michaels to the murders here and across the river."

"What about Finch's crucifix?" asked Gabe. "What about . . ."

"The hair," said Murphy. "We needed the hair, and we didn't find it."

"No question the hair would have clinched it," said Christianson.

Christianson's secretary knocked once and opened the door. "Your wife's on line two. Says it's urgent."

Christianson frowned and put his hand on his phone. "I have to take this," he said to Gabe and Murphy. "We'll talk more later."

Murphy and Gabe walked out of the chief's office. "You're right about one thing," Gabe grumbled in the hallway.

"That one thing would be?"

"Slick acting like a dick on this case. It's way more than his usual dick behavior. 'You heard me correctly, Nash.' Fuck him."

"Who died?" asked Castro as they walked into Homicide. Gabe ignored him and sat down at his desk.

"Too many loose ends," mumbled Murphy as she sat down at hers. "Too many holes." She grabbed the file, staring at the tab before opening it. Michaels, A. Romann. She flipped it open and shuffled through the mound of paper inside of it. She found a scrap of paper and puzzled over it. Four words. It suddenly came to her when she'd scribbled them. She picked up the phone and punched in a number.

"Sister Ella Marie?"

"How are you feeling, Paris?"

"Fine. Better," Murphy said. "Sister, how's your Latin these days?"

"You should know better than to ask that of an old school nun," DuBois said, laughing.

"Well, mine's a little rusty," Murphy said. She struggled to read her own handwriting. "What does *vita brevis ars . . .*"

"*Vita brevis, ars longa,*" said DuBois.

"That's it," Murphy said.

"Life is short, art is long," said DuBois.

"What the hell does that mean?" Murphy asked.

"Pardon?" said DuBois.

"Sorry, Sister. Does that phrase have some deeper meaning?"

"It means what it implies," DuBois said. "That art outlives humanity."

"Art outlives humanity," Murphy repeated.

"What's this all about?"

"Tell you later. It has to do with a case."

"Sounds interesting."

"That's one word for it. Well, thanks, Sister."

"Take care, dear," DuBois said. "Stop by and see me sometime."

"I will. 'Bye," Murphy said, hanging up the phone.

"Art, art, art," Murphy repeated, tapping a pencil on her desk as she stared at the piece of paper cradled in her other hand.

"Hey, Gabe, Murphy, wanna get some lunch?" asked Castro as he headed for the door.

"There's a new Coney Dog joint down the street," said Dubrowski behind him.

Gabe stood up to join them. Murphy waved them off. "Not hungry," she said. "Thanks anyway." She tucked the slip of paper back in Michaels's file and continued paging through the folder. The three men walked out, leaving her alone.

She took the file home with her.

"How's your head doing?" asked Jack.

"Stop asking, would you?" she said. "It's fine."

Murphy and Jack sat on her houseboat deck. Though early evening, it was still warm out. The mosquitoes were thick. A citronella candle burned on the table between their chairs. Murphy grabbed the can of insect repellant and sprayed her legs and arms.

Jack set his beer bottle down on the deck and leaned over from his chair to kiss her. She stiffened. "Baby, what's wrong?" he asked.

She didn't answer, didn't look at him, sipped her wine. "It's those dreams, isn't it?" he asked. "You're still having them."

"I wish you didn't have to go out of town," she said.

"You know I can't get out of this conference," he said. "I'll be back in time for the Fourth."

"Yeah, yeah," she said, finishing her wine.

"Want me to pour you another glass?" he asked.

"You think getting drunk might help?" she asked.

"Can't hurt," he said.

"Then bring it on," she said, lifting her glass.

He poured her another, set down the wine bottle and stood up. "I'm sorry, baby. Gotta go," he said. He bent over and kissed her on the cheek. "If it's a horseshit conference, I'll slide out and take an early flight back."

"Fat chance," she said. He turned and left. She heard his car pull out of the parking lot, and the sound depressed her.

She sipped the wine and watched the river. A party barge floated by. The railing along the deck was strung with blinking white lights. The sound of laughter and music drifted across the water. She kept swatting; the repellant wasn't doing much. "Damn skeeters," she mumbled. She blew out the candle, stood up and went inside with her wine.

She took a long shower, scrubbing hard to get the oily bug dope off her skin. She rested one hand against the shower stall, enjoying the hot water running down her hair and face and body. She thought about picking up the phone and calling him, to talk. She chastised herself for thinking about him. She stood in the shower until the water turned cold. She turned it off, toweled dry and wrapped herself in her robe. She walked over to the phone on her nightstand. She hesitated for an instant and then picked it up. Punched in his number.

"Paris. I was thinking about you. Are you alone?"

"Yes."

"Where's Jack?" asked Erik.

"Chicago. Medical conference."

"He shouldn't leave you alone," he said.

"I'm fine," she said. "He's got a life."

"Do you want me to come over?"

She paused. So tempting. She was lonely and more nervous about the night than she wanted to admit. It would be her first night alone since getting back from Castle Danger.

"Why don't I come get you, if you don't feel right about me spending time there."

"No," she said.

"Then what do you want me to do?" he asked. "Tell me."

She wanted his company but felt guilty, and at the same time resented the guilt itself.

"Paris?"

"Come over." She hung up and tossed the phone at the foot of the bed.

He pushed her down onto the bed and peeled her clothes off so quickly, she didn't have time to help. She took it slower, moving her hands up his chest as she slipped off his T-shirt. She gasped the first time he entered her. "You are so tight," he said appreciatively.

It had been a long time since she had made love to anyone other than Jack; Erik's body seemed so foreign to her, and that made it exciting. They were both athletic, a tangle of tanned and sinewy arms and legs and backs. He lost his hands in her hair. She ran her hands over his back and shoulders. Muscular and smooth.

Her mind was empty and clear as long as they were in motion. When they were finished, it all came rushing back. Fears about Michaels. Fears about her marriage. A new layer of guilt over what she'd just done. She stared at the ceiling as if she were watching some movie only she could see.

"He really did a number on your head, that bastard," Erik said. He was on his side, staring at her troubled face. Her clock radio was turned low, to a jazz station. The sax was barely audible, competing with the sound of a speedboat cruising down the river.

"I'm fine," she said. Her voice was emotionless. She rolled away from him to face the patio window.

"Stop saying that," Erik said. "You sound like a busted tape recording. 'I'm fine. I'm fine. I'm fine.' You aren't fine. Your head is all messed up."

"Nothing's wrong with my head," she said, still facing the window.

"Great. You invite me over, we screw and then I have a conversation with your back. Forget this shit. I don't need this." He sat up and swung his feet over the edge of the bed.

She turned her head. "Where are you going?" she asked, immediately hating how needy that question sounded.

"I think I should leave you and Michaels alone to work out your differences," he said.

"What do you want me to do?" she asked angrily. She sat up in bed.

"Talk about it," he said, swinging his legs back on top of the bed and turning to face her. "Look at me and talk about it. Talk to me."

"Okay, Mr. Therapist. You want to hear it?" she said. She grabbed the pillow from his side of the bed and hugged it in front of her. "I haven't slept well since I got on this case. I wake up in the morning dead tired. When I do sleep, I have these weird-ass dreams. They started even before Castle Danger. Now I have them twice a night, sometimes more. Twisted dreams. He's on top of me, raping me. Did I share enough, or do you want more?"

She tossed the pillow on the floor, swung her legs over the bed and hopped out. She ran into the bathroom and turned on the faucet. She splashed cold water on her face until it felt numb, and then scooped water into her mouth until she felt full. He walked up behind her and slipped his arms around her waist. She resisted the urge to shove his arms off her.

"I'm sorry," he said, his face buried in her neck. "I didn't mean to push you. You're acting so strange, so distracted. I'm worried about you."

She clutched the edge of the bathroom sink to steady herself. "You're right," she said lowly. "I'm not fine, but I don't know how to fix it. I mean, I'm so obsessed I brought the file home. Tell me that isn't sick."

"All right. Then let's use that. Let's sit down and go through the file together," said Erik. "He's not a demon, but you've made him out to be one. Let's pick him apart."

"An autopsy," she said.

He opened a beer and she poured herself another glass of wine. They sat on the bedroom floor—he in his boxers and she in her robe—and rifled through the thick file. Each took possession of a stack of paperwork. For several minutes neither said a word. The patio doors leading to the deck were open. No breeze blew in, but the mosquitoes had thinned out. A motorboat sped by and then another. A busy night on the river.

"Jennifer," said Erik, breaking the silence between them. He took a sip of beer as he held up the sheet of paper.

"What?" asked Murphy. She put down some crime-scene photos.

"I didn't know his wife's name," he said.

"Yeah. Jennifer," she said, grabbing a forensic report.

"His daughters?" he asked.

"Stephanie and Alexandra."

"Oh yeah, here they are," he said, picking up two photos, their most recent school portraits. "Pretty blond girls." He set them down and held up a yellowed newspaper clipping.

"What's this?"

"We have a file on his mother. Found dead in the swimming pool."

"You don't think he killed her, too?"

"No, no. Suicide."

Murphy picked up the wrinkled scrap of paper with the Latin scribbled on it, set it down on the floor in front of her and smoothed it out with her hands. *"Vita brevis, ars longa,"* she mumbled, taking a sip of wine.

"Arthur," Erik said, holding up a copy of Michaels's driver's license.

"What did you say?" she asked.

"Romann was his middle name. His first name was Arthur. Didn't you know that?"

"Yeah. I never gave it much thought. He used the initial. Lots of people go by their middle names because they hate their first."

"All the kids at school would have called him Art the fart," Erik said, chuckling.

"Art," she repeated. She stared at the scrap of paper in front of her and smiled a tight, thin smile. "Life is short, art is long."

"What?" Erik asked.

"He's still alive," she said. "Michaels is still alive."

"Paris?"

"When I talked to him over the phone, after we found the bodies in the carriage house, he told me to remember *'Vita brevis, ars longa.'* That's what he said."

"Forgive me; my high school didn't offer Latin," Erik said. He stared at her.

"It means art outlives us," she said. "Only he didn't mean sculptures and paintings. He meant Art with a capital *A.*"

"Paris. Come on. That is a stretch," Erik said, dropping the papers he'd been studying.

"You don't know him," she said. "I do."

"Did, Paris. *Did.* You *did* know him, and not for that long. Now he's dead! Come on. Give it a rest."

"He faked his own death," she said. "Maybe that's why he came back, so we could see him die."

"He drowned," Erik said. "You're the one who pushed him in!"

"He was a good swimmer," she said. "He could have followed the shoreline and crawled up into the woods."

Erik stared at her incredulously, and his disbelief infuriated her. "Why don't you go home?" she snapped. She stood up. She swayed a bit. Her head was light from the wine and the anger. Her face felt hot, flushed.

"Paris," Erik said, looking up at her from the pile of papers on the floor.

"Go," she said.

He stood up and stepped toward her. He lifted his arms to grab her shoulders and she pushed them down. "Please," she said. She picked his jeans and shirt up off the floor and threw them at him. "Get dressed and go home."

This time the bright, otherworldly light was missing. The room was dark, a change from the earlier visitations. The only thing that was casting light was his face as he bent over her. As before, she couldn't make out his features right away. They were a blur. He again flashed a knife in front of her face, slipped the blade under the bodice of her thin nightgown and slit it down the middle with one pass. He crawled on top of her and turned his head to one side, burying his face in her hair. This time he wore no clothing, nothing to melt away as in the previous dreams. The weight of his body was unbearable. She could feel his heart beating, matching the rhythm of her own.

She struggled to see his features. "Look at me," she said. "Look at me." He laughed into her hair; his breath felt like steam from a hot iron. She fought hard. The hardest she'd ever fought. She beat his back with her fists and clawed at it with her nails. This time it seemed to work. He lifted his body off hers slightly, and she was relieved. She looked into Michaels's gray eyes. But they weren't human eyes. They were the bug eyes of a fly. He put his mouth on her cheek and licked her. She could smell him, smell his cologne.

She screamed and bolted upright in bed, awake and alert. She could still smell him. She felt the side of her face. Wet, from his tongue. He's really here, she thought. He's on my boat.

She was dizzy and her head was throbbing. Too much wine. She fumbled around the top of her nightstand for her cell phone. She knocked over an empty wineglass. It shattered on the wood floor. She heard muffled ringing. On her hands and knees she crawled around on the bed until she found it buried in the covers. She froze with it in her hand, then slowly lifted the phone to her ear.

"Hello," he said. "Sorry to wake you from such a dead sleep."

"Where are you?" she asked. "Where?" With her free hand she yanked open the nightstand drawer and reached inside for her purse. Not there.

He laughed. "Come find me," he said. "I want you to find me."

She slid off the bed and went for the light switch, but stopped. This was her boat. She could get around better in the dark than he, but she needed her gun. She threw the phone on the bed and ran toward the closet. She tripped over his file in the middle of the floor, scattering its contents. She yanked open the closet door and felt around for her purse. Still couldn't find it. She felt along the closet walls, pressing against her suits and dresses and knocking them down. No one there. She needed a weapon. Something. Her hand touched a wooden hanger. She wrestled it from a knot of clothes. Better than nothing.

She picked up the phone. "Where are you?" she said. He laughed again. "Why aren't you dead?" she asked. He stopped laughing; he didn't like that question.

Murphy ran down the steps to the galley. She heard a paddleboat go by. Clearly heard it. She looked into the living room. The patio doors to the deck were wide open. She was sure she'd shut them before going to bed. She slowly walked toward the open doors, looking to her left and right around the galley and living room.

She remembered the wooden dowel she kept in the track of the patio doors for extra security. She set the phone and the wooden hanger on the galley counter. She walked over to the patio door, bent

294

over and picked up the rod sitting on the floor next to the track. The pole was the size of a broom handle; it felt good and solid in her hand. She stepped out onto the deck. She gripped the rod with both hands, ready to swing it like a bat. The moon illuminated the deck; there was no one there. She heard thumping along the boat's waterline. Murphy held her breath, walked to the railing and looked down. A large log was floating in the black water, bumping against the boat. Slowly, she exhaled. She stepped back inside, shut the door behind her and locked it. She retrieved the phone and raised it to her ear.

"Still there, Michaels?" Murphy said.

"This is taking way too long," he said. "I'm getting bored with this game. Maybe I should come find you. Come fuck you. Fuck you hard, the way you like it."

"Don't do me any favors . . . Art," she said. "Or should I call you fly boy?"

"You're too smart for your own good," he said. "Don't you know dumb women live longer? It's a medical fact."

"Why did you come back?" she asked.

"Be it ever so humble . . . ," he said. He laughed loudly. He sounded different, more unhinged, even hysterical. He kept laughing. She took the phone away from her ear to try to hear where his laugh was coming from. Nothing. She looked up at the ceiling, straining to listen. She thought she heard creaking. Was he still in her bedroom? She lifted the phone back to her ear. He'd finally stopped laughing. She heard only his breathing. Keeping the phone pressed to her ear, she set the dowel down on the galley counter and pulled open a kitchen drawer. She felt around until her fingers touched the handle of her largest knife. She lifted it out.

She took the stairs back up. She walked slowly, with the phone in one hand and the knife in the other. When she reached her bedroom, she threw the cell phone on the bed and walked into the master bathroom, her right arm raised and ready to stab. With her left hand she grabbed the edge of the closed shower curtain. She took a breath and ripped it down. Plastic curtain rings clattered to the floor. No one there.

She walked to the patio doors leading to the deck off her bedroom. She grabbed the handle and slid the door open. She poked her head outside. Nothing. She slid the door shut and locked it.

She reached for her phone on the bed, lifted it to her ear. He'd hung up. She dropped the knife on the bed and punched in Gabe's phone number. Her hands were shaking. "Gabe," she whispered into the phone.

"Murphy?"

"He's on my boat."

"What?" asked Gabe.

"Michaels is on my boat," she said. "Or at least he was."

"Be right over," he said.

She heard something downstairs. Footsteps. She picked the knife up again. "Hurry," she said into the phone. "Please." She heard Tripod barking next door; stranger on the dock.

Every light in the houseboat was on and Murphy's living room and galley were filled with plainclothes and uniformed cops. They'd gone through every closet and cabinet, looked under and behind furniture. They'd roused neighbors on each side of Murphy to make sure the caller hadn't taken refuge on their decks. They'd waved their flashlights under the cars in the parking lot and tromped around the bushes lining the lot.

Murphy and Gabe stood alone in her bedroom. He was in sweatpants, sandals and a white T-shirt turned inside out. "Are you sure someone was here?" Gabe asked. He saw Michaels's file and its contents scattered in the middle of her bedroom floor and crouched down to pick it up.

"What a stupid question!" she snapped.

He sighed, threw the folder on the end of her bed and looked at

296

her. Barefoot and in her robe. Hair like a nest of black snakes around her face. Then there was the knife on her bed. The broken wineglass next to the nightstand. The torn shower curtain in a heap in the bathroom. What the hell was she doing with Michaels's file all over her bedroom floor? He didn't even want to ask. If she wasn't a cop, thought Gabe, she'd be cuffed in the back of a squad headed to the psyche ward.

She walked out onto the deck and he followed her. "You've been having these dreams," Gabe said. He waved a moth away from his face. "Mix in a little too much wine and that bedtime reading you brought home from the cop shop, and you've got a ghost lurking around your boat."

"I did not dream this up," she said. "I am not drunk and I never said it was a goddamn ghost! Didn't you hear a single word I said? Michaels was here. Michaels. On my boat. He left and ran down the dock. Tripod was barking."

Sandeen walked into the bedroom and through the open patio doors. "Bergen found your husband's cell phone in the parking lot," he said. "Figure some pervert stole it from your hubby's car and then used it to rattle you. The asshole hit redial and lucked out, maybe watched you while he was jacking off in the bushes. Probably dropped it and ran when he heard us coming."

"So the dog was barking at someone in the lot," said Gabe.

"He doesn't bark unless there's a stranger on the dock," she said.

Sandeen's eyes met Gabe's.

"Get prints," she said. She turned her back on the two men and looked out at the Mississippi. She knew what they were thinking; she knew what she looked like. Cops laugh and tell stories when they get back to the station from calls like this. Calls where crazy women living alone see bogey men in their bedrooms.

"Sure. We'll get prints," Sandeen said tiredly. "Whatever you want, Murphy. Whatever you say. It's your show." Sandeen left them alone on the deck and went back downstairs.

"I know it was him," she said, as much to herself as to Gabe. She suddenly realized that she had a hangover. She leaned against the railing with both hands and focused on the downtown lights lining the waterfront across the river. "He was here, on this boat. He didn't get the phone from Jack's car. He took it right off my kitchen counter."

"Get a grip, Murphy," Gabe said sternly, folding his arms across his chest. "There's no way in hell it was Michaels who called you. No fucking way. You got an obscene phone call, a heavy breather getting his rocks off. That's all."

"You're wrong," she said. Gabe sighed, but didn't say anything in response.

She brushed a mosquito off her cheek. The night air felt like a sauna and smelled like dead fish. Under her robe, she could feel beads of sweat trickling down between her breasts. She felt like taking another shower, a cold one.

"Let's check his house tomorrow," she said.

"Why?" Gabe asked.

"Be it ever so humble," she said softly.

"What?"

"Humor me," she said.

"Jesus. You don't think he's there, do you? " Gabe asked.

"I think he might have stopped there, tried to get in, retrieve something. I'm sure he's long gone after tonight's little game. He'd be too smart to hang around. If we can find evidence that he's alive . . ."

"He's not," Gabe interrupted.

She took her hands off the rail, squared her shoulders and walked inside. Gabe followed her. "If we don't find shit, I'll keep my paranoid delusions to myself from now on," she said. "Deal?"

"Deal," Gabe said. "Now go back to bed. Try to get some sleep. I'll have a couple of uniforms hang in the parking lot until their shift ends."

"Don't bother," she said. "Thank everyone for me and then get them the hell off my boat. Tell them the nutty, drunk bitch has settled down." She shut the patio door, locked it and gave it a pull to make sure it was locked.

Gabe started to leave, but stopped at the foot of the bed to pick up the knife. "How about I put this away for you?" he said, eyeing the massive blade.

"Top drawer, to the left of the sink," she said. She walked over to the broken wineglass and bent down to pick up the pieces. The room started spinning. She grabbed the edge of the nightstand and closed her eyes.

"Did you find your gun?" he asked.

"Yeah," she said, without looking up.

"Where was it?"

"In my purse, under the bed. Right where I left it. Why? You want to take that away from me, too?"

"Don't be a smart ass," Gabe said. "What about Michaels's file? Through with it?"

"Take it," she said. "I've had enough of him for tonight."

"Right about that," Gabe mumbled. He picked the folder up, tucked it under his arm and walked down the stairs.

"Lock the living-room patio door on your way out and put that wood rod in the track," she yelled after him. "It's on the kitchen counter." She tossed the broken glass into a wastebasket next to the nightstand and then grabbed the edge of the wastebasket, fearing she was going to vomit. She stood up slowly and held her forehead.

Bergen was waiting at the bottom of the stairs, smirking. Gabe wanted to punch him. "Jesus Christ," Bergen whispered, eyeing the blade in Gabe's hand. "Look at the size of that mother."

Gabe threw the knife in a drawer and dropped the wood rod into the patio door track.

Bergen shook his head. "A butcher knife. A bat. What the fuck did she need us for?"

"Shut the hell up and let's go," Gabe said.

"What's that file under your arm?" asked Bergen, following Gabe outside.

"None of your business."

THIRTY-EIGHT

"U nreal," said Gabe. "The crap keeps raining down on us."

Murphy walked into the chief's office twenty minutes after her partner. "Thanks for joining us," Christianson said, looking at his watch.

"Sorry," she said, sinking into a chair next to Gabe. She'd overslept and gotten to work late. Her head ached. All day she'd felt like her limbs were stuck in low gear no matter how fast she tried to move them.

"You didn't miss anything," said Gabe. "Chief was getting to the good stuff. The part where we drop our pants and get fucked in the ass."

Murphy raised her eyebrows; Gabe usually kept his tongue tamer around the chief. She looked across the desk at Christianson. They'd asked to meet with the chief to propose another sweep through Michaels's mansion.

"They want access," said Christianson. "Family heirlooms, legal documents and the like. We can't keep them out forever."

"Who wants access?" asked Murphy. "What are we talking about here?"

"Michaels's relatives. We're letting them into the house on Monday," said Gabe, glaring at Christianson.

"The hell we are," she said. Christianson looked down and shuffled some papers on his desk, avoiding her eyes.

"Yeah," Gabe said, slapping his hands on the arms of his chair. "It's a regular shit tornado."

Christianson looked at his watch again. "Are we finished? It's almost seven. I'd like to get some dinner tonight."

"I'd say we're finished," Gabe said. He stood up and walked out, slamming the door behind him.

Murphy stared up at the ceiling, willing herself to stay civil. She returned her gaze to Christianson. She leaned toward his desk and spoke in a low tone. "Who in the hell is coming down on you? Huh? One of those assholes up on the hill? The mayor and his cronies? Who?"

He didn't answer.

"God dammit!" she said, slamming her hand on his desk. "We've got a right to know who's pulling the strings."

He set the papers down on his desk, folded his hands together and looked at her. Murphy thought his face looked as pasty as the papers on his desk, and wondered if it was the case that was grinding him down or something else. "Murphy, they can get a court order," he said.

"Let them," she said, throwing up her hands. "Force them to get one. It'll buy us some time."

"Time to do what?" he asked.

"Give us one more shot at the house, one more pass through to see if we can find something," she said.

"The hair?" he asked.

"Maybe," she said.

He lowered his eyes and fingered the same stack of papers, straightening them so the edges lined up. "Nash tells me you think Michaels is still alive, that you got a call from him last night. Maybe even a visit," he said. "Hard to believe, but a lot of things about this case have been tough to swallow. Really tough."

A knock.

"Yes," he said tiredly. Christianson's secretary poked her head into the room. "Your wife again. Line three."

"I'm on my way home."

"She says it's important."

He glanced at the blinking light on his phone. "I don't give a damn what she says. Tell her I'm in a meeting."

"I did, sir. She says it can't wait."

"Yes it can," he said sharply. The secretary closed the door.

Christianson reached across his desk and picked up the photo of his sons. He studied it for a few seconds, running his fingers over the edges of the frame. He sighed heavily and set the photo down so it faced Murphy. "Good-looking boys, aren't they?" said Christianson. "Got my damn lantern jaw. That hair, though, that's my wife's side of the family. All the kids on her side have it."

She frowned, thrown off guard by his sudden self-absorption. She picked up the photo and studied the three youths, all in hockey jerseys. All blond. All with familiar gray eyes. She inhaled sharply and set the frame down, turning it away from her.

"How could a father do what he did?" Christianson asked, rubbing his forehead with his hand. "To kill the mother of your children, their grandmother, and . . ." His voice trailed off. He swiveled around to face the window.

Murphy stared at the back of the chair, her mouth open. It took her a full minute to form the question. "How is she related to him?"

"Cousins," he said, still facing the window. "First cousins. Very close. She refuses to believe Buzzy . . ."

"Buzzy?"

"That's her nickname for him. Buzzy. She refuses to believe he did it. Absolutely refuses. Others in the family admit it's possible, probable. They saw his temper. The drinking. Of course it doesn't matter to them; they still want a whitewash job. Family reputation comes before everything. My wife, she's different. She sincerely believes he is . . . was . . . incapable of murder."

"Chief . . . ," she said.

"I didn't know the guy very well, and didn't care to," Christianson continued. "The little I did know of him, I didn't like. He was a mean drunk. Told my wife she married a loser. Told her that at our wedding reception, and he was one of the groomsmen. Bastard. He brags that his family got me to St. Paul, into this office. That's bullshit."

"You didn't need to tell me all that," Murphy said. She stared at her fingernails and then the carpet. She wished Gabe would come back in, the secretary would walk through or the phone would ring. This was more than she ever wanted to know about her boss.

"I didn't handle this case any differently," he said.

"I know you didn't," she said a little too quickly.

A long silence. She picked the photo up again and looked at it. Very handsome boys. Big grins, like they'd just won a game. Would they grow up to be drunks, wife beaters or worse? Would it be inherited, passed down like the blond hair and the money?

"Chief?" She set the photo down. "Ben?"

Christianson swung his chair back around to face her.

"Ben," she said. "How do you want your sons to grow up? How do you want them to turn out? Like him or like you? You can stop them."

Christianson shook his head.

"It's in your power to stop them," she said. She spun his nameplate around on his desk so it faced him. "You're the chief of police. You've got the power. Not them."

"Power," he repeated. A long silence. He was thinking. His eyes went from the photo to the nameplate. A grim smile stretched across his face. "You and Nash take as many people as you need and get over there. Do it now. Spend the weekend there if you must. I'll sign off on the overtime. Come next week I'll be clean out of excuses and they'll have shopped around for the right judge."

"Can't you stall them any longer than that?" she asked. She stood up to leave.

"It would be like stepping in front of a freight train," he said. "I don't have enough power to survive that."

They took an unmarked squad, one of the last cars in the lot. The thing was a hot box and the air conditioner was busted. Gabe turned on the ignition and rolled down all the windows. "What'd the chief say?" asked Gabe. "How'd you get him to go along with this?"

"Tell you later," she said. She slapped a light on the hood. "Come on. Let's rock. It's the pedal on the right."

"What's the rush?"

"This operation's got a time limit and I want a good head start," she said. He squealed out of the parking lot and headed toward the freeway. The sun was a low, orange glow on the horizon. She looked in the rearview mirror as they got on the Interstate 94 ramp headed west. "Where's the rest of our crew?"

"Castro had to take a quick pee," Gabe said. "Bladder infection."

"Why is everyone sharing with me today?" Murphy asked.

"Huh?"

"Never mind."

Traffic was heavy with the start of the weekend. They took the Lexington Avenue exit and headed south toward Summit. Murphy kept checking the rearview mirror, wondering when the other Crown Victoria would materialize behind them. She figured Castro and Dubrowski would be help enough, but she changed her mind when they got to the house.

"The tape," Murphy said. They stood at the bottom of the steps leading to the side door off the driveway.

"Yeah. Yeah. I see it," Gabe said. "Maybe it fell off."

"Bullshit," she said. She drew her gun and started walking up the steps, but Gabe put a hand on her shoulder.

"Keep your ass right where it is until I radio for backup," he said.

Gabe ran back to the car. Castro and Dubrowski pulled up behind him and got out. Dubrowski walked up the driveway.

305

"What's the story?" asked Castro, leaning into the open passenger window.

"I called for backup," Gabe said.

"Why the hell do we need backup?" Castro asked.

"Tape's broke," Gabe said, hanging up the set.

Castro pulled his head out of the window and started for the house. "So where's Murphy?" he asked.

Gabe looked through the open car window and saw Dubrowski standing alone at the bottom of the steps, eyeing the loose yellow tape.

"Perfect!" Gabe said. He jumped out of the car, slammed the door shut and drew his gun. "She went inside by herself. Damn her."

Michaels's house was warm and quiet. With the place sealed tight for days, the air had grown musty and dead. It smelled like the inside of an old purse.

She quickly surveyed the modernized kitchen and saw there was no place for him to hide amid the open stainless-steel shelves. She kept walking, looking to her left and right and back to her left. The early-evening sun wasn't strong enough to filter through the heavy curtains that hung from every window on the first floor. The house was dim, getting dark, but she decided not to turn on any lights. The thick oriental carpets cushioned her footsteps. When her shoes hit expanses of bare wood, she walked a little slower. She entered the cavernous dining room. One long gleaming table, big enough for a banquet, surrounded by more than a dozen chairs. She bent over and looked under the table. A forest of chair legs. She stood up straight and looked around the room. The drapes. She lifted them away from the wall and looked behind them. Nothing but cobwebs.

She heard the floorboards squeak behind her. Her feet froze. She held her breath and turned, gun ready. Gabe, with Dubrowski and Castro right behind him. All had their guns drawn. Gabe looked pissed. He pointed to the floor. He wanted her to stay put, until backup arrived. She shook her head and pointed to the ceiling. Gabe shook his head, forming a silent "No" with his mouth. She ignored him and walked toward the staircase.

"Fuck," Gabe said under his breath. "Let's do it." He motioned Dubrowski and Castro toward the library and followed Murphy up to the second floor. By the time they reached the top of the stairs, they could hear more sets of feet on the first floor. Their backup.

"Goddamn about time," Gabe whispered to Murphy. He was at her elbow. She tipped her head toward the first door on the right. He nodded. Both had their guns raised as she gently pushed the door open with one hand. They figured it was one of the girls' bedrooms. Small, square and yellow. Posters of female soccer players taped to the walls. Poster of a shirtless male guitarist taped to the ceiling over the frilly bed. Gabe opened the closet. A solid wall of clothes. He shut it. Murphy got on her belly and looked under the bed. Dust bunnies. Soccer shoes. A flattened soccer ball. A stack of teen magazines. A lone stuffed animal, a loon. Murphy stood up and motioned toward the door. He walked out ahead of her.

The hallway bathroom. Gabe and Murphy stepped around the broken pieces of mirror. Crime-scene investigators from the first search of the house left the shards where they were. "What the hell was this about?" Gabe said, speaking low, scanning the mess on the floor.

"Maybe he didn't like what he saw," she said, looking behind the shower curtain.

The next door opened to a grim guest bedroom, a furniture museum with matching Victorian pieces that were heavy, dark, deeply carved. Even the velvet bedspread looked like a dusty antique. "Welcome to Our Home" read a needlepoint pillow on the bed. This time she checked the closet and he looked under the bed.

"Nothing," he whispered, standing up.

"Out-of-season coats," she said, gently shutting the closet door.

"Murphy," he whispered as they walked down the hallway to the next bedroom. "I don't think there's anyone home. This is another wild . . ."

"Don't say it," she said.

Uniformed and plainclothes cops went through every room in the house, from the basement to the attic, and checked the carriage house and the yard.

"Murphy. Thanks for another exciting evening," said Bergen, holstering his gun. He stood in the kitchen between Murphy and Gabe, under a ceiling rack of hanging pots.

"Drop dead," she said.

"Hey, I appreciate the overtime," Bergen said. "I'm working on a new motor for the bass boat." He walked through the side door, following a stream of other cops who were laughing or grumbling on their way outside.

"No roaming Romann," said Dubrowski, shuffling tiredly into the kitchen. "Not even his ghost."

"The tape was busted when we got here," said Murphy.

"I know it was," said Dubrowski. "Probably fell off. That shit happens." He holstered his gun and looked at the kitchen wall clock. "Hey, my shift is long over. It's Friday night, a payday and life is good. Want to grab a brew?"

"Usual place?" Gabe asked. Dubrowski nodded. "We'll meet you there," Gabe said. Dubrowski followed the line out the door, leaving Murphy and Gabe standing alone in the kitchen.

"Thank you," she said quietly.

"No problem," he said, snapping his holster shut.

"Sorry I shook you off in the dining room," she said.

"It worked out."

"You're a man of few words tonight," she said.

"I'm wiped out," he said, digging in his pockets for the car keys.

"Mind waiting while I do one last walk-through?" she asked.

"Christ almighty. Don't you ever let up?" he said. "We're coming back first thing in the morning to rifle through that pile of boxes in the attic. Murphy, the man is not here. He's at the bottom of Lake Superior. You know what else? The hair isn't here, either. We're gonna waste a nice weekend digging around this stuffy morgue looking for evidence that doesn't exist. Phantom evidence."

She looked wounded.

"Oh, fine. You hit the second floor and I'll take down here," he said. She smiled. "Afterward, you're coming to the bar with me and you're buying the first round. For everybody. Deal?"

"Deal," she said, heading for the stairs.

"Should have my head examined," Gabe said. "Should have her head examined." He flipped on a light as he walked into the dining room. Empty. He flipped off the light and walked to the library. He flipped on a light and stared at the wall of shelves filled with books from floor to ceiling. He pulled the pack of Winstons out of his pocket. One left. He lit it, inhaled deeply and walked closer to study a row of westerns.

"Hmmm," he mumbled. "What we got here? *Shootist. Hanging in Sweetwater. Day the Cowboys Quit. Last Days of Wolf Garnett.*" He stopped to pull a copy of *The Black Mustanger* off the shelf when he noticed a vertical sliver of light between two stacks of shelves. The cigarette dropped from his mouth.

"Clever son-of-a-bitch," Gabe breathed.

"That's me," Michaels whispered behind him.

Gabe reached for his gun.

Michaels slipped off his right glove and felt for a pulse. "Still alive, you hardheaded cop bastard?" He pulled the glove back on, and wiped both gloves and his gun on Gabe's shirt. He'd pistol-whipped him hard, twice, and there was a lot of blood, but head injuries were deceptive. They tended to produce a lot of blood regardless of their severity. He thought about one of the knives in the kitchen. The big carving knife. He didn't want to take the time. Not yet. He hooked his arms under Gabe's armpits and dragged him into the safe room. Michaels dropped him in the middle of the room and looked down. He didn't want to look at that ugly puss while he was doing the bitch. He

309

grabbed one of his wife's fur coats and threw it over Gabe. Maybe he'd finish her partner off in front of her. The thought excited him.

He took the stairs to the second floor, slowly and deliberately. He avoided walking directly in the middle of each step; that's where most of them squeaked. He thought about what he was going to do to her. Rape her and then kill her and then rape her again. He'd brought condoms, though it was probably unnecessary. Everyone thought he was dead, even his own family. They'd never trace the crime to him, never even consider it. He'd take some things from the house, break some stuff. Arrange the corpses cleverly. Make it look like burglars surprised the two cops and killed them. Such a tragedy.

He'd have to remember the hatbox. Couldn't leave that behind. Then it was off to Europe to join his daughters, create a new identity. They'd understand in time. Even if they didn't, tough. They'd have to live with it.

The buzzing in his head was so loud, he wondered if it would give him away.

Murphy walked into the hallway bathroom and crouched down to study the hunks of mirror on the floor. Mixed in was a broken drinking glass. She figured he must have gotten drunk and thrown the glass at the mirror. She carefully picked up part of the broken glass by its edges and examined what was painted on the side. Some sort of bird. She put the piece in her left hand and with her right picked through the scraps of mirror to look for another piece to match it up with.

On the floor, she saw his disjointed reflection in the jagged fragments.

He grabbed the top of her hair with one hand and with the other jammed a gun into her neck. "Should we do it on the bathroom floor, or take it to the bedroom?" he said. He yanked her up by the hair.

She held on to the broken glass in her left hand, cupping it so he couldn't see it. "Why aren't you dead?" she said.

"Shut up! Using two fingers, unsnap your holster," he said. She hesitated. "Do it!"

She did.

"Good girl. Now take it out. Two fingers. Slowly. Slowly. Set it on the counter. Good. You're a quick study. You're going to learn a lot more before the night is through."

"Go to hell!" she said.

"Shut up, bitch. No talking. Save that tongue for my cock."

He kept the gun on her neck and, from behind, wrapped his left arm around her waist. He pulled her against him. "We've danced this dance before, haven't we? This time you're going to be the one left for dead." He pulled her into the hallway. "One foot in front of the other and walk toward my bedroom. Slowly. You know where it is. Baby steps. That's it."

"Your dye jobs keep getting worse," she said. He'd colored his hair black this time.

"Yeah. Yeah. I'll tell my hairdresser," he said. "Keep moving."

He kept his arm around her waist and the gun against her neck. He smelled like sweat and whiskey; probably hadn't showered or shaved for days. She could feel him getting hard as his front pressed against her back. He was getting off on this, and it made her sick. She wondered where Gabe was, if Michaels knew he was in the house.

As if he'd read her mind: "By the way, Gabe won't be joining us tonight," he said in a low voice.

"What have you done with him, you asshole?"

"I'm afraid he's suffered a severe head injury," he said. "Bleeding badly. The doctor predicts he might not make it through the night."

She stopped walking. "Where is he?" she asked. Michaels laughed. She decided to make her move, gun or no gun. She took the broken glass she'd been cradling in her hand and ripped a jagged, red line across his left arm.

"Bitch!" he snarled. He released her and wrapped his good arm around the bad. He dropped the gun. She dove for it. He kicked it away, grabbed the back of her head and plowed his knee into her face. She fell against the wall, blood running from her nose. He bent over to retrieve the gun and she crawled to her feet and ran for the stairs. He fired a shot into the ceiling; plaster rained on the floor. She stopped, inches from the stairs.

"Arms up or the next one is in your back," he yelled. "Kill you now or kill you later. Your choice. Makes no difference to me. I don't mind fucking a dead woman."

"Someone is going to hear, call the cops," she said, raising her hands in the air.

"Old house is pretty solid, walls are thick. Neighbors are all gone for the weekend," he said. "Besides, your friends were already here. They aren't coming back. This is the last place the dumb shits will check.

"Now turn around and march your pretty ass back here," he said, training the gun on her. "You're gonna pay for this arm."

She turned and walked toward him, arms raised. "Keep coming," he said. "Coming. Stop." She was less than two feet from him. He took a step toward her, swung his arm back and slammed the side of his gun into her mouth. She fell backward.

"Stand up and peel off your T-shirt." She didn't move. "Now," he said, pointing the gun down at her face.

She wiped her split lips with the back of her hand, stood up and pulled her shirt over her head. "Give it," he said. He stretched out his bleeding left arm. She tossed the shirt over it and he held the arm close to his chest. "Arms up again," he said.

"I hate white sports bras," he said, studying her chest. "Boring. I like to see black lace against a woman's skin."

"Sorry to disappoint," she said. She swallowed a mouthful of her own blood.

"It's what's underneath that counts, right? Let's see what's underneath." Grimacing, he reached over with his left arm and unzipped the front of the bra.

312

"I hate your fucking guts, you sick puke," she said.

"I love it when you talk dirty to me," he said. He pushed the white material aside and with the gun barrel, traced the curves of her breasts. "Lovely."

They were standing across from the bathroom. He saw her eyes dart to the counter, her gun. "Bad idea," he said. He shoved the gun into her left breast. "Downstairs. We're gonna check on your partner, see if he's still bleeding, still breathing."

"Keep both hands on the railing while we're walking down," he said. He was one step behind her the entire way down and kept the gun buried in her back.

"Stop," he said. They were at the bottom. "To the library."

They stepped into the library. "A safe room," she said. "How long you been in there? Did you sneak into the kitchen at night to eat, like a cockroach? Wait. Wrong insect."

"Move," he said, pushing her farther into the library. His arm was starting to throb. "Stop," he said. "I'm not ready for you yet." Grimacing, he reached his left hand into the left pocket of his jeans and pulled out some handcuffs.

"Turn around," he said. He threw the cuffs at her. She caught them and looked at them; they were Gabe's. "Snap one over your right wrist," he said. "Do it!" She did.

He looked at her face and scowled. "You're a bloody mess, and whoever sewed up your forehead did a crap job. You look like the Bride of Frankenstein."

"Know a good plastic surgeon?" she said.

"Gotta clean you up," he said.

"How considerate," she said.

"Can't screw you the way you are now," he said. "I'll get blood all over myself. Walk, toward the kitchen."

He pushed her into a bathroom in the hallway between the kitchen and the dining room. "Turn it on and get in," he said, nodding toward the shower stall. She turned it on and felt the water. "Get in," he said. She stepped in. "Snap the other end of the handcuff over the showerhead," he said. She paused. "Do it, unless you want your brains running down the drain," he said, aiming the gun at her head. She obeyed.

He shook her bloody T-shirt off his left arm and, with his teeth, pulled the leather glove off his left hand. As she stood with one hand stretched over her head, he roughly rubbed her breasts with his bare hand. With his gloved right hand, he jammed the gun into her back. "Nice," he said. Blood from his arm dripped onto the shower floor and washed down the drain. "Very nice. Is it the cold water, Paris, or is it me? Please tell me that it's me."

"Drop dead," she said.

"If you don't like it, shut your eyes and pretend it's somebody else's hand getting you off. Ever do that with your lover?" He kept rubbing her breasts. "Ever shut your eyes and pretend he's somebody else? Maybe you pretend it's me. Ever dream about me?"

"Shut up," she said. "Shut the hell up."

"I hit a nerve," he said, smiling. "Good."

He pulled his hand away, set the gun down on the counter and got a first-aid kit from under the sink. He lifted the lid and dug out a roll of gauze.

"Where's Gabe?" she asked. "What have you done with him?"

"Don't worry about old Gabe," he said, wrapping the bandage around his arm. "Gonna take care of him in a minute. Worry about yourself." He taped the ends of the bandage and slipped the leather glove back on his left hand.

He opened a drawer under the bathroom counter and pulled out a large pair of scissors. She stared at them. "No peeking," he said, setting the scissors down on the counter. "You'll ruin the surprise." He figured he could still get his souvenir, but he'd have to be careful, take a small section from the back of her head.

This time she read his mind: "If you cut it they'll know it was you," she said.

314

"I won't take enough to flag them, and they won't catch it because they won't be looking for it," he said.

"Yes they will."

"No they won't. I'm dead. You drowned me. Remember?"

"You'll never get away with it," she said. "Never."

"Close your trap," he said. "Close your pretty fucking trap." He walked over to the shower, reached up and turned the showerhead so it hit her in the face. He grabbed the gun and the scissors off the counter. He opened and closed the scissors in front of her face. "The fly shall marry the bumblebee," he said, grinning.

"Bastard!" she screamed through the water.

"I don't want to hear you," he said. Michaels walked out of the bathroom, shutting the door behind him.

"Bastard!" Her voice bounced off the marble walls.

The water was ice cold, and she was glad for it. It eased the throbbing in her face. The shower was higher than a standard one, but she could reach the oversized head when she stood on her toes. She grabbed it with her free hand and tried to turn it. Getting a good grip with her left hand was hard, especially with the water running. It wouldn't budge. She stretched as tall as she could and hung on to the shower pipe with her cuffed right hand for leverage. "Damn," she sputtered. She kept straining. Her hand kept slipping. She relaxed for a moment, turned her head and tried to catch her breath as the shower pounded her.

She reached up and tried it again. "Righty tighty, lefty loosey," she muttered. "Come on." It moved. Water shot out where the pipe met the showerhead. She kept turning. The head popped off and dropped to the shower floor.

She opened the door and ran out of the bathroom, the free handcuff dangling from her right wrist. She stopped in the hall and listened. She could hear him in the kitchen. She recognized the noise; she'd done it a thousand times in her own kitchen. He was putting an edge on a knife.

She dashed for the stairs and took the steps two at a time.

"Bitch!" she heard him yell at the bottom of the stairs. He was on her heels. She ran into the bathroom, crunching over the broken mirror. A shot rang past her ears and slammed into the bathroom wall.

"Looking for this?" he said.

She threw up her arms and swung around to face him. He was standing in the doorway, her gun in his hands. "Don't do it," she said. "You'll get life for killing a cop."

"Life in Europe, with my daughters," he said, raising the gun. "That's what I'm gonna get."

"Your daughters? Are you crazy?" she said. "Don't you remember?"

"Remember what? What the hell are you talking about?" He looked mystified.

"They're gone!" she yelled. He still didn't get it. What she said wasn't registering. "Your daughters. Your daughters are dead!"

"Liar!" he yelled, raising the gun higher. "Lying bitch!"

"You killed them," she said. "You! We found their bodies at the lake. There were four bodies in the carriage house. Four rotting corpses."

For the first time in days, the buzzing stopped. Shocked out of his head, like with a stun gun. He lowered the gun and took a couple of steps backward into the hallway. The color drained from his face; it was coming back to him. A terrible epiphany.

"You killed your own daughters," she said. "Your pretty blond daughters."

"Shut up!" he wailed, waving the gun toward her. "Shut the hell up!"

She heard footsteps downstairs. Voices. They'd come back. She knew what she wanted to do, but she didn't have much time. "Did they put up much of a fight? Did they beg for their lives?" she asked, speaking low. "Or don't you remember?"

He fell to his knees, crying.

"You don't, do you? You don't remember."

"Stop!"

"You don't even remember murdering your own daughters," she said. "You make me sick."

"I do remember," he said softly. "They cut their hair. I told them never to cut their hair. Never."

"Did you want to do other things to them?"

"What are you saying?"

"Even worse than killing them. Did you want to? What stopped you?"

"I wouldn't," he said, shaking his head. "That's what my mother tried to do to me. I wouldn't let her. I wouldn't do that to my daughters."

So that's what had happened between mother and son. She felt a flash of pity and brushed it aside. "You killed your own daughters," she said. "How can you live with yourself?"

"I can't," he said. "I can't live." He slowly stood up, the gun still in his hand.

"Nothing left to live for," she whispered. "Nothing."

"Nothing," he repeated, putting the gun to his head. "Nothing left."

"Do it," she said. "I would. In a heartbeat. Do it."

"Murphy? You up there? Murphy!" Gabe, at the bottom of the stairs.

"Don't come up here!" she yelled. "He's armed. Don't come up!"

"You don't have much time . . . Buzzy," she whispered.

His finger was on the trigger.

"Shut your eyes and pretend you're shooting somebody else," she said. "Pull, Buzzy. It's the only way to redeem yourself. Pull."

"I can't."

Gabe was running up the stairs.

"Say the rhyme, Buzzy. Finish it and pull."

"I can't."

"You can. Say it."

"Fiddle-de-dee, fiddle-de-dee, the fly shall marry the bumblebee. They went to church and married was she . . . I can't . . ." He choked back a sob. "You finish it. I'll pull if you finish it."

"The fly has married the bumblebee," she said.

Gabe was at the top of the stairs when he heard the gunshot, saw Michaels's brains splatter against the wall, saw the big man fold on the floor. Bergen and Dubrowski came up behind Gabe and stopped. "Holy shit," said Bergen, looking at the body in the hallway and the red running down the wall. "Holy shit."

Gabe pulled out his cell phone and called for paramedics, even though he knew Michaels was gone. Murphy walked out of the bathroom. Gabe looked at her battered face and her open bra and ordered a second ambulance.

"Give us a minute," Gabe whispered to Bergen and Dubrowski. They stayed back while Gabe stepped over the body and walked toward her, holding the back of his bleeding head. "Murphy? How you doing?" he asked. "How bad is it?"

"I look worse than I feel," she said. She looked down and with shaking fingers, zipped up her bra. When she looked up, Gabe was staring at her, a worried expression on his face. "He didn't get that far," she said. "Okay?"

"Yeah. Okay. It's just . . . Jesus. We found your bloody T-shirt in the bathroom downstairs. We thought . . ."

"How are you?" she asked.

"Sore as hell."

She started shivering. "You're soaked," Gabe said. He took off his sweatshirt to give to her and saw his own blood smeared all over it. He turned it inside out and draped it over her shoulders.

"Why did they come back for us?" she asked, pulling the sweatshirt tight around her wet body.

"Missed me at the bar," he said. She nodded.

She studied the bloody wall. "I'm surprised he had the balls," she said.

Gabe stared at her.

"I tried to stop him," she said, turning to meet Gabe's eyes. "I really did."

"That's not what I heard," Gabe said in a low voice.

She didn't answer, pretended not to understand. Sirens wailed in the distance. She crouched next to the body and saw that his gray eyes were open wide. "Did you know . . ." her voice trailed off.

"Know what?" Gabe asked.

"Did you know that suicide is considered one of the worst of the mortal sins?"

THIRTY-NINE

"How's your partner?" asked Jack.

"His new girlfriend is coddling the hell out of him," Murphy said. "It's almost too sickening to watch. I'm afraid to say it, but she may turn out to be wife number four."

"More power to him," said Jack, raising his beer bottle in tribute.

She and Jack were on the deck of her houseboat, watching the rockets light up the sky across the river in the first of three nights of Fourth of July fireworks over the State Capitol building. The summer night was hot, but the humidity was down and so were the mosquitoes. She kept the patio doors and all the windows open to cool off the houseboat.

"I wish Gabe would reconsider that early-retirement bullshit," she said. "What's he gonna do with himself all day? Fish?"

"Give him a break, baby," said Jack, taking a bump from the bottle. "This case really knocked the wind out of him."

"Me, too," she said. She reached up and reflexively touched her face. The bruises were fading and her nose wasn't broken, but her mouth was sore and the stitches on her forehead still troubled her. Bride of Frankenstein.

Jack knew what she was thinking. "If it bothers you that much, let me set you up to see a plastic surgeon," he said. "I know a few who aren't homicidal maniacs."

"Had my fill of plastic surgeons for a while," she said. She carefully sipped her wine; it made her lips burn. "Maybe I'll talk to one later, if I can find a nice lady doc. Hell, a scar on my forehead might add a little character."

"Oh, please," he groaned, polishing off his beer. "I am not going to touch that; too damn easy."

She laughed.

"At least you don't have to worry about that lawsuit," Jack said. He bent over and retrieved another beer from under his lawn chair. He popped off the cap. "You surprised his asshole uncles backed off?"

"Hell no," she said. "Imagine having that gruesome hair collection dragged out in front of a jury. Poor Finch's red hair, all braided and everything. The ash brown hair from that Minneapolis murder victim. Roxanne Magnuson's auburn hair. His wife's blond hair . . ."

"Even his wife's?"

"Uh huh," she said. "We found Rue's sad, brown braid. All of it stashed in that safe room of his."

"Had pretty much every shade covered, except black," Jack said.

"Except black," Murphy said in a low voice.

"He didn't cut his daughters' hair?" Jack asked, taking a bump off his beer.

"They got their hair cut short in Europe, to copy the Danish girls," said Murphy. "That probably helped freak him out." From what Murphy and Lake County officials could piece together, the two girls had begged to come home early from soccer camp, so their mother arranged for them to take a connecting flight to Duluth and a cab to the cabin. They walked in on their father in the carriage house standing over the bodies of their mother and grandmother. He smashed his daughters' skulls with the same shovel he'd used on their grandmother.

321

"What about that drowning stuff? You think he planned that?" Jack asked.

"I think he planned to disappear, but not like that," Murphy said. "I think he almost got his clock punched by the lake and that made him even crazier."

"Figured out how he made it back to the cities without someone spotting him?"

"Nobody was looking for him," she said. "He had a dye job on top of a dye job, and he was driving some junker motorcycle he'd picked up. The big thing is, nobody was looking for him. He was supposed to be dead."

"You knew he wasn't," Jack said.

"Yeah, I knew."

He leaned over and patted her thigh. "My baby is smart."

"You are so drunk."

"Yeah, but you're still smart."

She laughed again. "Stop. You're making my face hurt."

"Hey, smartie, what was all that fly and bee stuff?"

"Something with his mother," she said.

"Always boils down to hating your mother."

"He didn't hate her," Murphy said.

A rocket exploded in the sky, releasing a display of red, white and blue in the shape of a sunflower.

The phone rang in the galley. It jarred her. She still half expected a call from Michaels, even though it was impossible. He'd shot off half his own head. In her report, it was a straight suicide. Gabe knew otherwise. He'd made it to the top of the stairs and heard the words she and Michaels exchanged right before he pulled the trigger. Gabe said he didn't care. Said he was glad. He told her she'd saved the justice system a lot of time and the taxpayers a pile of money. Still, he'd treated her differently these last few days. Like she was a cocked gun. She wondered if she had played a role in his decision to retire.

The phone kept ringing. She tried to ignore it. "Should I get it?"

Jack asked. He set his bottle down and started to get up from his chair.

"Sit. I'll get it," she said, motioning him down with her hand. She stood up, set her glass down and walked into the galley. "It's probably my mom calling for the hourly update on my health."

Erik: "Paris?"

"This isn't a good time."

"I was on the phone with the Lake County coroner, wrapping up a few loose ends," Erik said.

"Any surprises?"

"No. The grandmother and two girls died of blunt-force trauma to the head and Jennifer Michaels was strangled."

"Anything else?"

"How you feeling?"

"I'm not suppose to say 'fine.' Right?" she said.

He laughed. She liked his laugh. Liked his hands on her. Liked Jack's hands on her, too. The status of their marriage was still uncertain. They weren't back together. Not really. Did that give her license to sleep around? She pushed the answer and the guilt to the back of her mind.

"Jack's home?" Erik asked.

"This morning," she said.

Then why he really called: "When can I see you again?" Erik asked. "I really want to see you again."

"I don't know," she said.

"I think we have something good going here."

"I don't know." She hung up and set the phone down on the counter and went back out onto the deck.

She lowered herself into the chair and picked up her wineglass. Empty. She grabbed the bottle to refill it when it suddenly occurred to her it was the 1997 Cabernet Sauvignon Michaels had rejected during his visit to her boat. She stared at the label and then poured another glass.

"Was it your mother?" Jack asked.

She paused. "Yeah."

She took a sip of the wine and remembered Michaels had said it wasn't complex enough. She smiled to herself; she was alive to drink it and he wasn't. She sipped again. "Plenty fucking complex."

"What?" asked Jack. "What did you say?" Thunderous explosions in the sky, like cannons going off. Multiple clusters in green, gold, blue and red rained down showers of sparks. The beginning of the grand finale.

"I said the fly was killed by the bumblebee," she said softly.

Cold Blood

This book is dedicated to my sons,
Patrick and Ryan,
with all my love.

Acknowledgments

I'd like to thank David for his continued support; Ryan for his expertise on knives; Patrick for rescuing me from computer problems; Marilee Votel-Kvaal, Ann Norrlander and Rita Monsour for their medical knowledge; Tom Dooher and Joseph Monsour for their auto tips; Kristina Schweinler of city licensing for background on St. Paul bars; and Esther Newberg and Leona Nevler for their hard work.

Learning Curve

Two of them pinned the tall boy's arms against the wall of the school building. Two others did the punching; one would step back and take a breath and the other would take over. They started with the head and worked their way down. Steam boiled out of their mouths as they whispered curses in the fall air. He wouldn't have hollered for help. Wouldn't have given them the satisfaction. They gagged him anyway. Stuffed his mouth with a jockstrap. It tasted salty with someone else's sweat and urine and made him feel filthy. A dirty animal. Down the hill behind them, the bonfire crackled and sputtered, and teenagers talked and sang. A radio blared the Talking Heads. "Burning Down the House." The tall boy tried to concentrate on the music and on the sparks darting into the air, send his pain floating into the night sky.

They punched him in the crotch, and he felt as if a flaming log had shot up the hill and buried itself in his gut. He gulped. Almost swallowed the jockstrap. The one holding his right arm laughed. "Not the balls. That's lower than low." They let go of him. He folded in half and fell to the ground. He coughed up the gag and a tooth chip and a mouthful of blood. Don't cry, he told himself, but he did. Big, heaving sobs.

One of them kicked him in the side. "Woman. Should have earrings in both ears. Fucking baby."

"No," said another. "He's a f... f... f... fucking b... b... b... baby." The four of them laughed.

He curled up on the ground, covered his head with his arms. The grass felt cool on the side of his face. He wished he could bury his whole body in the coolness. Disappear into it. Melt away.

"I think he peed in his pants," said the fat one. He bent over and took the tall boy's baseball cap off his head and put it backward on his own.

"He always smells."

"No. He did. He fucking pissed all over himself."

"Let's call his old man to mop it up."

That hurt him more than the punches and kicks. He propped himself up on his elbow. He lifted his head; it felt heavy. A block of concrete on his neck. He tried to open his eyes; they were already swelling shut and all he could see through the slits were shadows. He wanted to tell them something. Get one insult in. What came out was a growl. "You b... b... bastards."

The fat one pushed the tall boy's head down with his shoe and kept it there, as if he were propping his foot up on a rock. "Did you s... s... s... say something, d... d... d... dickhead?" They all laughed again.

Someone down the hill saw them. A teacher's voice: "Hey, what's going on up there?"

"We're outta here," said the fat one. He took his foot off the tall boy's head. "Come on!" He threw the tall boy's baseball cap on the ground.

Three of them ran to the car. The fourth, the one with the most arm patches on his letter jacket, leaned over and whispered in the tall boy's ear: "Listen good, Motorhead. Talk to her again and I'll kill ya, you creepy son of a bitch." He grabbed the ear. "One more thing. You're fuckin' out of uniform." He ripped off the earring, tossed the gold loop in the grass and went after the others.

2

On Monday, the tall boy went to school. His hand repeatedly went up to his left ear to finger the bandage. That tiny part of him, the torn earlobe, throbbed more than his entire body. He kept to himself all day; he always did anyway. Nothing had changed, really, except now he had a burning hate where once there was emptiness. He preferred the hate to the emptiness; it filled him up and gave him purpose. He had to find a way to get back at them. Sweet Justice would be patient and clever; he was a smart motorhead. Whatever happened would be their fault.

What goes around comes around.

He knew she was sitting there during lunch, at her usual table with her girlfriends. He longed to look at her. Longed to let her know that he blamed her. She must have said something to them. Maybe she told them to do it. Yes. She was also guilty. At first he thought she was different from the others. Thought she was good. Another Snow White. He was wrong; her beauty had fooled him. *Bitch.* She was as mean and shallow as the rest of them. Sweet Justice would nail her someday, too.

What goes around comes around, beautiful.

"Jesus. What happened to him?" asked one of the girls in between bites of a sandwich. "He get hit by a truck, or what? At least he lost the jewelry. Band-Aid's an improvement."

The other girls at the table laughed. All but one. The tallest, and the only one with black hair. "Leave him alone," she said.

The girl with the sandwich: "Got the hots for him? He make ya cream your jeans? Thought you had better taste than that."

"The creep asked her to homecoming," said one eating yogurt with a carrot stick. "I heard him. During choir. You should've seen his face when she turned him down. I thought he was gonna bawl right there on the risers. Right during 'Ave Maria.'"

"Shut the hell up," said the dark-haired one. She grabbed her lunch bag and left the table.

The other girls watched her go. The one with the yogurt ran the carrot around the inside of the carton. "She broke up with Denny.

3

Big fight. This morning. Saw them in the parking lot." She paused for drama, and to take a lick off the carrot. "She ain't going to homecoming."

The bell rang and the students got up, some leaving their trash on the table. A janitor pushed a broom into the lunchroom. He picked up apple cores and napkins and tossed them into the garbage cans as he went along. The tall kid stared at the custodian until their eyes met. The man nodded. The boy got up, threw his lunch sack into the garbage. He walked past the janitor and said in a low voice, "Later, P... p... pa."

1

Bunny Pederson would be alive today if her best friend hadn't picked peach for the bridesmaids' dresses.

"I'm a fucking pumpkin," said Bunny, standing in the ladies' room at the bar and scrutinizing her hips in the mirror. She swayed drunkenly, grabbed the countertop for support and burped. Something fruity came up; too much Asti. She swallowed it back. Raised her arms and sniffed under her pits. Damn deodorant was quitting on her. She turned around and looked over her shoulder to scan her butt.

"Peach is good on you," said Katie Stodel, the other bridesmaid and a twig of a woman. She brushed a few strokes of blush into the hollows of her cheeks and dusted between her breasts.

Bunny grabbed the dress at the hips and tugged down. It crawled up again and bunched under her bodice. "Black would have been better. Slenderizing."

"Black? For a wedding?"

"A fall wedding. Everyone does it."

"Not in Moose Lake."

"This town should join the twenty-first century." Bunny hiccuped.

5

Katie dropped the blush compact in her handbag and tightened the drawstring. She and Bunny had matching purses made from the same material as the dresses. "She went cheap on the flowers, but the music was nice. I love J.D." She started humming "Sunshine on My Shoulders."

"John Denver's a wuss. She should've gone with my pick."

"The vocalist didn't know it."

Bunny loosened the string on her bag and reached inside. She pulled out a folded piece of paper and waved it in Katie's face. "I got the words right here." She opened the paper and started singing "Can't Help Falling in Love," but stopped after "fools rush in" to burp.

"Was Elvis as drunk as you when he sung that?"

"Shut up." Bunny hiccuped again, dropped the paper on the wet counter. She picked it up, shook it off, folded it. Tucked it back in her purse. "Chad and me, we had that song at our wedding dance. Made the DJ play it four times."

"Yeah, and look what it done for you. How long you been divorced?"

Bunny flipped her the bird and pulled a tube of gloss out of her bag. She leaned closer to the mirror and applied another layer to her lips. She stepped back and saw the wet counter had left a waterline across her abdomen. "Great. Now I'm a soggy pumpkin. Screw this. I'm sliding into some jeans. Drive me home?"

"Stick your stomach under the hand dryer. Come on. Do it and let's go."

Bunny ignored her, kept looking at her reflection. Someone had slapped a NO FAT CHICKS bumper sticker to the top of the mirror. Bunny's eyes kept wandering to the sign, as if it was meant for her. "This hairdo she picked out. Jesus Christ. What porn magazine did this come from?"

Katie was offended; she'd helped pick out the do. "It's from *Modern Bride*."

"Try *Modern Slut*." Bunny reached up, pulled out a few bobby pins. The brown pile atop her head came cascading down. She bent over and shook her hair and stood up again. She looked in the mirror and groaned. Medusa. "Gimme your brush."

"Didn't bring one. Use your comb."

"It'll never get through this mess. Take me home. Please?"

"They're cutting the cake. German chocolate. Can't you wait?"

"Forget it. I'll walk."

"The dress is fine. Stay."

"I'd stay if it wasn't peach. Peach in October. Might as well be orange."

"What should I tell Melissa?"

"That she has shit taste."

Bunny shivered and held her sweater close as she clicked through the parking lot. Should have worn a coat, she thought. Shouldn't have had that fourth glass of Asti Spumante. She felt sick. She ducked between two pickup trucks, bent over and vomited. She straightened up, leaned her back against one of the trucks and reached into her purse for some Kleenex. She wiped her mouth, blew her nose, tossed the tissue to the ground. The night air was hazy. Neighbors were burning leaves in their yards. Something else was smoking. What was it? She sniffed. Bratwurst. Burning leaves and brats. She loved the smells. They smelled like Friday night in a small town. Bunny inhaled deeply and immediately felt better. She brushed some hair off her face. Hoped she didn't get puke on it. She

7

considered turning around and going back into the bar, but she couldn't stand the dress a minute longer. She wrapped her sweater tight around her body, shoved her evening bag under her armpit and kept going. A short walk, she told herself. Less than a mile.

Halfway there the heels started to hurt. She kicked them off and picked them up. Peach pumps. When would she wear those again? Waste of money, and she didn't have money to waste. Two kids to support on a crappy waitress job. Chad was late with his child support. Again. He should have shown up Thursday morning with the money and to take the boys duck hunting. Here it was, Friday night. No Chad, no check. Come morning she'd have to drive down to St. Paul and bang on his door. She knew he was struggling. Still, he had money for a new snowmobile. Why couldn't he pay on time for his sons? She was always short of money and the boys always needed things. They were growing out of their sneakers faster than she could buy them. Winter was around the corner. They'd need new boots and coats and snow pants, thought Bunny. Hockey skates. What about hockey skates? Last year's wouldn't fit either one of them. Little Chad was going to need new goalie pads for sure. Both boys' helmets were still good. The sticks, too. Where did she put those sticks? They weren't in the garage. The basement?

Home was a couple of blocks away. She could see the porch light. That dim bulb teenager she'd hired to baby-sit was probably out there smoking. Better not be her pack he was puffing. A cigarette would be good right now, thought Bunny. She couldn't fit her Marlboros and matches into the stupid little bag Melissa made her carry down the aisle. Another waste of money. Won't they all be pissed when the matron of honor returns in jeans and a sweatshirt? Tough shit. Tacky bar reception anyway with tacky bar food. Who

8

serves onion rings and buffalo wings at their wedding? Besides, thought Bunny, it's all Modern Bride Melissa's fault for picking peach. Peach dresses. Peach shoes. Peach purses. Even peach nail polish.

Some women turn thirty and panic because their lives aren't headed in the direction they'd hoped. When Bunny hit thirty earlier that fall, she hardly noticed. Her life was exactly what she'd expected. She saw it unfold ahead of her years ago, in high school. She could pinpoint the exact time and place and circumstances of the epiphany: between second and third period, in the girls' bathroom, while she was sitting on the pot reading the instructions from a drugstore pregnancy kit. As long as it took for her to pee on the stick and wait for it to change is about how long it took for her to let go of any grand plans for the future. She married a month before she gave birth and was pregnant again before she turned twenty. She lost the third; that didn't surprise or upset her. Got her tubes tied at twenty-five—smartest thing she ever did, she told friends. She didn't tell herself that working at the restaurant was temporary, until something better came along. Bunny knew nothing better ever comes along, especially in small towns.

Her low expectations were always on the money. She expected Chad to take off and he did. Anticipated the heartache and was relieved when it finally came. He was too much for her. Too handsome. Too decent. Too well built. Too desired by other women. Bunny never got what everyone else wanted, only what no one else wanted. Leftovers. Some nights she'd be in bed next to him, listening to him snore, watching his chest rise and fall with each breath. She imagined she actually loved him and he loved her. Then she'd snap out of it, wonder if she should kick him out and get it over with.

9

She let him dump her instead because kicking him out would have taken planning and Bunny wasn't good at planning. She was better at watching things head her way and letting them happen.

Open. *Chink*. Close. *Chink*. Open. *Chink*. Close. *Chink*. He couldn't keep both hands on the wheel. Too nervous. Too jumpy. Not too high, though. He steered with his left hand and with his right pushed the switch on his stiletto. The blade shot out of the handle. A snake's tongue. Pointed and straight and narrow. He closed it and the snake's tongue darted back inside. He loved the *chink* sound it made. Metallic and mechanical at the same time. Open. *Chink*. Close. *Chink*. Open. *Chink*. Close. *Chink*. His forehead itched under his baseball cap. He reached up and scratched it with the knife handle. Scratched and scratched until it burned.

"Dammit," he muttered. He dropped the knife in his lap and turned the cap around so it was backward. On the back of the cap in embroidered script: *Elvis Has Left the Building*. He picked up the knife. Open. *Chink*. Close. *Chink*.

When he spotted her walking on the side of the road, he had that thought he always had after a bad day. After too many pills. After too many nights on the road. Alone and driving, driving, driving. A white-hot thought that burned his brain and warmed his body. The thought went this way: a small movement of the wrists and hands. No greater than the effort it takes to wave good-bye. Shoo away a wasp. Twist the gas cap off a car. Flip open a jackknife. A small, controlled movement. That's all it would take to flatten someone. A quick jerk of his steering wheel to the right and they would be finished. Gone. All they ever were. All they ever hoped to be. All their high-and-mighty dreams.

10

Crushed. Erased with the slightest movement of his hands. So breakable, the human body. Doesn't take much to do a lot of damage. Cripple. Kill someone.

Open. *Chink.* Close. *Chink.* She could be that someone. Open. *Chink.* He saw her weave a bit. She was drunk. He liked drunks. They made it easier. She dropped something. Shoes? She picked them up and kept walking. The dress was a perfect target. When his lights hit it, it glowed. A walking neon sign. HIT ME! He passed her slowly, took a right down a side street. He wanted to circle the block and drive by her again. Do a little calculating. Close. *Chink.* Open. *Chink.* Give it more consideration. Pop another pill. They always made him smarter. Braver, too. He closed the knife for good, shoved it in his pants pocket. He flipped on the interior light and looked over at the passenger's side. Shit. The top had come off the bottle. Pills all over the seat. He eyed the mess, hunting for the yellowish Adderall tablets. He picked out one and popped it in his mouth. Chewed. It tasted nasty, but chewing worked the amphetamines faster than swallowing whole. He grabbed his Coke cup and sucked on the straw. Watery dregs. How many was that tonight? Two? Three? Doesn't matter, he thought. As long as he felt wired for action. Gotta fly high this weekend to make up for the week. The week had been a black hole. Most of his work weeks were black holes; his life disappeared into them. Vanished without a trace. He flicked off the dome light.

He wouldn't think about flattening someone in a car. Cars were weak. Couldn't be trusted to handle even the smallest smack. His Ford truck could take it. It had taken it before. Trucks were his safe world. Didn't matter if he was driving them or working on them. Trucks recognized his talent. Bent to his will and skill. His red F150 had an extended cab and eight-foot box covered by a sturdy

11

topper. Brush guard across the front that protected the lights and grill. There'd be limited damage to the vehicle. Nothing he couldn't fix himself. If she went up on the hood, she might take the windshield with her. Again, no big deal. He'd get the hell out of town quick. Fix it when he got home. The surface conditions were right. Hard, dry road. There'd be no tracks. He'd drive away. Check the papers in the morning for her name. She probably deserved it. He figured most people deserved to get run over for one thing or another. Maybe it was for something they did that morning. Maybe it was for something mean they did years ago. Could be they forgot what they did wrong; that didn't make it right again. He wondered what she did. Decided he didn't care.

It would be a good night for Sweet Justice, coming as it did on the heels of a black hole week filled with mean people.

"The shop's limited on floor space."

"We're vendor downsizing."

"Does anyone wear dress shirts anymore?"

"Got flannel? Don't bother me if it ain't flannel."

"Read the sign. No solicitors. Take your shitty shirts outta here."

They were shitty shirts, and he knew it. That's what the side of his truck should read, he thought. GET YOUR SHITTY SHIRTS HERE. He pulled at the collar of his oxford. Stiff and new and scratchy. He hated wearing his own merchandise; all the salesmen had to pay for their own samples and it was a drain even at cost. He was too tall for most of the stuff and it never fit right, but he'd run out of clean clothes and didn't want to waste quarters at a Laundromat. He undid another button at the neck and the button came off in his hand. He tossed it onto the seat with the pills and muttered, "Shitty shirts."

He circled the block and saw her in his lights again. Fat ass taking up more than its share of the road. That dress. What was she, some old prom queen? Probably thinks she's hot shit. She deserved it, all right. He was coming up on her fast. His only hesitation was checking the rearview mirror to make sure there was no one behind him, and there wasn't. He clenched his teeth, tightened his grip on the steering wheel. Then something amazing happened. She stumbled and fell flat on her face. He couldn't believe how much she was helping him. "Now!" he said out loud. He gunned it and yanked the wheel to the right. He smiled at the satisfying *thump-thump* as the front right wheel rolled over her. Then the back right one. Another *thump-thump*. Solid sounds. He could feel them through his steering wheel. He said, "Perfect!"

He slowed and checked his rearview mirror. A smear on the side of the road. He punched off his lights and peeled away. He took the next right, drove a mile down the country road. He pulled over and turned off the engine. "Damn!" he said, and pounded the steering wheel with his fists. "Damn!" He threw his head back and exhaled while a shudder started at the top of his head and rippled down to his toes. He was panting. His heart was zooming. Patching out. Burning rubber. Such a rush. Such a high. Better than the best blow. Better than racing down the highway with all the windows rolled down and the needle pushing past eighty. Past ninety. Past a hundred. The prom queen didn't even squeal. Didn't have time. Lying drunk on the road one second, squished dead the next. He wondered how her face looked right as he nailed her. Longed to see that surprise. Mouth hanging open and pressed into the tar. He wished he could have heard her last words. Wondered what she squeaked as the life was pressed out of her. "Shit!" or "Help!" or "Fuck!" or maybe, simply, "No!" Did she

13

cry out for her ma or her pa or her lover? The eyes. He bet her eyes were so wide when he rolled over her they looked pure white, as if the pupils had popped out. He figured the prom queen had to be dead. Get back on the road and keep going, he told himself. Keep driving. Stopping is never smart. Someone could see him, see his truck pulled to the side. He hadn't checked carefully; there might be something caught on the tires. A bit of material. Someone could spot it. He told himself to savor the moment only a couple of minutes longer.

He wondered what else ever gave him such a high. Thought back to the last time he felt this good. Wasn't about pills or the road or his wheels. God, that was fun. An even bigger high than this high. That was glorious. He was a real fuckin' superhuman superhero. On top of a mountain on top of the world. He'd never get that back. Or could he? Maybe the dead prom queen could pull double duty. He punched his steering wheel again. "Hell, yeah!" he said. That'd serve Sweet Justice fine. He popped open the glove compartment and fished around for his sharpest knife. Decided the wire cutter would work better.

He pulled on some gloves. Worked quickly but carefully; he didn't want blood on his clothes. Kept his eyes peeled for other lights. If someone stopped, he'd tell them he found her there and was taking her to a hospital. Only two cars drove past. One right after the other while he was sliding her into the back. Their headlights scared the shit out of him, but neither car slowed. He figured the whole town was sleeping or out drinking. That was all there was to do in small towns late at night. He took out a bag of sand, part of the truck's winter gear. He emptied it over a spot of blood on the road. He pulled off the gloves. Checked the road one last time with his flashlight. He'd almost left her shoes. He picked them up and tucked them inside the tarp with the body.

He didn't sleep at all Friday night. The Adderall did that. He gassed up the truck at a station off Interstate 35. Used the bathroom to wash his hands, wash the wire cutter, check his clothes. Grabbed a Coke. Paid for it and the gas. The tired clerk hardly gave him a look when she rung him up. He stepped outside and walked around the truck. He didn't see any blood or cloth on the tires. Noticed a sub shop next door to the gas station. He wasn't hungry. The Adderall did that, too. He leaned against the side of his truck, unscrewed the cap off the Coke and took a long drink. He had the driver's window opened a crack; a Judas Priest CD was pounding inside the car. Every once in a while he patted his jacket pocket to make sure her finger was still there, wrapped in plastic.

2

He wanted to hear what people were saying about the prom queen. Did they assume she was dead? Kidnapped? He decided to spend Saturday morning making sales calls in town. He wouldn't be an unusual figure; he'd called on most of the shops before. He walked into a clothing store with a box of individually packaged shirts and asked the clerk if he could see the store owner. The girl went into the back office. Toward the front of the store, two women were picking through a rack of Halloween costumes and talking about the missing woman. He listened while taking the shirts out of the box and stacking them on the counter.

"Spider-Man," said the fat one, holding up a nylon outfit of red and blue. She checked the price tag. "On sale. Twenty bucks. Size ten. Could fit your youngest."

"He was Spider-Man last year," said the skinny one. She kept shuffling through the rack. "What do you think happened to her?"

The fat one pulled out a Batman costume, stared at it for a few seconds and put it back. "Sleeping it off somewhere. I heard she got drunk as a skunk at the reception."

The skinny one held up a skeleton costume. "This one's got a rip. Maybe they'll knock off a couple of bucks."

The store owner came out of the office and shook her head. "Sorry. Not unless it's wool or flannel. Winter's on the way."

He scooped up the shirts and dropped them back in the box. "Thanks anyway." He slipped out the door and went to the truck.

By Saturday afternoon, he was congratulating himself. Hauling the body around with him was brilliant. The body would keep. He'd wrapped it in a tarp and it was cold enough outside to prevent it from rotting right away. The topper kept everything dry and out of the open. He wouldn't bury her until the cops had searched the area. Then he'd put the prom queen someplace they'd already covered. A place they'd never find her.

Bolstered by the amphetamines, he even had the guts to stop at a diner for coffee. He watched from the restaurant window while a sheriff's deputy walked down the sidewalk toward the truck. He held his breath and squeezed his coffee cup with both hands. The deputy walked right by without a glance. He exhaled and loosened his grip around the mug. He saw the waitress heading toward him and busied himself with the menu.

"How about a warm-up?"

He slid the cup toward her and she filled it. He raised his eyes as far as her name tag. "Thanks, B... B... Bonnie."

After his coffee he got a room in a motel outside of town. Water stains on the ceiling. Matted shag carpet. Sagging bed. Television with free cable that didn't work. Reminded him of every other motel he had ever stayed at while working sales. His first job was right after high school, peddling wholesale party goods. Plates, cups, napkins, streamers, balloons, piñatas. Great samples. Cheap

17

for him to buy and useful. He didn't do dishes the whole time he had that sales job. He and his old man would laugh as they sat down to dinner. "What are we celebrating to-night?" his pa would ask. They'd pull out birthday party plates or baby shower plates or Halloween plates. Then a string of other sales jobs, each ending with him getting fired or quitting. The one right before the shitty shirts was the worst—commercial cleaning supplies. He'd stand in bathrooms and squirt urinals with blue liquid or pink goop in an effort to convince janitors that his chemicals cleaned piss off porcelain better than some other guy's products. He would never be a good salesman no matter what he sold. Didn't have the personality for it. Couldn't look people in the eye and bullshit with them. Backed down as soon as someone said "no." He stuck with sales only because he loved riding around in his truck.

He threw his suitcase on the bed, opened it, rummaged around inside for her purse. He'd left her shoes wrapped up in the tarp with her body, but he wanted to check her handbag. Wondered what secrets were contained in a dead woman's belongings. He loosened the drawstring and tipped the bag upside down on the bed. Bobby pins. Lipstick. Kleenex. Comb. Couple of quarters. Three tiny vials; perfume samples. He opened one and sniffed. Lily of the valley. He put the cork back in and threw the bottle on the bed. Something was stuck in the bottom of the bag. He reached inside and pulled out a square of folded paper. Finally, he thought, a little mystery. He opened it. Immediately recognized the lyrics. "Can't Help Falling in Love." He'd come all this way to run over an Elvis fan when he could have had his pick of them back home. He refolded the paper and slipped it back in the handbag. He thought about throwing away the lipstick, perfumes and bobby pins, but instead returned them to the purse. He

put the quarters and comb in his pocket. He inspected the
Kleenex. Clean. Put that in his pocket, too. He tightened
the drawstrings on the purse and stuffed it into a dirty
sock. He threw the sock back in the suitcase and closed
it.

He went back into town for an early dinner; he finally had
an appetite. By then, the flyers were up. He walked past the
drugstore and saw the pharmacist taping one to the
window. He read it through the plate glass. MISSING, it said.
Below that was her photo and right beneath her photo, her
name: *Bunny Pederson*. He hadn't heard her name while
walking around town and it never occurred to him she had
a name other than the nickname he'd given her. The poster
gave her height and weight—no wonder he'd strained to lift
her into the truck—and age. Only thirty? He thought she
was older than that. Time hadn't been kind to Bunny
Pederson's face or figure. Were she alive, she'd probably be
one of those loser women who'd consider sleeping with
him. A washed-up prom queen. The poster said she was
dressed in a peach bridesmaid's dress and shoes. Carried a
peach purse. Television is going to love that, he thought. A
disappearing bridesmaid. That would be her new nickname: the bridesmaid. She was last seen leaving a wedding
reception at a bar. That's where the whole town was Friday
night, he thought. CALL THE MOOSE LAKE POLICE OR
CARLTON COUNTY SHERIFF'S OFFICE. Below that, what he
was waiting for: volunteers were meeting in a church
basement to prepare for a Sunday morning search of the
woods and fields in the area. He checked his watch; he
could still make it.

* * *

19

He steered the truck into the church parking lot. Jammed with news vans; he'd read the media right. His heart raced. Already, it was starting. He patted his jacket pocket; the finger was still there.

3

"Pull!" said a husky female voice.

The clay pigeon thrown from the trap veered to the right. She aimed the barrel over the orange saucer and swung to the right, getting ahead of it. She counted to three in her head and squeezed the trigger. The disk exploded into a black cloud.

"Nice hit," said her shooting partner. The crack of other guns and the smell of gunpowder warmed the cold fall air. A busy Saturday at the range.

"Your turn," she said.

"Pull!" he said. His pigeon flew to the left and seemed to hang in midair for a moment, as if caught in an updraft. He pointed the barrel over the target and squeezed. The shot nicked off a sliver of orange and the rest of the disk fell to the ground. "Finally. A hit," he said.

"Barely," mumbled the teenage boy behind them. He was sitting in a chair keeping score. He ran the trap by pushing a button on a box he held in his palm. An extension cord connected the box to the concrete bunker that expelled the clays.

The man looked over his shoulder. "What'd you say, kid? Working on your tip?"

The boy grinned and started to say something, but it was lost in the rattle and whistle of a train crossing the nearby tracks.

"A chip's still a hit," the woman said over the noise. She slipped a shell into the chamber and pumped it forward. "Pull," she said. Another throw to the right. She started the barrel pointing behind the pigeon and swung it smoothly ahead until it was past the disk before squeezing the trigger. It shattered; another square hit.

The man slid a shell into the chamber, pumped and raised his shotgun. "Pull." He followed the target with the barrel. He closed his right eye and squeezed the trigger. A miss.

"Lost," said the scorer.

"What am I doing wrong here, Paris?"

She took off her safety glasses and shoved them into the pocket of her shooting vest. "First off, are you shutting one of your eyes?"

"Yeah. Sometimes."

"Don't. This is a shotgun, not a rifle." She pulled out her earplugs.

"Okay," he said. "What else?"

Paris Murphy walked over to the gun rack behind the teenager, leaned her gun against it and went over to her husband. A gust of wind rattled the trees on either side of the range and sent more leaves floating to the ground. Murphy regretted leaving her gloves at home and tucked her numb hands under her armpits.

"You're behind the pigeon when you should be in front of it." She stood behind him. Jack Ramier was tall, but his wife nearly matched his height. She was slender, with a narrow waist and hips, but had large breasts and a runner's

22

well-defined legs. She had long black hair, violet eyes framed by thick lashes and olive skin—traits from her Lebanese mother and Irish father. Her complexion was flawless except for a crescent moon scar on her forehead— a souvenir from her job as a St. Paul Homicide detective.

"And your form is all wrong," she said. She bumped the back of his legs with her knee. "Bend those knees, Jack. Relax. You're not performing surgery." Jack was an emergency room doctor at Regions Hospital downtown. "Put your left foot slightly forward. Keep your feet shoulder-width apart." She put her hands on his hips. "Lean forward a little at the waist."

"You're getting me hot, wife."

"Not in front of the kid."

"This isn't fair. You handle a gun all day long."

"Stays in my purse ninety-nine percent of the time."

"You've had training."

"I've given you training."

"I'll say you have." He turned and winked at her. He had curly brown hair and brown eyes that never failed to get her attention.

"Watch that muzzle control," she said lowly. "Wouldn't want your gun going off prematurely. Save something for tonight."

"I got plenty of ammo," he said, and they both laughed.

"You finished or what?" asked the boy behind them.

"We're finished." Murphy rubbed her hands together. "I'm cold, Jack. Give him a couple of bucks and let's go inside. Sun's going down anyway."

Jack pulled three ones out of his pocket and handed them to the teenager. He set his gun next to his wife's.

"You sure the chamber's empty?" she asked.

He picked up his gun and checked. "Chamber empty. Safety on."

23

"Good."

He set the gun back on the rack. "I'm a quick study." He shoved his glasses and plugs into his vest pocket.

"Yeah. Right. Don't quit your day job."

He smiled and followed her into the South St. Paul Rod and Gun clubhouse, a building that resembled a ranch-style house with a deck attached. The Mississippi River snaked in front of it and railroad tracks cut behind it. It was a block off Concord, a long street connecting the city of St. Paul and the suburb of South St. Paul. The gun club shared the neighborhood with a furniture liquidator, a used-car lot, a beauty shop and a Dairy Queen.

Murphy checked the bulletin board inside the clubhouse door. Covered with handwritten index cards and flyers: "Beretta AL390 Gold Mallard 20 GA. $725." "Custom Docks. Call for an estimate." "4×10 Utility Trailer made by Cargo. ALMOST NEW. Drop down ramp. $900." "Lab choc. M. AKC Exc. bird dog. $2,500." "FOR SALE. Remington 870. Nice clean gun. $450." "German Wire-Haired Pups. AKC. Exc. Blood Lines. MAKE GOOD HUNTERS/FAMILY PETS. $500."

"Decent price," Murphy muttered. She grabbed a bar napkin and wrote down a phone number.

"Shopping for a gun?" asked Jack, looking over her shoulder.

"A dog."

"Since when? You're not home enough. Your place is too small. A dog would go stir-crazy on that dinky house-boat. It'd chew the shit out of everything."

"Stop hyperventilating." She shoved the napkin into the pocket of her jeans. "We'll discuss it over a beer."

It didn't take much to turn their discussions into arguments, and that's why they periodically separated. In their eight years of marriage, they'd lived apart as much as they'd lived together. Jack stayed in the house they'd bought together when they first got married. She had a houseboat on the Mississippi River, moored across from downtown at the St. Paul Yacht Club. They kept trying to make their marriage work and were most successful in the bedroom; they never argued about sex.

All the tables were taken; they found two stools next to each other at the bar. "What can I get you?" asked the bartender. He was a big man with curly red hair, a red beard and a red flannel shirt. He could have passed for a lumberjack.

"Grain Belt," said Murphy.

"St. Pauli Girl," said Jack.

"No imports."

"Grain Belt then."

The bartender set two cans on the bar. "Sign up for the big shoot?" He thumbed toward a flyer behind the bar: MINI JACKPOT TRAP SHOOT.

Murphy took a bump off her beer. "You betcha."

He eyed Jack. "You that ringer she been threatening to bring in?"

Murphy laughed and then coughed and held a napkin to her face; she felt beer coming up her nose. Jack glared at her. She cleared her throat. "No," she said. She blew her nose and took another sip of beer. "This is my husband, Jack. Jack, this is Gunnar."

"Gunner?"

"Gunnar," said the bartender, without smiling. He walked to the other end of the bar.

"Isn't that what I said?"

"No. Gunnar is Norwegian or something. Gunner is . . . I don't know . . . a good name for a hunting dog maybe."

"Back to the dog, are we?"

"I'm the only one in my family without a dog." She had nine brothers, no sisters.

25

"Your siblings are nuts. You can't eat dinner at their houses without swallowing a pound of fur. Rawhide bones everywhere. Yards all tore up. They live in giant kennels."

"I'll be sure to pass that compliment on to my brothers—and their wives." She frowned and brushed the hair from her forehead with her fingertips. She wasn't comfortable with bangs. Jack said he found them attractive, told her she looked like Cleopatra. She used to wear her hair parted down the middle and pulled back. She got bangs over the summer to help cover the scar, a constant reminder of the fight she'd gotten into with a killer.

Jack popped open his beer and took a sip. "Forget the damn dog. Dog's a bad idea."

She didn't answer. She turned in her stool to see who she knew in the bar. The room had paneled walls, a low ceiling and was cloudy with smoke. Four guys in camouflage jackets were at a table playing cards and puffing on cigarettes. She recognized a couple of them. Retired towboat crew. Her family used to run a bar along the Mississippi that served river workers. The two men saw her and nodded. Another table was filled with guys in blaze orange caps. They were hunkered over a map, planning a deer hunt. Murphy was envious. She wished Jack was more of a hunter. Maybe she could get out this season with her brothers.

She turned around to sip her beer. The television behind the bar was turned to the news. Gunnar walked over to switch channels when a female reporter came on. She was standing in front of a church, interviewing a tall man. "Stop," Murphy said. She strained to listen. "Turn it up."

"One of your cases?" asked Gunnar.

Murphy didn't answer. She stared at the screen. The reporter was talking about how the tall guy was a traveling salesman who'd volunteered to join a search party. They were looking for a Moose Lake woman who'd disappeared Friday night after a wedding. "A bridesmaid who vanished," the reporter said. She emphasized the word *bridesmaid* to show it made the story different. Special.

Jack watched his wife's face. "What is it, Paris?"

"I recognize him."

"From where? Work?"

"No. Can't remember exactly. But not work."

"Fuckin' tall as a house," said Gunnar. He grabbed a bar rag and wiped the counter.

Murphy studied the man while he continued talking to the reporter about why he'd volunteered, how he'd wanted to help. His face was pale and smooth and his eyes dark. His lips were full. Almost a woman's mouth. He had black, slicked-back hair. In a strange way, he was attractive. Seductive. He looked like a vampire from a black-and-white movie. His left ear was weird. Looked as if he had two lobes. Some kind of accident? More familiar than his face was his voice. He had a trace of southern drawl, and a stutter. She could tell he was concentrating on his speech, pausing at words that were threatening to turn into a problem. Who did she know with a stutter? No one came to mind.

"Hey!" yelled one of the deer hunters. "How about some ESPN instead of this crap?"

"Yeah. Yeah. Keep your shirt on." Gunnar walked over to the television and switched channels.

Murphy rubbed her arms; she had goose bumps under her sweatshirt, but not from the cold. Talking more to herself than to Jack: "I know him. How do I know him?"

27

Jack drained his can and set it down. "How about some dinner, babe? Something from that Mexican market down the road. I could go for some beans and rice."

"I've got stuff in the fridge," she said. She took one more sip of beer and slid off the bar stool. "Let's get the guns and get outta here."

4

The school bus rattled down the road, kicking up a cloud that trailed behind like a phantom. The bus lurched to a halt and the dust ghost disappeared into the gravel. Thirty-three people in jeans and sweatshirts filed out, calling out the number each had been assigned before boarding the bus.

"One."

"Two."

"Three."

"Four."

"Five."

Men. Women. Seniors. Middle-aged folks. A couple of teenagers. A few had water bottles strapped to their waists and candy bars shoved in their pockets; they were the ones who'd done this before and knew they'd get thirsty and hungry out in the field. They squinted in the fall light and wrinkled their noses. The air smelled of skunk. All wore coats or down vests over their sweatshirts and some donned mittens and stocking caps. The sunshine was deceptive; it was raw outside. Gusts of wind bent the tall grasses and blew the remaining leaves off the trees. It could have been

29

December instead of October. Last off the bus was a sheriff's deputy, a short, husky woman. "Number One takes the ditch along the road and the rest of you follow him in order," she said.

The civilians lined up in firing-squad formation at one end of the meadow. They stretched their arms out so they'd be spaced apart evenly. Number One was the tallest in the crowd by two heads. The ditch was knee-deep, but when he stepped into it he still towered over the deputy and half the others in the group. The deputy studied his feet. "Hope those are decent boots," she said. The ditch was swampy.

"Sorels," he said. "I know how to d... dress, ma'am."

"Guess you do," she said. She noticed his baseball cap. A suede brim and *E.P.* embroidered on the front. "Those your initials?"

"Elvis Presley," he mumbled. He shoved his hands into the pockets of his leather jacket and averted his eyes.

He's a weird one, she thought. She turned her attention to the rest of the group, eyed the row of volunteers. She wished she had someone as tall as Number One anchoring the other end, and the middle for that matter. The middle man kept the line straight. No matter, she thought. It was the second day. Missing people cases go bad after two days. Same as fresh fish in the fridge. After two days, the missing become the dead and clues turn cold. It would be a miracle if they found anything useful out here.

"Ready?" They all nodded. "Let's go," she said. The line started moving. The deputy walked behind them, surveying the evenness of the line. The speed. "Slow down, people," she hollered. "This ain't a race. Wait for the middle to catch up while they go through that brush. Take your time." No one talked. They kept their eyes down as they walked, searching for something. Anything. A strand of thread from her dress. Footprints. Bobby pin from her hair.

A crow landed on a tree stump ahead of the line, eyed the humans heading toward it and cawed. A woman— Number Fourteen—looked up. "No bird-watching," said the deputy, and a few in the line laughed. Then another stretch of walking and no talking in the line. The sound of boots crunching down dried grass and leaves. A menacing noise. The sound of an invading army. Halfway across the field, Number Seventeen caught the toe of his boot on a rock and fell on his face. He stood up and spit out dirt and weeds. The line stopped while he brushed off.

"You okay?" asked the deputy.

"Yeah, yeah," he said, red-faced.

The line continued moving. They'd nearly reached the end of the meadow when a yell went up.

"Found something!"

"Everyone stop. Now," said the deputy. She ran to Number One. He had his right hand raised like a kid at school and his left pointed to the ground. Her eyes followed to where he was pointing. She squatted down. Couldn't believe what she saw.

"Shit," she breathed. A finger. Peach polish on the nail.

"Stay where you're at!" she yelled to the line. Then, so only he and those next to him could hear, she said lowly, "Good eye, Number One." The deputy stayed hunched over the finger while she radioed for help.

Number Two, a pretty blond woman, kept her place in the line but turned her back to the finger. Stared up at the sky.

"You okay, ma'am?" Number One asked in a low voice.

"Sorry I'm such a baby," she whispered.

"N... no," he said. "You're doing fine."

She turned to face him and touched his arm. "Thank you."

31

He lowered his eyes and nodded. His heart raced. He tried to keep from breathing fast. Tried to keep from grinning. He covered his mouth with his hand, pretended to cough. Don't grin, he told himself. This wouldn't be the time or the place for grinning. It would peg him as a creep, and it would tip them off.

5

Sunday afternoon Jack relaxed on the deck off the living room while Murphy chopped and mixed in the galley. Every time they had a quiet moment, she wondered if she should tell him about the affair she'd had over the summer. The urge to confess was overwhelming; she blamed it on her Catholic upbringing. That morning she'd gone to the cathedral without him. All during mass she'd thought about their marriage, their problems. She scanned the pews in the cavernous church. Saw couples worshiping together. Families. The fact that he wasn't next to her in the pew spoke of one of their differences.

When she was growing up, Sunday mass and meals were a big deal for the Murphy clan. She and her mother would be up before church preparing the feast. They'd make Lebanese flatbread from scratch. The first loaf out of the oven would be theirs. They'd spread butter on the hot bread and wash it down with mint tea. The smell of baking would fill the house and rouse the males out of bed. They'd all attend morning mass together, filling up two pews. After church came a family meal that seemed to last all day. Jack was raised differently. He was the only child of two University of

Minnesota professors. They seldom went to church and rarely cooked. Jack's childhood memories of Sundays involved sleeping late and going out for brunch at a restaurant. Murphy didn't relish visiting his parents in their upscale St. Anthony Park neighborhood. Their house was too quiet and the copper pots they had hanging in their kitchen were covered with dust. Murphy thought there was something sacrilegious about buying nice cookware and using it solely for decoration. Jack was equally uncomfortable in her childhood home. Holidays were especially crazy with her brothers' wives and children added to the mix. More than one Thanksgiving she'd found Jack sitting alone on the back porch. "Too much noise," he'd mutter.

She watched him sitting on her deck, his feet up on the rail and a Sunday paper next to his chair. She went over to the refrigerator and stood in front of it, hand on the door handle. She ordered herself to go out on the deck and spill her guts. She stood still for a moment, and then pulled open the door and reached for the tomatoes. She told herself she'd unload her conscience on another day. She slammed the door shut and returned her attention to something she could control: the food.

She was glad she had all the ingredients on hand for tabbouleh:

Half cup of bulgur (cracked wheat)
Four cups of chopped parsley (no stems)
Two medium tomatoes, diced
Half cup of finely chopped green onions (including tops)
Quarter cup of finely chopped fresh mint
Quarter cup of extra virgin olive oil
Quarter cup of freshly squeezed lemon juice
One teaspoon of salt
Half teaspoon of pepper

She covered the cracked wheat with lukewarm water and let it soak until it was soft—about twenty minutes. She drained it and squeezed it with her hands to get out as much water as possible. She tossed the bulgur with the other ingredients and chilled the salad in a covered bowl while she made the rest of the meal.

They ate in the galley; it was too cold to dine on the deck. After lunch, he sprawled out on the couch to watch the Vikings game while she cleaned up. The galley was separated from the living room by a counter. He scrutinized her camel statues, figurines and pillows. "Where'd you get that big wooden one?" he asked. It had a leather saddle and was nearly a foot tall.

She was loading the dishwasher and froze with a plate in her hand. "What'd you say?" She was glad he couldn't see her face.

"Never mind," he mumbled.

She heard snoring a few seconds later and was relieved. She finished loading the dishwasher. The camel was a gift from Erik Mason, an investigator for the Ramsey County Medical Examiner's Office. She hadn't thought Jack would notice a new addition to her collection.

That night Murphy and Jack sat up in bed; he was in his boxers and she was in an oversized Old Navy tee shirt. She had the remote and switched from one channel to the other. The tall guy was all over the ten o'clock news; every station led with him. He'd uncovered a clue during the search, and now the Moose Lake cops knew it was murder. Murphy stopped at one station. The reporter tipped her head toward the tall guy, as if the two of them were sharing a secret. "And what did you find?" The way she asked the question—slowly and dramatically—made it clear she already knew the answer.

The guy paused and swallowed. The camera closed in on

his face. He was looking off to the side, as if he was shy, and rubbing the brim of a baseball cap he held in his hands. "A finger. Her p... pinkie, I think."

"A final question," said the reporter. "Is there anything you want to say to the person or persons who did this to Bunny Pederson?"

For the first time he looked up and into the camera. "Turn yourself in and tell the p... police where you buried her, or you'll never be able to sleep at n... night."

The reporter: "Will you be able to sleep tonight, after that horrible find? Expecting nightmares?"

He smiled, head lowered again. "I'll be fine, ma'am."

"Thank you, Mr. Trip. Back to you in the newsroom, Blake."

"Trip." Murphy said. "Why is that name so damn familiar?" She switched from station to station until she finally caught his full name: Justice Trip. "Bastard's everywhere," she said. "Dammit. I wish I could remember."

Jack grabbed the remote and pulled it out of her hands. "Why'd you put a set up here when you've already got one downstairs? I don't like a television in the bedroom."

"Fine. Then don't put one in *your* bedroom." She grabbed the remote back and switched to another channel. Justice Trip on that news station as well. She studied his face; that weird earlobe. She said suddenly, "Wait. I know how I know him. Sweet Justice." She threw the remote at Jack and hopped out of bed.

"Babe. It can wait," he yelled after her. "Who gives a shit?"

She thumped down the stairs. He heard her opening and closing cupboard doors and throwing stuff around while talking to herself. "Where is it? I just had it out." She ran back upstairs and climbed under the covers; it was cold downstairs and her feet were icy. She tucked them under Jack's legs.

Jack looked over her shoulder while she flipped through the slender volume. "What's this?"

"St. Brice High yearbook."

"You went to school with him?" Jack nodded toward the television. Trip was still on the screen, but Jack had hit the mute button.

"Yup." She pointed to his photo. In the sea of grinning teenage faces, Trip's stood out for its dark seriousness.

"What made you think of him? You don't see any of your old high school friends."

"All-class reunion coming up. Anniversary of the founding of the school."

"You're going without me, I hope."

"Without you," she said. "But I would have remembered Trip regardless. Hard to forget. He asked me to the homecoming dance one year."

"Didn't know your standards were so low."

"Funny." She elbowed him in the ribs. "Didn't go with him. Didn't go at all that year." She stopped paging for a minute and stared straight ahead. Remembering. "The guy I should have gone with . . . Denny . . . we had a fight. Made up after homecoming. Were planning on prom. He died that winter. With three other boys. Car accident. They'd been drinking. Roads were slick. Went off a curve and into a lake." She turned to the first page of the yearbook and showed Jack the dedication. A photo of four boys in letter jackets. Grinning. Arms thrown around each other's shoulders. Below that, lines from Longfellow:

We see but dimly through the mists and vapors;
  Amid these earthly damps
What seem to us but sad, funereal tapers
  May be heaven's distant lamps.

37

Jack: "Four kids. Big loss, especially for a small school."

"Horrible. I'll always regret missing that homecoming dance with Denny."

"What was the fight about?"

"Denny and his buddies beat up Sweet because he asked me out."

"Sweet?"

"Trip's nickname. One of the nicer ones. Another was Motorhead. Trippy. Freak."

"Nice school you went to."

"Small schools don't have a lot of choices when it comes to cliques. If you don't fit into one of a handful of groups, then you don't fit in at all. Sweet was one of those kids who fell between the cracks. His creepy personality didn't help him out. Check out what he wrote in my yearbook." She turned to the last page and pointed to a neatly printed message in the upper right corner:

What goes around comes around, beautiful. Sweet Justice.

Jack's eyes widened. "Damn."

"Yeah. I'm sure he blamed me for the beating. I never had the courage to talk to him again, tell him it wasn't my doing."

"Maybe the reunion."

"I don't think Sweet's one of those sentimental alums who misses the old gang."

"What was your nickname?"

She turned to the section of the book with individual student photos and pointed to a line under hers: "A.k.a. Camel Rider, Potato Head and Betty."

"I get the first two. What's with Betty?"

"Private joke between me and Denny. He was a closet *Flintstones* fan. He'd shut the door to his bedroom after

38

school and watch. He told me I was his Betty. I gave him a *Flintstones* coffee mug. He kept it in his car. Filled it with change. I know it sounds stupid, but I wanted it back when they recovered his car. It was gone. Probably sitting at the bottom of the lake." She closed the yearbook and set it on her nightstand.

Jack shut off the television and handed her the remote. "Put this away, too. Bedrooms should be reserved for screwing and sleeping."

"In that order?" She threw the remote on her nightstand.

"Bet your ass in that order."

"Talk's cheap, baby." She slid down so she was flat on her back. He reached over and shut off the bedside lamp. He peeled off his boxers and leaned over her and pulled her tee shirt over her head. Jack crawled on top of her. She loved the weight and warmth of him; it was like being buried in sand at the beach. Hot and heavy and wet.

A passing barge pushed waves against the boat, but they didn't notice. The rocking seemed part of the rhythm of their lovemaking.

6

What a rush it had been. Being fawned over. Fought over. "I get the first live shot . . . Bullshit. I was here first . . . I set this up before you got here." Treated with respect. Treated like someone with a mind. Called "Mister" every time he turned around. "You're doing fine, Mr. Trip . . . Thank you for your time, Mr. Trip . . . How can we reach you later, Mr. Trip?" He was finished with all the television interviews by a little after ten o'clock Sunday night. Finally got to pull his hat back on. They didn't go for his hat. Told him to take it off for the on-camera interviews. They said they couldn't see his face when he had the hat on. He took it off to please the reporters. Especially the pretty women. All his life—with one exception—just the homely ones went for him, and then only when they were lonely. He'd slept with a lot of ugly, depressed women. He liked being liked by attractive women, and being liked by more than one person at any one time was a complete novelty.

The only other time he'd been showered with that sort of group approval was when he found that little girl's necklace. A few years earlier. A Wisconsin town, outside of Eau Claire. The maintenance engineer for a manufacturing

40

company said he'd buy a couple of five-gallon buckets of degreaser and a bunch of mops if Trip would help comb a farmer's cornfield for a missing kid. Reluctantly, he went along. A hot August afternoon, and the corn was tall. He'd bent over to tie his shoes in between the rows and found the child's jewelry. Then the cops found the kid. Alive. Then it started. Newspaper interviews. People stopping him on the sidewalk and shaking his hand. Strangers in the bar slapping him on the back, buying him beer. At first he was terrified of the fuss. Tried to numb his nerves with booze and pills. Took someone out one night when he wasn't prepared. He wanted to leave town right away, but there were too many reporters waiting for interviews. He didn't want to raise suspicions. He got scared when a cop noticed his cracked windshield the next day, but a couple of people stood up for him. Said the crack had been there all along. He'd never had anyone stand up for him like that. Not since Snow White. That's when he warmed up to the attention, discovered it wasn't so bad if it was positive. The town's mayor, who owned a trophy shop, even gave him an award with his name engraved on it. A bowling trophy. The message said: *Thank you, Justice Trip. You bowled us over with your help.* Probably a leftover from a bowling tournament, but Trip didn't care. He'd never before won a prize for anything.

Most of his thirty-six years, he'd been afraid of any sort of attention. Self-conscious about his height—nearly seven feet—he walked hunched over. He stared down because looking up never got him anything but whispers and stares. Even in kindergarten he was big, and he was so afraid to draw attention to himself he'd pee in his pants rather than raise his hand and ask to go to the bathroom.

41

He finally trained himself to go without water all day. Everyone expected him to play basketball when he got older, but he got tangled in his own legs. He was smart, but doing well in class would have drawn attention. He worked at mediocrity and kept his grades to Cs. Worst of all was the teasing about his stutter. The more the other kids teased, the worse it got. He'd try to go all day without talking. Then he'd hear: "What's wrong? The c... c... cat g... got your t... t... tongue?" When he'd come home from school crying because of the mean kids, Pa would tell him they'd get theirs. He'd say, "What goes around comes around."

His pa was tall, too, but he carried it well. Trip didn't know what his ma was like; his pa had burned all her pictures right after Trip was born. All he knew was her name. Anna. Whenever he asked about her, his pa would say, "Ran off with your big sister. That's all I know." Same words every time. All Trip knew about his big sister was her name. Mary. Two names. Anna and Mary. The only history Trip ever had of his immediate kin. When he was ten, he found a photo in a kitchen drawer, under the paper liner. Nothing written on the back. He assumed it was his sister. Black hair. Nice skin. Dark eyes. She was in a frilly dress. His pa found him holding the picture, ripped it out of his hands and shoved it in the sink.

"That my s... s... sister? That Mary?"

His pa's answer was to turn on the garbage disposal.

Most days he and his pa got along. They were both neat. Kept the house fine. Neither one could cook worth a damn; ate a lot of TV dinners and instant oatmeal. Certain holidays, such as the Fourth of July and Flag Day and Halloween, his pa dressed in a white jumpsuit and passed out Fudgsicles from the front porch while "All Shook Up" blared from the cassette player. He'd make Trip wear a

42

cowboy outfit: hat, vest, bandanna, spurs, holster, plastic six-shooter. That way his pa had his two favorites on the porch: Elvis and cowboys. The routine was supposed to be for the neighborhood kids, but the women came around, too. Pa charmed them. Called them all "ma'am," whether they were junior-high girls or grandmas. His pa craved an audience the way Trip feared it. He was relieved when he finally outgrew the cowboy clothes.

Trip couldn't decide if his life would have been better or worse if he hadn't spent his childhood in the shadow of Graceland. His pa sold bootleg Elvis Presley paraphernalia at a strip mall in Memphis, right across the street from Graceland. Bumper stickers. Snow globes. Shirts. Hats. Action figures. Backscratchers. Salt and pepper shakers. The shop was a weird place to be when Elvis was alive. Always full of tourists talking about *The King. The King. The King.* When he was real young, Trip thought they were talking about Jesus because he'd heard about The King of the Jews in Sunday school. He thought Jesus starred in *Jailhouse Rock* and sang "Love Me Tender," and wondered if The King was crucified and went to heaven, why was he still living in the big house across the street. The shop got weirder after Elvis died, and busier. His pa struggled to keep up. The stock of souvenirs multiplied nearly overnight; floor-to-ceiling snow globes and backscratchers. The stuff flew off the shelves, but the fans doing the buying weren't happy anymore. They were all bawling when they came into the store, and his pa would bawl with them. Trip didn't like any of it; he hid in the stockroom. His pa would yell for him: "Make yourself worthwhile." The store became a jumbled mess.

Then his pa hired Snow White.

Cammie Lammont had skin the color of eggshells and black hair that reached down to her butt. She walked into the shop carrying a suitcase and wearing sunglasses and a wide-brimmed straw hat; she could have been a starlet on the run from her fans. Her dress was spray-painted on. She was nearly as tall as Trip, but she carried herself like a queen. Nose in the air. Back straight as an ironing board. She ripped the Help Wanted sign they'd posted in the shop window and brought it over to his pa. "Meet your help," she said, and slapped the sign on the counter. When she took off her sunglasses, the expression on his pa's face was strange. A combination of surprise and fear and curiosity. She moved in with them. Took the spare bedroom. She couldn't cook and she didn't know spit about Elvis, but she managed the inventory and did the bookkeeping. She saved the shop. His pa gave her a baseball hat on her six-month anniversary. She eyed the cap with suspicion. "What's this E.P. stand for?" Trip thought his pa was going to pass out.

She was Trip's first crush, and she knew it. She'd laugh and tell him, "For all you know, I'm old enough to be your mama." Cammie was one of those women who slathered on the makeup and kept her age a big secret. She told him she'd run away from home because her ma's boyfriend tried to get into her pants, so Trip suspected she wasn't that much older than he. Still, she didn't dress or act much like a teenager and she had a hard edge. She didn't laugh or smile much, but she was good to him. Called him "Sweet Justice" or "Sweet." She didn't mind his stutter. Told him she used to stutter. He didn't believe her; to his ears, she articulated like a radio announcer. They'd go to movies together. Cartoons. She loved anything by Walt Disney. One night some older kids from school saw the two of them together. She caught them giving Trip dirty looks. She grabbed his ass in front of them and kissed him hard on the mouth. One of them dropped his popcorn. Trip loved her for it. She took him to a motel after the movie. He was fourteen. Not long after, Cammie and Pa had an argument. Trip heard them yelling at each other one night, then Cammie crying. Trip rolled over and went to sleep. Cammie was one for dramatics. He figured the fight was over the bookkeeping. They always fought over the bookkeeping. Pa thought Cammie was doing a little skimming; he kept her on anyway. Whatever she was holding over his pa's head, Trip was glad for it.

She was with them about a year, until she was struck by a car one autumn night while walking home from the shop. She'd left Trip's pa behind to close up. Dark side street. No witnesses. Paramedics said she might have lived had they gotten to her a little sooner. Had the driver stopped and summoned help. The police never caught who did it. The only clues were two quarters wiped clean of prints. One placed on each side of her head. Cops guessed whoever killed her left the money as some kind of final insult, like she was a two-bit whore or something. Trip imagined the accident. Played it over and over in his head. In his mind's eye, she was run over by a car filled with jealous teenagers like the ones at the movie theater. Sometimes they were headed to a dance and other times they were coming back from a football game. Always ended the same, though. Snow White sprawled on the street. Coins tossed out of a car window. Laughter coming from the car as it squealed away.

His pa was as broken up as he was. Trip wondered if they'd had another fight that night and that's why she stomped off. When Trip asked him what had happened, the response was nearly the same as when he asked about his missing ma: "Ran off. That's all I know." His pa shipped her body down to Baton Rouge, where he said she had

45

family. Trip wanted to go to the funeral but his old man told him they were headed in the other direction. They sold everything and moved to Minnesota—about as far north as they could drive without leaving the country. They kept a few Elvis souvenirs. A snow globe with a miniature of Graceland inside. A box of cigarette lighters engraved with a line drawing of Graceland. A clock with The King's swinging legs as the pendulum. A green street sign that said *Elvis Presley Boulevard*. Trip made sure he took her *E.P.* hat; it carried her smell. Herbal shampoo and Charlie cologne.

His pa got work cleaning a Catholic high school in St. Paul. The principal gave Trip free tuition. Wasn't any better or worse than public school in Tennessee. Like back in Memphis, the other students teased him about his stutter. They had the additional ammunition of his pa being the janitor. His accent was the biggest, easiest target, however. Between classes, the meanest ones yelled stuff down the hall in an exaggerated southern drawl. *Yew-all* this and *yew-all* that. *How yew-all doin', b... b... boy? Yew-all eat g... g... grits, b... b... boy?* He worked on it and toned down his accent, but there was nothing he could do about his stutter. He'd had it all his life, since he could remember. Even in his dreams he stuttered. In elementary school, the nurse tried to get Trip some speech therapy, but his pa wouldn't go for it. Said it would be a waste of time because stuttering ran in the family. Nothing to be done about it. Trip wondered what his pa was talking about; he didn't know any relatives who talked like he did.

At home, Trip hid under the hood of a truck. All the neighbors in the trailer park brought their beaters to him and he worked on them until they purred. He loved it. Trucks didn't care whether he could dribble a basketball or what he sounded like when he opened his mouth. All they

46

recognized was his skill and genius at work on their engines and bodies. Behind the wheel of a truck, up so high off the ground, he didn't have to look anybody in the face. The money he earned fixing trucks he spent on his own trucks, and on drugs and knives.

He loved fancy knives. Sharp and flashy, the way he wished he could be in public. His pa thought the knives were a waste, wanted him to get into hunting. "Buy a shotgun. Something worthwhile," he'd tell Trip. His room had piles of catalogs with knives and swords and daggers in them. He ordered hundreds of them so there were always packages with wonderful surprises arriving at his door. Samurai swords. Battle-axes. Throwing knives. Daggers with dragons carved on the handle. Machetes. Folding knives. Stilettos. Bowie knives. A set of jackknives with Confederate officers etched on the handles, including General Robert E. Lee. He surrounded himself with his collection; they were his closest friends since Cammie. They hung on the walls of his room and rested in different wooden cases under his bed. At night, he'd spend hours getting stoned and listening to Black Sabbath and getting those blades sharper. Loved putting a good edge on a blade while listening to his music. Sharp metal and heavy metal.

7

Murphy got up before Jack to go for a run. Pulled on some sweats and a stocking cap and her shoes. Went out onto the dock, shutting the door quietly behind her. While she stretched she searched the decks of her nearest neighbors and saw signs of cold weather preparations. Covers draped over grills. Patio flowerpots emptied. Those who were planning to stay the winter but didn't have well-insulated houseboats were already wrapping their exteriors in plastic. She'd recently beefed up her insulation to avoid doing that this year—one bit of practical maintenance she'd managed to accomplish. She wondered which of her neighbors would tough out another winter on the river and which would lock up their boats and get an apartment downtown. The cold didn't get to them as much as the isolation. Even in the summer, not many people lived on the river full-time. In the winter, the numbers dropped to a hardy few. The wildlife artist and his photographer wife would stay; they utilized the scenery for their work. The architect would stay; his well-equipped boat even had a Jacuzzi in the master bath. She hoped Floyd Kvaal and his three-legged dog, Tripod, would stay another winter. Kvaal was a garage-door salesman and a musician. In the summer, he paddled his canoe around the neighborhood and played the sax. Last winter, the neighbors took turns having him play at their houses.

She finished stretching and thumped down the dock and through the parking lot. Took one of her usual routes. North across the Wabasha Bridge, glancing down at the Mississippi as she crossed it. The leaves on the trees lining the river were orange and yellow and rust. A gray morning. Cold and windy. She ran through downtown to the State Capitol mall. Fallen leaves crunched under her feet. Back south down Wabasha. For variety, she took a left at Kellogg Boulevard and cut through the riverfront park to run across the Robert Street Bridge. She looked downriver as she ran. Jammed with barges. Soon enough they'd be gone, chased south by the ice. She hung a right on Plato Boulevard and watched for trains as she went across the railroad tracks. North up Wabasha and a left onto Harriet Island. A couple of weeks had passed since the Twin Cities Marathon. It had been a good race for her—she'd come in at 3:41—but it left her sore and she was having trouble going back to a regular running schedule.

She started walking when she got to the yacht club parking lot. Thumping toward her boat, she spotted her copy of the *St. Paul Pioneer Press* in the middle of the dock. The paper carrier was getting better; at least it wasn't floating in the water this time. She bent over to retrieve it, stood up, inhaled the river air. What did it smell like today? Some days it smelled like dead fish. Other days, motor oil. On rare occasions, like something fresh and clean. She didn't mind. Murphy loved living on a working river jammed with barges and towboats. Sure there were speedboats and paddleboats and rowboats, but they all knew to steer clear of the metal behemoths that ruled the

Mississippi. She couldn't imagine living on a body of water without the barge traffic. Too quiet and boring. She tucked the paper under her arm, walked into the boat, heard the shower upstairs. Damn. He'd beaten her into the bathroom. She'd have to put a shower in the downstairs guest bath one of these days. She turned on the coffeemaker and scanned the paper while the pot dripped. There he was again. Justice Trip. On the front page, above the fold. She stared at his photo. "Sweet Justice," she said. She poured herself a cup and sat down at the kitchen table to read the story. Trip was a shirt salesman. He traveled around northern Minnesota and western Wisconsin selling shirts to clothing stores in small towns. He'd helped during a search years ago. A Wisconsin town. A missing girl. He found her necklace in a cornfield. The cops concentrated their search and found the child at the edge of the field. Dehydrated but alive. It made him feel good, he said in the story, and he wished this search had the same happy ending. "But it doesn't look good," he said.

"No shit," Murphy said.

Jack walked downstairs while digging in his ears with a Q-Tip. "Talking to yourself? You're losing it, lady." He bent over and nibbled on her neck. He saw the front page spread out on the table. "They're sure making a big deal out of him."

"Something isn't right; these stories aren't the whole story," she said, more to herself than to Jack.

He walked over to the coffeepot and poured a cup. "How so?"

"The way Sweet's portraying himself. It's as if he's talking about someone else. Some character he made up."

Jack leaned against the counter and sipped his coffee. "I'm sure we'd all exaggerate, try to make ourselves sound better in the newspaper."

"Genuine good guys are embarrassed when people call them heroes, especially on the front page. Sweet's wallowing in it. Promoting himself. He was never that way."

"That was high school. People change." Jack took another sip of coffee.

"Look here. He's talking about how he feels a connection to this Bunny Pederson because she was an Elvis fan. Who says she was an Elvis fan? And he hates Elvis. Heavy metal was his music He's constructed this bizarre fantasy world."

Jack set his coffee cup in the sink. "Her music tastes aside, anything else new about the unfortunate owner of the finger?"

Murphy folded the paper and set it down. "They ran out of stuff to say about the disappearing bridesmaid. Sweet's the latest angle, you know."

"On that cynical note, I'm outta here." He pulled on his jacket.

"What about breakfast? I've got omelet fixings."

"Nope. Early shift. By the way, that showerhead is leaking."

"I'll add it to the list," she said. "Right after the paint job and new deck railing and a second shower."

"I've offered to help. I spend enough time here."

She shook her head. "It's my own damn fault." She'd saved for repairs at one point, but blew it all on upgrading her galley. She had to have a great kitchen. "I'm a big girl. I'll figure it out."

He kissed her on the cheek and left. The sound of the door slamming made her feel sad. Another weekend spent together and not a word uttered between them about their relationship. She couldn't remember what they'd talked about. What they'd said to each other that mattered. Lately they both kept moving and doing because when they

51

weren't in motion, they had nothing to say to each other. It used to be the silent moments they shared were intimate and comfortable. Now they were awkward. First-date awkward. Not a good sign for the marriage, she figured. Something had changed, and she decided it was her fault. The affair had hit her harder than she expected. She was spending too much time thinking about it, analyzing the word itself. *Affair*. Had it lasted long enough to be called that? She and Erik had slept together only once. If it wasn't an affair, what was it? She avoided thinking about the other *A* word. *Adultery*. Whenever it crossed her mind, she told herself it wasn't adultery because she and Jack were separated at the time and working on getting back together. Like they were now. It seemed as if they were always working on it. What did Erik say? *If it takes too much work, maybe it isn't there.* She had to admit she missed him. Missed his hands on her. His mouth. She ran her finger around the rim of her coffee cup. "Damn you, Erik." She shivered, cold in her damp running clothes. She'd have to turn up the temp on the boat; winter was on the way.

She ran upstairs, pulled off her clothes and turned on the shower. She stepped into a lukewarm spray; a new water heater moved up a notch on the home improvement list. She heard ringing while she was drying off. She twisted the towel into a turban around her wet hair and went into the bedroom to search for the cell phone. She fished it out from under the covers. "Murphy."

The Homicide commander: "Got a little job for you this morning."

"Let's hear it." She braced herself. Commander Axel Duncan was new to the job but not to the department. He'd worked in Vice for years. Since moving to head Homicide he'd shaved his beard, cut his wild blond hair and stopped dressing to pass for a drug addict, but he was still behaving like a loose-cannon undercover cop. His act wasn't translating well in Homicide; he summoned his detectives at all hours to send them off on strange missions. Some of the other cops called Duncan "Yo-Yo."

"That Moose Lake case," he said. "They haven't been able to reach her ex. Baby-sitter says he took off with the kids Friday night."

"So?"

"So he's a West Sider. Check out his place. See if anyone's seen him or his kids. Sniff around the garage. Maybe he's a sentimental fool and took part of her home in the car trunk."

"They're looking at him for this?"

"Maybe."

"Don't suppose anyone's explored the nine hundred other possibilities." The state had a medium-security prison in Moose Lake with nearly nine hundred male inmates.

"All the naughty boys have been accounted for."

"Good." Then a question for which she already knew the answer: "Have we got a search warrant for the ex's place?" Duncan rarely worried about legalities, rules, jurisdiction.

"For what? We're not searching jack. We're poking around. That's all. Poking around."

She paused and then asked, "Is this official or unofficial poking?" That was code for: *Are you going to get both our butts in trouble with this one?*

He ignored her question. "You're from that end of town. You can canvass it in your sleep. Shit. With that big fucking clan of yours, he's probably one of your relatives and you don't even know it. Get on it, Potato Head."

She didn't want him calling her that, but she let it go. With Duncan, it was best to let it go. He was always ready for a fight. "What's the address?" she asked.

8

Murphy didn't need to write down the address. It wasn't far from the Murphy family home, where as a kid she'd claimed the root cellar as her bedroom to escape the rest of the beehive. That's how she'd earned the title "Potato Head." A family nickname. She didn't want anyone using it except relatives and a couple of close friends; Axel was neither one. She thought he was a pain in the ass. A hot dog and a show-off.

She pulled out of the yacht club parking lot and went south on Wabasha Street. She took a right on Water Street and passed the Great River Boat Works, where yachts and speedboats and houseboats were on blocks and lined up behind a fence, waiting for repairs in the yard. She took a left on Plato Boulevard and a right on Ohio Street and snaked up the winding hill. She hung a right on George Street, crossed Smith Avenue and drove into Cherokee Park.

Chad Pederson lived in a compact bungalow off the park. Murphy circled the block once and then drove down the alley. She parked her Jeep in front of a garage a couple of houses away from Pederson's. Before getting out of the car, she opened her shoulder bag and checked her service weapon, a .40-cal. Glock Model 23. When she didn't wear a belt or shoulder rig, her purse doubled as her holster and had a special sleeve to carry her gun. She walked down the alley, surveying the trash cans huddled next to all the garages. The cans were empty; the neighborhood had recently had a garbage pickup. If Chad Pederson had disposed of any evidence in the trash, it was already at the dump. A cedar privacy fence enclosed Pederson's backyard, but there was a gate from the alley. She peeked through a crack between the fence boards and then opened the gate and walked in.

Against the back fence was a garden the size of a doormat; it was a tangle of dead tomato vines. On one side of the yard she saw an aluminum playground set with two swings and a slide. On the other side was a tree with slats of wood nailed onto the trunk; the rungs led up to a wooden platform set between the lowest branches. A fort. Her brothers built lots of them when they were kids. A deck ran alongside the back of the bungalow. Tucked into one corner of the deck was a doghouse—a miniature of Pederson's bungalow—with a sign nailed across the top. *Spike's Place.* A couple of shallow holes in the dirt against the fence had to be Spike's handiwork. There were no suspicious mounds or patches of fresh sod, and she'd expected none. She'd never come across someone stupid enough to bury his ex in the backyard. She remembered one genius who'd dumped his wife in the lake behind their house. Another kept his girlfriend in a trunk in the garage. Better check the garage, she thought.

The service door was open a crack. She put her ear to it and listened. Nothing. She pulled out her flashlight and pushed the door the rest of the way with her hip and

55

walked inside. She sniffed. No suspicious smells. She flicked on the flashlight and ran the beam around the garage. No car. No trunk, either. A snowmobile sitting on a small trailer took up half the two-car garage. Tools hanging from the walls. Kids' bikes and rakes pushed against the side. She shined her light overhead. A plastic snowman and a set of reindeer tucked into the rafters. A bunch of hockey sticks. Couple of shovels. She turned off the flashlight, stuffed it in her purse and went back outside.

Both the garage and the house needed a coat of latex; white paint was flaking off in spots. Murphy could sympathize; her boat needed a paint job. She walked onto the deck and peeked through the sliding glass doors. No signs of movement. She knocked on the back door and listened. No response.

A big voice from next door: "They went duck hunting."

Murphy turned to her left; a man was standing on his deck looking over the fence at her. He'd returned from his own hunting trip. He was dressed in camouflage and had an armload of shotguns in camouflage cases. He was fat and all the green he was wearing and carrying made him look like an army tank.

"How'd you make out?" Murphy asked.

"Got our limit." Three boys in camouflage came up behind him on the deck, their arms empty. He looked at them as he struggled to open the back door. "You lazy turds. Go help your mother unload the car."

"I gotta pee," said the littlest.

"You can hold it. Go help your mother." The three boys turned around and stepped off the deck.

"No school today?" Murphy asked.

"Kids have been off since Thursday. Teachers' convention. They should have been back in school today but I let them play hooky so we could hunt longer."

"When did Chad leave for hunting?" Murphy asked.

The man pushed open his back door. Two big dogs ran up the deck steps and shot through the door ahead of him. "He was having a hard time getting off work. Said he wasn't leaving until after work Friday. Was gonna swing by his ex's house and pick up his boys and go."

"Know when they're due back?"

"He was talking about taking today off, like we did. Send them back to school tomorrow." The man set his guns down against the side of the house and looked at her. "You the new girlfriend?"

"No."

He smiled. "Too bad. Chad's a good egg. Deserves a babe." His wife came up behind him, arms loaded with gear. She was as big as he was and was also dressed in camo. She pushed past her husband to get into the house.

"Know where they were hunting?" Murphy asked.

"Chad's buddy has got a cabin. Not sure exactly where. You social services or what?"

Murphy heard barking from inside the man's house, and then his wife: "Fred! Get these filthy animals out of here!"

"Gotta go," he said. He picked up his guns and walked through the door.

Murphy went to the front of the Pederson house, stood on the porch, peered through a couple of the windows. An elderly voice: "Nobody home. Went duck hunting." Then a hacking cough. Murphy turned and saw Pederson's neighbor on the other side of the fence. The elderly black woman was wrapped in a heavy sweater and sitting on a porch swing. In her lap was a white poodle dressed in a matching sweater. Murphy swore to herself she'd never own a dog that wore sweaters.

She smiled as she walked up the old woman's steps. "Hello."

"You're a cop," said the woman. She coughed again. Her skin was as gray as her hair. She had a cigarette between her boney fingers and was holding it away from her so the ash wouldn't drop on the dog. She wore red lipstick; it was smeared all over the cigarette butt. "Paris Murphy, right?"

"Yeah. Do I know you?"

"Mrs. McDonough. Recognized you from your mom and dad's joint." More hacking. "I saw you punch a fella after he pinched your ass. You were a tough little shit."

"Tell me about this Pederson. Is he a decent neighbor or a jerk?"

"Chad. He's a nice kid. Moved down here from up north. Juggles two jobs to make his child support."

Murphy took her notebook out of her purse. "Where's he work?"

"Machine shop in Minneapolis. Third shift. Tends bar during the day at that titty club on West Seventh Street."

"I know the place," said Murphy, writing in her notebook. "Ever see him lose it with his kids or his ex or anyone else?"

"Never met his ex." She stopped talking to pick a dog hair off her tongue. "Cute kids. A little wild."

"Does he yell at them a lot? Slug them? Hear any racket over there?"

"That stupid monster, Spike. Barks at everything that moves. Scares the living shit out of my baby." She scratched behind the poodle's ears and kissed his head; she left a lipstick mark on his fur.

"What else about Chad?"

"Quiet. Shovels my walk in the winter. Won't take a dime from me. Sent tomatoes over all summer. Big Boys. Real meaty." She paused to take a drag off her cigarette, coughed, took another pull. Then it occurred to her: "Christ Almighty! That's his ex on the news, isn't it? You're not thinking he killed her. No way he did it."

"Know how I can reach him?"

"He's at a friend's cabin. No phone. No electricity. Outdoor crapper." She coughed so hard she dropped the cigarette. A gust of wind made her shiver and pull her sweater tighter around her thin body. "I think he's nuts. Especially this time of year."

"He ever mention the friend's name? Where the cabin is located?"

"Nope. If he did, I'd remember." More hacking, then: "The body's going, but the mind still works. Your folks, Sean and Amira, they still alive?"

"Alive and kicking," Murphy said.

"Tell them Tootie says hello."

"I'll do that. You take it easy, Mrs. McDonough." She closed her notebook and slipped it back in her purse.

"Try tonight on Chad," she said as Murphy stepped off the porch. "He'll be back tonight. Probably bring me a duck all cleaned and ready for the oven." She bent over and picked the cigarette off the porch floor and took another puff. "No way in hell he killed her."

Murphy checked her watch. Close to lunchtime, and she could go for a bar burger and fries. She took Smith Avenue and crossed the High Bridge over the river. She hung a left on West Seventh and drove a couple of miles. There used to be several strip joints in St. Paul, but one by one they were shut down by neighborhood activists. One on the East Side was now an Embers restaurant in the front and a bingo hall in the back. Another on University Avenue had been converted into the police department's Western District Office. The West Seventh club was one of the last two left in town.

She took a left and pulled into the parking lot, turned off the Jeep and slipped her keys in her purse. She slid out of the car and shut the driver's door. Surveyed the parking lot. Not many cars. From what she remembered, the place had the biggest lunch crowd on Fridays. She hiked her purse strap over her right shoulder and walked to the entrance. The front windows were painted black with white silhouettes of nude women. After stepping inside, Murphy stopped for a few seconds so her eyes could adjust to the dark. The place looked the same as she remembered from her days as a uniform. The bottom half of the walls were covered by wood paneling and the top half by barn-red paint. Large oil portraits of nude women provided the main decoration for the place. The bar was on one end of the room and was circled by stools. The other end was the stage. Murphy saw a nude dancer swaying to Tina Turner. A boney blonde with dark pubic hair shaved into a narrow V. A glass wall separated the performers from the rest of the bar. The city didn't allow establishments with nude dancing to serve liquor. As a way around the rule, the strip joints divided their clubs and put up the walls. They had separate outside entrances for the performance and bar areas. So the women could still receive tips, slots were cut at the bottom of the glass walls. Men slipped the bills through like they were sliding deposits to bank tellers.

Murphy took a stool at the bar. Unzipped her jacket and set her purse on her lap. Most of the dozen customers were sitting at the foot of the stage. A guy in a booth against the wall was getting a lap dance from a skinny brunette in a bikini. Murphy didn't see anyone she recognized; it would be easier to ask questions. She didn't expect trouble regardless. Strip clubs tended to have middle-aged patrons—including lots of married men—and those customers kept a low profile. Rarely made trouble. The police got more complaints about bars frequented by the younger crowd; they'd spill out of the clubs and pee and puke on people's lawns.

An older woman with big arms and a pink face walked to Murphy's end of the counter. Her silver hair was braided and coiled in a circle on top of her head. She wore a tee shirt that read: *Cleverly disguised as a responsible adult.* "What can I get you?"

"Burger and fries."

The woman scratched the order on a pad.

"Anything to drink?"

"Diet Pepsi."

"No Pepsi."

"Diet Coke?"

"Coke we got. Want that now?" Murphy nodded and the woman turned around to fill a glass with ice.

"Chad not working today?" Murphy asked.

The woman poured the pop and slid the glass to Murphy. "Duck hunting. That's why I'm up front instead of in the kitchen." She nodded toward the dancer onstage. "I'm not big on this stuff." She left to hand the order off to the kitchen. Murphy looked at the stage again. The dancer's routine had switched from simple swaying to squatting with her knees splayed wide and then standing. Squatting. Standing. Squatting. Standing. The bartender returned with a towel. Started wiping the counter.

Murphy sipped her Coke. "I suppose Chad deserves a day off."

"That he does," said the woman. "Works his hind end off for those boys of his. Hockey equipment ain't cheap. The older one is a goalie. Know what goalie pads cost? My daughter's got two goalies. Thank God her husband makes good scratch."

61

Murphy took another drink. Set it down. Stirred it with the straw. "You'd think Chad's ex would help out more."

"Don't know a thing about her," said the bartender. "Never heard Chad say a word against her. Who knows? Maybe she's playing him for a sucker." The woman stopped wiping and eyed Murphy. "You Chad's new squeeze?"

Murphy: "No."

"Friends, huh? Chad's got plenty of those. He needs a woman who can cook for him."

Murphy tipped her head toward the woman onstage. "Doesn't he socialize with any of the ladies here?"

She wrinkled her nose. "The dancers? No way. Not his type."

A guy in a suit took a stool to Murphy's right. He had a drink in his hand. It smelled like whiskey. Strong stuff for lunch, Murphy thought. His eyes were bloodshot. Tie askew. He had short red hair and freckles. Old enough to be in the bar, but too young to be hitting the booze so hard so early in the day. He raised his right index finger. The bartender eyed him. "I think you've had enough," she said.

The guy turned and said to Murphy, "The responsible adult thinks I've had enough."

"I'd have to agree," Murphy said. She sipped her Coke.

He stared at Murphy's chest. "You should be up there, baby." He thumbed toward the stage; the boney blonde had been replaced by a chubby blonde, also with dark pubic hair. She turned her back to the crowd and bent forward, looking between her legs while hanging on to her ankles.

"No," said Murphy. "That's not my kind of dancing."

"You wouldn't have to dance," he said. "All you'd have to do is get naked and stand there and they'd slide you wads of cash. Know why?"

"Why?"

" 'Cause you got a rack." With the word *rack* he slammed his right hand on the bar.

"Thanks," Murphy said dryly.

"No. I mean it. I could talk to the manager. I know the manager." He threw his left arm around her shoulders and leaned into her right ear. "Listen. Here's the plan." He stopped talking and frowned. "I forgot what I was going to say."

Murphy pushed his arm off her. "You were going to ask the bartender for a cup of coffee and a sandwich."

He nodded. "Good idea." He raised his finger again. A male bartender—a tall black guy in a square haircut—approached him. The drunk pointed to his glass.

"No way, buddy. You're done," the bartender said, and walked to the other end of the bar.

The female bartender set a plate of burger and fries in front of Murphy, and a bottle of ketchup. The drunk picked up the bottle and squirted a puddle of ketchup on Murphy's plate. Set the bottle down.

"Hey!" said Murphy. He picked a couple of fries off her plate, dipped them in the ketchup and started eating them. She slid the plate in front of him. "Put this on his tab," she told the female bartender. "He needs it more than I do."

"I'm sorry," said the woman. "I'm gonna get someone over here to deal with this joker." She walked over to the tall bartender and whispered something in his ear. He nodded and picked up a phone under the bar.

"I got what I need," Murphy said to herself. She pulled some bills out of her purse, threw them on the bar and hopped off the stool. Threw her purse strap over her shoulder and went out the door. She was reaching in her purse for her keys when she heard someone behind her. She turned. The drunk redhead. He had ketchup on his chin. "What the hell do you want?" she asked.

He stepped toward her. "I think you know." He pressed her against the side of the Jeep and cupped her left breast over her jacket. "You gotta be a hooker, coming into a place like this by yourself. With tits like these. What do you charge for a knob job, huh?"

She pushed him off of her and he fell against her again. Reached around and cupped her buttocks with his hands. "Come on, baby. This your day off or what?"

"My friend," Murphy said. "You picked the wrong ass to grab." She pushed him off of her with both hands, stepped behind him and slammed him face-first into the Jeep. She grabbed each of his wrists in each of her hands and pulled his arms behind him.

"Murphy. Need some help?"

She looked over her shoulder. Two uniforms. She recognized both of them. The male bartender must have called them. "Yeah. Take this asshole to detox." She stepped away.

The bigger of the two uniforms held the drunk's arms behind his back while his partner cuffed the guy's wrists. They flipped him over so he faced them. He looked at Murphy. "Why'd you call the cops, baby?"

Murphy was wiping the front of her jacket with a wad of tissue. The guy had ketchup on his hands and had gotten some on her. "I am the cops," she said.

"Shit," the drunk muttered.

The two uniforms walked him over to their squad. They eased him into the back while Murphy watched with her arms folded in front of her.

64

"Wouldn't have squeezed her tits if I knew she was a cop."

"You squeezed her tits?" said the big uniform. "Jesus Christ. You're lucky to be breathing. We saved your life, dumb shit."

9

Chad Pederson wasn't a wife killer. Murphy did more checking when she got back to the station. Made a few phone calls from her desk. He had nothing in the way of a record. "Damn waste of time," she muttered as she threw down a pen and leaned back in her chair.

Chuck Dubrowski and Max Castro walked into the office. They were veterans in Homicide and had been partners so long they looked alike—big arms, bushy eyebrows, gray hair, thick necks that seemed sunburned even in the middle of winter. When Dubrowski learned he needed glasses, he went out and got the same wire-rimmed frames as Castro. He said it was a coincidence, but Murphy enjoyed giving him grief about it. Today they wore matching sweatshirts under their blazers.

"Wild-goose chase," Castro muttered, tossing a notebook on his desk.

Dubrowski poured himself a cup of coffee and collapsed into his chair. "Yo-Yo and his bullshit."

"What happened?" Murphy asked.

"Get this," said Castro, sitting down. "Duncan hands us this address on the North End. Some guy getting death threats."

"The North End?" asked Murphy. "I know where this is going."

"Yup," said Dubrowski. "Anyway, I tell Yo-Yo who we're dealing with, that we all know this head case. He says there could be something to it; maybe somebody is really threatening the guy this time. I tell Duncan to send a uniform. Castro says we should call head case's social worker. The asshole says if we don't take the call, he's gonna write us up. Fuck him."

Castro: "So we drive out there to make Duncan happy. The head case is sitting in his front room with a crucifix. He's got his noggin wrapped in aluminum foil so the aliens can't tap into his mind. Waves his cross around and says he won't talk to us because we're part of the conspiracy. Says we're ghosts from another planet and we're helping UFOs abduct people."

"Ghosts? That's a new twist in his story," Murphy said. "But then why does he keep calling us?"

Dubrowski: "Hell if I know."

Murphy: "Ghosts don't go out during the day, do they?"

Dubrowski: "I didn't write this guy's script for him."

Castro got out of his chair and walked over to Murphy's desk. "Anyway, we're coming back to the cop shop and Duncan calls us." He folded his arms across his chest. "Guess what he says? Says to make sure we do up a detailed report. That's the word he used. *Detailed.*"

Murphy: "You're shittin' me."

Castro: "I shit you not."

"Think it would do us any good to talk to the boss?" Murphy asked.

"He's got his own problems," said Castro.

Murphy knew he was right. Months earlier, Chief Benjamin Christianson had been accused of hindering her investigation into a prostitute's death. The murderer—the man who'd given Murphy the scar—was a surgeon and a cousin of Christianson's wife. The doctor killed himself before his arrest, but that didn't end the mess. The mayor wanted the chief's resignation and Christianson was fighting it. Adding to the tumult: a city council plan to move police headquarters from downtown to the lower East Side.

"What about going to the union?" said Murphy.

"We already talked to Sandeen," said Dubrowski. Pete Sandeen, another Homicide detective, was a union steward. "He says we should hold off. Give Yo-Yo time. I say it's time to kick his ass."

Castro walked back to his desk, sat down and waved Dubrowski over. "Come on, Casper. Let's put our alien heads together and do up a *detailed* report on Reynolds Wrap Man."

Murphy had to give them a hard time about their shirts before they went to work. "Hey, cute sweats. Where can I get one? Then we can all match."

Castro opened his desk drawer. "I already grabbed one for you."

Murphy thought he was joking, but he pulled a shirt out and threw it to her. She caught it and held it up. The upper left side of the shirt was embroidered with a St. Paul Homicide detective's badge and circling it, the words: *To the living we owe respect. To the dead we owe the truth.* "I like that," she said. "Where'd this come from?"

Castro: "The union. Sandeen made them up. Says it'll promote unity and team spirit and all that other crap. He's trying to come up with a different one for each division. If he can't get rid of Yo-Yo for us, at least he can dress us pretty."

* * *

Murphy wanted to find out if her mission was Yo-Yo's idea or if the Moose Lake cops had asked for help. She walked into Duncan's office before going home that night. He was on the phone with his feet up on the desk. He motioned for her to sit down in the chair across from his desk, and she did.

"Did he have anything on him when you picked him up?" While cradling the phone between his ear and shoulder, he was playing with a paper clip. Unbending it. A mound of straightened paper clips on his desk, as well as foam coffee cups, piles of paper, a half-eaten bagel and a copy of *Popular Science*. "No kidding? Any of them been fired?"

He wore an oxford shirt with sleeves rolled up, dress pants and a tie—Christianson ordered all his commanders to wear ties—but his clothes looked as if Duncan had slept in them for a week. He had sneakers on his feet. Murphy recognized the brand. Pricey running shoes. The tread was worn. Did the slob actually exercise? The blazer he'd brought to work was on the floor next to his desk and there was a dirty stripe across the back; he'd run over it with the casters of his chair.

"I'll ask my detective. She's back from the house. Sure. Sure. Happy to help out. Glad the s.o.b. turned up."

Murphy realized he was talking about Chad Pederson. She couldn't believe Moose Lake was seriously looking at him for this. Everything she'd learned about Pederson told her he wasn't the killer. What did they have on him? She got a sick feeling in the pit of her stomach. Had Yo-Yo cooked up some theory and sold it to the cops up north? Duncan craved being in the middle of all the action. She hoped he hadn't dragged her into the middle with him.

He picked up a cup and speared it with a paper clip. "Tell you what. Here's an idea for you." He pulled his feet off the desk, knocking a pile of papers to the floor. "Why don't I send her up there?"

"Shit," Murphy said under her breath.

"She's the best we've got. Real easy on the eyes, too." Duncan winked at her and Murphy smiled. He swiveled his chair around to glance out the window while he talked and she flipped him the bird behind his back.

"No. No. Not a problem." He spun his chair back around and hung up the phone. "Pack your bags, Potato Head."

Murphy: "What did you tell them? I haven't even briefed you yet. Jesus Christ. I don't think he did it. Doesn't have a record. Neighbors love his ass. Works like a dog. He was duck hunting with his kids."

"That's the bullshit he laid on the authorities up there. Here's what really happened: Pederson shoots his ex after she leaves the wedding reception, dumps the body, grabs the kids and takes off. Maybe he really does take them duck hunting; it's a good excuse to disappear for a while. He brings them back to the ex's house days later and acts all broken up, pretends he didn't know she got croaked."

"Motive?"

"Hated paying child support."

"Why did they find a finger? Where's the rest of her?"

"Animals probably snacked on her; one of them ran off with a hunk of her and dropped it. The rest of her is out there somewhere."

"This is the story you've sold to the Moose Lake police?"

"Carlton County sheriff. But the police up there are on the same page." He picked up a sheet of paper and started folding it into an airplane.

Murphy got up from the chair and paced in front of his desk. "You've got nothing to base this on."

"Pederson had a trunk full of shotguns when he pulled into Moose Lake this afternoon. A couple of them had been discharged." He tossed the paper airplane toward a wastebasket in the corner and missed. "On top of that, he had a vicious dog. Almost took a deputy's arm off. I would've shot the thing."

She stopped pacing, stood behind the chair she'd been sitting in, grabbed the back of it with both hands. She knew he was waiting for her to go ballistic; she saw the expectant expression on his face. She sat back down and rubbed her forehead with her hands. She caught his eyes locking on her scar and she brushed her bangs down to cover it. In a low voice she said, "He was duck hunting."

"If he's innocent, it'll all come out. He's got major fucking holes in his story. If you think you can plug them with what you got down here, go right ahead, if that's what you wanna do." Duncan leaned back and put his feet up on the desk again. "But if that is what you wanna do, it makes me wonder. That little bump on the head. That making you soft, Murphy?"

She sat up straight in the chair. Her eyes narrowed and darkened, seemed to go from violet to black.

He smiled and took another shot at her: "They got an opening in the Public Pretender's Office."

That's what Homicide called the Ramsey County Public Defender's Office. She wanted to bolt out of the chair and tell him to go fuck himself. Leave the room. Slam the door behind her. He'd love it, though. A big scene in the office. She didn't give it to him, but she was disappointed with the weak argument that finally came out of her mouth: "This is out of our jurisdiction."

"Don't worry about jurisdiction."

"It's not our case."

"Now it is. Get your butt up there, Potato Head."

71

10

He'd decided not to weave any lies because he feared he'd lose track of them. Instead, he left out the bits of his life that were unsuitable for a savior. He didn't tell them he lived in a trailer park or that his father was his roommate or that he was considered a loser in high school or that he'd never gone to college. No one questioned the missing details; all the reporters wanted to concentrate on was his previous hero experience.

He met one last newspaper reporter for an interview over lunch Monday. She said she was doing a feature on him for the next day's paper. He ordered a burger and fries and she bought herself a Diet Coke. He was grateful for the food; it gave him something to fiddle with. He kept stumbling over what to call her because her last name sounded like a first name—Jill or Jane or Jan—and her first name was a fella's name. Terry or Tommy. He gave up and called her "ma'am." His pa had taught him to fall back on "ma'am." She was barely five feet tall and couldn't have weighed ninety pounds. Cute. Smelled good. Lilacs. He tried to imagine himself in bed with her and decided they'd look ridiculous. He was clumsy at sex no matter who he was with, but it was the most awkward with the short ones. He was having trouble concentrating on the interview itself. Exhausted after the weekend, he'd hit a wall and needed to pop another pill. The body in back of the truck was another distraction. Minnesota Octobers were unpredictable; any day the cold snap could give way to a warm spell. He had to get rid of the bridesmaid.

An hour into the lunch interview he was staring at his plate and repeatedly dipping the last fry into a spot of ketchup. "What p... paper you with again?"

"*Duluth News Tribune.*" She sounded irritated. She closed her notebook, clicked her pen and shoved both in her purse. "I got everything I need. Why don't you get some sleep? You're wiped out." She slid out of the booth and threw enough cash on the table for her drink. Trip watched her leave and tiredly ran his fingers through his hair. A few strands fell into his plate.

His cell phone rang. He'd shut it off Friday night and had turned it on again that morning. He pulled it out of his jacket and flipped it open.

Wade Murray, his regional sales manager: "Hey, big shot. Why the hell haven't you been picking up?"

Trip: "Busy."

"Yeah. I noticed. Why didn't you give the company a plug?"

"B... b... been wearing the shirts on TV."

"So what? Who knows where they came from? Next time they shove a camera in your mug, the first words outta your mouth are *Pinecone Clothing Distributors.*"

"Sure."

"How'd you do up there?"

Trip: "Great."

A pause. Murray knew Trip was lying; he never did great. "When you heading back to the Twin Cities?"

"A couple d... days. Thought I'd d... do some cold-calling south of Duluth."

"We got a sales meeting early Thursday. I want you here for it." He hung up.

Trip closed the phone, shoved it back in his pocket. He threw some bills on the table and slid out of the booth. Went out the door. On his way back to the car he heard sirens. He stopped in the middle of the sidewalk and scanned both ends of the block. His heart raced; three squads were coming down the street. His eyes went to the truck and back to the squads. Were they on to him? How? They zoomed past him. He wobbled as he walked the rest of the way to the Ford. He wondered where they were going; wherever it was, he wanted to steer clear of them. He pulled his keys out of his jacket and dropped them in the street while opening the door; his hands were shaking. He picked them up, opened the door, slid into the driver's seat. As soon as he shut the door his cell phone rang again. Should have left the thing off, he thought. Probably Murray again. He pulled it out and flipped it open.

"Yeah."

"Son?"

"Pa."

"When you coming home?"

"Soon. How you f... feeling?"

"Horseshit."

"How's your blood sugar?"

"Too damn high."

"How high? Nurses b... been there yet?"

"Come and gone. Bitches. Especially that fat blond one you favor."

They *were* bitches, but he and his pa couldn't pick and choose. The free homecare service was contracted by the county. The fat blonde, Keri Ingmar, was a longtime

74

neighbor in the trailer park who'd enrolled them in the program. She was ten years older than Trip. Stupid as a rock. She'd been supplying him with his drugs since he was in high school. She'd been sleeping with him since then, too. It used to be the drugs were separate from the sex. Over the years, as Keri grew older and Trip grew less willing, the sex became part of the payment for the drugs.

"Hang in there, P... Pa. I'll try to cut it short." He felt guilty for being gone and at the same time was glad he wasn't there. His pa wasn't a well-behaved diabetic. He ate what he wanted. Didn't keep up with his insulin shots. Ignored the sores on his feet until he had to have a big toe amputated. The nurses fought with the old man to get his socks off during their visits. His pa didn't want them to check his feet because he was sure a leg would be the next to go, and he was probably right. His eyesight was failing—another side effect of his refusal to cooperate with medical treatment—and the old man wouldn't admit it. Pretended he could see perfectly well. All the while he kept pissing in the bathroom wastebasket instead of the toilet.

"Sweet."

"Yeah?"

"You look real sharp on TV."

"Thanks." Trip was amazed his old man had taken a break from his western channel to catch the news.

"They pay you anything for that?"

"No."

"Don't worry about me. Take your time up there. Sell some shirts. Make some money. Do something worthwhile."

"Later, P... Pa." He closed the cell phone and tried to put home out of his mind. The whole scene in their trailer was getting too depressing. The fat blond nurse was getting to be the highlight of Trip's week, and that in itself was pathetic. He wished she didn't live so close; sometimes he felt trapped by her. His pa knew Trip was sleeping with her; he'd asked Trip to keep the bedroom door open so he could listen. The old man said it was the only action he'd get for the rest of his life, but Trip knew that was a lie. His pa was sleeping with her, too. That's why his old man told him to take his time. Trip didn't care. He couldn't leave Moose Lake yet anyway; he had work to do that night.

Trip went back to the motel room after lunch and relaxed on the bed with some magazines and a six-pack. He popped open a can, took a gulp and paged through a couple of knife catalogs to see if there was anything new. The bowie knife with a running stag etched on the six-inch blade was nice, but the handle was imitation antler and he wanted the real thing. The gladiator swords didn't interest him; he already had a whole rack of those. He wondered if his pa could use the cane; the carved cobra head pulled out to reveal a sword. He pictured his old man tooling around the trailer park with a sword cane and laughed.

The motel room was chilly. He cranked up the thermostat, peeled off his clothes and stepped into the shower. Good and hot. He ducked his head under. He massaged his scalp with his fingertips; his pa told him he needed to get the blood circulating in his head. When the stream turned lukewarm, he turned off the water. Trip saw black strands in his palms and tangled around his fingers. More hair on the shower floor. He'd been losing hair since he graduated from high school. It depressed him; he figured he'd be bald by the time he hit fifty. Just like his old man. Didn't seem fair.

The room was warmer by the time he toweled off and collapsed into bed. His feet hung off the edge of the mattress. He tried to turn on the television with the remote. The screen stayed black. Batteries were dead. He got up and turned it on manually and fell back against the pillows. He was surprised and happy to see what was leading the six o'clock news. Bunny Pederson's ex-husband had been picked up for questioning on her disappearance and suspected murder. Trip never imagined someone else would get blamed, and so quickly. He figured they'd eventually find the body—she'd be a collection of bones. There'd be weeks of investigation while they followed tips and leads that led nowhere. Then they'd give up. Beaten. They'd never say the word. *Beaten*. But that's what they'd be. That's how it had worked before. This was even better. "Perfect," he said. He popped open a second can and took a long drink. He studied the man on the screen. Handsome. Well built. Probably a jock in high school. Captain of the football team or some such shit. Chad was his name, according to the television reporter.

"I didn't do anything," he said into a microphone, and he slid into the backseat of a sheriff's car. In the background, the cops were loading a bunch of shotguns and a barking dog into a van. A deputy was holding a couple of crying boys by the hands. Trip figured they were the Pederson kids.

He thought: *Things are looking up for Sweet Justice*. He wondered if he should dump the body where the cops could find it and really seal the jock's fate. No. They took the jock's guns; they thought he shot her. If they found the body and figured out she'd been run over, that might somehow exclude the ex-husband as a suspect. The cops would probably figure out that it was a truck that did it and maybe this Chad didn't have a truck. No. Better play it safe. He'd bury her that night while the cops were focusing their attention on the jock. He took another sip of beer and popped the top off his pill bottle. Fished around with his finger until he found what he needed. His favorite. The

Adderall. Full of energy. He'd need energy tonight. He chewed the pill and washed it down with another sip of beer. He was hungry. Knew he'd better eat before the amphetamines did their thing and took his appetite away. He decided to go back into town for dinner. Load up on some food. More energy for tonight. He'd try that bar where the wedding reception was held. Where Bunny Pederson was last seen alive.

11

"Public Pretender's Office my ass. Stupid jerk." She drove home from the station Monday night muttering to herself while making a mental list of who she needed to call before leaving and what she needed to pack for Moose Lake. She pulled into the parking lot and saw a sapphire Jaguar convertible. Erik Mason's car. "Not what I need," she said to herself as she shut off the Jeep and pulled her key out of the ignition. She slid out of the car with her purse and slammed the driver's door hard. As she ran to her boat she heard Tripod, her neighbor's three-legged dog, barking like crazy. He was the yacht club's fail-safe alarm; he went off whenever there was a stranger on the dock. She thumped down the dock and saw Erik standing by her boat. She would have recognized his figure from across the river: tall, athletic, short walnut brown hair. Jack was a rower and had a muscular upper body. Erik, a runner, was a bit trimmer—and more preoccupied with his own looks. He spent a lot of time in the gym. He was also more interested in money. Spent too much time at the track. Murphy figured the horses paid for the Jag. She liked that dangerous edge to Erik, and his looks matched his personality. She thought he resembled an older James Dean. Her husband—safer and more playful than Erik—looked like a younger James Caan.

"Horseshit timing," she said, and rushed past him to open her door. He followed her into the galley; his arms were filled with flowers. "What if Jack was here?" she snapped. "You can't just show up. Jesus Christ." She threw her keys and purse on the kitchen table and turned to glare at him.

"I checked first. No silver Beemer in the lot. Got a vase?"

She pointed to a cupboard and ran upstairs. "I've got to go out of town for work," she yelled from her bedroom. "I appreciate the thought, but they're going to be wasted. And what if Jack sees them?"

"Tell him they're from your mother." Erik set the flowers on the table and followed her upstairs. She was stuffing a tangle of bras and panties and socks into a duffel bag that was sitting on her unmade bed. "When are you going to tell him what happened over the summer? You should. Get it all out in the open."

"No," she said flatly. She went into her closet and pulled a jean skirt off a hanger. Some running gear—stocking cap, sweats, shoes—were in a heap on the closet floor. She picked them up. Maybe she could squeeze in a workout; Moose Lake had some great trails.

"That's it? No? Didn't it mean anything?" Erik was on her heels and she almost knocked him over when she turned around. "Answer me."

She stepped around him and tossed the clothes on the bed. "I don't have time for this." She yanked open a dresser drawer and pulled out three sweaters and two pairs of jeans and tossed them on the pile. She went into the bathroom, scooped a handful of toiletries out of the medicine cabinet and went back to the bed with them. Her cell phone rang. "Dammit!" She dumped the toiletries in the bag and rifled around the sheets for the phone. She found it under a pillow and picked it up: "Murphy."

Jack: "Babe. Want to meet for dinner at that Italian joint on St. Peter Street?"

Murphy frowned at Erik while she talked to her husband. "I can't. They're sending me up north. Moose Lake."

Jack: "Why?"

"Long story," said Murphy, cradling the phone on her shoulder while shoving clothes into the bag. "Call my folks. They're expecting us for dinner tomorrow night."

"You won't be back by then?"

"I don't know. Maybe not." She tried to close the bag; the zipper was caught on a bra strap. "Gotta go. I'll call you."

Jack: "Love you."

She paused. Erik was staring at her; he knew who was on the other end of the phone. "Me too," she said. She hung up and threw the phone on the nightstand.

"Want some company for the ride up?" Erik asked. "I've got a couple of days off."

"No," she snapped. She disengaged the bra strap and finished zipping the bag shut.

Erik sat down on the bed. "Stop moving and talk to me." He put his hand on the bag to keep her from leaving. "What about us?"

She hated that pleading tone in his voice and the hungry look in his eyes; she thought he might as well wrap his arms around her ankles. "I don't know. I told you a couple of weeks ago I don't know. I'm no closer to figuring this thing out. Jack and I are still married, you know. I still have feelings for him."

"You have feelings for me." He grabbed her wrist and

81

pulled her next to him on the bed. She opened her mouth to argue and he planted his mouth hard over hers. His left hand cradled the back of her head and his right moved down to her left breast.

"Damn you," she breathed, trying to push him away with both hands. "Don't tie me in a knot right before I have to leave town." He released her and she stood up. The smile on his face. Smug. Self-satisfied. He knew how to stir her up.

"Admit it," he said. The smile disappeared. "You care about me."

From manipulator to wounded puppy; Murphy didn't know which made her angrier. "Give me some time. Breathing room. Space." She pulled the bag off the bed.

Erik stood up and shoved his hands in his pants pockets. "That's the line I usually use."

Murphy ran downstairs and took her keys and purse off the kitchen table. She opened the fridge and took two bottles of spring water for the road.

Head lowered and hands still in his pockets, Erik walked downstairs. "I'll leave the flowers in some water. They'll last. Call when you get back."

"Fine," she said. Suddenly, leaving town for a few days seemed a wonderful idea. She opened the door to leave and turned to toss him her spare key. "Lock the place up behind you." He caught it and grinned. "Don't get any ideas," she said. "I want that back."

As she walked to the parking lot, she wondered what was going on with Erik. They'd known each other for years. She was familiar with the sly, dangerous side of him; it was what first attracted her to him. The timing had been good for them, too. They'd both been assigned to the prostitute's murder—she as the lead detective and Erik as an investigator for the ME's office. Erik supported her through the tough case and believed her when she first raised the surgeon as the main suspect. Jack, who hated her job anyway, thought she was nuts. He went out of town for a medical conference in the middle of things. Part of her was still angry with Jack for that. Erik stuck by her, too, in the internal affairs investigation that followed the surgeon's suicide. The doctor had killed himself with her gun. But this clingy, needy stuff with Erik was new and unsettling. If that was her lover's flip side, she didn't want any part of it. What did they have in common anyway? Good sex. They'd trained for the Twin Cities Marathon together. They both enjoyed cooking. Sex and running and food. Not enough for a long-lasting pairing. Sometimes she feared all she and Jack had in common was sex.

She opened the back of the Jeep, tossed the bag inside, slammed it shut hard. Sliding behind the wheel, she took a deep breath and told herself to relax. She went through downtown and turned onto Interstate 35E heading north. She'd missed rush hour; traffic was light. Moose Lake, a town of two thousand on the way to Duluth, would be well under a two-hour drive. She slipped a compact disc into the CD player. Billie Holiday's "Night and Day" filled the interior of the car with smooth horns. She took a long drink of water and felt better. Time to forget about Erik and Jack and her leaky showerhead.

As soon as she got out of the metro area, the drive took on a north woods feel. She passed a few red barns and white farmhouses, but mostly the highway was lined with hardwoods and pines. The interstate sliced through lakes and rivers and towns with names that conjured up the forest: Pine City. Snake River. Willow River. Sturgeon Lake. Moose Lake would be coming up after all those. What did she know about Moose Lake? She'd passed it a hundred times while headed to the North Shore. She'd taken the exit into the town on a few occasions. Once to interview an inmate at the state prison. Another time she ran a 10K there. A weekend in May. Moose Run, it was called. Rock hound Jack dragged her there one July weekend for Agate Days. The town dumped 150 pounds of agates and $100 in quarters in the street mixed with gravel; with the blast of a siren, everyone dove in to dig for rocks and money. The silliness of the event charmed her. She'd been in enough small towns to know she'd never work in rural Minnesota. The odd missing bridesmaid case aside, there wasn't enough murder and mayhem to keep a cop busy. If she had to pick a place to retire to, however, Moose Lake would top the list. It was one of those places that had at least one of everything. Flower shop. Pet store. Dentist's office. Doctor's office. Funeral home. Drugstore. JCPenney catalog store. Hardware store. Grocery. Hospital. Movie theater. The community was nestled in an area checkered with lakes, streams, rivers and forests. She couldn't see what else a person needed.

She was south of Moose Lake when her work cell phone rang. She looked over at her purse sitting on the passenger's seat. Let it ring, she thought. She didn't want to talk to Erik or Jack. Maybe it was her mother. It might be the cop shop. She reached over, fished it out and answered. "Murphy."

Duncan: "Don't sound so excited."

After the scene she'd left behind on her houseboat, talking to Duncan didn't seem so bad. "Actually, I'm looking forward to this little trip," she said.

"Know where you're staying?"

"Not yet." She planned on scoping it out when she got to town.

"I do. I already made reservations for you at the Americ-Inn right off the freeway. Got you a room with a Jacuzzi."

"I'm afraid to ask why."

"My way of trying to apologize. Plus they had a weekday special. Okay?"

Odd but well-meaning gesture, she thought. Yo-Yo wasn't such a jerk after all. "Okay."

"Sorry about that crack about your head. Actually, that scar gives you an air of mystery."

"Cut the crap, Duncan. Should have quit while you were ahead."

He laughed. "My life story."

She took the Moose Lake exit. The hotel was part of a growing tourist development right off the highway. A gas station and sub shop shared the intersection. She parked the Jeep, took her bag out of the back and walked in. A blaze crackled in the lobby fireplace. The clerk at the front—a skinny blond woman with hair pulled back into a ponytail—slid the key card across the desk to Murphy. "Breakfast in the morning. Served right here in the lobby. Coffee. Juice. Cereal. Toast. Fruit. Waffles. Danish. The whole nine yards. Comes with the room."

"Thanks." Murphy took the card and grabbed a trail map from the counter. A quick run at dawn would be good.

"You can get on one of the trails right off the parking lot," said the clerk.

Murphy pointed toward the moose head mounted over the fireplace. "That real?"

"Who knows? I hate it regardless. Scares me at night. His eyes follow you."

"Which way to the pool?" Murphy asked, and the woman sent her down the hall. Murphy poked her head into the room. Hot and humid. High, wood-beamed ceiling. Through the sauna window she saw two fat men sweating it out. Two fat women sat in the hot tub; probably the fat guys' wives. The pool was unoccupied. She'd have to go for a swim later. She walked to the edge of the pool and peered into the water. At the bottom of the pool, written in tile: MOOSE LAKE. She went to her room, slipped the key card into the lock and pushed open the door. She turned on the light and gasped. A two-room suite with a whirlpool and a fireplace. "Shit," she muttered. She threw her bag and purse on the bed, a four-poster. The setting gave her an idea. *Why not?* She pulled the cell phone out of her purse and punched in his phone number. "Hey, babe," Murphy said into the phone. "Are you up for a one-night vacation?"

Murphy pulled down the bedsheets, turned on the gas fireplace, filled the ice bucket and set it next to the tub. She called the front desk. "A tall, handsome guy is meeting me here."

The woman laughed. "Does he have a brother?"

"His name is Jack Ramier. If he gets here before I get back from dinner, give him a key card."

"Gotcha."

Murphy checked her watch. It would take nearly two hours for Jack to drive up. He'd already eaten and she was hungry. She grabbed her jacket and purse. Remembered a bar off the main drag that served dinner.

12

Murphy spotted Trip the instant he stepped into the bar. His height caught her eye first, then his gait. Eighteen years had passed and she still recognized his walk and posture. Slow. Hesitant. Head down. A giraffe tiptoeing past the lions. He was by himself; that hadn't changed with the years either. In high school, he'd sat alone. In the library. At the lunch table. In his truck. Never a friend at his side. She saw him turn his head away when the hostess started talking to him; he was still having trouble looking people in the face.

The woman led him to a table toward the front. A round table with six chairs around it. The hostess probably figured she was doing him a favor, giving him legroom. The big table made Trip seem even lonelier. Murphy was in a booth in back. A few other tables and booths were occupied. A young couple. A middle-aged couple. Three men in jeans and flannel shirts. Probably farmers. Four duck hunters in camouflage loudly replaying the day's shoot. A family celebrating Grandma's birthday. Home-made cake in the middle of the table. Pointed hat on the old woman's head.

The room was dark, long, narrow and had a low ceiling. She figured she could order and eat dinner and he'd never notice her, but that would make her feel like she had something to hide. She contemplated standing up and walking over. Extending her hand. Joining him for dinner. Would he remember her? Sure he would, she told herself, and that's why she was hanging back. He would remember that she turned him down at homecoming. That her boyfriend and his pals beat the hell out of him for talking to her. That she never offered an apology. Could he still be holding a grudge? Would it mean anything if she said she was sorry now? Pushing her even more than her guilt was her curiosity. What was he trying to do by reinventing himself? Was he after attention or something else? She had to know. She grabbed her purse and jacket, slid out of the booth, stood up and walked over.

His back was turned to her. His posture when he was seated was as bad as when he was standing. As crooked as a comma. His black mop was worse than she remembered; she could see his scalp through the thin hair at the back of his head. She walked to the other side of the table to face him. He was paging through a menu, bending over it like a man huddling over a campfire.

"Hello, Sweet." She extended her hand.

He glanced up. Ignored her hand. His eyes widened and then narrowed. In the span of a few seconds, she could see his expression go from recognition to surprise to hate. After all these years, he still blamed her. That made her sad and uncomfortable, but above all else, curious. What kind of man was Sweet Justice?

"D... d... do we know each other, ma'am?" Trip asked. His gaze shifted back and forth between her face and the menu.

He's playing a game, she thought. She lowered her hand

but flashed him her biggest smile. "Justice Trip. I can't believe you've forgotten me. Paris Murphy. It's been eighteen years, but I thought you'd still remember. St. Brice's?"

"High s... school. Sure."

His mouth was half open, as if he wanted to say something more to her. Murphy braced herself. Expected him to finally rip into her after years of stewing over the beating and her imagined role in it. Trip only stared. Not at her. Past her. She decided not to say anything about it. Let it be for now.

"How've you been, Sweet? You look good."

His eyes fell again. "So d... do you, Paris."

"I'm eating alone," she said. "Mind if I join you?"

"Suit yourself," he said.

Not an enthusiastic reception, but she'd take it. She draped her jacket over the back of a chair, set her purse on the floor at her feet and took a seat across from him. Despite his thinning hair, she still saw a trace of his high school handsomeness. Dark. Brooding. But that earlobe. Two gobs of flesh hanging down like teardrops from the side of his head. Why didn't he have that fixed? Was it some kind of badge?

The waitress came by. A skinny young woman with short hair the color of strawberry Jell-O and a silver stud in her nose. She handed Murphy a menu. "You changed tables."

"Is that okay?" Murphy asked.

"Whatever. Separate checks?"

Murphy was going to buy Trip dinner but decided against it. "Yeah. Separate."

"Something to drink?"

"Glass of red wine," said Murphy. "House Merlot is fine."

The waitress to Trip: "What about you?"

He was fingering the menu. "Whatever's on t... tap."

"Miller? Bud? Pabst?"

"Miller."

The waitress left to get the drinks. Murphy propped her right elbow on the table and rested her chin in her hand. Waited to see if Trip could manage a question. His head was bent down. He was studying the menu again. Finally he glanced up.

"You m... married? Kids?"

She was surprised that was his first question. Figured there was no reason to lie about it. "Separated. No kids. What about you?"

Head down again. "No. I'm not m... married." A long pause, then he asked the question she thought would have been his first one: "What you d... doing up here? Live in Moose Lake?"

If she wanted to get the maximum amount of information out of him, she had to hide what she did for a living. "No. Still live in St. Paul. Come up here every year for the fall colors. A little vacation. What about you?"

He set down the menu and picked up the salt and pepper shakers. "Work. Up here for w... work." He had a shaker in each hand. Tapped one against the other. Looked at them instead of her.

"So what do you do for a living?" she asked.

"Sales."

"Oh, yeah. I read that in the paper. Shirts, right?"

He set down the shakers. "Dress shirts."

"You've certainly been big news lately."

"Guess s... so." He raised his eyes and smiled.

"You're a regular hero," she said. The waitress brought their drinks. Murphy took a sip. "How does it feel to be a hero?"

"Good," he said. He took a sip of beer and set it down. Stared at the stein. Ran his right index finger around the rim. "Actually, feels g... great." He added what sounded to Murphy like a hollow afterthought. "I like h... helping the c... c... cops." He took a long drink. Wiped his mouth with the back of his hand.

It wasn't about being helpful, she thought. It was about getting attention. He was as puffed up as a rooster. She took another sip of wine. "Must have been horrible when you found that poor woman's finger."

He leaned back in his chair and stretched his legs out underneath the table. "I've g... got a mighty s... strong stomach." He finished off his beer and looked her straight in the eyes for the first time. Grinned. Murphy found it a creepy, self-satisfied smile. An idea darted into her mind. Trip and the missing bridesmaid. Was there something more to it?

The waitress returned with her order pad poised. "Walleye's on special. Fried or baked. Comes with fries or baked potato and coleslaw or garden salad. All you can eat. Seven ninety-five. Ready or should I come back?"

Trip jumped in before Murphy could answer. "Fried chicken."

"Half or quarter?"

"Half. Fries. Coles... slaw."

The waitress looked at Murphy. "For you?"

"The baked walleye, please. Baked potato and garden salad."

The waitress left. Murphy took another sip of wine and drummed her fingertips against the side of the goblet. Even though he had already ordered, Trip was back fiddling with the menu. She'd have to keep the talk flowing. Slide in some questions without arousing his suspicion. "Newspapers said you helped find a missing girl, too."

He saw the waitress, set down the menu and raised his empty glass. "Found her n... necklace. That led the c... cops to her."

"Alive?"

"Yeah." The waitress set another stein in front of him.

"What do you suppose happened to that bridesmaid? Who'd do such a thing? She's got a couple of little kids."

Trip took a long drink of beer. Set the stein down but kept his hand wrapped around the handle. "The ex d... did it."

She took a sip of wine. Tried to act surprised. "What? You're kidding?"

"Saw it on the n... news tonight." He took another long drink, almost finished the second stein. "Guy looks like a s... stupid jock."

Trip still hated athletes. Another leftover from high school, she thought. The waitress slapped their salads and a basket of rolls on the table.

"About t... time," Trip grumbled to no one in particular. He pulled the rolls toward him, took three of the four, put them on his bread plate. Slid the basket in Murphy's direction. He started spooning the coleslaw into his mouth. Murphy thought he was swallowing the stuff without chewing.

She unfolded her napkin and set it on her lap. Picked at her salad. Took a sip of wine. Tossed out a chilling question: "How does it feel? I wonder."

He bumped off the rest of his beer and raised his glass toward the waitress. "How does what f... feel?"

"Killing someone. Murdering someone. Wasting them. What's that like?"

He ate a roll in two bites and as many chews. Nodded toward the table of men in camo. "Ever go h... hunting?"

"Think it's like shooting birds?"

"No. Not d... duck hunting." The waitress brought him another beer. He grabbed the mug by the handle and lifted it. "Ever go d... deer hunting?" He took a long drink and set the stein down. "Ever hit a d... deer with your car?" That creepy grin again.

Murphy was ready to jump up and leave. She needed a break. She pushed her chair away from the table. Took her napkin off her lap and set it on the table. "Got to visit the ladies' room. Be right back." She grabbed her purse, stood up, walked to the bathroom.

He watched her go and thought: *Bitch. Beautiful bitch responsible for the worst beating I ever had.* He reached up and touched his earlobe. Seeing her gave him the same jolt as the one he'd gotten once while he was wiring a new light switch in the trailer. He'd touched the hot lead and felt a charge that ran right up his arm. Pain and excitement mixed together. After that shock from the light switch, he'd been tempted to touch it again. Had it really been that bad or had he imagined it? Of course, he was too smart to touch it again; he was too smart to fall for her again.

Trip pulled his pills out of his jacket pocket and, under the table, emptied them into his left palm. Surely he had something left for Paris Murphy. He couldn't see in the dim light of the bar. He reached over and slid the votive candle closer. Better. He poked around the tablets and capsules with his right index finger until he found the white ones. Scored on one side. Stamped with the word "Roche" and an encircled "2." He'd paid Keri about five dollars apiece for them. They came in a bubble pack, but he'd popped them out and dumped them in with the other pills. He hadn't tried them on himself yet. Keri told him they went great with beer; took the drunk to a new high. He couldn't remember the drug's real name. She called it a lot of different things. "Roofies." "Roachies." "Date rape pills." He didn't want to rape Paris Murphy; but if he got her stoned, maybe someone else would. He'd heard it made women lose their inhibitions, practically rip off their own shirts. Even if it didn't do that, it would make her dizzy and drowsy. Maybe she'd get behind the wheel. Pass out. Crash her car. He scanned the room to make sure no one was watching. A table of people had started singing "Happy Birthday" to an old woman and everyone else in the bar seemed to know her. Turned to watch and sing along.

Happy birthday to you. Happy birthday to you.
Happy birthday, dear Hazel. Happy birthday to you.

He reached across the table and dropped a tablet in her glass of wine. The drug had no taste or odor. He'd wolf down his dinner and leave. She'd get sick after he was gone. Blame it on the food or the flu. She'd never suspect a guy from high school. A guy she hadn't laid eyes on in nearly twenty years. She had no idea how much he hated her. Was one pill enough? What would two do? Three? He picked two more tablets out of his palm. Dropped a second one in the glass and then, to be sure, a third. That should do it, he thought. Keri had told him the pill was ten times more powerful than Valium. He poured the rest of the pills back in the bottle, screwed the lid back on, shoved the bottle back in his pocket. Slid the candle back to the middle of the table. He studied her wineglass and prayed the pills would dissolve quickly.

The waitress set the chicken and fish dinners on the table. "Will the lady need another glass of wine?"

"Doubt it," Trip said with a small smile. "I think that'll b... be enough for her."

94

Murphy washed her hands and splashed water on her face. Eating dinner with Trip was making her sick. He had the table manners of a pig and the conversation skills of a rock. The few full sentences he'd managed to utter gave her the creeps. She dried her face with a paper towel and looked in the bathroom mirror. How had she held up since high school? She leaned closer to the mirror. Except for the stupid scar on her forehead, her face was good. No lines yet. She took a brush out of her purse and gave her dark mane a few strokes. No gray hairs yet, either. She dropped the brush back in her purse and hiked the strap over her shoulder.

She walked out of the bathroom. She looked across the room and saw Trip pick up her glass, swirl the wine around and set it back down. What the hell was he trying to pull? He didn't see her watching him; he'd started attacking his food. She stepped next to the table. Set her purse on the floor. Trip was tearing off strips of chicken with his fingers and rifling them into his mouth. She sat down. Put her napkin back on her lap. Picked up her fork and knife, cut off a piece of fish and popped it in her mouth. Chewed and swallowed. She glanced at her glass. She wanted to ask him what he'd been doing with his hands on it, but decided to get some conversation going first. What in the world did she and Trip have left to talk about? Then it came to her: "Going to the all-class reunion?"

He set a chicken bone down. "What?" Licked his fingers.

"Didn't you get an invite in the mail? I can send you a copy." She put her hand on the wineglass, saw him nervously eye the goblet.

"No. No. I saw it. I d... don't know. I wasn't p... p... planning on it." He picked up a leg. Cleaned the meat off in a couple of bites. Threw down the bone.

95

She started to lift the wine to her lips. He looked at it again. She pretended to sip and set the glass down. Had Trip slipped something into her drink? "You should go. Everyone will want to hear about how you helped up here. If it was me, I wouldn't miss a chance to wave it in their faces." She saw he was studying her face. Searching for signs that she'd tasted something odd or that whatever he'd slipped into her drink was working.

His eyes fell again. He wiped his mouth with the napkin. "Maybe I will g... go. When is it?"

She wrapped her hand around the goblet again. Picked it up. Put it to her lips and then set it down again. His eyes followed the glass like a dog's eyes following a steak bone. "Saturday night," she said.

"This Saturday? You g... g... going?"

She smiled. "Wouldn't miss it." She wanted to throw the wine in his face and slap some cuffs on him, but she had no proof. She didn't see him do it. He could always say someone else had altered her drink. His behavior was also making her wonder about his involvement with the missing bridesmaid, and she didn't want to get his back up until she could poke around that case more.

She wanted to say something about the past to see if he really had held a grudge for nearly two decades. If he did, the scars went deeper than the torn earlobe. Could one beating change someone, turn them into something they wouldn't have otherwise become? Maybe it triggered something that was already there, waiting to surface with the right provocation. Perhaps other traumas had marked him after high school. Regardless, there was a dangerous edge that wasn't there eighteen years ago. The Trip she knew wouldn't have doctored a woman's drink.

She wrapped her hand around the goblet and watched him watching her do it. "Sweet. I always wanted to tell you."

"Tell m... me what?" He wasn't listening to her; he was preoccupied with her wineglass.

"What those boys did to you. It wasn't my fault. I didn't know until afterwards. When I found out, I felt horrible. Didn't have the courage to say anything. I always wanted to say—"

"I d... don't know what you're t... t... talking about," he said, interrupting her. For an instant, his eyes left her glass and locked on her face. He knew exactly what she was talking about. He didn't want to give her the chance to apologize.

"You know, Denny wasn't so bad if you'd gotten the chance to know him. He was just another kid. Not so different from you."

"I wasn't a b... bully. I wasn't a big b... baby. Didn't still like stupid c... cartoons in high school."

Murphy was stunned. How did Trip know Denny watched *The Flintstones*? Only she knew that. She stared at him but he wasn't paying attention to her anymore. He was scanning the bar for the waitress. He spotted the strawberry head and waved her over.

The young woman walked over to the table. "Another beer?"

He pointed at Murphy's glass. "On second thought, m... maybe I should l... let the l... lady catch up. Why don't you p... polish that off and I'll buy the n... next round?"

Murphy checked her watch. "Know what? I gotta go. I'm supposed to meet someone." She pushed the wineglass away. Stood up, pulled on her jacket. Picked up her purse, opened it, pulled out some bills and threw them on the table. "I'll see you on Saturday." She turned and left.

The waitress was still standing over him. "Another beer?"

"No. The check."

The waitress ripped it off her pad, set it on the table and walked away. He stared at the wineglass. She hadn't had enough. Waste of good drugs. He checked his watch. Still early. He'd go back to the motel and rest before his late-night errand.

13

Murphy was never so relieved to dump a dinner date. She practically ran to her car while digging her keys out of her purse. She opened the driver's side, threw her purse on the passenger's seat, got in, slammed the door shut. She started up the Jeep and shot out of the parking lot, turned onto the main drag. She slipped in a CD. An upbeat instrumental by Leo Kottke. The twelve-string guitar massaged her nerves during the short drive back to the hotel. She rolled into the parking lot and her cell phone rang. She hoped it wasn't Jack backing out of their romantic evening. She turned off the CD and pulled the phone out of her purse.

Duncan: "Don't get too comfortable."

"Don't tell me I have to turn around. I'm all settled in." She didn't want to tell him her husband was on the way up.

"No, no. But you might be spending less time there than I thought."

Something's up, thought Murphy. She guessed the theory he'd sold to the sheriff was beginning to unravel.

Duncan: "The ex-hubby's story is starting to check out. The cops up there finally caught up with this friend of his."

Murphy smiled to herself; she was right. "The buddy with the cabin?"

"Name's Ozzie something. Starts with a Y." Duncan shuffled some papers on his desk. "Yates. Ozzie Yates. Claims he was in the car with Pederson from the time he left St. Paul until he picked up his kids and went hunting."

"Where's this Yates been this whole time?"

"Still at the cabin. Pederson left him there to take his kids back home. Yates had a motorcycle he was working on up at the lake. Was gonna ride it back to the cities."

She couldn't resist: "Told you so."

"The sheriff's got more checking to do. Could be Oz is lying for his pal."

"I'll bet you lunch he's not."

"You're on. Give Carlton County what you got, see what you can do to help. Might as well spend the night. Here's the plan. Unwind tonight. Go to work in the morning, then head back. How's that sound, Potato Head?"

"Duncan." She thought about challenging him on the Potato Head issue, then reconsidered. Leave well enough alone. "I'll check in with you before I leave town. And hey, thanks for the nice room."

"No problem. Enjoy."

"I will." She hung up and shoved the phone back in her purse. She spotted the silver Beemer in the parking lot and checked the Jeep's clock. She didn't want to think about how fast he'd driven to get up there. She pulled her keys out of the ignition, shoved them in her purse, slid out of the car and slammed the door. Told herself to punch out of the job for the night. Put Trip and that horrible meal they'd shared out of her mind. Jack sure as hell wouldn't want to hear someone may have tried to poison her. She walked through the lobby.

The clerk was behind the front desk, leaning on the

counter and flipping through a magazine. "Your hubby *is* a looker. Sure he ain't got a brother?"

Murphy smiled. "Sorry. Only child."

"My luck. Most of my dates look like that." She nodded toward the moose head.

Murphy laughed and went to her room, slipped her card in the lock. Pushed it open. Jack was standing in the middle of the room with a bottle of champagne in his hand and a big grin on his face. He'd just walked in himself. Under his jacket, he was still in his scrubs. Murphy shut the door.

"Where were you?" he asked. "I was getting worried. Thought you'd dragged me up here to stand me up."

"Went out for some dinner." She looked at his crotch. "Wasn't it uncomfortable driving all the way up here with that in your pocket?"

"I've had a continuous hard-on for you since we got married. I hide it well is all."

"How many traffic laws did you break on the way up here? Add any new speeding tickets to your collection?" She pulled off her jacket and purse and tossed them on a chair.

"Believe it or not, I even had time to stop by your boat and grab a couple of accessories." He pulled a champagne glass out of each pocket. "I saw flowers in the galley." He said it in a way that required an explanation.

"My mother," she said, and immediately hated herself for the lie.

"What's the occasion? Did I miss something?"

"You didn't miss a thing." She wanted to get him off the subject. "When are we going to get a new set of flutes?" She pulled the glasses out of his hands and set them on the nightstand.

He took off his jacket, threw it on a chair. He saw the

101

ice bucket on the floor next to the tub. "How'd you know I'd bring champagne?"

"You're that kind of fella." She walked over to the tub and turned on the water. It would take a while to fill. She peeled off her top, dropped it on the floor and walked toward him.

"The kind of fella that will drive for two hours with a hard-on to meet his wife?"

"Exactly." She pulled his shirt over his head and threw it on the floor. "Know what I love about doctor duds?"

"What?" he said.

She loosened the drawstring on his pants and slipped them down. "No buttons or zippers."

They finished undressing and fell into bed. He kissed her, his tongue darting past her teeth. His mouth moved to the hollow at the base of her throat, and then to her left breast. When he bit her nipple, she arched her back. He entered her. Moaning, she wrapped her legs around him and gently raked his back with her nails. He saw her eyes were half shut and slowed the pace of his thrusts. "I don't want you to come too soon," he breathed in her ear. "I had to wait. So do you."

They saved the champagne and Jacuzzi for last.

14

Trip knew the park was open year-round, but he was counting on the office being empty late at night. The entrance was a half mile east of Interstate 35 at the Moose Lake exit, off County Road 137. He pulled down the road that ran next to the building and saw a sign posted out front that made the campground an even better hiding place: DUE TO STATE BUDGET CUTS, OVERNIGHT CAMPING HAS BEEN ELIMINATED FROM THE DAY AFTER LABOR DAY UNTIL MEMORIAL DAY WEEKEND NEXT YEAR. He left the truck running, got out and walked up to the park office window and peeked inside. Dark and empty. He got back in and drove around the arm blocking the entrance. He drove a few more yards straight ahead. A right would take him to the picnic grounds and beach. A left to the campground and boat landing. He took the left. Headed for the south end of the park.

The campground was made up of three loops coming off the west side of the road. The east side of the road was lined with woods and a farmer's field. Even if the campground was open, it would probably be near deserted on a cold Monday night in October. Still, he decided to be safe and make sure no campers had ignored the sign and pitched a tent. He took the first right off the road and drove past campsites 1 through 10. Empty. He took a right turn and exited the first loop. The second right off the road rounded past sites 11 through 18. Again, not a single car or tent. He hung a right and got off the second loop. He went down the road toward the last and largest loop. The third right turn circled 19 through 35. A dull glow radiated from a building containing the showers and toilets. No one around. He hung a left and took the road back to the first set of campsites.

He pulled the truck into number 5, the closest to Echo Lake. He punched off the lights and turned off the engine. He wanted to pop another Adderall, but his stash was getting low and he needed to ration the stuff until he got home. He wished the park was more uniformly wooded. It used to be old farm fields and it was in the process of turning back into a forest. Many of the trees looked more like tall bushes. The few mature hardwoods had dropped most of their leaves. The rest of the park was pines.

He thought about the options. If he drove around he could probably find a garbage dumpster or a big trash can for day visitors. Chances were there wouldn't be anyone in the park until the weekend. Still, there could be a weekday visitor, or the dumpster pickup might be anytime during the week. No. He wanted the body to stay well hidden for as long as possible. Until it rotted. He could walk to the end of the fishing pier and dump her into Echo Lake. He had chains and bags of sand and salt—the truck's winter equipment—that he could use to weigh the body down. What if it wasn't deep enough at the end of the pier? No, the lake was too risky. The pond in the northern half of the park? No. Definitely too shallow, and there were beavers living there; they might disturb the grave. Better to bury her in the woods. He had a shovel, another piece of winter gear. Flashlight. Where'd he put it? He reached over to the glove compartment, flipped it open and felt around. Sunglasses. Owner's manual for the truck. Couple of jackknives. Bowie knife. Stiletto. Wire cutter. His one-hitter kit. Damn. No flashlight. He grabbed the stiletto and shut the glove compartment. He played with the stiletto while thinking. Open. *Chink*. Close. *Chink*. Open. *Chink*. Close. *Chink*. He reached under the driver's seat and felt some highway maps and a phone book. No flashlight. Leather gloves, though. He'd need those. He grabbed them and sat up. "Fuck. Now what?" he muttered. Open. *Chink*. Close. *Chink*. He couldn't bury her using his truck lights; he wanted to walk the body into the woods so he wouldn't leave a trail of tire marks. Come morning, the tracks he'd left around the closed gates could be blamed on teenagers screwing around. Tire marks going into the woods would raise suspicions. He peered through the windshield. The moon was full. Maybe he could manage without a flashlight. He shoved the stiletto in his jacket pocket and pulled on the gloves.

As he opened the driver's door and got out, he heard rustling in the bushes surrounding the campsite. Holding his breath, he gently closed the truck door. He pulled the stiletto out of his pocket. Open. *Chink*. More rustling. Son of a bitch, he thought. Had someone followed him there? He turned, flattened his back against the truck, held the stiletto in front of him. In the moonlight, he couldn't distinguish substance from shadows. An icy gust rattled the trees. Had it been a breeze he'd heard? The wind settled down. He stood still. More rustling. No. Not the wind. He exhaled slowly and tightened his grip on the knife. A ball of fur on four legs waddled out of the bushes. It stopped, sat up on its haunches and stared with beady eyes. "Fucking 'coon," Trip said. He picked up a rock and threw it at the animal. It didn't budge. He threw another. It growled at him and bared its teeth. "Get the f... f... fuck out of here." It turned and went toward the road.

Trip closed the stiletto and slipped it in his right jacket pocket. He walked to the rear of the truck and opened the back. A flashlight rolled out and hit the ground. "Great," he said. He picked it up, turned it on and shined it over his cargo. Under the pile of boxes and packaged shirts he saw a corner of blue plastic. The tarp. He set the flashlight on the tailgate, grabbed the edge of the tarp with both hands and pulled. It hardly moved. Bunny Pederson was a cow, all right. He pulled harder and the body inched out. Was the tarp caught on something? He gave a good yank. The blue cocoon slid out and fell to the ground with a thud. A pile of boxes and shirts tumbled out after it. He picked up the boxes and shirts and threw them back. He shined the light on the ground to make sure nothing else had fallen out. He reached inside the truck, pulled out the shovel and threw it next to the body. He trained the flashlight on the tarp. A good wrapping job, he thought. Nice and tight. A giant candy bar. He bent over and sniffed. No stink yet; he could thank the cold spell for that. He wondered if she'd bled all over the truck bed, or if the plastic had contained it all. He ran the beam up and down the tarp and didn't see any dark stains. He'd check the truck later. He shoved the light in his jacket pocket, wrapped his arms around the middle of the cocoon and hiked the body onto his right shoulder like a rolled-up carpet.

"Oh, man," he grunted. He held the body in place with his right hand and with his left pulled out his flashlight. He shined the flashlight in front of him and walked three steps before he realized he'd forgotten the shovel. "Fuck." He set the body down and went back for the tool. He picked up the shovel—a wooden-handled spade—and wondered: *How am I going to carry all this shit?* He thought for a few seconds, shoved the flashlight back in his pocket. He unbuckled his belt, ran the end of it through the shovel handle and buckled it again. The shovel dangled down the side of his leg and banged against him when he walked, but it worked. He went back to the body. Awkward with the shovel, but he managed to bend over and hike the cocoon back up on his shoulder. He stood still for a minute, making sure of his balance. He pulled the flashlight out of his pocket and started walking again. He'd visited the park before, even camped there a couple of times to spare the expense of a motel. He had a pretty good idea of where he wanted to bury her. He walked north on the road out of the campground. Every ten minutes or so he had to stop and adjust the body's position on his shoulder. The gusts of wind seemed to grow stronger and last longer. He was grateful for the gloves but wished he'd packed a wool cap. His *E.P.* hat wasn't warm enough. The Minnesota fall felt worse than any Tennessee winter. The hat belonged back in Memphis as surely as he did. After less than a quarter of a mile on the road he took a sharp right and went east into the woods, where there were no trails or other attractions for fall visitors. The ground was hard. The digging was difficult and he worked up a sweat. Even had to take off his jacket. He buried her, tarp and all, in a shallow grave.

Trip was throwing the first shovel of dirt over the body when ranger Bob Kermitt turned in to Moose Lake State Park. Clueless tourists who hadn't been reading the newspapers didn't know many state campgrounds were closed until Memorial Day weekend. They'd pull up to the office, read the sign, get pissed off and drive around the arm. Some didn't even read the sign. They stuffed money in the self-registration lockbox and drove around the arm, never questioning why the thing was down. Since the day after Labor Day, park staff had been monitoring the campground, even during the week. If someone had pitched a tent or parked an RV, they were told to leave. If they left money in the lockbox, it would be returned. Kermitt wanted to check his live traps for raccoons as well; the day staff had probably forgotten to do that and he didn't like leaving the animals caged for an entire day.

He didn't mind working the night shift on occasion; it broke up his week. His day hours were filled with what he called "glorified housekeeping and baby-sitting." He scrubbed the outhouses around the picnic grounds and trails—there were still a lot of hikers taking in the fall leaves. Picked up trash. Sold souvenir tee shirts. Cut the grass. Gave directions. Asked park guests to *please* stop leaving food out for the raccoons. *Please* stop dumping trash down the outhouse holes. *Please* don't rinse diapers in the lake. *Please* leash your dogs. *Please* don't let your kids run wild on the dock. He told his wife he should change his name tag to *Ranger Please*. He looked forward to November, when the visitors would taper off and he could catch up on some of the maintenance he never had time to do in the summer and early fall. Painting picnic tables. Repairing broken grills and fire rings. Removing dead wood. The park would get busy again after the first good snowfall, when winter visitors came in with their snowshoes and cross-country skis.

All in all, Kermitt thought he had a good job. He enjoyed being outside; it kept him fit and trim and tan. The state benefits were great, especially the pension. A few more years and he could retire. Spend time with the grandkids. Do a little fishing. Make more trips to Vegas with the old lady. Maybe they'd even make it to Hawaii.

Kermitt pulled up to the office, got out of the pickup. He dug his keys out of his pants pocket and opened the lockbox. He shined his flashlight inside. Empty. He slammed it shut and locked it again. As cold as it was, he didn't expect any illegal or clueless campers. Monday nights were dead even before the cutbacks. Still, there was always the odd slacker and screw-off. He looked up at the sky. A full moon, as white and as bright as a snowball. Full moons brought goofballs out of the woodwork. He decided to take a tour of the campground and leave the live traps for last. The raccoons could wait a little longer.

Free of his load, it took Trip a fraction of the time to get out of the woods. He ran most of the way—shovel in one hand and flashlight and jacket in the other. He wanted to get back to the motel for another hot shower, another beer. Unwind. Treat himself to a couple of tranks. Those baby-blue Valium tablets. He came out of the trees and got on the road. A raccoon darted across his path and startled him. "Fucking 'coon," he said. He stopped and followed it with his flashlight as it crawled into the weeds. He leaned against the shovel to catch his breath. He inhaled; the night air smelled of dry leaves. A blast of wind chilled his body, still damp with sweat. He shivered and put his jacket back on. He picked up the shovel and started jogging again. He took a right turn off the road and started down the loop containing campsite 5. Then he saw it. A pickup with its headlights on, parked behind his. A park ranger walking around Trip's truck, shining a flashlight into the cab windows. The ranger had his back turned and didn't see the beam from Trip's flashlight. Trip flicked it off, shoved it in his left pocket and crouched behind a low bush on the edge of the adjoining campsite. Trip heard the ranger yelling as he peeked inside the truck. He couldn't make out the words at first; they were muffled by the breeze. The wind died down.

"Hello? You can't spend the night. Campground is closed." The ranger walked to the back of the truck.

"Fuck," Trip said under his breath. "Fuck. Fuck. Fuck." He'd left the gate open. If there was blood on the bed, the ranger could find it.

The ranger reached inside the truck, rifled around, pulled something out. He held it upside down by the heel while he trained the flashlight on it. Trip's palms felt cold and wet under his gloves. He wasn't breathing anymore. He was sure his heart had stopped beating. He thought: *Is this how it feels when you're drowning?* He couldn't believe he'd missed it; it had fallen out of the tarp. Her shoe! The ranger found her fucking peach shoe! The entire town of Moose Lake—the entire state—knew what the bridesmaid was wearing when she went missing. Peach dress. Peach purse. Peach shoes.

The ranger was still rummaging around in back of the truck. What else was he grabbing? How long had he been snooping around? Trip studied the ranger's figure. No one was ever as tall as Trip, but most men were thicker. Stronger. The ranger was big. He couldn't see his face; he was probably some young guy. Trip wondered if he could take someone stronger and younger. The ranger headed back to his truck with the shoe. Trip figured he was going to radio for help. Couldn't let him do that.

Another gust came up, whistling around the bushes and pines. Trip dashed out from his hiding place. The ranger's fingers were wrapped around the door handle of his pickup when Trip came up behind him and bashed the back of his head with the shovel. The *clang* of the spade rose above the sound of the wind in the trees. The ranger's head bounced once against the driver's-side window of the pickup. He dropped the shoe and the flashlight and fell against the door. He slid to the ground. Facedown in the dirt and moaning, the ranger blindly raised his right hand and brushed it against the side of the pickup. He was trying to pull himself up. Trip raised the shovel up over his right shoulder and brought it down hard with a *thud*. The ranger wasn't moving, but Trip struck his head a third time to be sure. Gray hair was matted with the blood. He wasn't a young guy. He was old, same as Trip's pa. That made him angry. An old man shouldn't be out here, he thought. He raised the spade and brought it down again. A sickening sound. Crunching and soft at the same time. Trip dropped the shovel and stood over the still figure.

Trip had never killed someone this way before. Had never gotten so close to one of his victims while they were still breathing. Still moaning and groaning. Fighting for life. This wasn't like running someone over with a truck, so high off the ground and impersonal and efficient. This was messy and personal. Hard work. Scary. Trip was perspiring under his hat. His armpits were clammy. He was panting. Couldn't get air into his lungs quick enough. That drowning feeling again. He wanted to get the hell out of the park. Get away from the mess. He hopped over the body and ran to his truck and pulled the door open. The shovel and the shoe. He forgot the shovel and the shoe. He ran back and picked them up. Rubbed the back of the spade against the dirt to get the worst of the blood off. Wondered if there were brains on it. The ranger's pickup lights were on. Should he shut them off? No. Leave it alone, he thought. The ranger's flashlight was next to his body and it was still shining; the beam illuminated the man's bloody head. Trip was spooked by it; the flashlight was accusing him. He kicked it and it rolled away; the beam flickered and died. He remembered his own flashlight. Where was it? Did he drop it? He reached into his jacket pockets. His right one. Empty. His left. There it was. On the way back to his truck, he stumbled over the ranger's leg and fell in the dirt, right next to the body. It freaked him out; he made a startled noise that sounded like a pig's squeal. He scrambled off the ground, picked up the shovel and the shoe. He checked his pockets. Flashlight still there. Checked his head. Hat still there. Did he drop anything else? He scanned the ground with the beam and saw only the ranger's body and the ranger's flashlight. Good. He flicked off the light and shoved it back in his jacket. He ran to his truck and threw the shovel and shoe in back and shut the gate.

When he pulled out of the campsite he managed to back up without hitting the ranger's pickup, but he did run over the ranger himself.

15

He was shaking as he sped out of the park. Vibrating like a car going faster than it could handle. He wanted to escape the sound the shovel had made with that last hit. It reminded him of something. A kitchen sound. An egg cracking? A mallet hitting a tough steak? No. His pa used to buy fryers whole because they were cheaper that way. He'd chop them himself into serving pieces with a meat cleaver. Sloppy and messy. That was the sound. Meat and bone being broken. Crunching and squishing. It'd be a long time before he could handle a raw chicken again. He needed to downshift. Needed his pills, and they were in the motel room. He'd calm himself with the next best thing: his music. His discs were in a case on the front passenger's seat. He grabbed one without looking at it, popped it in, cranked the volume. When he realized the CD he'd picked, he had to laugh. *The Grave Digger*. Dark and evil German power metal. The guitars and drums pushed the broken bones and meat out of his mind. His first instinct was to keep driving. Keep the pedal to the floor and tear out of town. What about his stuff? He couldn't leave his stuff in the motel room. The purse was in his suitcase. Should have buried the bag with her, he thought. The risk hadn't been worth it to get a peek at a handful of her cosmetics and the lyrics from an Elvis song.

He headed for the motel; he'd pack his stuff and leave. Then he remembered he hadn't paid the bill. Skipping town without paying would attract attention. The motel owner, an old woman, lived in back of the office. Trip checked his watch. Midnight. Too late to wake her; that would arouse suspicions. He could slip the money under the door. No. That would seem odd. He could check out at dawn; the owner kept early hours. He pulled into the motel parking lot and sat behind the wheel with the lights off and the music on and his brain working.

The purse and her shoe. The only objects tying him to her. The shoe was in back of the truck. The purse was in the suitcase. He'd left no witnesses. No one saw the truck run her over and no one saw him in the park except for the ranger, and he was dead. What had changed since he buried her? Had he dropped any clues that could steer the cops in his direction? He'd gotten rid of the biggest piece of evidence—her body—and it was well hidden. He'd left another body behind in plain view. He should have buried the old guy. Still, they would have found his car and probably a mess of blood and brains on the ground. Once the ranger's body was discovered, the cops might set up roadblocks. Stop cars and trucks. Couldn't let them see the shoe or the blood on the shovel. The shoe would be easy to lose. He'd clean up the shovel. Washing the entire truck bed wouldn't be a bad idea. Check everything out. Make sure the bridesmaid's body hadn't leaked anything while it was bouncing around back there. Something to do while waiting for sunrise; he sure as hell wasn't going to get any sleep. He turned his lights back on, pulled out of the motel parking lot and headed to town. He knew there was a self-service car wash in Moose Lake adjacent to a gas station.

Three bays, all of them empty. He steered the truck into the middle one, punched off his lights, turned off the engine. He opened the driver's door but before he hopped out, he took off his baseball cap and set it on the passenger's seat. He didn't mind if he got his clothes wet, but he didn't want to mess up his hat. Didn't want to ruin his leather gloves, either. He pulled them off and threw them on the seat. He got out of the truck, slammed the door behind him. Walked behind the truck and pulled down the bay door. The streets were empty and the gas station was closed for the night, but he didn't want to chance anyone seeing what he was doing. He opened the truck gate. The shovel and shoe—partners in crime—fell out together. Lying on its side against the gray concrete floor, the peach pump resembled a dead tropical bird. How to get rid of it? He looked around the bay and saw a trash can. Too obvious. The drain might work. A narrow trench that ran nearly the entire width of the floor and was covered by sections of grate. He bent over, wrapped his fingers around one of the sections and tugged hard. It didn't budge; screwed in. He tried the next grate. It lifted out easily. He set it aside. Using two fingers, he picked up the shoe by the tip of the heel and carried it over to the drain. He dropped it in, watched it settle in the muck, replaced the grate.

The shovel. He lifted it up by the handle. Wet spots all over the spade. Blood. A few clots of something red and raw and glistening, like bits of uncooked liver. He dropped the shovel on the floor directly over the drain and walked to the power hose mounted on the wall. He scanned the sign over the hose. It listed spray settings: *Tire*

Cleaner. Engine Cleaner. High-pressure Soap. Suds 'n' Brush. High-pressure Rinse. High-pressure Wax. At the end of the list: *Warning. Grip wand tightly due to 1000 lbs. pressure. We are not responsible for damage.* He turned the knob to *High-pressure Soap* and plugged the machine with a dollar's worth of quarters. He pulled the wand over to the shovel. Sprayed the blade with soapy water. Pink dripped down the drain. He kept shooting the blade until the water ran clear. He flipped the shovel with his foot and sprayed the other side. Ran the wand up and down the handle. His time ran out. He walked back to the knob. Turned it to *High-pressure Rinse.* Four more quarters. He sprayed the blade and handle until the water shut off. He picked up the shovel and inspected it. Clean as a spoon out of the dishwasher. He set it upright against the wall. Plugged the hose with more quarters and took the wand over to the gate and sprayed it down to give him a clean working surface.

Now the hard part. He started reaching in and pulling his merchandise out of the truck. The unopened boxes filled with individually wrapped shirts were easiest. He slid them out of the truck, held them up, examined the cardboard cubes on all six sides for bloodstains. Each of the five sealed boxes was clean. He threw them inside the cab. He leaned in and grabbed the two opened boxes out of the truck. The cardboard was clean on the outside. He carefully lifted out the polybagged shirts inside and held them to the ceiling light. Clean. He put the shirts back inside, folded the box tops shut, set the cubes inside the cab. Now all the loose stuff. One by one, he pulled out two dozen packaged shirts. The shovel must have rested on top of them because six of them were smeared with dirt and traces of blood. It looked like red food coloring against the clear plastic. He set the clean ones on the floor, propping them upright

116

against the wall, and stacked the dirty ones on the gate. Then one by one, he picked up each bloodied package with his left hand, holding it by a corner. With his right, he worked the wand. He used the gentle *Tire Cleaner* setting. The high-pressure sprays could rip the polybags and he didn't want to ruin his samples; he'd already paid for them. As he finished each package, he propped it against the wall to dry next to the clean ones. By the time he was done, he had a row of shirts sitting upright on the floor as if on display. Instead of a garage sale, he thought, it would be a grave digger's sale.

He had to crawl inside to reach the truck's winter gear: jumper cables, a set of chains, a towrope, one bag of rock salt, six sacks of sand. As he pulled out each item, he held it up, examined it from all angles. Set the clean stuff against the wall next to the shirts. The edges of two bags of sand had dirt on them; he couldn't tell if it was plain dirt or dirt mixed with brains and blood. He washed the edges with the *Tire Cleaner* setting and propped the bags against the wall.

The truck bed itself. Should probably spray the sides and ceiling of the topper, too, he thought. He plugged the hose with coins and turned it to *High-pressure Soap*. He shot foamy water inside the truck and watched as it poured out of the bed and ran down the floor drain. He didn't see pink. Only dirt. When his time ran out, he plugged the hose again for the rinse. When it stopped, he hung up the wand and scanned the bay, hoping for a towel dispenser. Nope. He wished he had some rags to wipe the bed dry. He studied the row of shirts, picked out the ugliest one. He ripped the package open and took out a yellow oxford with navy blue and white vertical stripes. He pulled out the stickpins, removed the plastic from around the neck and the cardboard from the back. He ducked under the topper and leaned in to wipe the bed. When he was finished, he balled up the wet shirt and its packaging and threw them into a corner of the truck bed. He wanted to get a good look. Where was his flashlight? He checked his jacket. Still in his left pocket. He took it out and turned it on and ran the beam around the inside of the bed and ceiling of the topper. Clean.

The winter gear went back into the truck first; he shoved it all against the rear of the bed, including the shovel. He stacked the merchandise on the bed. Did it in rows so it appeared neat and professional. Sealed boxes in back. Then the unsealed. Then the loose shirts. He ran the flashlight around one more time. Satisfied with his job, he flicked it off and shoved it in his left pocket. He slammed the gate shut. Might as well wash the outside of the truck, he thought. He reached into his pants pockets. Bills. No more quarters. He peeled three one-dollar bills off and fed them to the change machine mounted against the wall. Twelve quarters. Enough for a wash, rinse and wax.

When he was finished, he stepped back and admired his truck. It always looked so good after a wash and wax. Shiny and new and invincible. He wiped his hands on his pants legs. Went behind the truck. Opened the bay door. Scanned the street. Still quiet and empty. Went to the driver's door, opened it, got behind the wheel, slammed the door shut. He turned the ignition and started to back out of the bay. As he pulled out he saw a sign on the outside of the car wash: *Thank You for Your Dirty Business.*

He checked the clock on the dashboard. Still too early to wake the motel owner. He felt safe and calm after washing the truck and sorting through his merchandise. He thought he could snooze a little and still get out of town at dawn. He pulled into the motel parking lot exhausted. He

118

pushed open the door to his room, dropped his jacket on the floor and collapsed on top of the bed, his shoes still on.

At first light, he rolled out of bed and shuffled into the bathroom. He unzipped his pants and peed for what seemed like half an hour. As he was zipping up, it occurred to him that he could have gotten blood on his clothes. He looked down at his pants legs. Didn't see anything. They were dark so if there was any blood, it wouldn't be visible. He checked the bottom of each shoe. Clean. If they had had any mud or blood, it had probably come off while he was washing the truck. Satisfied he was clean, he decided against changing. Better shave, though. He looked like a bum. He turned on the television and watched the early morning news while he lathered. Nothing on the ranger. Either his body hadn't been discovered or it had been found, but the media hadn't yet learned about it. He shaved in front of the bathroom mirror with an ear still keyed to the news. He toweled off his face. Packed up his stuff. Switched channels a few times. Still nothing on the ranger. He turned off the set and walked out of the room with his suitcase. He set it on the floor of the cab on the passenger's side; he didn't want to mess up his neat merchandise arrangement in back. He peered through the office window. There she was behind the counter, wearing the same polka-dot dress as when she checked him in Saturday. Hair still knotted in a bun at the back of her head. He rapped twice on the door with his knuckles.

"Come in," she said. She had a singsong voice.

He turned the knob and opened the door.

"Watch your head," she said.

Trip walked inside. He was used to people reminding

119

him to watch his head. Ducking through doorways had become second nature. His posture was so bad, he didn't have to duck too much. "Morning," he mumbled.

"You're an early bird," she said.

The coffee was still dripping into the crusty pot she kept behind the counter. "Smells g... good," he said. He was hungry; his stomach growled. She pulled the pot out even though the coffee wasn't done dripping. Some splattered on the warmer and sizzled. She poured some into a foam cup and handed it to him.

"Thanks." He sipped. Exactly what he needed. Hot and strong.

"Sorry to see you go." She set a box of gas station donuts on the counter and lifted off the cover. "Help yourself."

He took a chocolate glazed. Ate it in two bites.

"Take more," she said, hands on her hips. "Sure was fun having a celebrity around."

He popped a powdered sugar one into his mouth. Chewed three times. Took another sip of coffee to wash the donut down. He set the cup on the counter, licked his fingers.

"Do me a favor, Mr. Trip?" She pulled a newspaper out from under the counter. The Minneapolis *Star Tribune*. "Sign your picture? Please?"

He grinned. "No p... problem." He checked his pockets for a pen. She slid one across the counter. He picked it up and signed at the bottom of the front-page color photo: *Good luck. Justice Trip*. She took the paper from him. He tried to hand the pen back to her.

"You keep it, Mr. Trip. It's got the name of the motel and the phone number. You're always welcome here."

He pulled out his wallet. "What d... d... do I owe you?"

"Got a special rate for heroes," she said, and winked at him. "Half off."

He took three twenties out of his wallet and thought: *God I'm going to miss the attention.*

He started up the truck, turned on the radio, pulled on his baseball cap. He searched the stations and hit one with the news. A male voice: "The Carlton County Sheriff's Office has not named the park employee, but may identify him at a press conference set for later today. It is the first murder of a state park worker in decades. In other news this morning . . ." More station scanning, and then a female reporter: "Moose Lake authorities have refused to release the apparent cause of death. The Ramsey County Medical Examiner's Office is conducting the autopsy. More information may be released at a press conference today. We'll be there with a live report. Now for the weather . . ." He switched stations again and found nothing more on the ranger. He turned it off. He wondered what the cops were up to, why they were holding back. He opened the glove compartment to take out his worry beads. His stiletto. He rifled around; it wasn't there. Then he remembered he'd shoved it in his jacket after the raccoon encounter in the park. He reached inside his pockets. Flashlight still in his left. He pulled it out and threw it on the passenger's seat. Dug around inside his pockets. Nothing more in his left. Nothing in his right. Where was it? Had he dropped the knife somewhere in the park? "Fuck no!" he moaned, and beat the steering wheel with his closed fists. "No!" He remembered checking his jacket for the flashlight after he fell over the ranger. His stiletto was gone from his pocket by then. Had it fallen out when he tripped? No, he'd checked the ground around the body. So where had he dropped it? Probably near the grave when he took off the jacket. He had to go back for it. The dead ranger would

121

draw an army of cops to that park; one of them could eventually come across the bridesmaid's grave—and his knife right with it. He'd used gloves that night, but his prints would be all over the knife from the hundreds of other times he'd handled it. Might as well have wrapped his signed confession in the tarp along with the dead woman. He had to get the knife back. He could feel that panic starting again, that clammy drowning sensation. He'd packed his pill bottle with his clothes, but had shoved the remaining few of his favorites into his pants pocket. He fished out two Adderall tablets and popped them in his mouth.

He took Highway 137 and drove past the park without slowing. The cops were still there, of course. Yellow tape crisscrossed the entrance and there were sheriff's and police squads parked along the highway. Only two television news vans so far. He went a couple of miles past the park and pulled onto the shoulder. He checked his rearview mirror. No one behind him. He shut off the engine. The pills were working; his mind was racing around an idea. Parts of the park were bordered by private farmland. He could cut through a farmer's field to get to the woods. Sneak in while the cops were in the south end of the park gathered around the campground. It would take them a while to start spreading out, work the rest of the park. He'd be in and out in no time. Could he do it in broad daylight? No. Stupid idea. Someone would surely see him. Wait until dark? No. He'd probably get lost. Plus the cops would still be sniffing around the park. If they caught him sneaking through the woods at night, they'd really have reason to suspect him. He thought about the knife again. His prints were the only identifying mark. Otherwise it was a mail-order piece. Cheap. Mass-produced. Could belong to anyone. They needed to suspect him and get his prints to compare them

122

to those on the knife. He'd never been arrested for anything before. Never had his prints taken. The big question: Did they have a suspect? If he was lucky, there was another Chad-type scapegoat waiting in the wings. He heard a helicopter overhead and looked through his windshield. A Twin Cities television station. He could see the call letters from the ground. A news van shot past him on the highway on the way to the park. He wanted to get the scoop on what was going on. He'd wait a bit and then swing back to the park. Give the news crews time to get there, get some inside information. He'd stop and chat it up with them. They all loved his ass. Maybe he could get on television one more time. Yeah. He was starting to get pumped.

16

In the morning Jack went out into the lobby and loaded a tray with bagels, cream cheese, fruit, juice, coffee. He saw a box in the foyer and bought her a *Duluth News Tribune*. He went back to the room. She was still sleeping. He laid the food and newspaper out on the table and turned on the tub faucet; the sound of the water didn't wake her. He sat on the edge of the bed, kissed her eyelids. "Paris," he said in a low voice. "Time to get up, my desert flower."

Her eyes fluttered open. He looked down at her and traced the scar on her forehead with his index finger. "Maybe you should see a plastic surgeon. You're so beautiful."

She pulled his hand away from her face. "But not with the scar."

"That's not what I meant."

"What did you mean then?"

"Nothing." He stood up. "I'll get out of here."

"Wait. I'm sorry. I'm super sensitive about that stupid mark. Can't you stay a little longer? Talk? How about some breakfast? I can't eat all this."

"Quicker you get your day going, quicker you can get

back." He leaned over, kissed her on the mouth and crossed the room to shut off the tub. "Thought you'd want to get another soak in before you check out of the Taj Mahal."

"Thank you." She sat up. Felt bad about snapping at him. "Don't forget to phone my folks about tonight. Tell *Imma* we'll make it another night," she said, using the Lebanese term of endearment for mother.

He pulled on his jacket. "Why don't you call?"

"Too early to call now and I'll be too damn busy later. Besides, my mom enjoys visiting with you over the phone."

"And visiting and visiting." He pulled his car keys out of his pocket. "Sure you won't be back in time for dinner?"

"Even if I am, I'll be tired." She lied. Murphy suspected her folks had invited the two of them to dinner to meddle. Whenever she and Jack split, her parents made it their mission to get them back together. Sometimes their interference made reconciliation harder instead of easier. He walked to the door. She rolled onto her side and watched him leave. "Love you."

He was in a hurry, didn't answer. Pulled the door open and walked out.

She flopped onto her back, stared at the ceiling, replayed the night. As usual, the sex had been great. Afterward, she'd tried to talk but he'd rolled over and gone to sleep, so she'd turned on the television. That was becoming their routine as well, and it pained her to see it happening. They used to cuddle. Rehash the day with each other. Lately, the list of what they could discuss without fighting had shrunk. Some days, she thought the neutral topics could fit on the back of a postage stamp. He'd grown to hate her job. Feared any day she'd be the next patient wheeled into the ER. She'd start describing an especially tough case or problem at the cop shop. He'd raise his arm as if he were fending off a blow and say, "Give the Cliffs Notes version."

She respected his work as much as he resented hers. He was a top doc in town. Led the effort to make Regions Hospital a Level 1 trauma center. Still, he hoarded the details of his day at Regions like they were buried treasure. If he was especially stressed out over something, she'd ask and he'd say, "You don't want to know." They'd stopped talking about the future; planning was a wasted exercise since their life together was uncertain. The subject of children was a land mine. If the timing seemed right to one of them it was wrong for the other. She suspected the real reason neither was ready for kids was they didn't want to bring children into a marriage destined to end in divorce. She knew one night of spontaneous romance wouldn't fix everything, but she'd hoped to see a glimmer of their old relationship when she invited him to join her at the hotel. Instead, she saw more of what was wrong with her marriage.

She kicked off the covers and sat up, swung her legs over the side of the bed and stood up. She glanced at the breakfast table. Typical Jack. Neat. Methodical. Precise. Bagels stacked into a tower on one plate. Cream cheese stacked on another. One of each kind of fruit in a bowl. One of each kind of juice and milk, cartons lined up in a straight row like soldiers. She wished the time he took laying out the food had been spent in bed with her, talking. She was surprised she'd been able to lure him up to Moose Lake at all; he didn't like messing up his routine. The bed was what drew him, she thought. He'd never sleep with another woman, but in a way she felt he was cheating on her by having sex and bolting for St. Paul. On the other hand, there was a part of her that wanted to get rid of him first thing in the morning. Maybe they were both only in it for the sex. She turned on the Jacuzzi and stepped into the bubbling hot water. While she was soaking, she wondered if there was a way she could fit a whirlpool on her boat, along with a fireplace. She leaned back in the tub and her cell phone rang. "Go away," she said. It stopped ringing and then started again. Had to be Yo-Yo. She stepped out of the tub, wrapped a towel around her wet body and took the phone off the nightstand. "Murphy."

Duncan: "Morning, Potato Head. Catch the news?"

"Damn," she said. She grabbed the remote and turned on the television. "Now what?"

"I think we can completely rule out our pal Chad."

Murphy stopped channel hopping when she got to the news. A helicopter shot showed a body in the woods being lifted onto a stretcher. Murphy turned up the sound. The cameras switched to a male reporter standing at the entrance to Moose Lake State Park. The gate was blocked with yellow police tape. She turned up the sound and all she caught was: "Back to you in the newsroom."

"Who's the dead guy?" Murphy asked. She reached for a cup of coffee and took a sip. Cold and bitter. She downed it in a couple of gulps and shuddered.

"Park ranger. Robert Kermitt."

"When? How? Who found him?"

"Got croaked last night. Head bashed in. Body run over. Couple of other parks workers found him this morning. I would have called you earlier, but the cops up there haven't asked for our help on this one, especially since the one St. Paul connection is heading south."

Duncan was talking fast; he always talked fast when he was on to something big. Murphy knew he was saving the best for last. "What else?" she asked.

"The parks people found something with the body. Inside the ranger's jacket. I talked to the sheriff and police chief up there. They're keeping it out of the news."

"Something tying the ranger's murder to Bunny Pederson."

"That's my girl," said Duncan. "How does a peach shoe sound?"

"Sounds like the ranger caught someone dumping the bridesmaid. Couldn't have been the ex and his pal?"

Duncan: "Not unless there's a third person involved. The cops were keeping an eye on Pederson and his buddy all night."

"Good." Murphy had never laid eyes on Chad Pederson, but she found something endearing about a man who took his kids duck hunting and gave elderly neighbors tomatoes out of his own garden. "Still want me to talk to the cops here?"

"Sure. Give them what you got as long as you're up there. It'll reassure them Mr. Chad ain't their man. Then it's not a wasted trip."

Murphy thought the last twenty-four hours had been a waste personally and professionally. She ran her fingers through her tangled hair. Tried to move her mind from her marriage to work. "I'll head on over to the park. They'll still be processing the crime scene. Scouting around for the bridesmaid's body." She picked up a bagel and took a bite.

"You okay?" he asked.

Was her voice betraying her turmoil? Was Duncan that perceptive? She decided it didn't matter. Time to get down to business. "Fine," she said shortly. "Tired."

"Make sure you call before you head back to St. Paul, in case something else pops."

"Sure, Yo-Yo." She bit her lip; it had slipped out.

"What?"

"No. No. I won't leave before I call. Later." She hung up before he could say anything else. Shoved the phone in her purse. She dropped the towel and stepped into some

128

panties and a sweater. She'd brought the union sweatshirt with her; it was huge. She'd wear it over her sweater instead of her jacket. Her stomach growled. More food. She walked over to the breakfast table and saw the *Duluth News Tribune*. Unfolding it, she wasn't surprised to see yet another story on Justice Trip. She sat down at the table and read it. Still making a big deal about volunteering for the search party. More fluff about how he felt an emotional tie to Bunny Pederson. Had he known her, he said in the story, they could have been friends. "Give me a break," she muttered, folding the paper. She grabbed another bagel and took a bite. She wondered if a dead ranger would finally push Trip off the front page. She thought about the uncomfortable meeting with him the night before. The way he'd picked up her glass and swirled the wine around. The way he'd repeatedly glanced at her drink and quickly averted his eyes. She was sure he'd dropped something in it. She should have challenged him on it, but all she wanted to do was get away from the creep. Trip and the bridesmaid. She kept thinking there was something more there. A connection, and not the bullshit kind Trip was selling to the newspapers.

Checkout time wasn't until noon, so she left her things in the room. She wanted to get to the murder scene. The park entrance was a half mile east of the hotel. On her way in, Murphy passed a caravan of squad cars and television news vans parked along the shoulder of Highway 137. She knew the call letters from the Twin Cities and Duluth stations, but there were several others she didn't recognize. The murder was big news, and for good reason. She couldn't remember the last time a park employee was murdered on the job in Minnesota. Rangers wore uniforms, but their

129

work wasn't supposed to be as dangerous as cops' jobs. When she pulled up to the office, Murphy spotted a familiar beat-up pickup truck parked in the lot adjacent to the building. She scanned the back bumper of the heap to make sure and saw the telltale sticker reflecting the owner's attitude toward most other human beings: "Some People Are Alive Only Because It Is Against the Law to Kill Them." Cody, the *Pioneer Press* police reporter. Murphy drove up to the police tape blocking the road and flashed her badge out the window. A deputy stepped up to the driver's side of the Jeep and right behind him was Cody, with his shoulder-length brown mop and John Lennon glasses. He wore a down vest over a sweatshirt, but Murphy figured his signature Hawaiian shirt was under there somewhere. He was at the deputy's elbow while the officer checked her ID. "Murphy. What are you doing here? Got a St. Paul angle to this ranger slaying? Tell them to let me in. Come on."

The deputy looked to be in his late twenties, about Cody's age. Even with his hair shaved into a crew cut, it was obvious he was a redhead. Freckles spattered his face like measles. He handed Murphy's badge back and turned to yell at Cody. "Get lost!"

Cody was wired. Too much coffee and news. He had a notebook in his right hand and a pencil in his left. "She knows me. She can vouch for me. We work together in St. Paul. Tell him, Murphy. Tell him you know me."

The deputy: "I don't give a shit who knows you. Go away. Go far away. Take that piece-of-shit truck with you."

Murphy: "Sorry, Cody. Stay behind the tape with the rest of the pack." The deputy untied the tape to let Murphy through. "Who's here? BCA up yet?" she asked, referring to the Minnesota Bureau of Criminal Apprehension.

130

"Everybody and his uncle. BCA. Sheriff. Police chief. Bunch of squads. Ramsey County ME is doing the autopsy. In fact one of their guys happened to be up here on vacation. Came by right away. Nice of him."

She paused. Rural communities often asked Ramsey County to do autopsies in murder cases. Murphy figured Erik wouldn't be on the case, though. He was off work. "Yeah. Nice." Damn Erik, she thought. He'd followed her up and then heard about the ranger. Figured she'd be here. He must have spent the night in town. She didn't want to imagine what could have happened if he'd ended up at her hotel.

"Which way?" she asked.

"Hang a left after the office," he said, pointing toward the road. "You'll pass a boat landing. Keep going. Watch the signs. Campsite five. First loop off the road. Can't miss it."

She noticed the deputy's eyes were red. "Knew him?"

The deputy leaned inside her window and spoke in a low voice; he didn't want Cody to hear. "He worked hard. Treated people fairly. Hell of an angler. Pretty good poker player, too. Taught me a few things. Couple more years and he could have retired. The whole thing sucks. I want to personally nail the bastard's hide to a tree."

"You'll get him," she said.

He noticed her Homicide sweatshirt. "Catchy slogan."

"What's your mailing address? I'll send you one. Our union rep came up with them." The deputy's face brightened. He reached into his jacket pocket and handed her a card. "Sean Mahoney," she said. She tucked the card in her purse. "My dad's name is Sean. A good Irish name. I'll ship you a shirt as soon as I get back to the cop shop."

"Appreciate it." He stepped back from the car, waved her through. Murphy looked in her rearview mirror as she pulled away and saw Cody following the deputy inside the office, yammering the entire time and waving his notebook around.

Murphy pulled over to the side and parked the Jeep on the road leading to the campground. Figuring it was already jammed with cars, she didn't want to park at the campsite itself. She walked south for several yards, took a right off the road. Headed down the first loop into a sea of uniforms. BCA's crime-scene team crawling around the ranger's truck. A guy snapping pictures of the ranger's body. Another guy kneeling in the dirt making a cast. Cops and deputies poking around bushes and weeds. A couple of parks workers standing around, probably the ones who found the ranger. Then she saw him. He was the only one crouched next to the ranger. She contemplated turning around and getting back in the car. Too late. He looked up and saw her. He smiled. She told herself she was a coward for wanting to run from him. He stood up and walked toward her, peeling off his gloves as he went. He moved slowly and deliberately. His eyes never left her face. He reminded her of a lion who'd spotted his next meal. She hated to admit it, but that predatory quality intrigued her. Excited her. She didn't want that right now; she was already confused.

"Surprise," Erik said, and stuffed his gloves into his jacket pocket.

She crossed her arms over her chest. "Are you trying to piss me off? I can't believe you followed me up here."

He stopped next to her and leaned into her ear. "This isn't the space you wanted?" he whispered.

She took a step away from him. She didn't want his hot breath on her neck; she enjoyed it too much. "I'm not going to be here too long," she said, pulling some sheets of paper out of her purse. "I'm handing over a few notes and then I've got to check out of my room. Head back to the cop shop. Where did you spend the night?"

"Not with you, unfortunately. Lunch?"

"Don't have time."

"Not even for lunch?"

"I've got to get back." She looked past him. "The sheriff around? Who's in charge?"

"Come on. I'll introduce you to Mr. Warmth." He led her to a big man standing next to the ranger's pickup truck. "Detective Murphy from St. Paul PD," said Erik. "Sheriff Winter." He looked like his name. White hair. White mustache. Ice-blue eyes.

He extended his hand—as big as a catcher's mitt—and she shook it. "What you got for me on this Chad Pederson?"

Murphy could tell he was impatient. He had better things to do than listen to a detective from St. Paul with a marginal connection to the case. She handed him her notes. "Here's everything I got. I'm sure you've already cut him loose."

Winter grunted. "Probably halfway home by now. Tore up about his ex and madder than hell we picked him up for questioning, especially in front of his boys."

Murphy: "How are his kids?"

"Unglued. They're staying up here with Grandma. For now. Pederson wants them, but child protection is giving him the third degree."

"Why?"

"Why the hell do you think? 'Cause we thought he killed their mama. Hope we didn't mess things up for him." Winter's eyes narrowed. "Tell your boss thanks for all his assistance."

Murphy opened her mouth to apologize for Duncan, but felt strangely defensive. "He was trying to help. You must have bought into it if you picked Pederson up."

Winter's face reddened. "Yeah. Well." He looked at the notes she'd handed him. "Good. This is good. County attorney thought we were too quick to rule Pederson out. This clears the decks on that issue."

She had questions about the ranger's murder and the connection to Bunny Pederson, but she figured Winter wasn't the one to ask. She handed him her card and he stuffed it in his jacket. "Call me if you want anything else," she said, and turned and headed to her car.

Erik went after her. "Thought you couldn't stand Yo-Yo. Why'd you pass up a chance to slam him?"

"Duncan's not so bad."

"Since you're in such a generous mood, how about granting me an audience?"

"This isn't the time or the place."

"I'll meet you at the hotel," he said. "We've got to talk."

"What about your dead guy?"

"He's got his own ride down to St. Paul. Where're you staying?"

They stopped next to the Jeep. Murphy wasn't ready to talk about their relationship—she was still angry he'd followed her to Moose Lake—but she did want to hear what Erik knew about the case. "Fill me in on the ranger's murder?"

"Sure."

"AmericInn," she said. She opened the driver's-side door and hopped in. "Meet me in the lobby. Under the moose head." She slammed the door.

On her way back to the hotel, she saw Trip standing by the side of the highway talking to Cody. A news van parked in front of Cody's beater truck pulled away and she steered

134

the Jeep into the space. She turned off the car and shoved the keys in her purse. Looked down at her sweatshirt. Ran her fingers over the embroidered badge. Now Trip would know what she did for a living. Good, she thought. Let's see what kind of reaction that gets. She opened the door, hopped out, walked toward Cody's truck. Trip and Cody were leaning against the side of it, talking. She noticed the reporter wasn't taking notes; this wasn't an interview. Trip's back was turned to her, but she could see Cody's face. He was aggravated. Seemed Trip was finally wearing out his welcome with the press.

"Hello again, Sweet," she said. Trip turned and looked at her face and then glanced down. He didn't notice her sweatshirt, she thought. She'd have to talk to him a little longer.

Cody checked his watch. "I'll leave you two to catch up. I've got a press conference." Murphy and Trip stepped away from Cody's pickup. The reporter got in his truck and pulled away, following a stream of other cars and television vans headed to town. The two of them were alone next to her Jeep. They stood three feet apart—closer than strangers stand, but not as close as friends.

She forced a tight smile on her face. "Was Cody trying to wring one more quote out of you?"

"I was on my way out of t... town. Saw all the reporters. Thought I'd check it out."

"They all know you now."

"Yeah, yeah."

He was still looking down, but she could see he was blushing. He loved all the attention, she thought. This didn't feel right. Not any of it. The way he enjoyed the publicity. His behavior in the bar.

Another breeze rippled the trees and sent leaves falling between them. She pulled one out of her hair. Trip's gaze moved up to her face and then her forehead. The scar. She thought she detected a small smile on his face. Then she saw Trip take in her sweatshirt. Watched his eyes widen and his face whiten. He quickly looked down. Fiddled with the baseball cap in his hands. She'd rattled the shit out of him and she was glad.

"You d... didn't tell me you're a c... cop last night," he said.

"Didn't think you'd be interested," she said. "Sometimes it puts people off."

"So you're a d... detective. In St. Paul. Interesting work?"

"Has its days."

"What b... brings you to the park?" He was pushing a rock around with the tip of his right shoe, trying hard to act casual.

"I heard the Moose Lake cops had a murder. Thought I'd check it out. I know a couple of the deputies."

He stopped pushing the rock around and froze. "The r... r... ranger? Know anything more about it?"

"I can't talk about it."

He started pushing the rock around with the other foot. He was trying to hide it, but he was nervous and afraid, and it had something to do with the ranger's body. She didn't believe he'd stopped outside the park to bullshit with the reporters. Killers return to the scene. Could Trip be the killer? Her amorphous suspicions jelled into a theory, and it sent a chill through her body. It all added up. The fact that he found the bridesmaid's finger. The way he enjoyed all the attention. His presence outside the park. His startled reaction when he saw her sweatshirt. She tried to beat down her own theory. Couldn't be Trip. Not somebody she went to school with, somebody she knew. In the same instant she warned herself that she didn't know him. Not really. That business with the wineglass proved it last night.

Last night! Did he have time to do it last night, after their dinner? She needed more. She had to make sure he showed up at the reunion. She pulled her keys out of her purse. Saw her business cards, pulled one out and handed it to him. "Call me if you can't find your invitation."

He took the card, put it in his pocket. "Sure you'll b... b... be there?"

"Absolutely." She glanced at her watch; almost checkout time at the hotel. "Gotta go. How far away you parked? Need a ride to your car?"

"Got my wheels right here," he said, pointing at his Ford parked across the road.

"Nice," she said, and took a mental photograph of the truck.

"Was good seeing you again, Sweet." She walked up to her car door, opened it, threw her purse inside. Over her shoulder she said, "Should have asked you last night. Can I still call you Sweet, or did you outgrow that nickname?"

He'd pulled the baseball cap on his head. "No. Pa s... still calls me Sweet."

"Good." She got in, shut the door, turned the ignition.

As he watched her drive away, he studied the make and model of her car. He said under his breath, "What goes around comes around, beautiful."

17

Erik was pacing impatiently under the moose head when she walked into the lobby. He looked pointedly at the clock behind the front desk. "Sorry," she said. "I saw Justice Trip on the way back and stopped to talk."

He frowned. "Why does that name ring a bell?"

She sat down on the couch in the lobby. She was overheating in the sweatshirt. She pulled it off, tossed it on the arm of the couch, ran her fingers through her hair. Had she forgotten to brush it this morning? Pretty soon she'd be coming to work looking like Duncan. She rubbed her forehead with her fingertips. A headache. She needed to eat something. The bagels in her room would be hard as rocks by now and they'd already cleared the breakfast food from the lobby. She saw a basket of fruit at the front desk.

"Toss me an apple," she said.

Erik carried the basket over and set it on the coffee table in front of her. "Told you we should have had lunch. I'm starving, too." He sat down next to her, peeled a banana, ate it in three bites. He tossed the skin on the coffee table and grabbed an orange. "Who's Trip Justice?"

She picked up an apple, wiped it on her sweater and took a bite before she answered. "Justice Trip," she said, wiping juice from her chin with her hand. "He's that tall guy who's been on television and in the newspapers for finding the finger."

"Oh yeah."

"I went to school with him. I bumped into him at a bar last night; we ended up having dinner together. Listen to this. I leave to use the john and when I start heading back to the table, I see him messing with my wineglass."

"You think he put something in your drink?"

"I wasn't sure last night. Didn't take any chances. Didn't touch it. Now I'm sure he tried to slip me something. He's acting so bizarre."

"How so?"

"Hanging around outside the park for no good reason this morning. Then his eyes bug out when he sees I'm a cop. On top of all that, he isn't the person he's pretending to be in all the news stories."

"Rewriting his own history?"

"More like giving himself a personality makeover. In the stories, he acts the part of this noble do-gooder. Volunteering for this search party and that. Helping the cops by finding clues. He's really a mouse. He's doctoring up even dumb little stuff about himself. Claims he's a lifelong Elvis fan, same as the bridesmaid. But he never—"

"Whoa. What did you say?" Erik stopped peeling the orange.

"The bridesmaid. Bunny Pederson. He says she liked Elvis and so did he and they could have been soul mates or some stupid crap like that." She took another bite of apple, chewed, swallowed.

"Paris." He touched her arm. "That's a tidbit only the cops up here know."

"What?"

"She had the lyrics to an Elvis song stuffed inside her purse when she went missing, but that's not general knowledge," said Erik. "As far as I know, nothing that was in her bag has been made public. A couple of her friends from the wedding party know what she was carrying, but that's about it."

"Shit," she said.

"Think he's the one?" Erik shoved an orange section in his mouth.

"I've been thinking he could be," she said in a low voice. "Explains the finger turning up minus the rest of her."

"He planted it."

"Kills her, cuts off the pinkie, ditches the rest of her somewhere. Then he volunteers for the search party so he can 'find' the finger. Could have been carrying it. Waiting for the right time to drop it."

Erik nodded. "The condition of the pinkie. Pretty damn pristine for sitting out in the woods. No insect bites. No animal bites. Winter wondered if the finger had been removed by a raccoon or something. No way, I told him. The cut was clean. Baffled the hell out of us. Who would have suspected the guy who found it? Brilliant and ballsy in a way."

Murphy: "Brilliant and ballsy. Two words I'd never use to describe Justice Trip."

"But why? What's the motive?"

"So he could be king for a day? I read the stories about him. He played hero before and loved it. Helped hunt for a missing girl outside Eau Claire."

"Think he killed her, too?"

"No, no. They found her after Sweet found her necklace."

"Sweet?"

140

"His nickname." She took another bite out of the apple. Chewed and swallowed. "Which song?"

Erik: "What?"

"Which Elvis song in her purse?"

"Why?"

"Curious. Bet it was 'Can't Help Falling in Love.' "

"How'd you know?"

"Every couple has it at their wedding."

"I wouldn't know. Never been married." He stared at her and she quickly looked away. "You'll need more than an Elvis song. Hell. He could say he overheard somebody in town talking about it." He popped two orange sections into his mouth.

"I know." She took another bite of the apple, chewed, swallowed. "What about that cast they took?"

"Tire tread. A partial. They're trying to figure out if it's the killer's or whoever camped there last."

"I saw a sign. Thought camping was done for the year."

"A few people have been sneaking in anyway." He picked up a second orange. Started peeling, adding to the garbage pile on the coffee table.

Murphy: "Car?"

"Looks like it was a truck." He pulled an orange section off, stuffed it in his mouth, chewed twice, swallowed, wiped his mouth with his hand.

"Sweet drives a truck," she said.

"So does half the state." He rifled more orange sections into his mouth. Chewed and swallowed.

"What else they find?"

"A print. On the bridesmaid's shoe. Some black hairs. The BCA lab boys are doing their thing." He shoved the last piece of orange in his mouth.

"Sweet's losing black hair a strand a second," she said. "But if he's as devious as I think he is, he's never been

141

caught doing anything. His prints and DNA aren't in the system." She chewed her bottom lip. "My only question is timing. I saw him last night. We had a late dinner."

"How late?"

"Seven or so."

"He would have had plenty of time to do the ranger." Erik swept the mound of orange and banana peelings off the coffee table and into the wastebasket. "What's your game plan, lady? Gonna run your theory by the locals?"

"I'm not saying anything to that prick Winter until I've got more. That's for damn sure." She ran her fingers through her hair again. "God. Somebody from high school. How weird would that be if he is the killer?"

He wiped one hand on his pants. "A guy I went to high school with is in prison."

"Murder?"

"Nah. Big-time embezzlement. Credit union."

She tossed the apple core in the wastebasket, picked up a pear. Polished it on her sweater sleeve. "When do you suppose we stop keeping tabs on the kids we went to high school with?"

"What do you mean?"

"You might not stay in touch, but you're always keeping score in your head. *I hope I'm doing better than he is. I'll bet I look better for my age than she does.* It's only four years out of your life. What's the big deal about high school?" She took a bite and chewed. The pear was hard and green.

"Here's my theory on that: High school's important because the person you become then is the person you stay for the rest of your life."

Murphy: "Bullshit. People change. Grow."

"Not all that much. Some traits and habits amplify or lessen when you become an adult. But the whole package is still the same."

"That guy you went to school with. Was he a thief in high school?"

"Bet your ass he was. Stole my calculator. Was this Justice character a creep in high school?" She didn't answer. "I'll take that as a yes. See what I mean?"

She shook her head. "I still don't know if I buy it."

He threw up his hands. "Hey. That's my theory. Take it or leave it."

She sat back in the couch with the pear in her hand. "I'm wiped out."

"Me too," he said. He leaned back and shut his eyes.

Both sat still on the couch for a moment. Murphy wondered when she'd last had a conversation this long with Jack, especially about work. She'd even forgotten about the stupid bangs covering her forehead. She touched them. They were all screwed up, but Erik hadn't once looked at her scar. She had to keep reminding herself that he'd followed her up there and that it pissed her off.

Murphy nudged him in the side with her elbow. "Wake up. We better get our butts moving." She stood, tossed the pear in the wastebasket. Picked up her sweatshirt and purse off the couch. Erik opened his eyes and yawned. "Talk to me while I pack," she said, and he got up and followed her down the hall. She was excited. Someone interested in her job. In her ideas. She slid the key card into the lock and pushed open the door. Threw her purse and sweatshirt on the bed.

"Nice room," he said, and sat on the edge of the four-poster while she stuffed her clothes into the duffel bag on the end of the bed.

"Tell me more about the case," she said, bending over to pick up her socks and jeans off the floor.

"First tell me about last night," he said. She stood up with the clothes in her arms. Erik was holding a champagne glass

143

in each hand. "Jack?" he asked, searching her face for a response. She dropped the clothes and nodded. "Jack," he said again. Not a question this time. A statement. Then angrily: "Jack!" He hurled one of the glasses against the fireplace. It shattered against the brick. He dropped the other glass on the floor. Bolted from the bed. Grabbed her hard by the arms. "You didn't want my company last night but you were happy to summon Jack. Run to me when you need a shoulder to cry on. A pal. Then go fuck Jack. Is that how it works?" His voice was low and deep. He was struggling to contain it. "Stop doing this to me. Stop doing it to Jack. Make up your mind."

She'd never seen him this furious. She struggled to push his hands off her, but he only gripped her harder. "You're hurting me," she said.

"No," he said. "You're hurting me." He pulled her to him and kissed her roughly on the mouth. He cradled the back of her head with his left hand. With his right, he pressed the small of her back; he wanted her to feel his hardness. He eased her backward onto the bed and fell on top of her. His mouth covered hers again and then moved to the curve of her neck. His left hand stayed tangled in her hair. His right moved up under her sweater. Cupped her left breast over her bra. Slid under her bra. He pushed her knees apart with his and moaned as he rubbed his crotch against hers.

She could still smell Jack's cologne on the sheets. "Erik," she said. "Please."

His hand moved from her breast to her stomach. Slid under her jeans and panties. "Please keep going?" He sounded groggy. Lost in the passion.

She raised her voice. "Stop. Get off me. We can't do this."

"Sure we can." He pulled on her left ear with his teeth.

144

Even louder: "No!"

"Damn," he muttered. He withdrew his hand from her panties. "*No* forever? Or *no* right now?"

"I don't know," she said.

"Let me help you make up your mind," he said into her ear. His right hand moved back to her breast; he squeezed it as hard as he could over her sweater. "Break it off with Jack or I'll do it for you." The lion coming in for the kill. "I'll tell him we slept together. So help me God I will."

"Bastard!" she said. She tried to push him off with both hands but he grabbed her wrists and pinned them against the bed. He kissed her on the mouth while she cursed him. "Bastard!" He released her wrists. She rolled him off of her and stood up. Her legs felt weak and wobbly; she grabbed the bedpost for support. He sat up on the bed, smiling. She drew her right hand back and slapped him. The smile was still there. So was the lion. She drew her hand back again and he grabbed it and pulled her onto his lap and kissed her on the mouth. He wrapped his arms around her and she buried her face in the crook of his neck.

"You son of a bitch," she murmured. "I hate you."

He rested his head between her breasts. "Paris. I have to know if we have anything together. Life's too short. I want to enjoy you in public. I want to look ahead with you. Make plans. I'll tell him if you don't. I mean it."

"Tell him what? That we slept together once?"

"There's more to it. More to us. I know there is."

She wrapped her arms around his neck. There was more, but she couldn't put a name to it. Maybe it was simple lust. Whatever it was, it made her guilty and miserable. Behind his back, she held up her left hand. She half expected the gold circle to crack and fall off her finger right before her eyes. She untangled her arms from his neck and got up off his lap. Turned her back to him while she talked. She

145

couldn't look into his hazel eyes. Not while the lion was awake. "I can't write off eight years of marriage so easily."

He got up off the bed and walked over to her. Stood behind her. Twined his arms around her waist. "Give it up, Paris. If it's this much work, it ain't there. Move on."

She tried to push his arms off her but he wouldn't budge. She gave up and rested her arms over his. "I have to try."

"Try what? Try hoping for a miracle? Let me ask you. Is he trying as hard as you are?"

She didn't respond.

"Is he?"

In a voice that was barely audible, she answered, "No."

"That's what I thought." He dropped his arms from her waist and walked to the door. She turned to watch him go. "I'm heading back to St. Paul. Ranger Bob pulled the plug on my little holiday. If they find the bridesmaid, she's on my plate, too. I'll be a busy man this week." He put his hand on the door handle. "Make a decision." He opened the door and left.

She went to the bed and finished packing her duffel bag. She picked up the surviving champagne glass off the floor, tossed it in the wastebasket. She'd have to get a whole new set. What good was one champagne flute? She'd never find a match for it. Then she sat on the edge of the bed and buried her face in her hands. The glass was from their wedding day.

18

While he sat in the truck watching all the news vans pull away, he took the pill bottle out of his suitcase. Trip hadn't learned anything from the reporters. They were all cold to him. Too busy to talk to him. They'd used him up; on to the next big thing. Fuck them all. Every last one of them. See if he'd ever give them another story. With shaking hands, he fished a couple of downers out of the bottle and swallowed them. He needed to come down after seeing her outside the park. She had a scar on her forehead; he hadn't noticed it last night in the bar. That mark pleased him. Something had caused her pain and damaged her and he was glad. She was still stunning, though, and that disappointed him. All these years he'd imagined she'd turned into a dried-up hag with gray hair and yellow teeth. Worse than seeing that beautiful face in the light of day was seeing that detective's badge printed on her shirt. She was lying about being on vacation. If she was working on the Moose Lake case, there had to be a Twin Cities angle since she was a St. Paul detective. The bridesmaid's ex was from St. Paul. Maybe that was it. That didn't explain why she was at the park after the ranger's body was discovered. Did the police see a St. Paul angle in that case as well? Or had the cops somehow connected the two cases? How? If they had, it wouldn't be good for him. It could mean he'd left something else behind. He'd picked up the shoe the ranger found. What about the other shoe? No. He'd shined the flashlight around before he pulled out of the campsite. Had he dropped it in the park while carrying the body? No. He would have noticed. The shoes were big, bright objects. Not like the dark, compact stiletto. He was sure the other shoe was buried with her in the tarp. He'd left nothing else behind besides the stiletto, and maybe they wouldn't even find that. Even if they did, it wouldn't immediately lead to him nor would it tell the cops the two cases were related. If they found her body, then they'd figure out why the ranger had been killed. That still wouldn't lead them to him. He decided he was safe.

He started the truck and pulled back onto the road. He was afraid it would take too long for the downers to kick in. While he drove, he opened the glove compartment with his right hand and pulled out his one-hitter kit. The wooden container was the size and shape of a pack of unfiltered Camels. He flipped open the hinged top with his thumb. Inside, a stash of Colombian weed on one side of the divided box and a brass smoking pipe on the other. He shifted the box to his driving hand and with his free hand pulled out a pipe the size of a cigarette. He dipped the pipe into the weed, ground it in, pulled it out, put it between his lips. He pushed in the truck cigarette lighter. When it popped out, he grabbed it with his right hand and lit up. He inhaled deeply. The end of the pipe glowed. He held the smoke in his lungs as long as he could. He coughed and the truck swerved a bit. The buzz was starting. "You don't cough, you don't get off," he muttered to himself. He put the pipe back in the box, closed the kit, returned it to the glove compartment. He felt much better.

He checked the gas gauge. Might as well top off the tank before hitting the highway, he thought. He drove to the station off the interstate. He looked up and down the road as he held the gas pump. No police blockades or anything. He was relieved. Maybe the cops figured whoever did it was long gone. He went inside and paid for the gas. Went next door to the sub shop and bought a couple of sandwiches and a pop. He slid into a booth and ate so fast he didn't taste anything. Still hungry. He bought a bag of chips and a third sandwich and shoveled the food in. His cell phone rang while he was wiping his mouth. He pulled it out of his jacket.

"Yeah."

His pa: "You sound tired, Sweet."

"I'm ready to c... come home."

"How'd you do? Sold a bunch of shirts?"

He lied: "G... g... got all sorts of orders."

Pa: "I knew that job would be worthwhile. So when you heading back?"

Trip figured his old man wanted to schedule one last blow job from the fat blond nurse. "I should be home before d... dinner."

"Dinner tonight?"

"Yeah."

A pause. "Good. Okay then." He hung up.

His pa sounded let down. Tough. Trip wanted to get home. Get his head together. Find out about this reunion thing. Perfect opportunity for Sweet Justice. He started sucking down the last of his pop and turned his head to glance out the window. A state van had pulled into the parking lot. He tried to read the writing on the side. Minnesota Department of Corrections. The van was empty. How long had it been there? Where was the driver? He heard a voice at the counter and tried to check it out without being obvious. Two men in navy blue uniforms with DOC patches on their shoulders and a bunch of hardware hanging from their belts. Prison guards getting sandwiches. Big sons of bitches, Trip thought. Almost as tall as he and a lot more muscular. Military haircuts and hard-set mouths. The bigger of the pair eyed Trip while he was waiting for his sub. Trip wondered if he was close enough to smell the pot. He dropped his eyes and picked at some stray lettuce on his tray. He pictured himself behind bars. Imagined that all the in-between stuff could be skipped—arrest, charges, trial, conviction, sentencing—and that the two guards could grab him and take him back with them. The guards paid for their lunches and went back outside. The big one glanced at Trip's truck, got back in the driver's seat of the van. The other one got in, slammed the passenger's door. They pulled out of the parking lot and headed toward the prison. For a second, Trip thought he was going to vomit. He sat in the booth staring straight ahead, empty pop cup in his hand. Time to get the hell out of town, he thought. He'd pushed his luck long enough. He slid out of the booth and went to his truck.

Trip leaned back in the driver's seat as he got on I-35 heading south. Traffic was light. He steered with one hand. Wished the other had the stiletto in it. He slipped a disc into the CD player. *Master of Puppets* by Metallica. The screaming guitars provided balance to the downers and the one-hit. The sensation was similar to sitting on a seesaw with someone who weighed the same. He and Snow White did that in a park. Sat on an old wooden seesaw. Each took an end. Sat perfectly still. Held their knees up so their feet were inches off the ground. He didn't know how long they were there; could have been a minute or half an hour. They looked straight ahead at each other; she was the only female he could ever stare at for any length of time. She broke the spell. "No sudden moves, Sweet," she'd said. She quick hopped off and his end slapped down on the ground. Landed hard on his ass. She laughed and laughed. So did he.

"No sudden moves," he said, and pounded the steering wheel to the beat of the drums. He'd make a sudden move on Paris Murphy. Knock her hard on her ass at the reunion. So hard she'd never get up again. How would he do it? He had to be careful. Taking down a cop would be dangerous. He'd already taken down one uniform. How different was a ranger from a cop? The ranger didn't have a gun, but a cop always carries one. He didn't see one on her. Probably under her sweatshirt or in her purse or even strapped to her ankle. He'd seen that in the movies. No. He couldn't take her up close the way he'd taken the ranger. Fooling with her Jeep Grand Cherokee was a possibility. Still, that was complicated. Took planning. He'd have to find out where she lived. Could he simply do it his usual way? He'd just nailed Bunny Pederson; flattening someone else so soon was risky. He liked spacing them out more. His face had been all over the news. If he showed his face at the reunion and someone at the party died the same way as the bridesmaid . . .

No. He'd have to do something different with Detective Paris Murphy. He eyed the pill bottle sitting on the passenger's seat. He hoped the fat nurse was still hanging around when he got home. The plan he'd almost executed in the bar wasn't such a bad idea. Next time she'd drink her drink; he'd make sure of it.

19

Her cell phone rang while she was loading her bag into the Jeep. She pulled it out of her purse. "Murphy."

Duncan: "Jesus Christ. Every time you pick up the phone you sound worse than the last time."

She silently cursed his perceptive ear. "Need to crash in my own bed."

"You sure that's all?"

"Let's not go there right now."

"That dick Winter give you a hard time? Something else going on?"

She appreciated Duncan's concern, but wasn't ready to spill her guts about anything personal. They didn't know each other well enough. "Winter was a jerk. I gave him what I had and hit the road. Throwing my stuff in the Jeep right now." She slammed the back gate and walked around to the driver's door. Opened it, got in, shut the door. "Please tell me I can head back to the cop shop. I already checked out of the hotel."

"Go straight home. Catch up on your Zs. Drag your butt into the station house tomorrow. You put in your eight and then some."

She leaned her head back in the car seat. "Thanks."

"For the record, Potato Head, Winter said you put together a real nice package for him. Stuff from the neighbors. Stuff from his work. Confirmation there were no cop calls to his place. The whole bit. Backs up his duck hunting story and shows he's no homicidal maniac."

She wondered if she could run her theory by him. "Speaking of homicidal maniac, I've got a wild idea about who the killer could be."

"Love wild ideas. Hit me with it."

"Tell you what. Let me present it in person. I'll get cleaned up at home and then come in with it. How late you gonna be there tonight?"

"Late as you want. Is your suspect for real? Should we run it by Winter? Maybe they should pick him up."

She regretted saying something to him this early. "Slow down, Duncan. I don't have enough yet. Got some legwork to do. Besides, my suspect isn't going anywhere. In fact, I expect to see him Saturday night."

"It's somebody you know? I can hardly wait to hear this. Only thing is, if it ain't a burning emergency, maybe you should save it for the morning."

"Why?"

"You sound like shit."

She decided he was right. She needed to pull her thoughts together, write it all down. There might be some holes in her theory. Her brain wasn't completely focused on work right now. "Know what? I think I will sleep on it."

"Good. Catch you tomorrow in the A.M. Later, Potato Head."

She hung up and slipped the phone in her purse. One of these days she'd have to tell him to lay off on the Potato Head talk. She started the Jeep, pulled out of the parking

153

lot and turned onto the interstate. She was on automatic pilot during the drive home. For once she wished she had a partner so she could ask him to take the wheel. She inserted a compact disc into the CD player. Nat King Cole's "Unforgettable" filled the interior like warm bathwater.

Traffic was light coming out of Moose Lake, but got heavier as she got closer to the Twin Cities. She checked the clock on the Jeep. A little early for rush hour. She took a downtown exit. Cut through downtown. Crossed the Wabasha Bridge and went home. She saw Jack's car in the yacht club parking lot. What was he doing there? She wasn't ready to tell him anything. She pulled into a parking spot, turned off the engine and sat for a minute. The beginnings of three different speeches ran through her mind. *I'm sorry I cheated on you. I'm sorry but if you don't try harder, we're through. I'm sorry but I'm tired, need to be alone to-night.* That last one sounded the best. Gave her some time. Okay, she thought, speech number three. She had no idea what she'd say after that first sentence, but figured something would come to her. She grabbed her keys and her purse and slid out of the driver's seat. Slammed the door. Went around back and opened the gate to get her bag. She walked down the dock and noticed a pair of mallards bobbing in the water. She had some stale flatbread. She'd toss it out to them later. She opened the door to her houseboat and walked in, her mind a jumble of Jack and Erik and ducks and bread.

He was standing in the living room looking out the patio doors. He was still dressed in his scrubs. Some days she wondered if he had any other clothes. She dropped her bag on the galley floor and tossed her keys and purse on the kitchen table. He didn't greet her. Something was wrong. "You lied," he said, his back still turned to her.

154

"What?" she asked.

"The flowers. I called your mother. Told her we weren't going to be over for dinner. I asked why she sent the flowers."

Murphy looked at the bouquet on the kitchen table. Covered her mouth with her right hand. With her left, she grabbed the back of a kitchen chair for support. She didn't say anything. Not one word came to mind. None of her speeches would work. Her brain was a blank sheet of paper: white, flat, flimsy, useless. The house was silent. Outside, she heard the sound of a speedboat. She wished whoever was piloting it would stop by, interrupt this, take her away.

Jack: "Who?"

She didn't hesitate; no point in hiding it any longer. "Erik Mason."

His back stiffened. He knew Erik. They'd worked together on different medical committees and projects over the years. "How long?"

"Does it matter?" She didn't want to go into details. This was too painful.

He turned around to face her. He poked his right index finger in his chest. "It fucking matters to me. How long?" She didn't answer right away. Louder: "How long?"

"Since the summer. That night you left for the medical conference. It was just that once. I was so wound up over that case . . ." Her voice trailed off. She didn't want to give excuses.

He took a step toward her. "Are you blaming this on me? This is my fault somehow?"

"No," she said in a low voice.

He took another step toward her. "Do you think I ever cheated on you? Slept with another woman, even when we were separated?"

"No," she said.

"Did I ever hit you, abuse you in some way?"

A mean, spiteful question that stung her. She shook her head. "No. Of course not."

"Was I a lousy lover?"

She looked into his eyes. He was genuinely concerned that their sex life was the problem. It mystified her. Didn't he realize it was the one thing that wasn't at issue? "You're a wonderful lover. You know that."

"I don't know anything anymore." He ran his fingers through his hair. "Why, then? Why?" She didn't answer. A long silence. Then: "Do you love him?"

The one question she dreaded. She looked down. Covered her forehead with her right hand and with her left still held onto the chair back. She felt as if the kitchen chair was the only thing keeping her from falling through the floor into an abyss. A special hell reserved for unfaithful wives. "I don't know," she said. She looked up with tears in her eyes. Then the only words she found useful from her prepared speeches: "I'm sorry."

He rubbed his face with his hands and said through them, "Me too."

She let go of the chair back and was surprised to see her legs still worked. She walked across the galley into the living room. She tried to wrap her arms around him but he pushed her away and turned toward the river again. The fall sun was starting to fade on the water. Come night, the Mississippi would be as black as ink. She spoke to his back and found the words easier than when she faced him. "I still love you and I think you still love me," she said.

"Nice words," he said.

She ignored it. "But we don't get along. We can't even live under the same roof. What kind of marriage is that?"

"One I thought we could save," he said sadly.

"We still could," she said. "You . . . we need to work harder at it."

He turned and faced her. He grabbed her shoulders. "Tell me something. Did you fuck him upstairs, in the same bed where we made love? On the same sheets? Or did you have the courtesy to change them?"

Hateful words that made her cringe and feel even guiltier. Dirtier. It had been in the same bed, on the same sheets. Her only response was a plea: "God, Jack. Please. Stop." .

He pushed her backward onto the couch and leaned over her. She dug her fingers into the cushions, bracing for another verbal assault. "You and Erik can both go to hell. We're through. Take this souvenir with you." He pulled her to him, kissed her hard on the mouth. She tried to pull away from him; he was frightening her. He grabbed each side of her head with his hands and held her mouth to his. Almost a minute went by. He withdrew his mouth, but not before biting her bottom lip.

She yelped and fell back against the couch. "Jack!"

He stood up and walked out, slamming the door so hard it shook the galley cupboards.

She touched her mouth with her right hand. Looked at her fingertips. Blood. Jack was usually a steady, calm man. Whenever they fought, he usually walked out before things got ugly. What he'd done was mean and angry, and his parting words unnerved her. Were they really finished? Was it really over? She got up off the couch and went to the kitchen table for her purse. Pulled out her phone. Took a deep breath and exhaled before punching his number.

"Erik?"

"Calling with good news?"

"Jack was here."

"You told him?"

157

"Yes." She pulled out a chair, sat down, rested her elbows on the kitchen table. "He went ballistic."

"You surprised?"

"I'm worried. If he shows up at your office, could be a scene."

"If he wants a battle to the death, this is the right place for it."

"Not funny."

"Don't worry. I'll behave."

She touched her bottom lip again; it was starting to swell. "You're not the one I'm worried about."

"Jack will behave, too. I know him; he's a gentleman."

She didn't want to tell Erik that the gentleman bit her. She stood up and went to the refrigerator, opened the freezer, dug around inside. Grabbed the ice cube tray. Empty. Pulled out a Popsicle instead. Shut the freezer door. Sat down again. "Be careful. He's not himself."

For the first time, he sounded serious. "I'd be a changed man if I lost you, Paris."

"He's the one who did the dumping, Erik," she said in a low voice. "He told me we're finished."

"Good. Somebody had to make a decision."

It wasn't the decision she'd wanted or expected, but she didn't want to tell Erik that. She peeled the paper wrapper off the Popsicle. Covered with crystals of frost. She licked it. Banana-flavored. The thing was probably six months old. She put it to her lip.

"Want some company tonight?" he asked.

She didn't want to see Erik. She was still trying to grasp the idea that her husband had just walked out. "I need to decompress. This thing with Jack, it was pretty intense."

"All the more reason I should be there, lover."

"No." She didn't like him calling her "lover." Suddenly everything he said was wrong. "Besides, I've got work stuff to keep me busy. Got to collect my thoughts on the Moose Lake case. Put something down on paper to show to Duncan."

"The tall creep still your man?"

"Yeah." She glanced at her duffel bag sitting on the kitchen floor. "I haven't even unpacked yet."

"Call if you change your mind."

"Okay."

"I love you, Paris." She didn't respond. He didn't seem to mind. "Call if you need anything."

She hung up and set the phone down on the table. She wasn't sure she'd ever be able to say those three words to Erik and mean it. She stood up and tossed the Popsicle in the sink. Felt her lip. Still swollen. Her cell phone rang. She answered quickly, hoping it was Jack calling. "Murphy."

Her mother: "Honey. Are you back in town?"

"Yes, *Imma*." Murphy leaned against the kitchen counter. Concentrated on steadying her voice. The last thing she needed was her mother's meddling.

"Why couldn't you and Jack come to dinner tonight if you're home?"

"Ma, I'm dead tired." That wasn't a lie; she was drained.

"Who sent you the flowers?"

"I don't need this right now."

"That's why you're not coming. You and Jack had another one of your fights."

"No, no." She turned around and rested her head against a cupboard. "Everything's fine, Ma."

"Bullshit."

Murphy stood to attention. Her mother never swore. "*Imma*." Murphy paused, holding the phone to her ear. They'd have to find out eventually. Might as well spill it now. "Jack found out I saw someone over the summer." She couldn't find the courage to say she "slept with someone." Her mother would know what "saw someone" meant.

"Someone. Who is this someone? Another cop?"

"Not a cop. A guy I work with from the ME's office."

"A guy you work with? You're risking eight years of marriage for a guy you work with?"

"Ma, don't make it sound like that."

"Like what? What does it sound like? Cheap? Come over and let's talk about this, daughter."

"Ma. *Imma*. There's nothing to talk about. It's over."

"You and this guy?"

Here comes the explosion, thought Murphy. "Jack left me. For good."

Amira gasped. "Jesus, Mary and Joseph!"

Murphy knew her mother was making the sign of the cross. She heard her father asking questions in the background. Heard her mother say the word "divorce." Suddenly he was on the phone: "Get your ass over here pronto young lady!"

Her father's language didn't jar her; he swore all the time. "I can't, Papa. I'm bushed." She knew that wouldn't satisfy her father, so she pulled out another excuse. "I've still got to go to the station. Tie up some loose ends from a case. File a report."

"File tomorrow. We got supper all ready for you. We'll talk about it over *koosa*," he said, referring to a Lebanese dish of zucchini stuffed with rice and lamb. "There's not a problem that can't be solved over *koosa*."

Murphy's shoulders sagged. She couldn't fight both of them. Besides, her refrigerator was nearly empty and she was famished. "Okay. Give me an hour." She hung up and shoved the phone back in her purse. She picked up her duffel bag and carried it upstairs. Threw it on the bed. She wished she could collapse on the mattress next to it and sleep for twelve hours. She peeled off her clothes, walked into the bathroom, turned on the shower, stepped into the stall. She reached for the shampoo, squirted a gob in her hair, lathered and rinsed. She tilted her head back, let the spray hit her face and sting her lip. While she was toweling dry, she checked her face in the bathroom mirror. The swelling was barely noticeable. She studied her reflection. Wondered if she looked any different now that she'd been dumped. Did she look like a woman about to go through a divorce? Her mother once told her she could spot divorcées on sight. Said they had a tightness around their mouths. As if they'd tasted a bitter herb. Murphy thought that was a bunch of nonsense. She examined her own mouth. Searched for new lines. Nothing yet. She walked out of the bathroom, dropped the towel on the floor and got dressed in her jeans and a flannel shirt.

She went downstairs and opened a few cupboards searching for something to take to her folks' house. Nothing but canned goods and crackers. She needed to go grocery shopping. She hated showing up at their doorstep empty-handed. Made her feel like she was back in college, coming home to mooch a meal. She scanned the counter. Her eyes fell on the wine rack. Two bottles left. She pulled one out and held it up. Champagne. Hardly appropriate. She slipped it back in the rack. Pulled out the other bottle. Good. A clear Lebanese liquor. *Arak*. Distilled grape juice flavored with anise. One hundred proof. Perfect with any Middle Eastern meal. She twisted the cap off and sniffed. The licorice scent belied the drink's strength. She screwed the top back on. Peeled off the price—her parents never approved of how much she paid for anything—and set the bottle in a paper bag. She pulled on her leather bomber jacket, grabbed her purse and keys and the bag and left. While she was shutting the door behind her, she wondered if Jack was going to give back her keys. She walked to her car and thought about all the clothes and toiletries he'd left at her place. Would he want photos back? She slid into the driver's seat of the Jeep. On the floor of the passenger's side, his travel coffee mug. Something else that needed to be returned. She turned on the ignition and pulled out of the parking lot. His sunglasses were dangling from the rearview mirror by a strap. She thought: *This must be what it feels like when someone dies and their stuff keeps turning up. Memories to be boxed up and stored—or thrown away.* As she turned south onto Wabasha to head toward the West Side, she looked at the gold band on her left ring finger. She stifled a sob.

20

He pulled into the trailer park late Tuesday afternoon. At the entrance: MANUFACTURED HOME COMMUNITY. He thought the sign made the place sound nicer than it really was. Adding to the deception: the decorative boulders and fall mums planted at the base of the sign. This was not a neighborhood filled with flowers and rock gardens. The community was a collection of mobile homes with attached decks that were often as wide as the trailers themselves. Metal garden shed in every yard. Satellite dish on every roof. Patches of grass in place of big lawns. The only flowers were the plastic ones in some of the window boxes. The trailer park was on the northern fringe of the city. He parked in front of the house, got out with his suitcase. He decided he'd empty the back of the truck later. He was wiped out and wanted to crash for a couple of hours. The last half hour of the ride home, even his music couldn't fight the fatigue.

He pushed open the front door with his shoulder, stepped into the front room and almost knocked over Keri. She was bending over, trying to pull the old man's socks off. Frank Trip was sitting on the front room couch in his standard weekday attire—drawstring pajama bottoms decorated with cowboys riding horses, white tee shirt with a pack of unfiltered Lucky Strikes rolled up in the left sleeve, Vikings ball cap pulled over his bald head. On one side of the couch was the TV tray his pa used for every meal. Today it was covered with an ashtray filled with cigarette butts, Grain Belt beer cans, a jar of salsa, a bag of tortilla chips, a can of beef jerky strips, an empty ice cream pint. Rocky Road. In the middle of the mess was a Mason jar with his pa's dentures; they were soaking in their usual disinfectant of Jim Beam bourbon whiskey. The television was blaring; his pa couldn't see the screen clearly but seemed to think he could compensate by increasing the volume. *TV Guide* was on the floor at his pa's feet; it was from last summer. Trip had canceled the subscription and kept handing his pa the same issue; his old man didn't know the difference and the money Trip saved he used to order more knives.

"Jesus Christ! Get away from me! You're killing me! They're fine, goddammit! Leave 'em be! Tell her, Sweet!"

"I got to check them tootsies, Frank." Keri looked over her shoulder at Trip. Her hair was her biggest asset; she had a blond braid that ran halfway down her back. Even though she was in her late forties, she only had a few strands of gray. "How ya doin' there, Mr. Big Shot Hero? Long time no see." She looked at his crotch and then up at his face. She winked at him and he looked down, adjusted his grip on the suitcase.

She returned her attention to the patient. Frank was hanging onto his cane with both hands and jabbing at her like he was harpooning a whale. She played the running back, deftly dodging him. The right sock was already half off and dangling from his toes; the left one was around his ankle. They played the game every time she came over and she always won. She outweighed Trip's old man by a hundred pounds.

Trip sighed. "P... Pa, let the lady do her job. Let her check your f... f... fucking feet."

He waved his cane in Trip's direction. "You can both go straight to hell in a handbasket!" The tip of the cane grazed the Mason jar. It fell over and spilled whiskey on the tray and the rug.

"Shit, Pa." Trip dropped his suitcase in the middle of the front room and went into the kitchen to get a towel. The front room was in the center of the trailer. On one side of it was the kitchen and then Frank's bedroom. On the other side was a hall that led to Trip's bedroom, the bathroom and a spare bedroom. The ceiling was higher than in lots of trailers—nearly seven and a half feet—but Trip still felt perpetually cramped in the place.

Keri took advantage of the spilled jar as a diversion and pulled the right sock off all the way. "Gotcha!" She grabbed the left one and got it in one yank. Waved it victoriously over her head. "Hah!"

Trip walked back in with the towel and got on his knees to blot the carpet dry. Close to the floor, he could smell urine and wondered if his father was having incontinence problems on top of everything else. Next he'd be taking a dump in the middle of the front room.

Keri was on her knees next to him with Frank's feet in her lap. "They're good," she said, patting them. "As usual, all your fussing was for nothing. Toenails could use a trim, but I ain't doing them. You got to get to a podiatrist." Her sweatshirt had crawled up her back. Trip could see a white flash of flesh dotted with pimples and above the waist of her jeans, a tattoo of a frog. He was well familiar with the frog, as well as the lily pad a couple of inches below it. The sleeves of the sweatshirt were cut short, revealing her fat upper arms.

Frank: "Sweet can clip my nails."

"He can't trim shit," Keri said. "He breaks the skin and you're back in the hospital."

Trip looked at his pa's toes and grimaced. The nails were yellow and thick and curling under. That empty spot where the big toe used to be bummed him out. He had no intention of touching those feet. He stood up with the wet rag, righted the Mason jar. The teeth were under the bag of chips. Trip picked them up with two fingers and dropped them into the jar. He looked for the whiskey bottle; his pa usually kept it within arm's reach. He found it on the couch behind a throw pillow. Trip picked it up and emptied the remainder into the Mason jar. He'd have to make a liquor store run later. Pa had to have his Jim Beam.

Keri: "Got to check your blood sugar."

"You ain't poking me," Frank said.

"The hell I ain't." Keri set Frank's feet down and stood up. She folded her arms over her chest. Trip thought she had small breasts for such a large woman, and they were heading south with the rest of her aging body. She nodded toward the TV tray. "What's this crap?"

"Breakfast. Lunch. Probably dinner, unless my son gets his ass in gear."

"You can't keep eating crap. Gonna kill yourself."

"Good. Then I won't have to listen to your nagging." He turned the volume even higher on the television.

She shook her head and walked into the kitchen to get the glucose monitor. Trip followed her with the wet towel. Threw it into the sink on top of the pile of dirty dishes. The counter was covered with empty beer cans, opened bags of chips, half-empty cereal boxes. Hardened spatters of something orange. The remains of a fried egg sandwich rested in a skillet on the stove. His pa's housekeeping had declined along with his health; the place was always filthy when Trip returned from the road. He worried his old man would burn the place down on top of it. Trip suspected his pa couldn't see well enough to tell if the range was off or on. Trip had arranged once to have some neighbor ladies come in and cook while he was out of town, but his pa had refused to open the door for them. Told Trip they were trying to poison him with slop called "tuna hot dish."

Keri was bending over the kitchen table, fiddling with the blood glucose monitor. "He can't keep drinking like a fish, especially with his diabetes. You're gonna come home one day and he's gonna be dead on the couch."

"I know," Trip said tiredly. He started moving plates and cups from one side of the sink to the other so he could plug the drain and start filling the sink with water. The dishes were going to have to soak; he saw dried egg yolk from the week before. A couple of the whiskey glasses had Keri's lipstick on the rim. How could she lecture about his old man's drinking one minute and tip a glass with him the next? She was a two-faced bitch not to be trusted. How could he ask Keri about which pills to use on Paris Murphy without telling her what they were for? Maybe he'd have to stick with a known quantity. The date rape pills. He plugged the drain, squirted some dish soap in the bottom of the sink and started filling it with hot water. He swayed as he stood over the counter. He wanted to sleep for a week. He turned off the tap when the suds reached the top and transferred one mound of dishes into the water. Wiped his hands on his pants. Keri's back was turned to him; she was sorting his pa's pills on the kitchen table. Putting them in the plastic box with the different compartments. One compartment for each day of the week. Trip came up behind her, massaged her shoulders. Leaned into her ear. "G... got any stuff for me?"

"Later, Romeo," she whispered. "Let me finish up with that old bastard in there first."

He hated that nickname. Romeo. The way she always said it—with a little smile on her face—made him feel as if she was making fun of his abilities in the bedroom. He walked back into the front room, picked up his suitcase. On television, cowboys were shooting up a town. He didn't know why they owned a remote; the set never left the western channel. "P... Pa. Lower that shit." His pa waved him away.

Trip walked down the hall to his bedroom and threw his suitcase on the bed. The trailer was a steam bath. His pa must have cranked up the heat to eighty degrees without realizing it. Trip unzipped his jacket and pulled it off and tossed it on the bed. Took off his hat. Set it on the dresser. His head itched. He scratched it with his fingertips; a few strands fell into his face and he picked them off. Unbuttoned his shirt down the front and at the cuffs. One of the cuff buttons came off in his hand. "Shitty shirts." He tossed the button in a wastebasket. Peeled off the shirt. Tossed it on top of the bed. He was sleeping in the same twin-sized bed he'd had since he was a kid, with his legs hanging off the edge every night. He didn't care. A full-sized bed would take up too much space and he had to have room for his stereo and his knives. The mattress was covered with a bedspread from childhood. Cowboys herding longhorn. One of his pa's picks. The bedroom curtains carried the same pattern. So did the sheets and pillowcases. While the linen was little-boy Old West, nearly everything else in the room was heavy metal Medieval. Wall rack with four samurai swords mounted horizontally. Spiked mace, South African bush machete and battle-ax, each displayed on its own wall shelf. Metal shield etched with a writhing dragon hanging on the wall over the headboard. Two U.S. Cavalry Artillery Officers' sabers mounted crossways over the dresser. On top of the dresser, an assortment of daggers and knives. On the nightstand more daggers and knives, as well as a pewter dragon with a round clock set in its belly. He checked the clock. If he fell asleep now he'd probably get up in the middle of the night. Better to stay awake for a few more hours. Besides, he still had to fuck Keri to get his pills. Trip hated the way she made him pay twice: by giving her cash *and* sleeping with her. He figured his pa was paying *her* for the sex, and he found that ironic. Some days he'd like to pay her more for the pills to get out of the sex.

He decided to unpack and hit the shower; a shower would wake him up. He popped open his suitcase. The sock stuffed with the peach purse was sitting on top. He reached inside the sock and pulled out the bag. He'd look at it one more time and dump it later that night.

"Hey, Romeo. Playing with yourself in there or what?" Keri was standing in the bedroom doorway.

He threw the purse in the suitcase, slammed it shut and turned toward her. "All finished with P... Pa?"

"Frank's passed out on the couch. Sawing logs to beat the band." She walked over to him and wrapped her arms around his waist. Her biceps were bigger than his; her head barely reached his chest. She pressed her body into his crotch. Cupped his butt with her hands. "Feeling frisky?"

"Let me shower. I reek."

She buried her face in his tee shirt. "I like you kind of smelly and dirty," she said into his chest.

"I d... don't," he said, and untangled her from his waist. Her arms were sweaty. He was being mauled by a sticky bowling ball.

169

"Why don't I join you then?"

He took a couple of steps back from her. "What about P... Pa?"

"Told you. Sound asleep. He'll sleep for a few hours." She pulled something out of the front pocket of her jeans. Held up a pill bottle and shook it. "Timed it right. Gave it to him after he told me you were on your way home."

He snatched the bottle from her hand and looked at it. He didn't recognize the name of the drug, but he could see it wasn't his old man's pills. The pharmacy label had another patient's name on it. In all their years of doing business he'd never asked her how she got the pills she sold him. He figured she stole the bulk of them from her patients.

"Don't worry. Only gave him one," she said.

"What if we g... gave him a few more? What would that d... do? Make him sleep through the n... night?"

She threw her head back and laughed. "Sweet Justice! What have you got planned for us tonight, Romeo?" She stepped toward him and plucked the bottle out of his hand.

"Wait," he said, trying to grab it back.

"No freebies," she said, pulling the bottle out of his reach. She stuffed it back in her pocket. "I don't give a damn if you fuck me till the cows come home. Still gotta have some cash to go along with it." She put her hands on her hips and looked around. "Speaking of bedroom, I'll say it again. This is the weirdest room I have ever laid eyes on. What you planning to do with all this stuff? Start your own war?"

He didn't like anyone criticizing his collection. He lowered his eyes. Wanted to hit her in the worst way. Instead, he shoved his hands in his pockets. "N... n... nothing wrong with a few knives. Man can have a f... few knives."

She frowned and shook her finger at him. "Don't tell me you ain't got the cash to pay for the pills when you got all this expensive hardware."

He looked up. "You d... d... didn't answer my question. What would more p... pills do?"

"Tell ya what, Romeo." She pulled her sweatshirt off and dropped it to the floor. Underneath: a white cotton bra and a bulging white midriff. Over her right breast, another frog leaping over a lily pad. Her hair wasn't showing her age, but her neck was. More lines in it than he could count. "We'll discuss pharmaceuticals after the shower."

"How you g... got time for that? Don't you got more p... patients to see?"

"Frank was my last. I'm punched out. Taking some compensatory time off. Got the rest of the week free, clear through the weekend. Plenty of time for fun." She raised her right arm, revealing the puff of blond hair buried in her armpit. "Got a razor I can borrow? If you ask real nice, I might let you watch me shave." He didn't say anything, shoved his hands back in his pockets and looked away. "Why don't you start up the shower while I slip out of the rest of these duds? Unless you want to help me undress." She reached behind her back and started unhooking her bra. Trip left to start the shower.

The steam enveloped them and boiled over the shower door, filling the compact bathroom. The radio hanging over the shower arm was turned on. They couldn't make out the song because of static, but Keri swayed as if she could hear music. Goofy woman, he thought. Trip wondered what the two of them looked like, crammed together in the stall. The tall, thin man and the short, round woman. She stood in front of him, her back to him, while

171

she hogged most of the spray. He didn't care. Wanted to get it over with. She wanted her back scrubbed. He used a loofah sponge; he didn't want to touch her wet skin with his bare hands.

"Don't forget Mr. Froggie," she said. "He needs some bubbles, too."

Trip moved the sponge down to the small of her back and scrubbed back and forth a couple of times.

"A little farther south," she said.

He sneered and ran the loofah in large circles around her left buttock and then her right. Her rear end was starting to sag. He could hardly stand touching her when she was lying down with her body spread flatter. Even then he kept the sheets pulled up, the lights off, the shades drawn.

"The shampoo, Romeo."

He cracked one eye open and spied the bottle on the shelf above the showerhead; too high for her to reach. He put the loofah on the shelf and took down the shampoo.

"Squirt some in," she said, and she bent her head back so her wet hair hung straight down in front of him. He tipped the bottle upside down and squeezed a gob the size of a quarter into her hair. She reached behind her head and scrubbed; he was fiercely jealous of all the hair she had. Wished he had a fraction of it. "What kind is it?" she asked.

He put the bottle back. "Baby shampoo. G... generic."

"Baby shampoo? Ain't you old enough to use big-boy suds?" She laughed at her own joke and then choked and coughed on some water.

"Supposed to be g... gentle."

She kept scrubbing. "Nothing gonna save your hair, Romeo."

She was right. He saw a tangle of black hair accumulated over the drain from the last couple of showers he'd taken. Not a single blond strand had fallen since she stepped in.

"You're destined for a rug," she said, stepping closer to the shower stream and rinsing off the shampoo. "I got a girlfriend who works at a wig store. I'll ask her to keep her eyes open for a deal."

"No," he said. A wig would be an admission of defeat. The last slam against his virility. Might as well get castrated and get it over with. "No rug."

"Sure?"

"Yeah."

"Whatever. Where's that razor?"

He paused. He didn't want to be so close to her when she shaved her armpits. "G... got one in the medicine cabinet." He stepped around her, pulled open the shower door, stepped out, pulled it shut. He opened the cabinet over the sink, grabbed a disposable razor. Handed it to her over the shower door.

"Shave cream?" she asked. He took a can off the shelf and handed it to her over the door. He heard her squirt some. "Ain't you gonna watch? How about I shave my pussy for you?"

He shuddered at the thought of witnessing that. "I hear P... Pa banging around the kitchen." He yanked a towel off the bar, wrapped it around his waist, walked out of the steamy bathroom. He exhaled with relief as he shut the door behind him. He went down the hall and poked his head into the front room. His pa was still snoring and the television was still blaring. He wanted to shut it off or at least turn down the volume, but that might wake his old man and it was more peaceful when he was asleep. He went back to his bedroom, threw the towel in a hamper. The dirty clothes were piled high, plus he had a suitcase full of dirty underwear and shirts. He'd have to go to the Laundromat damn soon. He opened his top dresser drawer. Three pairs of clean boxers left and no tee shirts. He stepped into a pair of boxers. Opened the second drawer. One pair of clean jeans inside. Stepped into those. Third drawer. Two sweatshirts left. Grabbed the one with the oval Ford logo across the front and yanked it on over his head.

"Sweet! Sweet!" His pa bellowing from the front room. He sounded groggy, but he was awake.

Trip shuffled out of his bedroom and saw Keri in the hall, walking naked out of the bathroom. "Jesus Christ. Get s... something on. Pa's up. So much for your b... bullshit p... p... pills."

"I'm still waiting for a little help with the razor," she said.

He looked down at her crotch. Shave cream covered it. The sight made her even more repulsive to him.

She saw him frowning. "Don't like it? Fuck you then." She flipped him the bird, went back into the bathroom. Slammed the door behind her.

More yelling from the front room. "Sweet!"

Trip walked into the front room. "What you want, P... Pa?"

"Supper! I'm getting light-headed! All woozy."

Damn pills, Trip thought. All they did was make his old man tired and crabby.

"Okay, Pa. I'll whip you up s... something." He walked into the kitchen. The floor was sticky on his bare feet. For all he knew, he was stepping on dried piss. He needed his shoes. They were in the bedroom. He walked past his pa into the hall, started to step into his bedroom and stopped. Heard something in the bathroom. Stepped next to the closed door and listened. What he heard coming from the other side made him freeze. What he heard told him that after he'd left his bedroom to start the shower, Keri had opened the suitcase. What he heard was Keri singing. "Can't Help Falling in Love."

He opened the bathroom door a crack. She stopped

singing. "I knew you'd come back for some action," she said. "Hurry up. Hot water won't last forever." She returned to her singing.

The two-faced bitch was going to use the purse against him, he thought. "B... be right there," he yelled into the bathroom and shut the door. Trip went into his bedroom and pulled open his top dresser drawer. Under his boxers was a small cardboard box. He took it out and set it on top of the dresser. He lifted off the cover. Inside, a straight-edge razor. One of his antique finds. He picked it up, unfolded it, ran the edge across his thumb. Sharp. Hiding the straight-edge behind his back, he walked down the hall and looked in the front room again. His old man had fallen back asleep. He went up to the bathroom door. He set the straight-edge down on the floor and stripped, leaving his clothes in a pile in the hallway. He picked up the razor and opened the bathroom door a crack. All he heard was the water running and in the background, some indistinguishable music coming out of the shower radio. He slipped into the bathroom and closed the door behind him, locking it. She was still singing, but a different Elvis song. What was it? "Jailhouse Rock." She was playing with his mind, he thought.

She heard him and stopped singing. "Come on, Romeo. Hop back in. The water's still fine." He pushed open the shower door with his left hand and with his right held the straight-edge behind his back. "Got a surprise for me?" she said, turning to face him and putting her back to the shower. She had shaved her crotch clean, but there was some lather in spots.

He snapped the door shut. "B... better rinse off one more time," he said. She turned around to face the water. He wrapped his left arm around her body and with his right, brought the razor to her throat.

"Sweet!" she screamed. "Sweet!" Then no more words. Only shrieking and frantic struggling. She locked both her hands around his right arm and tried to pull it down. He feared he would lose his grip on her fat, wet body. He pressed the straight-edge hard and sliced it across her neck, from his left to right. She yelped and then gurgled. Blood sprayed across the shower walls and dripped down her front. He looked at the shower floor and watched the red liquid snake down the drain. She went limp. He backed up and let go of her. She collapsed on her back. A wet heap of blood and water and shave cream. Knees bent. Arms out. Eyes wide open. Mouth partially open. Raw rip across her throat. He stood over her, panting. His legs felt weak. He dropped the razor; it fell to the shower floor with a clatter. He pressed his left palm against the door and his right against the wall for support. He ducked his head under the shower. Let the stream massage the back of his skull. The water had turned ice cold, but he didn't notice. For several seconds, the only sound he heard was the shower. A gentle rain washing the blood down and around her neck. A red necklace. More blood. Still more. When would the blood stop? Then through the static, he heard a DJ on the shower radio: "*Only twelve hours left of our twenty-four-hour Elvis marathon. Phone or fax your requests for songs by The King. Here's one of my favorites off his . . .*"

She hadn't discovered the purse or the lyrics inside it. She wasn't playing with his mind. Keri had been singing along with the radio. Trip reached up and pulled the radio off the shower arm and slammed it against the wall. Batteries and plastic pieces scattered on the shower floor around her body. He pounded the wall with his right fist. "Nothing. Killed her for n... nothing." He looked down. One of the plastic pieces had landed on her right breast. Covered the frog so only the lily pad was showing. Didn't look right. He bent over and picked up the shard. Now both were visible. The frog and the lily pad. He stood up and studied the plastic shard. Wrapped his right hand around it. Squeezed until it hurt. He let go of the plastic and it fell into her hair. He checked his arms. Blood on his arms. He'd gone from neat kills with his truck to bashing a man's head in with a shovel to this mess: A woman's bare body pressed against his while he sliced her throat. Her blood on his skin. Too personal and up close and intimate. On the shower floor, blood was collecting around her body and under his feet. Her body was blocking the drain. He envisioned the shower stall filling with blood and water, drowning him. Imagined the two of them floating together in the chamber of pink water. Dead.

Banging on the bathroom door jarred him from his waking nightmare. "Sweet? Sweet? What the hell is going on in there?"

His pa. What could he tell his pa?

21

For a family of six, it would have been roomy. For a family of twelve, it was a sardine can. Now with everyone gone and her parents alone, it seemed cavernous. She worried it was too much for them to maintain, but the place was immaculate whenever she visited. Murphy parked on the street in front of the two-story Victorian and immediately noticed how even in the fall, the lawn was golf course green. All the leaves were raked and bagged and sitting in the driveway, waiting for a trip to the city compost site. Orange and maroon mums lined the sidewalk leading up to the front steps.

Murphy shut off the Jeep and sat behind the wheel for a minute. She pulled the keys out of the ignition and jiggled them in her right hand. Talking to them about it was going to be tough, she thought. Almost as tough as talking to Jack. Her parents loved their son-in-law. Loved the whole idea of him. A big, handsome doctor. Catholic. The son of college professors. No Lebanese blood in him, but a smattering of Irish. Native of St. Paul. Helpless in the kitchen, as was proper for any self-respecting male. What could she tell them about Erik? He was a big, handsome

Lutheran from Minneapolis. German and Irish and Norwegian and God knew what else. Sliced open dead people for a living. Drove expensive cars. Spent too much time at the horse track. Too much time at the gym. Could cook circles around the best restaurant chefs. No. They weren't going to be impressed with the résumé of the guy she'd slept with. The guy who'd helped end her marriage.

She put her keys in her purse and got out of the car with the paper bag. She walked up the front steps, opened the screen door. She scanned the porch, which ran the length of the front of the house. The aluminum lawn chairs were folded and leaning against a corner. The terra-cotta planters were empty and cleaned and stacked in a row against the wall. Her father hadn't yet taken the hammocks down in preparation for winter. When she was a kid, many hot summer nights were spent sleeping on the porch. Swinging from the three hammocks her father strung from hooks in the walls. She and her brothers did rock, paper, scissors to see who got to use them. The losers slept on the wood floor atop sleeping bags or—if they were crybabies about it—were banished inside. She was usually one of the winners; the rock was her good-luck charm. She walked up to the front door. Her parents hated when she knocked or rang, said the doorbell was for strangers, not family. She turned the knob, pushed it open, walked inside. Inhaled. Garlic and onions and lamb and tomato sauce.

"Hello!" she yelled. She looked around. As usual, wood floors spotless enough to eat off of. Furniture shiny and aromatic with lemon oil polish. Overstuffed front room furniture with crocheted doilies draped over the arms and backs. Starched lace curtains hanging from the windows. She noticed a basket of clean clothes on the floor at the bottom of the stairs. Without complaint, her mother continued to carry clothes baskets from the basement to the second-floor bedrooms. The Murphy sons had offered to turn the pantry into a main floor laundry, but Amira refused to surrender an inch of kitchen storage. She had to have shelves for her home-canned goods. Tomatoes. Green beans. Grape leaves. All grown in the backyard. Murphy pulled off her jacket and set it and her purse and the bag on the front room couch. She picked up the clothes basket and put her right foot on the first step.

Her mother walked out of the kitchen, wiping her hands on her apron. "Put that down, young lady." Like her daughter, she was large-breasted. Unlike Murphy, her hips were wide after carrying ten children and her skin leathery from years spent tending to her garden. She stood a little over five feet tall to her daughter's five feet ten inches. Her dark hair, streaked with silver, was in a bun behind her head, but tendrils were loose around her forehead. Her face was red and beaded with perspiration from the kitchen heat.

"I can carry it up for you, *Imma.*"

"I'm not crippled." Amira pulled the basket out of her daughter's hands and started walking upstairs with it. "I'm going to hop in the bathtub," she said over her shoulder. "Sit down and make your father wait on *you* for a change."

"Sure smells good in here," Murphy said after her.

"Yeah, yeah," said her mother as she reached the top of the stairs. Amira Murphy wasn't good at accepting compliments.

Murphy hung her jacket and purse in the front hall closet, picked up the paper bag, walked to the back of the house. She passed through the dining room, noticed the table was set. Not a good omen for the evening. The clan ate their casual meals in the kitchen at a table made of rough-cut oak and surrounded by a dozen mismatched wooden chairs. Formal family meetings—to plan a

180

wedding, announce a pregnancy, settle a sibling spat—were held in the dining room at a long mahogany table surrounded by matching upholstered chairs. The kitchen table was suitable for a backyard picnic; the dining room furniture belonged in a castle. She counted the place settings. Five. Who else had they invited? She was afraid to ask. She pushed open the swinging door into the kitchen. Sean Murphy was sitting at the table drinking coffee and flipping through the *Pioneer Press*. He looked at her over his reading glasses and smiled. "Daughter."

"Papa." Murphy crossed the linoleum floor, set the bag on the table. She threw her arms around him, planted a kiss on top of his head. He still had a full head of hair, though it had long ago turned from black to gray. He smelled of Aqua Velva aftershave and cigar smoke. He loved cigars. The cheaper, the better.

He pulled the paper bag toward him. "Hope this ain't some of that overpriced wine you waste your money on." He pulled the *Arak* out and smiled. "Good girl. Get us a couple of glasses."

Murphy went to the cabinets above the sink, opened a door and took down three juice tumblers—recycled jelly jars with cartoon characters painted on them. She set them in front of her father. He filled each a third of the way. "Should we wait for Ma?" she asked.

A dismissive wave with his right hand. "We'll be dead before she gets out of the tub. Get the water and ice for ours. She takes hers neat anyway."

Murphy took a bottle of spring water out of the refrigerator and a bag of ice cubes out of the freezer and set them in front of her father. He poured water into two of the glasses; the transparent liquid turned a cloudy white. He slowly slipped two ice cubes into each milky tumbler. She sat down next to him and each raised a glass.

181

Sean: "May neighbors respect you, trouble neglect you, the angels protect you and heaven accept you."

Murphy loved her father's Irish toasts made with Lebanese liquor. "Thanks, Papa." While they sipped, Murphy studied her father. Searched for signs of old age beyond his gray hair. As always, he seemed the same to her. Bushy brows jutting over blue eyes. Lantern jaw. Barrel torso. Big arms. Big hands. Big nose broken on three separate occasions when he stepped between fighting patrons at the family bar. Still, with every visit he seemed to move slower and reminisce more. He missed the bar. Talked with increasing frequency about opening another. Murphy knew it would never happen. Not at his age.

He pointed to the refrigerator. "Your mother made some *kibbee nayee*," he said, referring to the Lebanese dish of raw ground beef, bulgur, onions and spices. "Let's have a nibble before dinner." Murphy got up, put the ice and water back and took a plate out of the refrigerator. The *kibbee* was patted into a large round like an oversized hamburger. She set the plate on the table and went to a cupboard below the sink for a bottle of olive oil. She set the oil on the table. With the side of her right hand, she pressed a cross into the *kibbee* and poured olive oil into it. "Daughter. Where's the garlic?" The dip was a sort of mayonnaise made of lemon juice, garlic and oil.

"I didn't see it."

"It's there."

She pulled open the refrigerator and dug around. Found the thick, white sauce in a glass bowl covered with plastic wrap. Took it out. Set it on the table. Peeled off the plastic. Immediately got a whiff of garlic.

"Flatbread's on the counter," he said. Murphy turned to get the bread and her mother walked into the kitchen.

"Papa," snapped Amira. "Why is my daughter running around the kitchen like a maid?" Her hair was damp; she didn't believe in blow-dryers. She worked her long mane in a bun behind her head while she talked. She always chastised Murphy for wearing her hair long, but never wanted to pay for a haircut for herself. So she kept it knotted behind her head. "I told you to wait on *her*."

"I am," he said. "Now I'm waiting on her to get the bread."

"We're eating in the dining room," Amira said.

"This isn't eating," he said. "It's nibbling."

Murphy put the plastic bag on the table, reached inside, pulled out a round, flat loaf. Ripped off a couple of pieces. She sat down next to her father and each used a hunk of the bread to scoop up some oil-drenched *kibbee*. Amira tucked a couple of strands of hair behind her ears and took a seat across from them. She was wearing a short-sleeved housedress that zipped up the front. Even while working in the garden, she wore dresses. She believed ladies never wore slacks. In a bow to comfort, however, she always wore knee-high nylons and flat-heeled shoes. Amira tore off a hunk of bread, scraped some *kibbee* off the plate and dipped it in the pool of oil on top of the meat.

The three of them chewed silently for a couple of minutes. Murphy's father took another sip of *Arak*. "That'll put hair on your chest." Another sip, then: "What's this bullshit about a divorce?"

Murphy swallowed her food, took a sip of *Arak*. "Can't we save this for after dinner?"

"No," said her mother. She lifted her glass, emptied it, slammed it down on the table. "I don't want to ruin the digestion with bad talk. Let's settle it now."

"Nothing to settle, *Imma*. It's over. Jack and I are finished."

183

Her mother dragged her right palm over her left, as if she were dusting flour off her hands. "Finished. Like that. Eight years of marriage. Use it, crumple it, toss it in the toilet."

Murphy rubbed her forehead with her fingertips. "It's not like that. We tried, Ma. I tried."

"Have you talked to a priest?" Amira asked.

"Should have had babies right off the bat," said her father. "Kids are glue. Stick people together."

"I'm glad we didn't have kids," said Murphy.

Amira: "Bite your tongue, daughter. You should go to confession."

"If we had kids, then a split would be messy."

"So that's how it is?" Her father took off his spectacles, folded them and pointed them at her. "This is gonna be one of those nice, modern divorces? Send each other Christmas cards and birthday cards? What a load of crap. No such thing as a nice divorce."

"It won't be nice. Jack is pissed." She touched her bottom lip.

"Here's to Jack," said her father. He set down his spectacles, raised his drinking glass and polished off the *Arak*. Rattled the ice around. "Balls the size of an elephant."

Murphy was indignant. "Whose side are you on?"

Amira: "The marriage's side."

Murphy stood up. Her father pulled her back down by her arm. "Okay, okay. Tell us about Mr. Wonderful."

Amira: "The home wrecker."

Murphy finished her drink and poured herself and her parents another. Going to be a long night, she thought.

The doorbell. Sean ripped off another piece of bread and used it to scrape more *kibbee* off the plate. "Who the hell is bothering us now?" He shoved the meat and bread into his mouth and chewed.

Amira folded her arms across her bosom. "What's his name, this guy you work with?" The doorbell rang again. "He Catholic?"

Murphy stood up. "I'll get it."

Sean swallowed. Motioned her down with his hand. "Sit. Probably kids selling magazines for school. We could stock a library with the crap we ordered from your brothers' kids."

Murphy walked to the front of the house and opened the door. Two men in their early forties were on the porch, each carrying a six-pack. They stood well over six feet tall, had their father's fair skin and blue eyes. "Why'd you clowns ring?"

Her older brothers looked past her into the house.

"We figured you'd answer the door," said Ryan.

"Fireworks over yet?" asked Patrick. He was nervous, ran the fingers of his right hand through his hair. Both men had wavy ink-colored hair like their sister.

She stepped onto the porch and shut the door behind her. "Hell no," she said. "Haven't even started." She rubbed her arms; the sun was setting and it was cold outside. The early evening air smelled of burning wood from neighbors' fireplaces.

Patrick pulled a bottle out of his pack of Beck's and held it up. "Got an opener, Potato Head?"

"Yeah. Keep one on me at all times."

He set the six-pack down. "Was that sarcasm?" He took out a second Beck's, turned it upside down and used the top to pry the cap off the first bottle.

"Our orders were to talk you out of this," said Ryan. Patrick took a bump off his beer and nodded.

"Can't believe they called you bozos," she said.

"They figured we'd stand up for Jacko because we wear the same uniform," said Ryan. He and Patrick were both orthopedic surgeons and had a practice together.

185

Patrick raised his bottle. "To the medical brotherhood." He took another sip.

"I got a news flash for you guys," said Murphy. "I'm not the one who did the walking."

"I'm sorry, Potato Head," said Patrick.

"*Imma* told us it was your doing," said Ryan.

"I guess it's my fault," she said. "No. There's no guessing. It *is* my fault."

Patrick picked up his six-pack and tucked it under his left arm. "Let's assign blame inside, where it's warmer. Besides, I'm starving."

"Go ahead," said Ryan. He pulled his sister by the elbow toward the first hammock. "We're gonna go for a swing. Be inside in a minute. Don't eat all the *kibbee*, you sow." Patrick made an *oink* noise, went inside, shut the door behind him.

Murphy opened her mouth to protest but then closed it. Ryan was two years older than Patrick and much more serious. He undoubtedly took to heart his parents' request to intervene. She'd have to hear him out now or he'd hound her later.

They lowered themselves into a hammock. Ryan set the six-pack down between them. "Want one?" he asked. She nodded. He picked up a Rolling Rock, twisted off the cap, handed her the bottle. Picked up another one, opened it. They sat for a few minutes, their feet flat on the porch floor. They moved the hammock back and forth by bending and straightening their legs. She wrapped her arms around herself. He set his beer down, took off his jean jacket and draped it over her shoulders.

"Thanks."

He picked up the beer, took a bump. Cupped the bottle between his palms. "What's the deal with you and Jacko?"

All her brothers called him that; Jack hated it. Another thing about her family that aggravated him. She took a sip of beer. Switched the bottle to her left hand and ran her right index finger around the mouth of the bottle. "We're finished. He found out I saw someone else. Over the summer."

"Is that why you're finished?"

She paused. At first she felt insulted, then she told herself it was a fair question. "It didn't help. That's for damn sure. But you know we've been having problems for a long time. Haven't been able to live together without fighting."

He stopped moving his legs. "I know. I figured. I don't know."

"You figured we'd keep limping along." She switched the beer back to her right hand. Lifted it to her lips. Took a long drink. Wiped her mouth with the back of her left hand. "That's what I figured, too. But Jack's really mad. Hurt. This might be it for us."

"So who's this guy? Is it serious?"

"Erik Mason. Investigator with the ME's office."

Ryan nodded. Took another bump off his beer. "What about the second half of my question?"

She took a sip of beer. "I don't have an answer right now. I don't know. All I know is Jack walked out and I think this time, we're split for keeps."

Ryan finished his beer. Set it on the floor. Started swinging the hammock again. "Maybe that's not so bad," he said in a low voice. "Lately, when I've seen you with Jacko, I haven't been so sure about the two of you. I've watched you watching him. Reminds me of someone sitting on the edge of their seat in a movie theater."

"Waiting for the next scary scene," she said. She took one last sip, set the bottle down, pulled her brother's jacket tighter around her shoulders.

He stood up. "Let's go in. It's cold out here and I'm hungry." He started for the front door. She bent over, put the empties in the six-pack carton, stood up and followed him. Still cleaning up after them, she thought. He was holding the door open for her. She walked through and he leaned into her ear to whisper, "Let me do the talking or Ma will throw us all out before we get to the *koosa*."

She smiled and nodded, even though she had no intention of letting anyone do the talking for her. They were still trying to take care of her.

22

He stood in the shower with icy water needling his body and creating a puddle of diluted blood at his feet. His pa kept pounding on the door with his fist. Pounding, pounding. Trip wished the pounding would stop. Wished the bleeding would stop.

"Sweet! Sweet! Open up, goddammit!" Now a sharp sound. He was hitting the door with his cane.

Trip looked at his arms. The cold water had washed the red off. His feet were wet with blood and water. He reached for the shampoo. Squatted over her body. Wedged the bottle under her hips so it propped her up and cleared the drain. The blood and water started running down the hole. He stood up and rinsed his hands under the shower. Pulled open the stall door as much as he could with her body blocking it. Hung onto the door with his left hand. Lifted his left foot into the cold spray and held it there until it was clean and stepped out with it. Lifted the right foot. Watched the water drip from it. Set that foot on the bathroom floor. He shut the shower door. Let the water keep running. Keep sending the red down the drain.

Pounding with his fist again. "Sweet! What the hell is going on in there! This is my house! I want to know!"

He stood naked in the middle of the bathroom, dripping water onto the floor. He was so tired he couldn't think. He needed a good lie and he couldn't come up with one. Not even the kernel of one. The same sensation as reaching into a cereal box, feeling around, finding it empty. Not one nugget. Not even crumbs. He peered in the medicine cabinet mirror for inspiration. All he saw was an exhausted man with thinning hair matted to his head. He grabbed a towel off the bar and rubbed his scalp. Lifted it off his head. Hair all over the towel. He wrapped the towel around his waist and went to the door. Put his hand on the lock.

More knocking with the cane. "Justice! Open this fucking door right now before I break it down!"

He twisted the lock and opened the door. Stood silently in front of his pa.

"Sweet?" His pa's face didn't show concern as much as curiosity, and Trip found that unsettling. Minutes earlier, a woman had been screaming in their bathroom.

"She's d... dead, Pa."

"What? Who?"

"Keri. She c... cut herself real b... bad with the straight-edge."

"Killed herself? In our can?"

Trip jumped on the suggestion. "Yeah. Suicide. Yeah. She's been real d... d... depressed lately. About her weight and s... stuff. I walked in on her and . . ."

His father shoved him aside with his left arm and thumped over to the shower with his cane. He pushed open the shower door. The bottom of the door bumped against her body. Frank looked down. Squinted. Even with his poor eyesight he could make out the wound across her

190

throat. Deep, red, raw, oozing blood as water splattered it. The straight-edge razor on the shower floor. Pieces of something scattered all over the stall. Bent over to get a better look. The shower radio, busted in a bunch of pieces. Leaned closer. Saw the shampoo bottle propped under her body, letting the blood flow down the drain. He stood straight, turned, looked in his son's face. Trip thought he saw the corners of his pa's mouth curl up for an instant. Stifling a smirk. "Suicide my ass! You did the bitch!"

Trip took a step back from him and raised both palms defensively. "Pa. No. I didn't."

"Who in the hell kills themselves by slitting their own throat?" The old man closed the shower door. "Why'd you do it, Sweet? Why?"

It came to him; a noble reason with the added bonus of being partially true. "She was trying to k... k... kill you, Pa. She d... doped you up."

It worked. The old man's jaw dropped. Then: "What the hell? Why she wanna do that?"

Trip blurted out the first word that came to mind: "Money."

"What money? I don't got a pot to piss in, and neither do you."

"Your Social Security checks. She was gonna hide your body and make me cash the checks."

Frank's eyes narrowed. Suddenly his son was part of the plot. "How she gonna make you do that?"

"Blackmail." Trip regretted that word as soon as it left his lips, tried to switch gears before his pa asked the next obvious question. "Didn't you think it was weird the way you g... got all sleepy all of a sudden? She slipped you a sleeping p... p... pill. How do you suppose she gave it to you, P... Pa? Hid it in your food? Your beer?"

Frank thought about it. "She did give me a new pill

191

today, right before you got to the house. I knew it wasn't time for my usual meds. Vitamin. That's what she said it was." He shook his cane at the shower door. "Vitamin my ass. Murdering witch. Glad you did her, Sweet. I thank you for protecting your pa."

Trip was stunned at how easily his pa accepted murder. Even if it was murder with a palatable motive. He studied the old man. Saw more than acceptance in his expression. Satisfaction.

His pa pushed the shower door open again and looked down at the body. Said in a low voice, "Shows what goes around comes around."

"Pa?"

His voice sounded distant. Removed from the moment. "Reminds me is all."

"Reminds you of what, Pa?"

"Nothing, son." He pointed up at the showerhead with his cane. "Shut that off before we get a triple-digit water bill."

"What about the b... blood?"

"What about it? We'll rinse it all down the drain at once, when she's done bleeding like a butchered hog."

Trip stepped around him, leaned into the stall, shut off the water. "What do we d... do with her, Pa?" He started to shut the shower door. Didn't seem right to discuss it with her body bleeding right under their noses.

"Wait." His pa reached into his left pants pocket and handed Trip two coins. "Close her eyes and put these on them. Bad luck letting the dead watch you."

Trip fingered the money. "Thought you're supposed to use pennies."

"What did I give you?"

"Dime and a nickel."

"That penny stuff's an old wives' tale. Any coin should

do it. Except quarters maybe. Quarters are too big; probably wouldn't sit right on the eyeball. Besides, that's all I got on me except for some folding money. That sure as shit ain't gonna work."

Trip stood with the nickel and dime in his right palm. Remembered something about quarters and the dead. An echo from his childhood. What was it? He had goose bumps on his arms. Whatever it was, it was something bad.

His pa touched his shoulder. "Son. Wake up. Put them on her."

Trip kneeled on the shower stall lip, shut her right lid with his left index finger and held it down while he set the dime on it. Shut her left lid, put the nickel on it. He stood up and surveyed his handiwork. Silver on her lids was spooky. Made it seem as if her eyes were wide open and lit up from the inside out. A flashlight shining inside a jack-o'-lantern. "Pennies would have been b... better. More natural."

"Shut up about the stupid pennies. Close the shower if you don't like how it looks."

Trip pulled the door closed. "What are we gonna do with her?" He tightened the towel around his waist. Paced back and forth the length of the bathroom. Planted a hand on each side of his head, trying to press out an idea. Took his hands down. Black strands on his palms. Shook them off. "Could stick her in her car trunk and drive it a ways away. Leave it somewhere."

"She walked here. Her beater's parked in front of her trailer."

"Her trailer. What if we carried her back to her own trailer, dumped her in her own shower? I got a key."

"She'd be a big load to haul outta here. Wheelbarrow might work. We'd have to do it in the middle of the night. Nosy neighbors. Gotta watch for them. She's got that old bat living next door; never sleeps. No. Too risky taking her back to her place. Too many eyes around here."

"Gotta b... b... bury her or something."

"Need to dig a big fucking hole. Bobcat would come in handy." Frank chuckled. Thought that was funny. "Where the hell would we bury her? We ain't got no land."

"We c... can't leave her here."

His old man nodded. "She'd rot and stink up the place. Someone might smell her. Call the cops."

"The cops," said Trip. "Who knows she was here? Her b... b... boss?"

"Nah. I heard her on the phone. Told them some bullshit about visiting some boyfriend outta town. She sure as shit couldn't tell them she was fucking her client. I mean her client's son."

Good catch, Pa, Trip thought.

Frank scratched his chin. "So what do you do with a dead cow?" His eyes widened; he thumped his cane on the floor. "You cut it up and store it in the freezer." He thumped his cane again. "Yes sir. We got that great big chest freezer in the spare bedroom. There's a plan if I ever heard one."

The color drained from Trip's cheeks. Not only was the idea repulsive, but the enthusiasm his pa showed for it was sickening. This was wrong. All of it. From the minute he opened the bathroom door and saw his pa's face, it felt wrong. This man smirking over a dead woman, talking about cutting her up like a side of beef, this wasn't his pa. Not the one he knew. The bit with the coins. How did he know what did and didn't work? He'd done this sort of thing before. Covered his tracks after murdering someone. "Pa. I d... don't know."

Frank detected the horrified reaction in his son's voice. "I'm only trying to help, Sweet. What you've done here, it's a sin." He nodded toward the shower stall. "But what she was planning was worse. A bigger sin. And you're my flesh and blood. Flesh and blood comes first. I got to help you."

Unconvincing speech. Still, he didn't know what to say. How to confront the old man. He was in no position to judge anyone.

"Okay. What do we d... do first? Maybe we don't n... need to cut her. She c... could fit as is."

His pa nodded. "Let's give it a try."

"How do we c... carry her down the hall without m... messing up the carpet?"

"That blue tarp in the shed. Should be plenty big and strong. Don't even have to lift her. Grab the corners of the thing and drag her."

Trip dropped his eyes. The blue tarp. He'd buried the bridesmaid in it. "I threw it away, Pa. Had a b... big hole in it. How about an old b... bedsheet?"

Frank shook his head. "Blood might drip through."

"We'll wrap her neck in a garbage bag. Seal it with d... duct tape. Got a couple of rolls in the kitchen, g... good and wide."

"Now you're talking. You get the tape and bag and I'll get the sheet."

Trip watched his pa thump out of the bathroom and head down the hall. He couldn't remember the last time he'd moved so quickly and with such purpose. His old man was having fun. He'd done this before, or something close to this. Would he be shocked to learn about the bridesmaid? The ranger? Maybe not. What about the others Trip had flattened over the years? What about what happened in high school? Would it horrify his pa or make him proud? He brushed the thoughts aside. One thing at a time. He dropped the towel on the floor. Went into the hallway. Retrieved the clothes he'd left outside the bathroom door and slipped them on. While he dressed he watched his pa digging around the hall closet for an old sheet. He was humming to himself. One of Elvis's religious songs. "How Great Thou Art." He used to hum that song when he did household chores. When he had the strength to vacuum and sweep. As unbelievable as it seemed, this task of getting rid of a body had actually reinvigorated his old man.

Trip walked through the front room into the kitchen and pulled open a drawer to the right of the sink. The designated junk drawer. Stuck. Always stuck, crammed as it was with tools, glue bottles, rolls of tape, scissors, rubber bands, bottle caps. He yanked hard and it popped open. He reached into the back of the drawer and pulled out a roll of masking tape. The wrong stuff. He set it on top of the counter. Took out the claw hammer and pliers and screwdriver. Put those on top of the counter. Reached way back. Felt it with his fingertips. Slid it to the front of the drawer. There it was. A roll of silver-colored duct tape. He shoved the other junk back in the drawer and forced it shut. He opened the cabinet door under the sink and took out the roll of kitchen garbage bags. Ripped two bags off the roll. Held them up. They were a flimsy generic brand. Usually leaked. He pulled two more off the roll. That should do it, he thought. Shut the door. He went back to the bathroom. His pa was standing next to the shower stall with the door open. Staring at her body. An old sheet was draped over his left arm. Had cowboys on it. Trip never figured his old man would give up a set of cowboy sheets. Maybe that's all they had left in the closet. Maybe he couldn't see what he'd given Trip.

"Got the t... tape and garbage bags," Trip said, holding the tape in his left hand and the bags in his right. His pa didn't answer. Kept looking down at the body. "Pa? Having second thoughts about the p... p... plan?"

"No, no." That faraway voice again. "She reminds me of someone is all. Not her looks. Her position. How she's on her back, with her knees up. Any minute you expect she's gonna pluck those coins off her eyeballs, get right up, dust herself off, walk away. Like nothing happened."

His pa was acting weirder and weirder. Trip tried to dismiss it. Time to get down to business. Trip stepped in front of him and reached for the cold water handle to turn on the shower, rinse off the rest of the blood. His pa touched his arm. "Don't bother," he said. "Getting it wet again will make a bigger mess. We'll wrap her neck up real good as is. Clean up the stall later."

Trip stood still for a moment, not sure how to proceed.

"Go ahead, son. She won't bite. Not no more." His pa laughed.

Trip kneeled on the lip of the shower. He set the garbage bags and roll of tape on the floor. He studied her neck for a minute. Her throat was still bloody, although the oozing seemed to have slowed. The shower floor remained wet with water and blood. The plastic and duct tape would work regardless. He grabbed each end of a garbage bag and slid it under her neck. He wrapped it around a couple of times and tied the ends in a knot under her chin. He picked up another bag, wrapped it around, knotted it on the side of her neck closest to him. "I d... don't think she n... needs the other two."

"Good," said Frank. "Damn bags are expensive."

His pa hovered over his shoulder while he continued. Trip wasn't sure what he could and couldn't see. He unraveled two feet of tape from the roll and ripped it off with his teeth. He stuck one end of the tape on the far side of her neck facing the shower wall. Working toward himself, he slowly wrapped the tape around the bags, flattening it against the plastic as he went. He lifted her

197

head up by the hair on top of her head with his left hand and with his right, brought the tape around the back of her neck. He sealed the end, set the tape back down on the floor, sat back on his heels to admire his handiwork. Trip thought she resembled someone who'd been in a car accident and was wearing a whiplash brace.

Frank patted him on the back. "Good job. Couldn't have done better myself and that's a fact." He handed Trip the bedsheet. "I'll get out of here. Give you more elbow room." He went into the hall and stood in the doorway to supervise. He pointed to the floor with his cane. "Spread it out and drag her onto it. Don't lift her. You'll throw out your back. One cripple in the family's enough."

Trip nodded. He spread the sheet out as much as possible in the cramped space. He stepped into the shower, bent over the body, hooked the inside of his elbows under her armpits and lifted her a few inches off the ground. He stepped out of the stall with his left foot and then his right, dragging her over the shower lip. Her buttocks hit the floor with a soft thud. Trip slipped his arms out of her pits and let her head drop. Another thud. The coins popped off. He picked them up and put them back on her lids. Her legs were still in the shower, knees bent at the stall lip. He stood up straight; his back was aching from all the bending. He noticed the inside of his arms. Streaks of shave cream on his sweatshirt, from her pits. It repulsed him. He yanked off the shirt and threw it in the sink.

Frank: "What's wrong?"

"Nothing," Trip mumbled. He didn't want to touch her anymore, especially with his chest bare. Didn't want to feel a dead woman's skin against his. He bent over and picked up the corners of the sheet. Pulled straight out until her legs made it over the hump. Then he pivoted a bit and backed out toward the door. He scrutinized the bathroom floor as he went. Was relieved to see no blood. His pa stepped out of the way as he dragged her into the hallway. Another pivot and he walked backward toward the spare bedroom. The sheet was a little more difficult to pull across the carpet than the bathroom tile. "Pa!" he yelled.

"What?" His old man was behind him, walking toward the bedroom.

"The freezer empty?"

"Shit. Didn't think of that. Keep going. I'll give it a look-see."

"And make sure the blinds are shut in there."

He heard his pa thump toward the bedroom at the end of the hall. Again, he was amazed at how quickly he was moving. A man with a mission. Trip looked over his shoulder as he walked backward. Saw his pa open the door for him at the end of the hall. Trip pulled her through the doorway and into the bedroom. He let go of the sheet and wiped his forehead with his right hand; he'd worked up a good sweat. He leaned his back against the wall.

The window blinds were shut. The top to the chest freezer was open and his old man was feeling around with one hand. "Ice cream. Peas. Chicken patties. Couple tuna pot pies. Tater Tots. Something wrapped in aluminum foil."

"Guess what we're having for d... dinner?"

His old man laughed and started taking things out of the freezer. Trip helped. They piled the frozen food onto a card table sitting next to the freezer. Trip had traded the freezer for some work on somebody's truck engine. Frank held up one of the ice cream cartons and squinted. "What flavor?"

"Spumoni."

"When the hell did we buy that? Hate that shit. Dried fruit and nuts and such."

Trip smiled sadly. "Keri b... brought that for Italian night. Remember, a few weeks ago?"

His pa kept pulling stuff out of the chest and setting it on the table. "Yeah. I remember. Frozen pizza and spaghetti made with sauce from a jar." His old man stopped taking stuff out. Pointed to a sticker on the inside of the freezer door that was big enough for even him to see. "Which one is she?" The sticker was in the shape of a triangle. The top of the triangle showed which items could be kept frozen for three months: fish, ice cream, pork. Below that was six months: bread, duck, lamb. Nine months: beef and deer. At the bottom of the pyramid, what could stay frozen for a year: chicken, corn, peas.

His old man was laughing so hard he was bent in half. "Since she's a cow, I guess we can keep her in here nine months. What do you think, Sweet? We could cook her up next Fourth of July."

Trip didn't think it was funny. "What the hell is wrong with you? You b... been acting like a c... crazy old b... bastard."

His pa stopped laughing and straightened up. "I wouldn't talk, boy. Who sliced up a woman in the shower? Huh? Wasn't me." Trip didn't answer. He looked down at her body and then at the freezer. His pa read his mind. "You're right, Sweet. She'll fit without alterations. Good thing, too. That'd be a mess and a half to clean up. How we gonna lift her in, though? She's gotta weigh in at two bills."

More than the bridesmaid, Trip thought. "Let's g... get her right against the chest. I'll s... slide her up and hike her in." He pulled the sheet closer to the chest. Stood over her, a foot on each side of her. He adjusted his grip on the corners of the sheet and pulled her through his legs. Kept tugging and lifting until her head touched the chest. He stepped back and grabbed the bottom of the sheet and pivoted her body so she was resting against the chest, parallel with it. The coins fell out of her eyes, rolled onto the sheet. Trip bent over and picked them up.

His pa held out his right hand. "We'll put them back on after she's all tucked in." Trip gave them to his old man and he dropped them in his pants pocket. Frank looked down at her body. "I hate to say it, but you're gonna have to get under that fat ass of hers."

The idea made Trip shudder. He ran his eyes around the bedroom. The freezer was huge and took up most of the space. Besides the chest and the card table next to it, the room contained a set of folding chairs leaning against a wall. Car battery with a charger next to it, both sitting on a hunk of cardboard on the floor. A case of beer next to that. Two sets of busted stereo speakers stacked on top of each other. The closet door was open. Inside, down coats and jackets hanging from a rod. Snow boots and old shoes on the floor. Trip walked to the closet and pulled a winter coat off a hanger. Slipped it on over his bare chest, zipped it up. Pulled on the hood, tightened it around his head with the drawstring. Found some gloves in the pockets and slipped them on. "Now I'm r... ready."

He went back to the body. Kneeled at her side. Bent over like a man kissing the ground. Rammed his shoulder under her lower back. He slipped his right arm under her thighs and his left under her shoulders. He slowly stood up while sliding her against the chest. He felt her roll into the freezer. Heard a thud. Was never more grateful to hear a sound. Stood up straight and looked into the freezer while he pulled off the gloves and stuffed them back in the jacket pockets. Perfect landing. Right on her back. Her left arm was jammed against the side of the freezer and the right one was flopped over her chest, covering her breasts. A modesty in death she never had in life, Trip thought. Her left leg was bent at the knee but her right leg was sticking up over the top of the freezer. His pa grabbed her ankle, bent the leg at the knee and tucked it down. Then the old man walked around to her head. Took the coins out of his pocket. Handed them to his son. He reached down and set one each on her eyes.

Trip glanced at the floor. "No spills. Sheet's c... clean."

"I think we can wash it up and use it again," said his pa. Trip shuddered at the thought of having the sheet on his bed but didn't say anything. His pa patted him on the arm. "Good job, Sweet. Let's find any personal shit she left around the house. Clothes. Whatever. Throw it all in with her."

"What are we gonna do with her d... down the road? Can't keep her in the d... deep freeze forever."

"I'll give it some thought. Got some friends in the foundry business." Frank gave her one last look. "That is one big freezer. Swear to God we could still fit another body in if we had to."

"We w... won't have to," Trip muttered.

"Good," said his pa. He reached down and pressed the coins flat to make sure they'd stay. He withdrew his hands, reached up for the lid. "Night, bitch. Sleep tight." He slammed it shut.

23

She woke up Wednesday morning with the taste of her mother's garlic sauce still coating the inside of her mouth. Garlic hangover, her brothers called it. She loved the stuff but as a rule, she avoided eating it during the workweek. It usually took at least two days to get rid of the bad breath. She slid off the couch and went into the guest bathroom to gargle with Listerine.

Erik sat up and yelled after her. "Hey, garlic breath! Where you going so fast?"

She spit into the sink. "Thought I'd spare you." She took another swig right out of the bottle, swished it around her mouth until it burned.

"Too late," he said. "I smelled it all night. Next time bring some home for me so we can make each other suffer. Or maybe you should have your folks invite me to dinner."

She spit into the sink again. "I don't think I'm ready for that scene quite yet, and neither are you. Trust me on this." She looked into the bathroom mirror. Ran her fingers through her hair to work out the tangles. She took a brush off the counter and gave her mane a few strokes. She'd left her parents' house Tuesday night after a tense meal punctuated by shouting matches between herself and her mother. It would have been worse without her brothers' mediating commentary: *She hasn't been happy for a long time, Ma. They can't even agree on whether to have kids. She needs to find someone else.* Her father concentrated on eating, but occasionally came up for air long enough to throw gas on the fire: *Remember what happened to that divorced cousin of yours in Lebanon? Remind her she can't remarry in the Catholic Church unless she gets an annulment.* She got home and Erik called, begged to come over. He brought a bottle of wine. They sat on her couch talking and drinking wine until well past midnight. She started crying when she talked about Jack leaving. Erik held her until her shoulders stopped shaking. They fell asleep, both dressed in their sweats. Arms around each other. Didn't even make love. That was fine with her; she wasn't ready to sleep with him again. She needed a friend more than a lover.

She set down the brush, walked back into the front room. She leaned over and puffed a breath of air into his face. "Is that better?"

"Oh yeah." He pulled her down onto the couch. Kissed her hard. His tongue darted into her mouth, scraping past her teeth. He pulled it out. Lifted his mouth off of hers. "I didn't know Listerine made a garlic-flavored mouthwash."

She gently pushed him off of her and stood up. "Let me get the coffee going."

He grabbed her left wrist with his right hand. "It's early. We could still go upstairs." He smiled. "Get a little more sleep. Or no sleep."

Ringing from a cell phone on the kitchen counter.

She tried to pull her hand away but he wouldn't let go. "Erik."

"Ignore it," he said. More ringing.

204

"No problem," she said. "It's your phone."

"Shit."

She pulled her wrist out of his hand and went to the counter. Picked up his cell phone and tossed it to him. He caught it and flipped it open. Put his stocking feet on her coffee table. She turned around and started filling the coffeepot with water. Poured the water into the coffeemaker. Pulled a filter down from the cupboard, set it into the basket and scooped some coffee into it. Set the pot under the filter and turned on the coffeemaker. The smell alone made her feel more awake. She leaned her back against the counter and listened to Erik's end of the phone conversation. It sounded like work.

"Yeah." A pause. "Really? Where exactly?"

She turned around and took two coffee mugs down from the cupboard. Ringing from the other cell phone on the counter. She set down the mugs, picked up the phone and walked across the front room. Opened the sliding glass doors and stepped out onto the deck in her stocking feet. Closed the door behind her, in case it was Jack. She inhaled the cold river air before answering. "Murphy."

Duncan: "You sound chipper for a change."

She walked across the deck. Held the phone with her right hand and with her left, leaned against the railing. A flock of geese honked overhead. "What's up?"

"They found Bunny Pederson."

She took her hand off the railing and stood straight. "In the park?"

"In some woods near the campground. Wrapped in a tarp and buried in a shallow grave. Real half-assed effort at hiding her."

"An obvious cause of death?" Erik was probably doing the autopsy. She guessed he was on the phone at that moment talking about getting the body down to St. Paul.

"Wasn't gunfire. Winter says some kind of massive trauma. Ramsey County ME is doing the workup."

"Sexual assault?"

"Nope. She was fully clothed and all that."

"Except for the shoe they found on the ranger," Murphy reminded him.

"Except for both shoes."

"The other is missing?"

"Yup. Purse, too. Robbery gone bad maybe. Who knows?"

Through the patio door, she saw Erik grab the remote and turn on the television. She asked Duncan, "On the news yet?"

"That's how I knew."

She walked back to the patio door, slid it open with her left hand, stepped inside and shut it behind her. In the front room, Erik was pacing while talking on the phone and channel surfing with the remote. The sound was off. She didn't see any images from the woods, only a weatherman standing in front of a map. "So Winter didn't call you?"

"Hell no. I called him," Duncan said. "Bastard didn't give me anything more than he gave the media. Told me since we don't have a piece of the case anymore, we'll have to read the papers along with the rest of the world. Fuck him."

She switched the phone to her left hand, walked to the galley, picked up the pot and poured coffee into the two mugs. "Actually, we might have an interest after all." She set down the pot.

That intrigued him. "Your wild idea? Let's hear it."

She went to her refrigerator. Under a magnet was the invitation for the all-class reunion Saturday. "Let me pull myself together and come in with it." She heard Erik tell his office he'd be there in an hour and she followed his lead. "Give me an hour."

"I can hardly wait." A pause. Then: "Hey. Who's there with you? That good ol' Jack I hear?"

She wondered how the hell Duncan could be so nosy. "See you in a bit," she said, and set the phone on the counter. Erik had already hung up his phone and was in the bathroom; she heard him peeing. She set his coffee mug on the kitchen table. "Coffee's ready," she yelled to the bathroom door. "I'm running upstairs to shower."

Her eyes were closed and her face was turned into the spray when she heard him push back the curtain. "Hey," she said. "I don't remember inviting you."

"I'm not going to do anything. Just want to share the shower." He stood behind her and squirted shampoo in her hair. Massaged her scalp while working it into a lather. He took a step closer so she could feel his erection.

"Erik. I'm not—"

"I know, I know. You're not ready for this. I just wanted you to know I am." He backed away and squeezed the soap out of her hair. Suddenly the water turned cold. He laughed. "That's one way to get rid of me." He stepped out, grabbed a towel and left the bathroom to get dressed. She silently thanked the defective hot water heater and quickly finished rinsing off in the icy spray.

Erik stood behind her while she locked up the houseboat. He had a travel mug of coffee in his right hand; she'd set her cup down on the dock while she fiddled with her keys. In the background, the sound of Tripod barking. "When will he get used to seeing me?"

207

"He still barks at Jack." She bent over, picked up her coffee cup, stood up. Took a sip; it was already cold. She jiggled her keys, remembered her spare. "Where's the key I gave you?" He patted his pockets. "Don't tell me you lost it."

"No. Left it at home."

"I want it back."

"Will I ever get a set of my own?"

Murphy studied his face. Wondered if the wounded puppy was about to make another appearance. "Don't push it, okay?"

He didn't say anything. They walked down the dock together and to the parking lot. Their cars were next to each other; she thought her red Jeep seemed dumpy sitting next to his sapphire Jag. They stood behind the two cars, each with car keys in hand. The sky was gray and it was cold enough for gloves. Murphy scanned the clouds and wondered if they'd get their first snowfall in October.

"Will I see you tonight?" he asked, zipping his jacket up to his neck. "How about eating at my place? Let me do the slicing and dicing for a change."

"Sure you won't be running late with this Pederson workup on top of the ranger autopsy? I could grab some stuff after work and get dinner going." She felt safer on her own turf, although the shower visit showed her that even there, she had to work to keep him at bay.

"I'll let you know." He bent down and kissed her on the mouth. "Whoever does the cooking, no garlic. Deal?"

"Don't know if it's possible for me to come up with a garlic-free menu."

"Then for sure leave the cooking to me." He kissed her again and walked to his car door. Opened it. Turned and smiled. "I love you," he said. He didn't wait for a response. He got behind the wheel and shut the door. She stood still for a few seconds, feeling guilty she didn't say it back. She wasn't ready. Couldn't force the words out of her mouth until she was.

She turned and walked to her car while digging in her purse for a pack of gum. She couldn't find any. The guys at the cop shop were not going to appreciate her breath. She opened her car door, threw her purse inside, got in, shut the door. In her rearview mirror, she watched Erik pull away. She reached over and opened the glove compartment. Rummaged around. Felt something promising. Pulled out a roll of Tums. Better than nothing, she thought, and popped a couple into her mouth. She started the Jeep, pulled out of the lot while sucking on the antacid tablet.

She walked into Homicide, hung her jacket on the back of her chair. She'd tucked the reunion invitation into her purse before she left home. She wanted to show it to Duncan. She pulled it out of her purse and tossed it on her desk. Threw her purse in her desk drawer. Dubrowski and Castro were out on a call. She saw Duncan in his office with his feet up. His customary working position. He was on the phone. Evans Bergen, the night guy, was hunkered over his desk with a pile of paperwork in front of him. Short. Thinning blond hair. The youngest detective in Homicide and the biggest whiner. He looked up and nodded a greeting. Put his head down again. Murphy checked her watch. Amazing. His shift was over and he was still at the shop, finishing paperwork. Duncan must have gotten on his lazy ass.

She saw Sandeen at the watercooler. Tall. In his early fifties. Thick head of white hair. Longtime union activist. He'd guided her through the internal affairs investigation that followed the surgeon's suicide. He was wearing a Homicide sweatshirt. She walked over to ask him if he could spare one for the deputy she'd met at the state park. He finished his drink, crumpled the paper cup, threw it in the wastebasket. "How ya doing, Murphy?" She knew it wasn't a casual question. He was still concerned about her emotional state, especially since Gabriel Nash, the detective who'd worked with her on the surgeon's case, retired early over the summer. He'd been her mentor and on occasion, her partner.

She resisted the urge to brush her bangs and make sure they were covering her scar. "Fine. I'm fine."

He nodded. "How was Moose Lake? See any moose?"

"Moose head in the hotel lobby." She pulled a cup from the dispenser and poured herself a drink. "Hey. Got any more of those sweatshirts?"

He smiled. "Step into my office."

She followed him to his desk. "Met this deputy up in Moose Lake. Sean Mahoney. Real nice guy. Broken up about the ranger's murder. He liked the shirt. Told him I'd send him one."

Sandeen sat down and started opening and closing his desk drawers. "You wore the shirt on a case?"

She took a sip from the cup. "Sure."

"Great. Good PR for us." He pulled a sweatshirt from the bottom of a file drawer and handed it to her. "Extra large is all we got left."

She tossed the empty cup in a wastebasket and took the shirt. Held it up. "It'll work. Thanks."

"Hear anything from Gabe these days? He still seeing that nurse?"

She draped the shirt over her arm and sat on the edge of Sandeen's desk. "They've been spending a lot of time up at the cabin."

"Cabin? You mean that fishing shack of his in Hayward? That ain't no cabin."

"She made him put curtains on the windows."

"You shittin' me?"

"I shit you not."

Sandeen suddenly wrinkled his nose and looked around the room. "Hey, Bergen. You eating those damn garlic bagel chips again?" Murphy covered her mouth, hiding a grin and bad breath behind her hand. Bergen didn't even bother looking up from his paperwork. Flipped Sandeen the bird.

She noticed Duncan was off the phone. She stood up. "Gotta go talk to Yo-Yo. Uh. I mean Duncan." She was trying to stop herself from using the nickname; he'd been pretty decent to her lately. Murphy walked over to her desk. Picked up the invitation, shoved it in her pocket. Went over to his office, knocked once on the open door. He waved her in. Murphy noticed the pile of papers on his desk was getting lower; maybe he was actually getting organized.

"Our agent from the north bureau. Have a seat." He tossed a balled-up piece of paper toward the wastebasket in the corner and made it in. He was getting better at it. She sat down on the chair across from his desk, the sweatshirt still over her arm. "What's that?" he asked. She held it up. "Cool. Where can I get one?"

She was surprised Sandeen hadn't given one to him. She threw it across the desk and he caught it. "This one's yours."

He ran his fingers over the embroidered badge and logo. "Who made these up?"

"Sandeen," she said. He set the shirt down on a pile of file folders, stood up and started unbuttoning his oxford. Her eyes widened. "You don't have to put it on right now."

He pulled off the dress shirt and threw it over the back of his chair. He had a white tank undershirt. She noticed the bulge of his upper arms, the muscles of his chest. His gut was flat and hard and his waist was trim. Duncan's disheveled wardrobe masked an athletic physique. He saw her studying his body. Their eyes met. She quickly looked down and felt her face redden. She didn't see the corners of his mouth curl into a satisfied smile. He pulled the sweatshirt on over his head. Smoothed the front of it with his hands. "Thanks, Paris."

The first time she'd ever heard him say her first name. Hearing it out of his mouth jolted her—and pleased her. She didn't know why. She shook it off. "Want to hear this theory or what?"

He sat down again and put his feet up on the desk. Knocked some papers to the floor. "Hit me with it," he said, leaning back in his chair and putting his hands behind his head.

She started at the beginning, told him about her earliest suspicions when she saw Justice Trip plastered all over the newspapers and television, weaving a sanitized story of his life. When she told him about the dinner she and Trip had shared and her fear that he'd doctored her drink, Duncan took his feet off the desk and sat forward. Interrupted her narration. "I would have decked the bastard then and there. Sent his sorry ass straight to the county jail."

"I thought of that," she said. "Even if the wine tested positive for drugs, I didn't see him do it. He could have argued that in a public place like that, a bar, anyone could have dropped something into the glass."

Duncan shook his head. "Trying to kill a cop. The dumb fuck."

"He didn't know I was a cop. Didn't tell him that night. Saved the surprise for the next day." She recounted their uncomfortable meeting outside the park, Trip's lame excuse as to why he was there and his reaction when he realized she was a homicide cop.

212

Duncan patted his chest. "You were wearing a sweatshirt like this one?" She nodded. He laughed. "That's rich. Good job, Paris."

When she got to the part about Elvis, Duncan held up his right hand. "Wait a minute. Let me get this straight. No one knew about the lyrics in her purse except the Moose Lake authorities?"

"And a couple of people from the wedding party."

"And I assume they were told to shut up about it."

She nodded. "Correct."

"Nowhere else—on television or in the newspapers— did anyone say Bunny Pederson had a thing for Elvis."

"The only person who mentioned Elvis was Sweet."

Duncan frowned. "Sweet?"

"Justice Trip's nickname in high school."

"Yuck."

"Yeah," she said. "And get this. Erik Mason says the finger Trip 'found' was in such good shape, it didn't make sense. No animal bites or insects or anything. Wasn't chewed off. It was cut off."

Duncan picked up a pencil with his right hand and thumped the eraser end on his desk like he was tapping a drum with a stick. "Okay. Okay. Here's what we got. Stop me if I get it wrong. This weirdo salesman cruises into a small town, spots this bridesmaid stumbling home Friday night, kills her, cuts off her pinkie. Then he joins up with the search party Sunday and makes like he found the finger."

"Yup. Then late Monday night or early Tuesday, Sweet drops the shoe while carrying the body into the woods. Ranger finds the shoe."

"Mr. Sweetie finds Mr. Ranger and nails him. I'm on board with that. But what did your high school pal do with the body between Friday night and Monday night?" Duncan dropped the pencil on his desk, pushed his chair back and stood up. Paced back and forth between his chair and the desk. "Do you think he held her somewhere and didn't kill her until Monday night?"

"Doubt it. Where could he have safely held a live person while still bopping around town and doing interviews? Scenario A says she was killed Friday night and he temporarily stashed the body until he found a spot he liked for burial. Under Scenario B, she was buried in that park since Friday night and he returned Monday night—after our dinner together—for some goofy reason. Maybe to bury the shoes with her."

Duncan stopped pacing and stood behind his desk. "I don't like Plan B. Winter told me his people searched those woods thoroughly over the weekend. Dogs and everything."

"Scenario A wins the prize," she said. "Of course, the autopsies Erik is doing today on both bodies could flush both theories down the toilet."

"Another question." Duncan sat back down, drummed his hands on top of his desk. "Motive? Does this motive fly? Pretty extreme to go out and kill someone to generate some ink for yourself."

In a low voice, as if talking to herself: "He wouldn't find it extreme if he's killed before. Then it's taking it just one step further."

Duncan leaned forward. "Shit. You think this isn't the first time?"

Murphy thought about it. Eighteen years later, Trip still resented her for the role she played in his beating. It took a lot of pent-up anger to hold a grudge that long. "Tell you what. Let's see what the cause of death is on the bridesmaid. See if we've had other unsolved murders with the same MO, either in the Twin Cities or small towns. He's a salesman so he travels all over the state."

Duncan was all grins. A kid digging into a trick-or-treat bag. She threw another piece of candy into the sack: "I've got a high school reunion Saturday night." She pulled the invitation out of her pocket and threw it across the desk. Duncan picked it up. "Guess who else is going?" she said.

"Mr. Sweetie." He looked ready to jump out of his chair. "Need a date?" He handed the invitation back.

Murphy was going to ask Erik, but another homicide cop might be a better idea. "Sure," she said. "A well-armed date."

24

Blood and spumoni ice cream swirled around Trip's mind while he slept. A monstrous concoction. Pistachio green and cherry pink and vanilla topped by a red stream. All of it sprinkled with coins. Dimes and nickels and quarters and pennies. He could smell the pennies. Coppery. Or was that the blood? He woke at dawn Wednesday. Expected the odor of pennies and instead smelled bacon. Threw his legs over the side of the bed, sat on the edge of the mattress. Rested his elbows on his knees and his head in his hands. Realized he was naked. Why was he naked? He always slept in his underwear. His pa's cowboy bathrobe was on the floor next to his bed. Silhouettes of black longhorn cattle against red flannel. Why was his father's robe in his room? He struggled to sort the dream from the truth. Had he slit a woman's throat in the shower? Had his pa helped hide her in the freezer? Had they calmly collected her clothes and shoes and tossed them in the freezer with her, and then dined on chicken patties and peas? He couldn't accept it. Blamed it on the pills. He remembered he'd taken some pills to help him fall asleep. Felt groggy from them. He stood up. His legs were weak and his head felt muffled.

Stuffed with cotton balls. He feared what he would find, but he had to look. He stumbled down the hall to the back bedroom. His jeans and boxers were on the floor next to the freezer. Why? He put his hand on the freezer door. Opened it a crack. Felt a rush of cold air.

"Ask her if she wants some breakfast." Trip turned and saw his pa standing in the doorway, his cane in his right hand and a coffee cup in his left. His old man took a sip. "Go on," he said with a smirk. "Ask her."

Trip slammed the freezer lid. Ran past his pa, down the hall, to the bathroom. Fell to his knees in front of the toilet and vomited. Something yellow and stringy and bitter. The room reeked of bleach. Now he remembered. After dumping her in the freezer, Trip had stripped naked so he wouldn't ruin his clothes. Returned to the bathroom. Picked up the broken radio pieces. Opened a bottle of bleach and splashed it around the stall. Poured some on the straight-edge sitting in one corner of the shower. Turned the water on and let it run. Poured bleach on the bathroom tiles, pushed a towel around the floor with his bare foot. The towel was still in the bathroom; he saw it balled up in a corner, soaking wet. In the sink was his sweatshirt. He'd taken it off because it had her shave cream on it. The smell of the bleach and the sight of the sweatshirt made his head spin. He vomited again. Clawed some sheets of toilet paper off the roll. Blew his nose. Tossed the wad in the toilet. More of the night before came back to him. After cleaning up, he'd grabbed his pa's bathrobe from the door hook. Slipped it on. Retrieved the straight-edge from the shower stall, dried it off, took it back to his room and tucked it away in its box. Joined his old man in the kitchen. They ate everything they'd taken out of the freezer. Chicken patties. Peas. Tater Tots. Tuna pot pies. Even the spumoni ice cream. A gross feast, all washed down with shots of tequila.

He remembered sitting at the dinner table, getting drunk and spilling booze on the robe. They'd capped off their evening by pawing through Keri's purse and the stuff they'd emptied from her pants pockets. That's when Trip found the pills. The same ones she'd given his old man. The pills and tequila together were a mistake. He puked again. Hung his head in the bowl.

His old man had followed him into the bathroom after exchanging the coffee cup for the bottle of tequila. He walked over to his son, screwed off the cap. Held the bottle in front of Trip's face. "Take a swallow. It'll settle your gut."

"God, no." Trip rested his forehead on the toilet rim.

"You weren't shy about drinking it last night. Take it."

Trip took the bottle by the neck, put it to his lips, tipped it upside down. One. Two. Three gulps. Set it down on the floor. Sat back on his heels.

"Get up." His pa jabbed him in the side with his cane. "Damn bleach is what's making you sick. Come on. Get up and dressed. While you been snoring, I been cleaning this pigpen. Making you breakfast." More jabbing.

Trip wrapped his fist around the end of the cane. "Stop p... poking me with that damn thing!" Yanked it out of his old man's hand. It clattered to the floor, knocking over the tequila.

Frank held onto the towel bar for support. His eyes narrowed and went from his cane to his son to the tequila bottle. "Pick it up, boy," he said lowly. Trip reached for the cane. "No. The fucking bottle. It's the last of the booze." Trip righted the tequila. A puddle of it was on the bathroom floor. He picked up the cane and handed it up to his pa without looking at him. "Sorry," he mumbled into the toilet bowl.

His old man jerked the cane out of Trip's hand. "Get your ass up and out of here. I got eggs and oatmeal waiting for you on the table. Probably rubber by now." He pointed to the bottle. "Give it here before you spill the rest." Trip handed it to him. "Put some clothes on. I seen enough of your hairy backside to last two lifetimes." He stomped out of the bathroom, cane in his right hand and tequila in his left. Trip watched him go. For a second, wished it was his old man folded up in the freezer—cane and all—instead of Keri. He held onto the toilet rim with both hands and struggled to his feet. Swayed. Feared he was going to pass out. Gripped the edge of the sink. Hobbled to the back bedroom to retrieve his clothes. Stepped into his boxers and jeans with his back turned to the freezer. He kept wondering what she looked like all frozen, with coins on her eyes. He walked out of the room. Figured it would take a lot more liquor before he'd have the courage to open the lid and check it out. He went down the hall to his bedroom, opened his dresser drawer, took out his last clean sweatshirt. While he was pulling it over his head he noticed his suitcase empty and sitting on the floor next to the dresser. His dirty travel clothes were piled in the hamper. He didn't remember emptying the suitcase. Where was the peach purse?

His pa yelled from the kitchen: "Get your butt in here, boy!"

Trip ran his eyes around the room. No purse. Had to be with the dirty clothes. He went to the hamper, started throwing socks and shirts and boxers over his shoulders. Then he picked the basket up and tipped it upside down. Shook the clothes out. No purse. A shiver rippled through Trip's body. His pa had emptied the suitcase into the hamper while he was sleeping. Had he discovered the purse? He told himself to stay calm. The thing was probably in the pile of clothes. Needed to dig through it better.

His pa again: "What the hell you doing in there?"

Trip left the dirty clothes on the floor and headed for the kitchen. Walked in. His pa was sitting at the table. A plate of food in front of him and an ashtray with a smoking cigarette to his right. To the right of that, a syringe and needle. Every time she visited, Keri filled a bunch of syringes for his old man. She said he didn't see well enough to do it himself. Trip wondered how many prepared injections were left. When they were gone, he'd have to fill the syringes for his old man. Another nursemaid task Trip anticipated with trepidation. "After breakfast you better make a trip to the laundry," his pa said. He used a wedge of toast to shovel the last of his scrambled eggs into his mouth. Chewed and swallowed. Picked up the Lucky Strike. Took a long drag. Tapped some ash into the ashtray. "That mountain in your room is starting to smell as bad as your feet. Take that bleach rag in the bathroom with you. Throw it in with the whites."

Trip sat down. Touched his plate of eggs and bowl of oatmeal with his fingertips. Both cold and hard as marble. He stood up, took the plate to the microwave, set the dish inside, put the timer on thirty seconds. Leaned against the counter while his breakfast warmed. Saw the kitchen was cleaner. The dishes he had soaking in the sink last night were washed and put away. Counter was cleared of most of the junk. Floor was still sticky, but swept. His old man was wearing jeans and a flannel shirt for a change. Not pajamas. No baseball cap. Even with his cane and crappy eyesight, he'd been able to accomplish quite a bit. "You been b... busy, Pa."

His old man took a sip of coffee and nodded. "Yup." Took another pull off his cigarette.

The microwave beeped. Trip took out the plate and set it on the table. Looked down at the bowl of oatmeal. The instant cereal was gray and congealed. Decided to skip it.

Sat down. Six slices of bacon were draining on a paper towel in the middle of the table. Trip took a slice, shoved it into his mouth, chewed twice, swallowed. "You're c... cooking like your old self, too." Took another piece. Tried to make peace with his old man by cracking a joke. "If I d... d... didn't know better, I'd say stuffing f... folks into f... freezers agrees with you." Slid the second slice of bacon into his mouth.

Frank set his coffee mug down. Took one last puff off the Lucky Strike and crushed the stub into the ashtray. Took something from his lap and set it in the middle of the table. "And if I didn't know better, I'd say you killed that bridesmaid." The peach purse, with grease stains dotting the satin. His old man had found the bag, rifled through it while eating breakfast.

Trip's mouth hung open with the bacon inside it.

"Shut your mouth, boy. Keep chewing. I'll do the talking."

Trip chewed twice and swallowed. Coughed. Stared at the purse and started to say something: "I think—"

"You think! You think!" Frank slammed his right palm on the table, rattling the dishes and silverware. He picked up the purse, bunched it in his right fist, shook it at his son. "You ain't been thinking! That's the problem! You been fucking up left and right. Gonna land us both in the slammer. You slice that blond bitch open under your pa's roof and feed me that crap about Keri trying to kill me. Then I find this." He threw the purse down on the table. It knocked over an empty glass. Trip opened his mouth. His old man pointed a finger at him. "Shut the fuck up!" Trip closed his mouth and lowered his eyes. His pa sighed and his tone softened. "I know a man's got appetites, Sweet. Believe me I know. But you can't let your dick head lead you around."

His pa thought he'd raped the women, or that something sexual had happened. By the sound of his old man's voice, that made the murders more acceptable. Trip decided not to correct him. Not until he saw where this was going.

"Are you listening, boy?"

Trip kept his eyes down. "Yeah."

"Good. You better listen 'cause your pa knows more about this stuff than you think."

More cryptic words from his pa. Trip looked up. Locked his eyes on his old man's face. "Tell me. Tell me what you d... done and I'll tell you what I d... done." His old man averted his gaze. Stared out the window over the sink. Outside, the wind blew a bunch of leaves off the scrawny tree planted next to their trailer. Could his pa even see the tree? Maybe he could see a lot more than Trip knew. A long silence. The only sounds were the drip of the leaky sink faucet and the distant clang of a neighbor's wind chimes. "Pa?"

His pa continued staring out the window. Picked up a steak knife smeared with butter and dotted with toast crumbs. Tapped the flat side of the blade against the edge of his plate. The clink of the knife alternated with the drip of the faucet. *Clink. Drip. Clink. Drip. Clink. Drip. Clink. Drip.* The clinking stopped. His pa's faraway voice again: "You ain't ready to hear what I got to say. No sir." He pulled his eyes from the window. Trip studied the down-turned corners of his pa's mouth; he'd seen that expression once before.

"It's g... got something to d... do with what happened to Snow White." His old man's brows wrinkled with confusion; he didn't know Trip called her that. "What happened to Cammie."

Frank's eyes widened for an instant, as if he'd touched a hot pan. The corners of his mouth curled back up into their usual hard, straight line. "Maybe it does and maybe it

222

doesn't. Ain't your concern. Your concern is saving your own ass. That's my concern, too. Your ass is in jail, mine is in a nursing home. Eating baby food and smelling other people's piss." He picked up the steak knife again and pointed the tip at Trip. In a conspiring voice: "What'd you do, Sweet? Tell your pa so he can help you."

Trip's turn to look out the kitchen window. "You know what I d... did. Killed Keri. That's it."

"Bullshit!" His pa reached across the table, picked up the purse, threw it at him. It startled Trip. He caught it, juggled it like a hot coal, dropped it on the floor. He bent over and picked it up, set it in front of him. "How'd you do her?" asked his pa. "Why'd you do her?"

Trip's mind was swirling like the ice cream and blood from his nightmare. He needed a story that involved rape, or at least some sex. His pa found it a reason to kill. "I f... followed her out of the bar, fucked her in the p... parking lot. She got p... pissed about something. Maybe I wasn't m... man enough . . ."

That was good. His pa's mouth hardened; no one challenged his offspring's sexual talents.

"She s... started to walk home. I followed her in the t... t... truck. Tried to give her a ride. She flipped me off. Told me to g... get lost. Said she was gonna call the cops. Tell them it was rape. I g... got scared. Stepped on the gas. Ran her over. Kept her in the t... truck a couple of days, until I could figure out where to p... p... put her."

His pa nodded; it was making sense so far. "What was that business with the finger?"

He paused, wondering if this part would sabotage the sex motive. Then decided it wouldn't. "I cut it off and d... dropped it during the search."

"To feel important again, like the time with the little girl and her necklace?"

Trip dropped his eyes and didn't answer. Didn't want to admit why he'd done it.

His pa continued. "Why Keri?"

"She found the p... purse. Was planning to t... t... turn me in."

Then a hard question: "Any others?"

Trip looked down at the purse, stroked the satin. More slippery than he remembered.

"Sweet? How many others?"

Trip pushed aside the purse. Picked up a coffee cup, took a sip. Cold. Set it down. His pa slid the tequila bottle across the table. Trip took off the cap, filled a juice glass. Drank until the glass was empty. Poured another full measure, drank half of it. Held the glass between his palms as it sat on the table. The room was rocking, like the trailer was bobbing in the water. Couldn't tell if it was the booze or his pa's question.

"Sweet? How many?"

In a voice so low it was nearly lost in the wind chimes: "Lost c... count."

"Dear Lord." His pa rested his elbows on the table and buried his face in his hands. Trip wished he could see through the wrinkled skin. Was he mad or sad or shocked? He lowered his hands and folded them in front of him. Trip saw something he'd never seen before. Fear. The fun had gone out of murder for his old man. The father–son scheme was really the son's dark project. "All run over?" his pa asked.

Trip made a quick decision. He wouldn't tell his old man about the ranger. His pa had a respect for any man in any uniform. Saw them all in the same light as the sheriffs and marshals in his westerns. "Yeah. All r... run over."

"All raped?"

Trip was insulted. "No. Most was w... willing at first and

then changed their t... tune. Tried to run off and tell t... t... tales like that bridesmaid gal."

His old man nodded wisely. "Women do that. Yes, they do indeed."

"They d... do," Trip added. "The b... b... bitches."

"Since when? How long this been going on? How long you been keeping me in the dark?" He sounded angry and jealous of the news, like he'd found out he'd been excluded from a party held weeks earlier. Underlying both emotions was that fear again.

Trip finished the glass of tequila. Tried to pour more into the juice glass. Empty. Set the bottle down but kept his right hand wrapped around the neck and his left around the glass. They were something solid he could hang onto and hold. Everything else seemed to be bobbing and rocking. Maybe the trailer would sink and they'd both go down with it. Drowning might not be so bad after all. Not in cold water, though. Not the way those mean boys in high school had drowned. He wanted to die in warm water. Bathwater. Should he tell his pa about those boys? Another instant decision. "Started w... with high school."

A quick intake of air by his pa. "You killed a girl in high school? Your high school? I don't remember any girl..." His old man's voice trailed off. A revelation that topped the earlier revelations. In an amazed voice: "You? All four of them?"

That tone angered Trip. His pa didn't have trouble believing he'd run over women, but he doubted he could kill men. After everything he'd learned about his son, Frank still thought his boy was weak. Trip lifted the tequila bottle up and slammed it against the table, scattering glass around the kitchen and leaving a broken neck in his hand. His pa leaned back in his chair, both hands clutching the edge of the table. Trip waved the jagged neck at him. "I k... killed

225

that p... park ranger, too. Fucking s... smashed his head in with a shovel. Is that m... man enough for you?" His pa opened his mouth; now it was Trip's turn. "Shut the f... fuck up!" Trip bolted up from the table, knocking his chair over. He hurled the bottle neck at the window and missed. It hit the backsplash and fell into the sink. He felt his bare feet stepping on broken glass and he didn't care. "I'm n... never good enough for you. Nothing I d... do is right. I can't even k... kill to your liking."

Frank raised both palms in the air as if he were surrendering to an armed man. "Son. Son. Sit. Calm down. Jesus Christ." In an accommodating, condescending voice: "Of course I believe you. I'm glad you did those bastards in high school. Thought it was an accident is all. The cops said it was an accident. Slippery road and such."

Trip smiled and folded his arms across his chest. "No sir. Was n... no accident. Fucked with their s... steering."

A nervous smile stretched across his pa's face. "Clever son of a bitch. That's what you are. Did you know it would kill them? Was that the plan?"

Trip shook his head. "Wanted to m... mess them up good. Them dying was a nice added b... bonus."

"Damn straight. They were mean shits. Good for you." That sounded sincere to Trip's ears. "But why the ranger, son?"

"He f... found her shoe in my t... truck while I was burying her in the woods. Couldn't let him t... tell."

His pa understood that, or at least pretended to. Nodded grimly. "Self-preservation. Man's gotta do what he's gotta do."

Trip liked that, his pa calling him a man. He puffed out his chest. Suddenly he felt the pain from the broken glass. He hung onto the counter with his right hand and picked up his left foot. Checked the bottom. Big sliver. Pulled it out. Dripped blood on the floor. "D... damn."

"What'd you do?"

"Cut myself."

His pa stood up. "One minute, you fool. I'll get something for that. Got a temper worse than your pa's."

Frank left the kitchen. Trip kept his foot up. Watched the blood drip in neat, round dots onto the floor. The trailer wasn't rocking and bobbing anymore, but he didn't like seeing his own blood. He looked up. Watched the wind bend the tree outside. Listened to the chimes. Wondered if his old man was getting bandages or calling the police. His pa returned with a box of Band-Aids and Trip's loafers tucked under his left arm. He walked over to his son, stepping over the glass and crunching it with the tip of his cane. "Careful, P... Pa."

"I got shoes on. Got sense. Not like others in this family." He bent down and dropped the shoes at Trip's feet. "Wipe your soles off first, make sure there's no more glass on them." He stood straight, pulled a Band-Aid out of the box and started tearing the wrapper.

Trip held onto the counter, brushed the injured foot with his hand. Clean. His pa handed him a Band-Aid. Trip slapped it over the cut. Slipped his left foot into the shoe with a grimace. Lifted his right foot. Dusted it off. One shard fell to the floor. Stepped into the other loafer. He looked at the mess he'd made on the kitchen floor. Broken glass and blood. "I'll c... clean it up, Pa."

His pa stood next to the kitchen table. Absentmindedly picked a large triangle of glass off the plate of bacon. "What about work?"

Trip righted the tipped chair. Crouched down. Picked some glass off the floor and wiped his own blood off the linoleum with his hand. "Got p... plenty to keep me b...

busy right here. Got to c... clean up this mess. Empty out the b... back of the truck." He wanted to keep his eyes on his old man, in case he turned on him and called the cops. "I'll go in t... t... tomorrow. They won't care."

His old man sat back down at the table. Picked up another piece of glass. A round piece that came from the bottom of the bottle. Looked at his son. "All these people you got rid of. I'm worried."

Trip stood up. "Don't be. I'm not n... nuts, Pa. Stuff happened. Won't happen no more. I p... promise."

"That ain't what I'm worried about." He set the round of glass in his left palm and held it there, as if weighing it. "How careful you been? How you been getting away with it? I can see getting away with it once, maybe twice. But to lose count. How?" His old man didn't sound worried or horrified as much as curious. Maybe he wouldn't turn his own son over.

"All the accidents..." Trip stopped at the word *accidents*. He'd never before given a formal name to his acts. Decided he liked that label. "All the accidents were at n... night on empty roads. Used the t... t... truck. Never had much d... damage to speak of. Couple of c... cracked windshields. Dinged hood. Easy enough to fix."

His old man scratched his chin. "I remember you coming home with those. So the *accidents* were all out of town, during your sales calls."

"Mostly."

"And with the exception of those boys, you didn't know them."

"They were all s... strangers to me. Gals I'd just m... met."

His pa's eyes narrowed. "Met where?"

Trip had never met any of the people he'd run over. They were less than strangers to him; they were targets.

They weren't all women, either. Still, he had to come up with something. He could feel his pa's eyes on him. Blurted the first place that came to his mind: "Bars." As an after-thought, to make himself sound careful: "I made sure n... no one saw me l... l... leave with any of them."

His pa sat for a moment, digesting this. "Smart," he finally said. He tossed the round of glass on his breakfast plate. "You played it smart." He pushed the plate away and got up from the table. Picked up his pack of cigarettes. "Too much excitement this morning. Gonna plop down on the couch. Catch some *Gunsmoke*."

He watched him thump out of the kitchen with his cane and his smokes. His pa was trying to play it cool, but he was scared. Was he afraid of ending up in a nursing home or ending up dead? Trip couldn't tell. Didn't care. All he knew for sure was he had to find out what his old man was hiding so he could use it against him if he threatened to call the cops.

25

Trip didn't know a cop was already planning a visit to his house.

Murphy wanted to make sure Trip went to the reunion. Wednesday afternoon, she decided to personally deliver the party invitation. She knew from reading the newspaper stories about him that he worked out of his house when he wasn't on the road. She figured she'd catch him at home. She was just as interested in finding his truck home. She wanted to get a copy of the treads to compare to the cast from the Moose Lake campground. She also hoped she could talk her way into Trip's place. Get a look around. In high school, it was well known that Trip lived in a trailer court. He was the only kid who did. She flipped through the phone book at her desk and found him still residing there. His name was under his father's. *Frank Trip. Justice Trip.* Each had the same phone number and address. Probably made Sweet feel better to have his own listing. At his age, he had to be uncomfortable living at home with a parent. She remembered his father well. Frank was even creepier than his son. Always staring at the female students, especially the youngest ones. Spending a lot of time cleaning the girls' bathrooms and locker room. She closed the white pages.

Now she needed a camera to get a picture of the treads. Castro and Dubrowski, the gadget kings, had to have one. Surveillance was their specialty. Both were on the phone. She stood up and walked over to Castro's desk. Eyeballed the mess on top of it. Didn't see anything under the greasy lunch sacks, foam cups, newspapers and reports. He hung up.

"What do you need?"

"A camera."

He pushed his chair away from his desk. "For what? Different cameras serve different purposes." He bent over and pulled out his bottom desk drawer.

Murphy stepped closer and peered inside. A pile of cameras. Nikon. Panasonic. Minolta. Pentax. Polaroid. Saw a lens nearly as long as her forearm. Binoculars. Something that resembled a ballpoint pen. She pointed at it. "How about that one?"

"Not unless you're going deep undercover. Are you going deep undercover?"

"No. Need something small and easy to use. Want to take a couple of quick ones and shove it in my purse. Get the image back ASAP."

He fished around inside the drawer and pulled out a silver Nikon a little bigger than a deck of cards. "Digital."

It looked complicated. "How do I use it?"

"These little babies are really sweet and easy. A no-brainer. Turn it on, point and click. No little hole to squint through." He pushed the On button and tipped the camera so Murphy could examine the back of it. She saw what looked like a tiny television screen. "What you see on the screen is what you get. Don't even need to focus it yourself. Does it for you."

"Dummy proof," she said.

"Exactly." Castro held it up so Dubrowski was in the frame. "Here's how you zoom in for those intimate shots." He pushed a button marked with a T for telephoto and the small screen went in for a close-up. Dubrowski hung up his phone and looked over at them. "Smile, you ugly bastard," Castro said. Dubrowski gave him the finger and Castro snapped a picture. "Captured for all eternity, or until you erase him from the camera's memory."

"Got it," she said.

Castro pressed a button marked with a W and the image on the small screen seemed to back up, capturing Dubrowski and the empty desks around him. "Wide angle. Good for those crowd scenes. That special riot you want to remember."

"Seems simple enough."

He nodded toward his partner, who was back on the phone. "Even numb nuts over there could handle a camera like this."

He handed it to her. She studied it for a few seconds, backed up, aimed it at Castro. Pushed the T for a tighter shot. The screen framed his face. She snapped a picture. "Works great," she said. "How do you develop the pictures?"

"No film to be developed. Download to the PC."

She frowned. "And how do I do that?"

"Tell you what. I'll handle that part. After you take some shots, bring it back to the office. I'll download the photos. From there I can crop it, cut it, paste it, make a print of it, send it to someone in an e-mail. Whatever you want."

"Thanks." She shut it off, went back to her desk, took her purse out of her desk drawer and tucked the camera inside. It fit easily. She took her jacket off her chair and slipped it on. Threw her purse strap over her shoulder. Headed for the door.

"Last thing," Castro said after her. "Don't forget to turn the damn thing off and save my batteries."

She gave him the thumbs-up and walked out.

Trip had seen her red Jeep in Moose Lake. She didn't want him to notice her driving down his block, give him time to close the shades and hide. Murphy took an unmarked car from the department fleet. A silver Ford Crown Victoria. She rolled out of the cop shop parking lot and steered the car onto the freeway, heading to the north side of the city. She saw the entrance to the trailer park from the highway. She took the exit ramp. Pulled into the neighborhood of narrow houses, narrow streets, narrow yards. Studied the street signs. Found the Trips' street. Pulled over at the beginning of the block and shut off the car.

Their trailer was at the other end; she could see Trip's red truck parked in front. A fire engine. She dropped her keys in her purse. Checked her bag to make sure she had the invitation. There it was, ready to hand to him. Checked her Glock. Ready to go, in case. She pulled the camera out and put it in her jacket pocket. She slid out of the car, slammed the door shut, hiked her purse strap over her shoulder and started walking toward the Trips' trailer. The wind was in her face. She zipped her jacket up to her throat and buried her hands in her pockets. Heard wind chimes tinkling but couldn't see where they were hanging. While she walked she rehearsed in her mind. If his father came to the door: *Hey, Mr. Trip. Remember me? Went to high school with Sweet. Got this reunion invitation for him. Is that coffee I smell?* If Trip answered: *Here's that invitation. Hope you can make it. Sure had a nice time having dinner with you in Moose Lake. Is that coffee I smell?* Once inside, she'd keep the conversation friendly. Avoid talking about Moose Lake. She didn't want to scare Trip away from Saturday night's gathering or make his father suspicious. She figured if Trip was hiding something, his father was helping him.

She got to the front of their house. Their blinds were down and the slats closed tight. She took the Nikon out of her purse, turned it on, knelt down on the street in front of the truck, aimed the camera at the driver's-side front tire. The image on the screen was sharp enough to clearly distinguish the tread pattern. She snapped the picture. Went in for a closer shot. Snapped again. Aimed at the front passenger tire and took a photo of that. Crouching down in the street, she went around to the back of the truck. Took pictures of both back tires. She kept glancing at the windows of the trailer and looking up and down the street to make sure no one was watching.

While Murphy was taking photos, Trip was frying his pa sliced hot dogs and diced potatoes for a late lunch. He spiced it up with some chopped onions, salt and a dash of Tabasco sauce. Exactly the way his pa liked it. Trip was frantically waiting on his old man. Keeping him happy. Keeping an eye on him so he wouldn't pick up the phone. He'd even promised to clip the old bastard's toenails. To soften them, he had his pa's feet soaking in warm water and Dreft detergent. Trip sensed his pa picked up on the urgency in his son's attentions. It seemed to convert the old man's fear to contempt. Trip thought his pa was even enjoying it, taking advantage of the situation. He had Trip darting around the house for him like a pinball. Trip hadn't even had time to clear the breakfast plates off the table.

The potatoes were sticking. Trip scraped the bottom of the frying pan with a wooden spoon. "Better not be

234

burning those taters," his old man yelled from the front room. In the background, John Wayne's voice boomed from the television set in *Fort Apache*.

"Nothing's b... b... burning," Trip yelled back. Then in a low voice to himself: "Hope y... you choke on it." He decided he preferred a fearful father to a contemptuous, bossy one. He shut off the range and dumped the potatoes and hot dogs onto a plate. Walked into the front room with it and set it on the TV tray in front of his old man.

His pa took a pull off his cigarette. "Want me to eat with my fingers?" Trip went back to the kitchen and returned with a fork. Handed it to his pa. His old man jabbed a hunk of hot dog with it. "Foot soak's getting cold." He popped the hot dog into his mouth and chewed.

Trip bent over and dipped his right hand in the tub, the square plastic one he usually used in the sink for dishes. "Water's s... still warm."

His pa lifted a forkful of potatoes to his lips. "No it ain't. Cold as ice." He shoveled the food into his mouth. Stared at the television while he chewed. Grabbed the remote with his free hand and turned up the volume.

Trip sighed. "Pick up your f... feet then." His pa lifted his feet and Trip slid the plastic tub from under him. Stood up and carried the tub into the kitchen. Dumped the water into the sink. Set the bucket on the counter. Turned on the tap and felt it. He'd love to scald his old man. Boil some water and dump it in. Set his feet in it. Hold them in. *Hot enough for you, you old bastard?* He looked at the stove. The teakettle was on top; they used it to boil water for instant coffee and instant oatmeal and instant anything else they could find on store shelves. All he had to do was walk over, turn the burner to high. Wait for it to whistle. Dump it in the tub with some Dreft.

Slide it under his old man's feet and leave the room. Apologize when the old bastard burned himself. *Sorry, Pa. Should have tested the water. I feel terrible.* He'd heard diabetics could start losing sensation in their feet. Maybe his old man wouldn't realize the water was burning him until it was too late. Until the damage was done. Would it be enough to send him to the hospital and get him out of Trip's way? Would it push his pa over the edge, make him call the cops? He couldn't call if he was in a hospital bed, doped up. Trip shut off the faucet and walked over to the stove. Reached for the range knobs. Turned the one for the teakettle to high. Willed the electric coils to turn bright red instantly.

A knock at the door. "Shit," Trip said. "Who in the h... hell is that?"

"Door!" his pa yelled from the front room.

Trip tried to ignore it. Maybe they'd go away.

His old man again: "Door!"

Trip left the kitchen.

"Door!"

Trip walked past his old man to answer it. "I heard you the first two t... times. Ain't d... deaf."

"Could've fooled me," said his pa. He picked up the remote and lowered the volume. Squinted to see who was at the door while sliding his feet into his slippers.

Trip put his hand on the knob. What if it was a neighbor? Worse, the cops? He jerked his hand off the knob like it was a hot coal. Another knock. He turned on his heel and darted to his bedroom. Behind him, his father yelling: "What's wrong with you? Answer it!"

Hovering over his dresser, Trip inventoried the top. Picked out his sharpest yet easiest to conceal weapon. The switchblade. He slipped it in his right pants pocket and ran back out, shutting his bedroom door behind him. By the

236

time he got to the front room, Paris Murphy was inside, talking to his pa. His old man was standing by the open door, leaning on his cane and laughing. He turned and glanced at his son. "Look who stopped by."

26

Trip stood next to the couch. Put his right hand out and clutched the back of it for support. A homicide cop was standing in his trailer. In his front room. Steps away from a room with a freezer. Inside the freezer, a naked dead woman. His hand left the couch and reached down, felt the bulge in his pants pocket. He slipped his right hand inside and with the tips of his fingers, touched the edge of the folded knife. Her eyes met his and then fell to his right arm. Whistling, in the kitchen. He started and drew his hand out of his pocket.

"Is that tea?" she asked, her eyes leaving his empty hand to take in his face.

"Paris," he said, his eyes meeting her gaze and then dropping. "What d... do you want?"

She smiled. Took a couple of steps into the front room. Raised her right arm and extended a piece of paper to him. "I brought it by in case you couldn't find yours."

He frowned. "My what?" In the kitchen, the whistling from the teakettle seemed to grow sharper and louder.

"Reunion invitation."

The reunion Saturday. He'd forgotten about it. "Thanks,"

he said, and stepped forward to take the paper out of her hand. He wanted to get rid of her, chase her back outside.

She lowered her arm before he could grab the invitation. "Is that the teakettle I hear? I'd love some tea."

He looked down at the paper and then at her face. Was she up to something?

"Don't stand there, Justice," said his pa. "Get the lady some tea." Trip's eyes went to his old man's face. Frank cracked a small smile and shut the front door. Tipped his head toward the couch. "Sit, Paris. Sit a spell while Justice gets us some tea." He thumped over to the couch, sat down. Took the remote off the TV tray and turned off the television. He patted the seat cushion next to him with his right hand. "Sit. Tell us what you been doing all these many years."

Trip watched his father and thought: *He doesn't know she's a cop. If he knew, he wouldn't invite her to stay.*

Frank looked at his son. That small smile again. "Paris is a policeman. A pretty lady like this a policeman. Isn't that something, Justice?"

Paris Murphy isn't the sneaky one, thought Trip. His pa was the person trying to pull something.

"Tea sounds wonderful," Murphy said. She walked over to the couch, unzipped her jacket and sat down with her purse in her lap. Her eyes went from the son to the father and back to the son. The whistling in the kitchen continued, but Trip wasn't budging from his spot. Stood in the middle of the front room. A tall, pale statue. "Why don't I make the tea?" she said. "I'm pretty handy in the kitchen."

She started to stand up and Frank grabbed her jacket sleeve. Pulled her back down to the couch. "Justice can wait on us, pretty lady." He glared at his son. "Did you forget where the kitchen is all of a sudden?"

Trip started to cross the front room to head for the kitchen.

"Wait," said his pa. He lifted his plate of potatoes and hot dogs. "Take this slop with you." He leaned into Murphy's left ear and said in a low, conspiring voice, "Justice ain't much of a cook. Some days, I swear he's trying to kill me."

Trip yanked the plate out of his old man's hand and went into the kitchen. Slammed the plate on the counter. A few minutes ago his pa didn't think it was slop. A few minutes ago, the bastard was inhaling the stuff. His old man was putting on a show for Paris Murphy and Trip wasn't sure why. That crack about his son trying to kill him. Was his old man trying to plant that idea in her head—that Trip could murder his own pa?

The kettle was still whistling, the noise drilling a hole in his head. Giving him a headache. Trip went over to the stove and turned it off. He picked up the kettle and moved it to the counter. Opened the cupboards over the counter. All their usual coffee cups were dirty. He reached in back and pulled out three dusty mugs they hadn't used in a while. Two with *Far Side* cartoons on them. A third with some other cartoon on the outside and a dead fly on the inside. He tipped the bug into the sink. He scanned the food shelves. Pushed around some canned goods. Found an ancient box of Lipton tea bags still sealed in cellophane. He set it on the counter, clawed off the wrapper, tore off the cover, took out three tea bags. He dropped a bag in each of the cups and poured hot water over them. He stared at the steam rising from the mugs. Thought about how he'd almost poisoned her with those pills. Should he give it another try? No. Not here. Too chancy. They weren't in a restaurant this time. She'd know to blame the tea if she got sick. What if he put enough pills in so she died? Bad idea. She'd probably told the other cops at the police station where she was going. No. No poison. At least not now. That reunion offered plenty of possibilities, however. All those people. Old classmates. Old grudges. Jealous of each other's success. Still trying to get an old girlfriend or former flame in bed. Any one of them could be suspects.

He was glad she came by with the invitation. Another opportunity to get back at her. Plus like she had said earlier, the reunion would give him a chance to show off his hero status. How had she put it? *Wave it in their faces*. That's what he'd do. Wave it in their faces.

In the front room, Murphy sat on the couch next to Trip's father. She breathed through her mouth as much as possible to avoid smelling the booze and cigarettes. Another smell, too. Urine? She wished she could plug her ears as well as her nose so she wouldn't have to listen to Frank Trip's lame ramblings as he tried flattering her and flirting with her. "I always thought you were the nicest out of that whole crowd . . . You weren't homecoming queen? I'd have sworn you were . . . Your folks must be so proud of you . . . Bet you're the prettiest police officer on the force . . . What color are your eyes? They're Liz Taylor eyes."

He'd wave his hands around when he talked and then bump her left thigh with his hand when he set his arms down. As if it was an accident. It reminded her of the crap he pulled when he was a janitor at her school. He'd yell a warning and then roll his bucket and mop into the girls' bathroom. Feigned embarrassment when he caught someone still sitting on the toilet or standing in front of the mirror. It got to be a joke among the girls. When they heard him coming, one of them would lean against the door so he couldn't open it. Whisper a warning to the others. *Hurry up, the perve is here!* No one ever wanted to use the bathroom alone.

She was actually relieved when Trip walked into the front room. He balanced the mugs of tea on an old cookie sheet. He held the tray under his father's nose. "Justice," said Frank. "Serve our guest first."

"Oh, s... sorry." He held the tray in front of Murphy, his eyes down.

She picked up a mug. "Thank you." She looked at what was painted on the side and inhaled sharply. Struggled to hide her shock. She felt as if all the blood were draining from her body, being replaced with ice water. A *Flintstones* cartoon showing Betty and Barney standing in front of a cave. She felt under the mug. The one she'd given Denny had a chip on the bottom from bouncing around the car. She held the mug by the handle with her right hand and ran her left index finger in a circle around the bottom. She found the chip. The only way Trip could have that mug was if he took it from Denny's car. He'd been inside Denny's car. Why? To steal a mug full of coins? When had he taken it? She had seen it in the car days before the accident. Another cold wave washed over her. Trip had tampered with the car. Caused the crash.

She didn't want to give away her horror and anger. She tried to put on a calm face and voice. She blew on the hot tea and pretended to sip. No way would she ever drink anything Trip gave her. She studied her own hands. Felt reassured they weren't shaking. She tried to think of something to say. She glanced around the front room. "You keep it pretty neat for a couple of bachelors."

Trip's father picked up a mug. Trip took the last one. Set the cookie sheet down on the floor. Eased his tall frame into a recliner across from the couch. "I g... guess so." He held the hot mug between his hands.

She imagined herself taking out her gun and shooting Trip in the forehead. A clean, wide target. She could see the hole as she watched him. She blinked and turned to his father. "This reminds me of the layout of my house-boat."

Frank set his mug on the TV tray, picked up his cigarette, put it to his lips. "You live on a houseboat, do you? How big?" He took a drag and exhaled.

"Smaller than this. At least I think it is. I'd have to see the rest of your place to judge. How many bedrooms you got?" She took another pretend sip. Stifled a cough from the cigarette smoke.

Frank set his cigarette in the ashtray. Stood up. Leaned his left hand on his cane and bent his right arm at the elbow like a wing. Smiled down at her and winked. "Take my arm, pretty miss, and I'll give you a walking tour of our Graceland. Free of charge."

Murphy stood up, reluctantly set her mug on his tray. She wanted to take it home with her, but it could be evidence. She threw her purse strap over her shoulder. Looked across the room at Trip. His hands were locked motionless around his cup and his mouth was hanging open. Eyes as big as saucers. His father's suggestion of a tour obviously horrified him. Trip was hiding something. She looped her left arm around his father's right elbow and grinned. "Do you have a jungle room, too?"

Frank threw his head back and laughed. "Closest we got is Sweet's room. You could call that a jungle."

Trip bolted out of his chair, spilling tea all over the front of his legs. "Godd...dammit to h... hell."

"Son. Watch your language in front of a lady."

Trip ignored him. Ran into the kitchen with the mug, set it on the counter and grabbed a towel. Returned to the front room with it. Wiped his pants legs while he talked.

"Pa. Wait. This ain't such a g... good idea. Bedrooms are a m... mess. A regular d... d... disaster area."

"Speak for yourself, son. My room is fit for a lady." Frank paused and smiled suggestively at Murphy. "I mean fit for a lady's eyes."

Murphy wished she could knock his cane out from under him. She grinned at Trip. Thought her face would crack from the effort. "You should see my place. Regular pit, and I live by myself."

"Not married?" asked Frank.

"Separated," she said. "Getting divorced."

Frank started to cross the front room floor and headed to the kitchen with Murphy on his arm. "So you're available."

Trip suddenly remembered the mess on the kitchen table, and in the middle of it, the peach purse. He dashed ahead of Murphy and his pa, plucked the purse off the table. He opened the cupboard under the sink and pulled out the wastebasket. Tossed the purse into it. He looked up. Murphy and his father were stepping into the kitchen. He snatched a dirty plate off the table and scraped the leftover bacon and eggs into the trash and set the plate in the sink. He needed more garbage to hide the purse. He saw the bowl of congealed oatmeal on the table. Picked it up. Tipped the gluey mess into the trash and tossed the dirty bowl in the sink. Looked into the wastebasket. Still saw edges of peach material. The hot dogs and potatoes. He took that plate off the counter and tipped the scraps into the garbage. He looked down again. Perfect. No peach peeking out. He kept scraping food scraps into the trash and setting the dishes in the sink. Picked up the remains of glass from the broken booze bottle and chucked those into the wastebasket.

"Justice. Take it easy," said his pa. He and Murphy had stopped in the middle of the kitchen and were both gawking at his frantic cleaning efforts as he bent over the garbage can.

"Told you, P... Pa. It's a d... disaster." Trip stood straight and glanced at the two of them—his old man and a cop—arm in arm. Like best friends, and it made Trip furious.

"Son. Paris is available. Maybe you should ask her to this reunion thing."

Trip glared at his old man and his pa stared back. A long silence. Murphy cleared her throat. Decided to lay some groundwork for Saturday night. "Actually, I'm seeing someone. I'm going with him."

"A policeman?" Frank asked.

"Yes," she said. Murphy gently disengaged her arm from Frank's and stepped farther into the kitchen. She could feel her shoes sticking to the linoleum. She noticed the room smelled like alcohol.

"This here's where Justice works his culinary magic," said the elder Trip.

Murphy didn't see anything suspicious on the counters or table. She walked around the kitchen table and went over to the cupboards. Trip was on her heels. "You've got more shelf space than I do." She reached up and pulled open a cupboard while keeping an eye on him. Wanted to observe his reaction. He didn't flinch. Nothing in the cupboards he cared about. She scanned the shelves and shut the door. She saw the wastebasket between the kitchen table and the sink. Trip's eyes darted down to it and then away. She glanced inside it. Saw a broken liquor bottle. Was that what he was hiding?

"Excuse the m... mess," Trip said. He opened the cupboard under the sink, set the wastebasket inside and shut the door.

With the tip of his cane, Frank pointed to a doorway on one side of the kitchen. "My digs are on this end."

She eyed Sweet. He was glancing out the kitchen window; this part of the tour didn't worry him. She walked past Frank and poked her head through the door. The full-size bed was made. A set of longhorns mounted on the wall over the headboard. Western print on the spread. Matching curtains on the windows. Nightstand. Dresser. Lamp on the dresser that looked like a miniature covered wagon. Elvis clock with swinging hips hanging on the wall above the dresser. "Nice," she said.

"You've already seen our great room," said Frank. She walked through the kitchen and ahead of him into the front room. Sweet was a step behind her. "Guess it's not too great. Let's call it our 'okay room.' " He laughed at his own joke and followed her.

She pointed down the hall on the other end of the front room. "The jungle room this way?"

Sweet stepped in front of her and barred her way, planting a hand on each side of the doorway. "No, Paris. Really. It's t... too m... m... messy."

She read his face. *Fear.* In one of the rooms or closets down this hall, Sweet Justice Trip was hiding a terrible secret.

Frank slipped between the two of them. Leaning his right hand on his cane, he faced his son. Said in a voice that was low and loaded with threat, "Out of the way, Justice. Let me finish the tour. I want her to see the rest of the place. *All of it.*" Sweet didn't move. Kept both arms up. His father lifted his cane and with the hooked handle, pulled down his son's left arm. In a guttural voice, the older man said, "Get the fuck out of my way. Now." Murphy took a step backward. She thought the two men were going to start swinging at each other. Instead, Trip stepped aside and let his father pass. "This way, Paris," Frank said over his shoulder.

Murphy didn't look at Trip. She followed his father down the hall.

Standing and watching the two figures' backs, Trip reached into his right pocket and grabbed the switchblade. He paused. Plenty of time to pull it out, he thought. He let go of the knife and took his hand out of his pocket. Followed his pa and Murphy.

Frank pushed open his son's bedroom door, flipped on a light switch and thumped into the middle of the room. Turned around to face Murphy. She took a couple of steps into the room and stifled a gasp. A medieval arsenal. Knives and swords and daggers mounted on the walls and displayed on the dresser. Was this what Sweet didn't want her to see? She heard him behind her and turned around. He was standing with both hands in his pockets, surveying the room with pride. No. His room and its contents weren't the big secret. In fact, she sensed Sweet wanted her to say something complimentary. "Impressive collection," she said.

He blushed and averted his eyes. "Thank you."

"Bunch of expensive junk if you ask me," said his father.

She noticed a street sign on the one spot on the wall not covered with weaponry. It said ELVIS PRESLEY BOULEVARD. She pointed to it. "That from your souvenir shop back home?"

"Yup," Frank said. "Worst thing we ever did was sell that place. It'd be a gold mine now." Frank walked out and Murphy turned and followed. Trip was on her heels.

They went past the bathroom. The door was open. Frank pointed inside with the tip of his cane. "It's a small can, but it's all we need. No bathtub. Wish we had one. Got a shower though." He looked over Murphy's head at his son. Said slowly and deliberately, "That shower gets more than its share of use."

Murphy turned and glanced at Trip's face. Saw only anger directed at his father. She didn't like standing between the two men. Might as well stand between two snarling dogs. She stepped inside the bathroom. "Mind if I wash my hands?"

"Go right ahead," said Frank, his eyes still locked on his son's face.

She went to the sink, turned on the faucet and put her hands under it. She heard whispering and gave a sideways glance. Frank was standing in the hall at the entrance to the bathroom, resting both hands on his cane. Sweet was leaning his back against the wall and looking at his father, shaking his head. The elder man noticed her staring at them. She had to say something. "Any hand soap?" she asked.

"Above the sink," said Frank. "Help yourself."

That's what she wanted to hear. Permission to snoop. She pulled open the medicine cabinet. Quickly surveyed its contents. Saw only a disposable razor and shave cream. Bottle of Tylenol. Bottle of aspirin. Cold medicine. Bar of Lava hand soap. She took down the soap, shut the cabinet. Tore off the paper wrapper and looked for a wastebasket. Saw it next to the toilet. Tried to peer inside it without being obvious. Saw it was empty. She dropped the wrapper into the basket. She held the bar under the water and rubbed it into a lather with her hands. She set the bar on the edge of the sink. Rinsed. Didn't see a towel. Wiped her hands on her pants legs.

"Sorry," said Frank. "My boy needs to get to the Laundromat pronto."

"That's okay," she muttered, and stepped out of the bathroom. She glanced at the last door down the hall. "That the guest room?"

"Let me finish the tour," said Frank. He thumped toward

the door and put his hand on the knob. Turned and pushed it open. Went inside. Murphy followed.

"A freezer," she said. "Good idea. I've been thinking of getting myself a small one." Murphy walked over to the chest and put her right hand on the lid.

Standing in the doorway, Trip watched her back in case she turned suddenly. He reached into his pants pocket and wrapped his right hand around the switchblade. He pulled the knife out. Put it behind his back. As he opened it, he coughed to cover up the click it made when the blade locked. In his mind, she was already sprawled out on her back in front of the freezer. He could see her bleeding from a gash across her throat. Struggling for breath. Dying. Dying. Dead.

Murphy turned her head and looked into the hall. Sweet was hunched in the doorway. His left hand planted on the door frame. His right behind his back. A pained expression on his face. A trickle of sweat snaking down the middle of his forehead. He could have been a man getting ready for his own crucifixion. She directed a question at Trip to hear his voice. Listen for the fear. "How much does it hold?"

Trip seemed startled. Surprised she'd asked him a question. "What?"

"How much does the freezer hold?"

Sweet's mouth opened but nothing more came out. His father answered. "More than you'd think." Frank rested his right hand on top of hers. "Would you like a dish of ice cream? I think we got some spumoni." He rubbed his sandpaper palm over her fingers.

She slipped her hand out from under his. "No. Thanks." Something was in this room, maybe even in the freezer. Drugs were a good bet. Money possibly. Regardless, Murphy's instincts told her to get the hell out of there. Get away from Sweet. The murdering bastard. His creepy father and his creepy house filled with knives and swords. She could always come back with a search warrant after the reunion Saturday. She backed away from the freezer, opened her purse and pulled out the party invitation. Turned around and headed for the door. Sweet took his hand off the door frame and stepped out of her way. "Thanks for the tea and tour," she said, and handed him the invitation as she passed.

Sweet took the piece of paper with his left hand and nodded. Stuffed it in his left pants pocket. "I'll w... walk you out." She went ahead of him down the hall. Trip exhaled with relief. His right hand still behind him, he closed the switchblade, slipped the knife back in his right pocket. He followed her down the hall. Wiped both palms on his pants as he went; they were wet with sweat.

Leaning against his cane and standing in front of the freezer, Frank watched them go. He was disappointed. He'd hoped his son would take her in front of him; he would have found that exciting. Satisfying. Still, he'd had fun tormenting Sweet. He yelled after them: "Nobody wants ice cream?" He lifted the freezer lid a crack. His lips stretched into a smile as a frosty mist rolled out.

27

Two corpses left Erik no time for cooking. As Murphy expected, he was too immersed in autopsies to make dinner. She didn't mind; she wanted a break from him. "Give it up," she told him when he called her at the cop shop Wednesday night to suggest a midnight meal. "You sound tired. I've got stuff to do."

"Stuff?"

"Grocery shopping."

"Exciting. Sure you don't want my company?"

"I'll take a rain check," she said, and hung up. She was tired and hungry by the time she left the station and went to the grocery store straight from work. Her visit with the Trips had rattled the hell out of her and mystified her at the same time. She couldn't believe Trip had handed her the mug he'd taken from Denny's car. She wanted to put it out of her mind for a while. Seeing it had been a shock, and it sent her emotions through the ceiling. Maybe she was reading too much into a stolen mug. She had to admit Erik would be good at helping her sift through a pile of wild ideas to come up with a solid theory. This wasn't one for over the phone, though. She'd wait until they got together again, whenever that would be. After that surprise in the shower, a part of her wasn't in that big of a hurry to be alone with him. Maybe they could meet in a restaurant and talk on Thursday.

She steered the Jeep onto Grand Avenue, a tree-lined two-mile meander of trendy shops, restaurants and old homes that started at the western edge of downtown and ended at the Mississippi River. About a mile down Grand she hung a right into the parking lot of Kowalski's Market, a family-run grocery store loaded with imported cheeses, organically grown produce, cut flowers, fresh seafood, meats. Inside, she piled the cart with some basics. Steaks, chops, a roast, a chicken, oranges, celery, milk, butter, bread. A carton of eggs. She'd hit the farmers' market later in the week for more produce. Saw pumpkins for sale, but decided it was still too long before Halloween to buy one. The Greek olives looked good and so did the ready-made wild rice salad, but the line in front of the deli case was deep and her stomach was growling. She couldn't decide between Gouda and cheddar. Tossed both into the cart. She ate a Hershey's bar while standing in the checkout line and felt embarrassed when she handed the woman an empty wrapper to scan. Gnawed on a hard-crust roll in the car while driving back to the houseboat, brushing crumbs off her lap at every stoplight. While cramming food into the refrigerator, she ate some cheddar. Didn't bother slicing it. Peeled off half the wrapper and nibbled on the block. She wanted to wash it down with a glass of wine, but all she had left in the rack was a bottle of champagne. She thought about a liquor store run, but instead fell asleep on the couch watching television, the half-eaten cheese in her hand.

She woke early in the morning still fully dressed. Even her jacket and shoes. The television was on. Her back was sore from another night on the couch. She shut off the television, stood up and stretched. Felt something under her foot. She looked down. She was standing on the block of cheese. "I'm pathetic," she muttered, and bent over to pick it up. She brushed it off. Figured the five-second rule was long past, but put it in the refrigerator anyway. Tripod loved cheese. Threw her jacket over a kitchen chair. Falling asleep on the couch with her clothes on and a block of cheese in her hand. Slob behavior, she thought. Nothing repressed the slob in her like a good run. She went upstairs, pulled on some sweats and a stocking cap. Opened the bedroom patio doors and stepped out onto the deck. Cold and cloudy. She scanned the activity on the river and saw some rowers from the Minnesota Boat Club skimming the brown water in their shell. They'd just pulled away from their stucco boathouse on Raspberry Island, a wedge of land downstream from Murphy's houseboat. She'd tried rowing that past summer and tipped the boat. She wondered what it would feel like to tumble into the water on a chilly fall day. She shivered and went back inside, slid the door shut and dug around in her closet for a windbreaker and gloves. Found them on the floor. Shook off the dust bunnies. Put them on. Pulled on her shoes. Checked the treads. Worn down. She'd have to get to the mall sometime soon. She thumped downstairs and out the door. Locked up and tucked the key in her windbreaker pocket. Did some quick stretching on the dock while a V-shaped flock of Canada geese honked in the slate sky overhead.

Instead of her usual route along Wabasha, she headed for Lilydale, a road that followed the river and sliced through a thickly wooded regional park. As she pounded along the tar running path, she had trees and the Mississippi to her right, the street and steep bluffs to her left. Even on a gray day, the colors of the fall leaves seemed fluorescent. She saw another runner yards ahead of her and a bicyclist glided past her. Otherwise the trail was quiet. It would grow quieter as it got closer to winter until only a hardy handful braved the cold to use the path; she would be one of them. She tried to use the run to clear clutter from her head. She was successful at pushing the Trips from her mind, but her thoughts about Jack were tougher to put aside. Jack. His back to her, growing rigid with the news that Erik was her lover. His questions. *In the same bed where we made love? On the same sheets?* She hadn't heard from him since he walked out. She wondered if she should call him, but didn't have a clue what she'd tell him other than what she'd already said. *I'm sorry.* When it came to responding to Erik's declarations of love, she was equally incapable of finding the words. Lately, responding to his touch had also been hard. Jack dumping her had shifted her emotions. Unsettled them.

After twenty minutes she turned around and took the same path back to the boat. At the parking lot, she slowed to a walk. Wiped her forehead with the hem of her jacket. Saw Erik's car in the lot. What was he doing there so early in the morning? She'd have to get that spare key back from him; she didn't mean for him to start using it so freely. When she set her feet on the dock, she looked for her copy of the *Pioneer Press*. Didn't see it. Looked over the edge into the water. Dead carp. Oily log. No floating newsprint. She made a mental note to call the paper and bitch. Maybe she'd complain to Cody, to aggravate him. Reporters hated when people called them with delivery gripes. She pushed open her houseboat door.

Erik was in the galley, standing at the counter, wearing her "Kiss the Cook" barbecue apron over his slacks and dress shirt. His sleeves were rolled up. His tie, blazer and jacket were thrown over the back of a kitchen chair. He must have pulled an all-nighter and come right from work. He was cracking eggs into a bowl with one hand—a skill she could never master. He turned and looked at her, egg in hand. "Figured you were running. Made myself at home in the kitchen. Thought if I couldn't make you dinner, I'd make you breakfast."

"Thanks." She pulled off her sweaty stocking cap and gloves and stuffed them in the pocket of the windbreaker.

"What's with the cheese?" He held up the dirty block of cheddar with teeth marks on it.

She took it out of his hands, opened the refrigerator, set it inside. Took out a bottle of spring water. "You weren't going to use that in the omelet?"

He started whipping the eggs with a wire whisk. "No."

"Good," she said, shutting the refrigerator door. "It's dog cheese. For Tripod."

He stopped whipping and frowned. "Dog cheese? Never heard of such a thing. Where do you buy it? Petco?"

She opened the bottle of water and took a gulp. Wiped her mouth with the back of her hand. "Yeah. Petco." Took another drink.

"Still thinking about a dog?" He set an omelet pan on a burner, turned the heat to medium, tossed a small chunk of butter into the skillet.

She leaned back against the counter. "Jack thought it was a bad idea, me being gone so much and all. He's probably right." She started chugging the rest of the water.

He moved the butter around the pan with a fork. "I could keep the pooch whenever you're out of town. I could come here and watch him. Or I could move in." She choked on the water. Coughed and covered her mouth. "Is that a yes or a no?" he asked with a grin.

She gave him a sidelong glance, tossed the bottle in the wastebasket and headed for the stairs. "I'll shower real

255

quick." She sniffed and pointed to the toaster. "Toast is burning."

She ran upstairs, yanked off her damp clothes, turned on the water and stepped into the shower. Tried to process what Erik had suggested. He said it so casually. Was he kidding? He had to be. In the span of a few days, she couldn't split from her husband and allow another guy to move in. She needed more time. No, she thought. He had to be kidding. She pushed her worries aside. Squirted some shampoo in her hair and scrubbed. The shower was lukewarm; she feared her hot water heater was quitting on her for good. She stayed under long enough to rinse the soap out of her hair and by the time she was finished, the spray was cold. While she was toweling off, her cell phone rang. She dropped the towel, took her bathrobe off the door hook, pulled it on and went into the bedroom. The ringing stopped. "You suck," she said to the phone. She turned to go back to the bathroom and it started up again. She ran to the nightstand and picked it up.

Duncan: "So what should I wear to this deal?"

"What? What deal?"

"This reunion deal. I'm going through my closet here and I don't know if I have anything. Been a long time since I been out anywhere fancy."

Murphy sat on the edge of her bed and checked the clock on her nightstand. Still early. "Where are you?"

"Home."

She switched the phone to her left hand and with her right ran her fingers through her damp hair to work out the biggest knots. Stood up, walked across the bedroom, took a comb off the dresser and started dragging it through her hair. "Can we talk about it when I get to the shop?" She heard Erik coming up the stairs. "I just got out of the shower."

Erik reached the top of the bedroom stairs and yelled, "Come on! Omelet's getting cold, lover."

Murphy set down the comb and covered her face with her right hand. Waited. Knew it was coming.

Duncan: "That sure as shit ain't Jack."

"No," said Murphy. "It sure as shit ain't." Erik walked over to Murphy. Raised his brows and pointed at the phone. She put her hand over the mouthpiece and said in a low voice, "Work." He nodded, turned, trotted back downstairs.

Duncan was speechless on the other end and Murphy didn't want to help him out. Wished she could see him squirming. Finally he blurted, "Shit. Sorry. Didn't know. Since when?"

She was going to rip into him for being nosy, then decided he'd find out eventually. "We'll talk about it when I get in."

"I'm here for you, Paris."

"Appreciate it." She couldn't imagine leaning on Duncan, but knew he meant well.

"If you need some time off or something . . ."

"No," she said quickly. "Really. I'm fine. It's all fine."

"I like Jack. Really do. Hope it wasn't the job. Can be hell on a marriage. Ruined mine."

She opened her mouth to say it wasn't the job, but stopped herself. The job was part of the problem, and she had to give Duncan points for recognizing it. Every cop knew their work strained their marriage, but few admitted it out loud. "It was a lot of things," she said.

Erik poked his head upstairs again. Murphy nodded. "I gotta go," she said. "We'll discuss your wardrobe for the reunion when I get there."

"Do I need a tux? Should I rent a tux?"

"God no. Don't rent or buy anything. Wait till we talk."

"When?"

"An hour. Give me an hour." She threw the phone on the end of the bed, tightened the belt around her bathrobe.

Erik was standing at the top of the stairs with his arms folded across his chest and a spatula in one hand. "Who the fuck was that?"

"Duncan." She walked past him and headed down to the galley.

He followed her. "Why in the hell is he calling so early? What's this reunion thing?"

The kitchen table was set. The flowers he'd given her earlier in the week were sitting in the middle. The flowers that had helped end her marriage. She picked up the vase, set it on the counter, pulled out the flowers, tossed them in the trash. She turned and saw Erik watching her. He looked hurt. "They were dying," she mumbled, and took a seat at the table. She lowered her eyes, put a forkful of egg into her mouth. Chewed and swallowed. "Really good. Is that mint?"

"Mint and cumin." He took off the apron, threw it on the counter, sat down. Didn't touch his omelet. "The reunion?"

She took a sip of juice, wiped her mouth with the napkin. "My high school is having an all-class reunion Saturday night."

"Why are you taking Yo-Yo? What the hell is that about? Thought about taking me?"

He was jealous of Duncan, and that made her smile. "I don't know if you'd be much use to me. How good of a shot are you?"

"What?"

She picked up a triangle of toast and set it down again. Cold. "This is a work-related outing. Justice Trip is going to be there."

"Oh." He started cutting into his omelet with his fork. "Sorry I lost it. What's the plan?" He lifted a forkful of food into his mouth and chewed.

"Duncan and I are going to mingle. Maybe Sweet will take me for a turn around the dance floor."

"Be careful." He picked up a piece of toast, bit off a corner.

"I dropped in on him yesterday, at the trailer park."

"You went by yourself?"

"Me and my Glock," she said. "His father was there, too. He lives with his father."

"His pop as creepy as he is?"

"No, but he thinks he's hot shit. Kept getting touchy-feely with me."

He threw his toast down on his plate. "Great. That's great. You're by yourself in this trailer park with these two creeps and one of them is a killer and the other is trying to cop a feel."

"Don't pull a Jack on me, okay?"

His eyes narrowed; he didn't like the sound of that. "What is that? 'Pull a Jack'?"

"That's where you freak out whenever I tell you about my day. Don't do that to me. I'll stop telling you stuff, and I don't want to do that. I like that we talk. Jack and I couldn't talk."

He picked up his fork. "Then you promise me you won't compare me to Jack every time you turn around. I am not Jack. Deal?"

"Deal," she said. She took another sip of juice. Decided after his reaction to hold off on telling him about the *Flintstones* coffee mug. "What's the latest on the dead folks?"

"So far looks like the ranger got his head bashed in. My guess is the weapon of choice was a BFS."

259

"Come again?"

"Big fucking shovel."

Murphy nodded, picked up her fork. "He buries Pederson. Comes across the ranger. Kills him with the same shovel he used to dig the hole."

"Yup."

"Cause of death on Pederson?"

Erik took another bite of omelet, chewed, swallowed. "I'm gonna go out on a limb here and say BFT."

"Big fucking something."

"Truck. Big fucking truck. You pick up on that medical terminology real fast, woman. Want a job at the ME's office?" He pointed his fork at her. "I got a pair of gloves with your name on them."

"She was run over? That's it? Sexually assaulted first? Beaten? Any physical indications she'd done something to really piss someone off before she got nailed?"

"Nope. In fact, I'm thinking she was passed out on the road when she was run over."

"Tire marks on her? Any good?"

"Not as good as the cast from the park—and that was a partial."

She set her fork down and frowned. Killing four boys in high school out of anger and then running a woman over years later for no apparent reason. No pattern there. Was she wrong about Trip? Maybe he had nothing to do with the earlier crash and maybe he hit Bunny Pederson by accident, and then took advantage of the situation to play hero. The ranger got in the way. Could it be there were no others? No. Her gut told her there was more to it.

Erik studied her face. "Disappointed?"

She picked up her fork. "I was hoping for an MO that might point to other murders. Signs of pent-up anger let

260

loose. A simple hit-and-run, though. I don't know. Wish there'd been more out of the autopsy."

"If Justice Trip did it, and then hid her body and planted her finger. Well. Shit. I'd hardly call that *simple*." He rifled the rest of his toast in his mouth.

"What else?" She took another bite of egg.

He chewed, swallowed, took a sip of juice. "They found a knife near the grave."

"Prints?"

"On the handle."

"Match the one off the shoe?"

He nodded.

"What kind of knife? Hunting?"

"No. Not what you'd expect. Stiletto. Odd."

"I'll show you odd." She got up from the table and ran upstairs. She came back down with a slender volume in her hands. She sat down at the table, opened it and slid it over to Erik. "Check this out," she said, pointing to a photo.

He looked at where she was pointing. A yearbook picture of a kid with black hair and dark eyes. Under the mug shot: *Justice Franklin Trip. "Sweet." "Trippy." Ambition: to move back to Memphis. Likes heavy metal . . . working on trucks . . . collecting knives. Remembered for blushing a lot, being the tallest kid in school.*

"Collects knives," said Erik. "Shit."

"Yeah. I got a gander at that knife collection yesterday. His bedroom is a sword museum or something. And the way he behaved. His dad gave me a tour of their trailer and Sweet was on edge the whole time. He's hiding something in that mobile home. I'm sure of it." She closed the yearbook. "That tire tread from the park and the finger-prints. Can you get me copies real quick?"

Erik cut off another wedge of omelet and jabbed it with his fork. "On the sly maybe. Winter is being a prick about

261

releasing info, even to other agencies. Yo–Yo really pissed him off." He popped the egg into his mouth, chewed.

"Yeah. Duncan." She wiped her mouth with the napkin, stood up and took her plate over to the sink. "I better get to the cop shop before he does something goofy, like buys a tux for this reunion thing."

Erik stood up with his plate. "I'll say it again. Be careful."

She scraped the scraps into the trash. "I can handle Sweet."

Erik opened the dishwasher. "I'm talking about Yo-Yo."

She stopped scraping. Set the plate on the counter. "Give me a break."

"You think I'm kidding?" Erik started loading the dishwasher.

She walked to the table to retrieve the dirty glasses and silverware. "Duncan's goofy; I'll give you that. But he's got an honest heart. I really believe that."

Erik pulled the box of soap from under the sink and filled the dispenser in the dishwasher. "The guy's legendary. He lived on the street for years. The junkies were afraid of him. He's a fucking wild man."

She stopped in the middle of the kitchen with a fistful of silverware. "Then why did they put him in charge of Homicide? Why's he a commander?"

Erik pulled the silverware out of her hands and dropped them in the dishwasher basket. "You got me. Maybe Christianson doesn't give a shit anymore because he's on his way out. Maybe he needed to rein in the wacko before he turned into a real PR nightmare. I hear by the time they took him off the streets, he was shooting up. Mainlining serious shit."

Murphy handed him a couple of dirty glasses. Recalled Duncan pulling off his shirt. She would have noticed needle tracks. All she saw was an athletic body. No. She didn't believe it. "You're full of shit," she said.

Erik set the glasses in the dishwasher, shut the door, and glared at her. "I don't like how you're Yo-Yo's big defender all of a sudden. What's up with that? You don't even call him Yo-Yo anymore. It's 'Duncan this' and 'Duncan that,' and frankly I don't like it."

She smiled wickedly. "He is hot. I especially like the way he dresses. That 'slept-in' look really turns my crank."

"Fine. Make fun. Don't blame me when Yo-Yo gets the both of you tangled in some big fucking mess."

28

No way. Can't be true, she thought. While driving to work later that morning, she mulled over what Erik had said and wanted to dismiss it as jealousy. Duncan was odd, but he was also a good cop. She'd worked with him a couple of times back when she was in Vice. He'd received more medals and commendations than anyone else on the force. Taken more dealers off the street than anyone else. She turned into the cop shop parking lot, shut off the Jeep and dropped the keys in her purse. Glanced at the Glock in her bag. Thought about Saturday night. Duncan also had more kills than anyone else on the force, but not all of them were clean. A few years back, Duncan had had a midnight meeting with a dealer in a downtown apartment. The guy smelled a bust and fled the building before Duncan came up. Duncan saw him running down the sidewalk and shot him. He said the dealer had pulled a gun on him. No weapon was found. Only a lighter, and it was still in the guy's pocket. Duncan concocted some bullshit story that the piece had tumbled down the sewer. Internal affairs and the police-civilian review panel bought it and nobody questioned their findings. Nobody cared. The lone ranger had blown away another bad guy. Murphy closed her purse, stepped out of the Jeep, slammed the door and walked to the shop. Decided she'd have to go over Saturday night's plan in detail with Duncan. She was worried about more than his wardrobe.

She didn't bother tossing her purse and jacket on her desk. She walked through Homicide and into Duncan's office. He was getting in himself. Draping his suit coat over the back of his chair. Underneath, his usual rumpled shirt and crooked tie. The tie was out of season; it was decorated with Christmas trees and holly leaves. At least he'd stopped throwing his blazer on the floor.

"Hey, Murphy." He pulled at the tie like it was choking him, loosened it and then took it off. Curled his upper lip and dropped the tie on top of his desk in disgust, like it was a moldy sandwich. He pointed to the chair across from his desk. "Take a load off." He noticed her hands were empty. "Coffee?" He jogged out of his office before she could answer and returned with two foam cups. Set one down on his desk and handed her one. "Black okay?"

She took it. "Thanks." She set hers down on the edge of his desk. "Let's talk," she said. He watched her while she turned and closed his office door. Even though there were no other detectives in yet, they could be walking in any minute and she didn't want them to overhear her concerns about working with Duncan. He was having enough problems with his credibility in Homicide. She pulled off her jacket and hung it over the back of the chair. Set her purse down on the floor and sat down. Picked up the coffee cup and sipped.

He lowered himself into his chair and clasped his hands together, resting them on top of his desk. His face took on a serious expression. Furrowed brows and down-turned mouth. He spoke in a low voice. A priest offering counseling to a penitent. "I'm glad you feel comfortable coming to me, Paris. Like I said, I know the stress this job can place on a marriage. Have you talked to a shrink? I'm pretty sure our medical covers it. Nothing to be ashamed of. They tried to set me up with one once or twice. I didn't go, but that doesn't mean you shouldn't."

She set the cup down. Held up both palms defensively. "Stop. That is not what this is about. I appreciate it, but I can handle everything on the home front."

He smiled grimly and nodded. "That's what *I* thought. Then I come home one night and all the furniture is gone and so is the wife." He picked up his cup and sipped.

"Saturday night," she said.

His eyes lit up. The priest was elbowed aside by the excited boy. "Yeah. Saturday." He leaned forward. "Sure this Trip is going to be there?"

"Took an invitation to him yesterday afternoon. Visited him at the family estate. Lives in a trailer park on the north side of town with his dad."

"How'd that go? What'd you see? Anything sound an alarm?"

"Sweet was nervous as hell. All he wanted to do was get me out of there. Meantime, his creepy dad is giving me the grand tour of the place and hitting on me at the same time."

"Yeah?"

"Yeah. Sweet's bedroom took the prize. Enough knives and daggers and swords to outfit an army."

"This dude's gotta be the killer."

"He's been a killer going back to high school."

He frowned. "What do you mean?"

She took a breath. She didn't know it would be so hard to talk about it. "He served me tea from this coffee mug.

When I was in high school, I gave the mug to this kid. My boyfriend. Denny." She took another breath. "Denny and three of his buddies died in a car wreck. Lost control and flew into a lake. The only way Trip could have the mug is if he stole it from the car right before the accident."

Duncan's eyes widened. "Am I understanding you right?"

"I'm thinking the accident wasn't an accident. Sweet messed with the car so it would crash. Fucked up the brakes or the steering or something."

"Why would Sweetie take the mug? A sick souvenir?"

"Maybe. More likely he stole the mug because it was filled with change." She sipped her coffee. "One thing I don't get. Why was he stupid enough to serve me tea in the mug?"

"Did he know you gave your boyfriend the mug?"

"No."

"Then he didn't know it was a big deal. Plus he probably had it sitting around his house so long, he forgot where he got it from."

"Sweet remembered Denny liked cartoons. He made a crack about it in Moose Lake."

"Just because a guy remembers a goofy fact doesn't mean he remembers *how* he acquired that fact in the first place. Hell. I'm a fount of useless information. I have no idea why I know certain shit."

She took another sip of coffee and nodded. "Yeah. I buy that."

"And you know, it is possible he stole the mug and didn't mess with the car. Could be the timing of the accident was a coincidence."

"No," she said. "I'm sure he did it."

"Why are you sure?"

She thought about it. Her intuition and instincts had

always served her well in navigating cases. The times she'd ignored them had led to disaster. "I just am."

Duncan nodded. "Okay. We'll get something out of him at the reunion." He took a gulp of coffee. "Saturday night. What do I wear?"

"What you've got on is fine," she said. She pointed to the heap of silk on the desk. "Except a different tie."

He took another sip of coffee, held the cup between both hands. "What are you wearing?"

"A dress."

"A fancy one?"

"God no. We're not going to the opera. A cocktail dress."

"Then I should wear a suit." He slurped his coffee. "Gotta get a suit. A suit coat would hide my piece."

"Duncan." She paused. Clearly he was looking for an excuse to get dressed up. "Okay. Get a suit. But save the receipt."

"Good idea." He polished off the coffee and tossed the cup toward the wastebasket. It hit the wall and bounced in.

"Now let's talk strategy," she said.

"Strategy," he repeated. He leaned back in his chair and put his feet up on his desk. The running shoes were still part of his uniform.

"Wait," she said. She pointed to his feet. "Lose those, okay? I hate jokers who wear sneakers with suits. They think it's cute and it's not. Dress shoes, okay?"

He gave her the thumbs-up signal with his right hand. "Got it, Chief. Next?"

" 'Chief' is the operative word here. I'm in charge of this operation." She took another sip of coffee and set the cup back down on the edge of his desk. "No cowboy stuff." She braced herself for an angry comeback but he only nodded. She kept talking. "I'm getting a copy of the cast from the tire treads. Before I knocked on Sweet's door, I took some photos of his truck tires. We'll use those to compare. If we're still not sure we'll take the cast copy to the reunion and compare it to the actual treads on Sweet's truck. As far as getting Sweet's fingerprints, we'll have to be sneaky about it. Maybe give him a clean wineglass and take it back after he handles it."

"So we can compare it to the print off the shoe?"

"And the stiletto," she said.

He held up his hand to stop her. "Stiletto?"

She felt bad for Duncan; that bastard Winter was doing a good job of keeping him in the dark. "They found a stiletto near Pederson's body."

"Part of Sweetie's knife collection?"

She nodded. "Got prints off the handle." Then, so Duncan would know she wasn't talking to Winter behind his back: "Erik Mason told me."

He snapped his fingers. "Mason. That's who I heard when I called you this morning. Knew I recognized the voice. You two move in together or what?"

"No," she said, lowering her eyes. "I'm not ready to have anyone move in." She looked up, could feel her face growing hot. "Can we talk about my personal life some other time?"

"Sorry," he mumbled. "Been saying that to you a lot lately." He took his feet off the desk and stood up. Unbuttoned his left shirt cuff and started rolling up the sleeve while he talked. "I take it Mason is the one slipping us the copies of the treads and prints."

She stared at his left arm. No tracks. "Yeah. Erik," she said distractedly. "Keep it under your hat. If Winter found out, he'd be pissed."

"What time should I pick you up?" He unbuttoned his right shirt cuff.

"Seven," she said. "Cocktails and appetizers at seven, dancing at eight."

"Dancing, huh? I better warn you. I'm a damn good dancer. Better keep up." He rolled up his right shirt cuff. "Where's it at?"

She studied his right arm. Again, no tracks. "Reception hall on Summit Avenue."

"The one with the wrought-iron fence, right? I know the place. Nice joint." He sat back down, rested his arms on the desk and caught her studying them. A tight smile stretched across his face. "You heard that bullshit story, too." Her mouth fell open; she didn't know how to respond. "I'm surprised you swallowed it. A smart cop like you. How long would I have lasted on the streets if I was doing that shit? Who fed you that crap? Your new boyfriend? Tell Mason he can kiss my ass."

She stood up. The cordial meeting had turned ugly. "My turn to say it. I'm sorry." She picked up her purse, threw the strap over her shoulder and turned to walk out. She put her right hand on the knob, pulled the door open a crack.

He bolted out of his chair and was right behind her. Pushed the door shut with his right hand. "Not so fast," he said in a low voice. "That hurts, Paris. That really fucking hurts. We worked together."

She kept her back turned to him. She wondered how he'd guessed Erik was the one who told her; they must have crossed paths before. It didn't matter. Erik was the one who told her, but she was the one who believed it, even if for an instant. She said again in a low voice, "I'm sorry."

He planted his left hand on the other side of her. "Well 'I'm sorry' ain't gonna fix it."

They were standing too close. She felt trapped. Wished there was someone else in the office. At the same time she noticed he smelled good. Irish Spring soap and a cologne she recognized but couldn't place.

"Listen," he said. "I'm only gonna give you this speech once. I'm fucking sick of defending my undercover work. Sure I dressed like a dope fiend. Hung out with them. Acted like a dope fiend. But that's all it was. A fucking act, and a good one at that."

She turned and looked at him. He was genuinely hurt, and she felt bad. For the first time she noticed he had blue eyes. Not dark blue like hers. Light blue. Then she silently berated herself for noticing his eyes. Noticing his scent.

With her facing him, he suddenly realized how close they were and it seemed to embarrass him. He quickly took his hands off the door and lowered his arms. Took a step back from her. Folded his arms across his chest. "My record speaks for itself."

She didn't know what to say. Had no good excuse. "I'm sorry. I really am. I told Erik he was full of shit."

"But you had to see for yourself. Didn't you? Had to check out the junkie's arms. Look for the lines." He took a step toward her, turned both his arms and raised them so she could see the inside of his forearms. "Here. Take a closer peek. Push the sleeves up more if you want." She lowered her eyes and shook her head. He stepped closer. Raised his arms higher. "Really. I insist."

She grabbed each of his wrists with her hands and pushed his arms down. "Duncan. Stop."

He pulled his arms away from her and paced the width of the room once. "Jesus Christ. How about a little common sense? Would that tight-ass Christianson have put an addict in charge of Homicide?" He stopped walking and stood in front of her, even closer than before.

"No," she said. She couldn't keep from looking in his eyes. Bloodshot. Angry. Incredibly blue. If Jack was young

271

James Caan and Erik was old James Dean, Duncan was Robert Redford after a rough weekend.

"*No*. Fucking right *no*. Why do you think people spread that kind of manure? Hmm? Think that new boyfriend feels threatened?"

Her eyes narrowed. "What do you mean?"

He leaned into her left ear and whispered, "A smart cop like you, you know exactly what I mean."

"No I don't," she snapped.

He turned and walked to his desk, sat on the edge of it. Picked up her coffee cup and took a sip. Set it down. "You know, I'm the one who should be worried about who I'm partnering with. I hear that crazy doc not only blew his brains out in his own house with *your* gun, but did it with *your* encouragement. That right, Murphy? Did you egg him on? The poor, crazy fuck."

She gasped. How did Duncan find out? Only one other cop knew what had happened that night. Gabe had heard the words she and the surgeon exchanged before the gunshot, and he kept it out of the report. Did Gabe share her secret with Duncan?

As if he'd read her mind: "Did I ever tell you who my first partner was?"

"You bastard," she said.

"Yeah. Nash and me, we were like this." He held up his right hand, with his middle and index fingers twined together. "Every once in a while, when something is bugging the shit out of him and he can't dump on anyone else, he calls me."

"Why? 'Cause you're so good at keeping your mouth shut?"

"I *have* kept my mouth shut, against my better judgment." He stood up and walked toward her. "I told Nash he should've turned you in. It's one thing to take out a

272

dealer in a good, honest shoot-out. But to talk someone into suicide." He stepped in front of her, stood inches away. Pointed his right index finger in her face. "That is fucking nuts."

She turned, put her hand on the knob, pulled open the door. Felt relieved to walk out. Felt even more relieved to see Castro and Dubrowski and Sandeen sitting at their desks. Duncan stood behind her, a hand on each side of the open doorway. Said loud enough for the entire office to hear, "Know what else is nuts? Dumping a decent guy like Jack for a puke like Mason. If you ask me, Paris, you traded down."

She froze in her tracks. Saw the three detectives look at her and then Duncan and then her again. Her colleagues were waiting for her to return the volley. She spun on her heel to blast Duncan but before she could say a word, he threw her jacket at her. She caught it, and he delivered one last jab: "I'll pick you up at seven Saturday. I know where you live. Wear something hot for a change." He went back inside his office, slammed the door so hard he rattled pictures on the wall.

29

"Fired!" The word kept repeating itself. Over and over. Each time getting louder. *"Fired!"* At a stoplight, he covered his ears with his hands but it didn't do any good. The word was inside his head, not inside his truck. He grabbed a Manowar disc, *Louder Than Hell*, to drive out the loud word. His hands were shaking so much he dropped the CD on the seat. He picked it up again. Shoved it into the player. Cranked up the volume. Even the thumping of the bass guitar failed to drive the word out of his head. *"Fired!"* The light changed and he stepped on the gas. Squealed through the intersection.

Thursday had started badly and gone downhill, bottoming out with that word. "Fired." He'd tossed and turned and gotten tangled in his sheets Wednesday night. He couldn't sleep. He was worried about the visit Paris Murphy had paid to their trailer. Why had his old man invited her in? He feared his pa was going to turn him in to the cops. The pills he'd taken—some Tylenol with codeine he'd found in Keri's purse—didn't knock him out as he'd hoped. They only made him dizzy and tired and sick to his stomach. He'd gotten up in the middle of the night and taken two more. A few hours later, two more. Still no sleep. Only the room spinning and his stomach churning. When he rolled out of bed Thursday morning, he felt like he hadn't slept for days and was constipated on top of it. He sat on the pot reading the warning labels plastered all over the bottle. One was yellow and had a drawing of a sleepy eye with the lid half-open. "May cause drowsiness," it read. "Alcohol could intensify this effect." He knew he should have taken it with a shot of booze, but there wasn't any left in the house. Another label, also yellow: "Use caution when operating a car or dangerous machinery." The white label next to it had a drawing of a loaf of bread: "If medication upsets your stomach, take with a modest meal, crackers or bread." Wished he'd read that label the night before. He'd skipped dinner Wednesday; he was too busy cooking for his old man. Waiting on him. Listening to his lies about why he'd invited a cop into their house. *I didn't mean anything by it, son. Just being a gentleman. Fine-looking women get the best of me.* The final label on the pill bottle, another white one, made Trip laugh: "Caution. Federal law prohibits the transfer of this drug to any person other than the patient for whom it was prescribed." Out of curiosity, he checked the prescribed dosage and patient name on the bottle. "Take two tablets by mouth every four hours as needed. Dunkling, Mildred R." Poor old Mildred R. Dunkling was missing some pain pills, courtesy of Keri Ingmar. Trip set the bottle on the edge of the sink, stood up, pulled up his boxers. Constipated or not, he had to get his ass in to work. He should've checked in with Murray Wednesday but didn't. For sure he had to show up today.

He stood in front of the bathroom mirror. Looked even

worse than he felt. Turned on the faucet and let it run until it got hot. Opened the medicine cabinet and took down the shave cream and a disposable razor. The same shave cream and razor Keri had used. He wanted to throw away the razor, but it was the last one on the shelf. Dried cream on the handle. Dried hairs on the blade. Keri's hair from her pits or crotch. He shuddered and held the blades under the hot tap water. Whacked it against the side of the sink. Watched the tiny blond hairs disappear down the drain. Rinsed the handle. He bent over, cupped his hands under the faucet and splashed scalding water on his face. The burn felt good. Jarred him awake. He stood up, squirted a mound of foam into his hand and lathered his face. He dragged the razor across his skin. Cut himself a couple of times. The blade was dull after servicing Keri. He rinsed off the cream, turned off the tap and stood up. Studied the shadowy face in the mirror. A little more human.

He turned and looked at the closed shower door. He'd have to use it eventually. Might as well get it over with. He pushed open the door and reached inside. Turned on the shower. Stepped out of his boxers and into the stall. He faced the shower and ducked his head under. Bent his neck down so the spray kneaded the back of his head. Reached for the shampoo. Squirted a dab in his hair and put it back. While he worked it into a lather, he remembered the shit Keri had given him for using baby shampoo. *Ain't you old enough to use big-boy suds?* He squeezed the soap from his hair. She'd said there was nothing he could do to save his hair and that he'd have to get a rug. He looked at his wet, soapy fingers. More strands of black hair tangled around them. He pulled them off and dropped them on the shower floor. The bitch was probably right. Still, better bald than dead. He wondered when someone would notice she was

276

missing. She didn't have any family in town. His pa was right about the neighbors; they were nosy, especially that old lady next door to Keri. How many of them saw Keri walk to their trailer Tuesday? Her job would probably be the first to sound an alarm, however. When was she scheduled to work next? She'd said she had the rest of the week off. Did she say that included the weekend? Even if the cops came by her place, they wouldn't find anything unusual. Her car would be parked in front of her house. The trailer would be locked up. Everything would be in order, as if she'd left town with someone. His pa had said she concocted some story for work about visiting a boyfriend. Maybe he and his old man could add to the tale. Come up with a description. Send the cops after this phantom fella of hers. Yeah. Good idea, he thought. Only problem was it required his pa's cooperation and he didn't know if he could count on it. Didn't know if he could count on his old man for much of anything anymore. Kill a few folks and that family loyalty goes right down the crapper.

He heard his old man thump into the bathroom. He banged on the shower door with his cane. Trip hated the way his old man used it as a weapon. "What?" Trip yelled from the shower.

"Going into the office?"

"Yeah."

"I bagged up the dirty clothes. Make a run to the Laundromat when you get a chance."

Trip was going to do the wash Wednesday night, but he was too nervous to leave his old man alone. He was still nervous, but he had to leave the house sometime. His pa banged on the shower door again. "Yeah," Trip yelled. "I heard you. Laundry. I'll d... do it. Can't a g... guy wash his d... dick in peace?"

He heard his old man lift up the toilet lid, take a pee. Sure enough, he was hitting the wastebasket. Trip could tell from the sharpness of the tinkle. He opened his mouth to yell something and closed it again. Better leave the old coot be. Let him piss where he wants, like a mean, old, blind dog. His old man flushed. He knew not to flush. Suddenly the shower turned scalding. Trip backed away from it. "Pa!" he yelled. "Why the fuck you d... do that?"

He heard his old man laugh. "Wash your pecker with that." He thumped out of the bathroom.

Things sure as hell had changed between him and his old man. He'd have to find out what he was hiding; Trip needed some collateral. In the meantime he'd have to get to the office. For a change, work didn't seem like such a bad place to be. He assumed Wade Murray had some lingering respect for him. Not like his old man.

Trip's assumption was blown out of the water at nine-fifteen that morning, when he poked his head into Murray's office.

"When's the s... sales meeting?" Trip asked.

Murray glanced up from a stack of papers and frowned. "Come in. Shut the door."

Trip raised his brows. Ducked through the door, shut it behind him. Looked at Murray. He was a short, fat man with a washboard forehead. He always had sweat above his upper lip. He had short, black hair on the sides of his head, but the top was pink and shiny. So shiny, Trip wondered if Murray waxed it. Trip figured he'd better take notes; he'd be joining that club soon enough.

"Sit," Murray said, pointing to the metal folding chair on the other side of his desk. Pinecone Clothing Distributors had had an address at Riverview Industrial Park south of

278

downtown St. Paul for years, but the offices—a small room, a larger conference room and a greasy rest room—were furnished as if the company had recently moved in or was in the process of moving out. Folding chairs. Card tables. Empty boxes piled in corners. Murray and his sales force worked out of their homes and cars, and used the industrial park space mostly for meetings and to pick up samples. No warehouse; the shirts went directly from the manufacturer to the clothing store. Murray sat at a metal desk in the small room. The walls were bare except for a map of Italy. The edges were ripped and curling. Murray was always talking about a vacation in Italy. Trip figured it would never happen because it would require Murray to take a break from work, and he never stopped working.

Trip started to take off his jacket before he sat down.

"Don't bother," Murray said. "This won't take long." Trip lowered himself into the chair. Murray glared at him. "Where in the hell have you been?"

"On the road. Just got back to t... town."

"Why haven't you been answering your phone?"

Trip had left his cell phone in the truck all day Wednesday. "Must have b... been out of range."

"That's a load of crap." He looked at the top of Trip's head and frowned. "I suppose you've been wearing that on your calls."

Trip reached up and pulled off his *E.P.* baseball cap. Held it in his hands. "The sales meeting . . ."

"Was two hours ago. You blew it, pal. I've had it with your bullshit. You're fired. Turn in your orders—if you have any orders—and we'll mail you your last check."

Trip felt like someone had kicked him in the chest. "Fired? I'm fired? Why am I f... fired?"

Murray bunched a stack of papers in his right fist and shook them at Trip. "Because you ain't been bringing in

279

enough of these. Know what these are? Orders." He dropped the papers on his desk. "We are in the business of selling shirts. You want to save the world, get your face on television, in the newspapers? Fine. But if you can't bring in orders, we don't want you."

"I got orders," Trip said.

"How many? Where are they? Who are they from?"

Trip's jaw dropped. He studied the hat in his hands, hoping an answer would materialize on the brim. He couldn't think of a believable number. He couldn't produce any paperwork. Couldn't even make up the name of a customer. The only thing in his head was that word. "Fired!"

Murray folded his hands together on top of the desk. Stared at Trip. Waited for an answer. After several seconds of silence: "Yeah," Murray said, straightening the stack of papers. "That's what I figured."

"Can I g... get my money b... back from the unopened samples?"

"You gotta be kidding me." Murray pointed to the door. "Hit the bricks."

Trip stood up and pulled the cap back on his head. Went to the door. Put his right hand on the knob. He was exhausted. Could hardly move his arms and legs; something was dragging them down. Like swimming through a weedy lake. He opened the door. Turned to ask a question that was addressed more to himself than to Murray. "What am I gonna do with all those d... damn shirts?"

Murray was paging through the paperwork again. Didn't bother looking up at Trip when he answered. "You'll be the best dressed chump standing in the unemployment line." Trip started to walk through the door. "Hey," said Murray.

Trip took a step back into the room. Maybe Murray had reconsidered. "Yeah?"

Murray pointed up at the hat. "Always wondered. What's that E.P. stand for?"

"Elvis Presley," Trip muttered, and walked out.

30

Trip drove north through downtown and instead of steering onto the freeway, took meandering side streets toward home. He needed time to empty his head of the word. "Fired!" If the Manowar CD didn't do it, maybe a couple of the right pills would. He pulled into a liquor store parking lot and put the truck in park but kept the engine running. He pulled a bottle of pills out of his jacket pocket. Another find from Keri's purse. He hadn't even checked the label yet. Prayed they were something potent and wonderful. Amphetamines would be good, but he knew that was asking too much. Keri had warned him they were getting harder to come by. She'd said she had one patient on them—a guy with narcolepsy—and he was wising up to her pilfering. Trip needed something to lift him up. Take him someplace. Any place was better than where he was now. Listening to that word rattling around inside his head. He read the label. "Fuck," he muttered. They weren't even part of Keri's stolen stash. Her name was on the bottle. "Ingmar, Keri M." Below that: "Take 1 capsule by mouth every day. Prilosec 20mg capsules." He unscrewed the top and dumped the contents of the bottle into his hand to make sure she hadn't filled the container with something else. He recognized the purple capsules. He'd watched her pop them into her mouth when her stomach was bothering her. She told him they neutralized the acid in her gut. He was poised to toss them on the floor of the car, but stopped. Poured the capsules back, screwed the cap back on, returned the bottle to his pocket. The way his life was going, he'd probably need the pills. He shut off the engine and shoved the keys in his pocket. Hopped out of the truck and slammed the door shut. Headed for the liquor store. If he couldn't get stoned before he got home, might as well get drunk. He walked inside, headed for the whiskey section of the store. Spotted his old man's favorite. Reached for the Jim Beam. Some liquor might soften the blow. *Got fired, Pa. Let's do shots.* Trip scanned the shelves for his own numbing agent. Vodka? Gin? Tequila? Tequila would work. He took it down. Wished he could twist off the cap and chug it right there in the middle of the aisle. He walked over to the counter and set both bottles down. Saw some beef sticks on a rack in front of him and threw a fistful on the counter.

"That it?" The clerk was an old woman with greasy gray hair and crooked teeth.

Trip scanned the rack for more snacks. Grabbed two bags of salted-in-the-shell peanuts. A can of cheese balls. Set them with the other stuff.

"Breakfast?" the clerk asked with a chuckle.

Trip didn't answer. Tossed some bills on the counter. He remembered the laundry. Pulled a few more bills out of his pocket. "Give me s... some quarters."

He pulled in front of the Laundromat. Turned off the truck and slipped the keys in his pocket. He sat behind the wheel. Stared through the storefront windows. Only a couple of folks inside. He grabbed the bag of munchies off the passenger's seat and eyed the other two bags—the liquor—with longing. He looked in his rearview mirror and scanned the sidewalk. No one close. He pulled the tequila out of its sack and picked at the paper seal. He needed a knife. He reached over and popped open the glove compartment. Took out a jackknife. He stared at his one-hitter kit. A toke would be so good right now. Exactly what he needed. Still, he'd better save it for later. With Keri dead, his pills dwindling and his job gone, he'd have to conserve any and all mood-altering materials. He opened the jackknife and cut around the paper seal of the tequila bottle. Closed the knife and tossed it back in the glove compartment. Stared at the one-hitter kit again. Told himself to be strong. He shut the glove compartment. Screwed the cap off the tequila. Looked up and down the sidewalk again and then put the bottle to his lips. Took a long drink. So good going down. He took a longer drink. Put the cap back on. Slipped the bottle back in the bag and set it on the floor on the passenger's side. He opened the driver's-side door and slid out, taking the bag of snacks with him. He shut the door and went to the back of the truck. Opened the gate. His stomach churned. Behind the garbage bag of clothes were all the shirts. He knew exactly how many he had because, like the other salesmen, he'd paid for all his own samples. Five sealed boxes. Twenty-four shirts in each. Two opened boxes. Twenty shirts in each. Twenty-three loose shirts. Each boxed and loose shirt was individually polybagged and ready for sale. Plastic inside the collar. Cardboard on the back. Stickpins here and there. Then there was the one dirty shirt rolled up in a ball way back in the corner. He'd used that to dry the truck at the car wash. That made 184 shirts. What was he going to do with all those fucking shirts? He grabbed the garbage bag with the dirty laundry and pulled it out of the truck. Slammed the back gate shut and crossed the sidewalk to the Laundromat. Bag of clothes in his right hand and bag of snacks in his left.

Trip sat on a chair in front of the dryers, stared through the round windows at the clothes rolling around and gnawed on a beef stick. The last of his snacks. In the chair to his right were his jacket and a pile of food wrappers and peanut shells. He rifled the last inch of beef stick into his mouth, chewed three times, swallowed. He leaned back in the chair and stretched his legs out in front of him. Folded his hands together and rested them on his stomach. His belly was full and his head was light. During the rinse cycle, he'd gone back out to the truck and chugged more tequila. He decided the Laundromat wasn't such a bad place to be drunk. Outside was gray and cloudy. Through the store-front windows, he could see crumpled paper and leaves being chased down the street by the wind. Inside, it was warm. It smelled clean from the dryer sheets and detergent and bleach. Not like the trailer, with its stink of his old man's cigarette smoke and urine and whiskey. The two other people doing laundry—an old guy in baggy khakis and a young woman in tight jeans—had finished their loads and were gone. He had the place to himself. Nice and quiet. The only sounds were the hum of the dryers and the muffled thump of the damp clothes inside them. Not like home, with his father barking orders and waving his cane around. Television cranked loud with the noise of gunplay from yet another western show. Didn't that channel ever run out of cowboys?

The first dryer stopped. Trip stood up. Swayed. Dug his hands into his pockets. Even if the clothes were dry he'd be willing to keep plugging the machine with quarters to listen to the drone. No change in his pants. He picked up his jacket and checked. No change there, either. Only his car keys and Keri's stomach pills. His gut was starting to ache from all the junk he'd eaten. He took the bottle out, removed the cap and fished out a capsule. Swallowed it dry. Put the cap back on and shoved the bottle back in his jacket.

The second dryer stopped. Fuck it, he thought. Time to go home. Where did he put that garbage bag? Had he tossed it by mistake? No. Here it was, under his chair. He took it over to the first dryer, opened the window, bent over. Started filling the bag with warm, clean clothes. The room began spinning. He dropped the bag and ran to the bathroom in back of the Laundromat. Fell to his knees in front of the toilet and vomited. Tequila and beef sticks and peanuts and cheese balls. He figured the purple capsule was in there somewhere, too. He blew his nose on some toilet paper. Stood up. Hobbled back to the dryer and finished emptying it. Went to the second dryer next to it and started digging out clothes. He wished he could crawl inside with the warm fabric. He shut the dryer and stood up. Started for the door and stopped halfway there. He'd forgotten something. What? His jacket. He dropped the bag on the floor, went back to the chair, picked up his jacket, slipped it on. The room was spinning again. His right hand darted out and held on to the dryer. Shut his eyes for a moment and opened them again. The spinning had stopped. He picked up the bag and went out to the truck.

He walked through the trailer door with the bags of liquor cradled in the crook of his right arm and the garbage bag of clothes in his left hand. He dropped the garbage bag on the floor. Saw his pa sitting on the couch, asleep. The TV tray in front of him. Loaded with chips, dip and other junk. Ashtray with a smoking cigarette. A spent insulin syringe and needle. The television was blaring. The theme from *Bonanza*. Was it that late? Almost dinnertime. Trip picked up the bag and walked to his bedroom. Threw the bag in a corner. Set the booze on his dresser. Took off his jacket and threw it on the bed. Wanted to collapse on top of the sheets and take a nap. His head was still spinning from the booze, but not as bad as before. He was sobering up. Maybe he should reverse the trend, he thought. Best to break the news to his old man while he was drunk. While they were both drunk. He went back to his dresser and took the Jim Beam out of the bag. He'd save that for his old man. No good mixing tequila and whiskey. He took a knife off his dresser and cut around the whiskey bottle's seal. Set the knife and whiskey bottle down. Slipped the tequila out of its bag, screwed the cap off and took a long drink. Burped. His mouth tasted like tequila and cheese balls and vomit. He took another drink, swished it around in his mouth and swallowed. He set the bottle on the dresser and went to his bed. Sat on the edge and pulled off his dress shoes and socks.

His pa bellowed from the front room. "Where in the hell you been all day? Thought that meeting was just the morning. I'm hungry. Been eating crap all day."

Trip got up from the bed, grabbed both bottles and walked into the front room. Sat down on the couch next to his pa. Took the cap off the Jim Beam. "Why d... d... didn't you make yourself something? You ain't helpless. You been making me b... breakfast." He handed his old man the whiskey bottle.

"Nothing in the fridge." His pa took a coffee cup off the

287

TV tray, tipped it in his mouth to finish off the coffee and poured himself a drink. Set the bottle between his legs. "We need groceries." He guzzled the whiskey like it was water. "You left me here to starve."

"I'll g... get some groceries. Meantime, let's order a p... pizza."

"You drunk?"

"Getting there."

"When did you start?"

Trip didn't answer. He took a juice glass off his pa's tray. Looked inside it. A layer of something orange on the bottom. Probably orange juice from the morning. Trip filled the glass halfway with tequila. Set the bottle on the floor at his feet.

"Maybe you didn't hear me, boy." He set the cup down, picked up his cigarette. Took a pull and set it down again. "When did you start drinking? Middle of the day?"

Trip threw his head back and bumped off the tequila without tasting it. Shuddered. "Hell n... n... no. I was already good and d... drunk by the middle of the d... day. This here is my s... second wind."

"Why you drinking like this? Did you make it in to work?"

Trip filled the juice glass. "I m... m... made it in all right. In and out."

His old man picked up his cup, took another drink of whiskey. Set the cup down on the tray. Stared at his son. "You been fired."

Trip nodded. Sipped from the juice glass. He'd filled it too high and spilled some of it on his shirt. "Shit," he muttered.

"Shit is right," said his pa. "We in a world of shit now."

Trip set his glass on the TV tray. "What d... do you mean?"

288

"Expenses. Our lot rent for starters. How we gonna pay? That's three hundred a month right there. Electricity. Groceries. My cigs. My meds. Jesus. How we gonna pay for my shots and pills and such?"

Trip had stopped listening. He stood up. Swayed. Started to unbutton the shirt and stopped after the top button. "Who g... gives a shit? There's more where this c... c... came from." He loosened his necktie, yanked it over his head and threw it on the floor. Ripped the shirt open with both hands, popping the buttons off.

"What the hell you doing? You nuts?"

Trip pulled off the shirt, held it up in front of him and ripped it down the middle as if he were tearing a sheet of paper in half. "Fucking shirts. I h... hate these shitty shirts."

His pa frowned. Softened his tone while watching his son's erratic behavior. "Now don't be wasting stuff like that, son. We got to be frugal now that you're . . ."

"Now that I'm what? Fired? Fucking f... f... fired?"

"You ruined a good shirt is all."

Trip threw the shredded shirt at his pa. "We g... g... got shirts up the ass." Barefoot and dressed in his tee shirt and dress slacks, Trip stumbled out the door, went to the back of his truck, opened the gate and pulled out both of the opened boxes of dress shirts. He went back inside. Dropped the boxes on the front room floor.

"What you got there, son?"

Trip didn't answer. Ran back outside and grabbed two of the sealed boxes and brought them inside the trailer. After three more runs to the truck, his entire supply of shirts was on the front room floor. He looked at the sealed boxes. He needed a knife to open them. He ran to his bedroom and grabbed the first knife he saw on his dresser—the straight-edge he'd used on Keri. Sitting folded in its box on his dresser, waiting to get sharpened. He took it out, shoved it in his pants pocket and ran back to the front room. Stood in the middle of the pile of boxes and shirts. Scanned the room. Saw what he needed. He headed for the couch. Fell over a box on his way there. Crawled to his feet. Picked up the tequila bottle. Put it to his lips and chugged. Wiped his mouth with the back of his left hand. He carried the bottle over to the pile of boxes and shirts. He shifted the tequila to his left hand, bent over, and with his right took a packaged shirt out of one of the opened boxes. He stood up with a pink men's long-sleeve in his right hand and the booze in his left. "Wrinkle f... free. Athletic fit. Size s... seventeen." He drew his arm back and whipped the package at his old man like a Frisbee.

Frank caught it with both hands. Set it on the couch. "Son. Why don't you settle down? Take a nap. I'll order that pizza."

Trip took another drink of tequila and pulled a blue-and-white-striped shirt out of the box. "Size s... s... sixteen. Cotton-poly b... blend." Tossed it at his pa. The package hit him flat in the face.

"Stop!" the old man yelled, throwing the shirt to the floor.

Trip set down the tequila. Took out the straight-edge, opened it. Saw his pa's eyes widen.

"Afraid I'm gonna c... cut you, old man?" He laughed and bent over. Cut the tape on one of the sealed boxes. Closed the knife and shoved it back in his right pants pocket. Pulled open the cardboard flaps and took out a white shirt. Held it up. "Size fifteen. French c... cuffs. Perfect for a n... night on the t... t... town. A favorite with the ladies." He threw it as hard as he could. The corner of the package caught Frank above the left brow. The shirt ricocheted off the old man's head, knocked the coffee cup off the TV tray and landed on the floor. Frank felt something warm trickling down his face but was afraid to get up. Afraid what his son would do if he tried to leave the room. Hands shaking, he wrapped his right fist around the neck of the Jim Beam and raised the bottle to his mouth. He took a drink and set it down between his legs.

By the time he was finished, Sweet Justice Trip had hurled 183 polybagged dress shirts at his pa. They were all over the couch and on the floor at the old man's feet. Frank sat motionless on the couch. Blood on his face, fear in his eyes, a polybagged size seventeen blue oxford shirt in his lap.

31

Duncan finally got his big, dramatic scene in the office, and it was at her expense. Sandeen pulled Murphy aside Thursday afternoon. Told her she had grounds to file a complaint. "That personal shit is way out of line." They stood whispering by the watercooler. Duncan had kept his office door closed all morning, but opened it after lunch. Every so often he looked out the door.

"Want to forget about it. If I filed, we'd have a tough time working together." Her real fear was that Duncan would tell their superiors about her role in the doctor's suicide. "I hate to say it, but I want him with me Saturday night."

Sandeen pulled a paper cup out of the dispenser and filled it with water. "I could do it." He took a sip. With his other hand, he ran his fingers through his white hair. Smiled. "You could tell your old high school pals you like older men."

She laughed. "Appreciate it, but he's up to speed on this case. I'm not gonna let his big mouth blow it."

"Fine." He downed the water and tossed the cup in the wastebasket. "But if that asshole gives you any more grief, I want to know about it."

"You will," she said.

"Now I hope I'm not out of line here." He touched her left arm with his right hand. "I'm sorry about you and Jack."

"Thanks. I'm sorry you had to hear about it the way you did. And for the record, Jack did the dumping." She looked across the room and saw Duncan watching her through his office door. She turned her back to him and continued talking to Sandeen.

Later that afternoon, she sat down at a computer and did a Google search using Justice Trip's name, to see what would come up. She found some online newspaper articles she hadn't read before, including stuff from the Eau Claire *Leader-Telegram*. The story was a rehash of Trip's brush with fame in that community, recalling how his volunteer efforts helped police find a missing girl. She got to the end of the piece and was ready to exit out of the site when she noticed the newspaper's seven-day archives at the bottom of the page. She scanned the list of headlines to see if there was anything else on Trip. A headline about an old hit-and-run case caught her eye. She called up the story, a short piece about how the Eau Claire County Sheriff's Office was still trying to solve the crime. A father of four was struck and killed on a dark country road. He was walking home from a local bar. Like Bunny Pederson, thought Murphy. No witnesses. No vehicle description. No suspects. From the magnitude of injuries, the cops thought it was a truck. Again, like Pederson. Murphy noted the date of the accident and went back to the story on Trip. Checked when Trip found the girl's necklace in the cornfield. Went back to the article on the old hit-and-run case, to make sure she was reading it correctly. Yes. Trip was in the area at the time of the fatal accident. Maybe *accident* wasn't the right word, she thought. Was the father of four another one of Trip's victims? At the bottom of the story was a link to the Eau Claire County Sheriff's Office. She clicked on it and saw a summary of the case under the heading *Detective News*. At the end of the summary: *If you have any information, even if you think it may be insignificant, please call Sgt. Vern Gilbert.* She picked up the phone and punched in the number. Got Gilbert's voice mail. Left a message. Hung up. Put the cursor on the Print icon and clicked.

She went home from work with the printout of the Eau Claire website and the stack of tire tread pictures Castro had printed off the digital camera. She thought about calling Erik for copies of the tire tread cast and fingerprints, but she was afraid she'd start venting about Duncan. She didn't want to give Erik the satisfaction. Didn't want to admit he could have been right.

She resented that Duncan had dragged her and her home life into one of his door-slamming displays, but she figured it was just a play for attention. Public dramatics. She dismissed his criticism of Erik and his praise of Jack. He didn't know either one of them well enough to have meaningful insight. He had no idea what they were like off the job. She couldn't so easily write off Duncan's opinion of the doctor's suicide. Right after it happened that summer, she told herself it was self-defense. The murderer had her own gun trained on her. Told her he intended to rape and kill her. She had to do something. Talking him into suicide was the same as struggling over the weapon and winning. Shooting the bad guy before he shot her. As time went on, she had had doubts. Had she made a horrible mistake? Gabe had tried to reassure her she'd saved the taxpayers some money. If he really believed that, why had he confided in Duncan? She considered calling Gabe and then talked herself out of it. She was a big girl. She didn't need to keep leaning on someone else. But she wanted to know why he told Duncan. She fell asleep on her bed with the phone in her hand, still undecided.

Murphy didn't go into the cop shop Friday. She called Duncan's number in the morning and left a terse message on his voice mail: "I'm working the case at home today. Be here at seven tomorrow night." She hung up before she added what she really wanted to say: "Go fuck yourself."

She checked the clock on her nightstand. Too early to call Martin Porter, her buddy at Public Safety. She'd left a message for him Thursday. Wanted to run some questions by him about pedestrian traffic deaths.

She got out of bed, walked to the bathroom, reached inside the stall and turned on the water. Ice cold. She waited. Put her hand under again. A little warmer. She dropped her nightgown on the floor and stepped into the shower. Shivered in the lukewarm spray. Could it be she needed to turn up the temp on the water heater? No, she thought. Too easy. With her luck, the thing needed to be replaced. In between calls on the case she'd search the Yellow Pages. Did Erik know anything about plumbing? Doubtful. Like Jack, he probably preferred paying someone else to do it. She squirted some shampoo on top of her head and worked her hair into a lather. In the middle of rinsing, the water turned icy. She held her head under it as long as she could and frantically scrubbed to get all the soap out. Teeth chattering, she shut off the water. Stepped out. She had a cold headache. She pulled a towel off the bar and wrapped it around her shaking body. Grabbed another towel and rubbed her head. Thought she heard ringing. Was it in her frozen head? She stopped rubbing. More ringing; it was real. She dropped the towel wrapped around her body, yanked the bathrobe off the door hook and pulled it on. She wrapped the other towel around her head and twisted it into a turban. Ran into the bedroom while she tied her bathrobe belt. Where had she tossed the phone this time? Not on the nightstand. Not on the dresser. She pulled the bedspread back and found it under the sheets. She picked it up.

Porter: "Since when do you give a shit about pedestrians? They demoting you to traffic or what?"

"Marty, Marty, Marty. Why would sending me to traffic be a demotion? You have a serious self-esteem problem, my friend." Murphy liked teasing Porter. He was a cynical numbers guy in the Minnesota Department of Public Safety's Office of Traffic Safety. He wrote reports about accident prevention and continued to pilot his Harley at the speed of light, and without a helmet.

"You sound crabby. Am I getting you out of bed?" he asked. "I know how you homicide dicks keep bankers' hours while the rest of us are up early, doing real work. Want me to call back when you wake up, like at noon?"

She sat down on the edge of her bed. Pulled off the turban. Ran her fingers through her wet hair with one hand and held the phone with the other. "Shut up a minute. Let me do the talking. I want to run something by you, but first give me some answers to a couple of questions. Traffic-type questions."

"Traffic-type questions. I live for those. One second. Let me grab the latest edition of the Bible."

She got off the bed and went to her dresser for a comb. Went back to the bed and sat down again. "Which Bible is that?" She switched the phone to her left hand and with her right hand, started pulling the comb through her tangles.

"The only one in this office. *Minnesota Motor Vehicle*

Crash Facts." She heard paper shuffling. "Okay," he said. "Fire away."

"How many pedestrians are killed each year in Minnesota?"

"Way too easy. Don't even need the book for that. Last few years it's ranged from the low forties to the high fifties."

"We could say about fifty each year." She tossed the comb on her nightstand.

"Fifty. Yeah. That works."

"Who are these people? What can you tell me about them? Anything?"

"Actually, I can tell you quite a bit. People younger than twenty-five account for a big chunk of those killed. Guys are more likely to get flattened than gals. Am I boring you yet?"

"You never bore me, Marty." She switched the phone to her right hand. "Keep rolling."

"Fine. Let me know when you've had enough. While most of the fatalities are in urban areas, a decent percentage—better than a quarter—are in rural areas."

"Stop," she said. The newspaper stories about Trip said he worked as a traveling salesman servicing small towns in Minnesota and Wisconsin. "What do you mean by 'rural' exactly? That includes small towns, right?"

"We're talking small-town Minnesota. Communities with less than five thousand folks."

"Okay. How are most killed? What I mean is, what are they doing when they're nailed? Jogging along the side of the road? In a crosswalk pushing a baby stroller? Standing in the middle of the street?"

He sighed. "Ah. The myth of the blameless pedestrian. About a third of those killed were trying to cross a road where they *shouldn't* have been crossing."

"Meaning?"

"No signal. No crosswalk."

She sat back against the bed pillows, put her feet up and tucked her toes under the bed linen. "I suppose I shouldn't be surprised."

"No. But this next thing is moderately interesting. Of those killed who were tested for booze—and most are tested—more than a quarter had concentrations of alcohol over the legal driving limit."

Murphy thought about Bunny Pederson, drunk when she left the wedding reception. The father of four in Eau Claire had left a bar before he was hit. "Walking while intoxicated," she said.

"Probably more like stumbling while intoxicated," he said. "I heard a story about this one poor bastard. Driving drunk. Ran out of gas. Started walking. Passed out in the middle of the highway. He was wearing black clothes. A tuxedo, I think. So many cars ran over him, the State Patrol had trouble figuring out—"

"Enough," she said. "We're veering off course here."

"Trying to give you a little flavor is all. Is this what you want?"

"Yes and no."

"What are you looking for, Murphy? What's going on?"

"Let me ask you this, and it might be out of your area, so if you can't answer, that's cool."

"Want me to make up shit? I can make up shit if you want. I'm really good at it. Ask my wife."

"No. Don't make up shit. What happens when people, when drivers, hit pedestrians? Do they stop? Do they keep going? If they freak and keep going, are they usually caught later? Does someone usually see them? Get a license plate? How hard is it to get away with it?"

"I'm talking off the top of my head here. I don't have anything in front of me that supports this. But I think people usually stop; it's damn stupid not to. If you flee, you can get in a hell of a lot more trouble. Do some dummies keep going? Sure. Are they always caught? No. Since time began, there have been cases of fatal hit-and-run accidents without suspects and without clues. Happens all over the state. Hell, all over the fucking world."

"What if it's not an accident. How hard would it be for someone to do it on purpose and get away with it?"

"On purpose? Depends. They hit someone they know?"

"No. A stranger. For the sake of argument, let's say he hits a stranger."

He paused. "Okay, this is more good stuff off the top of my brilliant noggin. We all know it's a lot easier to get away with murder if you kill someone you don't know. Could be even easier if you're in a car. You're already in your getaway vehicle."

"Yeah," she said. "You've saved a step right there."

"Yeah. But you still have to be clever about it. Pick the right road. Drive a big mother vehicle. Do it at night. Watch out for witnesses. It would help if you knew what you were doing, had some practice. A professional hit man." He paused and then started laughing. "Get it? Hit man?"

"He's clever," she said more to herself than to Porter. "And he's had lots of practice."

"What? Who are you talking about?"

She posed the question her mind had been dancing around: "What if one man was responsible for a number of these cases in Minnesota and Wisconsin over the last, I don't know, ten or fifteen or eighteen years? What if the reason there were no suspects or clues is because he's gotten really good at it? Really practiced?"

Murphy pressed the phone to her ear. Waited anxiously for an answer or a reaction. Wanted to know how nuts her theory sounded. Finally Porter asked, "What are you thinking? Some sort of serial hit-and-run killer? Jesus. Someone would have noticed the numbers jump, connected the dots."

"Not if the deaths were spread out over the years."

"You're scaring me here, lady. Have you got someone in mind? Some evidence?"

"I don't have spit yet. Just some wild ideas."

"You gonna pull those old cases? Look for a pattern?" He sounded excited.

"I'm not at that stage yet. I don't want to sound any alarms until I have more. Keep this call off the record, okay, Marty?"

"Sure thing. That is fucking scary, man. If it's true." He paused. Murphy expected him to say it couldn't possibly be true. Instead: "Let me know if you want some help going over those records."

She pulled on some jeans and a sweatshirt and a pair of wool socks. She always found the best part about working at home was wearing rags while sounding professional over the phone. She went down to the galley, put a filter and coffee in the coffeepot basket. Poured in some water. Turned on the pot. She opened the door to the dock and scanned the expanse of gray boards. No newspaper. She was about to shut the door when she noticed a neatly folded paper in front of the door, right under her nose.

"They finally hit the mark," she said. She bent over and picked it up. Took it inside and slapped it on the kitchen table. She went over to the pot and poured herself a cup of coffee. Sat down and unfolded the newspaper. The cell phone rang on the counter. She got up and retrieved it. Sat down and answered it. "Yeah."

"Detective Murphy? Sergeant Vern Gilbert. Eau Claire County Sheriff's Office." He sounded like an older officer.

"Great. Thanks for calling back." She pushed the kitchen chair away from the table and put her feet up on another chair.

"This your home number? Hope I didn't drag you out of bed."

"No. No. Sitting down with my coffee and the paper. Speaking of the newspaper, that's what inspired me to call you. I saw something online in the *Leader-Telegram* about this unsolved hit–and–run. Went to your website."

"Hard case. The wife still lives in the area. Supermarket cashier. It's been a struggle for her. She almost lost the house. He didn't have life insurance of course. She says the toughest part is not knowing who did it. Wondering if it was a neighbor. Makes her look twice at everybody going through the checkout line."

"Sounds like you guys have done a good job of staying in touch with her. That's something."

"Your heart goes out. You know how it is. Anyways, you've seen enough I'm sure."

"Yeah. Seen enough is right."

"Anyways, you got something for us?"

"Maybe," she said. She paused, not knowing how much to tell him. An older cop might not buy into it, might write her off as flakey.

He sensed her hesitation. "Didn't you pick up on that tone of desperation from our website? We'll take anything. The case is colder than shit."

She felt sorry for him, and for the widow. "Fine. I'm gonna spill my guts on this thing, but you've got to keep it quiet. It's this wild theory I'm playing with and maybe if I lay it all out for you, it'll shake something loose in your mind."

"Let 'er rip," he said. "Both barrels."

"Remember that Justice Trip? The one who found the little girl's necklace?" He didn't answer; only silence on his end of the phone. Murphy wondered if they'd been disconnected. "Hello? Sergeant? You still there?"

"Fuck," he said. "I knew it. That spooky son of a bitch."

She pulled her feet off the kitchen chair and sat straighter. Held the phone tighter. "You were looking at him for this?"

"Damn right I was. Nothing to base it on but my gut and a cracked windshield."

"That sounds more than a little intriguing. You show me yours and I'll show you mine."

He laughed. "I've fallen for that one before. I'm a sucker. Anyways, here goes. This tall, spooky goof rolls into town, gets dragged into a volunteer search party. And I mean dragged. Whines like a big baby the whole time. I remember it well. 'It's t... too h... hot. Corn's t... too high. There's t... t... too many b... b... bugs.' He stutters you know."

"I noticed," Murphy said. She took a sip of coffee.

"Anyways, he lucks out and finds the kid's jewelry while he's bending over to tie his shoelaces. The media makes a big deal out of it. Makes him into Superman, and he eats it up. Somebody even gives him a fucking trophy. Wish somebody would give me a fucking trophy. In the middle of the circus, we get this hit-and-run. Then I notice. The hero has got a crack in his windshield that wasn't there the day before. I ask him about it. One of his dumb-ass fans, one of our local do-gooders, says, 'Oh, no. That's been there all along.' Stands up for the joker. Gets some others to say the same thing. One even gives me some bullshit about spending most of the night with him, showing him the town. I know that's a lie. The goof is not a social butterfly."

"They all cover for him?" She bumped off her coffee and stood up to pour another cup.

"I don't even know if they realized what they were doing. They were all swept up in the excitement. The reporters and cameras bopping all over town. I think they didn't want anything to mess it up."

"Are you shittin' me?"

"I shit you not. Swear to God. You gotta love that citizen involvement. Anyways, I talk to the sheriff and he tells me to forget it. Says the big guy can't be our man if all these people saw the crack there before, and if he's got an alibi for that night. Plus he didn't have dick on his record. I let it go, but reluctantly. My gut says he was involved."

She stood at the counter and refilled her cup. Took it back to the table and sat down again. "I think your gut is right on."

"Anyways, your turn. Show me yours, and don't be shy about it."

She took a sip of coffee. "You been reading the papers on this Moose Lake deal?"

"Yeah. Noticed the big hero jumped in again. Found the gal's finger. Guess once you get a taste of fame, you gotta come back for more. Anyways, they find the rest of her yet? I haven't been keeping up with it."

"They found her body in the state park up there."

"Too bad. Cause of death?"

"Looks like she got hit by a truck."

A long pause, then: "The hero?"

"That's what I'm thinking." She downed her second cup of coffee and stood up. Went over to the counter with the cup and poured a third. She was wired and she didn't know if it was the caffeine or the conversation. Regardless, she didn't mind the feeling.

303

"Wait a minute here," he said. "Are you thinking he hit her and then fixed it so he'd find the finger? So he could be Superman all over again? Get another fifteen minutes?"

She leaned her back against the counter with the cup in her hand. "Yup." She knew he'd have the most trouble wrapping his mind around that part of it.

"On purpose? So you're thinking he hit her on purpose?"

"Yeah." She sipped. Set the cup down. Walked back and forth in front of the counter with the cell phone pressed to her ear.

"That is one hell of a theory. Man." He paused and then said, "If that's the case, it really makes me wonder . . ." His voice trailed off.

She stopped pacing and picked up the cup again. "Wonder if he did your victim on purpose?"

"Yeah." Another brief silence while the idea sunk in, and then anger. "Bastard. Sick son of a bitch. Are you looking at him for any others?"

"Possibly. I've got some ideas. A buddy at Public Safety is ready to help me sift through old cases."

"If there's anything I can do on the Wisconsin end, let me know. Pulling records. Making calls. Whatever. I want a piece of this. I'd love to hang that spooky Superman by his fucking cape."

32

Spooky Superman passed out facedown on the front room floor Thursday night and woke Friday morning with a hangover. He raised his head and saw all the boxes and shirts around him and briefly wondered why they were there. When it came back to him, he groaned and set his head back down on the rug with a thud. "Fuck," he muttered into the carpet. He smelled that urine smell again in the rug and rolled over onto his back. Stared up at the ceiling. Noticed some water stains. Something was in his right pants pocket, jabbing his leg. He reached down and slid his hand inside. His straight-edge razor. He'd used it to open the boxes. At least he'd remembered to close it before shoving it in his pants. He pulled his hand out and threw his forearm over his eyes. He heard his old man bumping around the kitchen with his cane. Heard him talking. Trip's body stiffened. Was there someone else in the trailer? Had Paris Murphy come back to arrest him? He held his breath and listened. No. His pa was on the phone. He rolled back onto his stomach, cocked his head toward the kitchen and strained to hear the words.

"No. I ain't seen her since she left our place Tuesday."

His pa stopped talking, apparently listening to someone on the other end. Then: "That's what she told us, too. Yeah. Yeah. That's right. Sorry. Don't know his name." Another pause. "Don't know that neither. My guess is he picked her up 'cause her car is still parked in front of her trailer." A break again and then something that, at least for the moment, restored Trip's faith in his pa's loyalty: "I seen him hanging around her place before. Short, round fellow. Big ears. Walks with a limp." He laughed. "That's a good one. I don't know what he sees in her neither." He stopped talking, listened again. Finally: "That's all I know. Sorry can't be more help. Guess you'll have to get by without her this weekend."

Trip heard his father hang up the phone. He crawled to his feet. His head was pounding. He lifted his right hand and pressed his palm against his forehead, as if that could stop the thumping. It didn't. He weaved around the obstacle course of boxes and packaged shirts. Walked into the kitchen. His old man was sitting at the kitchen table, a cup of coffee and an ashtray in front of him and a cigarette between his fingers. To his right was a spent insulin syringe and needle. Trip saw a Band-Aid on his pa's left brow. That's where a package had cut him; Trip was hoping that memory from the night before was part of a bad dream. His old man looked up at Trip. "That was a fucking close one." He tipped his head toward the phone on the kitchen wall. "Know who that was?" Trip shrugged his shoulders. "Take a fucking guess." He took a drag off his Lucky Strike.

"Keri's w... work?"

He exhaled. "Damn straight. They're short. They want her to pull some extra shifts this weekend. They know we were her last stop Tuesday, and they know we live down the street from her. Guess who saved your ass?" Trip opened his mouth to answer but his old man didn't give him a chance. "Your pa, that's who." He picked up his coffee and took a sip.

Trip crossed the kitchen floor, took a mug down from the cupboard. Recognized it as the one Paris Murphy had sipped tea from. He shuddered and put it back, took a different one. Poured himself a cup of coffee. Noticed the pot on the counter was already half empty. His old man had been up awhile. Would have had plenty of time to call the cops. What did they call it? *Senior abuse*. His old man could have reported him for *senior abuse*. Did he? Would the police be knocking before he finished his coffee? Trip took a sip and stared at his pa.

"Why you looking at me like that?" asked his old man. "You got no call to look at me like that. I saved your hairy backside."

Trip took another sip. The coffee was strong and bitter and burned. Tasted like it had been cooking on the warmer for hours. He dumped the rest of it down the drain and set the cup in the sink. "Like what? How am I l... looking at you?"

"Like a dog that's been kicked for doing nothing."

Trip leaned his back against the counter and crossed his arms over his chest. "I ain't l... looking at you any which way. You're n... nuts."

"Oh, *I'm* nuts. That's funny coming from you." His pa raised his left hand and touched the Band-Aid with his fingertips. "How's your throwing arm this morning? Huh, son?"

Trip lowered his eyes. "I'm s... sorry about that. Didn't m... mean to get all w... wild and drunk like that. Was b... bummed out over g... g... getting fired."

His old man tapped a tube of ash into the ashtray. "I'm bummed out, too." He put the cigarette to his lips and inhaled. Exhaled as he continued. "Don't see me throwing stuff all over the house. Throwing shit at you. Speaking of which, why don't you clean up that mess you made during that fit of yours? Do something with those goddamn shirts."

Trip looked up. "We could divide them up. Each get half."

His pa took a long pull and blew smoke in his son's direction. "What am I gonna do with all those shirts? I don't hardly leave the house. Far as you're concerned, ninety-nine percent of them shirts don't fit your monkey arms."

Trip cracked a small smile. "How about a garage s... sale? Buy one, g... g... get one f... free?"

His old man crushed the stub of his cigarette in the ashtray. "Brilliant idea," he said dryly. "First off, how many folks in this trailer park have cause to wear dress shirts? Hmmm? How many of them got suit-and-tie jobs? Not too damn many. Otherwise they wouldn't be living in this dump."

"I l... live here and I got a s... suit-and-tie job."

"Past tense. You *had* a suit-and-tie job." His pa bumped off the remainder of his coffee. "Secondly, do you think it's a good thing to have folks coming by the trailer? Sneaking around and peeking around? You forget what we got in the back bedroom? We got to keep a low profile. Garage sale. Jesus H. Christ." His pa snickered. "How s... s... s... stupid can you g... g... get?"

Trip's jaw tightened. The echoes of school-yard taunts filled his head. He couldn't believe his own pa had made fun of his stutter. He'd never done that before, at least not to Trip's face. He'd always told him it didn't matter and that anybody who teased him was trash. They'd get theirs, he told Trip. *What goes around comes around.* How often had he heard that from his old man when he was growing up?

Didn't it mean anything anymore? Had it ever meant anything?

His pa got up from the table, turned his back on Trip and started to cross the kitchen floor. Trip took two steps toward him. "Don't t... turn your b... back on me, old man. Don't call me s... s... stupid neither."

His pa turned and glared at him.

Trip continued. "You g... got balls making fun of the way I talk. You c... could of g... got me help when I was a little k... kid and you didn't. The way I talk is your f... fault."

"So now it comes out. You blame me." He rested his left hand on the cane and with his right pointed a finger at Trip as if he were correcting a child. "I told you before. It runs in the family. Ain't my doing. Ain't nothing to be done about it."

"That's a l... lie. You're lying. Who s... s... stuttered in our family? Who?"

"Your sister." A grin stretched across his old man's face. "Of course, she did manage to fix it towards the end of her life. So maybe there is hope."

Trip's mouth dropped open. "End of her l... l... life?"

"As long as we're unloading, I might as well tell you. She's dead."

"My sister? My sister is d... dead? I never g... got to know her and she's dead?"

"You got to know her, all right. Know her and then some." His pa smiled a sick smile. "Like I got to know her."

Trip stepped backward until he felt the counter behind him. He needed to touch something solid because he sensed the rest of his world was dissolving. "What are you s... saying, old m... man?"

His pa's eyes narrowed. "You know damn well what I'm saying."

Trip's face whitened. "No." He pressed his back harder against the kitchen counter.

"Yeah, you do." His pa took a step toward him. "Like you, I have appetites. Only difference is I like to keep it in the family. That's why your bitch ma run off." Frank rested both hands on the handle of his cane. His posture and voice took on that of a kindly old storyteller, but the tale he recounted was horrific and real. "Your ma knew what was going on in your sister's bedroom, but she didn't say nothing. How could she? Shit. Mary was my daughter, too. I could do what I wanted. But when you were born, that was the last straw. Anna was praying for another girl and she got you. Said she didn't want to live under the same roof with another Trip male. Not even her own son. She couldn't stand the sight of you. She packed up Mary and took off. No loss. Wasn't much of a wife anyway. Couldn't cook worth a damn. Lousy in the sack." He smiled. "Not like Mary."

Trip's fists tightened at his sides. "You slept with your own d... daughter. My poor sister. How could you? Sick b... bastard."

"You're one to talk. Let me tell you something, boy. Anna only left because she was afraid you were going to hit on Mary, too." His pa paused to let that sink in. "As it turns out, she was right."

What was his old man saying? Suddenly it hit him like a punch in the gut. Trip realized who he'd slept with more than twenty years ago. He wrapped his arms around his stomach and folded onto the floor. Slowly. A giant melting down to a midget. "I d... didn't know. I wouldn't have d... done it if I knew." He wished he would lose his mind. Pass out. Black out. Anything to banish the image from his mind. His body tangled with hers.

His old man stepped closer. Jabbed him once in the side

310

with the tip of his cane. "That's right, boy. We're both sick bastards." Frank stood over him. The storyteller kept weaving his tale. "I didn't know what she was up to when she come back after all those years with that made-up name. Cammie Lammont. Stupid name. Those fancy clothes. Thought maybe she wanted to get a look at her little brother. Reconnect with family. She asked me to keep my mouth shut about the past and I told her I would. Figured I owed her that much."

Trip curled up into a ball on his side. Shielded his face with his arms. He didn't want to look at his pa anymore, but he continued listening to his old man's voice. The story wasn't over.

"Then one night we're working at the shop, the two of us. She's got Elvis cranked so loud on the tape player I can't hear myself think. 'Viva Las Vegas.' She's bopping and swaying those hips of hers. Teasing hips. I turn it down and tell her to knock it off. One last customer might come in. She stops dancing. Gives me this weird look. Goes to the door. Locks it. Walks back to the register where I'm going over the receipts. I'm in the middle of counting the quarters when she tells me. Says it ever so casual, like she's telling me we run out of snow globes and backscratchers and we have to reorder. She's sleeping with you. You. Her brother."

There. His pa said it out loud: Trip had slept with his sister. Hearing his old man say it jolted him. Forced him to uncurl his body. He wiped his eyes with his shaking hands and crawled to his feet. Turned his back on his father and clutched the edge of the kitchen sink, afraid he would fold again. He wished that he could puke. Wished that the single act of vomiting would somehow send the filth of his teenage sin down the kitchen drain. He heard the neighbor's wind chimes tinkling. He stared out the

311

window. The scrawny tree was being buffeted by the breeze, losing the last of its leaves. He longed to be one of those leaves. A dead thing floating away on the wind. His pa kept talking.

"I can't look at her I'm so mad. I look at this handful of silver in my fist. She keeps jabbering. Says she's gonna walk home. Gonna tell you she's your sister. Then she's gonna grab her suitcase and leave. Mess up your life the way I messed up hers. She walks to the door, unlocks it and walks out."

Trip bent his head down. Stared into the sink. Stained and dirty. Like the ceiling. Like his life. "You d... did it? Those quarters they f... found next to her. Your quarters from the t... t... till."

"Bet your ass."

"All these years I h... had an idea in my h... head of who did it. The ones who r... ran her over, I thought they were mean t... teenagers. Mean kids from around t... t... town. Jealous k... kids."

"Jealousy killed her all right," his pa said. His voice was so low it was almost lost in the wind chimes. "Not the kind you imagined. Was your pa's jealousy."

Trip raised his eyes to the window. One leaf left on the scrawny tree. Another gust of wind and it was gone. He turned to face his old man. They stood a foot apart. He asked in a voice barely above a whisper: "You mean you didn't k... kill Cammie to p... p... protect me?"

His old man's brows went up. "What?" He paused for a moment, confused. Then he threw his head back and laughed. "Son. Son. You a piece of work. Protect you? Hell no. I was jealous. Mary finally come back and she's sleeping with you instead of me." Frank turned his back to his son and headed toward the front room.

Trip gasped. No honor left for him to cling to, not even

the idea that his father had killed to protect him. Nothing clean remaining in his life story. His pa was a pervert. His ma never wanted him. His sister was his first lover. He couldn't breathe. The sound of rushing water filled his head. He was drowning right there in the kitchen. Suffocating in a shitty trailer parked on the edge of a cold city. Over the din in his head and the tinkle of the wind chimes in his ears, Trip could make out his pa's voice floating from the front room.

"Clean up this junk before I fall and kill myself."

Kill. The only word Sweet Justice Trip understood. He reached into his right pants pocket and pulled out his straight-edge. Flipped it open and held it behind his back. Walked into the front room, crushing boxes and shirts beneath his bare feet as he went. His old man was standing in front of the TV, squinting to see which western was on the screen.

El Dorado. Sheriff Robert Mitchum is hunkered down in the jail with his deputies.

Frank took a step closer to the set. "Damn," he muttered. "It's almost over."

Bullets pound the jail.

Justice Trip crept behind his pa and wrapped his left arm around the old man's chest. Frank dropped his cane and reached up with both hands to pull his son's arm off him. He said in a calm, firm voice, the voice he used when he was giving orders to his son: "No, Sweet." Then frightened: "No!"

Injured John Wayne falls through the jailhouse door.

Trip whipped his right arm around, pressed the razor hard against his father's neck and pulled it across his throat in one left-to-right motion. The blood spurted out. Like water from a garden hose when there's a thumb over the nozzle. His pa jerked and made a gurgling noise. Trip

313

backed up and let his old man fall to the floor in front of the television set.

Bad guy Ed Asner is released from his jail cell and steps around John Wayne's writhing figure to walk out the door, a free man.

33

For an instant, Trip felt as if the straight-edge burned in his hand. He dropped it on the rug. Expected to see it glowing red and setting fire to the rug. He looked down at the knife. Cold metal against the carpet. Nothing more. He checked his right palm. No blisters or burns. He'd imagined it. Stop imagining stuff, he told himself. Trip looked down at the body. "Pa?" Trip said in a low voice. The voice he used when he was trying to wake his old man and get him up off the couch for dinner. "Pa?" He waited. Expected his old man to sit up and tell him to clean up the mess. A third try: "Pa?" He went down on his knees next to the body. Bent his head. Covered his face with his hands. He stayed on his knees until they were numb. He kept his face covered and, behind his fingers, his eyes shut tight. He couldn't look at what he'd done. He was guilty. More than that, he was afraid of being left alone. He'd lived thirty-six years with this one human being. Frank Trip was cruel. Demanding. Abusive. A drunk. A molester and a murderer. He was all Trip ever had, and now he was gone. Slowly, Trip lowered his hands from his face. He breathed in and out twice and opened his eyes. Looked at his father's chest.

It wasn't moving. Why wasn't it moving? Trip fell forward and buried his face in his father's bloody flannel shirt and wept. He looked like a man prostrate in worship. The two-word prayer he uttered into his father's chest: "Pa, p... p... please."

By the time he was all cried out, Trip couldn't tell how much of the wetness on his face was from the tears, and how much was from the blood. He raised his head off his father's chest and sat back on his heels. Wiped the moisture from his cheeks with the hem of his tee shirt. Noticed blood on his tee shirt. He yanked it off and used it to wipe his face again. Dropped it in a ball at his father's side. The television was still on. Trip couldn't tell if the gun battle was from *El Dorado* or if he'd been crying so long another movie had started. He rose to his feet. Stepped around his pa and shut off the set. Saw there was blood on the screen and on the wall behind the set. It looked as if someone had taken a bucket of red paint and thrown it. Even tiny spatters on the window blinds to the left of the television. The windows! The slats on the blinds were open. His instincts kicked in; if nothing else, his father had taught him self-preservation came before everything. Trip stepped up to the window. Peeked through the blinds. The street in front of the house was empty. He lifted the blinds away from the wall and checked the window. No blood on the window. He set the blinds back against the window and closed the slats tight. Trip turned and looked down at the still body. Pool of blood collecting under his head and neck. More red paint. His pa had landed on his back with his knees up. The way Keri had fallen in the shower. "What goes around comes around," Trip muttered tiredly. He knelt down next to the body, this time not in prayer but out of curiosity. Was his old man really gone? He picked up his pa's right wrist with his left hand and felt for a pulse with his right fingertips. Nothing. He dropped the wrist. It made a soft, heavy sound when it hit the rug. A dead bird hitting the ground. He studied his old man's face. So gray. Was it that gray before, or was death draining his cheeks? The eyes wide open. Surprised. Trip knew he didn't have any change in his own pockets. He carefully slipped his right hand into his old man's right pants pocket. Still warm in the pocket. Trip extracted a handful of coins. Dimes and nickels. He picked out one of each and set them on the rug next to the body and shoved the rest of the change in his own pants pocket. He reached up and pulled down his pa's right lid with his right forefinger. He picked up a dime with his left thumb and forefinger and set the coin on the lid. He pulled down the left lid and set the nickel on it. He stared at the silver for a few seconds. The coins seemed to be holding. He picked up the straight-edge and studied the blade. Not as much blood on it as he thought there'd be. He closed it and stood up. Shoved it back in his right pocket.

He didn't want to mop up the mess yet. Didn't want to touch the body until it had turned cool. All he wanted to do was get clean. He stumbled over the boxes and shirts and went into the bathroom. Peeled off his pants and boxers and kicked them into a corner. He grabbed the Lava from the edge of the sink. He pushed open the shower door, reached into the stall and turned on the water. Didn't bother feeling for the temperature. Stepped in and shut the door. Hot. He started with his head and worked his way down. Didn't care what the pumice did to his hair or his skin. Clean. He needed clean. He started crying again when he got to his knees, but he kept scrubbing his skin with the bar of soap. He stood on his left foot and ran the

Lava back and forth over the bottom of his right foot. Then he switched and stood on his right foot while he rubbed his left sole. He dropped the bar on the shower floor and stood up. Bent his head under the spray. His body felt hot and raw. He reached over and turned the shower all the way to cold. Shivered while the water soothed the burn. He'd finally stopped crying, this time for good. He shut off the water. Ran his hands over his scalp to squeeze out the water. He studied his hands. No black strands this time. He looked down. The shower floor was covered with black hair. His baldness would be his father's legacy to him. He wondered what sort of monster he and Cammie would have produced had he impregnated her. Horrible thought. He shook his head until he was dizzy. Wanted to put it out of his mind. He had to clean up the big fucking mess in the front room. Think about that, he told himself. He stepped out of the shower, pulled a towel off the bar, rubbed his head. The towel smelled of mildew. He remembered he had clean towels and clothes in the garbage bags in his bedroom. He wrapped the towel around his waist and then took it off. Dropped it on the floor. His old man was dead. No one to yell at him for being naked. He went to his bedroom, dug around in the garbage bag. It smelled like dryer sheets. He pulled out some boxers. Stepped into them. Decided not to wear anything else as it might get bloody. Then he pulled off the boxers and tossed them on the bed. Figured he might as well clean the house naked.

He went into his pa's bedroom. Yanked the cowboy spread and bronco top sheet off his pa's bed, bunched them up in his arms and carried them into the front room. He dropped them next to his old man's body. "Clean up this mess you made, Pa," Trip muttered. He crouched next to the body, held his pa's head up with his left hand. With his

318

right hand, he twined the sheet around his old man's neck. The coins fell off but the eyes stayed closed. Trip set his pa's head down; his old man looked as if he'd fallen asleep on the carpet while wearing a winter scarf. Trip stood up. Laid the spread flat next to the body. Hooked his arms under his old man's armpits and dragged him onto the middle of the spread. His pa's knees were still up. Trip didn't want to try pressing them down; he was afraid of what would happen. Imagined them cracking or snapping back into the same position, and that would scare the shit out of him. Trip picked up one side of the spread and folded it over his old man and did the same with the other side, creating a lumpy ghost covered with cowboys.

He faced forward and towed the spread behind him, kicking boxes and shirts aside as he went. Dragged it down the hallway. He kneed open the door to the back bedroom and pulled the spread up against the freezer. His old man was a lot lighter than Keri. Skinnier. He figured they'd both fit. Trip dropped the spread, put his right hand on the freezer lid. He'd open it without looking inside. He said out loud, "One. Two. Three." He looked the other way and flipped it open. The lid hit the wall with a bang. Trip could feel the cold air pouring out. He bent down to pick up the cowboy ghost. Decided the spread would take up too much room. He unwrapped his old man. Didn't look at his face. Didn't want to know if the eyes had popped open again. Didn't want to touch his pa's skin or clothes, either. Looking off to the side again, he slipped his arms under the spread and stood up, rolled his pa into the freezer. The body made a strange noise when it landed inside. He'd heard that noise before, when he was throwing fresh meat into the freezer on top of frozen. Something soft hitting something hard. He stepped closer to the freezer, shut his eyes and reached up for the lid.

319

Pulled it down. "No," he said out loud. "Fuck n... no."
Trip opened his eyes a crack. The lid wouldn't close; there
was a six-inch gap. He could see the top of his pa's knees
poking up. He pressed down on the lid with both hands.
It closed a little more, but there was still a gap. He put his
back against the freezer and rested his hands on the lid, one
on each side of him. He hopped up; his bare butt landed
on the lid with a smack. He felt something give when the
lid came down; he didn't want to think about what might
have broken or cracked inside the chest freezer. He turned
and studied the lid. Closed tight. "Sorry, P... Pa," he said
to the freezer. He bent down, picked up the spread and
carried it out of the bedroom, shutting the door behind
him.

He went back to the front room. Dropped the spread on
the floor. The thing would have to be burned or washed;
there was blood on it. He ran his eyes around the room.
Didn't see any more blood besides what he'd already noted.
How would he ever get the stain out of the carpet and off
the wall? He still had the boxes and shirts to pick up. The
sight exhausted him. Was there anything left in the house
that could energize him? All the pills from Keri's purse
were downers. Stupid stomach pills wouldn't do him any
good. He needed to hang on to those Roofies. Maybe
some music. He walked over to his pa's TV tray for the
remote. He found it sitting next to the Jim Beam. He
picked up the bottle by the neck and raised it to eye level.
Still half full. He unscrewed the cap, put the bottle to his
lips and tipped it upside down. He put it down, took a
breath, brought it to his mouth again and took another
gulp. He set it back on the TV tray. Saw his pa's pack of
cigs. Picked them up. Reached inside. Pulled out a Lucky
Strike. He didn't like smoking, but he needed something in
his mouth. He threw the pack on the tray and put the

cigarette between his lips. Found the lighter. A keepsake from their souvenir shop.

He ran his thumb over the engraved image of Graceland. He missed Tennessee. Nothing keeping him in Minnesota. No job. No woman. No family. He could leave anytime. Tell the neighbors he and his pa were going back home. Hell, he didn't have to tell them anything. They wouldn't care. They didn't like his old man and they only liked him when he worked on their trucks. He'd mop up the trailer real good. He still had jugs of cleaner around from that janitor supplies job. Some of the stuff promised to neutralize blood. Then he'd pile his frozen pa and frozen Keri into the back of the truck. Pull out of town. Let the trailer park take back the mobile home. He could bury his old man and Keri somewhere between St. Paul and Memphis. No one would know. Keri's work would be looking for the phantom boyfriend. Back in Tennessee, there'd be no one keeping tabs on him or his old man. No family left to speak of; his pa had taken care of that. He'd leave from the reunion Saturday night. He still wanted to make it to that. Take care of Paris Murphy. *What goes around comes around.*

He flipped open the lighter, lit up the cigarette. Closed the lighter and tossed it on the tray. Picked up the remote. Held it in his right hand for a moment. He couldn't remember the last time his old man let him touch the thing. The edges were smooth, rounded. It felt comfortable in his hand the way a well-worn wrench or ratchet from his toolbox felt comfortable. Almost as familiar as an old knife handle, but not quite. He turned around, aimed the remote at the set and hit the power button. Another cowboy show. Another shoot-out. He'd never have to watch that crap again. He punched the channel changer until he came to MTV2. Through the blood-spattered screen, he saw Marilyn Manson shrieking and convulsing. His pa would have hated it. He cranked up the volume and dropped the remote on the couch. Decided maybe it wouldn't be so bad without his old man after all.

34

Murphy stared at the photos. "Think there's a match?"

Erik frowned. "If there is, I can't see it."

They sat across from each other at Murphy's kitchen table Friday night. He was in his stocking feet, jeans and a sweater. She was dressed in a tee shirt, sweats and a pair of slippers. The photos were spread out in front of them. All the pictures were printed on computer paper. A dozen of the sheets were the photos Murphy had taken of Trip's truck tires from different angles. One was a photo of the tire track found at Moose Lake State Park. "I don't know," she said. She picked up the photo of the tire track and held it by the edges in her right hand. "It's hard to read this thing. That's the problem. You sure you can't weasel a copy of the cast?"

"I'm lucky I got what I got."

"Who e-mailed it to you?"

"Winter."

"No way," she said. "How'd you get him to cough it up?"

"Told him I needed it for the autopsy report, which I do."

"Sure you do," she said dryly. "What about the finger-prints?"

"I'm working on it," he said.

"Good." She picked up one of her photos with her left hand and held it next to Erik's photo.

He reached across the table and touched her left ring finger with his fingertips. "Why haven't you gotten rid of that thing?"

She dropped both pictures on the table. "*That thing?* My wedding band?" She gripped it instinctively with her right thumb and forefinger. Twisted it back and forth but didn't try to take it off.

"Yeah," he said. "It bothers me. Makes me feel like I'm chasing after a married woman."

"You are," she said. The oven beeped. She got up from the table, pulled an oven mitt off the counter and slipped it over her right hand. She went to the stove. Bent over and opened the oven door. She pulled the oven rack toward her with the mitt.

"Has Jack called since the blowup?"

"No," she said. "I would have told you."

"Then what's going on?"

She checked the thermometer on the roast. "Almost ready." She pushed the rack back in, shut the oven door and stood up. "Nothing's going on."

"Do you have a lawyer yet?"

She leaned her back against the counter and sighed. "Know what? I'm not up for this conversation right now."

"You're never up for it. Don't play with me, Paris." He paused and then said it again. The words she had trouble saying to him: "I love you."

She opened her mouth but had no idea what was going to come out. Not those three words. Something else. A knock at the door. Relieved, she pulled off the mitt, threw it on the counter, walked to the door. "That's gotta be the liquor store."

She pulled open the door and took a step back. "Jack!"

Erik dropped the photo, pushed his chair away from the table and stood up. Turned around. Saw Jack standing in the doorway. Jack looked at him and walked through the door into the kitchen. He didn't shut the door behind him and a wave of cold air followed him into the galley.

"Speak of the devil," said Erik.

Jack looked at his wife and at Erik and then back at his wife. "Figured you two would be together on a Friday night. Smells good. What's for dinner?"

"You're not invited," Erik said. He walked away from the table and stepped in front of Jack. The two men stood a yard apart, facing each other. She smelled alcohol on Jack's breath and saw his eyes were bloodshot. She was afraid for Erik. She was afraid for both men.

"This isn't your house," Jack said. He looked over Erik's shoulder at Murphy. "And that sure as hell isn't your wife."

Murphy slipped between them. Jack was at her left shoulder and Erik at her right. She raised a palm toward each of them. "Back off."

Erik looked past her at Jack. "She's not yours. Not anymore. You dumped her. That makes her a free woman."

"Bullshit." Jack wrapped his right hand around her left wrist and held it up. "What's this, asshole? Looks like a wedding band to me."

"We were talking about losing that," said Erik. He looked at Murphy. "Weren't we?"

Murphy pulled her wrist out of Jack's hand. Looked

from one man to the other. Each was red in the face. Ready to explode. She took a couple of steps back so she was at their sides but not between them anymore. She didn't want to get flattened if fists started flying. She used the calm, low voice she reserved for hysterical crime victims and pumped-up junkies. "This isn't going to happen. Not tonight in my kitchen."

"Tell him, Paris," Erik said. He addressed his words to her but kept glaring at Jack. "Tell him how we were talking about losing that ring and finding you a lawyer and making plans for the future. Tell him."

"I don't believe that," Jack said. "She doesn't give a shit about you. You don't have a future with her."

Erik reached into his right pants pocket and pulled out his key to Murphy's houseboat. Walked up to Jack and held the key in front of his face. An exorcist armed with a crucifix. "Oh yeah? Look into the future. We're moving in together."

Jack snatched the key out of Erik's hand and tossed it over his shoulder. It went through the open kitchen door and landed outside on the dock. "There's your future! Get out, you piece of shit!"

Erik charged toward Jack. Murphy grabbed his left arm to stop him but he pushed her hand off him. He shoved Jack backward through the kitchen door. Jack tripped over the threshold but regained his footing on the deck. Erik followed him outside, stepped up to him and cocked his right arm back. He went for Jack's face. Jack deflected Erik's fist away from him with his left arm and took a swing at Erik with his right. Jack's fist slammed into the left side of Erik's face. Erik went down on his back, sprawled in the middle of the deck. Jack stood over him, fists raised and ready for another punch.

Murphy ran outside. "Stop it!" She crouched down next

to Erik; he was up on one elbow. "Stay down," she said, pressing his chest down with both her hands.

He pushed her hands off him. "Bullshit." He stood up and went after Jack again. Took another right swing and nailed Jack in the left eye before Jack could block him. Jack stumbled backward but didn't go down. Their brawl was working its way to the end of the dock. Murphy stayed with them, fearful one of them would end up in the dark water. Tripod was barking next door. She was sure a neighbor was going to call the cops. Her own address would end up on a police report about a domestic call. Both men went down, rolling around close to the edge. Jack delivered another blow to Erik's face, hitting his nose.

A voice boomed out of the night air: "What the fuck is going on here?" Duncan was walking down the dock, straight for Jack and Erik. He could see the two men fighting, their tangled figures illuminated by the streetlights that dotted the shoreline and by the deck lights on the boats.

Murphy had no idea what he was doing there, but she was happy to see him. Another set of hands to break up the fight. "Duncan," she blurted. "They're going to kill each other."

"Not on my watch," Duncan said. Jack was on top of Erik and had his right arm pulled back to deliver another punch. Duncan bent over and grabbed Jack's right wrist. Erik's nose was bleeding. "Get off him, Jack. You've made your point." Jack tried to pull his arm out of Duncan's grip but Duncan was too strong, and that surprised Murphy. "No," Duncan said.

Jack looked down at Erik with contempt. "Fine," he said. Duncan let go of his wrist. Jack rolled off Erik and stood up. Duncan put his right hand on Jack's shoulder and started walking him off the dock and toward shore.

Erik crawled to his feet and wiped blood from his upper lip with the back of his right hand. Murphy was standing at Erik's side, but couldn't stop looking at Jack as Duncan led him away. A gust of wind made her shiver and wrap her arms around herself. "Let's go back inside," she said, and pulled Erik by the elbow toward the boat. "Get some ice on that nose."

Duncan and Jack stopped next to Jack's Beemer in the parking lot. Duncan folded his arms over his chest. "How drunk are you?"

Jack shoved his hands in his jacket pockets and stared at the ground. "Not drunk enough." He looked up at Duncan and smiled grimly. "A couple of shots after work."

"Doesn't take much when you're already wound up," Duncan said.

Jack leaned his back against the side of his car and stared across the river at the lights twinkling downtown. A view he and his wife had enjoyed while in her bed on the boat. It angered him that Erik had made love to her in the same bed. Taken in that same view of downtown. "I can't believe she slept with that jerk."

"You can fix it," said Duncan. "But fists ain't the way to do it."

"Too late to fix it. I already told her I wanted out. I don't even know why I came back."

Duncan realized he was wrong, that Jack had left her and not the other way around. It made him feel even worse about what he'd said to her. He stumbled to find words for Jack while wrestling with his own guilt. "You came back because you still want her."

"Maybe if that scumbag hadn't been here we could have talked it through. But seeing him with her pisses me off all over again."

"Cool off. Give it a few days and give her a call. Apologize. They love it when you apologize."

Jack sputtered. "Apologize? For what? I'm not the one who fucked around. I don't care if it was one time. Might as well be a hundred."

So Murphy had slipped once—probably in a weak moment when that asshole Mason was ready to leap on it—and now her husband was hanging her for it. Duncan thought Jack should give her another chance; he would if he was married to her. "Just think about it. Sleep on it."

"Sorry you got roped into this. It isn't your problem." Jack touched his left eye; he'd have a shiner. "What are you doing here?"

"I've got to talk to her about a case. Put a steak on that eye when you get home."

"Thanks, Doc."

"Want me to follow you home?"

Jack shook his head. "I'm sober." He dug his keys out of his jacket pocket. Started talking as much to himself as to Duncan. "She hasn't been the same since the summer. Since that maniac banged her up and then killed himself in front of her. It's like that scar on her forehead is more than skin deep."

"It is." Duncan suspected Jack didn't know the whole story and he wasn't going to be the one to tell him. "She's been through a lot. Probably still going through it. She needs you to help her."

"I don't know if I can," Jack said in a low voice. "I wish she'd quit that horseshit job. Who in the hell is nuts enough to like police work, especially homicide?" Jack stopped himself. Mumbled to Duncan, "Sorry. No offense."

"None taken. We're all a little crazy up there, but especially my corner of the asylum." He slapped Jack on the back. "Go home. No bar stops. Straight home."

Jack opened the driver's side of his car, slid inside, put his hand on the door. "Thanks." He slammed it shut.

Duncan watched him pull away and walked back toward the dock. He felt pity for Jack and disdain for Erik. He didn't want to think about what he felt for Murphy; it would complicate everything. Besides, he figured all she felt for him was dislike. Duncan padded down the dock. Saw a key on the boards in front of Murphy's boat. Figured it was hers. He picked it up and shoved it in his jacket pocket. The door was still wide open. Duncan walked through it and shut it behind him. He opened his mouth to announce his presence and heard voices upstairs. Heated talk between Murphy and Erik. He turned to leave but changed his mind. Erik could still be revved up from the fight and he wanted to make sure Murphy was okay. Duncan stood in the galley and waited for someone to come down.

Murphy: "And what was that crap with the key?"
Erik: "What do you mean?"
Murphy: "Waving it in his face like that. You could see he was already losing it."

Duncan slipped his right hand into his jacket pocket and pulled out the key. Studied it. Guessed it was the key they were talking about. He put it on the kitchen counter. Leaned his back against the counter and kept listening.

Erik: "You're taking Jack's side in this. He's the one who barged in."
Murphy: "You and Jack are both assholes. Duncan is the only hero in all this. He kept you idiots from rolling right into the fucking river."

Erik: "Duncan again. Maybe you should dump me and invite
   him to move in."

Duncan smiled to himself. Murphy didn't hate him; she
liked him.

Murphy: "Shut up about Yo-Yo. Here. Lie back until the
   bleeding stops. Keep the ice on it."

The smoke alarm in the kitchen went off.

Erik: "Something's burning."
Murphy: "Shit. The roast."

Duncan looked at the stove. Smoke was seeping out of
the oven. He saw the mitt on the counter. He slipped it
over his right hand, went over to the oven, opened it.
Smoke rolled out. He coughed and pulled the rack toward
him. Murphy materialized at his back.

"How's it look?" she asked. She picked up one of the tire
photos and started waving smoke away from the ceiling-
mounted alarm. It stopped buzzing.

"It looks like you should order a pizza." Duncan stood
up and ran his eyes around the galley. "Got another mitt?"
She set the picture back down on the table. Went to the
counter, opened a drawer, pulled another mitt out and
handed it to him. He slipped it over his left hand, bent over
and picked up the pan. He set it on top of the stove, shut
the oven door and turned on the vent over the range. He
pulled off the mitts and threw them on the counter.
"Sausage and pepperoni?"

She stepped closer to him and asked in a whisper, "Jack
okay to drive home?"

"He's fine."

"Good. What did he say?"

"Not much."

She paused and then it occurred to her that he might have heard something he shouldn't have. "When did you walk in?"

"In time to keep your boat from catching fire." He picked the key up off the counter and handed it to her. "Found this outside. Assume it belongs to you or one of your boxing buddies."

She snatched it from him. "It's mine." She shoved it in the pocket of her sweatpants. She picked up the oven mitts and slipped them on. She took the thermometer out of the black roast and set it in the sink. Picked up the pan. She nodded toward the door. "Open it, would you? I want the stink outside." He opened the door. She carried the pan outside, bent down and set it on the dock to the right of her door. Stood up and pulled off the mitts. "Tripod can have at it when it cools off." She stepped back inside and he shut the door behind her.

"Tripod?" he asked.

She tossed the mitts on the counter. "Three-legged dog. He was barking while the boys were punching the shit out of each other." She turned, took a breath and leaned against the counter. Stopped moving for the first time since he got there. Noticed he looked more pulled together in casual clothes than he usually did in his office wear. Black leather jacket over a black turtleneck and black jeans. She wondered what he thought of her sloppy clothes. She brushed her bangs to make sure her scar was covered.

Erik came down the stairs holding a washcloth stuffed with ice to his nose. "Duncan."

Duncan saluted him. "Erik."

Erik tossed the cloth and ice into the sink. Touched

under his nose and checked his fingers. No more blood. "How'd you happen to show up in time to referee?"

"My good luck. Actually I've got some stuff to talk to Murphy about. Stuff about the case."

Murphy picked up a jean jacket that was hanging from the back of a kitchen chair and handed it to Erik. "Before you launch into it, let me see Erik to the door."

Duncan looked at Erik and saw his mouth harden. Erik took the jacket from her and slipped it on. Duncan stifled a smirk; she was throwing her lover out. Erik stepped into his running shoes parked by the front door. She pulled the door open for him. As he was walking out, Erik bent toward her to kiss her and she leaned away from him. Duncan turned his back to them, pleased she was mad at Erik. Duncan pulled his cell phone out of his right jacket pocket, turned it on and used the voice dial. "Pizza." He heard the door shut. He turned around and Murphy walked toward him.

"That's sad," she said.

"What?" he asked.

"You have the pizza joint on voice dial."

He laughed and then said into the phone, "Yeah. For delivery. A large sausage and pepperoni. Houseboat parked at the St. Paul Yacht Club." He paused. "I don't know. I'll meet you on the dock. How long?" He hung up and shoved the phone back in his pocket. "I'm sorry."

"For?"

"The deal in my office."

She put her hands on her hips. "So this isn't about the case."

"It's more about my groveling."

"You made up for it tonight. If you hadn't showed up, I'd have two wet fools sitting at my table right now."

"And a charred kitchen. Don't forget that."

333

"And a charred kitchen."

"Not bad for a Yo-Yo."

Her mouth dropped open. He'd heard her call him that. Then she realized he'd listened to more upstairs than he let on. She didn't know if she should be embarrassed or angry. She wrote off both emotions. She pulled out a chair. Sat down. "Tell you what. You can pay for the pizza." He took off his jacket and draped it over a chair. Pulled the chair out and sat down next to her.

He eyed the photos on the kitchen table. "Your photos of Sweetie's truck tires?"

"Yeah."

"Turned out pretty good."

"Castro's digital."

He picked up the photo of the tread mark found in the park.

"Winter e-mailed it to Erik," she said.

He held the tread mark photo in his right hand. His eyes ran over the photos she'd taken. He pushed them around with his fingers and, from the bottom of the mess, picked up one from the table. Held it next to the one from the park. "I'd say we have a winner."

She stood up and went behind him. "Really? Erik and I couldn't see it." She looked over his shoulder at the two photos as he held them next to each other. Rested her right hand on his right shoulder and leaned over. "Son of a bitch. You're right. That is a match." She realized how close they were. She wasn't wearing a bra. Her right breast was pressed into his back. The only thing separating them was her tee shirt and his thin turtleneck. She suddenly straightened and took her hand off his shoulder.

He turned his head and looked at her. "What's wrong?"

"Nothing," she said. She went to the refrigerator.

Behind her back, he was grinning.

She pulled open the refrigerator. "How about a beer?"

"Sure. The tread marks and tires should match even better after a couple of beers." He reached across the table and collected all the photos. Stacked them into a pile. "Wish we had a copy of the cast itself. We could take it to the reunion and compare it to the genuine article."

She pulled out a six-pack of St. Pauli Girl and shut the door. "Let's just worry about getting those fingerprints off of him tomorrow night. Getting some information out of him. Bring up those boys who died in high school. See what that does." She plucked a magnetized bottle opener off the refrigerator.

"You never told me why Sweetie did those boys."

"They beat the shit out of him for asking me to homecoming." She set the opener and beer down on the table. Was going to take a chair across from Duncan and told herself that was stupid and paranoid. She sat down next to him. "Now I'm thinking he killed a lot more people in between those four in high school and those two in Moose Lake. They were the tip of a big fucking iceberg."

"Why do you think that?"

"I made some calls today. He was a suspect in at least one other hit-and-run. In Wisconsin. I've got a buddy in Public Safety ready to help me plow through old Minnesota cases."

Duncan sat for a few seconds, digesting what she'd said. He shook his head. "Scary."

"Scary. Good description of Sweet. Of both Trips."

"The scary Trips," Duncan muttered. He pulled a bottle out of the pack. "St. Pauli Girl. Good choice."

"I'd offer you wine but I'm out and the liquor delivery guy probably got lost. Your pizza guy will get lost, too. They can never find this place. I don't get it. The

Mississippi is such a big landmark. It's not like I tell them to take a right at the big rock or something."

"Liquor delivery? You call me pathetic."

"Shut up. I've been busy."

She tried to hand him the opener. "Don't need it," he said. He grabbed a second bottle out of the pack, tipped it upside down and used the cap to pry the top off the first bottle. He set the second bottle down and saw her staring. "What?"

"That's how my brothers open a beer bottle in a pinch."

He took a sip of beer. "Is that how you see me? A brother?"

"I don't know how I see you, Duncan. We really don't know each other."

"We're not in the office. How about using my first name?"

"Axel."

"I like hearing you say it." He took another sip and set the bottle down. "Well, Paris. What are you going to wear?"

She popped the cap off her bottle, dropped the opener on the table. "I've got my marching orders. I'm to *wear something hot for a change.* Isn't that how you put it?"

"How long do I have to live that down?" he asked. "I said I was sorry."

"You guys." She took a sip. "You think that's all it takes."

"What can I do to make it up to you?"

"Cover my back tomorrow night."

"I think we're going to make a good team." He held up his beer in tribute.

"We'll see," she said, and clicked her bottle against his.

He put the bottle to his mouth, took a drink. Stifled a burp. Put the bottle on the table. "Can you dance worth a shit?"

"Hell yeah." She took a bump off her beer. "Can you shoot worth a shit?"

"Fuck yes."

"Then we'll make a great team."

35

One hundred and eighty-two polybagged dress shirts. The entire knife collection packed away in an old steamer trunk. Stereo and CDs. Metal chest filled with car repair tools. Elvis Presley clock. "Elvis Presley Boulevard" street sign. *E.P.* hat. Box of Graceland cigarette lighters. Graceland snow globe. Bunny Pederson's peach purse. Keri Ingmar's purse and clothes. Two frozen bodies encased in cowboy bedsheets. Bloody towels.

On his way to the reunion Saturday night, Trip took a mental inventory of what he'd packed into the back of his truck late Friday and early Saturday while his neighbors slept. The last he'd loaded, and the worst, had been the bodies. He'd again donned the hooded parka and gloves so he wouldn't have to feel their hard skin when he fished them out of the freezer. His father wasn't frozen solid like Keri; he still had some bend. He'd dropped his old man in the middle of the sheet with the bloody towels from the cleanup. Gathered up the corners diagonally and tied them. A neat package. Dragged the bundle down the front steps and lifted it onto the gate without much trouble. Pushed it tight against the other stuff. Getting Keri out had been a bitch. Couldn't lift her out of the freezer for anything. Couldn't get a good enough grip. He'd been terrified something would snap off. A finger or an entire arm. He'd finally pushed the freezer over on its side and pulled her out. Rolled her onto the sheet like a boulder. Strangely, the coins had stayed stuck to her eyes. She'd looked frosty. A hunk of meat with freezer burn. He'd thrown her clothes and purse on top of her. Remembered the bridesmaid's purse in the garbage. Dug it out, tossed it on top of her. Gathered up the corners of the sheet and tied them and then twined nylon rope around the works. Used the rope like a handle to pull her down the steps. Lifting her onto the gate had nearly killed him. Wedged her next to his old man. Two bundles wrapped in cowboys.

Didn't go to bed. He'd sat on the couch and watched television, occasionally dozing off. Falling asleep with the remote in his hand. A privilege only his old man had enjoyed. Every so often he'd gotten up off the couch and peeked through the front room window to make sure no one was messing around near the truck.

Before he'd left for the reunion, he eyeballed the front room one last time. If anyone looked closely they could find evidence of blood, but he figured he'd given no one reason to scrutinize the place. His plan was to drive carefully and stay sober and straight while on the road. Give no state trooper reason to stop him. Bury the bodies, the towels, the women's purses and Keri's clothes at night. Somewhere between St. Paul and Memphis. The only thing he'd keep were the assortment of pills from Keri. He'd dumped the entire stash in with Keri's Prilosec prescription—including the Roofies.

As he steered the truck down Summit Avenue, he slipped his hand inside his right jacket pocket and touched the bottle. Safely tucked away. He withdrew his hand from the jacket and felt the bulge in his right pants pocket. The straight-edge. In case. His hand moved to the controls on the CD player. He turned up the volume on "Evil Element" by Taste of Insanity. The guitar squeals ripped through the cab. He pulled at the neck of his shirt. He'd sifted through all the shirts and picked out one of the few with sleeves long enough for his arms. A pale gray shirt. Athletic fit. Fifty cotton. Fifty poly. Button-down collar. Perfect with his cuffed slate-gray dress pants. No tie. After getting fired from his sales job, he never wanted to see another tie. Instead of a suit coat he wore his best jacket, the gray suede bomber. The black leather belt and black dress shoes were his old man's. His pa didn't need them anymore.

He stopped on the street in front of the reception hall, an old mansion like the other mansions that lined Summit Avenue. The three-story stone house was surrounded by wrought iron. The fence was draped in dried vines and white Christmas lights. The front yard was illuminated by a coach lamp mounted on a post, and by ceiling lights on the open front porch. Trip could see a few people milling about on the porch with their cigarettes and cigars. The rest had to be inside; it was cold and windy outside and an icy drizzle was starting to slice the air in diagonal lines. Trip wouldn't miss the Minnesota weather.

All the street parking in front of the hall was taken on both sides of Summit. He turned down the side street that ran alongside the mansion. Was frustrated parking wasn't allowed on one side. Found a space at the end of the block on the other side. He made a U-turn and pulled into the space. He shut off the truck. Shoved the keys in his left pants pocket. Hopped out. Slammed the driver's-side door and pulled on the handle to make sure it was locked. He glanced at the topper. Nothing suspicious. He sniffed. No stink. As long as the cold weather held, the bodies would keep. He buried his hands in his pockets as he walked down the sidewalk. The wind was in his face; the rain felt like needles on his skin. Ahead of him, a man and a woman were walking arm in arm under an umbrella. They were probably headed to the same place. He wondered if he knew them. Was the man a jock who'd shoved his face into a locker? Was the woman a bitch who'd whispered with her friends? Pointed at him? Laughed at him? The couple crossed under a streetlight. They had gray hair. Too old to be his former classmates. Since it was an all-class reunion, there'd be a lot of people he didn't know. He didn't care. As long as one person in particular showed up. He kept walking. Wondered what she'd be wearing. Who this fella was that she'd have on her arm. Trip had more than enough pills. Maybe he'd waste both of them.

Trip paid the cover charge at the door and walked in. Didn't bother standing at the table inside the front door to fill out a name tag. Ignored the other tables filled with St. Brice High memorabilia. Yearbooks. Homecoming buttons. Programs from school plays. Football trophies. Basketball trophies. Hockey trophies. None of that had ever been a part of his life. That was some other world he'd heard about but never experienced. He saw people carrying their jackets, upstairs. He didn't want to leave his jacket in the coatroom. He wanted it handy so he could bolt when he wanted.

Most people were funneling into the largest room on the main floor, an area that originally must have been the mansion's front room and dining room. Trip followed the crowd. A fire crackled in the fireplace. Chandeliers hung overhead. At the front end of the room was a band setting up on a small stage. At the opposite end, against the back wall, was a cloth-covered banquet table filled with food. Trip thought it was typical Minnesota fare. Veggies and dip. Fruit. Cheese and crackers. Sliced meats and rolls. Meatballs simmering in barbecue sauce. He wondered whatever gave northerners the idea of polluting barbecue sauce with meatballs. In his mind, he was already home eating real southern cooking. Interstate Bar-B-Que would be his first stop. A slab of pork ribs with a side of beans.

People were coming upstairs from the basement with drinks in their hands. He went down. He told himself he needed a drink in his hand so he wouldn't look suspicious. So he had something to do besides sit. Everyone else went downstairs for their drink and took it back upstairs to the main floor. Trip stayed in the bar, a converted cellar with stone walls and a low ceiling. He sat at a table in a far corner with his back to the wall and his eyes trained on the floor. He raised his eyes whenever he heard a female voice at the bar; he didn't want to miss her. Though a parade of people passed through the basement, he didn't try talking to anyone and no one tried talking to him. His resolve to stay sober melted in the crowded reception house. For him it was filled with two kinds of people: those he didn't know, and those he knew and never liked. One pair of blondes in particular. He remembered them. Recognized them the instant they walked into the bar. Long, straight hair parted down the middle. They wore their hair the same way in high school. They weren't related but the pair's nickname was "The Twins." They did everything together. Both were cheerleaders. Shared their lunch bags with each other. Took the same classes. They stood behind him on the choir risers. They'd complain in voices too low for the teacher to hear but loud enough for his ears: "Can't even see with the f... f... freak in the way." "Wish the f... freak would move his f... fat f... fucking head." "The f... f... freak can't sing worth a shit." They were "The Twins" and he was "The Freak." He hated them. They were giggling as they left the bar with their glasses of wine. They didn't see him sitting there, but he was certain they were laughing at him.

He ditched the idea of trying to impress anyone with his heroic volunteer efforts. Nothing he could do would ever make them accept him, even after all these years. All he wanted to do was poison Paris Murphy and her boyfriend and leave town. He reached into the right pocket of his jacket and touched the pill bottle again.

36

She'd considered wearing something dumpy to piss off Duncan and then thought she'd show him up instead. Murphy stood in front of her bedroom dresser mirror and scrutinized her evening attire. A fuzzy three-quarter-sleeve black cashmere sweater with a high neckline and a low back. Fitted black satin skirt with a hemline that fell just above the knees. She wished she could dump the panty hose—they were too confining—but it was cold outside and the wrong season to go bare-legged. She turned sideways and examined her profile. Murphy hadn't worn the outfit in a while; the material hung a little looser on her than she remembered. She hadn't been watching the scales lately and suspected she'd lost some weight since the summer. She blamed it on the surgeon's case. The "stress diet" was always effective. She took a brush off her dresser top and gave her hair a few strokes. She brushed the bangs; she'd never get used to those things. Peering into the mirror, she studied her forehead to make sure the scar wasn't visible. She didn't want anyone seeing it and asking about it. Worse, someone staring at it while trying to act like they weren't.

She heard a knock at the door. She stepped into her black pumps and went downstairs. She pulled open the door and blinked. "Nice."

Duncan could have been a catalog model in the black wool crepe suit. Underneath the three-button jacket were a white shirt and a silver silk tie. Over his arm was draped a black trench coat. He stepped inside. "You like it? Went to the Mall of America this afternoon. Found the whole kit and caboodle on the clearance racks at Nordstrom's. Even the rain gear." He was grinning like a kid showing off his trophy fish. He reached into the pocket of the coat and pulled out some paper. "Saved the receipt and the tags. Like you said." He shoved the scraps back in the pocket.

"I think you should keep it," she said. He pushed back his blazer and showed her his gun hanging from a shoulder holster. "Keep that, too," she said.

He raised his brows. "Hey. You look great."

"Thanks." She eyed his coat. "Raining out?"

"Starting to."

"Let me get my black trench coat. Then we can match. Plus I need my purse."

"Why? Don't need to drag around any makeup or anything, do you?"

"I need to drag around my gun." She ran upstairs to her bedroom.

He watched her go and said in a low voice, "Hot. Hot. Hot."

She came back down, pulling the coat on as she went. "Did you say something?"

"Got to go." He slipped his coat on.

"We're okay. We've got time." She threw her purse strap over her shoulder. Fished a pair of leather gloves out of her coat pocket and pulled them on. Took her house keys out of her purse. "Don't want to be the first ones there."

He held the door open for her and motioned her outside with his hand. "I've got some fancy wheels to go with your fancy outfit." She stepped outside. He followed, shutting the door behind them. She locked up and dropped the keys in her purse.

"I thought I was going to drive," she said as they walked down the dock. She'd heard Duncan was a crazy man behind the wheel.

"Paris. Have you been listening to those naughty stories about me again?"

She was glad it was nighttime so he couldn't see her face redden. "No. No. I like my Jeep is all."

"I like my little ride. Come on. I'll keep the needle under a hundred."

The instant their feet touched shore the drizzle quickened. They pulled their coat collars up and dashed to his car. He opened the passenger's-side door for her. Even in the rain she had to step back and take in the car. "A black boat." She slid inside. Red leather seats and interior, like a bar lounge. He shut her door, went around, got into the driver's side. Slammed the door. Pushed the key into the ignition and started it.

"Nineteen seventy-six Cadillac Sedan DeVille." He pulled out of the parking lot. "Eight-banger. Automatic everything. Not a spot of rust. Bought her out in California from Jurassic Cadillac. Drove her back here. Check this out." He reached under the seat, fished out a fat tape and pushed it into the player.

"I don't believe it," she said. "It works?"

"Bet your ass." He turned up the volume. "*Small World* by Huey Lewis and the News. Nineteen eighty-eight. The last eight-track released by a major label."

"Why do you know that?"

"I don't know why I know that," he said as he piloted

346

the Cadillac north over the Wabasha Bridge. "I just do." He took a left at Kellogg Boulevard downtown. "What's the plan regarding the prints?"

"We'll keep our eyes open for an opportunity."

Duncan steered the car through downtown traffic. The streets and sidewalks were clogged with hockey fans. The Wild were playing the Red Wings at Xcel Energy Center. "This joint is down from the cathedral, right?"

"Yeah. Sits on a corner. Parking on Summit's a pain. You can probably find something on a side street. Might have to walk a ways."

The rain pattered on the windshield. "Good night for a walk," he said. He went up a hill and took a left onto John Ireland Boulevard, curved past the St. Paul Cathedral and got onto Summit.

"Thanks for doing this. Really. I wouldn't feel safe without someone watching my back."

"Yeah, yeah. Don't get all mushy on me." They drove past the hall. "Shit. Nothing on Summit."

"Keep going. We'll find something farther down. Here. Take the first right."

He turned down the narrow side street. "This isn't any good," he grumbled. "Parking isn't even allowed on this side. Trying to get me towed in my own town?"

"Hang a U-turn and park on the other side." They got to the end of the street. "Stop!" Murphy yelled. Duncan slammed on the brakes. Murphy opened the passenger's door and jumped out. Left the door open. Ducked her head back inside and pointed to a truck parked on the other side of the street. "This is Sweet's." She slammed the door and Duncan waited with the engine running. She looked up and down the block. Didn't see anyone coming. She ran across the street, stepped next to the truck and peeked inside the cab. Didn't see anything weird. Went around to the rear and looked through the topper window. "Shit. Can't see." She went back to the Cadillac, opened the passenger's door. Leaned inside. "Flashlight?"

Duncan reached under his seat, pulled one out and handed it to her. "What are you looking for?"

"I don't know," she said. She shut the car door, flicked on the light and went to the back of the Ford. Ran the beam around the inside of the truck bed. Jammed with stuff. Shirts. Boxes. A bunch of balled-up bed linen in that cowboy pattern the Trips favored. She flicked off the light and went back to the Cadillac. Pulled open the door, hopped inside and slammed it shut. "He's taking off, maybe right after the reunion." She opened the glove compartment and dropped in the flashlight. Shut it.

Duncan started driving slowly, searching for parking spots while he talked. "Suitcases?"

"Trunks. Boxes. Bedspreads. He's definitely taking a hike."

"What about Pappy?"

"Good question."

Duncan went around the block and got back on Summit. Saw a van pulling out of a space across the street from the hall. He did a U-turn and took it. "Guess some of your classmates did pretty good for themselves," he said, pulling into the spot between a Mercedes and a Range Rover.

"I'll bet there's not another car on the street with a working eight-track."

He turned off the car and pulled the keys out of the ignition. "Any other things we need to go over before we do this?"

"Don't eat or drink anything."

"You have got to be shitting me. I'm starving."

"He tried to dope me up at that restaurant in Moose Lake. He could try doing it again—to both of us."

He slipped the keys in his right pants pocket. Checked his left. Made sure he had his cell phone on him. "How about we keep an eye on our food and drinks? How about that?"

"Okay. But be careful. He's sneaky." She paused and then asked a question she knew he wouldn't want to hear. "When do we call for backup?"

"Not until we need it," he said.

"When's that?"

He put his hand on the driver's-side door. "When I say."

"Did you tell the bosses about this?"

He opened his door and set one foot on the street. "I am the boss."

37

Trip was on his third shot of whiskey by the time the two detectives crossed the street and entered the hall. By the time they paid the cover and hung up their coats and went down to the basement bar, he was on his fourth. Murphy asked for a glass of Chardonnay and Trip looked up. Recognized her from behind. The long, black hair. Like Snow White. The Snow White who'd been his dream. Who'd turned out to be his nightmare. The boyfriend had big shoulders. Big arms. Trip was sure they didn't see him; he was a shadow hunched in a dark corner. Still, he felt perspiration collecting above his lip and on his forehead. He took the bar napkin from under his glass and wiped his face. Dropped the napkin on the table. He reached into his pocket and pulled out the bottle. Keeping his hands under the table, he unscrewed the cap. Set the cap on his lap. Poured all the pills into his left hand and set the empty bottle on his lap. He couldn't see well in the dim light and with his hand under the table. He looked up. They'd already left with their drinks. He raised his cupped hand from under the table and poked around the tablets and capsules. They were sticking

350

to his sweaty palm. With his right fingertips, he picked out eight Roofies and dropped them into his pants pocket. Four each would surely do the job. That still left him with six. No sense in wasting good pills. He dumped the remaining Roofies and the rest of the pills back in the bottle, screwed the cap back on, put the bottle back in his jacket pocket. He wanted to hang the jacket up after all. His mission might take a while and even in the cool basement, he was sweating like a pig.

Murphy and Duncan spoke in low voices as they walked upstairs from the bar.

"See him?" he asked.

"Yup. In the corner, hiding," she said. They reached the top of the stairs and stepped into a small side room. It contained one round dining table surrounded by chairs. No one else was there.

Duncan looked over his shoulder to make sure Trip wasn't coming up behind him. "Why didn't you go talk to him?"

"Sweet and his father are big boozers. Give him time and he'll get loose. We'll mingle and munch and keep an eye out for him. When he comes up from the bar, I'll back him into a corner. Get him talking about old times."

"Sounds like a plan." Duncan looked through the doorway into the dining room. "I'm hungry. Come on."

"Go ahead," she said. "I'm going to plant myself near the basement doorway."

They left the room, Murphy heading for her post and Duncan aiming for the food. A table filled with memorabilia caught her eye on the way. She picked up a framed eight-by-ten photo of Denny and his three buddies. The same picture they'd used on the memorial page in the yearbook. Arms around each other. They should be here, she thought. She set it down with an even stronger resolve to nail Trip.

"Paris. Where's Jack?"

She turned to see who was behind her. Father Leo, the priest who'd taught religion at the school for years and who officiated at her wedding. She smiled. "How's retirement treating you?" She extended her right hand. He took it in both of his. She'd run into him several times over the years and to her eyes, he never aged. He had the same thick gray hair. Same wire-rimmed glasses. Same tall, lean figure.

He laughed. "What retirement? The archdiocese has got me running from one parish to the other. Teaching was more relaxing."

"The priest shortage?"

He nodded and released her hand. "Back to my original question. Where's Jack?"

She hesitated and then answered. "We're split."

"Again?"

"This time for good."

"Want to talk?"

"Nothing to say."

"Bull." He pointed to his collar. "If this is the problem, I'll take it off. Meet you for beer."

"We'll see," she said.

"I'm shuffling between St. Luke's and Immaculate Heart of Mary. Hearing confessions and saying a few masses. Call either rectory."

She saw Duncan coming toward her; he was talking on his cell phone. He looked excited. "Gotta go," she said, touching the priest's arm.

Duncan pulled her back into the side room. "Interesting development." He shoved his cell phone back in his pants pocket. "That was Bergen. A home health-care nurse is missing. Keri Ingmar. Her employer just called it in. Last time they heard from her was Tuesday. She was supposed to check in Friday, see if they needed help for the weekend."

"So?"

"The last patient she visited was Frank Trip."

"Shit," she breathed. In her mind's eye, she saw Frank's hand resting on the white lid. "The freezer."

"Say again?"

"Remember that visit I made to their trailer? Last stop on the grand tour was a back bedroom with this huge chest freezer."

"You think Nurse Ingmar is cooling her heels in the freezer?"

"Maybe. Sweet's father was pulling some kind of crap while I was there. Egging Sweet on. Tormenting him. Taking his time showing me the place when it was obvious Sweet wanted me out of there. We get to this bedroom and Frank puts his hand on the freezer lid. I thought Sweet was going to have a heart attack."

"Pappy didn't actually open it?"

"No. I don't know if he really intended to open it. I think he was rattling Sweet's cage. Definitely some weird shit going on between father and son. I bolted before they sucked me into their family feud. Planned to get in there with a search warrant after the reunion. Figured we'd find a dope stash in the freezer since Sweet was a pothead in high school. At most, maybe some stolen money. Never thought of a body. Too bizarre."

"The thing was big enough to hold a body?"

"Hell yeah. Three bodies."

Duncan pulled his cell phone out again. "We've got to get into that trailer."

353

Murphy spotted Trip coming up from the basement. "I see Sweet." He started taking the stairs to the second floor, his jacket draped over his right arm. "I'm going to follow him. You stay down here, in case he gets past me."

Duncan nodded while holding the cell phone to his ear.

She let a few people get ahead of her on the stairs. She didn't want him to see her yet. She got to the top of the stairs and saw Trip go into the coatroom at the end of the hall. She ducked into the women's rest room off the hallway so he wouldn't see her. She stood on the other side of the door. Figured she'd give him a couple of minutes to hang up his jacket and go back downstairs. She waited. Opened the bathroom door. Ran her eyes up and down the hall. Saw Trip's back; he was headed back downstairs. He was hanging on to the rails. He was drunk. Good. She ran into the coatroom. Scanned the racks lining the walls. Saw his gray suede hanging toward the end of a rack. She looked behind her; no one was coming in. She stepped over to her own coat, took out her gloves and pulled them on. Went over to Trip's jacket. Slipped her right hand into the left pocket. Nothing. Slipped her hand into his right pocket. Felt something. A bottle. She pulled it out, read the label and gasped. The patient's name: "Ingmar, Keri M."

He killed her, Murphy thought. He killed her and took her pills. She looked at the prescription. "Prilosec." Common acid reducer. Half the people in the office were on it. She opened the jar and spilled some pills into her gloved hand. Saw more than the purple capsules. Couple of Valium. Tylenol with codeine. Some capsules she didn't recognize. Some scored white pills she recognized immediately. Rohypnol. She counted them. Six. Was this his entire supply or did he have more on him? She dumped all the pills back in the jar, screwed the cap on. Slipped it back in his pocket. She wanted to arrest him with Ingmar's prescription in his possession.

She heard music coming from downstairs. Pulled off the gloves and slipped them into her purse. Headed for the steps. She'd take a spin with Duncan. Then take a turn around the dance floor with a drunken murderer. Let him know what she knew. Get him to spill his guts. If he didn't, she'd still slap the cuffs on him.

Watching her glide across the wood floor. Her black hair shining in the dim room like it had a light source all its own. Seeing her smile at her boyfriend. Her handsome, golden boyfriend. Knowing she was happy and having a good time. It all freshened his hate for Paris Murphy. Reminded him of the time he was doing a sales demonstration and splashed cleaning solution on a scab. It burned his hand down to the bone. This reunion was the same thing. Solvent poured on an old wound. Making it worse was the setting. A party crowded with her old friends. His old enemies. Most of them had aged well. The men still had their hair. The women, their figures. One person from their class had died since they graduated. Breast cancer. He heard a knot of women talking about it in low, reverent voices. He recognized the dead woman's name. She'd been a class officer and a volleyball player. It wasn't as good as hearing about a former cheerleader or football player dying, but it still gave him a twinge of joy. He was sure any misery that any of them had suffered over the years was a fraction of what he had tolerated in his hellish years at St. Brice's. Their fucking school. It had never been his school. Never. He folded his arms over his chest and leaned against the wall and waited for an opportunity. Every so often he uncrossed his arms and slipped his right hand into his pants pocket. Felt the pills resting alongside the straight-edge.

While they danced, Murphy told Duncan about finding the pill bottle. "Perfect," he said. He guided her around the floor during the old-fashioned waltz. "Sunrise, Sunset" from *Fiddler on the Roof*. At the same time, he monitored Trip. Didn't like what he saw. "The way he's glaring at you. He's gonna burn a hole right through you. Careful around him. Homicidal maniac."

"I know," she said.

"Sure it was that fight? It was high school, for God's sake. Wasn't even your fault."

"I think he's been stewing over it all these years, imagining I played some big role in the whole deal."

"Must have been quite a beating." He lifted her right hand over her head and spun her around once.

"It was bad enough that he killed those boys over it," she said as she finished the turn and returned her right hand to the palm of his left hand. She felt awkward doing the move with the purse over her shoulder.

Both his hands slid down to her waist and hers went to rest on his shoulders. "How sure are you of that?"

"My gut and the Flintstones coffee mug tell me I'm right," she said. "I need something to back it up."

"Forensic stuff after all these years? Hard to come by."

"I was hoping for something a little easier," she said.

"A confession?"

She nodded. The music stopped. They stood and clapped. Found themselves standing in front of the nearly empty punch bowl at the end of the banquet table. Duncan turned around, picked up a glass and ladled some of the dregs of the red drink into it. Handed it to her. She sipped.

So sugary it made her shudder, but she was thirsty. "You wore me out."

He poured a glass for himself. "You kept up. Very light on your feet." He gulped it. Set the empty glass on the table. The music started up again.

Murphy took another sip of punch. "Where's my other dance partner?" She stepped away from the table and looked across the room at where Trip had been standing. He was gone. "Shit."

Duncan ran his eyes around the room. "How'd we lose someone that big? Where'd he go?"

"His jacket," she said.

Duncan ran for the stairs. "I'll check the coatroom."

Murphy turned around and went back to the table to set her glass down. Saw Trip standing on the other side of the punch bowl in the narrow space between the back wall and the table. His right hand was over the punch. He was about to drop something into it. Only a glass or two left in the bowl and Murphy figured Trip was counting on her and Duncan drinking it. Murphy grabbed his right hand, digging her nails into his flesh. Put her open left palm underneath to catch the pills.

"Drop it," she said in a low voice. In the background, the band was playing "Unchained Melody."

He grimaced but didn't move. "Drop what? I g... got nothing."

At that moment, she figured she hated him even more than he hated her. "You've got a fistful of dope," she said. "Drop it."

He yanked his hand out of hers and dropped the pills on the floor. "Fuck you, b... bitch," he growled. With both hands, he grabbed the edge of the table and flipped it toward her, sending the bowl and glasses and platters of food crashing onto the wood floor. Murphy stumbled backward to avoid getting hit. She felt herself bumping into other people. Heard gasps and screams from horrified dancers. The other end of the room didn't know what was going on. The band kept playing. Other partygoers continued dancing.

Trip dashed through the first opening he could find behind the table. The kitchen door. Murphy pulled out her gun and dropped her purse on the floor. She hopped around the table and the spilled food and broken plates and ran after him. Trip knocked over a young woman in a white apron and tipped an empty bread rack on its side to block Murphy's path. She jumped over it, slid on the kitchen floor but regained her balance. Trip pushed the back door open and ran outside. She was on his heels. As she clattered down the steps she heard another set of feet running behind her. She looked over her right shoulder and saw Duncan at her back. She wondered why his gun wasn't drawn.

The three running figures were illuminated by yard lights as they cut across the leaf-covered lawn. The drizzle had turned into a hard rain. Steam poured from the detectives' mouths as they hollered and ran.

Murphy: "He's going over the fence."

Duncan: "The fuck he is." In two strides, Duncan passed Murphy. "Stop, you dumb fuck," Duncan yelled. "I'm a cop."

Trip had his right leg over the fence and was about to throw the left one over when he saw Duncan racing toward him. He hesitated for an instant and then tried to pick up his left leg. The pant cuff was caught on the bottom of the fence. He reached down and pulled; it wouldn't budge. He thrust his right hand into his right pants pocket and pulled out the straight-edge. Opened it and reached down to slice his pant leg free. Too late. Duncan was almost on top of him. Trip straightened up, cranked his right arm back and took a swing. Duncan tried to dodge the blade, but it caught him on the chin and he stumbled backward. A shot rang out. Trip dropped the knife with a howl and clutched his left shoulder with his right hand. He saw Murphy bearing down on him, her gun raised. "Don't move!" she yelled. Trip pulled his left leg as hard as he could. The cuff ripped off. He threw his leg over the fence and ran down the alley, his right hand clutching his left shoulder.

Murphy shoved her gun into the waistband of her skirt and climbed over the fence. She landed on the other side, pulled her gun out. Duncan was right behind her. She eyed his face when he landed on the other side of the fence. Blood was oozing from his chin. They ran after Trip. By the glow cast from a streetlight, they saw him turn right when he hit the end of the alley. "His truck," she said.

"I'm getting my wheels," Duncan said, and ran ahead of her. At the end of the alley he took a left on the side street and ran toward Summit. He dug his keys out of his right pants pocket while he went and pulled his cell phone out of his left pocket. Called for backup while dripping blood down the front of his shirt.

Murphy got to the end of the alley and took a right. Followed Trip down the side street. She squinted through the rain and the night as she ran. She couldn't see Trip ahead of her. She looked for his truck at the end of the block. Gone. "Damn," she muttered. She stopped at the corner and looked up and down the side street. Up and down the street that crossed it. Nothing. She turned and jogged back toward Summit. She wanted to catch Duncan to tell him to call for backup. As she ran, she rubbed her arms and pushed the wet hair off her face. She was soaked and cold. Her sweater and skirt were matted against her like a second skin. She got to Summit and scanned the street.

An empty space between the Range Rover and the Mercedes. Duncan's Cadillac was gone.

She heard the squeal of tires. It had to be Duncan. She scanned the side street. Didn't see anything. Then Trip's truck came rumbling out of the alley, took a mad left onto the side street and headed for Summit. She stepped into the middle of the road to stop him. He kept coming. She raised her gun. He kept coming. She dove between two sedans parked on the side street and jumped on the trunk hood of one. Dropping to one knee, she aimed for Trip through the cab window on the passenger's side. As the truck roared by, she pulled the trigger. She heard the crackle of shattering glass but couldn't tell if she'd hit Trip. The truck kept heading for Summit. It would take Trip downtown. To the highways. To freedom.

As the truck rolled into the intersection, a black bullet shot down Summit and broadsided the driver's side. The thunder of metal slamming into metal. A hubcap rolled down Summit toward the reception house and another wobbled down the side street past Murphy. "Axel!" Murphy slid off the car trunk, shoved her gun in her waistband and ran to the intersection. Broken glass and bits of metal crunched under her shoes. She heard sirens in the distance and her own voice drowning them out. "Axel!"

She ran to the Cadillac. The front of the car was crumpled and the windshield was shattered. She tried to open the driver's door. Locked or jammed. She pulled with both hands and yanked it open. Duncan was lying back in the seat. He was wearing his seat belt; it saved his life.

His eyes opened. "Sorry I'm late."

She reached inside and wrapped her right hand around his left. She eyed his body but was afraid to touch him. "Where does it hurt?"

360

"Everywhere." He laughed. "Ouch. My poor Caddy."

"Don't move," she said. His eyes started to close. "Axel. No. Don't. Stay with me. Talk to me. Where were you? You dropped out of the sky."

His eyes fluttered but stayed open. "Drove to the end of the block and took a U-turn. I heard rubber burning. Figured he was coming out of the side street. Gunned it when I saw him."

"Why? We would have caught up with him."

"Couldn't risk a chase. The way he used his truck like a weapon, he could've taken out a bunch of people."

"You never drew your gun."

"Not a fair fight. He didn't have a gun." His eyes started to close again.

She squeezed his hand. "Axel. Stay with me."

Two squads pulled up. Then a third, followed by a fire rig and two paramedic units. She stepped aside so the paramedics could work on Duncan. She ran over to Trip's truck. The driver's side was punched in. Paramedics were crawling all over the cab. "How bad is it?" she yelled to one leaning in the driver's side. She looked past him into the truck. Didn't see evidence that airbags had gone off. She figured Trip had been in so many accidents, he'd stopped replacing the bags or disengaged them. "Is he conscious?" She had to know if he killed Denny and his friends. Wanted to ask how many others he'd murdered. "I'm a cop. Can I talk to him?"

The paramedic pulled his head out of the cab. "You the shooter?" She nodded. "Between that and the crash, he's gone."

She didn't know why she asked her next question: "Which finished him?"

"ME will have to sort that one out." He ducked his head back inside.

Another paramedic, a woman, came around to the cab from the back of the truck. She was shaking her head. "Never seen anything like it."

The impact of the collision had caused Trip's truck to jettison half its load. Curled up in the middle of Summit Avenue—amid a pile of cowboy linen and bloody towels and packaged dress shirts and Elvis memorabilia—were two bodies. A partially frozen old man. A frozen middle-aged woman. The man was clothed and had a sheet wrapped around his neck. The woman was nude. She had a plastic bag and duct tape wrapped around her neck and coins embedded in her eyes. A dime in one and a nickel in the other.

38

Searching for the perfect surface, Murphy turned the pumpkin around and around on her kitchen table. She stepped back, pointed to a flat spot. "How about here?"

Sitting at the table, Duncan pulled the pumpkin toward him. "Fine." He raised the small serrated knife to stab the top and start carving. He had to use his left hand; his right arm was in a sling.

"Wait," she said.

He sighed and set down the knife. "This is painful."

"I want it nice," she said. She walked to the refrigerator, pulled out two bottles of Grain Belt, shut the door and set the beers on the table. "I think some alcohol will improve my artistic vision." She took a chair on Duncan's left. The chair to his right was occupied by his crutches.

He tried to unscrew the cap by hugging the bottle with the sling and using his left hand. The bottle slipped and tipped.

"Let me. Stubborn." She took the bottle, unscrewed the cap and handed it to him. Unscrewed the cap off hers.

"No more St. Pauli Girl?" he asked.

She took a sip. "Fussy s.o.b."

"You should be nicer to me." He took a long drink, set the bottle down. "I had one broken foot in the grave."

She set down her bottle and turned the pumpkin around with both hands. It was sitting on sheets of newspaper. "A couple of busted bones, a few bruises. You didn't even have your big toe in the grave. You can thank your fat-ass Caddy for that."

"Don't speak ill of the dead," he said, and took another sip of beer.

A knock at the door. "Trick or treat!"

Murphy stood up. Grabbed the bowl of candy off the counter and went to the door. Pulled it open. Three boys dressed as bums in ratty clothes. She dropped a Hershey's bar into each sack. "Who do you guys belong to?" Only the relatives of yacht club members bothered hitting the houseboats.

"*The Commodore*'s our grandpa," said the tallest bum.

"Don't fall overboard," she said.

The shortest bum saluted. "Aye, aye." The trio tromped down the dock. She heard them greeting the barking Tripod next door. She shivered in her jeans and sweatshirt. Another cold night, she thought, but at least it wasn't raining on the kids. She closed the door.

While her back was turned to him, Duncan had picked up the knife and cut off the top of the pumpkin, sawing quickly and sloppily with his left hand. He steadied it by wedging it between his body and the sling. "Axel," said Murphy, coming back to the table. "That looks like shit."

He pulled off the top by the stem and thrust his left hand inside. Started pulling out gobs of seeds and string and dropping them onto the newspaper. "It's already seven o'clock. Halloween is almost over. Who cares how it looks? Get it done and get it out there so the kids have something to smash."

"We have a different tradition out here on the river." She sat back down. "My jack-o'-lantern ends up feeding the carp."

Duncan noticed something in the newspaper and scraped away some seeds with his knife. "Here's an ad for some GWPs." He tried ripping it off with one hand and tore the ad down the middle. "Damn."

She leaned over and ripped around the torn ad. Picked it up and read it. " 'German wire-haired pups'. I've been thinking about a dog, too. Same breed, as a matter of fact."

"Great for pheasant. When they're on point, nothing prettier."

She set the ad on a clean spot on the table. "You hunt?"

"You betcha. Missed the opener. I was hoping to get out before the season ends." He glanced at the crutches. "Maybe it won't happen."

"We could go out together." She took a sip of beer. "I could hold you up while you shoot."

"Thanks a bunch," he said dryly.

Her cell phone rang. She looked over at the kitchen counter. Wondered if it was Jack or Erik. She'd taken a break from them since the crash and concentrated on nursing Duncan. His injuries weren't life-threatening and the only permanent reminder he'd have of the case was the scar on his chin. Nevertheless, she felt guilty about what had happened and responsible for helping him heal. After his release from the hospital, she'd stayed with him and camped out on his couch. After a couple of days, they'd moved to her boat for his recuperation. She still took the couch.

The phone kept ringing. Duncan wiped his left hand on the edge of the newspaper. "Want me to get it?"

"Forget it, Speedy." She stood up and walked to the counter, took a breath and picked up the phone. "Yeah."

Amira: "How's your friend, honey?"

Murphy thought the way her mother asked that question made it sound like Duncan was a kid with a scraped knee. "He's much better, *Imma*." Murphy smiled at Duncan.

Then her mother asked a question Murphy had been trying to answer herself: "Gonna take that job he offered you?"

From his hospital bed, Duncan had asked Murphy to join him on a new five-state task force he was helping form with other homicide chiefs from around the Midwest. Police departments throughout Minnesota, Wisconsin, Iowa and the Dakotas were being tapped. The detectives would cross jurisdictions within their own states and even cross state lines to work on high-profile felonies. The states and feds would reimburse the home departments for hours spent working on the special cases. Duncan told her that assigning her to the Bunny Pederson case had been his way of auditioning her for the job.

"I don't know, Ma," Murphy said into the phone. With her personal life a mess, it didn't seem a good time to overextend herself on the job. "Thinking about it."

Duncan eyed Murphy. The minute she hung up the phone, he jumped on her. "I don't believe you. It's the opportunity of a lifetime for a cop. You get to skim off the cream. The most challenging homicide cases." He jabbed the knife into the middle of the pumpkin and started cutting out a triangle for the nose.

Murphy sat back down. Picked up her beer bottle. "Sweet's case was challenging, and I couldn't tie up all the loose ends. Maybe I'm not good enough."

"That's a load of crap." Duncan started carving a crooked smile below the nose.

The unanswered questions would always bother her. The bodies that bounced out of the truck were clearly Trip's

366

handiwork. Evidence also credited him with the deaths of Pederson and Kermitt. The Eau Claire murder looked like his doing, but there was no forensic proof. How many others he'd killed while on the road would never be clear. Murphy was sure he'd murdered Denny and his buddies even though the only proof she had was the *Flintstones* mug. She got it back when they went through Trip's trailer. She kept it on her desk at the cop shop, a reminder of a high school love and a high school killer.

She took a long drink and set the bottle down. Picked at the label. "I couldn't answer the biggest question."

Duncan kept carving. "Motive."

"Why did he waste all those people? I know he hated Denny and his pals for beating him up. I get that. The ranger was in the park at the wrong time, saw Sweet burying Pederson or something. There's the motive for that. But why did he kill Pederson in the first place? To plant the finger and find it and play hero? Why did he kill Ingmar and that guy in Eau Claire and God knows how many others? His father. Why did he kill his father?"

Duncan managed to carve one fat tooth in the middle of the jack-o'-lantern's big grin. "Trip was a dope fiend with a fucked-up family life." He accidentally cut off the tooth. "Shit."

She took another sip of beer. "How fucked up did it have to be for him to slit his father's throat and stuff him in a freezer? What did his father do to deserve that?"

Duncan stabbed the pumpkin above the nose and started on the right eye. "Sweetie and his pappy were both pieces of shit. You couldn't even find anyone who liked them enough to claim their bodies, right?"

"I found a phone number for someone in Baton Rouge. I thought it was Trip's mother. Frank's ex. Anna. I told her Frank and Sweet were dead."

Duncan finished the right eye, a triangle the same size as the nose, and started on the left. "What'd she say?"

"She said, 'What goes around comes around.' Then she hung up on me."

He finished carving the second eye and popped out the triangle. "Sounds like a wrong number." He put the top on the jack-o'-lantern.

"No. That had to be his mother."

"Why do you think that?" He picked up his beer and finished it. The front of his sweatshirt and the sling were dotted with pumpkin string and seeds.

"Trip wrote that in my yearbook." Another knock at the door. Murphy got up from the table.

"Wrote what?"

"*What goes around comes around.*" She grabbed the candy bowl and headed for the door. "Must be their family motto or something."